THE

ONCE UPON A PRINCESS

SAGA

THE COMPLETE SERIES COLLECTION

Beauty's Curse
Beauty's Quest
Beauty's Kiss
Beauty's Gift

C. S. Johnson

Ebook Box Set ISBN: 9781943934-386

Paperback Box Set ISBN: 9781943934-362

Hardback Box Set ISBN: 9781943934-379

For all my kids at school–Brooks, Nolan, Rebekah, Satori, Mary, Andres, and Tyler, as well as Miles, Tate, Sam, and, for this one, especially Ethan–I taught in hopes you would learn to be brave, and you ended up giving me the courage I needed to write something new. You know how much I love irony. Thank you for making such a difference in my life.

This is also for another Sam. While this is not the usual story you've heard, you're too much of my own for me not to be grateful for you.

This book is published courtesy of

www.direwolfbooks.com

To Get *Awakening* (A Special Christmas Episode of The *Starlight Chronicles*) as a bonus for picking up this book,

Click Here

Or Download It At:
https://www.csjohnson.me/awakening

BEAUTY'S CURSE

PART I OF THE *ONCE UPON A PRINCESS* SAGA

❖　　❖　　❖　　❖

C. S. Johnson

Print ISBN: 978-1-943934-25-6
eBook ISBN: 978-1-943934-24-9

ONCE UPON A PRINCESS

Prologue

"Get up."

It was the pain in his uncle's voice, rather than the urgency, which forced sleep from Theo's eyes. A sense of warning immediately pressed into him, sinking his body into the hard surface of his sleeping pad, even as he sought for the strength to crawl out of it.

"Get up, boy," the command barked out again, this time accompanied by a shaking hand dripping with the warmth of blood. "Your brother's already getting the horses ready."

Theo felt the sense of warning flare into danger as the new information began to piece itself together inside his seven-year-old mind. Not only was it unusual for Thaddeus, his older brother, to be up before the sun, but ever since the hostile fairyfolk of Riverbed Valley had overtaken the mountainside, no one in all of the kingdom of Rhone thought it wise to ride without the protection of daylight.

Flames spurt out from the other room as Theo hurried to get his things together. While his feet were quick to take him across the small cabin his father and uncle had built together, the one his mother had furnished with her love as much as her embroidery, Theo's heart pounded only with the desire for time to stand still. The call to remember everything, every little detail of his home beat inside of him as a resounding instinct. It rippled through his body, from his heart to his mind, distorting time and perception.

How strange his hand should shake, as he grabbed at the small bread packets, tucked away in their usual cabinet. How had he never noticed the slump in the floors from the years of walking? Theo glanced at his Uncle Thom, wondering what could have happened, what could be so important at this time of night. But before he could say a word, he nearly stumbled at the sight of his uncle and his wounds.

Deep gashes, down both his arms and across his back, were surging rather than slipping with blood. Cuts and bruises were settled into the ebony of his beard.

"Uncle Thom," Theo gasped.

His uncle, always seemingly so fiery and strong, narrowed his gaze. "We don't have time to worry about it," he said, dismissing his battle wounds with an eerie calmness.

"But we have to get you some bandages," Theo insisted.

"We'll have to worry about it after we get to the church," Uncle Thom muttered, stoking the small flames of the fire. "Bring me your mother's tapestry, the one hanging there. And hurry."

Theo rushed over and prudently pulled down the tapestry; his mother had told him, long ago, how his father had won in one of his many successful tournaments, and given it to her. Woven into it was a scene from the legend of Queen Lucia, the Fairy Queen who fell in love with a mortal man, and had him prove his love and his worth by becoming a knight in her kingdom. Since then—or since the legend came about—it was said only those who were worthy of love and power would become knights. It was a favorite bedtime story of Theo's, and his mother indulged him so often with the tale, the landscape of his dreams often wove itself right into the tapestry, as he became a powerful knight and protected the kingdom like his father and uncle.

He carefully handed it over to his uncle, secretly hoping they would be able to wash out the bloodstains from his uncle's hands later. The selfish wish twisted into pain when his uncle began to tear it into strips.

"Wha–" Theo sputtered. "What are you doing? I thought you said we would take care of your wounds when we got to the church."

"This is not for me." Uncle Thom shook his head. "We have to destroy this, Theo," he said. He tossed some of the strips into the fire. "Look."

Theo would have rather shoveled out the stables than watch as the beautiful, blue-green eyes of the fairy Queen began to burn red. But curiosity got the better of him; he turned to face the fire. He blinked in surprise. The fire was burning green and pink sparks, like live flowers sprouting into flames.

"That," Uncle Thom explained, "is Magdust."

Theo stilled; suddenly, he knew. "Mother and Father are dead, aren't they?"

His uncle furrowed his brow. "It's complicated, Theo. But I'm sorry."

Theo grabbed the rest of the tapestry remnants from his uncle's hands and threw them into the fireplace. The scenery from his dreams fueled the fire and lit up the room, burning into reality and changing it all into a nightmare.

Then, bravely but uncertainly, he turned around on his heel, pushed the wayward tresses of his black hair back from his face, and marched out of the door.

At the freshness of the air, tears threatened to flow even more sharply, and he had to hide his face; for a long moment, he tried to pull himself together, even as his world and his home fell apart.

A hand on his back and a horse's snort jolted his hands off his face, allowing him to see his brother. Thad was looking down at him, his eyes colored with the same dark green determination; it was a heritage only a brother could share.

"Uncle Thom said we were to ride together," Thad told him. "You ride in the back, okay?"

Theo nodded. There was nothing else to do but follow orders; he would later think it was a small blessing in its own way, since he was unable to think of what had to be done himself.

"Hopefully, Butterscotch won't mind holding both of us," Thad said.

He is trying to comfort me, Theo understood bitterly. Thad was suddenly, at ten years of age, the leader in their home. And, Theo realized, that made him a burden. Before he could respond to his brother, the door to their house slammed shut for the last time as their uncle walked out.

In the soft morning light, creeping its way over the far mountains, Theo's hope crumbled. It was one thing to see his house burn, and his dreams destroyed; but it was entirely another to see his beloved uncle, his father's protector and best friend, stripped of his invincibility, slinking toward the outskirts of death.

In muffled curses and moans, Uncle Thom clambered onto his steed and came up beside them. "No matter what, boys," he said, "you will need to ride on to the church outside Havilah, the capital. I have a letter for them here," he said, sliding a rolled up and sealed message into the bounds of their horse's saddle. "No matter what, see they get it, and your grandfather will see to it that they take you in."

Thad and Theo both started to object, but with a wave of his hand, Uncle Thom commanded their attention once more.

"The fairies are after us," he intoned. "You need to get to the church. They have protection there. While we are in the forest, *do not* make a sound. For spies and sprites, commanded by that demon witch, Magdalina, are everywhere, and anywhere outside the church's ground is fair game to them. If they hear us, they will kill us."

"Like they killed our parents?" Thad asked, the anger cool but clear in his voice.

"Not quite," Uncle Thom said with a sigh. "I imagine it would be much worse for us." At Thad and Theo's stunned and confused silence, he nodded forward. "Be brave," he called, giving one last battle cry, as he kicked his heels and his horse sped off. Thad, sure of Theo's riding skill, hastened to set a close course behind him.

The wind whipped through Theo's hair, almost in a comforting way. But however well-meaning the wind, it only stirred the angry fires inside of him. As the trees flew by in passing, as the fairies nipped and brushed and bounced about in a hovering threat, as the monks and nuns hurried around the hallowed grounds of the church … as the last of his uncle's weakened confessions fell silent, Theo felt the rage burn on inside of him, into his skin and into his soul, marking him with a lonely fierceness and an empty, nameless hunger.

PART I

"Come away! O human child!
To the waters and the wild,
With a fairy hand-in-hand,
For the world's more full of weeping than you can
understand."

~ "The Stolen Child," Yeats

"Be strong and courageous. Do not be afraid; do not be
discouraged, for the Lord your God will be with you
wherever you go."

~ Joshua 1:9, NIV

ONCE UPON A PRINCESS

ONCE UPON A PRINCESS

1

She had never been one to waste her time; after all, she had so little of it left. But whether or not the weather cooperated with her was another matter entirely.

Rose looked up at the bleak sky, feeling the hood of her protective cloak sliding down from her face, exposing her nape at the end of her close-cropped hair. The wind tickled her skin, and rather than finding it charming and pleasant as she might have when she was younger, she found it taunting and terrifying.

Her gaze moved down from the crying skies to the sea, the rough and tumbling creature so keen on hogging every inch it could of the world's edge.

There was nothing to it, she decided. They would have to enter into the cavern during the rain. According to the map Ethan had found, the entrance to Titania's realm was not far down the cliff, and while it would be easier if the rain would stop and the tide would recede, Rose knew she could never count on life to make things easier for her if it could.

That was how Theo found her; looking down the edge of the cliffs, standing in the rain, and declaring all the world her enemy. No wonder she had insisted leaving the palace when she'd been thirteen, he thought. Even the grand palace would have demolished itself, had she been unable to fight her own way free of it. She was a warrior through and through.

Theo shook his head and pushed back the cover of his cloak. "I know that look," he muttered, coming up from behind her. "And the answer is no."

Rose would have normally grinned at the sight of her best friend following her out of the safety of the camp to talk. But ever since she and her group had finally found the location of the home of a powerful Fairy Queen, time seemed to crush into her a little bit more each day, pushing her into possible tomorrows long before her today's had finished.

She pursed her lips together. "Come on. I'm the princess, remember? I'm the one in command here, Theo."

He smiled at her. "You only pull rank when you know I'm right." Crossing his arms, he added, "It's only been two days, Rosary. We'll give it at least one more before we go barreling in."

He was not fooled by the calm look on her face; there would be a battle in getting her to agree.

He had known Rose—officially Princess Aurora Rosemarie Mohanagan of Rhone—for over ten years, ever since he arrived to work in the royal chapel, and he knew well her charms. It was impossible not to notice them, and knowing her well enough, it was impossible for him to fall for them— which, he knew, she both liked and hated on different occasions. Knowing her expressions just as well, Theo knew this time she hated it.

"Mary can protect us with a weather spell," she argued.

He had to admit, halfway begrudgingly, he admired her tenacity as she refused to back down. "Mary is still tired from our battle with the Eastern Warlords. We're all still tired, even you. The rest will be good for us. We have time enough for rest."

"No, I don't have time, Theo. My birthday is coming up." Frustration and fear crept into the pattern of her speech.

"And you can spare a day now, and we'll make up for it later."

"What if we don't?"

"You still have a whole year afterwards, Rosary." Patience melted away into concern at her words. He knew she was upset and afraid, and there was little he could do about it.

That was why he had come, though, wasn't it? The thought hit him with a disgruntled air. There were few reasons besides counsel and comfort that would cause one to bring a priest across continents and into battle. He was fortunate to have found a friend in the doomed princess of Rhone.

Theo watched as she started pacing, her knight's armor clanking quietly in tune with her stride. Time to reinforce the reason, he decided. "Sophia can't build much of a raft by the day's end. Why not send her to town with Virtue and some of the guards? She can surely go unnoticed here, even with your beast of a hawk, and she'll be able to see about a boat for tomorrow."

After a moment of silence, Rose smirked despite herself. "You and your logic," she muttered. She gave him a friendly punch on the shoulder. "Is there anything you don't use it for?"

"Some things," he replied, "that you know of well, and we share."

Rose felt a world pass between them inside his soft-spoken words, and found comfort in it. "Wanting revenge does tend to bind people together," Rose agreed, finally stopping in her tracks. She laid out her cloak and sat down on the ground. She pulled off her gloves, running her hands along the mossy ground. "Even people like you and me."

"You mean a princess and an orphan?"

She thought about it. "No, more than that," she said. "Not just that. More like someone cursed and someone raised by the church. But I guess that's wrong, too. You're not a priest. Not yet, anyway."

"All of mankind is cursed," Theo replied easily enough, sitting down next to her.

"I guess you sound like enough of one it's easy to forget," she teased back. She sighed. "It's not fair."

He looked over at her, and not for the first time, felt the pull of her presence. She was beautiful, even as she desperately tried to hide it. He didn't have the heart to tell her it was a waste of her time. With her chopped hair, the sunlight-kissed locks fluttered playfully, mysteriously; her eyes, as blue as the sky and unfathomable the sea, were framed by thick, sable lashes, and her lips, lips said to shame the reddest of roses, were as expressive and quirky as he knew her mind to be. Yes, he thought, life was not fair, even to the brightest among us.

Theo knew, having spent his adolescence in the palace, while Rose was angry at the curse placed on her at birth by the wicked fairy Magdalina, it was not the fear of a sleeping death that ailed her so much as the curse of relentless beauty. He smiled, recalling the day when an intended suitor, praising her with a song of her looks, had finally caused her perfected façade to fold.

Rose caught his smile. "What?" she snapped.

"I was thinking about the Prince of Crete," he said. "When he came, and you took his instrument–what was it? A mandolin or something?–and bashed him over the head with it, saying he should be ashamed he'd forgotten to mention how the pearly gates gleamed second only to your smile."

Rose laughed. "You remember his face? It was so red, I thought he was going to throw up."

"He looked like he'd just swallowed some pig slaw," Theo agreed. "But it was your mother's face which I still picture the best. She looked like she was going to murder you."

Rose giggled. "I guess that's one upside to Magdalina's curse. It's not like my mother's going to get away with murdering me. And neither will anyone else."

They fell back into an easy silence for a moment. Then Theo asked, "Is that why you like playing the mercenary knight?"

"It's not for just that reason," Rose assured him. She narrowed her gaze slyly in his direction. "You need the practice, remember?"

"Oh, I see now." Theo shook his head, trying to hide his grin. "Here I thought I was getting pretty good at being your squire."

"I told you months ago you were good enough to be a Rhonian knight," Rose reminded him. "Or did you just want to hear me say it again?"

"No, I wanted to hear you admit I'd beaten you in your battle testing." Theo smirked.

"Ha, it's always a riot with you. But anyway, Sophia's my official squire now."

"When she's not working on your armory."

"She likes doing that. And you know blacksmithing is very important to knights like us. She might as well practice and put it to use."

"She has been, and probably too much to really get in any knight training with the tournaments and the Eastern Warlord battles we've had recently."

"Which we might not have had to fight at all, if the Lead General hadn't been so demanding." Rose squeezed a handful of dirt and watched it slip through her fingers, a

15

mixture of dust and mud. "The people in Greece are already taxed enough. He had some nerve demanding more. Even people like Ethan and Sophia's family deserve better."

Theo nodded. "And you work for it. One way or another."

"I like fighting, but I would rather see justice done, whether it's on the battlefield or in diplomacy," Rose said. "And if I get paid for it, all the better for us."

"I know. Since you feel you will never have it for yourself."

Rose shrugged. "I guess that's true. I mean, I know Magdalina wasn't invited to my party, but it's not exactly my fault for the war between the humans and the fairies, is it?"

Theo thought about the Magdust and the fairies who had died as the humans had captured and killed them and the retribution the humans faced. "No, it wasn't your fault."

"It wasn't fair of her to curse me."

"It wasn't fair of them to kill my family, either," Theo agreed.

"When I am Queen of Rhone, we'll find a way to deal with Magdalina and her magic," Rose vowed. "I just need to break the curse she placed on me first."

"Yes." A fierce protectiveness surged through him. How the world would change without Rose in it, he thought. How much his own world would change. Despite the fatigue of the journey, a renewed sense of determination wormed its way through Theo. He sighed.

"What's wrong?"

"Nothing, or maybe everything. I've decided you're right, so you win this time. We need to get down to Titania's terrarium and find a way to dispel the curse on you."

Rose allowed herself a rare moment of hesitation. She thought about how weary their battle finishing off the Eastern Warlord had been, just a few days before, and how tired everyone in the party was, trying to get to the edge of the northern waters of the Aegean. She looked up at Theo, and saw the usual reserves of coolheaded strength, all wrapped up seamlessly in the sharpened angles of his face. He was her rock, the epitome of reason and faith mingled together. She knew he wouldn't have fought for the time off earlier if he hadn't thought it needed.

There was a warm glow that softened in his emerald eyes, as if he could read her thoughts. "It'll be fine, Rosary. There's not one of us that hasn't watched you shoulder someone else's pain these past four years, regardless of your curse or the amount of time you feel you have. And there's not one of us who wouldn't do the same for you, if you will let us."

She snorted and turned away, but his kind words struck her heart and brought a slim layer of grateful tears to her eyes.

"Let's go get Mary and see if Sophia can rig up a makeshift raft for us. If Ethan can get in on it, all the better. For all his map skills he seems to be more of an architect in the making." He stood up and reached down a hand for her.

Her palms felt smooth and strong in his own as he helped her to her feet, allowing Theo to feel the warmth of kinship.

"Okay. I thought I saw a fallen tree down there, by the edge of the forest. Sophia might be able to use that." Rose grinned. "You'll really let me win this time? Even against your better judgment? Despite your unconquerable logic?"

"There's a good reason you're 'Rosary' to me," Theo teased, chuckling a bit, yanking playfully at one of her sun-colored locks. "Go get everyone ready while I say my prayers."

18

2

***

"I can't believe we made it."

At Sophia's cheerful announcement, all of them turned and gave her varying degrees of a glare. Sophia giggled, the bandage bound around her left eye wrinkling as she laughed. The sound echoed throughout the underground cave, causing more of a disparity on Rose and her friends.

"If that's really how you feel, the next time you aren't sure of one of your inventions, give us a warning, will you?" Sophia's younger brother Ethan growled. He pulled his pack out of the remnants of the cavern's tidewater and tentatively began pulling out long scrolls of letters. "I'm going to punch you if your stupid raft ruined my maps."

"Faith is just as important as skill sometimes," Sophia reminded him. "And I'll ignore the threat, since we both know first of all, your maps are likely fine, and second, I would win in a fight against you."

"Theo's been teaching me some tricks," Ethan muttered darkly.

Sophia stuck her tongue out at him. Before she could offer a counterargument, Rose's faithful hawk, Virtue, interrupted by shaking the water out of his wings.

"Augh!" The two siblings both ducked and Ethan howled as a new layer of moisture hit his exposed map.

"That's enough." Normally, Rose did not feel the need to interject into one of Sophia and Ethan's squabbles. But now they were safely tucked into the cliffs of northern Greek isles, she needed to take account of what was needed to be done.

"Virtue," she called, holding up her right arm. Instantly, her long-time friend and gyrfalcon came soaring through the darkness of the cave her to her. Rose smiled and stroked him under his beak, gaining a soft coo in response. Virtue had been only one of two bright spots during the fateful night of her seventh birthday—an event otherwise circumvented in conversation and in Rose's memory. Virtue had been given to her by her father, and he had been with her ever since.

Just like the other bright spot, she thought, turning to look at Theo as he hauled the last of the soaking supplies from the cavern entrance.

Virtue cawed softly. "Hey buddy," Rose whispered. "Head up to the others. Ethan, do you have the letter?"

Ethan handed her a small sheet of one of his precious papers. In the shaded light, it was hard to make out his exact features, but the tenderness he had in holding the scroll revealed his disposition. Rose thanked him quietly for the help and he dutifully responded, but he retreated quickly.

I'll have to make it up to him later, she thought to herself, mentally making a note. Ethan did not part from his supplies lightly.

At twelve and thirteen years of age, Ethan and Sophia were the youngest in her crew, and the only ones Rose had largely conscripted. They were not too far from her own age, but still too young to be on their own. But it was better than leaving them to waste away in the family's workhouse, or worse, to be beaten to death by their drunk of a father, Rose thought.

Turning back to Virtue, she tied the letter around his claw, and at her mark, he launched back out into the storm and rain, keeping his flight sure and straight despite the torrid winds and prickly rain. "Fly safe!"

ONCE UPON A PRINCESS

"Do you want me to place a spell on him, so he'll be able to repel the elements?"

Rose grinned as she turned to see Mary fluttering out from underneath Ethan's long, hooded cloak. The small fairy shone out a light all her own, as if it reflected the kindness and uniqueness of her soul. Her red hair, cut short and unevenly on different sides of her face, brightened as she used a handful of her magic to dry off.

"No need, Mary," she said. "Virtue knows his own strength and bravery well, and the odds against him never seem to faze him." Her expression turned speculative. "Besides, we might need more of your power coming up here, to get into the portal."

Ethan returned with a new scroll. "According to the scroll we found, there's supposed to be a tunnel here which leads to the heart of island, and that's where the entrance to Titania's hideaway should be."

"And you're sure we can trust the Eastern Warlords?" Sophia asked. "They didn't seem too bright when it came to fighting."

"That's because a lot of them are scholars, and saw the chance for potential land and knowledge in fighting a war," Rose muttered absently as she looked at the ancient map. "We were lucky we fought them."

"I'm pretty sure they don't feel that way," Theo recalled.

"The Greeks in recent years have been more concerned with art than war," Sophia admitted. "The Warlords no doubt knew this and thought we wouldn't put up a fight."

"Or pay others to put up a fight," Mary chimed in.

"Or that," Sophia agreed. "I guess they were expecting an easy win."

"Easy win or not, a year's worth of fighting is still taxing. But this map is easily worth my weight in gold," Rose said.

"Well, that's fine, but we'll need some actual gold for more supplies on the way back to Rhone," Mary said. "I can't put a spell on all of you and the others, all the time."

"Why can't you just make more gold with your magic?" Ethan asked.

Mary put her hands on her hips as she fluttered over and hovered in Ethan's face. "You obviously haven't been around many fairies in your life."

"I don't think a lot of people have, Mary," Rose reminded her as she laid the map out on a nearby rock. "After all, your family is the only one who still remains friends of the crown of Rhone."

"Well, I suppose. But still," Mary said, turning her attention back to Ethan, "Fairy Magic is not magic to us; it is not learned. We grow with it. It is as natural as breathing is to your kind. But there are rules that go with it, and one of them we have is not to use our power for greed."

"What's the point of having magic if you've got limits on it?" Ethan muttered, inciting a small war as he went back and forth with Mary on the matters of magic and morals.

"Enough," Theo spoke up. "Which way do we go, Princess?"

It always slightly grated her nerves Theo was all proper with her in front of others. She knew he did it out of respect, but it was still jarring.

She pointed to the map and traced a lightened trail. "This is the way," she said. "Mary, take the lead. Ethan and Sophia, stay behind Theo and me."

Down the darkened cavern tunnels they went, with Mary flying consistently ahead of them. With her light to lead the way, Rose found hope bubbling up inside of her for the first time in years.

Even in the dark, Theo could see the excitement in her eyes, and he could feel it in the air; the lightening of her soul resonated with his own.

After several close passages, a broken bridge, and a few stops to double-check the map, the group finally arrived in a small, circular atrium. There was no window to the outer world, but the bright glow of gemstones and phosphorous sparkled against the cavern sky.

"We're here," Rose said, standing in the middle of the room. "This is it. This has to be it."

Ethan and Mary glanced back at the map. Mary squealed with delight. "I see it on the map! The name of the place just appeared, almost like it was … well, I guess it was magic."

"What does it say?" Ethan asked. "I can't read runes."

"It's the Crystal Gate," Mary confirmed. "The Crystal Gate which guards the throne of Titania, Queen of the Fairies." She flew over and placed a hand on the center of the room.

Rose felt the room shift, and she stumbled as power surged through the atmosphere. She reached out to catch herself, but she ended up catching Theo by surprise.

"You okay?" He gripped her arms, steading her.

"Yeah. Sorry."

"No problem."

The rumbling suddenly stopped; Rose looked up to see the stones and light all around were shining with bright light. Pillars of pure crystalline appeared, framing the room. They began to wash the floor with a flood of light, cause it to fade into nothingness.

"Wow," she breathed, as the portal opened up beneath her feet. She smiled up at Theo. "This is amazing."

ONCE UPON A PRINCESS

Theo was about to agree when all of a sudden the sand and stone beneath their feet dissolved. In an instant, all of them plummeted down into the empty hollows of the earth.

Rose felt the scream rise in her throat, but before any sound could escape her, a hard floor flew up to meet her.

"Ouch!" Rose yelped. She looked around to see her companions had all expressed similar sentiments, except for Mary, whose wings wavered gracefully as she took in her surroundings.

Rose briefly took a scouting glance; there were no reasons to suspect she would not be welcome. Mary had told her before the fairies under Titania's rule were not particularly vindictive, unlike those who were under Magdalina's power.

She felt a pressure on her arms and realized Theo still held her. "I'm good," she said, shaking him off as she stood up.

He grunted and stood up beside her. "This place is beautiful," he said. "Makes me think of Heaven."

There were rows of plants and trees, and flowers were everywhere. Great light beams, in all and every color, streamed down, adding magic to every detail. In the distance, Rose heard running water. Was it possible? she thought. A waterfall down here?

A moment later, she decided it was more than possible. Here, down in Titania's terrarium, in her own perfect and private world, it was a type of Eden, before any harm had come upon Paradise. And it was, in Rose's estimation, the ultimate place for fairies to live in peace and fun.

"Can't say I don't agree with you on that one, Theo." Rose looked to see Sophia and Ethan helping each other up. "Mary, what do you think?"

ONCE UPON A PRINCESS

"I think this is a dream," Mary said. Gleaming moisture lit up in her eyes as she swirled around. "This place is just glorious!"

"Well, thank you all for your praise," a new voice said. "It'll be nice to have something to brag about to Gloriana. Sisters can be the best of friends and the worst of enemies, especially when it comes to reputation."

Rose turned toward the voice, to see the small form of the Queen of the Fairies herself. Titania smiled. "Of course, you might know of that yourself."

She looked just as Rose had imagined her to be from all the paintings she'd seen of her, with her bright eyes and sparkling movements. But then, she recalled, it had been said Titania was quite proud. She would be the kind of person who only wanted the best of humanity's painters to sketch her delicate features, and with accurate, if not exaggerated, details.

Awkwardly, Rose bowed to the Queen. It was not something she regularly did, but having learned all the motions of proper behavior before her departure from court, it was passable for respectful. "Queen Titania."

"Yes," Titania agreed, while the rest of the others bowed.

From all around, other voices began to frittle softly, excitedly. Titania held up her hand, and silence ensued. "My friends and family welcome you, Princess Aurora of Rhone," she said.

Rose's eyes jerked up, and Theo had to muffle a laugh. If there was one thing the princess hated, it was to be surprised.

"Maybe I should call you Rose, instead?" Titania asked politely enough. She eyed Theo playfully before adding, "Or maybe Rosary?"

Rose felt warmth fly to her face. "Rose is fine," she said, summoning her calm demeanor.

Titania chuckled. "Rose it is," she said. "I have an affinity for flowers, if you can't tell from my home."

"If you know me, you must know why I am here," Rose concluded.

"We're just getting to know each other, Rose," Titania said with a sigh. "I haven't been introduced to your other group members."

Rose felt her mouth drop in involuntary irritation. Titania ignored her as she perused through the line of Rose's loyal compatriots.

"Well, this is a first," Titania purred as she looked at Theo. "I've never had a priest come and visit me. Are you going to try to convert me?"

"I'd promised not to take more time than necessary down here," Theo replied easily. He'd been in enough public alehouses and inns to know when a woman was flirting.

Titania laughed. "Oh my, gorgeous *and* funny. How would you like to stay down here for a while? You can take all the time you need to tell us about the love of God." She touched his arm companionably. "Contrary to what you might think, we are very cognizant of his reality."

"We're not here for that," Rose spoke up. "We're not missionaries."

"My princess has spoken," Theo said. He tugged his arm away from Titania as he added, "But thank you for inviting me. I appreciate it."

Titania pursed her lips. "I can see why you would appreciate a willing audience, given the impudence of your current one," she told Theo, glancing back to Rose. "My offer is open should you ever change your mind."

"Thank you." Theo gave her a brittle smile in return. He might have known when women were flirting, but he also knew how to say no. He was grateful when she just giggled girlishly and moved on.

Rose shot him a frown, and unable to answer for it, Theo looked away.

Mary dazzled the Queen with a quick show of her skill, and Titania, grateful for the display, clapped. "Wonderful! You are indeed a powerful one." She turned back to Rose. "You're right to keep such a creative artist by your side."

"I know," Rose replied. "Mary is the only one of three fairies who remain loyal to the royal family in Rhone; I do not take her friendship or her skills lightly." Mary straightened proudly.

Titania turned her attention to Ethan and Sophia. When she caught sight of Sophia's bandaged eye, she nearly wept. "You have both suffered so," she whispered. "Let me do what I can to help."

Rose and Theo exchanged interested glances as Titania called three other fairies down to her side, and they all pressed their palms against Sophia's missing eye. A *poof!* of magic wafted out from underneath their hands.

Sophia gasped as her bandage fell away. Rose, Theo, Mary, and Ethan all stared.

"Oh, you twit!" One of the fairies muttered. "It was supposed to match her brown eye."

"I thought blue would go better with her hair," another one said.

"I thought we were doing green," the last fairy whimpered. "Green's my favorite color, after all, and I'm the one who has seniority among us."

"It's brilliant," Sophia said, blinking her eyes and staring all around the hidden fairy world. "No matter the color! I can see again!"

"That's awesome," Theo cheered.

"Yes, that's great," Rose agreed, trying to be supportive. Inside, she had to fight off her impatience. Surely, if the Queen of the Fairies could bestow a new eye upon a girl, she could tell Rose how to break her own curse.

She watched as Titania whispered something soft and placed a small peck on Ethan's cheek, before turning back to her.

"Well, Rose, I am finished with the pleasantries," Titania announced. "I assume you want to get down to business?"

Rose nodded. "Yes. If you know who I am, you probably know why I've come."

"You seek answers."

"I only want one," Rose replied. "I've brought gold and gifts along with me, all in exchange for the knowledge of how to break the curse placed upon me by Magdalina."

"I see."

"Magdalina, who commands the realm of fairies surrounding the kingdom of Rhone, my home and future, cursed me when I was younger. She said I would prick my finger on a spindle of a spinning wheel when I was eighteen, and I would die."

Rose nodded to Mary. "And while other fairies before had gifted me with beauty, grace, and song, so that I might marry well and quickly, Mary tried to adjust the cursed spell at the time. She did, making it a deathlike sleep, rather than death itself. She has charged herself my nurse since that time, and vowed to be with me until the end.

"But I can't just let there be an end. Not like that. Ever since I found out the truth, I vowed I would find a way to be free."

28

Titania nodded. "I see," she repeated. "I have heard tales of you, Lady Princess, you know."

Rose said nothing as she tried to hide her surprise.

Titania continued. "Word has it that once you found out of your destiny, you insisted on getting your way. You rejected the potential suitors your parents had lined up for you to marry at twelve, in hopes an heir for the kingdom would be born before your death. You demanded to be trained as a knight, and learned how to read, not only in your native language but also in the Runes of the ancient Scandinavians, the Latin of the church, and Greek, for the country which owns the world's arts. You set off from Rhone at thirteen, with only your closest friend and a small guard, fighting for adventure and answers and purpose, despite your young years and the certainty of your demise. And you have accomplished many things these last years. You've waged war and made peace between nations."

She glanced at Sophia and Ethan, the former of which was trying hard to pay attention even as her eye's sudden sight astounded her, and the latter of which was gaping at the water nymphs playing in a nearby river. "You've saved lives and given hope to those who had none."

Titania cleared her throat, commanding the full attention of her subjects and guests. "I admire you for such decisions and such results."

"Thank you," Rose said, nodding her head.

Titania flicked her wrist, and a crystal ball appeared in her hand. "I have no need of the gifts you've brought me. I will help you, as you have helped plenty."

"You can help me?" Rose asked. Her heart beat wildly as anticipation burst like a dam through her countenance.

Titania washed her hand over the small crystal, and Magdalina appeared inside of it. Her black apparel, the deadly force of her staff, and the crowning tyranny of her atora all pierced through Rose's heart. Anger, hatred, and even a sliver of pity for the sorceress flashed through her.

"Here she is," Titania whispered. "My half-sister, the daughter of Queen Lucia, our mother, and a powerful sorcerer." She sighed. "We have, understandably, never gotten along."

"So you'll help me? You'll tell me how to break her curse?"

Titania sighed. "There are rules to magic."

As Mary gave Ethan a smug kick to the shoulder, Theo stepped forward behind Rose. He didn't like the sound of Titania's voice. One of his ominous warnings shot through him, and though it had been years since his uncle's death, the call of a coming premonition remained potent.

Titania waved away the crystal ball. "There are rules to magic, even for Magdalina. If she put the curse on you, she is the only one who will be able to tell you how to break it."

Rose felt the blood rush from her head. "So, Magdalina is the only one who knows?"

"Yes." Titania's eyes closed in regret.

Theo placed his hand on Rose's shoulder, trying to get her to stay focused. While he knew she would probably later chide him, he also knew he couldn't leave her alone in this. Not after everything they'd gone through to get this far. "What can you do to help us?" he asked.

"I will give you a gift," she said. "Magdalina is not a full fairy, like myself. She is half-human as well. As such, she has her own weaknesses, and you might be able to use that to your advantage. Your sword, please, Rose."

"My sword?"

"Hold out your sword."

Rose pulled out the sword she had tucked into the scabbard at her belt. She held it out proudly, momentarily thanking Sophia for the recent sharpening and cleaning.

Titania waved her hands over it, and magic spurred the hilt to grow metal vines, which laced around the sword's sharp edges, before burning into the blade. The fire faded, and a new sword appeared.

"What happened?" Rose asked.

"This is no longer your sword, but the sword of my great mother, Queen Lucia. She had her flaws as a Queen, but she was a skilled warrior." Titania smirked. "You might recall the story."

Theo surprised Rose by answering for her. "Queen Lucia fell in love with a man, and to show his love, he became the first knight of Rhone."

"There's a bit more to it than that," Titania huffed. "After he became strong enough, thanks to the Magdust he ingested, he wanted Lucia's throne for his own. He placed her in a special genie bottle, hiding her in the dark, away from everyone else and all light."

"I have never heard that part," Theo admitted, stunned by the dark turn of events the legend took.

Titania shrugged diffidently. "Well, you wouldn't have, would you? No one wants to hear their first knight and King managed to murder fairies and capture their Queen."

"That does take away from the Rhonian pride some," Rose agreed, "and paints us as the villains."

"Yes. But you are not your ancestors, and I am not my mother, am I?" Titania asked quietly.

Rose shook her head. "No. I can't change the past. But I can work for the future."

31

"Yes, you can. And I believe you will be able to use my mother's sword for good," Titania said. She arranged the sword in Rose's hands, making it cross over her heart. "Above all else, my mother sought worthiness. You, Princess Rose, have lived in loneliness, cursed and set apart by a witch's revenge. Yet you have the unfailing loyalty of a gifted fairy, the admiration of young children, and close companionship of a man of God." She looked around at Rose's companions. "I have a feeling my mother would have found you to be worthy.

"My only caution to you would be to watch where you place your love. My mother is trapped now, for all eternity, until she can be freed from her own self-imprisonment first, and then from her genie's bottle, all because she was not careful with her love."

"I'm not worried about that," Rose remarked dismissively. "Loving me would be too painful for anyone to bear. I have chosen not to love anyone. I will especially not fall in love. Ever."

Theo felt the familiar twist of pain inside his chest. He knew how loneliness, even self-imposed, could embitter the heart.

Titania giggled. "Love is something that is chosen and must also choose." She tried to stifle her laughter at the sight of Rose's face. "However, given your record, I would not bet against you. I do not envy Magdalina in that she has made you an enemy."

3

Rose had gone down to bury her fears, only to find it was her hope that died. Time was also playing tricks on her, and she didn't know if it resulted primarily or secondarily from the fairy world.

The return trip to their campsite was both smooth and silent. Or maybe, Rose thought, it was just that way to her. She could hear Theo guiding everyone along, while Mary murmuring her spells along the way, and Sophia was astounded to find her new eye could also see in the dark ("Wow! They really didn't know what to think! This is grand!") Relief to be back in the human world washed over her tepidly along with the sea spray and the moonlight.

"It's late." The words from her lips were harsh, bungled in her throat. They sounded alien to her, but the rest of her crew, with such loyalty and pity on their faces, nodded in agreement and hurried off to camp for the night.

Only Theo stayed behind. "I'll take first guard," he offered.

"You might as well get some rest," Rose told him. "I'm not going to be able to sleep."

"And leave you to all the glory, should Titania and her ilk decide to abduct us again?"

"She didn't seem that interested in keeping us," Rose muttered. "Well, except for you."

Theo shrugged. "Rather like a pet, I imagine," he dismissed. "I have better things to do."

"Like what?" Rose asked. "Waste your life on a fool's journey, under a silly girl's orders?"

"I have never considered saving your life to be the same as wasting mine, Rosary." He came and stood in front of her, the ease of his presence replaced by an unusual heat rather than familiar warmth. Rose had never before been bothered by the six inches he stood taller than her, but all of a sudden the shadow of his strength imposed itself on her.

The cursed beauty of the moonlight revealed the clarity and sharpness of his eyes as she gazed up at him. "What if you did waste your life though? What if?"

"If I have wasted my life, I have wasted it on you. Willingly." He took her by the shoulders. "And you're far from the fool you may feel like tonight. You're allowed to have doubts and fears like the rest of us, and leaders are supposed to make harder decisions. But God knows I have enjoyed every moment of being out here with you. Well, almost every moment."

"Like the time we were captured by the Gaullian forces?"

Theo smiled briefly at the memory. "I was referring to something a little more recently." He nodded down toward the cavern. "The last couple of moments have not been particularly enjoyable. I know you're upset."

"Really?" Rose pushed back and away from him.

"Yes. I am, too."

"I don't want your comfort or your pity," Rose spat. "I'm too angry."

"That doesn't seem fair," Theo countered. "Don't you pity me sometimes?"

"Why would I pity you?" Rose argued. "You don't know when you're going to die. You don't get to be a prize for some prince or just some scapegoat for an entire nation, even one as small as Rhone."

ONCE UPON A PRINCESS

"My parents died as a result of the fairy massacres," Theo reminded her. "At least you still have yours."

"Oh, yes, I have my parents, who are so economical in their treatment of me, they only see where I should marry well. I'm placed on display for the nation to come together and unite over my suffering, all while I am deprived of freedom."

"You have freedom," he said. "You might have had to fight for it, but you have it. Here and now."

"I am not free to live as I choose!"

"Neither am I," Theo argued. "I was sent to the church at a young age, and I have been raised there with the expectation I serve there until there is nothing left of me to give."

"You at least have your brother."

"You have a brother, too, and a sister as well," Theo reminded her.

"In name only. They've been largely kept hidden from the rest of the world, and taught in such a manner as to avoid my fate. But you can be open with your grandfather."

"Yes, my mother's father, who holds himself so closely to the love of God he has none to spare for the rest of us. It was only on his honor my uncle managed to convince him to take over raising us." He glared down at her, refusing to step down. "And he only managed to do that because my uncle died right in the middle of the church floor. I watched it happen when I was only seven. You can't tell me you don't pity me for that. Even a spoiled brat like you should be able to sympathize."

Some of the other guards nearby shifted tellingly in the distance. They were watching as the scene unfolded. Rose grumbled to herself. The last thing she needed was everyone to watch as she burst into tears. "Draw your sword," Rose commanded. "You've insulted my honor, so I challenge you!"

Theo complied easily. "I accept," he said, taking his sword out of his scabbard. He held it up high, prepared to do battle.

Rose did not wait for the count to charge. She sped in and unleashed her fury at him, and he met her blow for blow.

Their swords clanked and clanged in tune; over and over again, for how many hours or minutes, he could not say. The metal clashed and rang out as they dodged blows, lashed out attacks, and buckled under defense.

Theo watched as Rose's fury focused and burned, and felt his own lighten into silent laughter as the sunlight peeked out from the horizon's edge. He kept fighting, knowing Rose would only hate him for letting him bait her into battle.

For some time, they exchanged taunts and insults, curses and threats. Before long, Rose was calm and exhausted, while Theo was drained but happy.

He felt the tide of the battle turning in his favor. It was only at the sight of approaching riders he wavered.

"Hang on. Look," he said. "Rhonian riders."

Rose turned to see a small company of horsemen riding, carrying the flag of Rhone, with the symbol of her father, King Stefanos I, boldly resting on each of the riders and their horses. "They're from my father."

Theo nodded. "I wonder if something's happened?"

"I doubt it." Rose let her sword go limp. "I'll bet anything they were sent to make me come home."

"What makes you think that?"

"Virtue is able to carry messages just fine, as are other hawks and falcons from the kingdom. Why just send me a summons when they knew I would likely ignore it?"

"Good point. And speaking of good points … " Theo used her momentary distraction to duck down and kick her legs out from under her. She fell down on the ground, and he held his sword to her neck in triumph. "You're mine now."

Rose glared at him. "Cheater," she accused.

He smirked. "Hardly."

The riders sent out a trumpet call as they approached. Seeing Theo's gaze briefly divert, Rose took her opening. She lashed out a kick of her own, hitting his knee. He stumbled, falling as Rose jumped up.

"Sorry," she said unapologetically. "But I can't let my countrymen see me lose to a priest. We'll call it a draw. No prize this time."

Another trumpet blast came, and the riders were upon them.

He smiled to himself. "*Only* this once. Next time, you'll lose to me," he warned. But for the moment, Theo gave in and flagged the riders before he stood up behind Rose.

"My Lady," the leader of the cavalrymen greeted. "I am Captain Locke, of the cavalry of the kingdom of Rhone. We are looking for the direction of Her Highness, Princess Aurora Rosemarie Mohanagan, heir to the throne of Rhone. We were told she was last seen at the town a day's ride from here, west of the sea."

"I am Princess Aurora," Rose responded. She sighed to herself. It was clear, close up, the men could tell who she was; they might have been hesitant at a distance but Rose was well aware of her beauty's reputation. It did not matter if she was fresh from a battle; one look at her face, open to the sun and sea, was all the confirmation the men needed. "What is the message you have for me?"

"We have traveled many weeks," Captain Locke spoke. "We have several messages for you and those in your party."

"Well, give them to me," Rose insisted. "There is no need for formalities now, Captain. We are not in my father's court, and my company wishes to be off before the next year."

"Please, Your Highness," the captain begged. "We have traveled several extra days trying to locate you. I have orders from the King to escort you personally back to Rhone for the people's sake. The war between the fairies and the people has broken out again, bringing human bloodshed to the land."

Theo doubted the older man would be physically able to force Rose back to Rhone, should she object, but he did not want to point that out. That's why the man was going with the emotional appeal, he realized. There was nothing more sacred than a monarch's ability and conscientiousness in keeping the kingdom safe.

"Let me see the letter," Rose said with a sigh. It wasn't that she was despairing of her people's troubles; it was that most of the problems with the fairies seemed to be provoked by the humans. She silently wondered if the Magdust trade had resumed while she was gone. A look over at Theo prompted him to ask that all the other letters be given to him.

Captain Locke handed her the scroll from her father, and the rest went into Theo's arms. Theo watched her initially as she peeled off the wax seal, and began reading through it.

When she just frowned, he turned his attention to the bundle of mail the other riders had handed to him and saw one from Thad. His brother's untidy loops of letters sent a wave of nostalgia and homesickness through him. He heard Rose sigh and decided Thad's letter would have to wait until later.

"What's it say?" he asked. He glanced over her shoulder at the mess of words, and wondered briefly if the King had written the letter himself. Either that, or his scribe would need to retire. The scrawlish writing seemed to shake as he deciphered it.

Rose bit her bottom lip. "He wants me to come home."

"I figured that much out."

"To officially abdicate the throne. Or to get married."

Theo paused. *Maybe we should have waited longer for our battle this morning,* he thought. *He certainly felt a second wind coming on.* "Well … which, uh, which one are you thinking of doing?"

Her eyes blazed blue lightning into him. "Neither!" she snapped. She tore up the letter into tiny pieces, ignoring the disproving look from Captain Locke. "I'm not going home." She turned and stalked off, heading towards the edge of the cliffs.

Theo grimaced as he realized he had to take care of the messengers himself now. "Gentlemen," he said. "Please, come and make yourselves comfortable at our camp. It is just over there," he said, pointing to where he could see someone else had started a fire.

As Theo led the way over to the campsite, Sophia caught his eye. Her blue-green eye winked at him, and he nodded to her in reply.

"My Lords," Sophia came out and bowed deeply. "I am Sophia, squire to Her Highness, the Princess. It would be my honor to welcome you on her behalf."

The guards were surprised at the notion their princess had taken on a squire rather than a nurse or a maid but said nothing. Theo chatted with the men as Ethan handed out some of their food and drink rations, watching and waiting for a moment where he could read Thad's letter.

When he finally managed to steal away, he grabbed a bottle of ale and headed away from the crowd. He pulled out Thad's letter and began to read.

Dearest Brother Theophilus,

I hope this letter finds you well, and you are making progress in both your journey to find the fairy world for the princess and in your fighting skills.

I am happy to report my mastery of Greek is near fluent and comparable to my Latin skills. Thank you for sending me those pamphlets from the Greek peninsula. I am going to take my priestly vows soon, and Grand Father —my latest name for Reverend Thorne—is accepting of this, and dare I say proud, even though of course he would never admit to being proud of me. It's not like he can be, considering his youngest daughter was supposed to be a nun rather than marry our father. I have been given access to all the libraries the church has to offer as a result of my training, and I …

Theo smiled as his brother wrote on of his love of learning, the thrills of finding new information and how it fit into the old. Theo knew he wasn't so much different from his brother. Thad just liked reading as much as Theo, but Thad found a passion and pleasure in serving others Theo knew he would never have; in setting off with the princess, Theo had hoped to learn the ways of knighthood, to learn how to first protect and fight, rather than comfort and educate.

His eyes caught the end of Thad's rambling, and he nearly choked.

… found several letters of interest here in the church, and Grand Father does not know or else I would most likely be excommunicated. I

ONCE UPON A PRINCESS

found the letter our Uncle Thom wrote to him. Grand Father had stacked it with some of the other letters he'd received in lieu of confessions over the years. It was rather miraculous I found it (for all the man assures me each soul has value, he never seems to worry overmuch at what their bodies and minds are doing, and he has a generic letter of forgiveness sent out) but after reading it, I must talk with you as soon as possible.

I regret to ask you this, since it has been almost four years since you left, but when are you returning? In addition to this discovery, many things here are happening …

Theo felt his fingers tingle. His uncle's letter. How could he have forgotten? Though it had been over a dozen years ago, he recalled that night clearly. His old curiosity sparked inside of him, as he wondered what the letter had said. Maybe it had a clue to his parents' demise, he thought.

And instantly the door in his heart, the one behind which he had locked all thoughts and dreams of revenge, justice, and truth regarding his family's deaths, burst open and unleashed a tidal force of energy. The prayerful resolution to accept the past and move on shattered, bringing him back to the place and time where his uncle had died before his eyes. The possibility of new information swept over him, intoxicating him.

Thad was right; he had to go back, and soon. Thoughts of leaving the princess and the others stung him, but he had a task of his own to uphold.

Maybe Rose was right about my logic, he thought glumly. Sighing, he turned his attention back to the rest of his brother's letter.

Rumors have been circulating back to Rhone of tales of your adventures. While I do agree with you now it was best for the princess to have left, and indeed for the world, her father is in an outrage—he confesses to me some dreadful things—and he has begun seeking suitors out. This is most likely why the war has escalated, as the fairies are never happy to have any humans in what they have deemed their territory. Magdalina herself has been spotted by some of the travelers. Since the princess' eighteenth birthday comes after this year, that alone gives me enough reason both doubt and believe such rumors ...

Theo crumbled the paper, recalling Titania's words. *Only Magdalina would be able to know how to break the curse.* Rose is not going to like this, he thought. But on the bright side, he consoled himself, he would be able to stay with her, if he could only persuade her to head back to Rhone. And, he decided, it was that thought which would easily carry him through the unpleasant conversation which would soon come.

4

Mary made her way to Rose's side quietly as the cavalrymen dined and relaxed around the campsite. She knew full well their prejudice against her kind, and while her older cousins, Fiona and Juana, kept busy at the royal court, she could not blame the humans for their discomfort. Not entirely, anyway.

"Hi Mary."

Mary shuddered at the sadness in Rose's greeting. "I feel like you'd say the same at my funeral," she replied, coming up and hovering at eye level. "Come on, Rose. Cheer up."

"It's not easy to do that, Mary." Rose shook her head. "It's not like I just have to pull a switch and it will take care of itself."

"I can put a happy spell on you," Mary offered.

"No thanks." Rose sighed. "I appreciate the offer, though."

"I know you don't believe in using magic like that," Mary said slowly, "but there are deeper things than magic which work just as well, and you have all of them at your disposal."

"Like what?"

"Like friendship, for one," Mary asserted. "You need not bear this alone, Rose. Aren't I proof of that?"

Rose gave her friend a small pat on the head. "You're right. Thank you."

"And here comes another one," Mary said, gesturing toward Theo's approaching figure. "I've never seen him back down from a battle, whether it was for you or with you, or even both, as it was earlier, when he'd pushed you into it. Your fighting this morning kept a lot of the guards awake."

Rose frowned. Theo had purposely pushed her into battle? But why?

The answer came right after the question. To help her work out her trouble and frustration.

That scoundrel, she thought. But she smiled a moment later. "I hope they put money down on me."

"Some did," Mary assured her, as they both laughed.

That was how Theo found her—laughing again. He knew it helped; the early days of living in the church were unpleasant days, scars on his memory, only brightened and sharpened by the practical jokes Thad had encouraged him to participate in against their crotchety grandfather.

He smiled, hoping he wouldn't ruin it. "Mind if I join you, ladies?"

"Not at all," Mary said. "In fact, I think I'll leave you with Rose. I'm going to scour the woods for some berries before we head home today." She twinkled her wings and flew off.

"Why would she think we're going back?" Rose snorted.

"Why shouldn't we, Rose?" he asked her. The instant fire in her eyes almost made him flinch. Before she could unleash the verbal fury from her mouth, he cut her off. "Look, there's war escalating, and your father is worried about you and the future of the kingdom. And Thad sent me a letter to let me know there are suitors coming in from the surrounding kingdoms."

"That's why the fairies are attacking?" Rose asked. "Never thought I would say it, but good for the fairies."

"Rose."

She immediately regretted her words. "Sorry, Theo. I don't want to go home. It's horrible. Looking back on it, I don't know how I survived thirteen years in it. Defeating the Eastern Warlords and the Talonian Gypsies and the Gaullian

Giants—all of these things were easy in comparison to my stifling childhood. All the dressing up and manners and pampering, all the people bowing down in admiration mixed with pity, not for who I am or what I do, but for what role I play … I'll bet anything they feel better I'm not there, so they don't have to worry about me as a person. They only have to worry about the future as a kingdom."

"And that's exactly why you should go," Theo told her.

"What?" Rose frowned. "That doesn't make sense."

"Let them see you for who you've become without them." Theo began circling her, as he imagined it. "Many of them have heard the stories of your adventures. Let them see it. We have the riches and the reputation among the nations. Otherwise, why would suitors still come, even after you'd rejected them, or even frightened them off?" Theo gave her a teasing grin. "Come on, Rosary. I've never known you to step back from a battle."

"This is not an enemy that I can kill," Rose reminded him. "I have trained with the weapons of knighthood, but they have weapons that cut, slice, and wound, just in their words."

"You've also trained with logic, reason, and observation," Theo said. "You are more than their match with all your experiences."

But what if I'm not? What if I fail? What if you're wrong about me? Then what will you do? Rose closed her eyes, unable to bear the thought of Theo seeing her cry. "If—*if*—we go, we'll get there close to my birthday. And then I'll only have one year left before Magdalina's curse comes to fruition."

"All the more reason to go," he pushed. "Magdalina has been sighted around the kingdom's outskirts." He reached out and put her hand on her arm. "We can see if she'll remove the curse from you."

ONCE UPON A PRINCESS

Rose thought about it. "I doubt she'd do that," she said.

Theo pointed to the camp. "Maybe we can do something. We have your reputation for making peace between people, right? Maybe we can strike a deal with her."

"Make peace?" Rose blinked in surprise. "Magdalina has proved she has no interest in peace."

"There has to be something more that she wants. Maybe we can give it to her." Theo shrugged. "We will never know what exactly she does want if we don't try, Rosary," he chided gently.

He knew he was dangerously getting close to wearing her resolve down when she did not say anything against his remark. He pressed on. "If nothing else, would you consider doing it for me?"

"You?" Rose cocked an eyebrow. "Why would I go home for you?"

"Well, I haven't seen Thad in close to four years," he reminded her. "It would be nice to see him again." And talk with him about what he's found out regarding our parents' deaths, he added silently.

There was a long moment between them, as Rose searched his face. It was such a familiar face, she thought, resigned. Theo had been her best friend for many years, besides her ward and confidante. He had given up his home in order to follow her and fight with her. She almost smiled as she saw the small scar on his neck, the one he'd sustained in their first battle, as he'd put his newly learned knight skills to their first full-fledged test. The temptation to reach out and touch it, so close to his pulse, hit her unexpectedly.

Instead, she sighed, slumping her shoulders as she caved into defeat. "All right. We'll return."

Theo grinned. He snatched her up by the arms and twirled her around as he laughed. "Thank you."

Rose, despite herself, laughed as well. "I suppose I owe you something, after everything you've done for me," she conceded.

Theo frowned as he put her down. Rose fleetingly wondered if she'd offended him, but he just shrugged. "Well," he said as some of his cheer returned, "at least I kept my promise. I defeated you this round."

"Hey! This wasn't a battle," Rose objected.

Theo tugged playfully at a lock of her hair. "Everything's always a battle with you, Rosary." He turned and headed toward the campsite, calling back, "I'll start getting everyone packed up and ready to go."

Rose watched as he left, her pride scorched. She wondered what was wrong with her before admitting there was probably very little that was right.

5

"We need to head west." After a moment scrutinizing one of his maps, Ethan pointed up toward the rocky highlands. "Rhone is on the other side of that mountain. The castle should be just through the rest of the forest."

Further up the line of travelers, comments stirred.

"What did he say?" Mary asked. "We're going to rest?"

"Not quite," Rose told her, pushing her helmet's visor out of her eyes. "Buck up. We're almost there. Another day and we'll be there. Half-day, if we finish getting through the forest tonight."

She looked around to see the familiar forest of her youth. The tall trees shaded them from the blast of the sun; even wearing their full armor, it was a comfortable temperature. The fairies, so far, had allowed them to go through the woods without trouble while the wild animals and other supernatural creatures whispered around them. Rose would have thought it was humorous, if the horses they'd procured did not spook so easily.

Rose watched the scenery with sudden reverence. Here, during the daytime, she would take Virtue out for some hawking and hunting. The happy memories made her wistful. She regretted sending Virtue on ahead to announce her arrival, even as she knew he would have hated the necessary passage by sea.

"Your Highness," one of the guards spoke up. "It is too near nightfall now. I suggest we rest and head off in the morning, when it is safe."

"Safe from what? The fairies?" Rose scoffed. She held up her new sword, taking a brief moment to admire the elegant design once more. "I doubt they will give us trouble. I've got the sword of Queen Lucia, courtesy of Titania herself."

"That seems to be precisely a good reason for them to attack us, Your Highness," a messenger responded. "We mustn't provoke them."

"Excuse me," Rose snapped back. "Last time I checked, I was the heir to the throne of Rhone, and they live in our kingdom's land, freely. No one has banished them, no one has forced them out. If humans and fairies will live together, we must agree on how to proceed together. We will not attack them, but there is no need to fear them should they attack us."

The men shrank back onto their saddles, indistinctively muttering in a range of agreement.

"Easy," Theo muttered behind her. "Magdalina's ambition is still to be feared."

"Only if it goes unchecked," Rose replied. She watched as the men headed out before them. "Or maybe *especially* if it goes unchecked."

"They are merely being cautious," he said.

"Too cautious of the wrath of the fairies, not cautious enough of me." Rose flicked a stray wisp of hair out of her line of vision. "Ethan? Can you come here with the map?"

"Don't let your anger out because your pride gets trampled, Rose." Theo looked away as he adjusted the reins of his horse's bridle. "I know you're tired. Everyone is. We've been riding non-stop for days now, and out of all of us, Sophia and Ethan were the only ones who were able to avoid getting sick on the ship before that. Please take care to curb your temper."

"You're not my governess," Rose sniffed indignantly as he moved away.

"What is it?" Ethan asked. "Everything okay?"

"We're fine. And if we're not, we'll be fine. Let me see the map for this forest."

Dutifully, he presented her with the map of Rhone he'd found a few days prior in a town they had passed through. He pointed to the southeast corner. "This is where we are right now. We need to … "

Rose nodded noncommittally as Ethan continued to point out different paths available for them to take to Rhone's principal city, Havilah. While Ethan went through the easiest and the quickest paths, her attention turned to the Darkwood Forest.

The Darkwood Forest was home to Magdalina's forces. No human had breached it in many years, and certainly no one from Rhone. Located just inside the northeastern tips of Rhone's borders, it was about three days' journey from Havilah's palace.

Once the matter of succession was settled with her father, she would likely have to venture through the Darkwood Forest. The prospect was not comforting.

"What do you think, Rose?"

Rose blinked. "Huh?" She glanced up to see Ethan watching her.

"I was asking about which path you think would be best," he repeated, "given the various obstacles we would face in the forest."

"Oh. Well," Rose replied, as she regained her composure, "I think it would be best if we–"

"Augh!"

A piercing howl screeched through the sky, followed quickly by small explosions and horses rearing.

"Someone is in trouble." Rose pushed Ethan and his map aside as she flipped her visor down and drew her sword. "Stay here, Ethan. Wait for my usual signal."

"Be careful!" Ethan called after her.

Rose did not respond, only heading out, sword first. The rush of oncoming battle was potent after so many days just traveling. She could only hope it was a legitimate fight, not some kind of joke, or worse, some kind of drunken mistake gone even more wrong.

Rose was not disappointed.

A band of fairies had captured a grand carriage. Fairies danced in glee as they sliced through the horses' ropes and scared them off.

A large, powerful-looking fairy, whom Rose assessed to be the leader, laughed cruelly as he picked off the guards one by one, hitting them with spells or enchantments as they attempted to slice him.

"You think your little sticks are a match for the mighty Everon?" he taunted. The last of the guards stumbled, dropping his sword, as Everon used his magic to slit the ground beneath his feet.

Rose smirked as she ran. She would start with the fairies' leader, she decided. He was so preoccupied with the guard he hadn't noticed anyone else coming from behind.

Everon gave his prey a grisly grin as he called his power to his palm. The furious red glow transformed its shape, changing into a bulky, sharp blade. "I've killed many humans before you," he bragged. "And I'll keep killing them long after you're dead. Do you wish to beg for your life?"

Before the guard could answer, Everon laughed. "It's never changed my mind, but it is always amusing to me."

"Perhaps then, you will enjoy giving it a try!"

Everon turned to see Rose's sword just before it struck him. He doubled over, the blackness of his blood oozing from his shoulder to across his chest. His eyes narrowed, watching the small warrior before him.

As he lay on the ground in pain, Rose ducked and rolled, fighting with his minions, their power easily overcome by the grace and stealth of a well-taught opponent. As all of his followers began to flee, she turned back to face Everon.

She held her sword steady as she stood in front of the fallen guard, protecting him. "Last time I checked, humans were still allowed to enter into this forest," she said. "Take your goons and leave these people be."

"They're not from Rhone," Everon insisted. "They are fair game."

Rose, recalling the coat of arms on the carriage, could agree they were definitely not from the area. "Be that as it may, you do not have the right to attack them, no matter what Magdalina has to say about it. Especially if the King has invited them."

"I do not listen to the whims of the humans," Everon spat. "They are so inconsequential. Magdalina and I were here long before them, and we will be here long after they have passed."

"If they are so inconsequential, there is no need to bother with them." Rose readied her blade for another parry. "And you will not be here if you continue to attack them."

"No human sword can stand against mine," Everon hissed, as he stood up and called his power to his palm again.

But before he could lash out, Rose slashed her sword across his power, surprising him. He gaped at her as her sword cut right through, leaving his power to implode upon itself.

His fellow fighters gathered around him, and before they could avenge him, Rose held up her sword to a patch of sunshine. "I wield Queen Lucia's sword of light. You have no power here."

Everon bared his teeth against her, but in a flash of light, he disappeared.

Rose grinned at the power of her sword. Titania had said she was worthy of such a sword, and the sword had come through for her.

"I must thank you. You saved my life."

The guard behind her stood up as she turned around to face him. He pulled off his own visor.

She nearly gasped.

Rose was glad her own visor was still in place; he was undeniably the most handsome man she had ever seen. His intensely hazel eyes peered out at her through thick lashes, while the wind caressed his copper hair. A beard, a shade darker, was sprouting slowly but stubbornly on his cheeks and chin. She took in the rest of him in a quick second; he was tall, but only a few inches taller than her; his shoulders were wide and capable, obviously built for battle and, in later years, consulting on weighty matters. Rose judged him to be between five and ten years older than herself; at least a couple older than Theo, she decided.

Realizing he could tell she was openly staring, she quickly put her sword away. "No thanks needed," she assured him.

"I disagree." The man looked around as only a few of the others began to stir, while the others would never wake again.

ONCE UPON A PRINCESS

"All of my guards were overcome, and you were the only person standing between me and certain death."

"Your guards?" Rose asked.

"Oh. Yes." The man reached out an empty hand. "Please, allow me to introduce myself. I am Prince Philippos, from the kingdom of Einish."

Rose shook his hand. "Nice to meet you." She reached up and pulled off her helmet. "Princess Aurora of Rhone."

Shock crossed his face, but Rose would never find out what he was most surprised by—her beauty, skill, name, or how he suddenly had a life-debt to an heir of another nation—as two other figures came barreling through the bushes.

"My Lady!" Sophia panted, shining in her own, recently refurbished armor. Her weapon of choice, a large battle axe, parried with the low-hanging branches of the surrounding trees as she came to a halt.

Rose turned to face the other fighter, not even needing to see him to know it was Theo. "You were a bit late," she greeted him.

He took a moment to look from her to the prince and back again. And then he pushed up his own visor. "You know me, Rosary. I had to say my prayers."

"A priest and his prayers." Rose rolled her eyes before turning back to Sophia. "Sophie, run and get the healer's potions; see if Mary will come to help with the carriage." As Sophia ran off, Rose turned back to the prince.

"I'd heard tales of the exiled princess of Rhone," he said carefully, "but I never expected them to be true."

Rose smirked. "We'll see what's true and what's not. I suppose you headed to the palace as well?"

"Yes."

ONCE UPON A PRINCESS

"Prince Philippos … one of the suitors my father has been calling for, no doubt," Rose surmised.

"Yes. Please call me Philip." His eyes glittered with mirth. "My company and I have been traveling for several days. We had hopes of arriving in time for the princess' seventeenth birthday–your birthday, My Lady."

"Don't worry about the formalities, either, Philip. I saved your life. Call me Rose," she offered.

"Rose–" Theo interrupted her and then stopped.

"What is it, Theo?" she asked, surprised to see he was wearing a steely expression. *Is he sick?*

"Uh, please excuse me. I wish to help the others."

Rose was uncertain about his mood, but knew there was nothing to be done about it. She would have to confront him about it later, she decided. "You're excused," she said.

"Thank you," Theo said brusquely, before he turned and headed over to check the men.

"You might not want to be so informal," Philip told her as Theo walked away. "Some people would be too shocked by it."

"I'd wager that's their own problem, then."

"I didn't think princesses were supposed to place bets on anything," he replied jovially.

She laughed and asked, "Just what do you know about princesses? Weren't you the one who just told me that you didn't think the tales about me were true?"

Philip could not resist a grin of his own. "Well, you have me there, My La–Rose."

ONCE UPON A PRINCESS

6

Theo's heart murmured distractedly as he watched as Philip once more burst into laughter. The last day had been even more tiring than the previous parts of their journey back to Rhone, largely due to the prince's company, and for Theo, it was not just because three of his men of arms had been injured by a pack of Magdalina's fairy warriors. Prince Philip had taken over much of Rose's time and conversation—understandable, but not practical.

And not welcome, either, Theo decided. Without Rose's company and conversation, he had been bored to distraction, checking over the prince's men for medical or spiritual needs while Rose had talked directions, paths, and decisions over with the Prince.

Theo's posture remained steady and his gaze focused on the path ahead, as inside his mind, the only comfort came from forcing himself further into his plans for revenge.

He would see Thad as soon as he could, he decided. As they moved closer, Havilah's castle would occasionally peek out from the veil of hills and trees; Thad resided in the chapel next to the castle grounds, so close as to be adjoining.

One of Prince Philip's guards stirred on the horse beside him. "Sire?" his voice called out, in a loud and slurring sound, but it was clear to even Theo, who was not inclined to like the prince on sight as the others had, he was loyal and anxious for his master's wellbeing.

"You can relax, sir," Theo told the fallen guard. "Your Prince is well."

"Thank the heavens," the man muttered, before slumping down in his awkward seating on his horse once more.

Theo almost laughed, but instead, pulled the horse's reins, drawing it closer to his own horse. There was no need to let the poor man fall, Theo decided, even if he had been wary of the guard's master.

He turned back to the front to see Rose looking back at him. She gave him an approving look, which he drank in like life-sustaining water, before she turned away, turning back to Philip.

Rose felt wary enthusiasm growing as she began to see Havilah's prominent castle through the thinning trees. "We're almost there."

"Excited?" Philip asked.

The old music of the city called to her ears. The sound of street performers, sales clerks, and servicemen jumbled together with children's tears and cheers, ladies' chitter-chatting and animals' pitter-pattering. Homey smells of the bakery and the sweetness of the florist all rushed her senses, baptizing her in the essence of the home of her youth.

"A little, I guess," Rose admitted. "I haven't been home in four years."

"Only natural for you to have missed it in that case," Philip agreed as they stepped out of the woods. "Why did you leave? I've heard it said you couldn't stand it here. But it seems pleasant enough."

Rose laughed. "I'll agree it *seems* pleasant enough," she agreed. The lightness of her voice left as she continued. "But the people here, while they are busy and preoccupied with their lives, do little more than pity me, and my parents."

"You don't want their pity."

"No. Especially since it seems rooted more in their own sadness for themselves." She mimicked a fretting nursemaid. "'Oh, woe is me, for who will rule our kingdom should there be no heir after the princess?'"

"Pity is an easy emotion," Philip agreed. "But also dangerous. It's pretty easy to manipulate people who feel pity for you."

"I might be a living casualty of the war between my kingdom and Magdalina's loyalties," Rose said, "but my life still has value outside of my crown."

"I feel silly for not believing what I'd heard about you," Philip confessed. "You are obviously pretty resourceful, using the curse to your own advantage, and helping others with it. Though," he observed, "the ones you help are not your people."

They don't deserve it. Rose watched as the people began to notice her and Philip, and their respective crests. Several smiled and waved, while others burst into tears. She kept her eyes on the castle as it loomed ever more closely.

The royal palace was cut from the older traditions of stone and wood, built up majestically, and maintained throughout the years of its use. The intellectual culture at court insisted it was a hundred years or more, while the people nearby only concerned themselves with their rulers if they curtailed liberties.

One of which, Rose thought bitterly, apparently was the right to a surviving heir for the kingdom. And that was the trouble, she knew, of her visit. Her father's command slipped back into her mind.

Come home, Aurora, and marry, or abdicate your right to the kingdom rule.

Rose wondered if the people were giving her father reason to force her hand. She prayed a silent prayer, hoping that was not the case. It was one thing for her to assuage her father's worries; it would be another thing entirely for her to try to calm the fears of the people. Fears which were also her own, as her eighteenth birthday's deadline loomed closer and closer in her vison.

As if in answer, the clanking of the castle drawbridge rumbled as it fell, and trumpets and horns blared, as a thunderous voice fell across the sky: "Princess Aurora of Rhone has returned!"

Huge crowds of people gathered seemingly out of nowhere, crying out happily, expressing welcome, relief, and gratefulness to God for returning their princess to them safely.

And this is why my prayers are useless. Theo would chide her for her faithlessness, Rose thought, but there was a reason she needed him to be the one to believe in the things which angered her.

Why would God, who was said to be good in all forms, allow her to be cursed? Why would he not remove her curse from her, even as she asked and begged to be free from it? Rose turned to look at Theo again, wishing he could be by her side. While his answers to her questions were not enough for her–that was, when he gave them at all–there was something about having him around her that comforted her unspeakably, as though he was proof God, assuming he was real at all, had not completely abandoned her.

Rose was about to call out to him to hurry over to her, but she stopped at the conflicted look on his face. Theo was looking at the adjoining chapel to the side of the palace. He turned his gaze back to her. Rose realized that he was torn

ONCE UPON A PRINCESS

between following her or heading to the church, to see his brother and grandfather.

Their eyes locked for a long moment.

"Prince Philippos of Einish!" the thunderous voice announced in welcome.

"Rose?"

Rose jerked her head around. Philip waited expectedly for her to move forward into the castle. She glanced back at Theo, briefly, seeing he had headed out. "I'll be there in a moment," she said. "I need to check in with my crew." Before Philip could reply, she urged her horse on after Theo.

"Theo."

He stilled and turned back to her. "Yes, Your Highness?"

She pursed her lips at the formality. The bitterness it left in her throat wiped away any excitement she had to be home. "Come on, don't do that." Her horse stopped beside him. "Aren't you coming to court with me?"

"You are not the only one to return, Rose," he told her gently, though it sounded like an insult. "I am here to see my brother at the church."

"God will forgive you if you wait a while."

"Are you saying you wouldn't?"

Rose's lips quirked up into a smile.

"I'll be up shortly," he promised. "But I must see my family."

"What if you're not in time to escort me to see the King?" she asked.

His nose wrinkled. "I doubt your father will be ready to see you right away. We made good time. He'll most likely schedule a meeting with you through one of his servants."

"Theo … " It was most likely the truth, Rose conceded silently. But it still hurt.

"Sorry." After a moment, he pulled off one of his gloves and reached underneath the long sleeves of his chainmail. Rose couldn't see what he was doing, but a moment later, he reached his hand out to her. "Here."

Rose felt the smoothness of several stones slip against her palm, allowing herself to grip his hand in hers for a long moment, as if she was drawing out strength from him. She smiled. "Your rosary beads?"

"Yes." He winked. "So you can say *your* prayers." He took the reins of his horse once more. "I'll be there soon. Go check on the others, Rosary."

"I was going to do that," Rose called after him as she watched him head for the church stables.

"Where's he going?" Sophia asked, coming up beside Rose on her own horse. "Should I go after him?"

"You're not going to bail on me too, are you?" Rose asked.

"A squire stays by his master's side. Or *her* master's side," Sophia recited dutifully. "But on the off chance I would make things more uncomfortable for you, I thought to spare you." She paused as many people began to peer at them curiously. "I *am* a foreigner here."

Rose scoffed at the onlookers. "Spare me only the excuses," she instructed. "I'll need you and Ethan and Mary all with me in my quarters when you've finished seeing to the horses and Prince Philip's guards."

Sophia grinned. "Can I visit the castle's forage house?"

"Later," Rose promised with a smile. "After we meet with the King. I'll need to make living arrangements for you and Ethan."

"How long are we staying?"

ONCE UPON A PRINCESS

Rose glanced up at the crowds and the tall towers of her home. "We'll see." She glanced back at the space where Theo's shadow no longer lingered. "But probably too long."

ONCE UPON A PRINCESS

ONCE UPON A PRINCESS

7

Long before the church had become his home, Theo had always found comfort in his family. As he entered the chapel, the home of the kingdom's worship and the conscience of its leaders, he knew instantly his brother, Thaddeus, was close.

He took off his visor and smoothed his hair. The ebony locks were fickle in their formation. Trying to look presentable to God and kingdom proved difficult, but Theo hoped his spirit was contrite enough.

"Well, well. If it isn't Brother Theophilus," the old croaking voice called out, and he turned to see his grandfather, Reverend Thorne, coming out from the confessional.

"Hello, Reverend," Theo greeted, tempted but not foolish enough to title him "Grandfather." Theo was not surprised to see the old man who helped raise him had changed little in the four years he'd been gone. The same sternly pressed frock, the same look of general disapproval, and the same intense stare were all still there. Only more crinkles and wrinkles folded into his loose skin as he furrowed his brow. "I see you've been fighting lately."

"I'm serving as a knight now," Theo said. "Well, not officially, but the princess has taught me well."

"So you've forgotten priesthood, have you?" Reverend Thorne shook his head. "Well, I suppose it was a long shot to raise you right. You must have too much of your father's blood in you. But at least your brother turned out well."

Theo grimaced. "Where is Thad?" he asked. "I'd like to see him. I don't have much time at the moment. Princess Aurora"–the name felt foreign and uncomfortable on his tongue–"has just returned home and has asked me to accompany her to see the King."

"It's for the best you stopped here first," Reverend Thorne muttered. "Thad is in the back library of the church, reading. He is studying for his next catechism. But he will be able to show you where your deacon's frock is located, so you'll look decent for the princess' audience with the King."

"But I was going to go–"

"What?" Reverend Thorne snorted. "As a knight? Don't subject yourself to such a useless cause. While the King holds meetings daily with his guards and the council of knights, it has been many years since the King has come to the church. We are in disrepair, we are dying, and the kingdom is dying, from his neglect. If you want to make a difference, trust me, and go as a priest. You want his respect as a fighter? Well, this will make him fear you, and remind him we are called to serve God first, not kings."

Theo gritted his teeth together, trying not to growl. "I'll think about it," he grumbled. "In the meantime, I'm going to see Thad. It was nice seeing you again, Reverend."

His grandfather's face softened only slightly. "No need to lie to me in the house of God, son," he muttered, heading back the way he came. "Off with you."

Theo didn't need to be told twice. He hurried off, down the labyrinthine corridors of the church, looking for his brother.

Theo found Thad right where Reverend Thorne said, in the library. He was hunched over a desk, looking at several layers of books and manuscripts.

"Studying for pleasure or priesthood?" Theo called out.

Thad's gaze jerked up. "Brother!" he cried out, happily. He carefully arranged his papers, and then enthusiastically bounced his way over to embrace his younger brother.

Theo was surprised to see Thad had changed as much as the Reverend hadn't. Having spent a good deal of his life looking up to his brother, Theo finally surpassed him in both height and breadth. The priestly robes Thad wore were simple and soft, easily caving under Theo's armored embrace, and his hair was neatly trimmed. His brother's matching green eyes were rested and happy.

"I'm very happy to see you," Thad said, as he drifted out of Theo's returning hug. "You've certainly grown."

"You've grown shorter," Theo teased. "I can see over your head now."

Thad laughed, a heartwarming sound that reminded Theo momentarily of their mother's laugh. "God knows you needed to be taller more than I," he said, "with all the battles you've been fighting of late."

"True," Theo agreed.

"It just means I get the smarts," Thad added smugly.

"Well, I don't know about that … "

The two mocked each other and joked and talked excitedly for long moments, before Theo heard the bells chiming.

"I have to head out soon," Theo said.

"Where are you staying?" Thad asked.

"I was just going to come camp–uh, reside here," Theo said, realizing he would be going without his friends for the first time in months.

Thad pushed on, ignoring Theo's disappointment. "Wonderful. We'll have some time here later to discuss things," he said. "I assume with the celebration of Princess Aurora's birthday, she won't miss you for a few days?"

"I'm not sure if she'll need me around," Theo half-heartedly admitted.

Thad laughed, making Theo's frown deepen. "I'm sorry," Thad apologized, "but unless you've become paranoid, addicted to your knight's work, or your homesickness has already turned to roadsickness, I think it's time you admitted you're in love with her."

Vulnerability sliced through Theo's heart, and he felt visceral rage at his brother's perceptive intrusion on the most hidden secret—and closely guarded fear—of his heart.

"Your silence speaks volumes," Thad observed. "So I was right."

"Why would you think that?" Theo asked in the best neutral tone he could muster. "You haven't seen me, or her, in four years."

"Don't give me a time fallacy, Theo. You're forgetting I've known you your whole life, *and* I was the one who nursed your broken nose after you met her that first time."

"It wasn't broken," Theo huffed.

"Well, broken or not, it was pretty smashed in."

"I deserved it."

"You said as much when you'd met her. You never railed about how a seven-year-old girl could slug you, nor did you, for once, seek to return the favor. Which prompted me, at the time, to worry you believed yourself to be half in love with her already."

"People don't fall in love when they're ten."

"People don't tend to insult their future ruler and live to tell the tale, either."

"Well, I don't really tell that story," Theo muttered. "So let's talk about Uncle Thom's letter. What did it say?"

Any additional teasing Thad would have gladly dispensed to his younger brother disappeared at the change in topic. "Keep your voice down, would you?" Thad's voice dropped low for the first time. "The Grand Father doesn't know I've found it."

"Why would he worry about it?"

Thad stilled. "It's not entirely pleasant, for one," he finally said, "and you have to remember, Uncle Thom and Father didn't exactly get along with Mother's family."

"Well, what does he know of love?" Theo asked. "It's not like Mother wanted to go live in the convent over by the coast. She told us before, remember? She fell in love with Father and they got married."

"It's more complicated than that." Thad grimaced. "Father, uh, didn't exactly want to marry her."

Shock made him pause for a moment. "Well, he did, so that's all that matters," Theo said.

"Not quite." Thad reached into his frock and pulled out a faded, folded letter. "It's actually pretty bad."

The yellowed parchment was old, wrinkled and faded in his hands. For a brief second, Theo thought the paper had traces of pink and green patterns.

And then realization hit him, hard. "The Magdust," he said.

If Thad was surprised at Theo's comment, he did not say so; he just nodded. "Yes. From what I know–the Grand Father has mentioned it in some other letters I've read as well–she tricked him into marrying her. Uncle Thom had been out fighting when Father came home from battle–you remember, when he was wounded delivering the message to the King about the Farnish kingdom?–and met Mother, and got married to her. Uncle Thom probably didn't realize until a few years after you were born that something was very off about their marriage."

"I don't really want to hear this, Thad."

ONCE UPON A PRINCESS

"I know," he said, sympathetic. "But take the letter. Read it, and get it back to me. You've always been the one who wanted to make peace with their deaths, not their lives. And you are right; the results aren't going to change because some of the circumstances have."

Outside, Theo could hear the trumpets blasting again. More suitors arriving for the princess' birthday, no doubt, he thought disgruntledly.

"I really will need it back, in case the Grand Father ever does decide to go through his papers again," Thad told him.

"Okay." Theo words were as hollow as he felt. He looked back at Thad. "How did you get through, after learning this?" he asked.

Thad sighed. "You were younger than me, only seven, when our parents were killed and we were taken to the church. I remember some of what Uncle Thom mentions in the letter. And," he added, "I have been here all these years. Marriages are not usually made based on mutual affection, unless it is for the love of money and titles." He dropped his voice down to a whisper. "It would shock you, how many wives and husbands have confessed to me of affairs, prostitution, and illegitimate children."

"Are you cynical, then?" Theo asked. "Is that what you're trying to tell me?"

"Not cynical," Thad replied. "Just used to being sad."

"Is that why you have decided to stick to priesthood?" Theo asked.

"Is the princess the reason you have decided not to?"

Theo didn't take the bait. "I asked you first."

Thad gave a wan smile. "I'll keep trying," he warned. "But for now, my answer to your question is no. I like being here, Theo. I like helping people when they need it; I have brothers and sisters and children here, people who rely on me, look up to me. This place, while you have found it to be stuffy and quiet and boring, is structured and settling to me. This is no last resort for me, as many kings and even our uncle had thought it to be. This is home. I've learned to read and research and write. I need no marriage to look for love or magic, as I've found those here, in God and in books; supernatural love has called me here and bound me to this place, and I have chosen to choose it back, and celebrate it rather than escape it." He paused, nodding to the palace just on the other side of the chapel walls, where Theo knew Rose was getting settled in. "Surely you can understand that. All I long for is here."

"I can understand that," Theo agreed, "even if I have not experienced it yet." His hand reached for the rosary beads he kept around his wrist, only to recall he'd given them to Rose before she left.

The bells chimed again, followed by trumpets blaring, and Thad tugged on Theo's arm. "Why don't I accompany you to the princess? I'd love to see her again."

The wicked playfulness in his smile made Theo grumble, but he hurried after his brother nonetheless, grateful and groaning to be in his company once more.

ONCE UPON A PRINCESS

8

The maids bustled about in her old room, replacing the curtains to her window, pulling up and shaking out rugs, taking down all the sheets which hung over the furniture, and opening up her closets. She could hear every pronounced "*Tsk, tsk,*" every stifled hum, every muffled curse.

All the rushing around and unpacking made Rose feel even more like a stranger in her home. Not even just a stranger, she thought bitterly, but an unwelcome guest.

Mary laughed next to her, sitting on the edge of a teacup that one of the many faceless maids had brought it only minutes before.

"Are you getting a tea bath?" Rose asked.

Mary giggled. "I was thinking about it. This tea sure tastes good, though."

"I'll take your word for it."

"Come on, cheer up, Rose." Mary gestured around the room. "This isn't so bad, right? When was the last time you slept on a mattress this fine?" Mary flitted over to the bed and jumped on it as if to prove her point. "This is the first mattress I've seen in years that lets me bounce back that wasn't being bounced by a team of horses."

Rose smiled and ran her fingers over the fine silk sheets. "You have a point there," she conceded.

"And Sophia's in the adjoining room over there," Mary said as she pointed to a nearby door, "and Ethan is just down the hall. And of course, my cousins and I are near the throne room." She gave a sly grin. "And Philip's just a few floors below you, if you miss his company that much already."

73

"Mary!" Rose sputtered. "I don't care about that."

"You seemed to like him well enough. And he's handsome," Mary goaded. "I don't think it would be a hard thing, to marry him and to try to get an heir."

"He's definitely handsome," Rose agreed. "But I don't want to marry someone just to give the kingdom an heir. I could've done that years ago."

"Why didn't you?" Mary asked. "I know it's not ideal. I've given you everything I could, just changing the curse that Magdalina placed on you. But you're running out of time."

"I might be running out of time, but I haven't run out of options," Rose shot back.

Mary cocked an eyebrow. "Is there someone else?" she asked, too innocently for Rose's taste.

"No, of course not!" Seeing the maids glance her way, Rose stood up and turned to the maids. "All right, everyone, thank you. Please get out now."

The maids, all surprised to be stopped mid-task, bowed quietly and retreated out the door. Rose slammed the door behind them, already well aware of their discordant chattering. She turned back to face Mary, ready to denounce all thoughts of any earthly happiness, when she nearly jumped in surprise.

A girl, hardly more an inch shorter than her, stood staring at her from behind the door. With her long black hair, brushed to a bright sheen and hanging free, and her rigid posture, she could have easily passed for eighteen. Her dark eyes stared closely at Rose, examining her as if she was a new species of some sort. Her stare was not quite rude, but not so innocent that Rose missed the playful indignation behind it.

"Where did you come from, Isra?" Rose asked dryly. "Crawling about the tower passages again? The Queen won't like you getting your dress dirty."

The girl frowned at the cold welcome. "It's nice to see you too, Aurora," Isra said. "Nearly four years have passed, and you haven't returned any of my letters."

"I felt obliged to let you rot away in your perfect world, here at home," Rose replied. "My letters would have disrupted you from your studies."

"You really did not think your sister would have wanted you to write, especially after all the long treatises and the epic poems I wrote?" Isra's eyes went wide with an injured quality while Rose tried not to grimace at the thought of the many rolls of letters from Isra she had never read. "Ronan is hoping to hear of the battle stories when he gets back."

Rose frowned. "Where is our darling brother? Did he finally learn to stop following you into trouble?"

"He's making his rounds throughout the kingdom with a royal guard. It's part of his knight's training."

"Oh. Well, he'll have to wait to hear them later."

"I want to hear them, too."

"You're too young for them."

"I'm not two years younger than you."

"*I'm* too young for some of the battle stories."

Isra's chin came up, delicate and defiant all at once. "Theo didn't seem to think I was too young for them. I've saved all his letters."

"You leave him out of this," Rose snapped, instantly making a mental note to strangle her former squire the next time she saw him. "He wrote to you against my orders."

"We were such good friends before, Rora," Isra said, her voice beseeching her sister to recall the good times, even using her special sister name. "What changed?"

Rose nearly spit out, "I turned thirteen!" but she stopped herself. Her thirteenth birthday was the day the King had decided to try to marry her off to any one of a handful of suitors. After scaring most of them off, and angering the rest enough to leave, she'd decided to leave her home as well, and the burden of her curse became her own. Instead, she put her arm around her younger sister. "Nothing changed, Isra. The world just came crashing in on me, and I refused to let it hurt you."

Tears flecked into her younger sister's eyes. "So you hurt me instead."

Rose blanched.

Before she could say anything, Isra shook herself free from Rose's awkward embrace and erected the wall of pride inside of her once more. "The Mother Queen sent me here to tell you she and the King will see you in precisely an hour, down in the ballroom. They want the rest of the city to see you with their own eyes." She shook her head resentfully, adding, "I can't believe she couldn't just send a servant up here to your tower. Although, I suppose when it comes to you, I essentially *am* a servant to her."

Rose said nothing. Once she had been cursed, her mother and father had done everything they could have to help nullify the spell and protect her. The spindles on the spinning wheels were all collected and melted down, and with further taunting, the King ordered all the spinning wheels in the kingdom to be burned. Rose remembered thinking after hearing that, how much he sounded as though he could order the rest of the world's spinning wheels to be burned as well.

Finally, after a year of Magdalina's taunting, and unable to secure a way to stop the curse from coming true, the King decided they needed to have another baby. But unlike before, with Rose's birth, they decided to keep it a secret. They had the Queen shut away for weeks, ironically proclaiming a strange sleeping sickness, and a little over a year later, she gave birth to Isra and Ronan, a pair of fraternal twins. The knowledge of their birth was kept hidden, only known to the leaders of the church and the main household of the castle keep.

Because of the secrecy, Isra had grown up in Rose's shadow, watching as people showered her older sister with their love and pity, and in the shadow of the curse, as the King and Queen became more like living martyrs, persecuted and oppressed by the fact their first child's life would be cut short.

Rose could only wonder if Isra felt as used and useless as she did; it was too easy to see Isra was lonely. Isra was also the first member of the royal family to remain ungifted by fairy magic, as King Stefanos had been worried such magic might draw too much attention.

"If it makes you feel better," Rose said, "I've never liked the Crown Princess' tower."

"Why would that make me feel better?" Isra asked, wrinkling her nose.

"You'll get to enjoy it more, should I abdicate the throne and leave it to you."

Isra rolled her eyes. "You won't abdicate of your own accordance," she muttered. "It's been your dream to rule Rhone since we were little and we played make-believe. Remember? You used to make Theo play the King and Ronan would be your son."

"Some things are better off leaving to make-believe," Rose told her, wistful and saddened by the long-ago memories of long-ago hopes and dreams. "Some things only come true in make-believe worlds."

"All the world might as well be make-believe to me," Isra said. "I haven't been out of these walls since you were home last time. You should have taken me with you."

Rose sighed. "If it will make you happy, I will. Someday. I've got to get out of here again soon."

Isra's eyes narrowed in suspicion. "Did someone else tell you?" she asked.

"Tell me what?"

"About tonight."

"What is it?" Rose asked. "I figured it was some kind of tournament going on. I saw the jousting fields being set up."

"The King has decided to introduce me to the kingdom."

Rose raised her eyebrows in angry surprise. "Why? Tell me why," she demanded.

Mary, who had been lounging comfortably in Rose's bed, also shot up. "That's utterly irresponsible of him," she said.

Isra sat down in one of the nearby chairs and picked up the cold teapot. "Mary, since you're up, would you warm this for me, please?" she asked prudently.

Rose nearly knocked the tea out of her hands. "This is serious, Isra. Magdalina could come after you. I would have thought you would be safely wed before the King decided to present you to the kingdom."

"That's silly," Isra said. She flashed an appreciative smile at Mary, who just finished dazzling the teapot with a quick fire spell.

"Silly?" Rose yelled. "Protecting you from a fairy curse is not 'silly.' I would be the one to know!"

"It seems silly to me," Isra retorted. "Why would it really matter? Think about it, Rose. If Magdalina *did* learn about me later, when I have been married and I have children of my own, who is to say she wouldn't go after them? Or even *their* children?"

Rose hated to admit Isra had a point. "I was going to try to make peace," Rose whispered. She sat down in the chair opposite of Isra and put her head in her hands. "This complicates things."

"Make peace? With Magdalina?" Isra burst out laughing. "That's comical. She doesn't want peace. She wants the rest of us to be just as miserable as she is."

"Why is it all the evil people in the world want everyone to be unhappy?" Rose asked, not expecting an answer.

Isra gave her one as lifted the teacup to her lips. "Because it's easier to make everyone else miserable than it is to make yourself happy."

Rose smiled despite herself. "You've grown up while I was gone, didn't you?"

"Not enough so someone would really notice. And no one will, since you've come back." Isra sighed. "Tonight was supposed to be for me. The King didn't actually think you would come home, you know, after you routinely ignored his letters and you either fought off or found a way to escape his guards. He probably thought it would be an easy forfeiture of the crown."

"Our father has never known either of us very well."

"Speaking of which, we should probably go down and see him." Isra set aside her now-empty teacup. "Thanks, Mary."

"No problem," Mary replied with a smile. She suddenly giggled with excitement. "I'm going to get to see Fiona and Juana again!"

"I guess it's just a day for reunions," Rose muttered, putting down her own teacup, still half-full. Looking out at the nearby spiral on top of the church, she fingered the gift Theo had given her. His rosary beads hung from her wrist like a bracelet, but it seemed more like a talisman. She wondered how Theo was doing with his brother, and if he was on his way back to her yet.

ONCE UPON A PRINCESS

9

As Rose made her way down to the ballroom to meet with her parents, Theo hurried up through the chapel passageways and over the bridge. With his brother at his side, crowds easily parted for the well-known Brother Thaddeus and his strange, but also strangely familiar guard.

A loud bell sang out from the town center nearby.

"It seems the tournament games are starting," Thad remarked.

"I'm glad," Theo said. "I'll want a distraction later tonight."

"Why would you keep fighting?" Thad asked. "You're home. There's no need to worry about food or supplies or money. And you'll always have your reputation to carry to the next one."

"I like to practice." Theo walked through a pair of castle guards into the keep and spotted Rose coming down the stairs to his right. He straightened at the sight of her. "And Rosary likes the distraction."

"Rosary?" Thad asked, ready to tease his brother.

But he instantly recognized Theo's expression and turned to face the woman who had inspired it. Thad found even he had forgotten what a sight the princess was.

"She looks good with short hair," Thad muttered.

"Just don't tell her that," Theo said with a grimace. "Rose hates it when people compliment her beauty."

"After hearing it all her life, I'm sure it's tiresome," Thad agreed. "And beauty is fleeting, compared to what is in the heart and soul."

"That's pretty much how she takes it."

"Still, she's beautiful."

"Shut your mouth; here she comes."

Rose brightened up at Theo's presence. "Theo," she greeted him warmly, as though it had been a year since their parting, rather than the long hours it had really been. She reached out a hand to him before stalling.

"Princess." Theo bowed, thrusting his elbow into Thad's chest. He could hear her sigh, but he caught sight of his rosary beads tied up like a bracelet on her arm.

"Are you ready to go with me to see the King and Queen?"

"Yes. Thad offered to join us as well."

"Excellent." Rose smiled at Theo's older brother. "Theo's missed your company, and there's nothing like having a couple of priests around as witnesses." She wriggled her nose at Theo. "Even one who is not dressed like a priest."

"Especially for a princess dressed up as a knight," he agreed with a grin.

"Theo, is that really you?" Isra stepped forward.

"Isra!" Theo reached out a hand to her as well, taking it and giving her knuckles a friendly caress and a kiss. "You've become quite the lady while I was gone."

"And you've become quite the hero. Thank you for your letters." Isra looked over at Rose, who was clearly not happy she had been interrupted. "I know my sister didn't want you to send them, so I owe you extra thanks."

Rose blushed. "We can reminisce after we meet with our father," she said. "Let's go." She turned to Mary. "Mary, would you go and collect Sophia and Ethan? Please ask them to bring a sample of the treasures we've collected on our journeys. Tell Sophia to wear her sword, and Ethan to bring a small collection of his favorite maps."

"Yes, Rose!" Mary saluted. "I'll return shortly."

ONCE UPON A PRINCESS

"Why all the fuss?" Isra asked.

"It can't hurt to show some of my adventures have been rewarding to the kingdom." Rose shrugged. "Anything to keep them off the topics of marriage or abdication."

The walk to the ballroom took longer than she'd ever remembered or expected. With each step, she felt her heart press against her, climbing steadily into the space between her ears to beat rhythmically with the passage of time.

"We'll be all right, Rosary," Theo whispered, so only she could hear. She gave a shrug and then he added, "By the way, you look beautiful."

Her anger flared, which sparked enough bravery to see her through the last steps into the throne room.

"Princess Aurora of Rhone!" The announcement was declared across the room, but to Rose, it felt like it resounded throughout the world.

She made her way, with her friends and sister flanking her, towards the King and Queen, down the red carpet that went from one end of the majestic room to the other.

The throne room never failed to amaze, she thought, admiring the elegance of the high ceilings and inlaid trim. Even as a small child, she marveled at how it would display her power and rule one day.

King Stefanos I, her father, sat down on the right, having married into the throne. Her mother, Leea, while she was the true monarch by birth, made no secret of the fact she despised politics and left most of the trouble of ruling a nation—even one as small as Rhone—to her husband.

Leea met her daughter's gaze and smiled warmly, glad to have her home; the King, by contrast, frowned, no doubt knowing the difficulty ahead.

ONCE UPON A PRINCESS

"Welcome home, Princess Aurora," King Stefanos announced. "We have long desired to see you again."

She bowed and her party followed suit. As she knelt, she saw Sophia and Ethan, along with Mary and her fairy cousins, walk into the threshold of the throne room. Please let them wait for my signal, Rose silently prayed. The King wouldn't like it if they were interrupted, even if it was because of riches and tales of fame, adventure, or even war.

"Rise," Leea called, standing up. She headed over to Rose and hugged her. "My daughter is home."

The rest of the ballroom attendants erupted in cheers. Trumpets blared and music soared from the orchestra pit below the dancing floor. Banners waved and for the moment, crushed to her mother's bosom, Rose felt her world all but disappear among the many celebratory waves of color and happiness and chaos. She angled herself to see her father smiling on the throne, and felt a wave of relief. He had not moved, but any sign that his heart had was a good sign. After catching his gaze, she gave him a smile. He finally did move, and come over to stand beside his wife, and rumpled her hair affectionately.

Rose squeezed her mother tighter to her, a moment of perfection washing all over her.

And then it was over.

"We'll talk soon, Aurora."

Rose nodded but felt the bile rise in her throat. Was it all an act? she wondered. Or was it possible some affection was real? She wanted it to be real so much, it was too hard to determine if it was or not.

She turned to hug her mother again and caught sight of Isra's expression. Her younger sister, once more shuffled to the side, looked grim.

To her right, she watched as her father headed over to Thad, and shook his hand, whispering something to him as well. Rose wondered what he was telling Thad when the King turned to Theo, and blatantly stared at him with a cold glance. Rose saw a brief flicker of shock before Theo disguised his face.

Something is wrong.

Her mother unleashed her, and Rose looked up at her, trying to read her expression. But her mother had her eyes resting on someone else, and before she could stop herself, Rose turned to see one of the guards meeting her mother's gaze.

It was Roderick, she recognized, one of the four guards her mother had insisted go with her when she'd set out into the world at thirteen. It had been the only condition of her blessing. Rose almost smiled; Roderick had been the one she'd nicknamed "Redbeard," because of his bright ginger hair and shaggy beard. It appeared she should have been paying closer attention when her mother handpicked them for her service.

Anger struck her, making her feel exposed, as she realized she'd had her mother's spy in her midst the whole time.

But as she watched the guard, who was looking back at the Queen, their eyes speaking all the words which were forbidden, she suddenly wondered if he wasn't more than just her mother's spy.

"Mother?" Rose broke the silence between them, too irritated by the tender yearning in her mother's expression.

"Yes, darling?" Leea ran her hand affectionately down Rose's short hair, smoothing it out where the King had ruffled it.

"What's going on?"

Leea's eyes turned sad. "We've made you upset."

"A little," Rose admitted. "What's with you and Roderick?"

Leea sputtered. "Nothing," she said. "He's just a dear friend, and he has been writing to me, of course, while you've been out."

"I figured that much out." Rose decided to hold her mother's waywardness against her later, when there weren't so many people shouting and yelling. "What's going on with the throne? And Isra?"

Leea sighed. "You're just like your father, you know. Always wanting to get down to business right away."

"Pleasantries should not be needed between family."

"We are family, but we are in the business of keeping a kingdom," Leea reminded her. "And some of us *like* the pleasantries."

"Well then, how many days of 'pleasantries' am I going to have to put up with before we discuss the King's ultimatum?"

"We thought we would give you till your birthday to discuss everything," Leea mumbled. "It's only a few days away."

Three days suddenly seemed like an eternity. "I could make it to Magdalina's castle in that amount of time," Rose muttered.

"What? What did you say?" Leea asked, distracted once more by the gaze of the redheaded solider. "I didn't hear you."

"Nothing." Rose nearly rolled her eyes before she caught herself. "What are you going to do about Isra?"

"She's our distraction."

Stunned, Rose could only hug her mother once more. "Can I go now?" she asked.

"Pleasantly," the Queen told her. "Go back upstairs and dress for the evening. The tournament has begun, and you'll need to be here every night for the ball."

"Fine. But during the days, my time is my own."

Leea sighed. "You aren't going to embarrass us by participating in the tournament games, are you?"

"I wouldn't dream of embarrassing you." Rose detached herself from her mother, wondering if it would be the last time she hugged her and turned around.

The King had moved on to talk with some of his friends and consulting warriors. He didn't notice as she grabbed Theo and turned toward the door.

"Are we presenting the gifts tonight?" Sophia asked.

"I guess not," Rose told her. "Sorry for making you go through the trouble."

"What about all the stories?" Ethan asked. "Should I begin rounding up some minstrels and singers?"

"What for?"

"To compose songs about your travels." Ethan grinned. "Couldn't hurt to move in and win the people's hearts over."

"Ethan has a point," Theo spoke up. "If you're worried the King is getting pressure from the people, now is the perfect time to quell their fears." Rose exchanged a knowing look with Theo at his words; while she hadn't said it aloud, that was part of what she was worried over.

"We have some awesome stories," Sophia added. "I'll go with Ethan and get them started."

Rose nodded. "All right. Take some coins with you." She turned to Theo. "Come with me."

She led the way through the chaos of the ballroom entrance and the keep's entrance before ducking behind curtain and settling into a hidden corridor. Rose jerked Theo in behind her.

"What is it?" he asked.

"I need you to do me a favor," she said. "Isra told me, and the Queen confirmed it, that they're going to present her as the prize in the tournament, not me."

"Well, that's good, right?" he asked. "So you don't have to worry about pressure to get married. And you know Isra. She'll love the attention."

"This isn't good; this is a disaster!" Rose snapped. "What if Magdalina comes after her?"

Theo thought about it. "Well, they still have Ronan, right? I don't imagine they're going to reveal all their secret heirs. Or else Isra would have been against it even more."

"Stop thinking about Isra." Rose felt the temptation to slap him as she recalled he'd been writing to her while they had been traveling all around, trying to find a way to break her curse.

"I wasn't thinking about her, specifically," Theo objected. "I was trying to think about this from the King's perspective. If Magdalina comes to curse Isra, which she might not–"

"How could she *not* come after my sister?" Rose asked. "She cursed me, didn't she?"

"Well, yes–"

"Well, then, why let Isra go? She wouldn't just ignore her. And I can't let Magdalina curse her." Rose sighed. "I know you wouldn't let it happen, either."

"Of course not." Theo took her hand, momentarily shaking her out of her concern.

Without his gloves on, she could feel all the blisters and calluses of his hands and fingers; but she could also feel an aura of strength and capability as his grip tightened over her own small fingers. She watched as he reached out his other hand and placed it on his other.

"You know I would do anything for you or your sister."

Rose's eyes jumped up to his face, and Theo wasn't sure he should have said anything. Her eyes were wide and her lips were parted in a rare moment of honesty. The darkness of the surrounding passageway suddenly hugged him closer to her as the sudden urge to kiss her crashed through him.

"Rose?" A new voice drifted through the curtain as it was pushed aside.

Rose jumped, pulling her hand free of Theo's, and turned to face the new arrival. "Philip."

Prince Philip shuffled in, his tall figure imposing on the small space they shared. "I saw you come this way and thought I would follow. I didn't realize you were having a meeting with your subordinate."

Theo felt anger boil inside of him, suffocating him.

"We're trying to think of a plan for the tournament," Rose explained. "It turns out Isra is the one who is going to be featured, rather than me."

Philip nodded. "Are you worried about her?"

"Tournaments like this have happened before," Theo said, "where the King might offer his daughter, and the throne, as the prize."

"Sometimes it is not always a tournament," Rose added. "My father was assigned a task, for example." She turned to face Philip. "But I'm worried for Isra. My parents have kept her a secret from Magdalina, and never placed any fairy magic on her. I fear she will become a target for Magdalina as well as the many suitors."

Suddenly Rose frowned. "Did you know about Isra?" she asked Philip.

Philip sighed. "Please don't get upset, Rose," he said. "I knew."

"So you were coming for her?"

"My brother and your father have become close friends," he explained, "as the kingdom of Einish has been attacked by the Grand Isle Kingdom in recent years. The Grandians are determined to capture the isle of my home and kingdom. With your father's help, we have managed to keep them at bay. When we met at the Channel battle, I was introduced and he told me he had two daughters. When the time came to make offers, I would get the first invitation to prove my worth to Rhone." Philip's hazel eyes twinkled in the darkened corridor. "For we all know well how much Rhone concerns itself with worth."

Rose wrinkled her nose. "That's true," she conceded. "Well, then, I will request your assistance as well." Turning back to Theo, she said, "I want you to watch over Isra whenever possible. I don't want Magdalina to get to her, and your priesthood instruction will help. I'm sure my mother has a bunch of duties and formalities lined up for me, so I can't protect her at all times."

Looking over at Philip, she missed the shadow of disappointment as it crossed Theo's face. "Since he'll be with her, you'll have to protect Isra by warning off her suitors."

"I am one," Philip reminded her. "I doubt anyone will take me seriously; they'll only see it as a play for the princess' hand."

"Then *make* them take you seriously," Rose nearly shouted. "I'll not have my sister touted as some grand prize just so her ego can revel in it while our enemy sees her as an avenue of revenge."

She shook her head. "Magdalina has been seen around town. I can't let Isra be cursed as I am."

Philip looked solemn. "One day, when we have time, princess, I have a story to tell you."

"What?" Rose's determination flouted.

"I have a story to tell you," he said, "about myself and who I am. While I am staying at the castle, my crew and I meet at the Golden Fleece Inn following the daily activities. Perhaps one night, you would like to join us?"

Theo frowned. Was Philip trying to woo Rose? he wondered. From the confused look on Rose's face, he could tell she was thinking along similar lines.

"Protect my sister during this tournament, and I will be more than happy to hear your stories later, Philip," Rose replied.

She turned to Theo. With a single look, she said nothing and everything all at once. And then she lowered her eyes and pushed past him. "Now, excuse me. I have my own role to play."

ONCE UPON A PRINCESS

10

Rose had promised her mother she would do nothing in the tournament to embarrass her family, and she vowed to keep her promise.

By vowing not to lose any of the games she participated in.

"You're not seriously going to joust, are you?" Fiona the Fairy came clucking into the room as Rose was pulling her breastplate over her head.

Rose had to stop herself from telling Fiona to leave her. Out of all the fairies, Fiona tended to be more busybody than body. With her brown hair pulled up into a tight bun streaked with gray, and her long nose and stern expressions, Rose thought of Fiona as a type of mother hen, always trying to manage people or take them under her wing. She didn't always think it was a bad trait, but Fiona seemed to do it out of a desire to control things. And while Mary seemed to genuinely like her, and Juana had a deeply set compassion in her heart, Fiona was always planning plans no one would follow, spreading rumors which had at best doubtful origins, and offering solutions where she "miraculously" turned out to be the hero. That was largely why Rose didn't trust her.

However, it seemed to Rose that her mother the Queen had no such reservations, as Fiona was also her mother's confidante. After the Queen had mandated her presence at the rest of the tournaments nightly balls, Rose felt it best to make sure she had the upper hand when dealing with her.

If nothing else, Rose thought, the last four years had taught her about the necessity of strategy, and the danger of trusting emotions.

"Fiona." Rose forced herself to greet the tiny fairy amiably. "How nice to see you again. Mary and I have missed you."

"I could tell, by all the infrequent letters Virtue came back with. Or should I say without?"

Why is everyone so upset I didn't write? "I'm sure you could tell by the infrequency of the letters themselves how busy we were on the different battlefronts," Rose said as innocently as possible.

Fiona folded her arms across her chest. "Her Majesty sent me here to commend you on your performance in the ballroom last night, not to chitchat about your travels."

"I'm glad Her Majesty was relieved to see I remembered how to dance."

"She also commends you on your special attention to Prince Philip."

"Special attention?"

"You danced with him more than once at the welcome ball, and frequently talked and laughed with him. She is pleased, as is your father, which only makes My Lady happier."

"I met him on the way to castle," Rose explained with a shrug. "He seems nice enough."

And he is handsome and funny. The voice in her head made her sigh. She knew her parents must see Philip as a long-awaited answer to their fervent prayers, but she loathed to see herself do the same.

"I'm sure Isra will make him a lovely wife," she said.

Fiona sputtered. "But, princess, what about you?"

"Haven't you heard, Fiona? On my eighteenth birthday, I'm just going to prick my finger on the spindle of a spinning wheel, and fall into sleeping death."

"But *you* could marry Prince Philip, and secure the crown!" Fiona shook her head in distress. "Dear, dear princess, you need not worry for Isra's sake."

"I don't want to get married, Fiona," Rose told her. "Marriage is for people who have the time to find true love, like my mother and father." She carefully watched Fiona's face as it contorted and her mouth released a snort. She saw her opening and pounced. "I mean, after all, my mother is deeply in love with my father. How could I ever want anything less than what she has?"

Fiona patted her shoulder. "Dear, your mother is not as in love with your father as you would think. He frequently ignores her and leaves her alone while he attends to the matters of the nation. She is a beautiful bride, but he has no interest in attending to her love."

"So ... he loves her but she doesn't love him?" Rose asked, pretending to think this through.

"Well, it's more complicated than that," Fiona told her, "but all relationships are like that."

"So she loves him but he doesn't love her?"

"No, it's not like that. Your mother was offered in exchange for a task, remember?" Fiona asked. "Your mother's father tasked every available man in the nation to search out the Rose Ruby."

"And he found it?"

"Yes, of course. He went on a long journey to the Far East, and there it was. He brought it back, and presented it to the King, and he wed your mother that very day."

"Where's the ruby now?" Rose asked. "I've never seen it."

"Treasures come and go," Fiona muttered noncommittally. "But he loved your mother enough to go and get it."

Either that or he loved the idea of being King. The thought burned through Rose with a clarity as sharp as her broadsword. "And ever since, his love for her has grown cold?" Rose asked.

"Not exactly," Fiona muttered again. "But my point is, affection is not a proper requirement in a marriage for a girl like you or your mother."

"I see," Rose murmured.

Before she could ask about Roderick and the Queen's relationship, Mary and Juana popped into her room.

"My Lady," Juana cried. "I'm so happy to see you again!"

"Hello, Juana." Rose gave her a big smile as she saw the bouquet of flowers in her arms. "Did you miss me so much you brought me flowers?"

Juana giggled. "Oh, I should have thought of that myself, but these are not from me, my lady." She handed the large arrangement of assorted posies to Rose. "These are from Prince Philip. He asked me to send them to you this morning."

"Oh. Well, that was very nice of him."

"It's very sweet," Mary agreed. "First the dancing, and now flowers. He's trying to court you!"

It would take more than amusing company and flowers to break the lock around my heart, Rose thought. She wondered briefly if she hadn't been cursed, would she have allowed herself to get swept up in a romantic daydream?

Hopefully not, Rose decided as she arranged the flowers in a bowl. Curse or no curse, her mother's wandering gaze seemed to be proof a marriage made for reasons of greed and power would not result in a lasting happiness.

What do I want? Rose asked herself silently, as she finished putting on her armor and headed down to the courtyard. She didn't even really know what she wanted, she decided. She'd

ONCE UPON A PRINCESS

wanted the crown, if only to prove to others she was not going to die, or fall victim to some curse by a bitter half-fairy. She supposed she just wanted to be free, and that meant she had to be powerful enough to be free.

But there was another wish in her heart, she knew, and she would never let it go, or she would die along with it.

"Rose."

At the sound of Theo's voice, she perked up. "Where's Isra?" she asked him.

"Isra's sitting on the throne by the jousting yard outside," Theo told her, pointing out the window. From what Rose could see, a heavily veiled figure was sitting stylishly between the King and Queen. "They didn't announce it was Isra," he said. "They've only been using her title, 'Princess of Rhone.'"

"So this is a joust for *my* hand?" Rose asked. "Amusing."

"It seems they're playing the tournament game pretty deep," Theo told her, falling behind her as she moved forward. "My guess is they will announce you or her to be the prize, depending on what you decide with your father later."

Rose paused and thought about what Theo said. It was a good guess. "That's probably right," she said. "There's definitely power in being vague. Isra gets all the attention she wants, but she is never in danger. My parents get all the interested suitors to battle and rather than risk their honor, they'll risk my decision to stay and keep the throne or abdicate and succumb to the curse."

"You won't fall victim to the curse if I have anything to say about it," Theo promised.

"Thank you, but we can't worry about it right now. Go to my sister and stay with her."

"I was thinking of fighting," Theo remarked. "If I win, I could ask for my knighthood to be granted, officially."

"Not this time, Theo." Rose met his eyes, surprised to see the depth of the dark circles underneath the green emeralds. "You're the only one who can protect Isra from Magdalina."

"Thad could do it while I participate in the games."

"*I'm* going to fight," Rose told him. "Do you really want to find yourself fighting against me?"

"Scared of me?" he asked her, reaching out to tug a lock of her hair, as he'd done so many times before. Heat flared inside of her again at the affectionate touch, warming her from the end of her hair to the tips of her curling toes.

Yes. Rose quickly shoved that part of her mind aside. "No. But I'm scared for Isra." Her eyes went wide and misty as she added, "Please?"

Theo crumbled inside at her openness, but laughed it off. He'd have to find another way to handle the ache in his heart, he decided. "All right," he told her, before bowing and turning away. "Let me go and get my priestly robes, so your father won't even have to see me."

He was gone before Rose could ask him what he meant. "Thank you!" Rose called after him. She wasn't sure he heard her.

"Rose."

"Huh? Oh, it's you." Rose bowed to Philip politely as she watched Theo's back disappear into the crowds. She turned her face up to see the prince grinning down at her attire.

"I see I'm going to have some steady competition today on the field." Even through his neatly trimmed beard, Rose could see a hint of a dimple.

"I figured I'd help you scare off some of the competition," Rose said.

"You might have some luck in keeping the competition from competing," he said, "since no honorable man would willingly joust with a girl, let alone a princess."

"I don't let them see I'm a girl beforehand. I keep my visor down and my helmet on. And I use a different name when I battle."

"I suppose that's allowed," Philip contended. "But I wouldn't want to do you the harm."

"Then you'll let me do the harm to you?" Rose grinned. "I didn't think an honorable man would be given to throwing the match."

Philip's smooth cheeks turned red. "You've quite a wit, Your Highness."

"We'll have to see if it is as sharp as your lance," Rose retuned, already brushing past him to hurry off to the first match of the day. "Remember your promise to me. Look after the princess."

Philip smiled as he watched her speed past him. "I most certainly will."

ONCE UPON A PRINCESS

11

Isra sighed. She felt her eyes closing under the waning midday sun, its heat bearing down on her through her veil. "How much longer?" she asked, turning to her self-appointed guardian. Or, she thought, more likely, her sister-appointed guardian.

"Too long," Theo muttered behind her, before trying to hide a yawn.

She snorted. At least he didn't bother to lie to her. Well, then again, why would he? He was as much her friend as he was Rora's, Isra thought. Or was it Rose now?

The sight of her sister returning after years on the road brought none of the joy she'd had previous to her parting. It seemed like Rora had gone, and Rose had come back. Theo, however, was much more Theo than he had ever been.

She looked at him now. Even in the silly deacon outfit he'd gotten from the church, he looked the perfect mixture of dashing and dangerous. The white frock clashed with his dark hair and sun-washed skin, allowing all the battle scars on his hands, neck, and face to slide more easily into view.

Fortunately, her father, from what she'd seen, didn't look past the priest outfit. "I wonder if Rose looks past it, too."

"What was that?" Theo leaned closer to her as the crowd cheered for the triumphant warrior on the jousting field. "What did you say?"

"Nothing," Isra said. "Any sight of danger to my person?"

"Just expiring from boredom," Theo teased her.

"This is nothing new, you know." Isra sighed. "No one is actually paying attention. Or at least," she said as she slanted him a gaze, "no one worth paying attention to is paying attention to me."

He shrugged. "I'm sure Rose will fix that," he said. "In fact, there she is now."

"*She's* going to joust *here*?" Isra asked. Her lips pouted.

Theo watched with renewed interest in the games as a small armored figure, garbed in familiar colors, headed out onto the field with a horse's bridle in one hand and a lance in another. A rush of pride and admiration involuntarily rushed out from his heart. He knew he would never grow tired of her helmet falling half a head shorter than all the other warriors, or seeing her shoulders square themselves as she went into battle despite her disadvantages.

Isra shot up to her feet. "What if she wins? She can't make an offer for me."

"Well, the joust is only part of the tournament," Theo reminded her. "I think it's safe to say she'll opt out of the last day's trial."

"What is it?" Isra asked. "You never know with Rose."

"Fortunately, in this case, we do know her," Theo replied. "The last day has a singing challenge."

Irsa raised her eyebrows. "Well, that'll do it. I don't think there is anything in the world that would make Rose sing again."

"She's certainly managed to keep that vow as long as I've known her," Theo said with a grimace.

"The day she made that vow was quite comical, as I remember it."

Theo had heard the story from several different sources. On Rose's seventh birthday, the whole kingdom had seemingly turned out in celebration. He knew from later it

ONCE UPON A PRINCESS

was at the King's insistence, to show Magdalina her curse could not defeat their spirits.

Rose had always been a gifted musician; the pianoforte, the harp, and even the mandolin had been quickly conquered by her nimble fingers and overflowing love of music despite her youth. It had been said the angels bent near the earth to hear the dulcet tones, and the whole world stilled that it might hear of her voice; Theo did not doubt it, from the way people chatted about it.

When she was asked to sing for her audience at her birthday, Rose complied with a child's willingness to please.

As she began the second verse of her chosen song, she noticed everyone was weeping, and she stopped, finally seeing their sadness for what it was—pity.

She stopped mid-verse, and ran away from the crowds and her parents and everyone else, heading towards the castle chapel.

Only to run into me, Theo remembered, rubbing his nose.

Isra's laugh caught him off guard. "I forgot about that," she said. "That was the day she broke your nose."

"Making it bleed is not the same thing as breaking it," Theo muttered.

"What did you say to her that made her hit you?" Isra asked.

"She asked me why everyone pitied the princess and couldn't stand to look at her without crying."

"So you told her the truth? About the curse and everything?"

"Yes." Theo shrugged. "I didn't know it was her at first; after all, I had yet to see her. That was the first week I'd arrived from the church near my home. But after I told her the story of Magdalina and everything, I told her to stop

ONCE UPON A PRINCESS

worrying about it, since it wasn't her problem. And then, after she insulted me, saying I must be blind, since *she* was the princess, I laughed in her face. I told her the princess was supposed to be a model of beauty and kindness, and I didn't think that it was her."

"She wouldn't have liked that." Isra laughed. "No wonder she punched you."

"I didn't say I didn't deserve it. But what I did get out of it is nothing short of a miracle of grace."

"What do you mean?"

"People sometimes ask me why I believe in God," he said softly. "And part of is because of Rose, even if she scoffs at the thought of a holy and divine existence. That day, I insulted her and she punched me. When I got the call to go to the palace the next morning, I was fully expecting to be whipped. After all," he said, looking at her pointedly, "the King had wanted to keep a great many secrets, and I'd managed to spill his biggest one.

"But I learned I was to take my daily lessons with Rose, and I was to be assigned her council in the church. And that's not the most amazing part."

"What is?" Isra asked.

"I got to be her friend." Theo looked on as the horn blared, calling the riders to their posts. "Since then, she gave me her trust, and I have always sought to be worthy of it."

Isra watched as his hand covered the pocket at the side of his frock, where she could see a small scroll had been stuffed inside.

Before she could ask what it was, Theo continued. "And I'll never forget what she's given me, even if we have to say goodbye."

ONCE UPON A PRINCESS

Was he talking about Rose, or himself? Isra wondered. She was about to ask him when a loud *clang!* rang out from the field, and she turned to see Rose had hit her target while dodging the other warrior's lance.

The crowd cheered with wild enthusiasm as the spunky winner did several circles of jubilance. But Isra remained still as she watched Rose peek out her visor, looking up in her direction before her gaze drifted to Theo behind her.

"Do you think you'd win against her?" Isra asked.

"I don't know," Theo admitted. "We're pretty even when we fight. Jousting is about the same, since for all her small size, her speed and aim are hard to combat."

"Are you going to dance with her later?"

"Huh?" Theo frowned as he finally looked back at her. "Dance with her?"

"Yeah. Since you're stuck watching over me all day. You should dance with her later."

"Is there a competition?" he asked.

"Why does there need to be?" Isra asked. "You obviously want to join her."

"I wouldn't mind the fighting," Theo acquiesced. "I could use a distraction to stay awake." He glanced at her with a smile. "Not that you're not interesting to watch, Isra."

Isra laughed. "If I'm exciting to watch while I'm sitting here bored, you must be ill. Especially after all the fighting and traveling you and Rose and everyone did across the world."

"It sounds more interesting with all the exciting parts strewn together," Theo confessed. "I won't lie; it was much more enjoyable than being here. But the food is better here."

"I made Rose promise to take me one day," Isra said.

"I'm not sure how long she is staying this time." Theo looked down to see Philip taking his position on the jousting field. "And she might decide to stay yet."

"I doubt it. She seems to agree with you, that traveling is preferable." Isra hesitated before she continued. "Do you think you'd go off on another adventure and leave her here?"

Theo's hand covered his pocket again, pressing down on the letter he kept safe. He sighed to himself. Isra could be just as irritating as Rose, he thought. Especially when it came to perceiving his own secrets.

"I don't know." He pressed his hands together in front of him, trying to keep them occupied. "I don't really want to think about it."

That was as close to the truth as he could get.

"Okay." Isra sighed and relaxed back into her seat, just in time to watch Philip overcome his jousting adversary.

Theo watched as Philip took off his helmet and waved to Isra from where he stood. As Isra waved back and even smiled–though Theo doubted Philip could see it from the field–he decided to concentrate on his uncle's letter, the one Thad had given him. Otherwise, it was too tempting to worry about any princess falling in love with Prince Philip.

Sir,

My time is short, so forgive this quick note. We have not been introduced due to your objection to the marriage of your daughter Eleanora, but I am the brother of her husband. I regret to inform you of their tragic passing. I have evidence to believe they were killed as a result of their participation in Rhone's forbidden Magdust trading.

As I write this, I am preparing to send your grandchildren to you. As a member of the council of knights under King Stefanos I, I am frequently gone and feel unable to provide for them an adequate home. I beg you to receive them at the church, asking for your charity if not your approval. The boys are innocent and ignorant of their parents' activities. I have been around long enough to know that much. Thaddeus has just turned ten, and Theophilus will be eight in a few short months. I have not confided to them this and plea, as a final request, for you never to tell them. The boys are good-hearted and eager to learn; there is no gain to be had in spoiling their early years with the truth of their mother's transgressions and their father's insatiable greed, nor to tell them of their brutal execution by a dangerous fairy-man called Everon, Magdalina's lead henchman in the war against Rho—

The letter ended in a splatter of blood, well-worn into the parchment after all the years it had been kept safe by Reverend Thorne. Theo supposed Uncle Thom had failed to finish it, as he himself was attacked, probably in his own small house. Or maybe he had followed his parents to a drop-off site, where they had traded the illegal Magdust to strangers, and was caught as he headed to gather Theo and Thad to safety.

There were only two clear memories from what Theo could remember of that night: Uncle Thom dripping with blood, and the pink and green fairy dust patterns glowing in the hearth, as the tapestry, the one his mother proudly displayed in the home of their house, burned into ashes.

No, Theo recalled bitterly, there was another memory: Uncle Thom telling him to forgive his family, and to forgive those who killed them. He felt the raging desire for revenge burning inside of him all over again, as his noble uncle breathed his last, only hoping for the eternal security of his nephew's soul.

ONCE UPON A PRINCESS

It was, out of all of the memories he carried, the one he hated the most.

"Rose is up again. Oh, and look who she's up against. This should be interesting."

Theo jolted back to the present at Isra's words. He looked to see the final round of the joust had started. Rose was taking to the field on one end while Prince Philip pushed down his visor on the other.

"Should I stop her?" Theo asked Isra.

"Could anyone ever stop my sister?" Isra asked, standing up. "I'd better get Mary or Juana ready to go down there."

"You don't think she'll win?" Theo asked.

"Prince Philip hasn't lost a joust yet," Isra told him. "And he's stronger, and pretty fast as well."

Before he could say anything else, the horn blared and the riders were off. Theo watched as Rose took aim, ducked down, and kicked her heels into her horse's flanks. She was determined to win.

Theo's eyes squeezed in pain as their lances collided with their shields. A glaring *clank!* followed by the sound of metal banging onto the hard ground made him look.

Rose was lying on the ground, her armor punched in on the side, with blood oozing out from under her surcoat.

12

*

"I'll get him back for it tomorrow at the fencing duels," Rose insisted. "There's no need to baby me about it."

"Forgive me then, as my body does not appear to be able to enact your wishes," Theo muttered back. He held her hands lightly, pulling her gently through the various turns and spins of the dance.

"You could, at least, let me dance with Philip," Rose said. "I'd get him back early, in that case."

"There's nothing I want you to do less," he assured her. "If dancing with me will be the closest thing to resting you do tonight, I'll make you dance with me all night."

"Don't make me hate it."

He gave her a charmingly slanted smile. "You couldn't hate it any more than you do fighting with me."

"But I like fighting with you," Rose argued.

"Exactly. Dancing is just the form our fighting is currently taking."

"After I take down Philip, I'm going to come for you, Theo."

"I suppose I'll have to ask for my rosary beads back then."

"Yes, yes, don't worry. I'll give you plenty of time to say your prayers."

"I'll hold you to that."

"After you picked me up off the field today, I'm sure you'd be able to." Rose followed through a turn, allowing herself a moment to briefly blush. Theo and Isra had run down to see her as some squires and pages had helped her off the field. He'd plucked her up off the ground, not even waiting for her to pull off her armor. She'd felt the deep seriousness of his anger and frustration, all wrapped in concern, as he and Isra had scoured the castle for Mary. As much as her side had hurt from Philip's lance, her heart ached with pleasure as Theo clasped her to his chest.

"Anything to get you to cooperate," Theo said.

She gave him a glittering smile. "What happened to your cold-hearted logic?"

"It's in my other priestly frock."

Rose laughed as Theo twirled her again, and immediately regretted it. Many faces turned at the joyful noise, watching her, wondering about her. Even her father caught her eye.

She merely tried to smile back, but it was for nothing. He narrowed his gaze at her before turning his attention to Theo.

"He doesn't like me," Theo told her as he saw her quizzical expression. "He's probably still angry at me for telling you about Magdalina's curse."

Rose thought about what Fiona had told her about her father and mother and their marriage. "I don't think he's forgiven me, either, for asking."

"Some people do have problems with forgiveness," Theo said noncommittally.

"If you're talking about the situation between Philip and me, I can assure you it'll be fine. He'll gladly apologize by the time I'm finished with him tomorrow."

Theo grinned. "That's not what I was thinking of."

"What were you thinking of?" Rose asked. "Come on, you can tell me."

"I was thinking of my parents, to be honest." Theo didn't want to tell her the whole story. "I talked with Thad some yesterday and, well, was a little surprised to hear my mother had tricked my father into marrying her somehow."

Rose didn't miss a beat. There was no pity, there was no surprise. "My mother was a prize in her marriage," she offered.

"Is that what you fear?" Theo asked. "Being a prize for someone to win?" When she didn't answer, he sighed. "Anyone who loves you, Rosary, will always find you to be a prize. The trick for you would be to find someone who knows he could never be worthy of it."

Theo's quiet tone felt like a condemnation. "I don't know if I agree with that," Rose argued. "Queen Lucia found a way to make her man worthy of her love."

"Yes, but Queen Lucia also lost her freedom. She lost her heart to a man she deemed worthy, but did not respect her in return."

"All the better reason never to do something as foolish as fall in love."

"There are plenty of foolish things to do or not do, regardless of love. I'm pretty sure my mother used Magdust to get my father to marry her."

Rose looked vaguely surprised and deeply curious. "Did she use the enchantment herself, or did she bribe him with the money to be made in dealing?"

"I'm not sure," Theo acknowledged. "Does it matter?"

"If you are asking if it matters to me that your parents had an unhappy or falsely happy marriage, then no. Fiona told me my mother and father are pretty much only on speaking terms."

"People in your mother's position don't really marry for love," Theo reminded her.

"I agree. That's why I don't want to get married. I'll not marry for the sake of the kingdom. I'll only marry for love."

ONCE UPON A PRINCESS

"And yet you don't want to fall in love." Theo pretended to be in deep thought. "Hmm, I can certainly see the logic of that."

Rose nodded in the direction of her mother. "I'm pretty sure my mother is having some kind of affair."

"She wouldn't be the first, monarch or otherwise. Thad was telling me just yesterday there are apparently loads of people running around, being unfaithful."

"That doesn't keep you from getting married, does it?"

He gave her a smile. "I doubt I'll get married."

"Why not? You'd make a good husband," Rose said, surprising even herself at her comment.

"I only want to marry for love, too," he admitted.

"So? You're not cursed like I am. It'd probably be very easy for someone to fall in love with you. Look at Queen Titania. She was practically drooling all over you."

"Thanks." Theo laughed. "But I think I'll stick to mortals. I'd feel weird growing older while my fairy wife would stay young."

They laughed together before he added, "But in all seriousness, I have my own reasons for not wanting to get married. I have some things to do yet, and I wouldn't want to drag a bride or a family into the middle of it."

"Revenge is a sticky mess," Rose agreed with pride.

"And it's about to get stickier," he told her as the dance ended.

Her hands tightened affectionately around his as a new song started. "If you're going to make me dance with you, you're obligated to entertain me. Tell me what else you've learned from Thad."

ONCE UPON A PRINCESS

"I know who killed my parents," he said. "It was one of Magdalina's underlings. Some fairy named Everon. I don't know if he's still out there, or still alive—"

"Oh, he is," Rose interjected. "He was the fairy leading the attack on Philip's caravan."

Theo allowed the information to sink in. "He's still in the woods?" he asked. A heady storm of vengeance brewed deep inside, renewing its hold on him.

"Probably."

"I should go find him."

"Can you wait a few more days?" Rose asked. Her fingers laced themselves around his urgently. "I need you here yet."

Theo sighed. "Must I, Princess?"

What broke her was hearing her title, rather than any name he'd ever had for her; it was as if he was already trying to place some distance between them. She jerked her hands out of his, stopping in the middle of the dance floor. "Never mind. Just go. I know it's important to you, and I have to accept that it's more important to you than I am." She gave him a brittle smile and then turned on her heel and sped toward the nearest exit.

"Wait," he called after her.

He waited until they were clear of the room before he reached out and grabbed her hand. "Rose, that's not fair."

"*I'm* not being fair?" Rose asked.

"No, you're not." Theo maneuvered in front of her quickly, drawing her to the side of the room. "You don't know how long you're going to be here—"

"I have plans—"

"You don't know what you're going to do about your father—"

"He doesn't matter to me—"

"And you have no idea whether or not you'll cave in to marriage in order to keep the throne or not."

"That's not true! Don't you know me at all?"

"Don't you know *me* at all?" Theo asked. "Rose." He reached out, catching her face between his hands. "I honestly don't know, because *you* don't know. You can't deny me my revenge while you deny me your heart."

Rose felt the floor disappear beneath her. "What are you saying?" she asked.

"I'm telling you I've always been here for you. But I can't stand beside you if someone else will, or you decide you want to stand alone." He let her go. "Your father, the King, is making you make a decision. You need to make it. I'll wait for you; I'll stay beside you, as much as I can, for as long as it's my duty to do so. But there are some things that I just can't do."

"It's never been your duty to coddle me," Rose snapped.

"Should I forgo my revenge for you?" he asked.

"No! That's not what I want at all."

"Then tell me what you want!" Theo exclaimed. "Just tell me what you want me to do for you."

"I want you to stay away from me." The words were out of Rose's mouth before she could stop them.

Theo just stared at her, frozen. And then he bowed. "As you wish ... Rosary."

Before she could take it all back or reverse the command, he left her. Alone.

13

Rose wiped the bleariness from her eyes, silently cursing herself for the hundredth time since she'd woken up. After her argument with Theo, she had tumbled and turned all night in her covers, unable to find peace or any comfort in sleep. Despite Mary's keen work on her jousting injury, the pain in her side made the pain in her heart extra uncomfortable.

Her only comfort at the moment was knowing she was one more battle away from a well-earned nap. She turned with a mocking grin to face her last opponent. "Prince Philip." She gave a graceful bow. *At last.*

"You're not tired, are you, Princess?" Philip asked. "You've already gone several rounds."

"As have you," Rose shot back. "I can more than hold my own against you."

"Do your parents know you've been fighting in the competition?" Philip asked. "I'm just curious," he assured her, seeing the accusing look in her face. "I'm not going to turn you in."

No, he was too kind for that, Rose thought. "No, they don't pay attention to me during the day," Rose told him. "They only care if I embarrass them during the balls."

"Well, bad dancing is considered quite incriminatory in some circles," Philip replied, making her laugh.

"Atrocious," Rose agreed. "Right up there with the rest of the seven deadly sins."

"If we're going to focus on churchly rituals," Philip said, "I feel I should confess to you, I've never fought a woman in battle before."

"That you know of?" Rose asked teasingly.

Philip nodded. "I suppose you're right. That I know of."

"I would have thought the good people of Einish would have appreciated doubling their ranks with the women warriors."

"Our women fight every day," Philip told her. "Maybe not on the battle field with an ax or sword, but they fight every day, taking care of everyone who would cause their own destruction if left up to their own survival. The men and children of Einish all owe it all to the women when it comes to keeping civilization going. I have a high respect for them and all they do."

"I can respect that," Rose agreed.

"Then please let me assure you, I hold you in the same respect; even if I know I will not be worthy of yours." Philip bowed again, before holding his sword up in the starting position.

The battle chime sounded, and the fight began. Rose paced herself, realizing early on that her patience was a key factor in how well she did.

The point of a battle was to be ready to defend primarily; punishment was secondary. Patience was the difference in winning a battle and dominating the enemy, and Rose had enough experience in the past to know patience would pay off in the long run.

Philip lived up to her expectations. He lashed out a moment later, and at once, Rose began to read him as a warrior.

He had a nimble quality to his feet, she noticed, making it hard to follow him at times. But there was a drawback, of course; he was too much of a dancer, too willing to make the battle look good, rather than just win. While she admired him for his artistry, her practicality proved triumphant first. She scored the first point by slicing through his armor at the kneecap.

"Point," he huffed, obviously dismayed at losing a point in the first several minutes.

His strength would be her biggest obstacle. Sizing him up, he was quite tall and his shoulders were broad. But she'd had plenty of practice with Theo, so she wasn't worried about that—

She missed a step and felt Philip's sword slice through the leather of her surcoat. "Point," she conceded. "But you technically missed me."

"I'll try harder next time," Philip promised.

"Hmm," was all her reply was as the battle began again, and she took to analyzing him once more.

After a few more strikes and parries, she resigned herself to a longer battle than she'd expected. Philip was a hard soldier to fight, she decided, because he was handsome. He was strong and svelte, talented and smart; he had the look of a legendary prince fighting off demons, working to protect his lady love.

A resounding *rip!* distracted her from further studying Philip's enchanting fairy-tale face. Rose was surprised; she'd scored the next point by sheer chance. She managed to slice through one of his sleeves as he charged at her; she ducked and rolled away, her sword breaking from her grasp and puncturing the chainmail at his wrist.

One point to go for me. Rose pulled back to settle herself from her unexpected gain. Even good surprises will keep one off balance, Rose recalled.

As Rose and Philip circled each other in a short interim, cheers and jeers came from the surrounding crowds. Several people had bet money on the outcome, while others were there to support their respective knights. Rose caught a glance at Sophia, letting her know she would need her armor tended to once she was done.

"I enjoyed dancing quite a bit with your sister last night," Philip told her. "Isra is very charming."

"She is," Rose agreed.

"She speaks highly of you."

"I'm surprised."

"I'm not." Philip tugged down his ripped sleeve and adjusted his glove. "I am a younger brother myself, and I know well what the adoration of an older sibling feels like."

"Really?" Rose decided to move. She sliced her sword through the air. "What happened to your brother?" she asked. "Why is he not here?"

"He is recently married," Philip told her, trying to angle a successful blow himself. "To a beautiful bride and princess."

"I see."

"It is my hope to have similar success," he continued, paring with her jabs.

"Why? Is she a rich princess as well?"

"No, not really," he told her. "But she loves my brother considerably."

"How do you know that?" Rose asked. "She could have been lying."

Philip's brow furrowed underneath his visor. "You needn't sound so pessimistic, Rose."

"I have to be, being cursed and all."

"She was cursed, too, you know."

"What?" Rose frowned. "Who was cursed?"

"My sister-in-law." Philip dove forward and rolled as Rose pressed forward. "She was placed under a curse by an evil sorcerer. She changed into a swan every day, and it was only by the light of the moon each night she was able to become a human again."

"Really?" Rose faltered, accidentally allowing him an open blow on her; if she had not slipped at just the right second, she would have been hit. "How did her spell get broken?"

"I'd love to tell you the full story when we're finished here."

Rose felt her second wind come flying through her, as her relentless curiosity propelled her onward. "Augh!" she cried out, as she leaped over Philip and grabbed him by the throat, wrapping her sword around him as she pulled up his helmet, just enough to see the barest glimmer of skin.

"I submit," Philip muttered, his voice wavering only in the slightest. "For now."

I won. Rose felt a rush of happiness run through her and she looked up to the crowd. She watched as Sophia cheered for her, and Mary sent off her magical glittering confetti, and Ethan, ever with his coloring pad in hand, held up a poster he'd drawn of her triumph over a nameless warrior, face down in a puddle of blood. Grinning, she looked around for Theo before remembering she'd banished him from her presence.

And then the hollowness slithered in. This is what she had been so worked up about? Soothing her pride? Proving herself to be equal to a man in skill was one thing; finding out

119

she could be as arrogant and conceited as one in victory was another.

Rose lifted her sword from the side of Philip's neck. She stepped back and bowed her head, hiding the disappointment on her face. "You have my respect," she said. "Excuse me."

And then she turned away, put her sword in its scabbard, and headed off before her name could be announced as the winner.

ONCE UPON A PRINCESS

14

Theo expertly skirted around his grandfather's presence as he made his way through the old chapel as he looked for his brother. His brother had never been an early riser, Theo recalled, but then, neither was he. He grimaced as the noon bells rang throughout the small chapel.

By the time he reached the private quarters, the tolls of the bells had diminished into echoes.

He knocked on the door to his brother's small room.

"I'm in the middle of my prayers." Thad's voice called out with just enough of a yawn Theo had to grin.

"It's me."

"Who's me?"

Theo knocked again. "Would you just wake up, Thad? It's me, Theo."

"Oh. All right, hang on one moment." Theo had put his hands over his mouth to keep from laughing as he heard his brother scrambling around, trying to make himself presentable.

"Not shirking your duties as a man of God, are you?" Theo asked.

"Not at all," Thad murmured dryly, opening the door and rubbing the sleep from his eyes. "The psalmist says to make a joyful noise unto our Lord, and before noon, mine happens to be snoring."

"Try telling that to the Grand Father," Theo said with a snicker.

"I'm purposefully avoiding it; he'd think me to too loose with scripture. Hurry up and come in." Thad opened the door. Theo had to smother another laugh as he saw his brother was wearing his frock inside out.

Theo slid into the room and nearly fell over a pile of books. "Wow, I didn't know Reverend Thorne was starting a new library in your room," he said.

"Yes, yes, laugh it off," Thad muttered. "But how else do you think I'm able to hide things like Uncle Thom's letter?"

"There are more?" Theo asked.

"Of course there are letters of the dying," Thad explained, clearing off a small chair. "But there are also other things of equal interest. I found a manuscript of the old fairy legend of Queen Lucia just last month, for example."

"Queen Lucia?" Theo repeated. "It didn't happen to have the real story of her fate, did it? Titania was pretty adamant that her mother made some horrible decisions."

"I haven't finished reading through it, but it's proving to be interesting," Thad replied. "Magdalina's story is much more captivating at the moment, however."

"Magdalina's story?"

"Yes. Did you know she's only a half-fairy?"

"Titania mentioned something about that."

Thad continued excitedly. "She is the offspring of a powerful sorcerer and Lucia, apparently. The half-mortal blood in her body makes her immune to the weaknesses of fairies, and the half-fairy blood makes her extremely hard to fight against."

"I guess that would explain why she's not as tiny as Mary or the others, too."

"Yes."

Theo thought about it. "How would you defeat her? If she is able to undo fairy magic, and stronger than humans?"

"Are you asking this, or is the princess?" Thad asked.

Theo snorted. "This isn't for her. She's tired of having me around to do things for her. I was just asking because I was curious."

"Curious," Thad repeated. "What happened?"

"That's part of the reason I came to find you," Theo told him. "I read through the letter. Uncle Thom had horrible penmanship."

"Agreed."

"But he said that our parents were killed by Everon, one of Magdalina's minions. Rose said she actually fought with him in the woods. He was the one who attacked Prince Philip's carriage."

"I've noticed they've been getting along quite well," Thad said, running a hand over his chin thoughtfully. "I was at the singing competition part of the tournament last night. I saw her cheer for him after he performed. I heard a rumor she is hoping he'll win."

"That doesn't have anything to do with this," Theo grumbled.

"No, it doesn't, but I was wondering if that was the reason you are upset at her."

"I'm not upset at her for that!" Theo snapped. "She can be friends with whomever she wants to be friends with. And I don't care if she wants Philip to win the tournament. She can marry anyone else she wants, or she can smash anyone else's heart she wants. I don't care."

Thad just looked at him.

Before he could say anything of comfort, Theo shook his head. "She already told Philip and me all she wants is to protect Isra from Magdalina's anger."

"That's why she asked *me* to come to the singing round last night, then," Thad muttered. "I guess that makes sense if she really did banish you from her presence."

"She did not 'banish' me. Not exactly." Theo felt his hands go numb as he clenched them. "Can we go back to Uncle Thom's letter? We're getting off topic here."

Thad clapped his hands together. "All right, brother. Sorry."

"I'm sorry, too," he apologized. "Rose did give me some time off away from her"–that was the least painful way of saying it–"so I have been using that time out in the streets to try to see what I can find out about Everon."

"There would be a lot of gossip going around during the festival for the princess' birthday and the tournament."

"Exactly," Theo agreed. "Which is how I was able to confirm Everon was seen around here lately, and that he has been under Magdalina's command for several decades now."

"He is her son."

Theo went silent with shock.

Thad eyed him curiously. "I told you, I'm reading her story," he reminded him. "And she had a child with a powerful fairy King. She named him Everon." He leaned back against the wall. "Although I suppose by now the Everon we're looking for might possibly have children of his own, so the one the princess fought could be his grandchild or something like that."

"It seems too much of a stretch." Theo drummed his fingers against his knee absentmindedly as he thought it through. "Even though it's still hard to believe Magdalina had children at all."

ONCE UPON A PRINCESS

"Magdalina wasn't born the tyrant she is now," Thad said. "She was actually born with the name Malena. She later changed her name to fit her demeanor."

"Either would be fitting, considering both names come from Mary of Magdala, the woman who housed seven demons within her."

"The observation is sound, and it's good to see you remember the Greek language so well." Thad's tone softened to one of sympathy. "I think Magdalina wanted to take the hope of salvation out of it, especially after the fairy King disposed of her and Everon."

Theo said nothing in reply. Nothing could convince him the woman who cursed Rose deserved his pity, after seeing all the years Rose suffered as a result of her curse.

"The fairies seem to be a fickle lot when it comes to love," Thad continued. "Lucia went through several mates before Benedict."

"Benedict?"

"The man who became the first knight of Rhone. From what I have read, he was one of King Arthur's castoffs."

Theo smiled. "I see why you've been hoarding books. It sounds like you've been enjoying them a lot."

"I do like to read," Thad agreed with a shy laugh.

"Did you find anything about how to break Magdalina's curse?" Theo asked.

"There's only one legend said to be able to break through the spell of any magic," Thad replied. "And that's true love's kiss."

Theo sank into silence again. Rose had decided it would be too painful for anyone to love her many years before. She had set out on her adventures with the same determination she had reserved for keeping herself from falling in love.

ONCE UPON A PRINCESS

Thad caught his brother's expression and quickly added, "But it's not something that's been proven, of course. True love is not always proven with a kiss, and anyway, it seems just a little silly, right? Too easy, maybe?"

"Right," Theo muttered. "Too easy and too hard."

"Especially with all those enchantments about luring people into seductions and all that. I don't think it'll be very helpful to us. Now, if you want to *kill* anyone, I can help you out there," Thad continued, "as there are several proven methods to kill all sorts of creatures in these books."

"Even Everon?" Theo asked.

Thad's expression darkened into a contemplative brood. "Yes, even Everon," he murmured, heading over to one of his pile of books. "Let me just look here … for a moment. I think … I think I have a book which can help us."

It took several moments of Thad thumbing through the various texts and scrolls lying around his room before he plucked one up in triumph. "Ah-ha! Here it is." He handed the scroll to Theo. "Here you go."

Theo squinted at the small handwriting on the ancient paper. "What does it say? I can't read Old Anglo, especially in this small type."

"Right there." Thad pointed to a line of text. "Dragon's blood. There are some dragons with blood that can kill any magical creature." He reached around Theo's shoulder and pulled out a map. Theo caught sight of the faded atlas and, after briefly thinking Ethan would want to see about updating it, noticed it was covered with strange markings.

"What are those?" Theo asked.

"Oh, those. That's the Romani language," Thad explained. "I haven't broken the code of it, but I do know from the pictures here"–he pointed to the small sketches in the map's frame–"that a special cherub guards the deadly dragons."

"Cherub?"

"Yes."

"Like the angel in the scriptures?" Theo asked.

"Yes. Some say she is a lesser cherub, keeping captive the offspring of the deadly serpent from Eden." Thad's eyes glazed over. "I've heard the legend before."

"How do you hear so many pagan legends? You live in a church."

"All truth is God's truth." Thad's eyes twinkled. "And besides, I still enjoy a good pint of mead at the tavern like anyone else, Theo."

"Does the Reverend Thorne, the Grand Father, know of that habit as well?"

"I'm avoiding the conversation with him on it, but only because so much of his holy living is subject to cultural whims." Thad cleared his throat. "You'll have to go with me sometime. There are a lot of travelers who pass through Rhone–many trying to get to the bigger kingdoms around here–and will gladly tell you a tale or two for a pint."

"That's how you heard of the dragons?"

"Yes. The legend says there is a Garden of Thorns, where the dragons live, unable to escape to the other side. Wouldn't that be something to see, Theo?"

"I guess so. If you want to be a dragon kebob."

Thad laughed. "Well, if you look here, the exact location of this map says it is in the Romani territory. It's not too far a journey from here; it would be no more than four months by land, and even shorter if you crossed the sea."

"Certainly no journey is too far to travel for something that can help us kill Everon."

ONCE UPON A PRINCESS

There was a tense silence before Thad spoke up once more. "Are you sure revenge is the best option, brother?"

Theo sighed. "It is the only one I haven't completely tried."

"What of forgiveness?" Thad sat down across from him. "If you haven't forgiven him completely, you can't say revenge is all that's left."

"Enough." Theo stood up. "Everon didn't just kill our parents, Thad; he murdered them. Uncle Thom was mortally wounded by him. And it wasn't just the people in our family we lost, but also our home, even our destinies. Do you really think you would be here, at the royal chapel, if Father had lived?"

"If Father had lived, I might very well be capturing helpless fairies and crushing them into Magdust, much as he did."

Theo sighed. "I didn't mean it like that."

"Why not mean it like that?" Thad asked, his patience wearing thin. "You can't mean we were robbed of a perfect life, or even a normal life. No one automatically gets to have a normal life, Theo. No one is guaranteed *any* quality of life. We are allowed to make of it what we can, that is all."

"I know." Theo's fists churned as he sought to control his temper. "I know, Thad. I'm just upset about it. And I have been for years."

Thad put his arm around his brother. "I know. I get upset to see you this way. I don't want to lose my brother to Everon, too."

"Thad?"

"If I have any advice for you, Theo, it would be to seek to protect those you love, rather than seek to destroy those you hate." Thad sighed. "If you're going to ruin your life, I'd much rather it be for love rather than hate."

ONCE UPON A PRINCESS

15

Theo felt his brother's words haunt him as he left the church. As he headed back towards the castle, anger surged through him, along with doubt and fear and confusion.

Was it really so terrible to know what hate was? Theo wondered. Was it so abysmal to have nothing to live for besides revenge, when nothing seemed to calm the storm inside of him?

Theo was crossing the courtyard when he saw Rose. She caught his gaze and he faltered.

Was it so irrational to believe all the answers to his life's troubles lay at the end of a road filled with thorns and an angelic gatekeeper? Especially when the alternative was to watch his best friend, mentor, and princess pass away into everlasting sleep, loved by her people, used by her family, and possibly tended by a husband who would never know her as he did?

Rose began to move toward him. Theo didn't move.

The road of revenge offered nothing but loneliness, danger, and uncertainty. But surely being lonely was better than being completely helpless.

"Theo." His name on her lips called into his heart, and he wondered for a moment if he was not the one who was cursed, that he had unwittingly bound his heart to a woman who intended only to ignore the power of hers?

"Princess." He bowed respectfully, the motion still strange, yet oddly comfortable.

Rose bit her lip. She'd been unable and unwilling to sleep well the previous night. After her fight with Philip, she knew she needed time alone to sort out what she had to do. And while she had no clear choice or path to pursue when it came to marriage or abdication, she knew she had to apologize to Theo first.

Seeing him struck her; she watched him sauntering around, wondering how he never saw how the other women eyed him with more than a lingering glance. With his strong back straight, and his stride purposeful, only his eyes hinted he was somewhere else. They clouded over in unseen worlds, some that she shared, and others she knew nothing of.

She felt her tongue run dry. Why was it so hard to apologize, to say what needed to be said? Rose wondered. It wasn't like she had been right to treat him like a servant, when he was so much more than that to her.

Cowardice secretly won. "It's about time for my birthday celebration dinner," she said, avoiding the subject. "I was wondering if you would accompany me down to the banquet hall?" Her deep blue eyes settled into his. "Please?"

Theo hesitated.

"I've missed you."

Rose's admission was soft enough Theo was not entirely sure she knew she had said it aloud. After a moment of silence more, a moment of watching her misty eyes, he gave her a teasing smile in return. "You need someone to lead you in prayer, Rosary?"

She giggled before smirking back. "I did wear these strange prayer beads," she said, holding up her wrist, where the gift he had given her jangled cheerfully.

"What do you mean, 'strange?'" he asked, taking her arm and tucking it into his own.

"I've seen rosary beads before. Many of them are plain and the same color or material. You have a lot of different ones," Rose said.

"I'll tell you why, someday, if you'd like."

"Sure." Her eyes lit up. There was something special about the idea of 'someday.' She smiled. "It'd make a good campfire story for when we head out to find Magdalina."

Theo stopped short in his tracks. "*If* we need to find her."

"What are you talking about? Of course we have to go and … " The hall was silent with tense worry as Rose's gaze followed Theo's to the center of the ballroom. Though Rose had no memory of ever seeing her in person, there was no mistaking the towering horns of her atora headdress, the sharp folds of her black robes, and the authoritative rigidness of her staff.

"*Magdalina.*"

Rose pressed her eyes together and blinked, while the rest of the crowded ballroom collectively gasped in horror.

Magdalina turned around as Stefanos and Leea gaped at her. "I see, after all these years, I still managed to turn heads and render crowds speechless." She turned and took a step towards Stefanos. "Maybe I should see about starting a fashion line."

Rose watched her father recover. "Seems like a waste of your talent," Stefanos muttered. "You were always prone to mischief, not helping people."

"And you know well why that is," Magdalina shot back. "Speaking of which, where is your darling sunshine, Princess Aurora?"

Theo dropped Rose's arm and stepped in front of her.

Stefanos cleared his throat. "Haven't you cursed her enough?"

"It was not I who cursed her so much as you have," Magdalina muttered back.

Rose stepped forward, pushing past Theo. "I am here," she announced. Eyeing her enemy warily, she graciously tilted her head. "Welcome to my seventeenth birthday party, Magdalina."

Theo held his breath as Magdalina turned to face Rose. He silently prayed she would be okay; but as he watched the resolution on Rose's face, he was reminded all the time of the fearless boldness of Rose as she negotiated treaties between people and countries.

His breath released itself as peace settled onto him. He knew everything would be okay. Eventually.

"So this is the Princess of Rhone," Magdalina murmured as she came over to stand next to Rose. "Such a pity you cut your hair."

Leea nodded behind her; Rose bit back a sigh.

"But I suppose though it is not the style, it suits you," Magdalina admitted.

"Thank you," Rose said. "And while I don't know what your hair color is at all, I would say you've made your own style as well, with that headdress."

Magdalina was clearly taken aback by Rose's response. Theo stepped up beside Rose, grateful he had decided to wear his knight's armor rather than his priestly frock. His hand rested easily on his sword.

Magdalina was amused at his actions, dismissing him easily in her estimation. Her sneer aimed its venom back at the King. "I see you've raised quite a spirited child."

"My father did little to raise me," Rose said, surprising everyone with her interruption. "And I am no longer a child."

Magdalina looked down at her. "No, I suppose you are not," she conceded, "if you would speak with me as an equal."

"I would," Rose insisted. "Just as I would ask you to remove the curse you placed on me."

Magdalina's sneer curled sharply. "You would speak to me as an equal, but you are far from my equal," she observed. "My mother's sword at your side would confirm that."

"I would ask you to remove the curse as well," Theo spoke up. "I am not your equal, and I well know it, but I also know every sentient creature placed on this earth is capable of mercy."

"Capable of mercy?" Magdalina fumed. She looked at him. "What do *you* know of mercy?" He was about to answer her when she held his eyes, and thoughts of revenge came to mind, revenge over his parents' deaths. "I see you have had seen some religious schooling. I should think you, of all people, would find my curse is rather fitting. That a promised child should suffer for the sake of another's transgression?" She laughed as Theo's gaze dropped to the floor.

"Whose sins should my life atone for?" Rose asked.

"Why, your father's first, and your kingdom's second," Magdalina said. "Wasn't it obvious? Perhaps you are more yet a child than you realize. Indeed, if this is a question of mercy, it is mercy for others, rather than yourself, that prevents any removal of the curse."

Magdalina's eyes darted to the throne, where Mary and Fiona were hovering nervously. "I see it has already been altered. Pity. I would have thought death was more favorable."

"Is there no way you would remove the curse from me then?" Rose's patience was thin.

Magdalina shook her head. "No, I will not. Not after all the trouble I went through. I specifically sealed it with a blood sacrifice," she told Rose, holding out her wrist to show a slim scar.

The Queen moaned and fainted, and Stefanos glared at Magdalina. "Have you come to gloat then?"

"Why, no," Magdalina snarled. "Not at all. I've come to see if you've learned your lesson."

"What lesson?" Stefanos asked. "That your cruelty is too cruel? That for all the times my knights have sought your head, you've only gotten stronger and stealthier? That you would punish me through my daughter for the rise of the Magdust trade?"

"One would think you would be more concerned with your daughter than yourself," Magdalina retorted. "Maybe I am mistaken?" She turned and looked back towards the ballroom entrance. Rose followed her gaze and saw Magdalina's attention fall on Isra, who was accompanied by Philip.

"So what I am supposed to do?" Rose spoke up.

Magdalina turned her attention back to Rose reluctantly. "Well, you have a year left. What do you have to do?" she asked. "You are supposed to be a grown woman. What do you say you have to do?"

Rose felt the unspoken aspects of the question burn into her. *What do you have to do for your father? For your throne? For your kingdom? For anything but your own heart?*

Magdalina nodded, as if reading her thoughts. "I have been watching you, Princess; for all these long years, I have kept watch over you, seen you fight, felt your anger and sadness over your fate." She sneered. "And it is a good curse, too. I should never think to find its equal in all the realms of time. But nevertheless, you have transformed my curse into a blessing in its own right. I suspect," she said, her gaze flicked over to Theo, "there is even more to it than that."

"What are you saying?" Rose asked.

"I'll let you think about it on your own," Magdalina told her, an arrogant smile on her ghoulish face. With one last wicked look at Stefanos, she added, "Happy birthday, Princess Aurora," and disappeared in a flash of grisly, green light.

Rose sighed as the rest of the ballroom was torn between horrified silence and intriguing whispers. "Well, that put a damper on the evening."

ONCE UPON A PRINCESS

ONCE UPON A PRINCESS

16

The imposing nature of the door in front of her seemed to be a grand sort of metaphor. All the knocking over the years before she'd finally left came rushing back, along with the accompanying feelings of anger, neglect, confusion, and frustration. But now, at the moment when she was finally allowed inside, she could not bring herself to enter into its protected realm.

"Are you all right, Rose?" Philip came up from behind her just as she hesitated outside of her father's private council room. "I had just entered the room with Isra when Magdalina appeared."

Rose glanced over Philip's shoulder to see her sister's elegant features entertaining a mask of indifference. "I hope you didn't just leave her to come over here for my sake."

"Oh, no. I don't think I did. I hope I didn't." Philip scratched his head nervously, and Rose almost grinned at his boyishness. From all his manly ruggedness, it was endearing.

"I'm sure she'll forgive you," Rose told him. "But you might want to go see if you can coax it out of her sooner rather than later." She narrowed her gaze in a teasing manner. "Although from your pretty poetry yesterday, I'm sure she'll grant it to you. Eventually."

Philip gave a small smile. "I worry for you at the moment, Rose."

"Worry is not a practical response," she said, wishing she could will away her own worry just as easily.

"What would be, in the face of the unknown and terrifying?"

"Prayer," Theo spoke up, as he made his way to stand beside Rose.

"What did you find out?" Rose asked, turning to him.

"Magdalina is nowhere to be found, as we suspected," he said. "Thad is working with the other priests and elders on sealing the castle grounds by anointing them with oil. From all Sophia, Mary, and Ethan could discern, she came by herself, with no backup or guards."

"I know you must be disappointed," Rose murmured, sliding closer to him.

Theo allowed his hand to slip into hers, the familiar gesture of comfort suddenly made unfamiliar by the surprising recklessness inside her.

"It's all right," he whispered back, his breath tickling her neck. He straightened his posture and added in his normal voice, "Sophia and the others wish to accompany you to see your father. As do I."

"May I accompany you as you seek council with your father as well?" Philip asked.

Rose felt a wave of bravery crest over her. "I'm pleased to welcome any and all who would stand by my side during an audience with the King," she replied. "But he might dismiss you."

"You are our leader, Lady," Sophia spoke up, as she came around the corner. "Not even the King could dismiss me."

"That's right," Ethan agreed.

"Ethan and I aren't technically Rhonian, anyway," Sophia playfully reminded her, twisting a lock of her black hair, reminding Rose of her Greek roots.

"I have stood by you during worse days," Theo added. "For worse foes, and with worse weather."

"And I would like the opportunity to pay you back," Philip said, "for the debt of my life, which I owe to you."

"There is no debt," Rose muttered. "Indeed, I am tired of people who only feel attached to me by a sense of duty."

"Then I owe it out of friendship."

"I'd rather have earned it on merit than kindness."

"Kindness is its own merit," Philip said, giving her a wink.

"You have earned the title of our leader, Rose," Mary spoke up, as she led Fiona and Juana to the front of the door. "As well as our loyalty."

A moment passed as Rose looked down the line at her row of friends—a warrior and a priest, a blacksmith and an artist, fairies and humans, new friends and old friends. "Well, then," Rose replied, suddenly only worried her sentiment and her desire to cling to the moment would prevent her from moving forward. "This is the best birthday gift I could have asked for."

Turning, Rose fumbled with the door and forced herself through; no longer only for herself, but for those who would swear their fealty to her.

Stepping through the door, nothing seemed as real as it had when Rose had been dreaming. The walls were bare; the table at which the councilors and the King would discuss politics and campaigns long into the night was in need of repair. Several councilors regarded her from all angles around the table, while others did not seem to be able to look at her at all.

To Rose, the second most disappointing realization was how King Stefanos was the unapproachable father he had always been. The first most disappointing thing was realizing he was the first person who taught her that for anyone, loving

ONCE UPON A PRINCESS

her was too painful. Yet she did not, could not, blame him for that.

"Your Majesty," she mumbled, moving forward and bowing respectfully. Her party followed suit behind her.

Stefanos stood up. "Councilors," he called. "You are dismissed. I would speak with my daughter in private."

The councilors in the various chairs stood up and grumbled their compliance, though from their faces on the way out, Rose could tell it was reluctant. *They are worried he'll mess up.*

The thought comforted her.

After the door once more slammed shut, its echo resounding through the hollowness of Rose's stomach, she spoke. "Well, Father, if we are to speak freely, now is the time, at last."

"Aurora," he said, his voice weary and tired, "I'm sure you have a great many questions regarding Magdalina and everything else."

"I do."

"I cannot answer them. I can only say you are answering for them, and that is wrong."

"Yes, it is. You should have enough integrity as a ruler, if not a father, to tell me why Magdalina is punishing you."

"There are some secrets a ruler must take to his grave," Stefanos insisted. "All our great legends have secrets of their own."

"Not all of the secrets should stay hidden," Rose reminded him. "Even Benedict, the knight of our forefathers, is unable to hide from his life's work while he is in his grave."

He sighed. "One secret I will tell you. Your mother and I went many years without having a child."

"I know."

"But our fortune reversed itself; we received word that the God of Heaven had heard our prayers, and was sending us a child. You were a child of promise; you were not a cursed child."

Rose said nothing.

He continued. "We were so happy. So happy. And then, all of a sudden, with her curse, Magdalina stole all our hope and joy away."

"I was still there," Rose reminded him.

"Yes, but the dreams we had for you were not," Stefanos explained. "And so, because of this, I have put this day off as long as I possibly could."

He stood up from his chair at the head of his table, holding up a document scroll in his hand. Stefanos came to a halt in front of her. "Here."

Rose took the paper from her father and looked at it. "My abdication," she muttered, seeing the expectant document. "It looks different from what I'd imagined it would."

"Either that or you can marry a suitor here." Stefanos looked past her to Philip. "I see you've been making friends with some of them."

"And this is what you think is best for me?" Rose asked.

"Not for you, Aurora." Stefanos straightened. "The kingdom. Only you can save the kingdom now."

"What of Isra? Or Ronan?" Rose asked. "They are royal offspring as well. Ronan is the first male-born of the nation in three generations."

"Only you," Stefanos repeated. "You are the heir to the throne. You are the one who is gifted by the fairies, and you were the one prophesized to save the lineage from dying out. Even if Ronan or Isra take the throne, there is danger for them; you saw how Magdalina came in here tonight. There is no stopping her. You can't bring that upon your siblings, can you?"

But you would have me suffer for your own failings? Rose bit back the harsh reply to her father. "So you would have me get married, then?"

"Marriage is not the best option for everyone, Aurora," Stefanos said, sending a rush of mental sympathy to her mother. "But I feel in this case, it is the lesser of two evils."

"So by giving me this scroll," Rose remarked as she thumbed the flimsy parchment, "you are trying to scare me into making a decision? You would have me choose between abdicating the throne, and throwing the kingdom into irrevocable darkness, or you would have me marry, produce an heir, and be chained to someone for the rest of my life?"

"Those are the only options we've been given, Aurora," Stefanos told her. "We have been gracious enough to allow you to select which option. The time has come for you to make it."

Something inside of her broke. Rose furiously ripped up the scroll in her hands. "I choose to make my own destiny."

Stefanos huffed. "What good with that do? You only have a year left before the curse is fulfilled. Magdalina's power is still strong, and she will not remove the curse from you. What can you do?"

"I don't know," Rose admitted. "But I'll not trust my heart to a loveless marriage, nor abandon the kingdom of my blood."

"You already left once," the King reminded her.

"Because it had already abandoned me," Rose objected.

Stefanos sighed. "I need to get your mother in here," he said. "Let me send for her." He turned to Fiona. "Fiona, please send for the Queen." Looking back at Rose, he ordered, "Dismiss everyone else, and we'll have a family meeting."

"No." Rose turned and faced her friends. "These are all people who have stood up in support of me. These are my councilors, Father. I will not dismiss them."

"Dismiss them, please, Aurora. This is a family matter."

"You were the one who assured me earlier it was a kingdom matter. If I am to be a leader in this place, I need to start leading."

"This is outrageous," Stefanos muttered. "Fiona, get me the Queen. Now!"

The tiny fairy disappeared in a flash of light, heading out to fulfill her orders. Rose felt her fury rise up inside.

"*We* are leaving," she announced. "You've had your time with your councilors. I'll take some time and contemplate the options you've given us to consider."

Rose turned to see her friends' reactions vary from shock to determination to approval. She ignored her father as he called her back, and headed out of the room.

Philip approached her as the door shut behind them. "How about we discuss this over drinks?" he asked. "The Golden Fleece Inn has been treating my guards impeccably these last several days."

She had nowhere else to go. Staying at the castle would mean finding herself standing before the King again, and likely sooner than she would like. "Couldn't hurt," Rose agreed. "I could use a more lively setting than this dreadful castle has to offer. Everyone in?"

17

The Golden Fleece Inn was small compared to other pub houses close to the royal grounds, but it was warm and welcoming and bright, even at the late hour Rose and her comrades arrived.

They settled in, momentarily allowing the music and the fun to sweep them along, even as they all knew they had come to talk business. But even Rose, as she was caught up in the atmosphere and tempted by the warm mead, was content to give herself a small break from the dreary circumstances of their venture.

She sat down in a large chair close to the hearth, looking over at her newest confidante. "You never did tell me the whole story of your brother and his wife."

Philip's hazel eyes reflected the warm fireplace blazing inside the tavern as he glanced over at her. He lifted his pint to his lips, taking a quick drink. "I suppose I have yet to tell you the whole story," he agreed.

Sophia came down and sat at Rose's feet with a tankard of her own. "What story?" she asked.

"Careful not to drink the hard liquor," Rose warned her. "I'll need you clearheaded for the night and the morning."

Sophia laughed. "I'm Greek. We can hold our liquor."

Ethan came up behind her with some tea. "Only when you don't drink it," he scoffed.

"Bah, that's not true," Sophia cheerfully denied, giving her younger brother a quick punch to the shoulder as she laughed.

Rose locked eyes with Ethan and signaled him to watch over his sister. He nodded dutifully, but Rose had a feeling he was secretly laughing at her. Sophia was responsible, but she was also tough and stubborn, and thanks to her blacksmithing skills, easily able to wave a hammer around dangerously.

"My brother and his wife are newlyweds," Philip began, his voice rising up and down with the ease of a natural storyteller. "They are happily married and content now, but their courtship was anything but easy or smooth. When he was younger, my mother, the Widow Queen, began scheming to find him a bride after her husband passed. I had just been born earlier that year, and without the King, my mother feared leaving the kingdom in doubt of her ability to rule as much as the continuation of the lineage."

"I can relate," Rose huffed.

"Yes. Being a king or queen is all very well and good, but only if your people are happy and confident in your ability to rule."

"Either that, or they are so poor, so tired, so overworked, and so neglected of a proper education they don't have time to worry about rebellion," Sophia muttered bitterly.

Ethan reached over and put his hand on her shoulder.

"You're right about that," Philip agreed. "But Einish, even though it is a larger kingdom, or perhaps even because of it, has a good system in place. Our local lords and knights all work through their duties, getting checks along the way, and there are more checks to make sure of continuing confidence and integrity within the systems."

"I'm guessing the downside is that it relies a lot on that legacy for the next generations," Theo spoke up. Rose watched as he leaned against the wall, his large hands

ONCE UPON A PRINCESS

wrapped around a mug. She briefly smiled at the picture he made, both commanding and inconsequential all at once. It wasn't fair how he did managed such a feat, she thought.

Philip nodded again. "You're right. Our strength has always been our collective agreement on leadership, but without the leadership in place, we are weakened."

"So your mother needed to convince them she was doing the right thing, and your brother would be able to uphold the legacy as well."

"Yes. But we are not so practical all the time in Einish," Philip said. He smiled. "We indeed hold love and compassion among our highest virtues. To help this, my mother, having seen other kingdoms come to celebrate my birth, found that one had not, because the kingdom in question had just celebrated the birth of a princess."

He smiled at Rose. "It was about a year before you were born, if my memory is correct.

"Her name was Juliette, and my brother, Derick, seemed to be a good fit for her. Our kingdoms joined on the far end of our borders, so the idea was to have them meet each summer, in hopes they would fall in love."

Mary, who had settled onto Theo's shoulder, sighed wistfully. "How romantic!"

Philip's mouth curved into a twisted grin. "You would think. Both Juliette and Derick initially hated the idea, and each other as a result. It took them several years to go from being angry to playing angry."

"You said she was cursed?" Rose asked.

"Yes. Before long, a ruthless sorcerer, desperate to gain power, tried to take over Juliette's kingdom. When he failed, he captured her and put a spell on her, trying to get her to agree to marry him."

ONCE UPON A PRINCESS

"Seems a bit unnecessary," Sophia observed.

"Well, I can see the reasons for it," Philip admitted. "The sorcerer, Ruebart, would have needed her support to maintain control over her kingdom. If he had married her against her will, she could have easily pushed for a civil war of sorts."

"A fair reminder that popular people are forces to be reckoned with," Ethan observed, shuttering.

Rose, recalling Ethan's own past, quickly pushed the conversation forward. "You said he put a spell on her?"

"Yes. He placed a curse on her, transforming her into a swan every day. During the night, when the moon came out, she would transform into a human again, so he could pursue her as a potential suitor."

"How did she defeat the curse?" Rose asked.

"Well, Derick, who was finally able to admit to himself—and others—that he was in love with Juliette, began looking for her. When he finally found her, he rejoiced and, with the help of our mother, put together an engagement ball for her, hoping to proclaim his love to the world."

"And his love is what broke the curse?" Rose asked.

"Well, there were some complications along the way, but the curse was broken after Ruebart challenged Derick to a battle, and he lost."

"He lost?" Ethan asked.

"Meaning he died," Philip explained. He took another sip of his drink. "Juliette and Derick were married, the kingdoms were united, and I was sent off to see about finding my own bride." He smothered a chuckle. "I doubt I'll have quite the same level of adventure and suspense in my own story."

"Well, you never know," Sophia quipped. "If you're with us now, that might change some." She smiled. "We've had quite a few adventures before. And Ethan and I have only been with Rose for two years."

"I look forward to it." Philip relaxed back in his chair. "I'm not in any hurry to go back to my kingdom. For the moment, it's safe, and I am not needed, nor am I going to suppose I am missed."

"Why wouldn't you be missed?" Rose asked.

"Because Juliette and Derick are newlyweds, settling in, and all that," Philip said. "My mother has begun to pester them for grandchildren, but the kingdom is still glowing from the wedding celebration. I figure I'll have a few years before another incident must come to help the people maintain good faith in our rule." He frowned. "And there was never too much of my mother's attention left over for me to begin with. When you have a parent trying to run a kingdom, it doesn't allow much time left over for raising a child. Let alone two."

Rose nodded. "Yes, that's true. I'm sure my father just proved that to everyone earlier."

No one said anything in reply. Theo watched the light in Rose's eyes fade as she was no doubt recalling the scene in the castle.

His heart ached for her, and there was only one way he could help. "What do you think we should do about your situation?" he asked. "Anyone have any ideas?"

It was a few moments later when Rose spoke again. "I don't want to get married. And I don't want to abdicate."

"It's pretty easy to name what you don't want," Sophia agreed. "What *do* you want?"

Rose sighed. "Honestly, I want the curse gone. But Magdalina's already said that she wouldn't remove it from me, and Titania told us, she would be the only one who would know how to break it."

"But what if Magdalina is gone?" Ethan asked. "Would the curse be broken then, as it was for Philip's brother and his princess?"

The tavern's lively background music started to swell inside of Rose's heart as she looked at Theo. *Is it possible?*

"I suppose it's plausible," Theo admitted, answering her silent question. "She is only half-fairy. Her mortal blood would have bound the curse to you, and by killing her, it would break the seal."

Philip scratched his head. "I don't see the harm in trying," he agreed. "If nothing else, killing her would prevent her from harming Isra or the other heirs to the kingdom."

"People have been trying to kill her for years," Mary said. "It's not easy."

"But that's because they don't know what we know," Rose replied. "*We* know that she's half-mortal, which makes her immune to fairy magic and still more powerful than other humans." She pulled up her sword. "Lucia's sword should be able to kill her."

"And that wouldn't be all of it, either," Sophia spoke up. "You are unable to die since her curse has to be fulfilled."

"Yes." Rose shot up to her feet. "I don't know why I didn't see it before. If we kill her, the curse would be broken."

"Maybe," Theo cautioned. "*Maybe* it would be broken. We aren't sure it would work."

"But surely there's a way to break the curse," Ethan said. He looked over at Mary. "Isn't that a rule, that all curses can be broken?"

ONCE UPON A PRINCESS

"It's true, but it is complicated," Mary admitted. "You heard Titania. Magdalina is supposed to be the only one who knows how to break it."

"So we kill her to break it?" Theo frowned.

"What else could do it?" Rose asked. "What else could possibly break her curse, Theo?"

Theo recalled what Thad had mentioned earlier. *True love's kiss.* But he avoided her gaze. Between killing a half-fairy and finding Rose an acceptable suitor, he knew he would rather seek out Magdalina's wrath.

Rose began pacing in front of them. "That's it, then." Her mouth was a grim, determined line as she made her decision. "That's our plan."

"What, just go and kill Magdalina?" Mary's eyes were wide. "It's not something that's easily done, Rose. We'd have to go to her castle in the Darkwood Forest, fight her scores of guards, and then we'd have to trap her and prevent her from disappearing on us. And then to kill her, you'd have to make sure she wouldn't survive. Queen Lucia's sword can combat fairy magic, but it is the sword of her mother. Lucia would have been smart enough to place a spell on her sword to keep it from killing her own blood."

"What about something that can kill any magical creature?" Theo asked.

"Like what?" Mary asked. "There are different potions and spells for certain things, sure, but there's nothing that's guaranteed to kill a half-fairy."

"Not even dragon's blood?" he asked quietly.

Mary emitted a small squeak. "How do you know about dragon's blood?" she asked.

"Dragon's blood?" Rose asked, intrigued.

Theo nodded. "It's in a manuscript Thad found in the church's library. It tells of a place in the Romani territory where dragons live, protected and guarded, and their blood can kill any magical creature–especially immortals."

Mary's voice trembled as she spoke. "It's true," she admitted. "That would work. But few mortals know about it. It is forbidden to speak of it in our world. We fear it."

"But you have a manuscript telling of its location?" Philip asked. "Then all we would need to do would be go there, come back, and find Magdalina."

"And destroy her." Rose stopped her pacing and looked around. "How far away is the Romani territory?"

"Let me see if I have a good map with me," Ethan said, reaching for his pack.

"I can see if Thad will give me some more information on how to get there," Theo offered.

"Are you seriously considering this?" Mary asked. "Dragons are dangerous."

"Sophia said it earlier: I can't be killed. Magdalina's curse has to be fulfilled," Rose told her. "I have nothing to lose, Mary."

"My magic won't work against dragons," she warned.

"I'd still like you along for company," Rose remarked softly.

Mary sighed. "You have it, Rose, and you know this. But I will be a burden to you without magic."

"We have much more than magic," Rose insisted. "Remember? We have faith, loyalty, and courage. You told me that before. You'll never convince me these things have done less for the world than magic."

Mary sank into a humble silence.

Rose sighed. "All right. We're going to do the impossible, possibly one last time. Who's in?"

"As always, my lady knight, you have in me a squire and blacksmith, at your service," Sophia saluted.

Ethan raised his hand. "You are my rescuer and leader. You have my tracking, hunting, and map-reading skills at your disposal."

Mary sighed. "For what it is worth, you have the magic of my friendship."

"It's worth a lot to me," Rose assured her. "What about you, Philip? Will you go to the Romani territory, slay a dragon, and face life-threatening danger with us, all to help break the curse placed on me?"

"Magdalina could very well come after my people next," he said. "I look to you, Lady Princess," he said, "to join our kingdoms together against evil." He smiled. "And I welcome the task to defend you from your curse as well."

"All right. I'll go and inform the King. You each need to go and prepare to depart in the morning. Sophia, gather extra supplies from the forage house. Mary, see if Fiona or Juana would like to come with us and gather your supplies. Ethan, get some grooms to ready my team of horses. Philip, go and collect your tournament winnings from the royal treasurer. My father will not be happy, but he is not known to cheat anyone. The money will help pay for our passage."

All of them agreed, and finishing their drinks, headed out of the tavern.

"What about me?" Theo called out from behind her.

"What about you?" Rose asked.

"Did you want me to come with you?" Theo asked. "You didn't ask me."

ONCE UPON A PRINCESS

Rose stopped and placed her hand on his shoulder. "I'm sorry," she said, surprising him by her apology. "I didn't think I needed to. Throughout all the years we've been together, I have never needed to know if you would come with me. I just knew. But," she said as he tried to interrupt, "I know you have your own vengeance to pursue, and it is so close to where we are. If you want to stay behind, I understand."

He said nothing; he just looked at her, with that strange, enigmatic look of his.

He is going to make me ask, Rose thought, suddenly bitter. He is going to make me ask, just so he can say no and smooth it over with logic.

A thought popped into her mind. "Everon can be killed, too, with the dragon's blood."

He nodded. "I was thinking of that myself."

She sighed, impatient. There was nothing to be had, she decided. "So, will you come with me?"

He took her hand. "Where you go, I have always gone. Where you've stayed, I have stayed only a step behind. Your journey has always been my journey, and should you need me, I will be here for you."

Rose felt her heart nearly stop. "That was beautiful," she finally replied. "Thank you." I guess Philip's not the only one who is good at poetry, Rose admitted ruefully to herself.

"You're welcome."

Before she could say anything else, Philip came up beside her. "I've paid the bill, Rose," he told her. "Do you want us to meet you by the King's council room again?"

"What? Oh, uh, yes, that's a good idea," Rose said. She was still feeling the fervent beat of her heart as it clung to Theo's words.

She glanced around the room, as though seeing it for the first time. *How differently the world does look, when it is christened by hope.*

Looking from Theo to Philip, she grabbed them both by their arms. "Come on," she said. "We have work to do."

The music swelled around her and inside of her. A familiar tune caught her ears; it was the *Ballad of Queen Lucia,* an ode to her legend. And before Rose realized what she was doing, her voice broke free of its long imprisonment and soared along with the song.

> *Queen Lucia sought to love a special one*
> *Sir Benedict, his heart became the prize;*
> *He who was worthy of her love alone*
> *She saw as worthy in her own eyes.*

Rose, caught up in her own world, did not notice as Theo's fingers clenched around her arm even more tightly, nor did she notice how his breathing grew shallow as he lost the last of his carefully guarded heart was stolen.

Rose also did not notice on her other side as Philip, struck with shock at the pure clarity of her voice, nearly dropped her arm all together, as he stared at her in pure astonishment.

"What's wrong?" Rose asked, as she noticed both of Theo and Philip had stalled. "Did you lose something?"

"No," both of them said simultaneously.

As Rose turned back toward the door, returning to her plans as she pulled the two of them along, Theo glanced at over to see the unmoving wonder in Philip's gaze. One look at the prince, and Theo felt his initial wariness of the prince reignite.

Theo knew reality of allowing himself to dream of a life with the princess meant he had to acknowledge Philip for what he suddenly was: A rival.

ONCE UPON A PRINCESS

18

"The King has taken ill, Your Highness."

Rose snorted at her father's valet. "I'm not surprised. Can you announce me anyway?"

"I am under direct orders not to allow anyone through without permission."

"I see how this is going to play out already," Rose muttered. It figures, she thought. Her father would find a way to circumvent any serious attempt of hers to lead the nation. "He's lucky all those in my council are away fulfilling their assignments. Announce me, please."

"I'll see if he can speak first, Your Highness."

The valet's dour look did nothing to deter her. Nor would she allow him to trample over her. She had a plan, and she was going to stick to it.

The valet returned shortly. "The King will see you now, Your Highness."

"Thank you." Rose walked past the man and into her father's chamber. She felt the rest of the world fold back under the pressure of her father's majestic surroundings.

The King was lying in his bed, his eyes closed as he pressed his palms into his temples.

"Your Majesty."

"Aurora."

Rose grimaced. "I prefer Rose, to be honest."

"Rose?" Stefanos looked confused. "Your middle name?"

"More or less. I began using it after I left home the first time," she explained. "Announcing you are a traveling foreign princess, or even a traveler who shares the name, just invites

157

trouble. But now I prefer Rose. I don't recognize the person Aurora would have grown up to be."

"That's a shame, for she loved her country more."

"Rose has learned there are other places in the world where love exists, and it exists there without the tinge of unhealthy pity," she mocked.

"You dare defy me? Openly?" Stefanos accused. "I could have you flogged for that."

"I'd take it as proper punishment, if the insult were indeed open," Rose countered. "We are in your private bedroom, and you are feigning ill to make sure no one else would bother you."

"I'm not playing make-believe, for goodness' sake."

Rose smirked. "Shall I send for Reverend Thorne?"

"I'll not let Rhone live without a rightful ruler."

"I am the rightful ruler," Rose insisted. "You said it yourself. I was destined to save the kingdom, and I mean to save it from evil as much as from you."

"Ungrateful girl," Stefanos grumbled into his pillow. "You wound me with your words."

"Well, you've assured me of your purpose enough to know my words will not be fatal." Rose took a step closer. "I have an answer to your ultimatum. I am going to kill Magdalina."

"What?" Stefanos shot up straight in his bed, looking much more like a lonely, little boy than a king of a grand kingdom.

"My friends and I depart at dawn," she said. "We are going to go and find a way to destroy her. If we can kill her, we might be able to break the curse."

"I've tried for years to do just that. No one comes back alive. It's a fool's errand, Aurora."

"Rose," she corrected. "Magdalina told me I have made my curse a blessing in my own right. I have decided she is right, and I will test her on her claim. If her curse is to be fulfilled, she will be unable to kill me."

"You're mad."

"Determined." Rose smirked. "That is my decision."

"What if you should fail?"

"I needn't worry about the throne. Isra or Ronan can rule in my place. Both of your other children have been taught to fight and survive, and, while they are not supposed to inherit the throne over me, both can lead."

The King paused. "Do you like your siblings, Aurora?" Stefanos asked.

"Yes. Of course," Rose replied. "Why?"

"You would leave them to clean up the evil you leave behind?"

"No one is guaranteed a life without opposition or evil," Rose shot back. "The important thing is you teach them to watch for it, to recognize it, and to have the courage to stand up against it." She took a step closer. "One would think you would agree with me, considering my life has been all about answering for your own mistakes. This way, should I kill her, even if the curse is not broken, she will be unable to harm anyone else."

Stefanos frowned, anger crossing his features. He sat up and grabbed a quill and a sheet of parchment from his nearby desk. "I will let you go," he said, surprising her, as he scribbled furiously on the paper. "But only on one condition. You will sign a letter saying that, on the day after your eighteenth birthday, you will abdicate the throne."

"But if I break the curse—"

"Then you will be awake to tear up the contract," the King interrupted. He handed her the piece of paper. "There. Read through and sign it, and I will send you off with money,

159

supplies, whatever you need, and a guard to go behind you. Captain Locke will no doubt be eager to follow you once more. He hates town life."

"But–"

"Sign it. Sign it with the pen, and then seal it with your blood, Aurora. What can it hurt you? What can you lose?"

She looked at the paper and read the words; she blinked, as though they had been written in a different language.

I, Aurora, Princess of Rhone, give up the throne to the kingdom on this day, the day after my eighteenth birthday, and resign my say in all kingdom matters and the subsequent consequences.

Rose sighed. "Fine." With her scrawl of a signature and a drop of her blood later, she turned toward the door while Stefanos returned to his bed. She watched as he rolled up the scroll and tucked it into his sleeve. Suddenly, she frowned. "What do you mean by 'subsequent consequences?'"

"We'll know more clearly when it happens," Stefanos muttered. "I can't say for certain at the present."

"But you do mean that Isra will take the throne, right?" Rose asked. "She's the older twin."

"We'll have to see," the King repeated.

Rose faltered as she headed toward the door. "Just what did you do to Magdalina," she asked, "that made her hate you so?"

He was quiet for a long moment; Rose almost thought he wouldn't answer the question. "She blames me for the Magdust trade," Stefanos said with a sigh.

"Why would she blame you?" Rose frowned. "It's not like it is legal in the kingdom."

"Who is to say why she blames me? A king must take responsibility for his kingdom; that's all I can say to that."

"But you didn't take responsibility for any of this," Rose corrected. "I did. I wonder why."

"There's nothing more important to me than the crown and our family. She took you away and left the shell of the promise of my most dearly held wish. Who is to say Magdalina won't send her armies to kill Isra, too, taking all the royal children away from me and Rhone?"

He turned his face into his pillow and began to weep, something Rose never would have thought he would do.

ONCE UPON A PRINCESS

19

Thad was lighting the candles along the church pews when Theo walked in.

"When are you leaving?" Thad called out, his voice seeming louder than normal as it echoed through the empty sanctuary.

"I don't know how you know me so well," Theo said with a sad half-smile.

"I would have thought it was obvious, given our last conversation." Thad put down the flame he carried and headed over to his brother. "So tell me the plan."

Theo quickly told his brother of their plans. "Rose is determined to kill Magdalina," Theo explained. "She thinks the dragon blood will break the blood seal on the curse."

"As much as he would say in public he is against it, I think the Grand Father would secretly approve," Thad said. "So I will make arrangements for a special blessing for your travels in the morning."

"Rose won't come." Theo said it with a hidden bitterness. "She thinks God has abandoned her, left her to a cursed fate."

"So do all who see such times."

Theo sighed. "We'll probably leave out early, anyway. But thanks for the offer."

"The offer is not for you, brother," Thad replied. "Prayer is not for the people who would only pray for themselves." He smiled. "I will do what I can for you, and that includes, I will shamelessly admit, the comfort of praying for you here."

"I'm really happy to hear you say that, brother," Theo said with a sly grin on his face. "Because I have a couple of books and scrolls I need to borrow from you."

Thad's face fell.

ONCE UPON A PRINCESS

20

The sharp, cold morning air was in direct contrast to the warm pub and the soft bed she would leave behind, but Rose knew it was for the best. She was seventeen years old now, at last, on the brink of adulthood.

Her hair was freshly trimmed, her armor was polished, and her bags were packed. After finishing her preparation for her departure, she had spent the night looking out of her tower window, wondering if all the world was so peaceful at night.

She'd watched the sunrise peer out over the high, green mountains of Rhone, their color growing from the darkest of forest greens to shining emeralds, rivaling even the hue of Theo's eyes.

She turned to him now, as he mounted on his horse. "Do you remember the first day we set out last time?" she asked.

Theo fixed the straps of the pack he wore on his back, which held the precious manuscripts Thad had been reluctant, but resigned, to hand over. Rose was glad to hear Theo had managed to get Queen Lucia's story, as well as Magdalina's, in addition to as much information about the Romani language and history as possible. "Of course. You asked me if I was ready to begin training to be a knight."

"You replied by saying, 'I already am one, just an untrained one.'" Rose smiled. "I always liked that."

"I never told you, but that was the answer I gave to my grandfather, Reverend Thorne, when he inducted Thad and me into the church. Contrary to what most people think, there are a lot of similarities between priesthood and knighthood."

"Really?"

"Yes. Both seek to fulfill a higher calling on their lives, both do what they can, when they can, and both require ongoing training, patience, and growth." He grinned at her. "Especially where you're concerned, Rosary."

She laughed, glad to feel her heart lighten.

"Are you ready to leave?"

Rose turned at the sound of Isra's voice. "Isra. I didn't think you would–"

"What? Notice you were gone?" Isra rolled her eyes. "I've lived too long in your shadow, Rose. If you are gone, I run from daylight." She shook back her long, dark hair. "I also came to remind you to write to me this time."

"I will try," Rose muttered, already making up the necessary excuses in her mind.

"I know Theo will still write to me," she warned. "And I'm hoping Philip will, too."

"Philip?"

"Of course," Isra said with a teasing sigh and a small blush. "He's such a good poet, you know. I'm hoping to read some of it."

"I'll see that he writes to you then, if nothing else. I'm sure Virtue won't mind the extra letters." Rose glanced behind her to see her faithful falcon sitting peacefully on the back of her saddle pack.

"See that you do. You owe me, you know."

"For what?" Rose asked.

"For keeping an eye out for the King and Queen, of course," Isra told her. She lowered her voice. "The King told you, did he not, that there are secrets every ruler has kept, right? Well, I mean to discover them."

Rose bit back a smile, realizing Isra had been diligent to keep her watch on their father throughout the night, even to the point of spying. "You always were a better scholar than I was," Rose said, giving her younger sister an approving smile. "You'd probably make a much better queen, too."

"Of course I would. But that's only because I don't actually have to be the queen. People are always better at things they don't do than the people who do them."

Rose laughed and reached down and gripped her sister's hand in her own. "I promise, I'll take you with me on my next journey," she said.

"I'm counting on it, considering I will be likely committing treason for you in the coming weeks," Isra said. "You know how secretive the King is, and how blatant his apathy is for Ronan and myself. If he catches me in his study, he'll probably have no qualms about throwing me in the dungeon."

Rose was surprised. "I don't think he'd do that. He is very concerned with keeping the people happy."

"Mama says it is because he wasn't born into the throne. He wants to keep it very badly."

"Well, he will. He has me, and you and Ronan. One would think he would be content with three heirs."

"He doesn't like any of us, Rose."

"He doesn't know any of us."

"He doesn't want to."

Rose bit her lip. "I don't know what to say to that," she said, admitting defeat. "But if what you say is true, then you must promise me you will be extra careful."

"Only if you promise me the same," Isra demanded.

"I will. You have my word."

"Fine. I accept. And I will accept with the same enthusiasm and undercurrent of deliberate deceit." Isra smirked. "I can already tell you will find some kind of way to justify getting nearly killed."

"Don't worry for her, Isra," Philip spoke up, as his horse came up next to Rose. "I will be watching out for your sister."

Isra snickered. "Then I can rest much better," she assured him, "with the bare assurance your poetry will be the one to eulogize her."

"Absolutely," Philip promised, making Isra laugh once more. "If you feel I must, I shall write it ahead of time."

"So long as you write to me consistently," Isra said, batting her eyes in a flirtatious manner. "Goodness knows Rose is terrible about correspondence."

"I will," Philip promised. "I will write so much Virtue will need a whole day off to recover from his deliveries."

"Don't even think about making Virtue suffer any," Rose objected, reaching behind her to stroke her falcon's feathers while Philip and Isra laughed.

Sophia and Ethan came to meet them, mounted and ready. Mary, still sleepy, was curled up on Ethan's shoulder, under the protection of his dark hood. A small band of guards, including Captain Locke and Roderick, had gathered in the distance, waiting for her signal, no doubt once more sent out by the Queen.

"We're ready with the armor and weapons, Rose," Sophia called.

"Excellent. Ethan?"

"Food and supplies are accounted for."

"Good. I guess Mary's still tired."

"She was up most of the night talking with Fiona and Juana," Isra spoke up. "You can't blame her for wanting to spend time with her cousins."

"No, I can't," Rose agreed. "Hopefully her healing herbs and potions are all packed."

"They should be," Ethan told her. "I saw her put them in when I was getting the food stored."

"All right. We'll risk it, if nothing else. We should be safe till we leave Rhonian land." Rose turned her attention to Philip. "How's the money?"

"Plenty to go around," he told her.

"And Theo, I know you have the scrolls from Thad. Anything else you are in charge of?"

"All the prayers have been said," Theo said, nodding his head down toward her wrist, where the rosary beads he had given her remained carefully wrapped.

"Wonderful. All right then." Rose looked tenderly at each of the ones who had willingly trusted themselves into her care–plucky Sophia, with her iron will; gentle Ethan, young and precocious; Mary, faithful and also faithfully innovative; Philip, the newcomer, with a penchant for adventure, and apparently poetry; and Theo, her best friend and proven providence, his soul only marred by the desire for revenge, yet somehow brightened because of it.

These were her friends, her followers, her family. "Ready to go slay a dragon?"

ONCE UPON A PRINCESS

C. S. Johnson is the author of several young adult sci-fi and fantasy novels, including *The Starlight Chronicles* series, the *Once Upon a Princess* saga, and the *Divine Space Pirates* trilogy. She currently lives in Atlanta with her family.

PRINCESS ROSE
By Julia Mae Busko

171

ONCE UPON A PRINCESS

172

ONCE UPON A PRINCESS

AUTHOR'S NOTE AND ACKNOWLEDGEMENTS

Dear Reader,

Welcome to the new world of my new series. I've many more I wish to explore yet, but this is one of the easier ones to slip into. If you have enjoyed my *Starlight Chronicles* series, you might be surprised by the departure in my style; it's still there, of course, but the voice has changed.

But then, Rose is very different from my other protagonist. Hamilton lives in a world where he thinks he is able to hold off on growing up, even as he does, while Rose has learned to grow up very quickly, even as she can't.

Still, I am hoping you like her as much you've enjoyed Hamilton (or will enjoy, because obviously you're going to buy my other books now that you've read this). God works his magic in our lives in mysterious, ironic, silly, and seemingly frivolous ways as much through pain, and usually through people. And it's my blessing in getting to bring some of those people to life, even while reaffirming or challenging elements of yours.

I thank you so much for your support in recent months. Life has calmed down a bit; my goals are more focused, and my time is more flexible. There is nothing more I desire than getting to write more and to interact with you more.

Finally, I'm going to ask nicely if you would leave a review for my book. I'm not asking for you to blast it out over social media, or tattoo it on your chest, or write it on your car. Every review helps, and I do tend to read them, especially at my worst moments.

Please check back in with Rose in the next book in the saga, *Beauty's Quest (Once Upon a Princess,* Part II*).*

Until We Meet Again,

C. S. Johnson

ONCE UPON A PRINCESS

BEAUTY'S QUEST

PART II OF THE *ONCE UPON A PRINCESS* SAGA

C. S. Johnson

Library of Congress Control Number: 2017909188

ISBN-13 eBook: 9781943934263

ISBN-10 eBook: 1-943934-26-6

ISBN-13 Book: 978-1-943934-27-0

ISBN-10 Book: 1-943934-27-4

ONCE UPON A PRINCESS

For my kids. My older ones: Nolan, Brooks, Rebekah, Andres, Mary, Satori, and Tyler, and Rachel, too; my middle ones: Tate and Jake and Miles; and my younger ones: Sam, Johnathan, Malik, Gracie, and Ethan, and my other Rebekah. I might be a role model for you, but you are the ones whose expectations I strive to live up to.

This is also for my other Sam. Yours was the first face I could see in my imaginary audience, and I have neither forgotten nor begrudged you the accompanying catcalls.

This book is published courtesy of

www.direwolfbooks.com

ONCE UPON A PRINCESS

ONCE UPON A PRINCESS

PART II

"When I have fears that I may cease to be
　　Before my pen has gleaned my teeming brain …
And when I feel, fair creature of an hour,
　　That I shall never look upon thee more,
Never have relish in the faery power
　　Of unreflecting love—then on the shore
Of the wide world I stand alone, and think
　　Till love and fame to nothingness do sink."

~ "When I Have Fears that I May Cease to Be," Keats

ONCE UPON A PRINCESS

1

If there was one thing Princess Aurora Rosemarie Mohanagan knew, it was that she had no reason to fear death. But as she glanced down at the half-sunk ship, wrecked on the rocky coast below her, Rose admitted to herself—more than a little reluctantly—she was lucky she'd survived.

"It's a miracle we're alive, Rose." The small fairy perched on her shoulder echoed Rose's thoughts as they both looked toward the harbor.

Rose tried not to smile as she watched Mary, her small fairy friend, wring the excess water out from the folds of her dress. "You're right about that, Mary. But I don't know if *they* think so," Rose muttered, nodding down to the gruff sea captain and his crew. She watched them as they waded into the cove, pulling the storm-weathered bow of the vessel closer to shore. "Philip gave them quite a lecture."

"One they won't likely be forgetting anytime soon, either," Philip agreed.

Rose looked over to see Prince Philip of Einish, her newest friend and traveling companion, making his way up the rocky beach. His copper-brown hair glistened with seawater, the droplets sliding down his sunburned face and into his beard. "Oh really?" she teased. "What did you tell him?"

"I told him the truth," Philip assured her with a grim smile. "I told him he'd almost killed two royals, and neither country would be happy to accept his calls to port anymore should anything adverse happen." He stepped up next to her. "I'm sure neither your father nor my brother would object to keeping them from our countries' docks after their incompetence during that storm."

"Einish and Rhone do make quite a large profit from the sea-faring trade," Ethan, the youngest of the group, spoke up. He sighed as he looked at the soaking wet packs in his hand,

181

the remnants of his precious manuscripts and scrolls. "Even when Sophia and I were living with our family"—his lips tightened at the memory—"I'd never known my father to complain of an investment failing when it came to trading with either."

Rose agreed. The kingdom of Rhone, her home, was mostly landlocked, but the few harbors it had on the northern side of the kingdom were bustling with activity throughout the year. She remembered seeing several when she had been younger, on one of her grand tours of the nation, the feeling of awe as she surveyed Elis, Rhone's largest port, and she watched the people there, busy about the docks. She knew Philip's warning was no light threat.

Looking at the sullen expression on Ethan's face, Rose turned her attention back to the situation at hand. "Where is Sophia?" she asked. She lifted her hand up to shield herself from the streaming sunlight as she looked around for her squire. "I thought I saw her make her way to the shore a few moments ago."

"She is a good swimmer," Ethan reminded Rose. "She might just be lingering to see if she can help. Theo was doing that, too."

"Well, I know he was going to help with the burials for the two crew members who died." Rose's fists clenched again. The reality of coming so close to a watery grave made her shiver. "I hope they're not making him help dig graves."

"I doubt it," Philip said with a sad sigh. "I know the men are going to be given a burial at sea. Many feel it is more appropriate, considering they drowned."

"I suppose so," Rose grimly agreed. "If that's what they're doing, then Theo should be here soon."

"All in a day's work for a priest, right?" Philip asked, shaking the water out of his gloves.

Rose snorted disdainfully. "Just because he was raised in the church and knows how to perform rites and catechisms and the like doesn't mean he's a priest." She glanced over

ONCE UPON A PRINCESS

Philip's shoulder to see if she could spot her long-time friend coming up from the beach.

"He acts like it enough," Philip reminded her.

"But he's still not, so get it right." Rose stuck her tongue out at him before turning her attention elsewhere. "If he was a full priest, maybe he could have stopped the rain sooner."

"It wasn't that long of a storm."

"*To you*, maybe it wasn't that long of a storm," Rose muttered. "When that storm grew severe, it had to have been already raining for at least two weeks."

Mary chuckled, her small wings fanning Rose's face. "It just seemed like two weeks," she said. "It was really only about four days, Rose."

"I lost track of time as soon as the crew stopped listening to reason," Rose said. "Especially after those goons in charge of the ship were trying to puff the sails to catch *more* of the wind, rather than pulling it up." She gave Mary a tiny pat on her head, flicking Mary's dark ginger locks affectionately. "If you hadn't used your magic to find this island, I don't know what we would have done."

"We'd probably be swimming back to Rhone. Or maybe we could've tried to get closer to the mainland, where the Romani territory is. We've got to be at least halfway there."

"Don't think I wouldn't completely object to it, either. I suppose now we will have to find a way to get more supplies." Rose turned to Philip. "How much money do we have left?"

"A good bit. But Rhonian money is different from the money used in the Peloponnesian countries," Philip warned her.

"Too bad we don't deal in Magdust," Ethan said as he began to move higher on the rocks, looking for a place to air out the parchment he'd rescued from his drenched pack. "I'll bet *that* would get us some money pretty quick."

"Don't say such things." Rose's admonishment came swiftly but softly. "Especially when you're working with Thad's manuscripts." Theo and Thad's parents had been

ONCE UPON A PRINCESS

killed by Everon, Magdalina's son, in connection with the illegal Magdust trade in Rhone. Theo wouldn't have appreciated that comment, Rose thought.

"I was just trying to liven things up some," Ethan grumbled, rubbing his hand through his shaggy brown hair. "I didn't mean any harm."

"I should hope so," Mary scoffed. "I've had friends who have been killed and smashed into Magdust."

"What?" Rose was shocked. "You've never mentioned that to me." Mary was loyal to Rose and her party, and one of the only fairies, in all of Rhone who still supported the ruling family. Rose could not remember a time her life had not been touched with Mary's devotion.

Mary shrugged. "You know I have never held the Magdust trade against you, Rose. I wouldn't want you to think that, especially with Magdalina placing that curse on you."

"I would never think of you the way I think of Magdalina. Being a fairy has nothing to do with being evil," Rose assured her. She turned back to look over the edge of the rocky cliffs. "Mary, can you help Ethan with the maps and scrolls? They need to be dried."

"No problem," Mary murmured dutifully.

Philip came up next to her. "Can I help you with anything?"

"Yes," Rose replied. "Please take an inventory of our remaining supplies, and count how much money we do have so we can see about moving on toward the Romani territory."

"Sure thing."

Rose sighed softly as Philip headed back down to the shore. She was alone for the moment.

Rose inhaled deeply, feeling the salty sweetness of the air. The beach was beautiful, with its white sand kissing the sea with such tenderness. There was a calmness in the air she would have given anything to have had during the nighttime storms. Rose knew full well she should have been grateful, even relaxed, to be on such lovely, solid dry land after several weeks of traveling by sea.

ONCE UPON A PRINCESS

But she wasn't.

Another victory for Magdalina, she thought, feeling the full weight of the curse placed on her at infancy. Like all the previous royal heirs of Rhone, Rose had been blessed by the gifts of the fairies, Fiona and Juana, Mary's older cousins, at the celebration of her birth. But before Mary could give her a touch of magic as well, Magdalina showed up, angry at not being invited and bitter against the kingdom. It was then she had cursed Rose to prick her finger on the spindle of a spinning wheel and die on her eighteenth birthday, now less than a year away. Magdalina had then laughed and took her leave.

Mary had been able to alter the curse—death-like sleep would replace death—but that was little comfort to Rose. It was still the end of her life.

Rose looked down at her palms, her gaze tracing up and down the length of her fingers, as she wondered which one would betray her.

After seeing Magdalina at her royal birthday party just over three months before, and feeling every second as it counted down to her eighteenth birthday, Rose knew more than ever she had to find a way to break the curse. That had been the plan when they'd set off from Rhone.

Now, if she was going to get the dragon's blood she needed to take care of Magdalina, she had to find a way off this prison of an island—and fast.

She pressed her fingers into her temples, steeling herself against the fear that clutched at her heart; the terror squeezed the beauty of her surroundings out of sight, until only the ugliness of despair and the unknown remained.

"It'll be all right, Rosary."

Rose jumped at the sudden presence by her side. She looked over to see Theo had climbed up next to her. "I know," she said, aware she was half-lying. "But we are only about halfway to Romani territory, and we can't afford to be delayed long."

ONCE UPON A PRINCESS

"We've made good time," Theo told her. "We are on the island of Maltia, according to the men from the ship. There's a city on the other side of that peak over there." He pointed to a mountaintop in the distance. "We should be able to find a church there, according to some of the crew. I'll be able to see about securing us quarters. And hopefully, passage on another ship as well."

"Are you sure you can trust their information?" Rose asked, nodding back to the sailors. "After the confusion on the ship, I'd rather not."

"A lot of them are superstitious men." Theo shrugged. "But they are not as given to fancy when it comes to knowing their trade and its routes."

"We're not going to have to wait for them, are we?" Rose asked.

Theo gazed at her, his emerald-colored eyes complementing the comfort of the sea. "We don't have to wait for repairs, if repairs are even possible. According to a man who'd talked to Captain Locke, the Maltians have a special trade route for the Romani territory."

"Good." Rose sighed. "Now we just have to get the money for supplies and passage."

"We'll find a way to get it," Theo assured her. "Don't lose hope, Rose. This could be a good thing. Maybe we'll be able to find out more about the dragons."

"I'll try. No promises."

Theo smiled. "That's the Rose I know."

"Right now, Philip's checking supplies while Ethan and Mary are working on drying out the scrolls Thad gave us."

"They're not damaged, are they?" Theo's eyes were wide with sudden concern.

Rose knew Theo's older brother, who resided in the chapel in Rhone's capital city of Havilah, probably prayed just as much for the safe return of his manuscripts and scrolls as he did for the safe return of Theo and his friends. "I think Mary will be able to take care of it," she told him.

ONCE UPON A PRINCESS

"That's good." Theo breathed a sigh of relief. "My brother is a forgiving sort, but I'd hate to be the one who tests his limits."

As Rose laughed, a wink of light flickered in the corner of her eye. She turned to see Sophia, her thirteen-year-old squire, as she sloshed onto the beach below.

"Did you finish taking care of those who died?" Rose asked.

"Yes, both of them. The older was a man who had been seafaring since he was eight, and the younger not even a year behind Ethan."

Rose reached out and placed her hand on his arm. She started to say something, but she found she had no words to say. It took a moment before she felt him relax as he let himself be comforted. She knew his heart was shaken, and his body had yet to catch up to the shock of seeing the dead. Rose had a feeling he would never be completely familiar with it, no matter his education as a priest or his training as a knight.

He drew up his arm, allowing Rose's hand to fall into his. His fingers tightened around hers. "Thanks, Rosary."

Theo smiled a bit as he momentarily fiddled with the chain of rosary beads at her wrist; he'd given them to her shortly before they had departed from Rhone.

"We should start heading to the city. The rain's let up, but nightfall will be here before we know it."

"Yes," she agreed. "Let's get the others."

2

The darkness settled in as Rose became increasingly aware of the numbness in her legs. After weeks at sea, walking on land proved to be a transition her body was hesitant to make. She struggled not to scream in frustration when Theo delayed their progress by searching for the city cathedral and asking the nuns there for information and directions.

She only decided to forgive him when the church pointed them toward a small inn, one that was tucked away just beyond the cobblestone city streets.

"Maltia City Inn." Rose read the small sign hanging from the door. "Thank goodness we've made it at last."

"Do we have enough money to stop for the night?" Ethan asked.

"We should," Theo spoke up. "The sisters from the city's cathedral assured us the owner was very charitable toward tourists."

Ethan groaned. "Good. I just want to rest. We've been walking on sand, climbing up and over a mountain, and waltzing through the woods all day."

Rose knew Ethan was tired, but he was still trying to be strong. He hadn't mentioned the previous nights, when sleeping on the sea-tossed ship had proven nearly impossible.

She turned to see Sophia, sleeping peacefully as Theo carried her on his back. Mary even yawned, her body slumping slightly as she perched on Philip's shoulder. "Philip?" Rose asked.

"Theo's correct. We should have enough."

"Oh, sweet relief," Mary muttered. "I'd love to have a proper bed tonight."

"Don't get your hopes up, Mary. Let's go in and see what they have," Rose warned.

ONCE UPON A PRINCESS

As they walked into the inn, Rose felt a surge of gratitude as the warmth of fire washed over her. While the sun had been kind during the day, the coldness of night had blanketed the rest of the island with a salty, chilly breeze.

"Welcome." A man appeared at the door. "Can I help you?"

"Hello," Rose greeted. "We were going to book some rooms for ourselves and a small guard."

The innkeeper, an older man with flecks of silver in his hair, nodded. "It'll be a shekel a night, for each of you," he said. "That'll take care of you and your guard."

"Do you take Rhonian money?"

"Rhonian?" The man's eyes sparkled with a suspicious gleam. "You're from the country of Rhone?"

"Yes." Rose decided from his tone it was best not to mention she was its princess. "Is there a problem with that?"

"No, not at all. But not many visitors come from Rhone. Haven't had one stay here at all since the Rose Ruby incident," the innkeeper told her. "But I suppose it has been nearly thirty years since that."

"What happened?" Rose asked with a sense of foreboding.

She knew the Rhonian history of the Rose Ruby. Her own father had set out to find it in order to win her mother's hand in marriage and the kingdom's throne. But as she had discovered before, the Rhonian history was often incomplete.

"The Sultan of the Orlo Empire was visiting this very island when it was stolen. Some have said that a peddler stole it and made his way back to a small kingdom called Rhone."

"I see."

"We were never able to prove it, and it has since disappeared again," the innkeeper said. "But it is said to have great powers, able to bring down great men and kingdoms."

"That seems … unusual," Rose said, trying to hide her surprise. She'd known her father had to have given the Rose Ruby to the previous king in order to marry her mother.

What had happened to the ruby?

ONCE UPON A PRINCESS

Rose shook her head, telling herself to focus. She could solve that issue later. At the moment, she needed to focus on securing rooms for herself and her crew.

"But surely you still trade with Rhonian ships? Could you take Rhonian money for the night?" she asked.

"Let me see."

Philip handed him several coins from the small pouch he had at his side. "Here."

The innkeeper looked at the coins, carefully turning them over in his gnarled hands. "Well, I haven't seen Rhonian money in a long time," he admitted. "Their ships call to port only a few times a year. We use Maltian shekels here, but this will do if you have collateral." He glanced up at them with his aged eyes. "I can trade currencies from time to time with a friend of mine. Collateral will act as a form of insurance."

"Here, take my sword," Philip offered, reaching to unclasp his scabbard before Rose could object. "This should grant you enough money in the event we are unable to pay."

After examining the sword with careful hands, the innkeeper nodded. "We have a deal." The innkeeper took the sword and placed it under his desk. "Let me show you to your rooms."

As the man grabbed a torch and beckoned them to follow, Rose elbowed Philip. "You didn't have to trade in your sword," she said. "I could have—"

"Done the exact same thing," Philip interjected. "But you have the sword of Queen Lucia. There's no need to risk it. I have more swords back in Einish. Besides, we'll get it back once our payment is secure."

"Still, I wouldn't—"

"Wouldn't want to owe me anything?" Philip asked, teasing her. "Wouldn't want to have to say 'Thank you' to me?"

Rose narrowed her gaze. "Well, thank you." Then she stuck out her tongue at him. "See? It's not so hard."

"Isn't it?" he asked, making his point.

Rose sighed. "I'm sorry I said anything."

ONCE UPON A PRINCESS

"An 'I'm sorry' and a 'Thank you'? I must be dreaming." Philip laughed.

"Shut your mouth," Rose barked.

"*That's* more like the Rose I know," Philip bantered back.

Theo cleared his throat from behind them. "Are we almost to the room?" Theo asked, directing his question to the innkeeper in front of Rose and Philip.

Rose glanced behind her. The terse tone of Theo's voice surprised her.

He nodded toward the untidy black curls that fell over Theo's shoulder as Sophia balanced on his back. "Sophia's getting heavy."

"Yes, here we are." The innkeeper looked back at them as he handed his torch to Ethan. "Have you come for the tournament?" he asked.

"What tournament?" Rose asked.

He laughed. "I guess that would be the right question," he said. "Maltia has tournaments six times every year in celebration of its many conquerors."

"Conquerors?"

"Yes. Maltia is a small island," the innkeeper explained. "But we have a rich heritage, thanks to those who would conquer us. Many kingdoms have come to our shores in search of freedom, comfort, or new land, and found our island to be suitable for their desires."

"So you have tournaments in celebration?"

"Well, that, and to cover up governmental foul play," the man admitted, a little sheepishly.

"What kind of tournament is it?"

"We are celebrating our Aragonian heritage with the Bull Tournament."

"Is there money to be made?" Philip asked.

"Plenty," the innkeeper confirmed. "It is a high honor on Maltia to win in the tournament rounds."

"We are definitely here for the tournament then," Rose agreed, ignoring Theo's disgruntled cough behind her.

ONCE UPON A PRINCESS

"Ah, excellent," the innkeeper said. "I've picked out good rooms for you then, for these are fit for champions."

While the others pushed into the rooms and began to get settled, Rose extended her hand to the innkeeper. "I'm Rose," she told him.

"I'm Felise," he said, bowing gracefully over her hand. "It's a pleasure to meet you, My Lady."

"I'm no one special," she told him, dismissing the formal gesture. "Please just call me Rose."

"I'll call you Rose, but you're far from being no one special. It is a special woman who holds the loyalty of her followers." Felise smiled. "I'll look forward to seeing you again tomorrow."

"Yes. Thank you."

Rose waited until the innkeeper had completely disappeared from view before she shut the door. She looked to see Philip head out his door to help her three Rhonian guards settle in while Mary and Ethan were both snoring already.

She watched Theo as he put Sophia down for the night, tucking the coverlet around her. *Ever the gentle protector,* she thought.

He met her gaze, and Rose smiled. He didn't smile back. She sighed. *He's not happy about the tournament idea.*

"Rose," he said, coming up beside her. "I don't like the idea of entering a tournament here."

"We could use the money, Theo," Rose reminded him.

"I know," he said, his lips pursed together in dismay. "But I—"

"I'll be careful," Rose promised.

"I still think we should learn more about it before jumping into it."

"We will. We'll find out all the necessary information tomorrow when we look for passage on another ship." Rose smirked. "Weren't you the one who wanted to enter into a tournament while we were in Rhone?"

"The one in Rhone for you or your sister's hand was to protect you," Theo reminded her. "This one is for money and

ONCE UPON A PRINCESS

acclaim. The money we need, I'll give you that, but you know it's dangerous for others to know who we are, and why we're traveling."

"The money is reason enough to do it," Rose argued.

"What if we find passage to the Romani territory tomorrow?"

"We'll still need supplies." She was tired, and as her patience wore down, her insistence increased. Rose met Theo's gaze with all the stubbornness she could muster.

After a long moment, the silent battle raging between them, he frowned. "I'll see about passage to the Romani territory tomorrow," he finally said. "Then we'll make some plans."

"Good." Rose nodded calmly even as she inwardly rejoiced. It wasn't often she was able to win an argument with Theo. "Thank you for carrying Sophia today. You should get some sleep. You need the rest."

"It's not obvious, is it?"

She put her hand to his cheek, wanting to comfort him as much as she wanted to get him to smile. She traced the outline of his jaw. "You have dark circles under your dark circles," she told him. "With your coloring, you look just a bit too much like a demon rather than a man."

"A man who serves you," Theo added softly, leaning into her touch.

In the darkness with only the moonlight's shadow, in the quiet of the room, she felt her iron grasp on her self-control fade as her palm brushed against the soft bristles of Theo's emerging beard, the back of her fingers brushing his ebony locks, having grown only a bit longer since they'd started out on their quest. Her eyes fell to his lips in unspoken weakness.

Quickly, she patted his cheek once more and then dropped it, the stinging warmth still there. "I would hope it's easier to serve me than the devil. He doesn't look after his own the way I do," she said, her words sounding empty against the oncoming night. "Get some rest."

Theo nodded. "Good night, Rosary."

ONCE UPON A PRINCESS

Rose turned and hurried into her own bed, feeling strangely vulnerable and exposed.

3

"Well, that was easier than I thought it would be." Rose jingled the new mixture of Maltian coins in her pouch. "Not only did we manage to exchange currencies, but that merchant was nice enough to tell me about the tournament fees."

Philip snatched the money purse out of her hand. "I'll hold onto the money for now," he offered.

"Hey, come on," Rose scoffed. "I'm not going to spend it *all* while we're out. I know we need to take care of the entrance cost."

"We don't have much left, especially if we are going to be staying for the tournament. We'll need money for Felise and food as well as the entrance fees. Our group should have only a limited number of people enter into the tournament, just to be on the safe side."

Philip watched Rose as she swiftly did the calculations. "Three is enough to enter. If none of us wins, the rest can see about getting jobs. That way, we'll have a safeguard."

"This tournament is different since it is in the Aragonian tradition," Philip reminded her. "There is no big winner; they go by individual challenge, much as the Greeks did with their Olympic contests."

"What do you mean?"

"It is the rare person who is exceptionally gifted in more than one area," he explained. "A regular tournament might have points or levels to achieve to be declared an overall winner, but an Aragonian tournament just has several winners. It's part of the reason they have longer tournaments than other countries and regions."

"That explains why Felise is so welcoming to his tournament guests. Greedy fellow."

Philip grinned at Rose's objection to paying Felise more than a week's worth of room and board. "At least he seems like a nice, greedy fellow, rather than an arrogant one."

Rose reached out and grabbed his arm, pulling him towards the food vendors. "Come this way. We need to get some food while we're out. Tell me what else you know about Aragon."

Philip floundered for a moment as she linked her arm under his. "Sure."

As they walked through the market, Philip told her about what he'd experienced from Aragonian guests and ambassadors growing up.

He celebrated with her at news of the joust, explained the rules of the sword fighting contest, and worked through her confusion at the Aragonian tradition of running with the bulls.

"They really see who can run with bulls?" Rose asked.

"Yes," Philip said. "It's a test of endurance, but also a sort of celebratory fanfare to welcome people into competitive settings. Many contests also use it as a way to wean the field while still pocketing tournament fees."

"Good for business, then?"

"In many ways, since medical supplies and doctor's fees tend to go up with demand."

They were nearing the end of the marketplace as well as the conversation when she sighed.

Philip followed her gaze to see one of the city's grand harbors, with plenty of ships loading and unloading, ready to transverse the waves of the world.

It wasn't hard for Philip to know what Rose was thinking. She was very much like Isra in that regard, he recalled, thinking of how he had befriended Rose's younger sister during the short time he'd been in Rhone.

"I wonder if there are any ships headed out to the Romani territory?" Rose asked.

"We have a decent amount of coins left," he said, shaking the small pouch, much as she had earlier. "We might be able to afford passage without needing to go into the tournament."

"Theo said about as much, too." She wrinkled her nose. "I doubt it, based on the price we paid for the first ship. But I guess we'll find out when we regroup for dinner tonight."

"We have been on the road for close to three months," Philip told her. "The tournament is only a week. We have time to stay and participate, if that's what you want, Rose. We can spare a week. And it's not like it wouldn't be good. I know you didn't enjoy being cooped up in the ship for the last two months."

Rose only shrugged at his remark.

Seeing her ambivalence over the matter almost made him laugh. *She agrees, but doesn't want to admit it.* At her glare, he quickly changed the subject. "Where is everyone else?"

"The guards are working on trading any goods we no longer need, Sophia is working on finding a blacksmithing forge, and Ethan is exploring the city."

"And Mary's back in the room still," Philip added, "because you didn't want people to see her."

"Fairies are everywhere if you know where to look. But there are many who are hostile, like Magdalina and her son, Everon." Rose shook her head. "And anyone who sees a fairy like our Mary might also think we'd use her loyalty and magic to win."

"I agree with you," Philip told her. "Although I'm sure Mary was unhappy with the decision."

"She wasn't today, because she's still tired, but she will be tomorrow. She likes to stay by my side when I fight. To help if I have injuries." Rose rolled her eyes. "As if I were a child."

"In many ways, I imagine you are one to her, from what I've seen and heard," Philip replied. "She has been connected to you for many years, especially after Magdalina placed that curse on you."

"True. Mary was the fairy who altered the curse, so instead of dying instantly, I get to fall into a death-like sleep," Rose acquiesced. "But I prefer to have her as a friend, rather than a

ONCE UPON A PRINCESS

doctor or a substitute mother." She took a bite out of an apple she'd purchased earlier. "I've been taking care of myself for a long time. I don't want anyone thinking they have to."

"What about people who *want* to take care of you?"

"That's where it gets annoying," Rose said pointedly.

"But Mary and Theo do it anyway," Philip countered.

"That's part of who they are, not necessarily what they are to me." Rose took another bite of her apple. "Mary is a younger fairy than her cousins. She grew up with me. And as for Theo, I blame the church's influence. They seem to want the best for people, even if the people don't want it for themselves."

"He did go back to the church today."

"I figured he would."

"Maltia has a rich tradition of different heritages; many cultures have traveled here and conquered the island before letting it go—as long as they paid their taxes to the right people, of course. It's not surprising the Christian church should have laid roots down here."

"No, it's not," Rose admitted.

"There have been rumors that this is where the Apostle Paul stopped on his way to the lands of Castile and Aragon."

"That's pretty far from the Promised Land."

"It's farther than the Romani territory, where we're headed." Philip grabbed her apple and took a bite of his own as Rose narrowed her eyes at him.

"I guess you can have the rest," she muttered.

"I'm only teasing you," he said. "Here." He held out his hand, the apple easily within her reach.

Philip watched her expression grow darker as Rose studied him. He knew he was treading on dangerous ground. But if you want something, he reasoned to himself, it was worth it to risk regret.

"You're lucky you're so pretty," Rose finally told him, pushing the fruit aside once more. "I don't feel like breaking your nose over an apple."

ONCE UPON A PRINCESS

"You're too serious," he told her, his teeth biting into the apple again. "And you fear too much."

"What would I fear from you?" Rose scoffed as a breeze tickled through her hair, ruffling it affectionately.

Philip gently pushed back her wayward bangs. "That I would offer you my heart just as easily as the apple," he told her quietly. "And you would have a harder time refusing it."

Rose stepped back from him and wrinkled her nose. "I have no trouble declining such an offer." She pushed her hair down, as if to let him know just how easy it was to deflect such an offer.

He felt a sudden sadness at her retort, one that was more for her than it was for him. "I know. I'm guessing you've had plenty of practice doing that."

"What's that supposed to mean?" Rose shot back.

"I mean, you're used to denying your heart."

"That's not it at all," Rose insisted. From the sound of her voice, Philip knew her temper was rising. "I'm used to denying what other people *tell* me what I want. I know what I want. I want the curse removed from me, so I can rule my kingdom and marry or not marry whomever I please. Until then," she said, stabbing her finger into his chest, "I'm not going to worry about such things."

"For someone so generous and giving, it's surprising you would overlook the wishes of others in this matter."

"I'm protecting them."

"Are you sure you're not protecting yourself?" Philip asked gently. He had known Rose long enough to know she could put up a fight if it was warranted, but if there was another way to achieve her end, she would embrace it.

"The two are not mutually exclusive." Rose huffed. "I don't want to talk about this anymore. Find someone else to talk about it if you want, but I'm done."

"Understood." Philip gave her a friendly smile. There's always later, he told himself. Slow and steady would win the war against Rose and her defenses. "Let's go check out the armory over there. Maybe we can see about getting your sword sharpened."

Rose nodded. "Sounds good to me."

ONCE UPON A PRINCESS

4

"Augh! Don't hurt me, you beast!"

Rose and Philip walked into the inn just in time to see Felise ducking behind the partition, his arms waving wildly as he screamed. "Help! Save me!"

Rose was just about to call out and ask what was wrong when a gust of wind and a slew of feathers flew into her. Instinctively, her fingers curled and her arm straightened out, allowing the grand gyrfalcon to land properly. "Virtue. I can't believe you're here!"

"He's yours?" Felise poked his head out over the table's edge, just enough so Rose could see his moppet of white hair and terrified brown eyes.

Rose choked down a laugh as she watched the poor man. "Yes. Sorry about that. I hope he didn't give you any trouble." She came over and reached a hand to help pull him to his feet. "This is Virtue. He's my messenger falcon and hunting partner."

"He's too large to be housed in here," Felise told her tersely as he brushed off his robes. "There are stables out back you can use."

Rose smiled graciously. "Of course. I'll get him settled in right away."

"That's fine," Felise agreed. "But don't bring him in here again. I'm afraid he would scare some of my other guests." He walked briskly away, leaving Rose wondering if he really was only concerned for his guests—if he even had guests other than her party.

"I'll bet anything he's never seen a falcon like you," Rose murmured to Virtue, whose eyes seemed to laugh in reply. She stroked his wings before turning back to Philip. "Can you take our purchases up to Mary?" she asked. "I'll just be a moment with him."

"No problem," Philip promised, skirting around her and heading back toward their rented suite.

A sense of relief stole over her as she watched him disappear down the hall. She was eager to forget their earlier conversation in the market. The sight of him, with his rich copper hair and the darker shade of his beard softening the sharper edges of his face, his hazel eyes twinkling at her in sport and something else—something she knew well to avoid—unnerved her as much as the topic of her heart.

Rose knew it wasn't worth discussing; she'd debated the problem with others before, and it did no good in the end. How could they understand she knew just what it felt like to have no power, to long for love freely given, only to know the cost was too great to count?

Rose headed for the stables, faltering only slightly in her steps as she caught sight of the package neatly tied to her falcon's foot. "Seems you brought us a present from Isra, huh?" she asked. "I guess that's why Theo and Philip were so eager for me to send you out before we set sail."

Virtue let out a small screech, as if to confirm her guess. It would be like Isra to put the pressure for news on the ones who would listen, Rose thought. In her earlier years of travel abroad, Rose had never written to her sister, and never wanted to. It was easier to deal with leaving behind her childhood if she forgot her sister as well.

"Well, let's hope she included some money." Rose prepared to see a letter scolding her for not writing yet.

"It hasn't been that long since we left. She can't be that bored already, can she?" Rose wondered aloud, peeling the papers apart from Virtue's claw, revealing several letters, all addressed in the same precise, looped writing. When Virtue squawked in seeming reply, she continued, "But then again, I suppose not everyone has to deal with rough seas, a shipwreck, and running with the bulls, all within the same month."

Virtue took off once more, heading for one of the higher beams of the small stable. "Rest well," Rose told him, blowing him a kiss.

Feeling the vellum of Isra's letters beneath her fingertips, Rose felt a sudden wave of shame. Her sister, while Rose's opposite in looks, had never been her enemy, even if she had been a bit of a brat growing up.

Isra would have loved to be here, cheering us on in the tournament as much as she did in the last one, Rose thought. *Maybe I should have brought her along after all.*

With a renewed sense of sisterly affection, Rose deftly opened the seal, and tore open her sister's letter.

To my sister, Rose, Princess of Rhone and Heir Apparent to the Kingdom, and Other things which should sound majestic and royal to you as I write this with my governess watching me with her hawk-like eyes and blackened soul—

Okay, she is gone. Thank God. How does one remain so irritating, even when she does not have to be?

Sister,

I would have preferred writing "Rora," as that is who you have always been to me, but I wasn't sure you would have recognized the reference. I also would have preferred you had taken me with you on your journey ...

Rose laughed. The few days she had spent in Rhone had been busy enough, but her sister had managed to make some of it memorable. Of course, Isra had always been that way, Rose remembered. Though it had been Rose who had been gifted with beauty, grace, and song in the form of fairy magic, Isra was the one who seemed to have been born with charm, wit, and humor.

... but probably not for the reason you think. I am afraid I write to you with some troubling news.

ONCE UPON A PRINCESS

There has been an attempt on the King's life, and I am afraid it has shattered his nerves and possibly his mind. Only yesterday, he arrested the Queen Mother, and placed her in the palace dungeon, citing treason, believing her to have attempted to poison him. Fortunately, Ronan had just returned from his grand tour, and instead of being his usual pompous vermin self, was actually a decent brother and took me away from the castle under the cover of night. We are headed to a secret location at present, with several of the Queen Mother's guards and a handful of our staff, as the Queen fears for our livelihood.

"What? What in the world is going on in Rhone?" Rose wondered aloud. "How could the King do this to the Queen Mother?" She looked down at the date on the letter; it had been written about five weeks after she'd left, and over a month since then. "What am I supposed to do?"

"Rose? What's wrong?"

Rose jumped. "Theo. You shouldn't scare me like that."

Theo smiled kindly in a mild apology. "I'm surprised I was able to surprise you. What's wrong?"

"Someone tried to kill my father. And the King decided to arrest my mother for it." The words sounded strange, almost like she was describing a play or the plot of a novel.

"What? Why?" Theo asked. "That's awful."

"I know, right?" Rose shook her head. "Isra says someone attempted to poison him and his nerves are overwrought because of it."

"Sounds like it if he's going to put your mother in the castle dungeons. Unless—"

"What do you mean, 'unless'?" Rose snapped. "She's my *mother*. She doesn't have the guts to commit treason, let alone the desire. You know how she is, Theo."

"I know," he replied. "But you even told me when we were there that she might be having an affair."

"But—"

"That's treason to the King, and the kingdom."

"But the King doesn't care about that. He doesn't love her."

"How do you know?" Theo asked. "He might love her."

"How could he?" Rose asked. "He doesn't even love me."

"He still sought her hand."

"He sought power."

"Okay, if you assume he doesn't love her, then why would he wait until now to arrest her for it?"

"Because of the poison."

"Do you think the poison attempt was a real or is it possible it was staged to frame the Queen?"

"I don't know," Rose admitted. "Do you think he's arrested her in hopes I'll go back to Rhone?"

"It's possible." Theo ran his hand through his hair. "It wouldn't be the first time the King's done something unusual to try to provoke you into coming home."

Rose snorted. "That's true." She looked up at him, suddenly feeling much younger and much more frightened than she had in a long time. "Do you think my father would release her if I came home?"

"I don't know." Theo looked down, unable to meet her gaze. He saw the other letters in her hand. "I got a letter, too?" he asked.

"Oh, uh, yeah. Here." Rose handed him the other letters.

He took them, handling them with too much care for Rose's taste. Isra had been her younger companion for much of her life, but she was unfamiliar with just how deeply her sister's devotion was where Theo was concerned. She wondered, not for the first time, if Isra was writing love letters to him. She waited in expectation as Theo read his own letter.

Finally, he looked up at her. "What does the rest of your letter say?" Theo asked.

"Huh? Oh. Let me see." She nearly blushed, having forgotten her own letter. Rose glanced back down at the parchment.

Ronan has his usual company of men, while I have my nosy governess, Mrs. Winston, of course, who has just come back into my small room

ONCE UPON A PRINCESS

here. I am also glad to have Juana by my side, as Fiona decided to stay with our mother.

That's good, Rose thought. At least Mary would be able to place a locator spell on Virtue, so she could communicate with Isra.

As per my current location and condition, I am unable to continue informing you of the King's intentions; I can only say this attempt on his life has shaken him, so please be cautious. The Queen Mother was only able to tell me she didn't know who actually poisoned his food, but all my (and your) potential suitors have been sent away just in case there is an assassin in their midst. Personally, I am not all that sorry to see them go, as many of them were ugly or just plain boring. Even when I was veiled and it was assumed I was you, they would only talk of my beauty and my tragic curse. I can confidently assure you, you would have hated all of them nearly as much as I did.

Rose felt a reluctant smile flit to her lips. Isra couldn't have been in too bad of shape if she was able to make light of her situation.

Since Ronan and I have left, we have been declared traitors as well. We will not be able to meet you in Havilah, not until the King's anger has subsided or the real assassin has been found and properly imprisoned. In the meantime, I hope to seek out some answers myself. I think you would be proud of me—off on a journey of my own, working to solve mysterious happenings.

When you arrive in the Romani territory, please send word. Just in case you think you will be too busy, I will tell you it is a matter of the greatest urgency that you write to me. Your streak of moral stubbornness is irritating at times, but I am strongly certain the guilt will compel you to fulfill my wishes.

Ever Your Sister,
Isra

ONCE UPON A PRINCESS

"She would guilt me into writing her, when she knows I can do nothing for her," Rose muttered under her breath.

Theo looked up from his own letter. "What did she say?"

"I'm supposed to write to her once we get to the Romani territory, among other things."

"Can I read it?" Theo asked.

"Sure. Can I read yours?"

"No."

"What? Why not? I'm letting you read mine," Rose objected.

Theo grinned. "She specifically told me not to let you read any of her letters meant for me."

"You know better than I that God will forgive you for breaking a promise."

"Ah, but would the Princess of Rhone forgive me for such grievance against the Crown?" Theo asked.

"There's only one Princess of Rhone you have to worry about while we're here together. Let me see the letter," Rose shot back.

Before she could make a grab for it, he stuffed the letter out of her reach. "Rose, it's nothing to worry about," he said.

"Then what does she say?"

"Nothing of import. She did want me to know my father's been keeping close watch on Thad and my grandfather. They are tending to your mother while she's being held."

"I can't believe this." Rose put her head in her hands. "This is just terrible."

Theo's arms wrapped around her, drawing her close to him. He placed her head in the crock of his shoulder. Rose felt heat rush to her cheeks as his hand ran through her hair affectionately.

His breath tickled her ear as he whispered, "It'll be all right."

Rose felt her terror over her mother's fate dissolve as a new, sharper form of terror took over. Her body went rigid as Theo's embrace, gentle and comforting, burned into her

ONCE UPON A PRINCESS

blood, turning it into something more, and anything but innocent.

Before she could say anything, he continued. "Once we get to the Romani territory, we'll get the dragon's blood, and then we'll go back to Rhone and get everything sorted out."

"What if it's too late?" she whispered, burying herself in his shoulder, easing herself into his arms, loving his closeness even as she hated herself for needing it.

"Then you can do nothing to change it."

After a moment of considering it, Rose nodded. "You're right."

"It doesn't mean you can't mourn," Theo told her. "But we need to focus on one problem at a time. First, we have to get off this island."

"Then we need to find the dragon's lair," Rose recited, as they had a hundred times or more during their many walks along the ship's deck.

"Once we have that, we'll head back to Havilah and see what's wrong with Rhone and the King."

"Free my mother."

"And then go and take care of Magdalina."

"And Everon, too," Rose added. She glanced up at him. "You can't leave your vengeance out of it."

He smiled. "Oh, I know."

Rose smiled back despite herself. "You always put me first. Don't you ever think of yourself?"

She felt him go still, before he loosened his grip on her. He tugged a short lock of her hair, playfully, as he had done so many times before. "Oh, I do," he assured her, "but only when you let me."

Rose hit his shoulder back at his jest. "That's not funny."

"Don't worry," he told her. "I'll pay for it, if I haven't already."

He indicated the letters in his hand. "Let's go give Philip his letter, shall we? Oh, and Roderick, too."

"Roderick got a letter?" Rose asked. "From Isra?"

"No, someone else." Theo held it up. "Different handwriting."

"Maybe my mother?" Rose asked. She reached at the letters, but only managed to grab Philip's out of Theo's hands. "Let me see."

"Rose, it's not yours. Just give Philip his and I'll take care of the rest."

Before Rose could argue, she was interrupted by a voice from behind them. "Some mail came for me?" Philip asked. Rose and Theo turned just in time to see Philip come through the stable doors. He looked from Rose to Theo and arched a brow.

"The Queen has been imprisoned," Theo explained. "Isra has sent word."

Rose took another step back from Theo as she held out Philip's letter. "She sent you one, too."

"Thanks." Philip took the letter and stared at it for a long moment, gently turning it over in his hands. "I wasn't sure if she was really going to write to me when we set off."

"Isra likes to write," Rose said. "She'd probably make a good scribe or authoress if she wasn't a princess."

"I'll read it in a bit," Philip promised, sticking it beneath his armor. "I came to see where you were. The others have arrived."

"Already?" Rose frowned. "I would have thought it would take much longer, given most of us overslept this morning."

"We're just waiting for you." Philip gave her one of his charming smiles and gallantly held out his arm for her. "Shall I escort you, Rose?"

While Theo narrowed his gaze at Philip, Rose clasped onto him and nodded. "All right. But I want to hear what Isra wrote to you. Perhaps it will have some insights into where she is going and what else is happening I should know about."

ONCE UPON A PRINCESS

5

Rose welcomed the light of the inn's private dining room, a room Felise had allowed them to use free of charge. Rose had to wonder if Felise had been charmed, like nearly all men, by her beauty when he'd offered them the room; while the old man was clearly respectable, she could not see him appreciating the loss of any profit.

Philip led her to the main table, decorated with flowers as well as some of the food and drink they had bought earlier that day. Rose's stomach rumbled as she spied the freshly baked bread.

Before she allowed herself to eat, she looked around to see her traveling companions were all present, even the guards. She frowned at Roderick, the guard with the curling ginger beard who shared a special friendship with her mother. Rose had seen the intimacy between his gaze and the Queen's back in Rhone, and Rose was almost certain he was a spy for her mother, if nothing else.

I'll need to work that into a conversation soon, Rose reminded herself. *With the Queen in prison, Roderick owes me some answers, and I intend to collect.*

She turned to see Ethan's face gradually getting redder as Sophia talked to him. There was a bundle on his lap that he gripped tightly, his fingers white with protective pressure.

Rose looked up at Philip as he surveyed the room with her, and Rose didn't have to look behind her to be able to know Theo was there.

She cleared her throat, announcing herself. Despite her uncertainty, she straightened her posture. Next to Philip, she felt almost like a regal queen. He was good at commanding attention, she thought. Then again, he was a prince; that probably came naturally after all the years of having it nurtured in him.

When everyone turned to face her, she didn't falter. "Something terrible has happened."

"'Something terrible?'" Sophia repeated. "What is it? We are still going to compete in the tournament, right?"

Rose cleared her throat again, trying to make sure she didn't choke on the words. "There has been an attempt on King Stefanos' life," she explained. Sophia let out a small gasp and Ethan's mouth dropped open. Roderick and Captain Locke flinched, while the other guard, Lannister, looked shocked. Mary, who had been fluttering around in a cheery manner, stopped and sank down to the tabletop as Rose continued.

"My mother was thought to be the villain, and she has been charged with treason and imprisoned in the castle dungeons. Isra and my brother, Ronan, are heading to a safe location. Other than that, I don't know exactly what has happened."

"They've imprisoned Leea?" Roderick asked. "For treason?"

Rose cocked an eyebrow. "You mean Her Majesty the Queen?"

"Of course." Roderick blushed. He added in a sheepish voice, "We are friends, and we do not use formal titles."

"I see." Rose relented in her preferred line of questioning for the moment, deciding not to barrage him just then. "But to answer your question, yes. She's in the dungeon. My father thinks she tried to poison him."

"But why would the Queen attempt to kill the King?" Ethan asked.

"I don't know." Rose sighed. "I don't even know if she did try to poison him. It doesn't sound like my mother."

"Maybe she was mad at him for emotionally blackmailing you," Sophia said, "since he was threatening you with abdication if you didn't marry."

"I still doubt it." Rose crossed her arms over her chest as she began to pace. "But I have no clear answers."

"We need to get back to Rhone, and soon," Mary asserted.

"I agree. But we still need to stay our course," Rose insisted. "These new developments won't alter the fact I still need to stop Magdalina, and for that, we need dragon's blood."

"And for that, we need to get off this island," Philip stated. "That means we need money and supplies, which we might be able to get by participating in the tournament rounds next week."

"We've gotten a good start on that," Sophia said. "Ethan and I made our way down to the merchant area. There were plenty of smithing sheds for me to exam. I've even been commissioned by one of the blacksmiths down there for the tournament."

"Really?" Rose asked. "That's wonderful."

Sophia's eyes, one brown and one a mixture of blue and green, both twinkled. "I'm so excited. I'm finally old enough where people are starting to take me seriously."

"I'm happy you've found a good place to work for now. The sooner we can leave, the better."

"I'll earn enough for all of us to book our own rooms on the Romani trader ships!" Sophia vowed.

"I don't know if that's possible," Theo spoke up. "According to the priests I talked with, some of the passages are quite expensive, and we will still need to pay for supplies once we get to the Romani territory." He glanced up at Rose. "I hate to admit it, but Rose is right. We will need more money, and the tournament is the best option to get it."

Rose felt the rush of silent triumph.

"We have enough for three people to enter," Philip spoke up. "Rose and I got the coins exchanged at the banks this morning."

"I'm going to enter," Rose announced. "I hate traveling by boat, and if I have another month yet where I am forced to travel by boat, I might as well put my fighting skills to good use while I'm on land." She looked over at Sophia. "I thought you might like to enter, to try out your knighting skills. But with your job ... I guess Theo and Philip will be able to enter?"

ONCE UPON A PRINCESS

She turned to find Philip's dimple winking in agreement, while Theo shook his head.

"I can't," Theo said. "I've been asked by the church to help out with some of their duties. For each tournament, several of them get together to put up a medical ward near the city square for people injured or indisposed."

"And you said yes?" Rose asked. "That hardly seems exciting."

Theo smirked at her. "Well, taking care of people has always been my stronger suit than yours," he teased. "But there are two other reasons I agreed. There are extensive libraries and scholars around the chapel and its adjoining university, and many people cavort there throughout the day. It is a good place to gather information. I also thought Mary might like to come along. I know we've talked about making sure she is out of sight, but I can easily carry her in a pouch on my belt."

Mary smiled. "I might be able to help," she agreed.

"All right. That leaves us with one ticket for the tournament. Any takers?" Rose asked.

"I'll do it."

Rose wasn't as surprised as she thought she would be as Roderick stood up. "If I'm to get us back to Rhone quickly, I might as well do something more useful than babysitting you, Princess."

Rose nodded. "I can't argue with that logic."

Sophia giggled, causing Rose to shoot her an inquiring look. Sophia pointed to Ethan. "He was worried he was going to have to fight in the tournament, too."

"Ethan's welcome to help any way he wants," Rose assured them. She knew all too well how much Ethan tended to avoid the battlefield. His father had tried too hard and too soon to make his son into a warrior, Rose thought. She grimaced as she recalled the day she'd first met Sophia and Ethan. "He does not need to fight."

Ethan looked up at her, meeting her gaze and reading her thoughts; he blushed further, this time more out of anger

ONCE UPON A PRINCESS

than embarrassment. "I was more worried I wouldn't get a chance to attend some of the festivities," he contended.

"Especially the musical ones, right?" Sophia asked with a teasing smile.

"Keep your mouth shut," Ethan muttered.

Rose nearly laughed, recalling the days and the fights she'd had with Ronan and Isra over similar matters. Fearing Ethan might think she was laughing at him, she nodded toward the bundle in his lap. "What's that?"

Ethan hesitated. "I made this today, with the help of a girl." He unwrapped the package, revealing an Aeolian harp. The wood was unpainted and plain, but the strings were straight and secure, and Rose could tell Ethan had put a lot of hard work into making it just right. He'd always been good with building things, she thought, recalling his skill in making traps, snares, and nets for hunting and fishing.

"Looks lovely," she praised, causing Ethan to break into his first genuine smile all night.

"Penelope has been training on the harp for many years," he said. "I met her at one of the street shops. She showed me how to make it, and let me keep it once I was finished. She said she'd never seen such fine workmanship before, let alone on a first effort."

"Do you play?" Theo asked. "I remember learning a little bit with Rose and the twins," he said, "when we had our lessons in the palace."

"Isra was always better than me," Rose replied. "And Ronan was more interested in using the harp for a weapon rather than music."

"It was quite a weapon in his hand," Theo agreed. "Even when he tried to play."

Rose laughed. "Remember the time he—" She stopped, recalling they were supposed to be concerned about Ethan. "Uh, never mind. Do you play the harp, Ethan?"

He shook his head. "Penelope told me she would teach me if I came back and visited her this week. I was thinking of giving it a shot."

ONCE UPON A PRINCESS

"Well, we would be saving a lot of future money on minstrels and troubadours if you could do your own compositions," Rose said in a calculated tone. "I suppose it's a worthwhile venue for you to pursue. But you'll have to practice when you come back to the inn, so we don't waste our time or resources. If you can agree to that, I have no trouble with you learning to play the harp."

"I can do that," Ethan said with a brightened look. He stuck his tongue out at Sophia as she rolled her eyes. "It would be much more fun than fighting."

"You're never going to get any good if you don't step up and learn," Sophia argued.

"Rose just said this is a way I can help. I don't have to fight."

"You mean you don't have to be brave."

"Shut your mouth," Ethan snapped.

As the two began to bicker between themselves again, Theo reached out and placed a hand on Rose's shoulder. "I think Ethan will make a good musician," Theo said, raising his voice just enough to be heard over the argument.

"Of course he will," Rose said. "He has the soul of an artist. I would have to be the most dim-witted fool in the world not to put his talents to good use." She turned toward Philip. "Don't you think so, Philip? You would be the one to know, especially since you won my sister over with your singing and poetry before."

Rose watched as he faltered; there was a strange look on his face as he glanced around the room. Before she could ask him what was wrong, he shrugged and grinned. "Of course, Rose."

Rose nodded. She turned her attention back to her plans, still wondering what was bothering Philip.

6

Philip found himself pacing in front of the fire in the common room of the inn.

He was used to being lonely, he thought. It wasn't a surprise to find himself on the outer edge of Rose's company. After all, from what he had learned, Ethan and Sophia had been with Rose for nearly two years, and Rose and Theo had known each other since childhood.

But in seeing Rose's exchange with Ethan and Sophia, and her shared glances with Theo and Mary, he felt strangely bothered.

He added another log to the fire. "That's a first," he conceded to himself.

When Derick, his older brother, had grown up and fallen in love with his Juliette, Philip's devotion to him had changed from admiring him as a brother to having pride in not only his character, but his accomplishments. But seeing the steady, resolved longing and love in his now sister-in-law's eyes made him distinctively jealous and also strangely liberated.

He'd known in that instant Derick had a heart behind him full of a greater love than one he could give him. It was freeing, for it signaled that it was time to make his own life, and find his own love.

His mother's overwhelming enthusiasm at hearing he was headed off to Rhone to fight for the Princess' hand in marriage had made him wonder if he would win her heart, too.

Philip knew he hadn't been expecting Rose when she had met him, saving his life in the process.

He looked down at the letter in his hand from Isra. There were many things he hadn't expected, he thought.

Dear Philip, Prince of Einish, and Friend of my Heart,

ONCE UPON A PRINCESS

I'm sure my darling sister has told you, immediately as she does when she cannot control things, that disaster has struck the kingdom of Rhone.

I regret to inform you I am a fugitive of my country for an unforeseen amount of time, and Rose is a wanderer in search of her heart, but only so she might smite it. What a pair of interesting friends my sister and I have proven to be to you, and in such a short amount of time.

His lips curled, knowing Isra's humor. She had a gift, he thought, for describing the truth in such illustrative terms.

I hope you do not mind me telling you I am distraught over such a fate myself—not that I am destined to run away from my home, but that I am unable to make your acquaintance sooner. As I am in such need of pampering and care, I pray you will remember how this terrible news has affected me when you come back home, and forgive me for indulging my emotional upheaval. And of course, for compelling Ronan (you didn't meet him while you were in Rhone, but you will get to someday) to go along with my plans in the matter.

What was she talking about? He wondered. He was definitely prone to compassion; she would have known that. What exactly was she planning?

He shook his head, unable to answer his own questions. Maybe Rose would know.

Despite the lively escape in the middle of the night, and the aura of intrigue inside Havilah's castle, I have been rather lonely without your company, and the company of my sister and our friends. Though in some ways I cringe at the thought—there is something to be said for having someone only read your words, and having them only see a shadow of your whole self, lost to all the trappings and trimmings our upbringings and teachings have scarred us with—I feel my heart jump in anticipation at seeing you again soon. You have my greatest envy, sir, that you are off on an adventure with some of my most favorite people ...

Philip smiled. He only wished he felt he'd earned her jealousy. There were many things still keeping him outside of Rose's circle.

Juana, who you might recall is my own version of a nursemaid fairy, has placed a locator spell on Virtue, so he might find you and the others without fail. Please have Mary do one as well, and write to me once you get to the Romani territory. I look forward to your no doubt poetic response.

Ever Yours,
Isra

"Isra always was very prolific," a voice said, coming from behind him.

Philip nearly jumped, but seeing it was only Theo who stood against the wall near the hearth, he forced himself to stay still. He gave a small grin, trying to conceal the forced effort behind it. "Since, according to Rose, she was on the road as she wrote these, I imagine she is." He paused. "Did she write a lot of letters to you during your previous travels?"

"Yes," Theo admitted. "She was very lonely, I think."

"She admits she has been lonely since we left in my letter," Philip agreed.

"She was nearly inseparable from Rose when they were younger, even though it was not encouraged by their parents."

"Sounds a lot like me and my brother," Philip remarked. "Were you her close friend as well?"

"Of course." Theo smiled. "I meet Rose and Isra after I came to the palace when I was ten. My parents and uncle were killed by a fairy, and my brother and I were sent to live with our grandfather, who is a leader in the church in Havilah."

"And this fairy? Was it Everon?"

"Yes, it was." Theo's eyes sharpened with animosity.

Philip knew Theo would not welcome a line of inquiry in that direction. "And so, when you came, you lived in the church?"

"My grandfather's followers remain in the village church where I grew up. They sent us to him before too long. Thad was quite the practical joker while we were there."

"I'm sure you appreciated it."

"Not at first," Theo admitted. "When he continued it at the King's chapel in Havilah, I grew to see it as a blessing."

"Sounds like a good older brother."

Theo came and sat down in a chair beside the hearth. "Seems like it would be something we have in common."

Philip's mouth curved into a small smile. "Are you worried we have other things in common?" he asked. "Such as the adoration for the princess of a certain country?"

The anger and surprise in Theo's face was palpable.

"I know the timing is poor, but I hope you won't begrudge me your friendship despite the circumstances."

Theo eased back into his chair. "I suppose I can't blame you for such a reaction to her. Everyone loves her."

"My brother grew up knowing he would marry Juliette, and he hated her for many years before he realized he'd only hated her for making it easy to fall in love with her." Philip, taking his cues from Theo, relaxed. "Some people enjoy the chase as much as the prize."

"I'd hate to try to match your brother in a hunt, then."

Philip laughed. "I certainly never won against him. But then again, you might be able to give him a challenge. It's been several years since you met Rose and her sister. With that amount of patience, you might actually beat Derick."

"I don't want to talk about it."

"It must be hard, since Rose trusts you so much."

"It's not as hard as it looks, since she does." Theo turned back to the fire.

"Tell me about earlier," Philip suggested. "I've been traveling with you and everyone else for weeks, and I'd like to know more about the rest of the group."

"What do you want to know?" Theo asked, trying not to grumble.

"Tell me how Rose met Ethan and Sophia. I know they're brother and sister."

"We met them in Greece, when we first arrived. The Eastern Warlords were causing trouble for their town and some of the surrounding city-states. We offered our help to negotiate peace, and if we failed, to help fight."

"You ended up fighting, then?"

Theo nodded. "Rose has quite a reputation for making peace between groups," he said, "but in this case, we had to fight. She was not opposed to it."

"I'm a bit surprised."

"I'm not. She ordered when she was eight to be trained as a knight." Theo laughed at the memory. "She was the smallest warrior Rhone had ever seen, and it took her longer to attain her knighthood, but she demanded to do it fairly."

"Are we sure Stefanos is not just prone to fits of hysteria?" Philip asked. "After raising such a child, we might be more lenient in our judgment."

Theo's expression drained of all warmth and life at the mention of the King. "He has been good as a ruler, most of the time, to Rhone. But as a father … I struggle not to strangle him sometimes." He sighed. "It's because of him Rose doesn't want to marry."

"I didn't know my father," Philip admitted. "He died shortly after I was born. But I know something of Rose's pain—never knowing the pride a parent has for you and your accomplishments."

"At least you'll never know if you would have disappointed him," Theo pointed out. "Rose knows full well her father doesn't approve of her."

"She is very non-traditional," Philip said. "But I would think that's why people like her. She's not what anyone would ever expect."

"Rose and I and our team of guards had been on the road for two years prior. Rose was actually helping me learn the

ONCE UPON A PRINCESS

ways of being a knight from her training," Theo told Philip. "We'd had some other battles along the way, by the time we arrived in the Greeklands, I had shown enough skill she, in her own way, christened me a knight." He shrugged. "I was hoping to get it made official when we were in Rhone. The opportunity didn't present itself."

"I thought you were studying to be a priest?"

"I was raised in the church. Thad, my brother, has decided to take the vows, but I have not made the decision to do so."

"Will you?" Philip asked quietly.

"I've thought about it." Theo shrugged. "But there are a couple of things I must do before I think about that."

Philip watched as Theo's grip tightened on his sword and nodded in understanding. "I guess it would do no good to give yourself to God if you have revenge as a master."

"Revenge is not my master, but rather a goal," Theo corrected him absently. He shrugged. "But you're right that it is too much of a life at odds with the priestly vows of holiness, worship, and consecration. I have some time, anyway; my grandfather came into the priesthood late, after my grandmother died."

There were a few moments of silence between them before Theo spoke again, continuing his tale. "Rose and I met Ethan and Sophia when she needed a new shield. We were two knights against the world of the Eastern Warlords, but she lost a shield in the final battle." He shuddered. "She almost got carved up. It was the most terrifying battle of our lives for me.

"But when it was over, she stayed and negotiated the treaty, with me by her side. Mary fixed up her wounds, and mine, too."

Philip could easily picture Theo, transfixed with Rose's pain, ignorant of his own, as he watched her sign her name with her blood, bequeathing peace to the two countries from her pain.

"Sophia's family ran the blacksmithing business where we were. In lieu of payment, for it was a poor town, Sophia's

ONCE UPON A PRINCESS

father offered to give Rose a new shield. She agreed, and asked, since it would take some time, if we would be to stay with the family and help out the town some more while it was getting made. They were easily charmed by her manners and granted the request."

"That sounds like her," Philip agreed.

"So does the next part. On the next night, Rose and I were talking late into the night, as we tend to do from time to time," Theo muttered. "We heard a commotion, and headed out to see what was wrong. Rose saw Sophia's dad strike her across the head, yelling all sorts of obscenities at her. Rose headed out to help, but I pulled her back and took care of him myself."

"'Took care of him?'" Philip asked. "You mean you beat him up?"

"Not exactly." Theo's fingers tightened into a fist. "He was drunk. I knocked him out from behind with one swift punch."

"Good for you."

"Rose and Mary settled Sophia down and kept watch over her for the rest of the night. I stood guard in the kitchen, listening out for any other problems."

"Which came, I take it?"

"Yes. You've noticed Sophia's eyes are two different colors. She told Rose and me, just once, it was because he came looking for her while she was working. He hit her hard enough where she fell over, hitting her head on one of her workbenches."

Philip closed his eyes and shook his head. "I'm glad you punched him."

"Me too." Theo clenched his fist at the memory. "I'm glad that Tatiana's fairies were able to heal her, too. That morning after the commotion, while he woke up sober, their father didn't seem any more hospitable toward Ethan. He called for him before dawn, while we were still up, and made him go out to the stables. We found out later he was 'training' Ethan

ONCE UPON A PRINCESS

for battle, even though there was no longer a problem with the Eastern Warlords."

"Well, that has always been debated. It's better to be prepared for war, but in preparing for war, people often find it."

Theo snorted. "You might have a point, but I just assumed his father was too drunk from the celebrations to recall he was no longer at war. From what Rose and I could figure, it had been something he'd worked with Ethan on for several years."

"Ethan doesn't like combat."

"Probably because he has seen too much of it too early, and too closely."

"I can understand that."

"Eventually, Rose and I talked with the others in the father's workhouse and the forage. We found out less than satisfactory things. We came to an agreement about what to do. We traded her shield in for the two kids, and paid their father off enough of our own gold to go through quite a few months of drinking." Theo paused. "As for the others in the workhouse, many of them were already planning on leaving since the Eastern Warlords had been defeated."

"That was smart, to buy them off of the father. Hopefully, even if he felt cheated later, you would have been far enough away for him to find you."

"That was the idea. Rose saved them. She took Sophia on as a squire, and Ethan helped me and Rose to learn more of the Greek language."

"You already knew it though."

"Yes." Theo nodded. "Yes, I did. The church has tried for a long time to teach its own, and I was an avid student."

"So Ethan became your map reader, and Sophia the blacksmith and Rose's ward."

"They both belong to her," Theo said quietly. "She has been their champion since they came along with us."

"But you helped save them."

ONCE UPON A PRINCESS

Theo looked into the heart of the fire. "I might have helped save them from their father, but she is the one who has made our group into a family."

"All of you have made a special place for yourselves in your family." Philip nodded, understanding, as he looked deep into the heart of the flames. "I can only hope I will have the same privilege."

7

Theo made his way to his bed for the night and lay down, pausing only slightly to listen for the sound of Philip following suit over in the next room.

Turning to the small window above his bed, Theo peeked outside. The moon was almost full, but the night air was clear enough he could see the stars glittering in the icy sky. A discomfort settled inside of him, as the combination of light and darkness haunted him, like a secret half-revealed.

Theo had not enjoyed talking with Philip. Hearing Philip compliment Rose with such a loving tone made Theo's heart sting. Even if what he said was true.

But Theo knew that apart from competing for Rose's affection, they could be good friends.

The Prince of Einish was a bit of a surprise, Theo admitted to himself. An instant wave of sympathy moved him as he remembered Rose and her perpetual hatred for surprises. Ruefully, he admitted he should have considered more seriously her feelings on the matter before.

Many princes had come to the palace in hopes of securing a marriage contract. Once they saw Rose and her loveliness, it was easy enough to derail their plans. Rose's temper, intelligence, and absolute determination to make their visits deplorable would quickly offset their fascination with her beauty.

But Philip knew of Rose's fighting skills, admired her strengths, shared some of her deepest convictions, and even knew something of her loneliness. And he was a prince; maybe without a kingdom, but he had been born into royalty and bred to lead with power.

He would be a good match for Rose, Theo acquiesced. Everyone would be pleased with the match. Rose and Philip's friendship could probably blossom into love very easily. King

Stefanos would have a secure alliance with another kingdom. Queen Leea, for her part, would rejoice at the thought of planning a wedding. The kingdoms would be happy, too, since both Rhone and Einish would benefit economically and politically.

Everyone, even Rose, could be happy, he thought.

Except for me.

"Theo?"

He jolted upright in his bed. Was it possible he'd actually summoned her, bringing her to face him in the night? "Rose?" he whispered back.

"Are you awake?" Rose opened the door a sliver, her moonbeam eyes peeking through.

"Yes."

"I can't sleep."

He got up and went to her. "Have you tried lying down?" he asked, following her to the suite entrance hall.

"No need to be sarcastic," Rose muttered. "*You're* awake, too."

"I guess so." He grinned. "Well, you have me there." He followed her, tiptoeing through the sleeping guards and collections of various weapons and supplies.

When they managed to sneak out into the hall, Rose let out a sigh of relief. "Whew. I was afraid we'd wake someone up."

"Don't worry; I think everyone's still catching up from being shipwrecked."

"They'll need their rest," Rose said, leading him outside through a side door. "We only have a few days until the tournament begins."

"Well, if you're worried about rest, you might not want to practice your sword fighting skills against me this time."

Rose smirked. "Don't think I haven't thought about it. But I doubt it would distract me from my nerves at the moment."

"Why are you nervous?" Theo asked.

"Nervous?" Rose laughed. "I'm terrified."

Theo let out a laugh. "Of what?"

"Failing."

Theo laughed harder. She glared at him, and he wisely stopped. "Sorry," he said. "But for someone who is unafraid of death, the idea you're afraid of failing is laughable."

"I don't need to fear death." Rose leaned against the wall of the inn. "Not right now."

"I know you've figured Magdalina's curse will keep you safe until your eighteenth birthday," Theo said, "but there's no way to know that's correct. Not without killing you, anyway."

"It has to be true. How else do you explain all the times we've been able to cheat death and keep going on?" Rose asked.

"Mary's magic and healing potions, for one," he said, counting off his fingers. "And your skills in peacemaking, sword fighting, and leading. And my skills in providing counsel." He reached over and pulled up her sleeve, revealing the bracelet of rosary beads he'd given her. "Not to mention divine providence."

Rose snorted as she grabbed her hand back. "I shouldn't have asked. Your arguing skills are as sharp as ever. You might have been a good lawyer for the courts if you had grown up with a normal life."

"It's still possible. The universities throughout the continent would still take in an old man like me."

Rose rolled her eyes. "You're barely twenty."

"Past twenty now, Rose."

"Close enough."

"Yes, close enough. But I don't think I'd be happy as a man of law." He smiled, tweaking a lock of her hair affectionately. "Give me an abnormal life any day."

When she only smiled back, he added, "Besides, I don't think I'm as good as you when it comes to arguing, since you've managed to steer the conversation away from our original topic."

"What topic?"

"Why you're afraid of failing; why you're nervous." He leaned next to her, looking out at the city fires below and the starlight above. "Why you can't sleep."

ONCE UPON A PRINCESS

"We're taking a bigger risk than I thought we would be, by entering the tournament." Theo could feel her gaze on him as she continued. "It's not a lot of our money, but it's still a lot to sink into the entrance fees when we're not certain of a return."

"We calculated it all out earlier," Theo reminded her. "We're close to a quarter of the way to paying for the passage fees, if the information we have on it is correct. Without the tournament, it could take weeks to earn the rest."

"What if I fail?" Rose asked. "What will we do then?"

"Are you sure you're not afraid of bulls?" Theo asked. "Running with them seems a little bit different than your usual training, not to mention all the other trials."

"Philip, Roderick, and I talked about it. I'll be doing the jousting, while Roderick will take on the boar wrestling challenges. He says it won't be too hard for him, since he has had practice in training and other tournaments. Philip says Einish has had visitors from all over, including Aragon. He's going to help get me and Roderick prepared tomorrow, since every contestant has to participate in running with the bulls."

Rose paused before adding, "I'm very happy we decided to let Philip come along. I was worried he would slow us down, because he wasn't used to being on the road like us. But it's just been really nice, and he seems to be fitting in well with everyone."

Theo tried not to flinch at Rose's babbling praise of Philip. "He does seem eager enough," he agreed, before switching the subject. "And I'm glad you won't have to worry about learning a new skill in the span of three days."

"I wouldn't mind the challenge, and it might actually put me to sleep with all the effort required." Rose sighed. "But you're right. It would be too risky at this point. With my mother detained in Rhone, and my siblings in hiding, I need to get the dragon's blood and hurry home."

"We'll get there as soon as we can. There's no shame in getting your rest and taking care of yourself in the meantime," Theo told her gently.

Rose put her head in her hands, much as she had earlier. "But what will we do if our plans don't work?" she asked, this time with more urgency.

"Jump aboard a ship and take it over, and head out to sea as pirates."

Rose giggled. "Theo! Come on, I'm serious."

"You don't like the idea of Captain Rose? Rose the Fearsome, Pirate Mistress of the Seas?"

Rose laughed again. "I should have known better than to think you were joking."

"If it makes you feel better, I don't think it will come to that."

"Let's hope not. I would hardly want to break the curse and then have a war to deal with when I am Queen." She turned her gaze back out to the city marina. "Assuming I don't fail at that, too."

Theo fell silent in response. There were just some thoughts which were too dangerous to entertain at the wrong moment.

He finally reached out and took her wrist again, seeking out the chain of rosary beads. "I don't think I've ever told you this," he said. "Part of me was wondering if you'd notice. But I've collected my rosary beads since we've been on the road, back when you first left Rhone."

"I did notice, but I didn't really care. At least, not that much."

"I figured," he told her with a smirk. "But these are all mementos of all the times you made me say my prayers. This one"—he plucked up one of the bigger beads—"is from the town outside of the Gaullian camps, where we fought off those giant men and their monstrous horses."

"I've never seen such huge horses," Rose agreed. "Fortunately, the Gaullian forces weren't so tough to beat. Their size always convinced them it would be an easy battle, so not too many of them had the smarts for long-term fighting."

ONCE UPON A PRINCESS

"That was the first time I got scared for you," he told her. "You seemed like such a small little girl on a battlefield too big for her, and I was helpless to defend you."

"You've never been helpless when it comes to me."

I've always been helpless when it comes to you. The words went unspoken, but Theo could have sworn she heard them by the look she gave him.

"I mean, you've got quite a collection here," Rose said after a moment, drawing her attention back to the beads. "So God must have heard your prayers, right?" She laughed and slid down to the ground. "Come sit with me, and tell me more."

"As you wish."

He sat down with her and went through some of the first beads' tales, recounting many of the absurd, funny, and sad adventures of the early years of their travels, before realizing she was no longer asking questions or laughing at his stories.

Theo looked down at her face. At her closed eyes, her soft breathing, and her wayward hair, he felt a tender protectiveness stir inside of him. She might have fallen asleep, he thought, but she was no sleeping beauty. Her beauty, even at night as she slept, was wide awake, bringing a haunted radiance to life.

Watching her, he finally slid into his own deep sleep.

ONCE UPON A PRINCESS

8

"Get up."

Theo shot up in his bed, ruffled out of sleep, with eyes still half-blurry and his heart pounding, to find Felise standing over him.

"What's wrong?" he asked, grabbing Felise's arm, searching to see if he was bleeding or wounded. Terrified they were under attack or being robbed, he scrambled to be free of his coverlet, nearly falling over.

"Relax, boy. It's opening day of the tourney," Felise reminded him. "Now, let me go, would you? I've got money ridding on your group, and I have to get the others up."

"Huh? Oh. Sorry." Theo let the older man's arm go and tried to hide his shaking fingers from Felise's scrutiny. As Felise left the room, Theo let himself fall back to the pad.

It was nothing. This time.

The early morning his Uncle Thom died had started the same way. Even though it had been over a decade since that morning, it had forever changed Theo.

He clenched his fingers into a fist. His mind drew up a fuzzy, unclear face of Everon, Magdalina's offspring, the one who had robbed him of his parents and a normal life.

He put his hands together, clasping them in a helpless, unspoken prayer, trying to take inventory of all the steps and provisions he needed to acquire in order to have his long-sought revenge.

We need this tournament to be able to make progress in our journey, he thought. With Rose's calculations, they needed to place high in at least two categories to win enough money for the passage to the Romani territory.

But he knew there were other concerns, too. There was no telling how long it would take to find the guarded dragon's

235

lair once they arrived in the Romani territory, and it would be another month before they arrived there by sea, at best.

Rose has less than a year to go before the curse catches up with her, Theo calculated.

"You okay?"

Theo looked up to see Philip standing at his door. "Yes, I'm fine," Theo told him. "I was just praying. I guess."

"Well, today's the day we're going to need it," Philip agreed. "The tournament kick-off is in an hour, down in the city square. Felise tells me there's going to be a crowd, so we had better get going."

"Can't argue with that." Theo grabbed his tunic and his gloves, and then, recalling his promise to the leaders at the church, put them back down. He would go in his priestly frock, he decided, recalling the conversations he'd had with the Abbess at the cathedral the previous day.

Theo regretted his choice in attire as soon as he saw the look on Rose's face. It held a grim mixture of darkened relief, before the expression flickered away and she asked him if he expected many people to die on opening day.

"No, but I have no doubt there will be a lot of people praying for good fortune," he remarked easily, raising his eyebrow as he looked her over. She said nothing; she only rolled her eyes and went back to eating her breakfast.

He wondered if Rose would think of him later, praying for her success.

Ever since that night he'd fallen asleep on her shoulder, something had changed—no matter he had woken up a few hours later and carried her to bed, tucking her in gently, and waiting until her breathing had returned to its steady rhythm before returning to his own bed. She had been reluctant to make time for him since then.

Not that she needed to, he sternly lectured himself. But something had been off in the steady cadence of their friendship, and he could not say if it was nerves or embarrassment or even something else—mostly because "something else" was too unbearable to contemplate. He pushed free of his own thoughts as Rose and Philip discussed their upcoming events.

"Felise managed to get us a list of the events," Rose was saying to Philip. "Looks like jousting is going to be one of the later ones."

"Should give you plenty of time to recover from the running of the bulls, then," Philip agreed. "Felise said that's how they get a lot of people to pay a lot of money and then drop out of the competition, and I happen to agree."

"Sounds dangerous," Theo spoke up. "Do you have to finish in a certain amount of time, or before a specific number of others?"

"Nope." Philip grinned. "In true Aragonian tradition, you just have to survive."

"Oh." Theo shook his head. "Well, I have noticed there are quite a few people around here determined to get personal glory."

"Yes, it's good we're just here for the money," Rose muttered in reply as she sipped out of her tankard.

Theo held his ground. "It might be harder to win, not just because of physical demands but also personal ones. It would be easy to make enemies."

Ethan shuffled his feet as he ate his breakfast. "From my observations of the practice arena, Rose, you are in good form and standing among the competition."

"Let's hope so." Rose nodded. "We'll need a good amount of money to book passage on a ship out of here."

"I checked down at the docks yesterday on my way back from the city blacksmith quarters, as you requested," Sophia spoke up. "We might have a few options, even if you guys don't place well."

"Just be careful," Mary spoke up as she perched herself on Theo's shoulder. "My magic might be able to conjure up a small raft from a tree trunk, but there's no way to save everyone from the kind of storm that brought us here."

Felise appeared in the doorway of the dining hall. "There are my favorite competitors," he said in greeting, rubbing his

ONCE UPON A PRINCESS

hands together. There was a speculative gleam in his eye as he added, "How can I help you get to the arena today?"

Despite the tension between them, Rose and Theo exchanged a smile; both were able to guess that their prudent, well-invested innkeeper had no doubt placed substantial bets on their performances after witnessing their practice sessions.

"We're just discussing the running of the bulls," Rose spoke up. "It says on the program that it'll be in a couple hours at the main city arena."

"It'll start there," Felise said. "But it'll take you out and around the city, down the docks, up by the mountains, and back through the city square."

"It's that long?" Roderick asked, as he came into the room and joined them.

"It's a tournament," Felise reminded him. "This is the best and the brightest."

"But we're running from bulls. It's not exactly the smartest thing I've heard of."

"It's tradition," Felise said with a shrug. "It doesn't have to be smart, or logical, or anything. It just has to be intentional."

"I suppose that's fair." Rose shrugged. "It wouldn't be the silliest thing I've heard of."

"There are reasons for it," Felise said, "in the Aragonian tradition, that even Maltians, or Rhonians, will never understand unless we see it from their perspective."

"But we will." Roderick spoke up from the far corner of the room. "There are many Aragonians who have arrived at the docks in the last day."

"Don't fret about it," Felise chided. "Many just come to watch and laugh at the contestants; few will participate. They think it's entertaining to see foreigners tested in their home nation's sports."

Theo stood up. "We don't have much time. Is it possible the crowds will disrupt us?"

"Theo's right." Rose pushed back her chair. "Let's go."

ONCE UPON A PRINCESS

With the assistance of Felise and his chariot, they headed out towards the city arena together.

Fanfare radiated the city landscape, charging the crowds with excitement and emotional energy. People could be heard yelling and fighting passionately, all in a variety of languages. Rose almost laughed at the ones she was able to decode, but the new ones were almost frightening.

Philip came up beside Rose. "This is almost like your father's tournament," he told her, "except much larger."

"Yes, well, Rhone is a small nation," she reminded him. "And we are tucked out of the way. I imagine this is what it would look like if we were on the direct trading passages to the East."

"Einish is farther north," he told her. "But we are suited very nicely around the trade routes. This looks much like a port we have near my summer home, O'Lin."

"Look, Rose!" Ethan pointed eagerly. "There's a performer's tent, and they're looking for contestants." He looked over at her. "Do you think I would be able to enter with my harp?"

Rose pursed her lips together as she considered it. "Well, Penelope would be the better one to ask, since she is teaching you this week while we're in the tournament games. You might as well check it out."

"Can we afford it?"

"For you, absolutely."

"All right!" Ethan cheered, and Rose immediately decided she had made the right decision, even though she hoped it wouldn't cost her the remaining coins in her purse.

"Don't wait up for me," he called, hopping off the chariot and into the crowd. "I'll catch up later."

"No need to worry about it. Be careful," Rose called, warning him as he weaved through the thick crowds. "And meet us back at the inn at the end of the day."

She caught sight of Sophia, who was smiling to herself beneath her blacksmith cap. Her mismatched eyes met Rose's as she mouthed a silent, "Thank you."

Philip also nodded. "It's for the best for him."

"He's young yet," Rose agreed. "He might as well have some fun while he can. We have other things to worry about for now." She shifted out of the conversation topic and into another one. "Such as what is waiting for us at the arena."

"It's just over there," Philip told her, indicating the area to her right. She scooted over as she tried to get a better angle on her view and bumped into Theo.

Flushing red heat warmed her cheeks. Rose felt the tournament's worries slip away as the memory of the night she had fallen asleep outside with Theo came rushing into her mind.

Rose had woken up briefly to see he had fallen asleep, leaning into her. She had reached out and grazed her palm against the stubble of his coming beard, her disloyal fingers lingering around the softness of his mouth as she studied the rest of him. She was shocked to realize the boy she had gone adventuring with had blossomed into a man.

A compassionate, caring, and strong man.

At the quaking of her body and the shudder in her heart, she realized the darkness, even with all its secrecy, had failed to disguise the longing inside of her.

Reality snapped through her as the chariot tumbled over broken cobblestones. Theo grabbed her arm, steading her, and she glared at him. The hidden bitterness in her heart over her fate caused her to hate him in that moment.

"You okay?" he asked.

Rose only nodded and cleared her throat, struggling to convince herself he could not read her thoughts. Why did he have to make it so easy for her to want to be with him, when it was impossible? When it was too painful to even think about?

"Excuse me," she whispered.

At her narrowed gaze, he said nothing; Theo shifted over, and Rose determinedly fixed her gaze on the arena and her mind on the task ahead.

ONCE UPON A PRINCESS

From the sight of it, the arena was a good distance around, and the path around the heart of island civilization would be longer. Rose nearly groaned at the thought of running it all; she was not accustomed to running longer distances. Rose knew from her studies that retreats never worked in the long-term.

"Felise, can you stop for a moment?" Rose asked. "I want to see if I can see the trail from here."

"They have it blocked off," Felise informed her. "You'll see it when you're running it. Chances are, you won't even care when it comes to it. You'll be too busy fleeing for your life from the bulls."

"We'll see about that," Rose replied, already sliding around the handrail. "Just give me a moment. I'm trying to visualize it."

"Rose!" Philip cried out as she hopped off the chariot and into traffic.

The rush and bustle of the people and animals moving caused Rose to stumble, and she nearly fell over as a horse and its rider shied and reared.

"What in blazes are you doing?!"

The cry barely registered in Rose's mind as someone grabbed her arm and steadied her. She looked up to see Philip's hazel eyes lit with concern as he gripped her. Out of the corner of her eye, she saw Felise yank on the reins of the chariot's team and jolt to a stop.

"We apologize, sir," Felise spoke up, addressing the horse's rider, who had been the one to yell.

Rose looked behind her to see a giant man resembling a Gaullian warrior. He was large and broad, and his beard clung to his chainmail. His angry expression made his thoughts easy to decipher.

"Get your lady out of my way," he snarled at Philip. "I'd hate to get her blood all over Storm's hooves."

"At least my blood would be clean," Rose shot back, infuriated she'd been passed over.

"By the sound of it, you'd best get her to hold her tongue, too."

Philip frowned as Rose nearly sputtered in anger. "There's no need for insult, sir."

"The only need I have is to get to the arena." The rider puffed up his chest. "If I, the Great Marsor of Castile and Aragon, am going to win the Maltia's bullfight tournaments for the fourth year in a row, I need to be there for the opening ceremonies."

"There's nothing 'great' about being a brainless brute who insults people," Rose snapped.

"I'm not the one who was traipsing through traffic!" Marsor yelled back.

"Well, you are the one who is holding up traffic now," Philip pointed out. "We have apologized, needlessly it seems. Be on your way, sir."

"I'll not take orders from the likes of you." Marsor huffed. But the roars of others behind him drew his annoyed scowl into one of blatant hatred. "Mark my words, you'll pay for this." He spat on the ground between them before he urged his horse onward, allowing traffic to resume with growing sparks of fluttery conversation.

"Let's get back in the chariot, Rose," Philip said, guiding her along.

"I'm no one's 'lady,'" Rose muttered angrily, watching the crowds cover the path Marsor had created in his angry departure.

"I know," Philip said. "I'm sure he just is not blessed with good sense."

"That's Marsor the Strong, from the Aragonian kingdom," Felise told Rose, as Theo took her hand and pulled her into the chariot. "He's smart enough to have won this several rounds in this tournament, and others, for at least three years in a row." Looking at Rose's face, he added in a loyal tone, "You're right about his manners, though. Hardly fitting for polite company."

"How can such a horrible man be smart enough to win such a grand tournament as this?" Sophia asked.

"Determination doesn't require being smart," Rose guessed.

"He's a mercenary," Felise explained. "He's paid well to know how to win. The Aragonians are particularly good at battle, too, seeing as how a lot of their knights travel, looking for a chance to sell their services."

"I've heard they have leadership issues in Castile and Aragon," Theo spoke up, catching Rose's eye with a knowing look. They'd had some experience with some of their fighters before.

"To say the least," Felise agreed. "I'm glad Maltia is not like that. With our economy, we have too much to lose to cause trouble, and it's a good thing we know it."

There were advantages to trading rather than fighting, Rose silently agreed, recalling Rhone's policies on similar matters.

Felise interrupted her thoughts. "We're coming up on the cathedral," he said, indicating a large set of stairs, leading up a small hill overlooking the city square. "I'll pull over so you can get out, sir."

Rose looked up at the grand cathedral church; she was not surprised to see in proper daylight it looked grander than the one in Rhone, nor was she shocked to see it looked as distant and cold as ever to her.

A hand squeezed around hers. "Be safe today … Rosary." Theo's murmured request was a soft whisper against her nape, sending chills down her back.

Rose stilled as his hand left hers, and he exited. Before she could say anything, Theo waved his hand and Mary, poking her head out of a pouch tied to his belt, winked as she sent a flicker of sparks in farewell.

"Have fun," Philip called back, as their travel resumed. He turned to Rose. "Hopefully, we won't need to see them while we're competing."

"Yeah," Rose agreed. "The medical tents have to be depressing." She wrinkled her nose. "I think I'll pass on visiting if I don't have to."

"You can come and visit me," Sophia told her. "The smithing forage is on the other side of the arena, but it's always full of people. Most of them seem nice enough."

"I'll take your word for it," Rose told her. "I'll need to spend some time later preparing for the jousting competition."

"That's still two days away," Felise reminded her. "You'll have plenty of time to do other things." His greedy eyes glittered. "There's a reason the events are so spaced out and there are some restrictions on entering. Maltia turns out a nice tournament, but in the end, they are the ones who benefit the most, financially."

"Seems pretty fair," Philip said. "Einish does similar events and such for holidays and special occasions. This is the first time I've been to a place that holds specific cultural tournaments."

"The diversity of Maltia's history makes for excellent tourism," Felise said with a chuckle.

"So excellent profit," Rose noticed.

"Yes. And you and your team will be bringing me in some extra profit this year," Felise added.

"How do you know?" Rose asked. "You've only known us a few days."

Felise laughed. "I've seen you practice and take charge. Your followers are varied and intelligent, and very loyal to you. That's not something that happens by accident. They have great faith in you, and it is not blind."

"That's true."

"I've heard the stories of you, you know."

"What stories?" Rose asked.

"The stories of the exiled princess of Rhone, an unbelievably beautiful young woman who has trained as a knight and works as a mercenary and peacekeeper."

ONCE UPON A PRINCESS

A moment passed before Rose found her voice. "How did you figure out that was me?" Rose asked. "I never told you."

"There are none so blind as they who will not see," he quoted. "And I, My Lady, choose to look very closely at who I deal with." He laughed. "That, and your man, Lannister, is a bit of an easy drunk."

"Thanks for the warning," Rose muttered. "I guess I know who will be staying on Maltia if we can't afford passage for everyone."

Felise laughed harder. "It won't come to that, my lady. I'm sure of it."

"Why?"

"Because I actually bet money on it. I haven't lost a bet in years," he bragged proudly.

Rose smirked. "Famous last words, Felise."

9

Rose had never been good about admitting her more unpleasant feelings to herself, seeing it as a weakness at worst and an inconvenience at best. But as the tournament began, and city counselors called for the traditional running of the bulls, Rose was more than happy to admit she was nervous. With the combined smells of sweat, sunshine, and essence of bull, she was less willing to focus on how much she wanted to vomit. Looking over at Philip, she could see he was struggling to maintain his own composure, while Roderick, who was getting ready on the other side of her, seemed ambivalent to the smelly atmosphere.

Philip tapped her shoulder, and then pointed to the gates behind them. "That's where all the bulls are kept," he said. "I don't think it'll be as much of a chore as we'd feared, running from them."

"Not with this smell," Rose agreed with a laugh.

"Being this close tends to have that particular drawback. It should get better once we're all running," Roderick told her.

"That's good to know," Rose said.

The sun shifted as the clouds wafted gently over them. Everyone was waiting for the moment when the bulls would be released. In the audience, some were quiet and contemplative, others eager and unable to stand still.

Rose looked around at her competition and felt strangely out of place. How many others, she wondered, were here, about to run for something greater than money and fame?

She needed to complete this race, she knew. It was the only way she would be able to get off the island. It was the only way to get what she needed, to escape her curse, to restore her family, and to keep her crown.

The bell tolled fiercely, and Rose felt her feet start to move as the others around her shifted as one, before gradually separating.

The bulls behind them were released, and like a moving mountain of drumming rocks. Rose lost sight of Roderick as a large bull rammed between them.

"Keep steady," Philip called, reaching out a hand to steady her. "The bulls have been bridled with different armor types, so if they hit someone, it'll more likely injure them."

She grasped his hand as she ran, using her imbalance to propel herself forward. "I don't need your help," she cried out.

"You apparently do, since I caught you."

Rose huffed. "I do not!"

"Don't worry, Rose, we can save the flirtatious banter for later," Philip told her. "Some people say it is easier to run if you are talking, but I've never found that to be the case."

"Then just shut your mouth, won't you?"

Snort! A bull came up behind Rose and sneezed on her. "Ew!"

Philip laughed from up ahead of her.

"You wouldn't be laughing if it had been you!" Rose snapped back.

"I know, but it didn't happen to me," Philip called back.

There was a careless grin on his face. The sight of it made Rose angry. It was one thing to suffer at the arrogance of a friend; it was another thing entirely to be forced to suffer with his handsome face, too.

Rose jerked her arm out of his and increased her speed to run beside him. "Let's see how long it is until *you* get bull spit on you," she challenged.

"Deal."

The sincere solemnity of his voice made her laugh, momentarily lifting her spirit.

Rose and Philip continued to run forward steadily, the pounding of their feet hitting the old cobblestone roads of the older parts of the city, the dirty puddles of the poor district, and the wooden planks surrounding the marina.

"Ouch!" Philip suddenly jostled to the side, disappearing from Rose's sight as a bull broke between them.

"Philip?" Rose slowed down, looking for her companion.

A strike of thunder lashed out from behind her. Rose felt herself fly into the ground as something huge smashed into her.

The ground was hard beneath her knuckles and knees. A second crash came down on her back. Before she could wonder if it had been a bull, Rose realized it was a large boot of another runner.

Her vision went dark as her faced landed in a puddle of mud and moss.

A cruel laugh and the charging bulls behind her made her desperately surge forward, groping for the sides of the running trail as her ears roared with the sound of oncoming terror.

Between the stomps and rumbles of the bulls' steps, she was able to catch the sound of cruel, arrogant laughter. "That'll teach you to run into city traffic." The familiar voice summoned up a tidal wave of anger. "You should have stayed at home where you belong, you senseless woman."

"Marsor," Rose muttered under her breath. A bull brushed into her, slamming her into the wall, hard. Pain punched through her, as she continued to keep moving. She had to keep going. "I'll get you back for that!" she cried, wiping the last of the mud out of her eyes.

A renewed sense of determination burned through her. She would keep going. Not only to win the tournament prize, now, she decided, but to make sure Marsor paid his dues for almost killing her for vengeful sport.

Her fists clenched as she sped forward. The marina became a blur as Rose scanned the runners' backs for Marsor's beastly countenance.

"Rose!" Philip's call was muffled as it sloshed around in her mind.

For several long moments, as the mountains were stripped of the cityscape's remnants and were gradually replaced, Rose pushed herself forward. It did not escape her she had almost died when Marsor had deliberately barraged her. Rose could not believe he had the nerve to attack her merely because of an earlier accident.

No wonder he's won in this event for the last three years, Rose thought to herself. He's willing to sacrifice anyone who stands in his way or anyone who had the audacity to confront him.

"Rose, wait up."

All of Philip's cries and all of her life seemed to blur into simple colors, until only black remained, and emptiness settled into the great, hulking figure of the champion from Castile and Aragon.

Rose pulled out the sword at her side and unsheathed it. With careful assessment, double-checking to make sure there were no other bulls in the area, Rose angled it downward and scooped up a small load of bull excrement that had fallen on the path.

Aiming carefully, she pitched the mushy lump of dung forward, managing to hit the back of Marsor's head.

A few laughs from other runners trickled into Rose's mind, serving as a small reminder there was a bigger task at hand.

"What in the blazes?!" Marsor's thunderous roar came just as Rose finished replacing her sword in her scabbard.

She laughed, slowing down ever so slightly, trying not to let the euphoria of payback get to her.

Only when she stepped on an unfamiliar substance did Rose awaken from her vindictive stupor. She gasped and faltered, nearly falling over, as she failed to stop herself from running onto a trampled human body.

"I've got you again," Philip told her, grabbing her arm and pulling her forward once more. He looked at her shocked face. "You know, you really should be more careful when you're—what's wrong?"

"That was a person." Rose's eyes were wide with shock.

"Yes, there are some people who get trampled by the bulls and other runners if they fall," he said, his voice kind. "There have been several who have left the race already because of injury, and others who were not so lucky. There are some volunteers who are working to get them off the track."

"I didn't even notice." Rose glanced back, unable to see the body she had run over, the body she had pushed further into the ground. Guilt and remorse pressed into her.

"I noticed you didn't," Philip replied. "You were on a mission."

"Marsor nearly killed me," Rose explained, her resentment returning. "He made me angry."

"I saw," Philip said. "I was butted by a couple of bulls and other runners myself, trying to reach you." His grip on her arm tightened. "I was worried for you."

"I know my curse will protect me from death," Rose said with a slight shrug. "But it makes me angry that Marsor thinks he can just cheat like that, just so he can win and feel like I got rightfully punished because of our earlier incident."

"It's amazing how many people will use the moral high ground to take others down." Philip smiled. "I saw you toss the bull nuggets at him. Clever move, but he'll only get more upset if you antagonize him."

"Not clever enough," Rose remarked brusquely. "I'm sure if he was vicious enough to try to take me down, he didn't have any trouble doing it to others, too." She glanced around, startled to see how many people were slowing down and getting bumped and bruised from the bulls. Some fell to the side as the city square came into sight.

"I've heard that a good quarter of the people will not make it past the running of the bulls," Philip said.

"Didn't Felise mention that?"

"I don't remember." Philip laughed bitterly. "I'm looking forward to the end, myself."

Rose frowned as she cast a hurried look at her friend. He was sweating and huffing, with a tiredness about him that

ONCE UPON A PRINCESS

made his movements awkward and stagnated. "I think this is the least graceful I've ever seen you."

"Give it some time," Philip said, breathing deeply as he kept pace with her. "I'm sure I'll look worse before this day is over."

"Are you okay?" Rose asked.

That was when she noticed there was blood dripping down his side. Philip's eyes followed her gaze. "Don't worry about it," he told her. "I'll be fine. We only have a few blocks left."

"You're hurt!" Rose shot back. "We should stop."

"We will, in about six blocks."

Rose glanced up to see there were several patches of cheering crowds; several trumpets and horns blared out acclaim and celebration. Other runners were beginning to arrive in the arena.

"We can at least slow down," Rose argued. "The point is to finish and be alive, not to finish first."

Philip remained silent long enough for her to pull herself close to him and wrap her arm around his waist, carefully placing her hand above his wound. She balanced his weight against hers, shuffling her feet around to match his pace.

"Come on, Rose, I'm not helpless," Philip insisted.

"Just let me help you." Rose looked up at him through her lashes. "Please."

He rolled his eyes, but allowed her to help him. "Isra's taught you how to flirt, I see," he scoffed. "She does the same thing."

Rose grinned to herself. She had always been good at getting what she wanted.

As they came to the entrance to the arena, more cheers went up, and a few nuns in medical gear began to ask questions.

Rose shooed them away, telling them loudly she would take Philip to the medical station herself.

"Looks like we're going to go see Theo early today," Philip murmured.

Rose pursed her lips together. "You're not allowed to die on me."

"Not for a small thing like this," he assured her. "I would hate for our two countries to become embroiled in a war over a matter of a bull. I'd rather it was over you insulting me, or me telling you how beautiful you are." He looked at her squarely. "I know you hate it, but it's true, even now. Especially now. All of us look tired after the long run, some of us dirty and bleeding. But not you. You're just stunning." He ruffled her hair affectionately.

"I'd rather you didn't do that," Rose told him.

"What? Go to war with you?" he asked.

"No. Touch my hair."

"Theo does."

"So?" Rose snapped. "He does it to tease me, not to flirt with me."

"How do you know?"

"I just know!" Rose's voice nearly cracked.

"I *am* teasing you, just so you know." There was a softer quality to his voice that stalled her anger.

"You're making me uncomfortable."

"I'm the one who's uncomfortable at the moment," Philip reminded her.

"Which is the only reason I haven't dumped you onto the ground."

"For which I can only be grateful," Philip said with a small laugh. He sucked in his breath sharply. "Very grateful."

"Let's see if we can find Mary. She'll be able to help you with that better than I can."

254

10

"Thank you, sir. You've helped me more than I can say."

Theo handed the older man extra strips of cloth and patted him on his hunched back; he smiled to see the bandages flicker with Mary's signature work. "We are all meant to help each other," he said. "Take these and use them to rewrap your wrist as you need to. Please let me know if we can do more for you. We'll be here all week."

"Your prayers are enough, Brother," the man replied, nodding graciously. "God bless."

Theo waved as the man headed off into the crowds. "Thanks, Mary," he whispered down to the small fairy perched on the pillow beside the pallet at his feet.

Mary sighed. "I'm glad I was able to help him, but he sure liked to talk."

Theo grinned. "Maybe I should let you put the next overly talkative person to sleep."

"It might help us actually get through the line." Mary looked over at the gathering behind their station, where women and men alike were weeping over personal injuries or the condition of their loved ones—several of which, Theo knew, were likely dead already.

"Brother Theo."

Mary jerked back under the pillow as one of the other medics came forward.

"Abbess Aurelia," Theo greeted warmly. The older nun was the one who had recruited him for working with the medics for the week, and Theo respected her for it. The Abbess was one who took charge of her calling, often giving orders and advice to all who would seek it—and, Theo recalled with a small smile, many who were not seeking it at all.

"Take a break and head inside to help the kitchens serve food to our patients," she instructed. "I have come to offer you a respite from this station. We'll need more men down at the city's trench for burial later, too, if you can stay after sundown."

"I'll help out as much as I can."

"You and your fairy friend have done some good work today."

"Oh, uh … " Theo glanced over at Mary's hiding spot. "I, uh, well … "

"The Good Lord made all the earth," Aurelia told him. "And while humans know full well not to dabble in magic, I've no objection to the creatures he has created for the task."

Mary peeked out from under the covers. "You'd be among the few, Madame," she murmured.

Aurelia's eyes twinkled kindly at her. "I can understand your position, given we are surrounded by the superstitious as well as the obnoxious. But I thank you for making the sacrifice to come and heal these people. The Good Lord himself healed many while he was preaching, and goodness knows none of us deserve such mercy." Her nose wrinkled as she added, "Especially when some of us are too quick to find trouble again."

Theo silently agreed, thinking of all the people who had sought the excitement of running with the bulls, only to find the shallow grave of the city trench. "If there is anything else we can do to help, please let us know, Abbess."

"You're a sweet one. And I'll take you up on it later, no doubt. This is only the first day, after all. Six more will follow; seven, if a lot of people end up dying."

"I know we have a lot of people who still need help," Theo said, "but, hopefully, we will be able to manage."

Aurelia nodded. "We are here to help, and there are many who need help. This is the easiest way to make a difference."

"I wish we could get everyone to help us with our problems," Mary spoke up.

"You have need of something?" Aurelia asked. "Just ask, and we'll see what we can do."

"I've already talked to some of the monks and nuns here regarding passage to the Romani territory," Theo told Mary. "There are a limited number of open tickets for ships, but passage is pretty regulated."

"What about finding the dragons?" Mary asked.

"Dragons?" Aurelia repeated. "You're going to hunt dragons?"

Theo nodded. "We are on a mission for the crown of our home country," he explained. "We seek dragon's blood, in order to rid our home of an agent of evil."

"So you'll be looking for the Serpent's Garden, then."

Theo was taken aback. "You've heard of it?"

"There are some ancient manuscripts on the matter," she said, "and it is impossible to account for all the tales travelers bring to and fro. But the Thorneback, that's the dragon you'll find, if you know where to go in the Romani territory. There, they are guarded by Amalia, the Celestial Dragonkeeper."

"Abbess!" A shout from another worker interrupted the conversation. Theo and Mary exchanged looks as Aurelia called back orders. From her expression, Theo knew she was in agreement with his silent conclusion: They had to find out more.

"Is that a true story?" Theo asked, as the Abbess turned her attention back to them. "About Amalia, and the dragons in the Serpent's Garden?"

"Many around here know of the more legendary aspects of the tale," Aurelia admitted. "Even though our sources are sadly out of date. But if you're interested, and they'll help you, I'll be glad to give them to you in exchange for all your hard work for the church here this week."

"You'd give them to us?" Theo asked.

"Of course. Part of our job here on Maltia is to make sure we have sufficient copies of our collected manuscripts," she explained. "Some nuns and monks keep record of the present, but there's really very little need for information, when you think about it. The world needs more knowledge, and people need more wisdom."

"I know my brother, who is getting ordained as a priest soon, sees to some of the records back where we are from," Theo told her. "He prefers reading his books and scrolls." Theo almost laughed, but thinking of Thad made him homesick.

Thad would love this, Theo thought. Helping people, and then getting to read a bunch of ancient texts after he finished his tasks—yes, Thad would be right at home on Maltia.

Theo decided if he ever could afford it, he would send Thad to Maltia to study at their university.

"He's a smart one, by the sound of it. The world needs fighters and heroes and friends, but it also needs stories and history." She chuckled. "Where else, but on the other side of heaven, would we know why we fight for things, and why those things matter? You know as well as I do, Brother Theo, the world is a sadder place when we forget those things, especially if we can't even remember why we are sad."

"Many fairy kingdoms have similar practices," Mary spoke up, before blushing. "I'd forgotten that, myself."

A young boy, struggling to walk, came up beside the Abbess, his parents only steps behind. "Well, you'd best head off," Aurelia said. "I've got patients."

"Thank you, Abbess," Theo said, bowing his head as he plucked up Mary's pillow and set off toward the cathedral.

"Do you think she knows what she's talking about?" Mary asked. "About the Romani territory and so forth?"

"Yes," Theo said. "I haven't been here long, but she is an authority in this church as an abbess, and as a community organizer for this tournament. I've seen enough of her diligence and intelligence to trust her." He smiled. "And I've recognized the streak of relentless curiosity in her."

"Takes one to know one," Mary teased.

"Yes, agreed." Theo gave a small laugh. "I didn't think about that before, but you're right. We share that."

"As does Rose."

"I think Rose would like the Abbess. I'm hoping when things settle down, I'll be able to introduce them to each other."

"You might be able to do so sooner than you think," Mary said as she pointed out to the far left of the church's grand walls. "Here she comes with Philip now."

Theo spotted Rose, finding her immediately in the small parade of people heading towards the medical stations. When he realized she needed help, he ran over to her, quickly noting how she clutched Philip's waist, her fingers covering a large, dark pool of blood. "Rose!"

ONCE UPON A PRINCESS

ONCE UPON A PRINCESS

11

Rose felt her knees buckling more and more with each step she took. While she was strong, Philip was a large man; after several blocks, she was beginning to find it nearly impossible to move.

A few deep, steading breaths later, she resumed her march with as much effort as she could. Her pragmatism told her moving more slowly just made it that much longer before he could lie down.

Philip's labored breathing matched her own. And while Rose felt the twinge of pity in her heart for him, as he struggled to keep his balance and his consciousness, she was glad they were nearly out of breath. It would keep him from giving her more compliments.

Magdalina's curse would rob her of the majority of her life, but it had also ended up taking away much joy she might have found in good things like that, she thought bitterly.

Fiona and Juana, at her birth, had gifted her with grand beauty—hair like the sun, lips to shame the red, red rose, and eyes as wide and expressive as the waters of the earth—as well as the gift of grace and song, giving her the ability to still the world around her just by lifting her voice. Even though she had chopped her hair short and hid her other charms, people still found her beautiful.

Telling me I'm beautiful just makes me sad, Rose thought. Theo would call her beautiful from time to time, but it was usually to make her angry.

She suddenly wondered if Philip had complimented her in order to keep her pushing on toward the medic tents. After all, he knew her anger could energize her when uncertainty hit.

"I've been wondering if you've been taking after Theo in that aspect," she said aloud.

"What do you mean?" Philip asked.

They stopped and leaned against the cathedral wall as Rose scanned the area. "Nothing," she murmured. "I'm trying to see where we can go." She bit her lip. "This place looks crowded.

"Rose!"

The familiar voice of her friend steadied her as nothing else could have in that moment. "Oh, thank goodness," Rose muttered. "Mary!"

She turned to see Theo hurrying over, holding the pillow on which Mary sat.

"Come on, Philip," she said, drawing his arm around her body again. "Help's here."

Philip groaned at having to move, but brightened as Theo and Mary came up beside him.

"Philip, what happened?" Mary asked.

"I think one of the bulls ended up liking me too much," Philip said, trying to make light of his situation. When he gasped in pain as he tried to laugh, he shook his head. "Any help would be great, Mary."

"Rose?" Theo's steps faltered some at the sight of her, but recovered quickly. He reached under Philip's other arm.

"Thanks for the help," Rose said.

Theo just nodded as Rose, who used her free hand to feel Philip's forehead.

"Well, it doesn't feel like you have a fever," Rose said.

"I'm working on stopping the blood," Mary said. "Rose, if you and Theo can keep him still for a few moments, I'll have his wound sealed up."

Rose sighed with relief. "That's great, Mary. Thank you so much."

"Feels good to use magic more openly." Mary's wings fluttered in a small show of excitement. "I've been trying to be discreet all day."

"How has your day been?"

"Not bad," Mary responded. "We've had a lot of smaller injuries, nothing too serious."

ONCE UPON A PRINCESS

Rose eyed Theo, surprised to see one of the monks or priests must have given his ebony locks a quick trim. "Nice hair." She fought down an urge to reach out and touch it.

"Thanks," he replied absently. "You didn't carry him all the way through the bull run, did you, Rose?"

"No, of course not."

Philip laughed. "I'm much too heavy for that. We were in the last leg of the trip when a bull managed to gouge me. Just a bit," he added.

"He should be better in another minute," Mary said. "But you'll need to watch it for a few days. I've been healing people all day and there's a limit to my energy."

"Should be easy enough," Rose said. "Philip is competing in the sword fight tournament, but not till later in the week." Looking down at him, she added, "If we'll even need him to fight at all. I'm sure we'll get enough funds by then."

"There! That should do it," Mary announced.

"Thank you very much, Mary," Philip said. "It's not often I get roughed up in battle, especially one of this nature, but I can tell you with certainty I do not like pain."

"It has its purpose," Mary assured him, "but I agree with you." She wriggled her nose in distaste. "For a variety of reasons."

"I won't argue with you."

"And you'll not argue with me, either. You're going back to the inn and staying in bed until tomorrow." Rose turned to Mary, ignoring the exasperated look on Philip's face. "Can you stay with him?"

"You might as well," Theo told Mary. "I can take care of the burials by myself. You've done such good work earlier, too. You should really rest."

Mary nodded. "All right." She yawned and then smiled. "I could use a bit of a nap."

Rose laughed. "Good. Let's get Philip back to the inn and I'll tend to you both then."

"I'll be late getting back," Theo spoke up. "Can you manage him like that, Rose?"

"Yes, I've got him. Wait, what do you mean, you'll be late? Can't you come with me now?" Rose asked.

"I have duties here just as you do," Theo reminded her. "Abbess Aurelia just asked me to stay late to help out with lunch."

"She's the one in charge of the nuns," Mary told her. "And she'd mentioned she has some scrolls for us with information we need on the dragons."

Rose felt a slight wave of disappointment despite the good news. "Okay," she said, resigned. "Come back when you can. We'll be there."

Theo nodded and hurried up the cathedral steps. Rose turned back to the long walk to the inn. "I was hoping he'd help me entertain you some, Philip."

"Mary can do just as well, I'm sure," he said, smiling down at the small fairy, who blushed. "And we get to look forward to seeing Ethan and Sophia again soon, too."

"Doubtful," Rose said. "I know Sophia will be back late as well, since she'll be there getting ready for tomorrow's matches."

"And Ethan's with his Penelope," Mary informed Philip. "He might be late getting back, too." She giggled. "He was very eager to head out and see her this morning."

"I can imagine," Philip agreed. "There's something to be said for having someone to aspire to please." He used his free hand to pat at his chest.

"What's wrong?" Rose asked. She peered back at Philip, to see the edges of a piece of paper plastered between the folds of his tunic.

"Nothing," Philip said, a small amount of blush accenting his cheeks. "It's nothing."

"All right." She looked at him suspiciously. What was he hiding? Rose wondered.

After a moment, she decided to let the matter slide; they had other things on her mind. "On the way back, look for Roderick," Rose directed. "I haven't seen him since we left the arena, but I'm sure he finished before us." *Considering how much he seems to love my mother, that should be a given.*

"I wouldn't worry about him, either." Philip smiled brightly at her. "I imagine you'll have a lot to write about in your first letter to Isra."

"Well, I suppose I have some time to write her, if I'm going to be watching you and Mary rest, don't I?"

12

"Are you sure you can do this?" Rose could barely open her mouth to speak. The scent of sweaty, sinewy bull muscle had been replaced over the last two days with the filthy, corpulent thickness of boars. The rainfall during the previous night had done nothing to help dispel the perpetual cesspool enchantment placed on the city, and the early morning sea breeze had failed to fight off its foulness. She glanced around the small pen, one of the many that had been crudely constructed for the boar wrestling matches, as she sat in the stands with Roderick.

Roderick gulped down some ale from a large tankard. Roderick nodded, determined. "I'll be fine, My Lady. I grew up on a farm, you know." He looked around with a nostalgic expression. "One that was close to the Aragonian border."

"You came from Aragon?" Rose asked, her curiosity overcoming some of her stomach's tepidness.

"I was outside of its borders, but my mother took me into the cities to see my father from time to time. He was a knight of sorts himself, before he went off sailing for the young Queen of Castile and Aragon." Roderick looked out into the distance. "He was presumed lost at sea when I was eight."

"I'm sorry for your loss."

Roderick shook his head. "A boy who loses a father he barely knew does not lose that much, Highness."

"I suppose." Rose thought about her own father and how he had imprisoned his mother. And how her mother might actually be in love with Roderick. She wasn't sure if she could say she knew either of her parents very well all of a sudden.

She decided to keep her attention on Roderick. "When did you come to Rhone?"

"My mother received a small inheritance for me when my father was declared lost. She decided to go away from the

ONCE UPON A PRINCESS

area, back to her own family. We were headed for the Farnish kingdom, but we ran out of money when we reached Rhone. So we stayed. She remarried, and I joined the King's knights."

"When did you meet my mother?" Rose asked.

Roderick shook his head. "If you were not the princess, My Lady, I would not be having this conversation with you."

"Well, I hate to disappoint you, but I am the princess, and even though I don't typically order people around, I will in this case," Rose countered. "I'd rather you answered now, anyway. We're alone, for one. And for another, your competition starts in a few minutes. I need a distraction in the meantime."

"You're not the one who is competing," Roderick reminded her. He reached out and, almost in a fatherly manner, patted her arm. "You've always taken on so much responsibility for those around you. You needn't worry about me."

"Don't tell me what I already know." Rose shifted uncomfortably. "I'd hate to think my mother's *friend* died trying to get me out of a mess I made."

"You didn't make it. Magdalina did."

Rose shrugged. "I could have stayed at home."

"Doing nothing in the face of evil never helps anyone," Roderick replied, "and you are not one to do nothing, anyway."

"Quit avoiding the topic. Tell me how you met the Queen."

"She was at court when I came. We bonded over travel more than anything. She was having some of the castle restored, and she heard I had been born to an Aragonian knight. Over the years, she sent me there with some messages and such." He raked his fingers through his bright red hair. "I doubt she loves me, if you're worried about that. I'm more like a pet to her than anything."

The sadness in his voice was disconcerting enough Rose wondered if he loved her more than her mother loved him in return. "I'm not sure she would send a pet to protect me, on either this journey or the last one," Rose told him quietly.

ONCE UPON A PRINCESS

"Really, My Lady? I feel as though that is *exactly* as she would have it."

Before Rose could object, the trumpet blared, and Roderick was summoned to the center of the wrestling ring. She watched as the round bell sounded out and a boar was released into his circle. She knew he only had a few moments to tackle and subdue the beast.

"There you are."

Rose jolted in surprise. "Theo. What are you doing here? Don't you have morning mass or something?"

He handed her a decanter of water. "I thought I would come and cheer Roderick on. Give you a break, if you wanted it."

"I am on break," she muttered. "I joust tomorrow."

"I thought you might want to go train. Or maybe rest; I know you didn't sleep much last night." Theo's eyes held a shadow of accusation Rose decided she didn't like.

"I've had worse, and you know it. As long as Sophia has my lance ready for tomorrow, we'll be in good condition."

"You might want to go select a horse."

"They'll have horses ready for me tomorrow. Are you *trying* to make me leave?"

"No," he scoffed. His voice lowered as he said, "I just didn't think you'd like being here with Roderick that much. And it is wrestling. It's not something you've ever been particularly interested in." He looked up at her. "Just trying to watch out for you, Rosary."

"Stick to praying for now," Rose bit back. "We're doing okay." She counted off her fingers. "Roderick, Philip, and I all finished the running with the bulls. We were given some coins at the end, some of which Felise took so he could reinvest them—"

"Reinvest them?"

"You know, place more bets."

Theo, surprisingly, laughed. "He would, that sly fox."

The audience around them gasped in surprise, and then cheered. Rose and Theo turned to see Roderick had managed to pin the boar down to the dirt.

"All right!" Rose jumped up and clapped. "This is great." She turned back to Theo. "This will help some more. He'll get money for every boar he wrestles, and if he wins the most rounds, he'll get a bonus."

"Do you think he'll win?" Theo asked.

"I have my hopes," Rose said. "He was telling me about his childhood and everything, but I'm not sure of his competition in this matter."

"Marsor's over there," Theo said, pointing out another nearby wrestling pen.

"Is he? Where?"

"I know he made you upset, Rose, but you'll get your revenge. I heard one of his men say he's signed up for the jousting tomorrow."

"Good." Rose caught sight of Marsor, stretching beside one of boar pens. "I hope he loses."

Theo nodded. "I won't argue with you there. But do be careful."

"I am careful."

"You know what I mean."

"Do I? What *do* you mean?"

Theo sighed. "I mean that you get upset and you can lose your focus, or you can only focus on the problem he presents. It's not good battle tactics, Rose."

"Considering I'm the one who taught you most of what you know about battles, I'll take that as an insult."

"I learned a few things from watching you make those mistakes," he insisted.

Rose snorted in reply. "Why did you come here again?" she said, deliberately changing the subject. "Was it to aggravate me?"

"No. I definitely didn't want to argue, if that's what you mean."

"Well, you're doing a horrible job of it."

"You're too stressed to see I'm looking out for you just as much as you look out for everyone else," Theo said quietly.

Rose said nothing to that for a long moment. She thought about denying the need for it, but decided to let it go.

She had known Theo for a long time, and he had always told her the truth, even if it was unpleasant and not what she wanted to hear. Even the first time she'd met him, talked to him, and punched him in the nose for his blatant impertinence. That was what she had liked about him. Now was not the time, she decided, to show him she was still that seven-year-old girl with a temper.

"I met with some of the church members yesterday," he told her, changing the subject. "Some of them donated money to help our cause."

"They did?" Rose asked, brightening up at the mention of money. "Well, that was kind of them. You didn't tell me."

"I got in late again last night."

"Yes, you did. I would have thought that with the running of the bulls over, there would be fewer people dying."

"Fewer people dying, in a sense, sounds like less work. But there aren't so many deaths here. There would be fewer if the tournament organizers weren't so determined to injure people. Only the prayers are needed at the graves. But when people are injured, there's treatment and follow-ups and materials needed."

"I see. I hadn't thought about it like that."

"Well, that's what keeps me busy," Theo said. "Of course, I've noticed some of the others coming in later, too. Ethan met me at the door on my way in last night."

"I'm willing to bet it's his teacher that's encouraging him to do so."

"I have no reason to argue with you on that point."

"Aw, really?" she teased.

"Don't worry, I'll still argue with you about other things." He reached out and tugged playfully at her hair.

Philip's earlier accusation echoed through Rose's mind. She sighed and scooted away from Theo, suddenly feeling uncomfortable. Before she could decide whether or not to say anything, Roderick returned.

"Here you are, highness," Roderick said, handing her a fistful of coins.

"Great job, Roderick," Theo congratulated him.

"Yes, thank you."

"Let's make sure it doesn't go to waste," he said. "I want to get back to Rhone just as much as you."

Rose tucked the money into her tunic for safekeeping. "We won't," she promised.

"I'm going back in," he told her.

"We'll be here," Rose promised.

As Roderick turned away, Theo shook his head. "I should have known you would find a way to stay and watch."

"At least you're going to stay with me." Rose brushed the matter aside. "So you can make sure I stay here and cheer on Roderick, and not try to sabotage Marsor's efforts or something. You can think of it as a compromise."

Theo laughed. "That's an interesting compromise, Rose, where you win and I lose."

"But at least I've made it interesting enough for you to lose," Rose said. "Don't you agree?"

"And you think *I* should be the one in law."

"If you're that upset about it, you can leave." Rose sniffed indignantly.

"Now why would I want to leave you?" Theo asked. "This is the first time since the tournament began I've been about to talk to you, largely uninterrupted."

"Speaking of which … "

A round of cheering went out as Roderick defeated another boar. Rose and Theo joined in, as they realized they'd been so busy with each other they had neglected to watch Roderick's progress.

Rose reached out and hugged Theo, wrapping him in her arms.

In that instant, she forgot all about the putrid smell of the boar wrestling as she caught Theo's scent. It was the musky mixture of training and sweat, with the sweetness of his own skin.

"Rose?"

She couldn't answer, and that was the most humiliating part.

No, she thought. *The next part is going to be worse.*

"You know what? You were right." Rose pushed herself away from him, her fingertips firm against his chest. "I should go."

She brushed at some imaginary dirt on her tunic, buying the time to think of a good excuse to get away. "I forgot, I wanted to stop by the medic station and grab some medicine for Philip."

"So you want me to—"

"Stay here, yes," she interrupted. "Stay here and watch out for Roderick."

Theo's green eyes were sharp in the sunlight. "All right," he acquiesced. "I'll see you later."

"Yes. Thank you." Rose backed away and awkwardly raised a hand and headed out, too grateful to escape Theo's embrace to realize the thinning potency of the pigsty behind her.

ONCE UPON A PRINCESS

13

"What is wrong with me?" Rose wondered aloud as she made her way through the crowded city streets. She pushed her hair out of her eyes as she finally looked up to see Felise's inn.

She headed for the stables, not willing to trust herself to another's company. She had time, so she would go check in on Virtue. I haven't seen him in a while, she thought. *Going on a hawking break might just be the thing to take my mind off matters.*

Her gyrfalcon did not disappoint her; he fluttered over to her, landing on her suddenly outstretched arm. "Hello, Virtue," she purred. "I've missed you."

She headed toward the small, grassy area behind the barn. "It's not much of an outing," she told Virtue, "but it'll have to do for now. You'll be on your way soon enough. And probably carrying letters to Isra, since Philip seems to be worming his way into my head with her demands."

Isra and Philip hadn't known each other long, but Rose swore sometimes he had elected himself to be her champion. During the time he'd been recuperating and she'd watched over him, nursing his injury, he asked her to write to Isra a letter while he did. By the time he was nearly finished with his, she had barely started hers.

"I'd gotten quite the lecture on it, too," Rose muttered into Virtue's feathers. "Philip seems determined to send off letters to her soon. I'm hoping we'll be able to before we set off to the Romani territory. That way, you won't have to worry about being caged while we travel across the rest of the sea."

Virtue cooed in response. Rose grinned; she knew he didn't like traveling by sea any more than she did.

"I wish I could sprout wings and fly, too," she told him. "And then I would be able to escape the world, and everything unpleasant in it. I would truly be free."

She thought of this as Virtue took flight, circling the skies and drifting in and out of the clouds.

Would she be free, though? Would she truly be able to let go of the world, and everything in it? Rose thought of her friends, who had come with her of their own election, of their own accord.

Could she really leave them behind?

It's not like I have a choice, if Magdalina's curse will be fulfilled.

Virtue could be entrusted to Sophia and Ethan's care. They'd always wanted a pet, she recalled, remembering Sophia had mentioned her father had never allowed them to have one. And they would have each other as they grew up and took up their respective trades.

Mary would weep prettily and tend to her care, and the care of the castle, with the help of her cousins.

Philip had a kingdom of his own. He had a duty to his people, same as she did.

And Theo … Rose didn't want to think about Theo.

After meeting him in the church on her seventh birthday, she had demanded her father allow him to learn along with her. She'd watched him grow up as much as she'd helped him do so. He had followed her everywhere.

What would he do? Rose wondered. What would he do, if she succumbed to Magdalina's curse?

He would kill her for me.

Rose stilled at the thought. Yes, she thought. She was right. Theo would do anything in his power to help her, even if she was stuck in an everlasting sleep.

She nearly jumped as Virtue screeched, letting her know he was returning.

Instinct took over as she caught sight of him. Effortlessly, he landed on her arm less than a moment later.

"Good boy," she whispered, petting his brow and stroking his long feathers.

"That was so cool!"

Rose turned to see Ethan had returned from his own adventure. She greeted him with a small, teasing smile. "How was working with Penelope today?"

"I'm getting better with the harp," he said, his enthusiasm for his newfound skill glossing over the irritation of Rose's teasing. "Penelope is playing in a competition tomorrow night, and asked me to join her since the song I am working on is getting pretty good."

"That's wonderful!" Rose cheered. "That's great, Ethan. Even Virtue is happy for you." She laughed as the keen eyes of her falcon focused on Ethan.

Ethan grinned. "Can I hold him?" he asked.

"You know you can. You've done it before." Rose held out her hand. "Do you want to hawk some? I brought him out for some exercise. I don't see why you can't work on your skills, too."

"Sure," Ethan agreed, grimacing as Virtue jumped onto his arm. "His claws are sharper than I remember."

"You're not wearing your usual gear," Rose pointed out. "Here, take one of my gloves."

"Thanks."

"Tell me more about Penelope," Rose prodded. "Tell me why you like her."

"Because she likes me, of course," Ethan said with a laugh.

"Is that all it takes?" Rose asked softly. Was it possible that was all it really took for attraction to take root into a heart so that it might grow into love?

"But she's also pretty and kind and smart." Ethan blushed. "She reminds me of you a bit, if you were a few years younger."

"I'm flattered. I'll have to meet her."

"She lives in town here. Her family has a lot of musicians and troubadours. They make their living off all the tournaments and festivities here."

"I suppose it's easier than traveling around following the different tournaments."

"Penelope's family agrees with that."

"And she likes it?"

Ethan's expression faded. "She likes the music, but wishes she could play in a more classical setting. She doesn't like all the bawdiness and the inappropriate tributes."

"Something I agree with," Rose said as she recalled some of the more racy compositions she'd heard in the tournaments she'd attended. "Is she a composer?"

"She does, sometimes." Ethan glanced up at her with pleading eyes. "Do you think you could come to our performance tomorrow? You'd be able to see for yourself how good a player she is."

"And I'd get to see how you're progressing in music." Rose nodded. "I'd love to. Why don't we see if everyone can come?"

"I don't know if I want everyone there," Ethan murmured. "Penelope is used to performing, but I'm not."

"Oh. Okay. I'll come with Sophia then, unless she's working late again, and maybe Theo or Philip. Captain Locke and the other guards seem content to find their own amusement," Rose remarked, recalling her earlier conversation with Felise.

"That would be great."

"It would," Rose said with a smile. "I'm glad to see you're getting to have some fun. I know it's important for you, growing up."

Ethan blushed again, before he turned back to the falcon on his arm. "Okay, but can you help me now? I haven't done this in a while."

"Sure."

The stress melted from her shoulders as Rose helped Ethan remember how to hold Virtue and how to call him back. She watched Ethan's face glow with wonder as the large bird came back to alight on his arm.

"You're getting much better," Rose told him.

"Thanks," he replied. "I was worried when my father wanted me to learn how to hawk. I'm glad he never got around to teaching me."

Rose bit her lip. "Do you think you would like learning how to be a knight if your father hadn't insisted on it?" she asked carefully.

"I don't want to think about it." Ethan's tone was frigid.

"There are different types of bravery," Rose reminded him. "Types that don't have anything to do with fighting."

"Let's just focus on hawking," Ethan remarked.

Rose only nodded. She knew it was not her place to push.

After a few moments, she relaxed again. It was too easy to sink into the sunlight, to feel the briskness in the air. Rose lost track of time as Ethan sent Virtue up and around again and again, as she talked with the boy who was seemingly a lifetime younger than she was.

She even failed to see Philip as he came from the other side of the barn.

"Rose?"

Rose turned around. "Philip. What are you doing out of bed?"

"I've been stitched up well enough," he said, indicating his ribs. "Mary said it looked fine, so I could start moving again." He came up beside her and watched as Virtue landed on Ethan's extended arm once more. "I thought it would be best, since I only have today and tomorrow to warm up for the sword fights."

"I suppose," Rose conceded. "Still, please promise me you'll be careful."

"I'll be fine," he assured her.

"I know Sophia told me she'd work on your weapons," Rose recalled. "She's going to work on my lance and my sword tonight, too."

"You're jousting with both the lance and sword?"

"Assuming I make it past the preliminaries."

Philip smiled at her. "You will. You always do well with the joust."

"You're just saying that because you beat me the one time we jousted."

ONCE UPON A PRINCESS

"No, I've heard the tales, remember?" Philip leaned back against the barn wall. "I've been hearing stories of you for many years. I know you're a pretty strong jouster, for being one of the smaller ones."

"I'm of average height," Rose protested.

"Well, I mean compared to the others you joust. And that's good, to have that. You get more speed that way."

"Speed certainly helps. Once I pass the preliminary rounds, it'll be a two-round joust with the lance. If I win both against my opponent, I'll move on. If we tie, we joust with the sword until there is a clear winner, and then that person moves on."

"And whoever is undefeated at the end shall win."

"That's about it," Rose agreed. "I've never been in this big of a tournament before." She rubbed her shoulders. "I hope I'll be able to keep my strength up."

"You will. You know we're all counting on you," Philip said. "You've never let us down before."

"Thanks, I guess." Rose felt misery well up inside her again. "Hopefully, tomorrow won't be a first."

"I'd never known you to be so worried," Philip observed. "You're usually the one leading the charge."

"I know. I guess since I only have the rest of this year to defeat Magdalina, my nerves are getting to me. It doesn't help the King has imprisoned my mother and my siblings are in hiding."

"I suppose not," Philip agreed. His sympathy comforted her, for the first time. "That reminds me, I saw Virtue flying out here and I wanted to see if you were sending him back to Isra."

Irritation sparked inside of her. "Are you trying to court my sister?"

Philip surprised her by blushing. "No, not at the moment."

"But maybe later?" Rose pressed.

"Come on, Rose. Stop," Philip insisted. "I just want to send off my letter. I'm hoping she'll be comforted by hearing from you and the rest of us. She can't be having an easy time with everything, either."

"That's true," Rose admitted, feeling slightly shamed. They were all racing against time. There would be plenty of time to think about Philip falling in love later. "I should probably go finish my letter to her, then."

"Ethan and I can see to Virtue's care."

"Thanks." Rose waved to Ethan. "I've got to get everything ready for tomorrow."

Philip squeezed her hand. "It'll be all right."

"Of course it will. You guys are counting on me."

Time passed as Rose finished writing her letter to Isra. She didn't want to put in too much detail, but she felt Isra deserved to know what was happening.

Dearest Isra, Princess of Rhone, Daughter of Night, my favorite and only sister, and all the greetings you'd like, etc.,

In regard to your last letter, I do understand who "Rora" is, but she was the innocent girl who thought she was universally beloved, only to disappear once she realized she was universally pitied. Rose has been my preferred name since I set out on my own adventures, looking for any semblance of a real life I could. I doubt I would have any issues, should you call me Rora despite that. After all, Theo calls me "Rosary" from time to time—

Rose bit her lip. She didn't really need to add that, did she? And there was also no reason to tell Isra how alive and special it made her feel, was there? She crossed it out.

One day I hope you will tell me what you did to poor Philip. He has been trying to get me to write you back ever since I received your letters this past week.

She thought about describing how, despite Philip being injured during the running of the bulls, he had thought to write her. Rose decided against it; Isra might worry, if she knew the truth, and Rose knew firsthand how worry could interfere with getting done what needed to be done.

ONCE UPON A PRINCESS

While I know I cannot help you at present, I will strive to as soon as we can. We have been shipwrecked on an island, Maltia, and, since most of our provisions went down with the ship, we have entered a tournament here in hopes of recovering our losses. It is in the Aragonian tradition. Apparently our mother would love it, from what I have learned about her from one of the guards.

Felise, our kind but enterprising host, has welcomed us and given us some insight along the way. I expect, should all go well, we will be in Romani territory soon, though not soon enough. If things do not work out, Theo assures me piracy is still an option.

By the way, why is Theo forbidden to show me letters from you? Did you do that just to bother me?

I will write to you once we are in Romani territory. Until then, be safe. I look forward to your next letter, which will no doubt be soon.

Your sister,
Rose

That was enough, Rose decided. It was short, informative, with just the right amount of sympathetic and suspicious; Isra would love it.

She headed out, deciding to rub it in Philip's face she had completed her duty to Isra. As she was passing the dining hall, she saw Theo helping Roderick into a chair.

Before she could come through the doorway, she heard her name and stopped.

"Rose will be okay with the amount you earned," Theo assured the clearly shaken man.

Rose felt her mouth drop open, unable to believe Roderick—Roderick, one of the burly, quiet men who had followed her all along the coast of the continent—was close to tears. She squinted at him, as though she was not sure what she was seeing was really there. Yes, she realized, shocked. There was no mistaking the sheen of unshed tears.

Rose watched quietly as Roderick spoke.

"My Lady won't like what he did, though."

"I don't know if I would tell her," Theo told him, as he grabbed a scrap of cloth from a nearby table. "At least, not just yet. Here. If the blood is leaking, this should help."

Rose tilted to the side to see Roderick's right hand contorted strangely, bound up in a fistful of bandages.

"I've had my fingers broken before," Roderick protested. "No need to baby me. Just get me some strong spirits, would you?"

"I doubt you had your fingers broken on purpose, and by someone who saw you as a threat."

Rose ducked around the door as Theo hurried to get a glass of ale.

Roderick huffed. "It's not me who is the threat. The only evidence that Aragonian oaf has any brains left is how he recognized me as her ward."

Marsor. He had attacked Roderick, out of some kind of sick revenge against her. Rose put her hand over her mouth, though whether it was to keep herself from crying out or from getting sick, she could not say.

"It was a good thing he didn't get a hold of my winnings, at least," Roderick continued. "Thank you for keeping them for me."

"It was no trouble," Theo said. "I'm sorry I lost track of you at the end of your last round. If I'd caught up with you sooner, I could have saved you from his attack."

Roderick shook his head. "He had more strength than I," he said as he gulped down his drink.

"I heard from his men, he'd only made it through six rounds." Rose could hear Theo moving around. "No doubt he was jealous of you."

"Of course," Roderick said with a puff of pride. "But the man's a fool. He'll get his comeuppance."

Oh, I will definitely see to that, Rose thought angrily.

"You're probably right about making sure My Lady doesn't hear. I'm not at my best, to be sure. And I'd hate to fail Leea in protecting her." Roderick choked. "The Queen has so much to worry about these days as it is, and I can't help her."

ONCE UPON A PRINCESS

"Was she the one who wrote that letter to you?"

Rose peeked out enough to see the surprise on Roderick's face turn into resignation. "Yes," he admitted.

"Has Captain Locke or Lannister heard anything from them?"

As Theo changed the subject, Rose almost leapt out and interrupted, wanting to know what her mother would write to Roderick, and why she wouldn't write to Rose about it first. She steadied herself a second later, but it became harder to stand still as she continued to listen.

"No. They're keeping an eye out for a good ship down by the docks, as the Princess suggested. But there hasn't been any Rhonian ship to come by this way, and no letters through hawk."

Rose could almost see the determined look on Theo's face. "It'll be all right."

"Leea is my best friend, you know," Roderick admitted quietly. "She's always been lonely. Stefanos has largely ignored her since the princess' birth, and Magdalina has taken her children away from her, either by curse or by proxy. In the end, she had no one but me and her fairy friends."

Rose suddenly felt a rush of sorrow and shame; she'd never thought about how difficult it must have been for her mother to live with her curse. No matter how determined Rose was never to fall in love, she knew it was nearly impossible for her mother to stop loving her. As much as she never let herself dream of it, either, Rose wanted to have children of her own. It was the greatest robbery Magdalina could have done to her.

"You must be very special to her," Theo comforted.

"She and I bonded after Stefanos sent his brother away to marry the Aragonian duchess. Hebert was her best friend before I came along. I don't think he liked leaving her either, especially at his brother's command. He and Stefanos disagreed a lot."

"If she is anything like Rose, I can imagine leaving wasn't easy on her, nor you."

Rose felt her face flush over, happy at the compliment even as she began to feel guilty for listening in on their conversation.

Theo sighed. "Let me go get Mary, and see if she can fix you up some more. I don't know if this will be enough without her. You should get some sleep after she checks you. Rose will have Sophia and Philip to help her with the jousting tomorrow. You need rest."

"What if she needs more help?"

Rose already knew the answer Theo would give.

"I'll do it," Theo told him. "I'm sure I can excuse myself from under the Abbess' watch for a—"

Rose blocked out his words as she silently hurried away, crushing Isra's letter in her fists as anger settled into her bones. Theo's kindness, Roderick's faithfulness, and Marsor's treachery weighed in on too many places in her heart. For the moment, she chose to focus on the problem she knew how to solve.

Marsor would suffer greatly for his actions, Rose fervently decided.

14

Rose felt a surge of satisfaction as she heard the distinctive crumbling of her opponent's shield as it hit the ground behind her.

"Yes!" She reared her horse in triumph, waving her lance into the air as the announcer declared her to be the victor for the eighth time since she'd taken the field. The audience roared with excitement.

The announcer himself seemed to be leading the cheering charge. "Everyone is going wild for the antics of our new favorite—the short, spunky knight who can fell any foe and do it with flair!" he cried out, his voice barely projecting into the roaring stands.

Rose opened her visor and winked over at Theo, who wore a smirk on his face just for her as she came over.

"You know your horse is going to tire out faster if you keep doing the showy tricks," he told her, as he handed her a fresh lance.

When Theo had informed Rose he would be helping her alongside Sophia in the morning, rather than Roderick, Theo had not given her a specific reason. It was not hard, especially after hearing the conversation between Theo and Roderick, to figure out Philip and Mary were tending to Roderick. And while she was not happy with the decision to keep her from the truth, she felt a small, secret happiness at the thought Theo would be coming; they had rarely been apart for each other's tournaments.

"Then we'll get another horse," Rose assured him. "They have plenty of extra."

"This one seems to suit you well," Theo argued playfully.

"I can't have too many more rounds. I've only got to last a few more before beating Marsor, anyway, right?" She nodded in the direction of his camp.

Theo suddenly gripped her arm. "You're not seriously more concerned about him than winning, are you?"

"Of course not," Rose lied. She wasn't sure if he believed her. "That's him coming this way, isn't it?"

"Rose … "

"No, that's really him, isn't it?"

Theo glanced over his shoulder. Rose could tell as he sighed what the answer to her question was. A burst of anger and bitter excitement rushed through her. She snapped her helmet's visor down and reached out for her shield.

"Here you go, Rose!" Sophia cheered. "I just finished putting a new shine into it."

"Thanks, Sophie." Rose saluted her. "I'm glad you're here today."

"Work has been fun in the forage," Sophia said. "But nothing compares to working alongside you, Rose."

"That's good, because no one does better work than you," Rose commended.

"Good luck in this round."

Rose looked to see the Marsor heading onto the field. She turned back to Theo. "What's the best strategy for this one, do you think?"

"He's left-handed," Theo told her. "When he carried his flag earlier, he took it with his left hand and secured it in his right."

"But he's jousting right-handed?"

"To hide his strong side, perhaps," Theo guessed. "His shield will be harder to dislodge."

"Got it. Thanks."

"Be careful." He leaned in closer. "Marsor has a foul temper, and he's a known cheater. And he apparently has several reasons to hate you."

"Good," Rose muttered. "I won't feel bad about giving him more."

"Seriously, watch yourself out there."

The concern in his eyes was touching, even if it exasperated her. "Are you going to say your prayers?"

"Of course." He took her wrist, his grip tightening over the spot where she wore his rosary beads.

Rose jerked back, pulling on her horse and headed to the field.

Marsor looked over at her. "So we meet again, little girl."

Rose said nothing, gritting her teeth.

"I look forward to dethroning you in this event. Perhaps then you will learn your lesson, and stay home. Let the men handle the important things."

Rose still said nothing. Years of being derided as a woman knight had prepared her for his scorn. She'd counted on it, even.

Marsor laughed a loud, brutish laugh. "Finally, a decent response from your sharp tongue; the silence is welcoming. If defeating you in jest is as easy as defeating you in the joust, I'll win for sure."

The wall of her patience caved as her skill was called into question. "You'll only manage to do so if you cheat!" Rose lifted her helmet. "You've already proven you're only a bully."

"So say the losers!"

"So say your victims!" Rose corrected. "I intend to bring them some semblance of justice."

The horn blared for the first round to go. Rose slapped down her visor and took off, pushing her horse for speed. She felt her palms sweating underneath her gloves as she stared down at the great, bulky figure who blocked out the rest of the world behind him.

This was the man who had trampled her. The one who had nearly killed her over an inconvenience. The man who saw winning as more important than living. The man who had punished her guard for his loyalty to her.

Marsor's lance was heading for her, targeting her lower torso. *Of course he would aim for the kill.*

As her horse thundered down the lane, her lance out strong, her shield tight, she took careful aim of her own. Rose tucked herself close to her horse, stabilizing her lance and allowing her speed to increase.

Bracing her shield, she shifted her weight to her lance, aiming for his right side. It was the weaker side, despite what he might have wanted her to think. With Theo's observation, she had insight into Marsor's weakness, despite what he might have wanted. "This is for Roderick," she muttered, forcing herself to shift any fear behind her.

There was a resounding *clash!* as Rose's lance met with Marsor's shield; instantly, the pressure of her horse's gallop pushed Rose's lance behind the shield. Marsor cried out in pain, scrambling to avoid any injury.

Rose easily pushed the glancing blow of Marsor's lance aside she passed; with his wild, jerky movements, she didn't have to turn around to know he slid off his horse.

Cheers went up from the crowd as she reared in her horse and turned to see Marsor had fallen indeed, and he was gripping his left arm in pain.

She slowed to a trot as she came up beside him. She lifted her helm off. "One more round, and you'll be finished," she told him.

"Oh, I doubt that," Marsor snarled. "You cheated."

"No, actually, I didn't," Rose said. "You might use brute force, but some of us still use our brains. If you have any, you might want to consider forfeiting now." She spurred her horse forward, a sense of righteous happiness pulsating through her. She could hear him yelling at his squire and the various assistants available on his end.

One more round, she thought. That was all. And then she didn't have to worry about him anymore. Hopefully, he would be too humiliated to show up at all for the rest of the tournament.

Theo came up to her and handed her a new lance. "Don't aggravate him, Rose," he warned her.

"Why not?" Rose asked, suddenly angry at being cast as a villain despite her valiant efforts. "He was the one who trampled me—"

"Please don't make this about what happened—"

"—and broke Roderick's hand yesterday."

Shock darted across Theo's face and left him speechless.

Rose frowned at him. "You really didn't think I wouldn't find out, did you?" She had hoped to bite into his very soul, and Rose could see she had succeeded as he fumbled for words.

"Rose—"

"I have to go," Rose smoothly interrupted. She pulled her helmet back on. She steadied her shield and her lance as much as she did her heart and her anger.

She would deal with Theo and Roderick later, she decided. She had more important things to worry about.

Marsor was in a rage. Even through the small opening of his helmet, Rose could feel his anger towards her. Good, she thought. *Good.*

The trumpet sounded, and they were off once more.

Rose saw no reason to adapt her strategy from the previous run; she took careful aim and sped forward.

It was only at the last second she saw the gleam in his eye; his lance slipped several inches lower as she met him. "Stop!" she yelled, as the tip of his lance bore into her horse's side.

The horse reared up in pain and surprise.

Rose felt her lance slip from her grip and she tumbled down from her saddle. Her shield arm gripped onto her reigns, but her horse, too surprised from the pain, was determined to run off. She felt her fingers slip a second before she rolled to the ground.

Marsor just laughed as the audience collectively gasped.

The trumpet sounded, declaring the end of the match.

"You monster!" Sophia screamed as she ran out to the field, with Theo close on her heels. She picked up a rock from the ground and threw it at Marsor. "You disgusting beast!"

Rose felt Theo dislodge her from her shield and grip her arm. "Are you okay?" he asked, his voice desperate.

"Are you going to tell me 'I told you so?'"

ONCE UPON A PRINCESS

Theo helped her up, steadying her. She could feel him tremble slightly before she shook him off. "Theo," she muttered. She lifted her visor. "I'm fine," she told him. "Just upset." She nodded to Sophia. "I'll see to her; would you see to my horse, please?"

Theo had no time to reply as she swept past him. Rose came over next to Sophia, who argued fiercely with Marsor.

"It was an accident, I swear," Marsor insisted, smugness written all over his face.

"That was no accident, you despicable creature."

Rose stepped in front of her. "Sophia, ready my sword," she ordered.

"But—"

"And a new horse, please." Rose met her gaze, silently promising she would take care of the problem for everyone. "Now."

"Yes, Rose," Sophia muttered, obviously unhappy. But she shuffled her feet and turned around, determined to give Rose's sword an extra sharpening before handing it over to her leader.

Rose turned her full attention onto the brute in front of her. "Sophia is right. You are despicable. To hurt an animal rather than face a fight fairly."

"I will not be denied my prize," Marsor shot back.

"Your prize is not worth the pain of an innocent party," Rose spat. "I will see you on the field."

"We will," Marsor agreed, a sinister gleam in his eye. "For a tiebreaker."

She said nothing as Marsor spit on the ground indignantly, before turning around and heading back to his post.

Rose hurried over to Theo. "Is the horse okay?" she asked.

"She'll live," he told her as he worked to hold a bandage over the wound. "It was a glancing blow on her shoulder muscles, though. I'm not sure she'll be able to compete again."

"Use our winnings from the last round to buy her," Rose told him. She reached over and stroked the horse on her

ONCE UPON A PRINCESS

nose. The large eyes looked at her in sadness, and Rose felt a wave of guilt pass over her, but she allowed herself only a moment to share in the horse's pain. "We'll have to see if Mary can help her."

"Here's your sword, Rose," Sophia said, slapping the newly-sharpened sword into Rose's glove.

"I know it was awful," Rose told her. "And I know you would rather be the one to punish him for it. But I give you my word, I will see that he pays—in both blood and pride."

Sophia's eyes blinked with tears, but she hung her head and said nothing.

"Be careful," Theo murmured as Rose stepped up into a new horse.

"Just stick to your prayers," Rose snarled. "Since they are apparently so effective."

At Theo's hurt expression, she felt a wave of regret. But there was nothing to be done. She watched for a brief second as he turned on his heel and walked away.

"He means well, Rose," Sophia said quietly.

"I don't care," she shot back. "This is not the time for romanticized notions that God will protect us from evil, when we just saw it in action."

She spurred the horse onward before Sophia could reply, or Rose could even see if she would dare to.

The tiebreaker round would be unpleasant, Rose knew. The objective was to draw blood. Whoever bled would be declared the loser.

Marsor was already the loser in her mind. He had broken his honor in order to gain more—such a thing would only bring about his end.

The new horse was as docile as the previous one, which made Rose all the more angry. She watched from her post, her sword and shield ready, as Marsor pulled out his own weapons. The sheen of the sun on his blade struck her eyes.

But not before she saw a strange, pink and green powder falling from the hilt.

ONCE UPON A PRINCESS

The trumpet sounded once more, and they were off. Rose lifted her sword high, getting ready to strike.

Marsor charged toward her, meeting her fury with malice. His sword arched up high before he brought it down.

"Augh!" Rose cried out vehemently as she swung out. She braced for the force of resistance.

Her sword clashed loudly against Marsor's, seconds before the metal of his sword broke.

Rose did not have time to observe anything else as her horse sped past. She reared him in, hearing Marsor's befuddled shouts, and turned around.

Her sword had cut through Marsor's, causing his blade to fall back on his leg. A large gash gushed blood freely as he sat on his horse, stunned and in pain.

She saw Sophia cheering as a tear managed to escape her lashes; she saw Theo with her wounded horse, his expression a cross between relief and anger as he looked on Marsor's stricken figure. He glanced back at her, and then looked to Marsor.

Something was wrong, Rose realized.

It was time to investigate.

She marched over to Marsor, her sword at her side. "Well, that settles that," she declared.

Marsor threw her a murderous gaze. "You cheated," he accused. "My sword is made of the strongest material this side of the Great Sea. There's no way your sword could have beaten mine."

Rose glanced down at the sword. The pink and green residue glittered once more, and she suddenly recognized it for what it was. "You've been using Magdust!" she announced.

The crowd, now silent, gasped.

Catcalls, anger, and calls for disqualification poured out a second later.

Marsor jumped up, momentarily forgetting his injury. "It's not true," he objected, before turning back to Rose.

ONCE UPON A PRINCESS

She stuck her sword blade straight at him in warning. "I have been given the sword of Queen Lucia herself," she told him, watching as his eyes crossed as they stared down the tip of her sword. "It is more than capable of standing up to your sword's foul corruption."

The jousting judges called for order behind them.

"Looks like you're going to get a proper punishment. I know the Magdust trade is costly and illegal."

"You'll pay for this," Marsor grumbled.

"I'm already paying," Rose informed him. "How I would love to slice you up for your cruelty not only to my horse but my friends! Now that justice has found you, I feel the cost of restraint; I feel nothing but disappointment that I couldn't kill you and send your evil soul to the devil myself."

She turned and walked away, her fists clenched her sword and shield more and more tightly as she walked away, even though her mind screamed at her, telling her to go back and secure the full amount of blood due her.

Rose felt her steps slow as the argument grew louder. But she pressed on. The silent argument within her pressed into her more.

It was too easy to let him live.

It would be harder to deal with regret if she killed him.

He might hurt someone else.

His pride was defeated, and his person was in pain. That would have to be enough.

Marsor hurt the innocent and cheated several hundreds of others, most likely.

She could be thrown out of the tournament.

He deserved it.

She deserved to be the better person.

Rose sighed as she finally made it clear of her post. It was over.

"Look out!"

Rose heard Theo's call just in time; she heard the whisper of sloppy footwork behind her. She sidestepped Marsor's awkward advance and thrust up her shield in time to protect herself from getting sliced with his broken sword. She returned his attack, lashing at him.

Her sword bit into him, again and again, as her anger burst free of her self-control.

She cried out as he finally dropped his sword and crumbled to the ground, weakened too much to stand. Rose felt her sword rise for the killing blow and did nothing to deter it.

Marsor's face twisted with terror.

She felt a violent satisfaction as she swung down.

Clang!

Rose gaped as her sword met with another.

She looked up to see Theo had intervened. "That's enough, Rose," he said. "It's all okay now."

"Theo!" Rose roared. "What are you doing? He's a cheater, using Magdust. He hurt my horse and Roderick, and countless others!"

"Exactly," Theo told her. "Every one of those people deserve to have him answer for all his crimes, not just the ones against us."

"Augh!" Rose thrust her sword into the ground in front of him. "Fine. Have it your way."

She hurried away, knowing it was pity she saw in his eyes as he looked at her.

15

"Thank you," Theo murmured kindly to the jousting judge, as he handed Theo Rose's winnings. As he pocketed the coins, a mixture of exhaustion and resignation cloaked him. It had been hours, surely, he thought, since the joust had been over, but his job was over for the day. "Lady Rose thanks you for today's … adventurous joust."

"We should be the ones thanking her. I've never seen such participation and excitement from the audience. Who knew a woman rider would be so amusing to them? It's positively decadent." The judge guffawed before he nodded and dismissed Theo.

Theo decided it was for the best he had been the one to receive the winnings. Rose would not have taken kindly to the judge's remarks, even if it would not have been the first time hearing such things.

Once Rose had walked away, no one else had wanted to joust. Many were more concerned with justice more than the entertainment, as Marsor had been hauled off by officials. One of the judges had let Theo know Marsor would be punished for unfairly attacking his opponent, but with Rose's fury, more of his behavior was also being called into question.

The audience, Theo realized, preferred such an ending to the day.

Sophia came up beside him. "We're all cleaned up here."

"And Rose's horse?"

"She'll be able to walk, but not far, in the bandages I've put on her."

"Will the inn be too far, you think?"

"I can run and get Mary," Sophia offered, "if we get stuck."

"Thanks."

"Don't look so glum," Sophia said. Theo glanced at her. From her expression, Sophia could have been talking to herself as much as she had been talking to him. "We won, didn't we? And Marsor is out of the way. All we have to worry about is tomorrow, when Philip will be fighting."

"That's all we have to worry about?" Theo shook his head. "I don't think so."

"Okay, so Rose is upset, I know." Sophia sighed. "She's just angry at what happened. I am too. Although, I do think you were right to stop her from killing him. I hope they decide to execute him publicly for hitting her horse." Reaching over, she rubbed the horse's nose with clear affection. "Although death might be too kind for a brute who would hurt an animal like you," she cooed, talking to the horse.

"Rose won't thank me for stepping in."

"She has always overlooked many of your kindnesses," Sophia told him softly. "And you never hold it against her."

"What are you saying?"

Sophia snorted. "Please don't pretend you're going to start holding her accountable to you. That's laughable. I know you well enough to know you will brood needlessly when it comes to Rose."

"I suppose," he said. Isra had told him once that his love for Rose was always painfully obvious to everyone except Rose, who would never see it, and he would never be direct about making her look.

"So, how much money did we get?" Sophia asked, deliberately changing the subject. "I wasn't really paying attention."

"Enough to make up for getting you out of work many times over," Theo assured her, "even with subtracting the cost of a horse from it."

"That's good. We should have enough for passage soon, right?"

"If my calculations are correct, we have enough now," Theo said.

"That's great!" Sophia cheered. "Philip doesn't have to worry about competing."

ONCE UPON A PRINCESS

"Well, we'll likely need supplies too, don't forget," Theo reminded her. "I'm not sure of what kind of prices we'll face for those."

"Surely, we're well off enough," Sophia argued. "We still have some Rhonian coins for when we get to the Romani territory."

"Not enough to get us back to Rhone."

"Maybe we can stop off in Einish," Sophia retorted. "Philip's surely got an allowance."

Theo laughed. "Perhaps," he agreed. It wasn't a bad idea, he thought.

They walked with their new horse through the city streets. Sophia chatted easily, telling Theo of her work in the city forage, how Ethan was getting along with Penelope and his music, and other things; Theo largely disregarded her until she mentioned Philip and Rose were going to go see Ethan perform later.

"Perform?" Theo asked.

"Yeah, Rose said she'd asked Philip if he wanted to come, since he was working on getting ready for tomorrow's event. She told me it would be a nice way for him to relax."

"That was kind of her," he replied, his tone neutral, while his heart twisted.

"Yeah. Ethan didn't want a bunch of people there, or I'm sure she would have made sure we all went."

"Understandable," Theo agreed. He thought about it. "Sometimes it is hard to allow the people surrounding you to see you change."

"You're not still worried about Rose arguing with you earlier, are you?" Sophia's eyes sparkled with concern. "You really mustn't. She was provoked."

"Yes, I know. She's been stressed for a long time, and getting shipwrecked and sidetracked has only added to it. But it is not the nicest thing to know how limited one is when it comes to comforting her." As an afterthought, he added, "Or at least, in calming her down."

ONCE UPON A PRINCESS

Sophia took ahold of the reigns. "Go on," she ordered. "Go and talk to her."

"I'm not one to let her rejection get in the way of my duties," he said. "And she'll most likely be gone by the time we get back to the inn, if she's going to see a performance."

Sophia sighed. "Just go and find her." When he hesitated, she doubled down. "No, really. Theo, she takes care of all of us. You're the one who makes sure she's taken care of in return. If you need to go make sure she's okay, then go see if she's okay. It's fine. I can handle Lightning here."

"Lightning?" Theo inquired.

"You know, the horse." Sophia shrugged. "I figured the name suit her, since she can really gallop."

"She *was* able to," Theo reminded her. "There's no guarantee she'll be able to run again, after her injury."

"Mary'll be able to fix her up," Sophia insisted. "You'll see."

"Well, I certainly hope so," Theo agreed, allowing himself to grin as he stroked the newly-named Lightning. "Let's hope she gets better like lightning, too."

Sophia giggled before exclaiming happily, "Look! There's the inn now."

The horse nudged him softly, and he agreed the mare might have had a point. "All right. I'll go and fetch Mary for you, and then I'll go and talk to Rose."

"Good." Sophia smiled, satisfied. And then her mismatched eyes moistened. "You and Rose are the closest things I've ever had to real parents. I hate to see you both sad."

"That's why we're working to break the spell Magdalina has placed on her."

After a moment of silence, Sophia nodded. "All right. Go on and get Mary, then."

16

The tavern was full of cheery music and brightness; Rose found it was easy to lose herself in all of its joyfulness and enchantment. Despite the commotion earlier, she had managed to walk off a good deal of pain and anger. And while shame still lingered, she was determined to ignore it for Ethan's sake.

"What are you thinking about?" Philip asked, handing her a tankard of ale.

"Nothing, really," Rose answered. "And it was glorious, before you interrupted it."

"I'm lucky to be alive, then."

"Yes," Rose said pointedly. "You are." She nodded in the direction of his wound, and even as he brushed her off, she noticed he was still sitting more stiffly than usual.

He took a sip of his own drink before asking, "Where's Ethan?"

"Getting ready over in the musician's corner," Rose told him, gesturing toward the far end of the brightly lit tavern. "As I understand it, the competition will be announced and then they'll get started."

"Thanks for inviting me tonight."

"Well, I know you're a big fan of the arts," Rose replied easily. She grinned. "Maybe you'll be inspired to write Isra some more poetry."

"I might," he admitted. "But I'm not sure she'd like it. You don't like it."

"It's not practical," Rose said with a shrug. "And I've had too much of it in my direction over the years."

"From Theo?" Philip asked.

"What? Why would ... no, not from Theo," Rose sputtered back. "Goodness, no, never from Theo. No, I had a large variety of suitors who came to see me."

Philip laughed. "And you criticized them for praising your beauty?"

"There's no point in celebrating what people see when they can't see what's behind it."

Philip did not say anything for a moment. Then he looked over to see Ethan making his way over toward them, carrying his harp in one hand. In his other hand, he held fast to a pretty young lady with olive skin and glossy, auburn hair.

"Poetry is better suited to people who live it, rather than spout it with no understanding," Philip told Rose. "And it looks like we might just have such a sight coming our way."

Rose glimpsed up as Ethan came to a halt. "Rose," he said. "This is Penelope, my music instructor."

At the introduction, Penelope blushed. "Pleased to meet you, My Lady."

"And this is Philip." Ethan waited while Rose and Philip inclined their heads in greeting before he asked, "Did Sophia come in yet?"

"No, not yet," Rose said. "She might not come at all. We had some issues on the jousting field earlier."

"You're the lady knight who defeated Marsor the Beast?" Penelope asked.

Penelope was young yet, Rose noticed, even though she had been dressed for a formal occasion. She had almost thought Penelope to be closer to her age, but the innocence of her large, chestnut eyes betrayed her real age to be closer to Sophia's, or even Ethan's.

"That's right," Rose confirmed.

"You are practically everyone's hero, My Lady."

"Please, call me Rose." As Penelope began to tell her how everyone was more than pleased to hear of Marsor's defeat, and the subsequent findings of Magdust and several witnesses to his dishonorable methods, Rose wondered if anyone watching had seen that there was a greater enemy inside of her than there had been on the field. Yes, Marsor was a cheat and a liar, with no respect for life, but she had been unable to control her collected anger.

ONCE UPON A PRINCESS

Rose knew full well she was not a true hero; she was just the better competitor. Even Theo, she knew, would be unable to defend her after how she'd treated him earlier.

"—so fortunate that he's being deported."

"Deported?" Rose repeated.

"Yes, uh, Marsor has been sentenced to be extradited back to Castile and Aragon, and he has been completely disqualified from the tourney," Penelope told her.

"That's good, I guess. I'm certainly tired of seeing him."

"It will be good if the courts there are able to take him up on his charges. There's a battle for power in the country, as the two territories are still not used to having a united kingdom."

"I've heard," Rose muttered, before changing the subject. "So, Ethan tells me you're a composer as well as a performer."

Penelope smiled. "I hope to establish a reputation by the time I am old enough, so I can wed into a royal court as a player."

"Consider this an audition, then," Rose told her. "If you're good enough, we can find a court for you where you can perform."

"What?"

"Did Ethan not tell you? I am the Princess of Rhone, a small kingdom on the other side of the continent." Rose, satisfied Ethan had not told her, was willing to help make Penelope's dream come true without such a cost.

She nodded over to Philip. "And this is Philip. He is the Prince of Einish. Between the two of us, we'll be able to find a place for you in our courts."

Penelope looked stricken. "Surely, you are jesting."

"No. Why would I lie about that?"

"I heard the rumors," Penelope said, clearly uncomfortable. "I didn't think they were true."

"What's wrong?" Rose asked. "We're allowed to be here."

ONCE UPON A PRINCESS

"Maltians have a complicated history with rulers," Penelope explained. "They would fear that you would seek to conquer the island."

"I'm not here for that, I can assure you."

"But why else would a prince and princess be here, of all places?"

"We were shipwrecked," Ethan reminded her. "I told you about it earlier this week."

"But … but …"

"I didn't give you stage fright, did I?" Rose asked, suddenly realizing she might have overset the poor girl's nerves.

"Uh. No. But Maltia is dangerous for royalty. They have kept their government here for many centuries now because of how kings and queens had sought to conquer the island."

"No need to worry then, Penelope." Rose took another sip of ale. "We're not here to conquer anyone."

Penelope's eyes were still hesitant as she changed the subject. "Well, then, I'd love to sing for you, Your Highness."

"Rose, please."

Penelope looked aghast, glancing from Ethan to Rose to Philip. She squared her shoulders. "All right … Rose. I hope you enjoy tonight's performance."

"I'm sure I will," Rose assured her. "I'm looking forward to seeing what Ethan has learned." Ethan blushed, and then excused Penelope along with himself, as the call to begin the entertainment trumped out from the tavern's small stage.

"That was certainly nice of us to offer her a position in our courts," Philip murmured.

"I'll say."

"You know, it might be better to keep quiet about who we are," Philip said.

"I'm not worried about it."

"I noticed."

"Are you worried about it?" Rose glanced over at him. "You were the one who revealed us to the crew of the ship we came in on, weren't you?"

ONCE UPON A PRINCESS

Philip paused. "Yes, well, I didn't think it could give us problems. But now, with a troublemaker such as Marsor detained because of us, it might be better not to mention it. A lot of people bet money on him, and could pass on their anger over losing to us and our kingdoms."

"I didn't think of that," Rose admitted. "Even if I think it is unlikely to happen. I'll have Sophia pass along the message to keep it secret, just in case."

"Thank you."

The strain in his voice was obvious. "You have to admit, though," Rose said, "it was a small price to pay for her dream to come true."

"If it's warranted. I can't tell you how much Einish would be remiss if she turns out to be a terrible musician."

Rose punched his shoulder. "She will *not* be terrible." Rose looked back over at where Ethan was standing with Penelope and sighed. "Ethan is clearly taken with her."

"Ethan has to grow up, just as we did, and let go of fantasy to find reality. Does even one of your romantic daydreams from thirteen still matter to you?"

Rose felt her face burn. It was her turn to answer with unfamiliar brusqueness. "No."

A moment passed in silence. Then Philip realized the full gravity of her words, and his. "Oh, Rose, I'm sorry. I forgot with your curse—"

"I'll be right back." Rose got up and headed out the door. "I'm going to see if Sophia's coming."

She pushed past some of the crowd as the music started, hoping desperately she wasn't accidentally skipping Ethan's performance.

Rose found her way outside and ducked around the side of the building. She took a deep, steadying breath of the fresh night air. It had to be this prison of a place, she thought. It was just too stressful being on this island.

"Rose?"

She groaned as he came up beside her. "Not now, please, Theo."

"What's wrong?"

"Nothing."

"Nothing you want to discuss."

Her eyes glared at him, sharp in the darkness. "Yes."

"Did Philip make you mad?"

"I don't want to talk about it."

"I'm not always going to play safe with you, Rose," Theo reminded her, coming to stand beside her. "You've been anxious lately."

"It's just the tournament."

"No, it's not."

Rose said nothing. Theo had known her for the majority of her life. He was probably more right about such matters than she wanted him to be. Finally, she spoke. "What do you think's wrong?"

He tweaked a lock of her hair. "I don't want to talk about it," he said, mimicking her.

"That's so rude."

"So what?" he asked. "You were rude to me earlier."

"I didn't want to be."

"But you were."

"So what?" This time it was her turn to repeat his words in a mocking tone.

He sighed and leaned back against the wall. "We have the money we need for passage. According to the scrolls the Abbess has given me, we need to book harbor into Poiyana, a port in the Romani territory close to the mountains. She says in the spine of the mountain's highest tops, there's a sliver of land guarded by Amalia, the Dragonkeeper."

"Do we have a ship secured?"

"I'll talk to Felise about it later. The Abbess might know something, too."

"All right. So we just have Philip competing tomorrow, and we'll have money for supplies."

"Sophia has some, too, from working. We might be able to find work aboard the ship, too, to help offset the costs of travel, if needed."

"It wouldn't be the first time we needed to do that," Rose agreed. "Sounds like we're on track with our plans to get off this island."

"Yes, thank God."

She looked over at him as they sank into silence. His body was relaxed against the building, but she'd known him long enough to know he was mulling over something. As much as she wanted to press, she didn't; she wasn't sure if this was an attempt to discuss what happened earlier, or if they were silently agreeing to let it go.

"Once everything is over," Theo finally said, "we should come back here. Maltia is very beautiful, don't you think?"

"'Once everything is over?'" Rose repeated.

"Once we break the curse, once we deal with Magdalina and Everon."

"What if we don't?" Rose asked quietly.

"And what if we do?" Theo hesitated briefly. "What if we break the curse? What would you want to do?"

"With the rest of my life, you mean?" Rose asked. "I don't think about it. Thinking about such things only makes it harder to do what needs to be done."

"Only sometimes." Theo stepped closer to her. "But it wouldn't hurt to have contingency plans."

Rose laughed. "That what you're calling it?"

"Come on. Just tell me one thing you'd like to do once the curse is broken," he nudged.

"I want to clear my mother's name, for one."

"I meant something fun."

"I already told you, I don't know. I don't think about it, so I don't have to worry about missing something if I end up sleeping forever." She frowned at his sigh. "What will you do? If you manage to kill Everon?"

"I'd be a knight in your court." Theo put his hands behind his head, using them as a pillow against the stone. "But I'd find a way to keep traveling, like my father and uncle did."

Her breath caught at the mention of his family; Theo rarely mentioned his family; she knew he did not like to talk about them.

Rose was relieved when he continued. "I think Thad would like this place. I was thinking about him earlier this week, while I was at the church." He glanced over at her. "I might write down all your legends. I will bet I could get Thad to store them in the church, just like the rest of the letters and manuscripts my grandfather has in there. I can see it now; generations later, as the Rhonian subjects would find out all your acts of courage and daring."

"There was nothing particularly courageous or daring about today's work." There, Rose thought, she brought it up.

"I didn't do the courageous thing either, by not telling you what happened to Roderick."

"I was mad about the other things more than that."

"But not for your own self." Theo shuffled his feet. "You weren't upset at what he did to you. I noticed while you were screaming, you were more upset at Roderick's injuries and your horse—Sophia has christened her 'Lightning,' before I forget to tell you—and his general dishonesty."

"What does it matter?" Rose asked. "I still needed you to rein me in."

"And I did," Theo reminded her. "Temptation is nothing new, Rose. And temptation is not sin. You did not kill him in your battle. Yes, you fought with him, and he was maimed a bit here and there, and you fought with yourself, but you were defending yourself from his own treachery first."

"I hate how I treated you."

"*I* hate how I treated *you*."

Rose finally looked at him. "Are we terrible friends?"

"Sometimes."

"Does it bother you?"

He flashed her a grin. "I'll take being your terrible friend over not being a friend at all any day, Rosary."

She brightened. "I guess we need to work on that some before you write your book about it."

ONCE UPON A PRINCESS

Theo smirked. "That's the nice thing about being a writer, I guess. No experience is wasted, and no experience needs to be presented in its raw format."

"True." Rose shook her head, resigned. "I never thought trying to get dragon's blood would be this complicated."

"We've had quite a few surprises along the way," Theo agreed. When she only nodded, he continued. "For what it's worth, I think you would make a good heroine. And since I'd be the writer, I'd get famous for it, too."

"You would not," Rose huffed.

"Sure I would."

"No one would believe it."

"I would, and my kids would, and that would be enough."

"Your kids?"

"Sure. Why not? It's not like Thad's going to have any kids; at least, not anytime soon, with the priestly vows he wants to take." He chuckled. "Maybe after his retirement, right? In the meantime, I'm my family's best hope for passing on the family name."

There was nothing she wanted to think about less than Theo's children. Especially if they would inherit their father's ebony hair along with his piercing eyes, his sense of humor or his honorable graciousness.

"Is that something you would want? Children?" Theo asked.

"I told you, I don't think about what happens if the curse is broken," Rose snapped.

"Come on, Rose. Just one thing. One small, fun, frivolous thing."

"No."

"What about singing? Would you sing again?"

Her eyes narrowed. "I'm not singing again, ever."

"You did at the tavern in Rhone."

"I did not."

"You did too. It was the first time I'd ever heard you sing. I'm not likely to make that up."

ONCE UPON A PRINCESS

Rose was about to argue when she did recall, angrily, she had let herself sing in a rare moment.

"I'd like to hear you sing again," Theo told her.

"I owe you nothing, especially after returning to Rhone for you."

"That's not fair, Rose," Theo objected. There was a small scowl on his face. "Frankly, I thought you sang beauti—"

"Don't even say it." Her voice was tart and stripped of all warmth as she cut him off.

Theo raised his eyebrows in surprise, but his mouth closed in compliance.

She breathed out slowly for a long moment as silence stilled the night around them. Rose was ready to ask him to come inside when he spoke up again.

"You want to be free," Theo told her. "But you don't even allow yourself to dream of it, even with small things, like singing a song."

A new wave of anger, both at him and at herself, washed over her. "If I am free, I am free to refuse," she muttered.

"It's not a matter of freedom, but fear."

"I am not afraid!"

"Aren't you?" Theo asked quietly.

"No."

Rose waited to hear Theo argue with her. But he said nothing.

"I should go back in," Rose said quietly. "Ethan's counting on me to be there."

"Do you want me to—"

"Rose, are you coming back inside?" Philip appeared behind them, all of a sudden. "Ethan and Penelope are going on next."

"I'll be there in a minute," Rose called back.

"All right. I'll be at the table," Philip promised. "I'll grab you a fresh drink, too."

"Thanks." She smiled and waved, before turning back to Theo. "What were you asking me?"

"Uh, nothing," he replied. "I was just … I wanted to know if you … needed me to do anything for you."

"I don't."

"Okay. Then I'll see you back at the inn. Good night."

Rose said nothing as she headed back inside the tavern.

17

Theo clenched his fists as he headed down the street. Rose might have dismissed him, he thought bitterly, but he did not have to go back to the inn right away.

He headed down the alleyways and made a few turns, finally arriving at the church.

The majestic cathedral was even more beautiful in the evening light. The strength found in its stained-glass windows and gothic arches welcomed Theo.

While mass was over, he knew the Abbess would be able to find him something to keep him preoccupied.

And there was always prayer, he reasoned, peeking into the chapel. He saw some of the priests had gathered at the front of the chapel. Must be some kind of meeting, he thought.

There was a sudden stirring on the back of his neck, and he stopped. Without another moment's hesitation, he hurried forward into the large chapel, rushing past the pews. The closer he came to the group, the more the smell of healing herbs and blood sunk into him.

"What happened?" he called.

"Brother Theo, is that you?"

"Abbess?" Theo looked around, stalling, as he heard her voice echo in the large chamber.

"She's over here," one of the priests called.

Theo felt dread and confusion unite inside of him, producing an entirely new fear. He hurried toward the group. "Oh, Abbess."

Aurelia was lying on the floor, her hands folded delicately over the large gash in her side. She sucked in her breath as he sat beside her.

"Get more bandages," Theo ordered, scowling at the slow-moving priests. "We'll need to stop the bleeding."

"Don't worry," Aurelia told him softly. "I know whom I have believed, Theo." She smiled bravely, even as she was shaking. "And the other sisters are coming with more bandages already. They should be here soon."

"I want to know who did this."

"It was a man who had been judged and condemned," Aurelia said. "Your lady would know him as the man she defeated earlier."

Theo' closed his eyes in shameful disbelief. "Marsor."

"Yes." Her eyes flickered wanly. "The church sometimes holds prisoners, especially if we can arrange for a special ship to deport them."

"Are there any others who need help?"

"I don't know."

"There are some who have already passed," a monk spoke up softly from behind Theo. "We held him captive in the catacombs, beneath the church. He forced his way out and began attacking."

"This is awful." Theo shook his head in pain, recalling the people he'd met while helping out in the medical tent.

"You must hurry now, Theo," Aurelia said quietly.

"Stay with me," Theo said, arranging her skirts over her wound and pressing down into them.

"There's no need for you to worry," she said. "Felise will know where to take you and your friends."

"What are you talking about?"

"He's coming for her." She eyed him carefully. "Your lady."

"Rose is in trouble?" *If I had only let Rose kill him earlier …*

"Yes." Aurelia nodded. "You know as well as I do that he has contacts. Hurry and get her; take his ship and get her off the island. She'll be safe that way."

"But—"

"The sisters are coming for me," Aurelia told him. "Go with God, Brother."

ONCE UPON A PRINCESS

Theo grabbed a priest beside him. "Hold this down," he ordered, showing him how to dam the blood trickling out of Aurelia's body.

With one last helpless look, Theo let Aurelia go. "I'm sorry," he said.

"It's not your fault," Aurelia insisted, pushing him away as forcefully as she still could. "Please, Theo. Go and take care of your own. Felise may need your help, too."

"Thank you," Theo said. He bowed over her hand and squeezed it affectionately. "I will never forget you, Abbess."

She smiled, and Theo watched as several other nuns came, carrying everything from bandages and medicine to food and rosary beads. Aurelia's ashen face disappeared as a sea of nun headdresses and murmuring twitters pushed Theo back.

He threw a desperate glance at the crucifix hanging on the back wall of the chapel, praying Aurelia and Rose would both be saved, before hurrying out of the church.

Shock pulsed through him, giving him speed and strength as he headed toward the inn. He didn't know how much time passed since Marsor's escape.

His hope faded as he caught sight of the smoke. The inn was on fire.

As the flames consumed the inn, some people were running into the building with buckets of water, while others were fighting in the streets.

The heart of the fire beat from inside of the inn. Theo could feel its power as he approached.

"Felise!" he called out. "Felise, where are you?"

Theo ducked inside a door, immediately placing his hand over his mouth, as he tasted smoke.

Hurriedly, he swiftly made his way through the rooms, many of which were already empty. Dread fueled his movements, as he made his way systematically through the building, searching for others.

"Theo!"

Theo jerked around to see Sophia hurrying toward him with a bucket. "Sophia, thank goodness you're alive."

ONCE UPON A PRINCESS

"Felise is in the stables," she said. "I put him there after Marsor showed up." She nodded toward the barn and added, "Mary's in there as well, trying to get Lightning healed up quickly so she'll be able to move."

"Good work. Rose will be happy to know her squire's taken care of everything."

"Thanks," Sophia replied with a grin and then a grimace. It was then Theo noticed for the first time Sophia had a black eye. "He hit you, didn't he?"

"I managed to get my own punches in quite well," Sophia assured him with a rueful expression. "When Marsor didn't find Rose, he set fire in the kitchens and had some of his men spread it. He said something about looking for her."

"He wants revenge," Theo agreed.

A creaking noise behind them made Theo shake his head. "I'm going to finish checking the rooms," he told her. "You get out of here, now. Go and get Felise. I need to talk to him, and then we need to get out of here and find Rose."

"Okay. Be careful!" Sophia called back as she tossed her bucket into a section of the fire and hurried away.

"I will."

He made the promise to an empty audience, but Theo's determination never wavered.

As the wooden structure creaked and heaved and hawed, Theo searched through the rooms and pulled a couple of people out of harm's way. Among them was a drunk Lannister.

"What are you doing?" Theo cried. "You're supposed to be on guard!"

"The princess is out for the night," Lannister reasoned. "And she doesn't care we're here to guard her, anyway. She doesn't need it."

"She needed it tonight."

"Well, tonight's the exception."

"You're lucky I got you out."

"Yes, I am. Thanks," Lannister said in a slurred voice, before he went limp. His eyes were bleary and listless. "I thought that I was going to die."

"You might have, if you didn't get out," Theo told him, as he hoisted his disheveled form up onto his shoulder once more, as he headed to the stables. "Come on, move!"

"Hello?" An older man's voice called out from the far corner of the barn.

"Felise." Theo looked up at him and squinted. "Are you okay?"

"He's okay," Sophia called from the other side of the room. "I've got Virtue packed up, too, and Mary's out here as well."

"Mary?" Theo called.

"Here," Mary replied. There was a small yawn in her voice and Theo wondered if she had been sleeping when the fire started.

"Where's Captain Locke?" Theo asked.

"He is fine, as am I," the old man stuttered. "Captain Locke is just out front, helping to direct the people away from the fire."

"Oh. Good." Theo nodded. "That'll help."

Felise remained unmoved by the good news. "They burned my hotel," he moaned.

"At least we'll live to see better days. The Abbess might not be so lucky."

"Did Marsor really attack the Abbess?" Felise asked.

Theo forced his voice past the lump in his throat. "Yes."

Felise balled his wrinkled fingers into a fist. "I had a feeling he was telling the truth about that."

"The Abbess has her sisters attending her. She said that you would know what to do."

"Marsor's on the loose," Felise said. "That means there's a boat at the docks you and the Princess can use to cross to the mainland."

"We're allowed to use his passage?" Theo asked.

Felise nodded. "The city council will see to Marsor for his actions tonight."

ONCE UPON A PRINCESS

"You know where it is?"

"Yes."

"Good. Let's go find Rose then. Stay close to us."

"I've no intention of doing anything else," Felise promised. "The Abbess has always commanded me to provide for my guests."

18

Rose gave Philip a smug look as the last notes of Penelope and Ethan's song fell silent inside the tavern and cheers erupted in its place. "See? I told you she'd be a good player."

"I'll admit, you were right about that," Philip said, as he stood and applauded. "I still think you got lucky about that, though."

Rose laughed. "Hopefully, I'll get lucky again and you'll relinquish any offer for her to play in your court."

"We should probably let her chose."

"You're just saying that because you know she'll want to come to Rhone."

"Hey, I'm just trying to be fair to her. Although, if you did get her to go with you, it would give me an excuse to come visit more often," Philip remarked thoughtfully.

"Rose!" Ethan called. "Did you see? We won!"

"I had no doubts," Rose assured him, giving him a congratulatory hug. "I loved your encore, too." She turned to Penelope. "You both did great."

Penelope's young face flushed with modest pride. "Thank you very much," she murmured.

"We've decided you're welcome in either of our courts," Philip assured her gallantly, making Rose grin and getting a beaming smile from Ethan.

"Thank you!" Penelope cheered. "I can't wait to tell my parents. They're going to be so happy—"

A *crash!* broke through the remnant of applause. Rose glanced over her shoulder to see what had happened. At once, her eyes narrowed in fury as Marsor stepped through the broken doorway.

Curiosity turned into rage. "Philip, get your sword ready," Rose ordered. "It looks like you're going to have a warm-up before tomorrow's competition."

Philip nodded. "I was hoping to get some more practice," he said as he drew his sword.

"Where's the Princess of Rhone?" Marsor bellowed into the crowd. "I was told she was here."

Rose felt her heart squeeze. "Right here," she called.

Marsor's gaze found her. "I have a score to settle with you."

"Really? I'm pretty sure we settled it earlier, when we found out you were using Magdust *and* cheating at your events."

"Listen to this *princess*!" Marsor raged. "What does a privileged little girl like this know about fighting?"

The crowds were now staring at the two of them, uncertain of how to respond. Some began to shift out of the paths of the two warriors. Rose watched as Philip tried to motion several out of the way; she noticed many of them had fixed their eyes on her.

She sighed to herself in frustration before forcing herself to push past it. She wondered if there was a way she could buy Philip time to get the people out to safety. Recalling the gossip about her the last time she'd fought Marsor, it was hard to say if that would be possible.

"I'm only privileged if you have never had the chance to learn how to fight fairly," Rose finally retorted. "And I'm pretty sure you have had the opportunity, considering Maltia has always had rules for those who enter the tournament games."

"You would never beat me in an unfair fight," Marsor challenged.

"It might surprise you to know I've had a lot of unfair fights," Rose assured him as she drew out her sword. She motioned to Philip to guard Ethan and Penelope.

"Then prepare for another one!" Marsor bellowed.

"It would be my pleasure," Rose muttered back, as he ran toward her, knocking over chairs and pushing people over.

Rose never missed a beat as he slashed his sword down on hers. She ducked and lashed out a leg, causing Marsor to stumble.

ONCE UPON A PRINCESS

At his fast pace, Marsor flipped over and found himself on the cold, hard floor. Rose smashed her sword against his while he was on the floor, knocking the weapon out of his hands.

He growled angrily, but Rose kicked his blade back from him before turning back to the others.

"Get out!" Rose called, as she hurried to block the others from Marsor's revenge. "Everyone, get out!"

Marsor struggled to get up. His lip was already bloody from the fight.

"Rose!"

Rose glanced over at the door briefly. She saw Philip waving at her. "We need to go," he called out.

"What happened to Ethan and Penelope?" Rose asked, suddenly concerned.

"They're outside, helping Theo and Sophia with the supplies."

"I've got *him* taken care of," Rose insisted, pointing down at Marsor. "Come here and help me bind him up, so the authorities can take him back to his cell."

"He has supporters—"

"Attack!" Marsor cried out.

Rose waited, straining her ears against the crowd. For a moment, there was nothing.

And then, she heard it.

Outside, she could hear the tramp of footsteps, as clanging swords were drawn and battle cries called out into the rioting night.

Well, this is going to be pleasant. Rose shook her head. If the fighting didn't stop quickly, many people would likely be in danger.

"You're mine!" One of Marsor's allies flaunted his sword over his head as he charged at Rose; she momentarily recognized him as one of the knights she'd jousted the day before.

"Not today!" Rose responded, grounding her feet as she blocked the blow. She slashed out in retaliation, only allowing

ONCE UPON A PRINCESS

herself briefly to take her eyes off her competition in order to make sure Marsor was still down.

"Ha!" She whacked the sword out of his hand and pushed him away, just in time to face another attacker.

She ducked and dodged, twisted and turned, and finally managed to break through the doorway. She slammed it behind her.

"Here, Rose," Philip called. He dug a fallen sword into the bolster. "That'll hold them."

"Through the door, anyway," Rose said, as she looked up to see others crawling out of the second story windows.

Philip grinned. "You got me there."

"Rose," Sophia called. "We're over here."

Rose turned to see her squire and several members of her company tucked into an alleyway nearby.

She made her way to them, Philip close behind, occasionally engaging in quick battles with the drunken rioters joining in.

"Tempers are flaring," Ethan said warily, as Rose finally made it over to them.

"Okay. Tell me what's going on," Rose said. "Obviously, Marsor escaped."

"The cathedral has been attacked," Theo spoke up. "Along with the Abbess."

"Is she okay?" Mary gasped. Her shocked expression was quickly replaced by concern. "She was such a kind lady; I hope she wasn't hurt."

"She's worthy of her title and power, to be sure," Theo agreed. "I don't know what will happen to her." He turned away as he explained, "She was bleeding when I left."

"Why did you leave?" Rose asked. "You could have stayed and helped her."

At Theo's expression, Rose immediately regretted her pragmatic tone.

"She told me to go. She told me Marsor escaped, and he was coming after you."

Felise spoke up, surprising Rose. "I have been instructed to protect you, Lady Princess," he said. "There is safe passage for you at the docks. We must hurry and get you aboard."

"What?" Rose shook her head. "I won't leave these people while Marsor is attacking them."

"He is likely doing it in order to provoke you to battle," Theo warned her. "Removing you from the island might help the city."

"The only other alternative is besting him and his followers in battle," Philip spoke up. "And before we're done with that, it is possible a lot of others will pay the price."

"We look to you, My Lady," Sophia assured her.

A moment passed as Rose heard more people running away and screaming. Rose grimaced; there were always so many uncertain things about battles and wars, she thought. It was impossible to act with complete assurance.

She was still the one who would make the call. The blood of the guilty and the innocent would be on her.

Rose finally decided. "All right. Here's what we're going to do. Lannister and Captain Locke, find some horses and ride around the city, telling people to hide in their homes or find shelter till morning. Make haste around the city and head toward the docks; see if you can help the city guards. Once you're at the docks, find the ship and join us."

"Yes, My Lady," Captain Locke said.

Theo elbowed Lannister. "Are you capable of this, sir?" he asked.

"Yes," Lannister mumbled, his eyes awake and sober at the surrounding cries.

"Good." Rose turned to Felise. "The rest of us will split up and take different routes to get to the docks."

"The church has a detained port," Felise said. "It's on the far side of the marina, close to the edge of the bay."

"How long till the crew can get prepared to sail?"

"It's a bigger crew, since it's for a prison transport that was going to happen in the morning," Felise considered. "It should be ready to set sail once the order is given."

ONCE UPON A PRINCESS

Rose turned to Captain Locke and Lannister. "We will all be there in an hour, or we will sail without you."

"Understood," the captain assured her, before they took off, Lannister stumbling behind his leader's forceful stride.

"Now, Sophia and Ethan, you find the most direct route and tell the captain to start getting ready to ship out," Rose ordered. "Theo, you and Roderick go back to the church on your way to the ship. See if the Abbess will take Lightning for us, as a gesture of goodwill for her hospitality."

"Aw," Sophia moaned. "I was hoping we could take her."

"The ship likely doesn't have the supplies for a horse," Rose reminded her. "She'll be in good hands if the church can take her in. Right, Theo?"

"Yes," he agreed.

"What if they can't?" Sophia pressed.

Felise spoke up. "I'll take the horse to the church stables myself, Princess. The Abbess will not refuse a gift from me."

"Call me Rose, please," Rose insisted. "The last thing we need is for people to believe I am a princess. I would not want to bring vengeance or shame upon my people."

"Understood, My Lady."

"That's probably why there is so much activity," Penelope spoke up. "Many fear another ruler on Maltia. The island does not wish to be conquered anymore, even though we celebrate our history's cycle of conquest and freedom."

Rose nodded politely before she turned to Roderick and Theo. "I think it would be best if Theo and Roderick protect you on the way there, Felise. Can you manage on your own afterward?"

"Of course," he assured her. He took her hand, briefly. "It has been my pleasure to serve you, My Lady."

Rose bowed her head, quickly acknowledging his graciousness. But then she leaned up and gave the old man a quick kiss on the cheek. "Should you ever come to Rhone, you will be most welcome," she promised.

"Thank you." He took Lightning's reins from a reluctant Sophia. Rose almost smiled as she heard Sophia warning

ONCE UPON A PRINCESS

Felise to watch her injured side, as Mary had only had a few moments to heal it.

Rose turned to Theo. "Philip and I will take the long route," she said. "But we'll be sure to be there in an hour."

"We cannot leave without you," Theo reminded her.

"It's still for the best we hurry," Rose murmured. "Let's go, Philip."

But she faltered, watching as Sophia and Ethan hurried off, followed by Penelope. "I should have told them to escort her home."

"It's fine, Rose," Philip said. "They'll watch over her, and we can trust the guards at the marina to see her home when it is safe."

"Good idea. Are you ready to fight some more?"

"I'm all healed up," Philip assured her. "I'm going to release Virtue with our letters before we start."

Rose sighed and tried not to roll her eyes noticeably. "Okay."

As Virtue took to the sky, and Felise had Lightning secured under his lead, Roderick waited patiently, guarding the alleyway.

Rose turned to Theo. *Now is the time to say anything, if you're going to.*

Before she could open her mouth, he cut her off.

"I'll see you at the ship, Rose," Theo said. "Be careful."

Even in the dark evening light, with the moon hiding behind a veil of clouds, the crystal green clarity of his eyes gave her encouragement. "You, too."

Rose watched as he hurried off, grabbing Roderick on the shoulder, and beginning to cover Felise from the various fighters and other frightened figures running around in the streets.

"Rose."

Philip's voice forced her to refocus. "Yes?" she asked.

"Are you ready to go?"

"Oh … yes. We need to find Marsor," Rose said, "and see if we can't draw him down to the docks. There's no point in

ONCE UPON A PRINCESS

getting him to cease his behavior if he doesn't believe we're out of his reach."

"Sounds like a good idea," Philip agreed. The cool steel of his sword flashed as they headed out from the alley.

ONCE UPON A PRINCESS

19

By the time they arrived at the marina, Rose was secretly relieved Marsor was nowhere in sight. As she stood up on her tiptoes to see where Philip had gone, Rose had to wonder if Marsor would even be able to see her among all the crowds. Though there were various fires burning brightly around Maltia City's port, it was hard to see him through the plush of people.

"Rose," Philip called out.

"Over here," she replied.

He came over to her, jostling through the people on the dock. "We're close to the port. One of the ship's captains told me we need that one," Philip said, pointing to the small ship buoying calmly in the waters, near the end of the bay.

"Right where Felise told us it was," Rose noticed. "Good."

"I think I see some of the others." He squinted and a moment later, let out a happy shout. "Yes, there's Ethan and Sophia," he said. "And I do see Captain Locke already aboard."

"Excellent."

"We might get through this without finding Marsor," Philip observed, "but at least we will be on our way, and the people will be safer."

"Do you really think they will be?" Rose asked. The hesitation was clear in her voice.

"He was fighting you," Philip reminded her.

"I'd rather let him."

"Never one to take the easy route, are you?"

"It's never been given to me to take," Rose replied. She looked down at her hands, her fingers. She clenched them tight. "At least, not without greater cost."

"Many people would have trouble recognizing that."

"I think more likely many would prefer not to."

Philip laughed and slowed down to a fast walk beside her. "You will be a great queen one day, Rose."

"Well, I certainly hope so—"

"There's Theo and Roderick," Philip exclaimed. "They're coming our way, and quickly, too. That should be everyone, right?"

"Yes. Run on ahead to the boat, and tell them to begin preparing to ship out. I'll wait for Theo and Roderick."

Philip nodded and jumped ahead, while Rose allowed herself to slow to a stop.

The instant she did, a shadow lunged out from behind her, throwing a thick arm around her throat. Her hands reached up to hold off the onslaught, causing her to drop her sword.

"Marsor," Rose spat out as she gasped for air.

"Princess," he greeted. "You might have escaped me before, but this time you'll be finished."

Rose managed to wriggle out of his grasp, surprising him. She ducked away and circled him carefully, weaponless but still watchful.

I need a plan, and quick!

"Rose!" She could hear Theo call out from behind her, but Rose knew she didn't dare take her attention off Marsor for more than a second.

"I see your friends are all around," Marsor sniveled. "Good. They can see you die."

"You don't seem to know me or my friends very well," Rose said, backing away from him.

"I see you are retreating. That can't be a very good sign for you."

"If you're that worried about me, just come and get me. I'm just a silly girl, after all."

"You've been nothing but a pain since the day I almost ran you over," Marsor agreed. "Normally, I wouldn't have even paid you the slightest bit of mind. But you humiliated me, had me cast out from my tourney. You *will* pay."

"You're the one who was cheating, with Magdust, of all things. You might want to consider this a lesson for the

ONCE UPON A PRINCESS

future. If you're ever allowed back here again, considering what you've done."

Almost there.

Marsor reached out with a small punch. Rose let it hit lightly in her side, before she retreated once more.

She grimaced slightly; the hit landed harder than she'd wanted. "I guess finding out I was a princess was what convinced you that I needed to pay the most."

"Princess or not, you're still a pain," Marsor insisted, lashing out a kick. "But it did explain the disgusting amount of moral superiority. It's bred into you royals, isn't it?"

Rose felt her feet hit the edge of the dock. It was time to wait.

"Rose!" Theo's call came once more, and she allowed herself to look for him, knowing Marsor wouldn't pass up the opportunity to strike.

"Augh!" he cried, rushing at her.

Rose darted to the side and stuck out her leg. His body slammed into her as he tumbled over.

A second later, she heard a distinctive *splash!* It told her, without looking, Marsor had fallen into the water. The smaller, successive sloshes told her he didn't know how to swim.

She stood up and brushed herself off as Theo made his way over to her.

"Are you okay?" He took her arms and held her steady.

"I'm better than Marsor is," she mumbled, not wanting to look behind her. The splashes were slowing and softening.

Theo glared at the figure behind him. "I'll get a rope," he offered. "The Abbess would want us to show him mercy. Though I am even tempted to disagree."

"The Abbess is all right?"

"She is recovering," Theo said. "It will be a while before she is completely out of danger. But her color was back when we passed through."

"I'm glad." Rose gave Theo a smile.

ONCE UPON A PRINCESS

He smiled back, just as Marsor's hand reached up and grabbed Rose's ankle.

Rose felt the dock rush into her as she landed face-first. She squirmed and kicked, but Marsor had a firm grip.

"Rose!" Theo's hands gripped her arms as he held her.

"Don't let go," Rose called back.

"I won't," he promised.

"I've got you now!" Marsor cried, coughing on the salty water.

"Hold her still." Rose and Theo glanced to the side as Roderick came up with Rose's sword in hand.

Rose felt Theo's grip tighten as his feet dug into the wooden dock. "Got it," he said to Roderick.

Roderick held the sword high and sliced it downward.

Marsor's cry of revenge became one of pain. Rose nearly collapsed into Theo as Marsor's grip suddenly disappeared. She glanced back to see blood streaming out of Marsor's hand and into the water.

"That was repayment," Roderick informed Marsor, "for what you did to my hand."

Marsor's eyes glared with an angry fire as his grip on the dock wavered. "Once I get out of here, you'll wish I'd killed you ..." He broke off into a string of obscenities and threats interrupted frequently as he struggled to stay above the surface of the water.

"I doubt he'll even manage to get out of there," Theo assured Rose, as he steadied her and began leading her away. "His armor looks pretty sturdy. The extra weight will work against him."

"I'm just glad his followers didn't join him," Rose said, glancing around to make sure there were no other surprises. "That would have been bad."

"It seems a lot of them have met their match in the Maltian City guards. The city's council sent out several warriors to break up the fights. Hopefully, with Marsor ... preoccupied, that'll be the last he'll cause trouble for Maltia."

ONCE UPON A PRINCESS

"Hopefully." She smiled up at him. "That was good timing, playing along with my distraction."

"It was too much like that time in Greece, near the northern cove of the Aegean," Theo told her. "I remember that one."

"I wondered if you had."

"I did. Still not used to seeing you in danger, though."

Rose sniffed. "I got out of it, same as last time."

Theo nudged her shoulder. "This time was a little more of a surprise. Let's get onboard before another war breaks out."

"No arguments there," Rose said. "Here's the ship now."

Philip waved down at them from the bow. "Good work, Rose," he called out. "I see you've once more been declared the winner."

"I wasn't the one who cheated," Rose called back, nodding back toward Marsor as he continued floundering in the marina waters. "It was a win from the start."

She turned back to Theo. "I am glad to be leaving, and that our plan in back on track. But I'm not looking forward to another month on the sea."

"It shouldn't be that long." Theo waved his hand toward the city. "Besides, it should give us a break from all the adventure we've been having lately."

"Well, that's true," Rose admitted with a reluctant smile.

Theo reached into his tunic and pulled out several squashed rolls of vellum. "Don't worry. I have some reading for you to catch up on, courtesy of the Abbess." When she slumped over, he smiled. "It'll help with the next part of our planning."

Rose sighed.

ONCE UPON A PRINCESS

20

The next month was marked with the cadence of routine, both in the winds of the sea and the repetitive nature of the day. While there was plenty of good weather aiding them this time, Theo knew Rose was happy once more to see land. He watched her as she leaned out into the surf and the wind.

"Don't fall out of the ship, Rose," Theo said, as he came up behind her.

"I'm being careful," she assured him, though he still had to wonder if she recognized her own recklessness.

"It's getting late. We will still likely spend the night aboard."

"Ugh, don't tell me that. Not now. Not when we're this close."

"You've been able to cope well enough," Theo reminded her.

"Getting off Maltia was preferable to dealing with a vengeful villain," Rose reminded him. "But just over a month back on the sea is enough rest. I think I have a right to be excited to be here."

"Yes, because the awaiting dragon's lair is definitely more welcoming."

"At least we're back on track, after all the detours." Rose shrugged. "And with all the reading and studying we did, we're more prepared for this next step. You know, the original one we were planning for."

Theo grinned. "It wasn't all bad, to stop off at Maltia."

"Yes, yes. Meeting new people, helping them fight off a villain, I know."

"I meant more that we were able to get the information about the Thorneback, and know where more specifically to go and how to get there."

Rose glared at him. "Sophia's gotten some good information from the men here, after she charmed them. She has a name of a guide who's supposed to be close to the Poiyana port, a man named Nikolai. And as you said, there was information on the dragons from those scrolls." She turned back toward the small strip of land. "I'm feeling pretty good about everything."

"Exactly how does this make you feel good? Enlighten me."

"I feel better knowing about the enemy beforehand, for one," Rose told him.

"I'll give you that," Theo complied, smiling.

He watched her carefully. Her blue eyes had darkened with gloom in the past month, and while they were no less beautiful, he was glad to see she was much happier. Her hair was longer, too, once more, and it seemed as buoyant as her spirit as it bounced in the breeze.

"Second," she continued, "I'm more than sure a dragon won't smell quite as foul as Marsor did."

"Again, I'll concede." Theo laughed. "I suppose that was the worst thing about Marsor for you, was it?"

"No. The worst part of him was that he went after innocent parties. At least I am sure the dragon will only worry about me. There's no need for it to attack anyone else."

"I wouldn't be so sure of that."

"I'll make sure of it. I'll face it alone."

"That's definitely not going to happen."

"Why?" Rose turned to him with a narrowed gaze. "You think I need the protection?"

Theo gave her an easy smile. "As much as I'd be lying if I said no, that's not the main reason. I want to go with you. Remember? This is not just about Magdalina's curse on you. I came for my own chance at revenge."

Rose frowned, but she relented. "I suppose you're right. About the revenge part, anyway."

"Magdalina's son is not a full-fledged fairy either. The dragon's blood is my best bet in killing him."

"I won't argue with you on it." Rose gave in. "As usual, you have convinced me."

ONCE UPON A PRINCESS

Theo was just about to ask her why it bothered her so much when he was right when he heard the approaching footsteps.

"It's good to know you won't be arguing with Theo over the matter of seeing the dragon, Rose," Philip greeted. "It gives me hope you'll relent and allow me to come along as well."

"Why would you want to come along?" Rose asked.

Theo frowned as Rose voiced his own question. There was no reason Philip needed the dragon's blood, he thought.

Philip raised his eyebrows. "For the adventure, of course," he said. "You don't travel halfway across the great seas of the world to sit back and wait around outside the Serpent's Garden."

"But it could be dangerous."

"No more dangerous than you've faced before."

"More dangerous than you've faced."

"That's all the more reason, isn't it?"

"To go with us? No, it's not."

"I'm not your escort, Rose," Philip argued. "I'm your friend, but I'm here of my own volition. If you do insist on going without me, I could just undergo the task on my own. Working together would prove to be both easier and safer for all parties."

Rose frowned. "I'm not going to argue about this now," she said.

Theo watched as Philip grinned.

"It is a great honor you would bestow upon me," Philip said, "to allow me to accompany one as lovely as you in peril, Princess."

Rose and Theo both turned and glared at him. A long moment passed as the three of them remained silent.

"I'm going to get everyone else ready. We'll be there soon," Rose finally said. She looked back toward the horizon. "Though not soon enough."

Theo waited until the echo of her footsteps had dulled before he turned to Philip. "She doesn't like that, you know."

ONCE UPON A PRINCESS

"What?" Philip asked. "Doesn't like what?"

"She doesn't like people telling her she's beautiful or lovely or any of that."

"It's not the words so much as the person saying it," Philip protested. "She knows I have great respect for her mind as much as her beauty."

Theo felt his temper spike. "She still hates it."

Philip softened. "If you want to tell her she's pretty, you'd probably be safe in doing so. You've known her for many more years, and know her better than I do."

"Which is how I know she finds it uncomfortable," Theo insisted.

"Sometimes it's okay to make people uncomfortable." Philip gave him an enigmatic smile. "Like I said, if you want to tell her that yourself, you're probably one of the few people that are able to do so without making her upset at you."

"It's not that," Theo argued. "I just don't want to see her hurt."

"She's already been hurt."

"By those words."

"Not by the words, or the truth of them," Philip said, shaking his head. "But by the callous people who've used them."

Theo said nothing, only glaring at him more openly.

Philip eased back. "It would help her much more," he said, "if she were to hear it from the people who matter to her, rather than avoid it."

"That's not how she views it."

"Are you sure?" Philip's voice was soft, but still stung.

Theo felt his fists clenched. "I'm sure."

"Am I making you uncomfortable?" Philip asked.

"No," Theo lied.

Philip smiled, clearly amused at Theo's expense. "We've had a similar conversation before," he reminded Theo. "And I think it's fair to say that Rose is the one who will determine

ONCE UPON A PRINCESS

what her feelings are in these matters, and how to deal with them."

Theo scoffed. "You don't know her like I do."

"I know her pretty well," Philip insisted.

"Rose doesn't let her heart override her duty," Theo said. "If you knew her at all, you would know that."

Philip shrugged. "People change, all the time," he said. "And sometimes, they do it while no one is watching."

Theo said nothing, not trusting to respond as irritation fought to overcome his patience.

"I've seen Rose lead with her heart plenty of times," Philip added.

"Only for others," Theo muttered back, recalling how Rose would not dream of a future for herself, even though she had worked hard to give him one. She had worked for Sophia and Ethan as well, and even given her time and care to Philip and Mary.

But there was no future for her as long as there was Magdalina. There were no dreams, no joy, not even a song in her future, as long as the half-fairy sorceress was alive.

Philip shrugged and finally relented. He turned away and headed down toward the stern of the ship, leaving Theo all alone.

21

"That's the guy we're looking for, right there," Sophia said, pointing to the man with the large eyes, long hair, and scruffy beard. "His name is Nikolai Colombo, and he's the one who knows the way to the Serpent's Garden."

"What else did you learn about him?" Rose asked, as she walked in full strides beside her squire.

"That he was a trader of furs, but exclusively works with taking people to see Amalia, the Celestial Dragonkeeper."

"He probably charges a lot of money," Theo remarked from behind them.

"You know it." Sophia nodded, turning to smile back at Theo's discernment.

Ethan sighed. "Do we have enough money for that?" he asked. "It doesn't look like this place holds as many tournaments as Maltia City."

Sophia nudged him. "Come on, my dear brother," she said. "Cheer up. You'll see Penelope again. She agreed to come to Rhone, anyway, right?"

"Not soon enough," Ethan muttered under his breath.

"Ethan, come here," Rose called. Ethan shuffled over toward Rose, the expression on his face grim and determined.

Theo smiled; he had a feeling Ethan knew what to expect from Rose.

"You'll have plenty of time to compose a new song for her. She'll be happy to know you've been practicing enough for that."

"Okay," Ethan agreed. But he caught Theo's eyes, and the two exchanged a knowing look. It wasn't enough for Ethan, Theo observed.

He found himself looking at Rose, admitting he could more than sympathize with Ethan. *Time and distance don't always matter so much when it comes to the heart.*

ONCE UPON A PRINCESS

Philip came up beside them. "Captain Locke and the other guards are shopping through the market," he said. "Keeping an eye out for news and goods, and possibly lodging if we need it."

"And if we can afford it," Sophia added.

"We should see if there is a church nearby," Theo said.

"Always with the church," Rose said with a sigh.

"It's a good place to find reliable help more often than not," Theo argued. "Those who seek, Rose."

"Those who object, Theo."

"You wouldn't know quite so much about Magdalina or her origins, or even the Serpent's Garden, if it weren't for the church."

"If God would have just removed this curse from me," Rose bit back, "we wouldn't even be here."

Theo sighed and shook his head.

Didn't Rose see it? Theo wondered. Didn't she see how much more of the world she saw and how much better of a ruler she would be? Didn't she see she could be free to be herself here?

"That's enough bickering, you two," Sophia interrupted. "Nikolai's slowing down."

"Good," Ethan muttered. "We've been following him long enough."

"We had to make sure it was actually him," Mary spoke up from underneath Ethan's hood.

"Mary's got a point," Rose agreed.

"We could have just asked the man himself two hours ago, when we first got off the ship," Ethan insisted.

"Now, now. Time has not dulled your excitement for journeying, has it?" Philip teased.

"Maybe not my desire for adventure, but more like my leg muscles. It's hard to walk after we've been on a ship for the last several weeks."

Theo smiled as Ethan and Philip, and then Mary, began arguing. He turned back to Rose, only to see her watching Nikolai. The man was quite a sight, with a stocky build

ONCE UPON A PRINCESS

draped in furs, tethered with rope that doubled up as a utility belt. He carried a walking stick in his right hand with the sureness of a warrior going into battle with his sword. "Are you worried he'll refuse?"

Rose winced. "I didn't see you there," she said. "You surprised me."

"I'll be sure to avoid it in the future," Theo assured her. "I know how you hate surprises."

Rose arched an eyebrow at him. "You know I have legitimate reasons for that."

"I'm teasing you, Rosary." He reached out to tweak her hair, like he'd done innocently so many times, but he faltered when she recoiled.

"Well, don't. I don't want you to." Rose then turned away.

Theo sighed. "I'll be happy to go and talk to him for you," he offered.

Rose was silent for a moment. Theo could see she was mulling it over, and he made no attempt to stop her. He hoped that once they were on the road, she would feel better. Or at least, she would relax some. Her restlessness was understandable, but hardly like her.

"Maybe it would be better for Philip to go," Rose said. "He's the one carrying the money, after all."

"I'd be happy to," Philip said, stepping forward. He grinned at Rose. "Although I hope you know I'm not acting as your royal announcer."

Theo frowned. Was Philip *trying* to make him upset by teasing Rose, especially in a manner he would have done himself?

He relaxed a bit when he saw Rose roll her eyes and send him off. But the question of Philip's intentions gnawed at him.

During the trip from Maltia, Rose and Philip had easily conversed on different kingdom topics at mealtimes, sparred diligently together on their mock battlegrounds, and had studied with Theo and the others over the manuscripts from Thad and the Abbess.

ONCE UPON A PRINCESS

He'd listened to her stories about growing up with Isra and Ronan, fought with her about sending letters, and accepted chastisement for frequently checking for Virtue or any other hawks carrying messages.

Philip had done nothing overt to suggest that he was angling for Rose's hand, or even her heart.

But he was still a candidate for both, wasn't he? Theo knew he was only kidding himself if he thought Rose wouldn't have to worry about marriage at all, especially if she was able to break her curse. And as each day passed, he realized, Philip was becoming more and more of a clear match for Rose.

A dark shadow crossed over him, interrupting his thoughts.

"You're the ones who are wanting to go see Lady Amalia, are you then?"

Nikolai's voice carried the weight of duty and the strength of certainty.

Theo and Rose looked at each other. He gave her a small smile, despite his mood. He knew when she looked for his support.

"Yes," Rose spoke up, turning to face the mountain of a man before them. "We're looking for the Serpent's Garden."

"Trying to get some Thorneback blood, are you?" Nikolai asked. "That's what most of them want when they come. I've never had anyone win over a dragon to give them blood."

Rose frowned. "What do you mean?"

"Dragon's blood is rare as they come," Nikolai said. "And that's for good reason. Do you know how many people die trying to get it? That's the reason I ask for my pay upfront. There's no point in getting half of a sale of a drop of dragon's blood if you don't survive getting it in the first place. And that's just half the nuts I talk with."

"Surely the rest of them are more fiscally minded?"

Nikolai's chest rumbled with muffled laughter. "The other half are worse. They never even plan for getting there. The mountains are rough and the trails can be dangerous. Then there's Amalia herself," he said, his voice caressing the name with reverence. "If you can stop staring at her and survive the dragon, there's still the matter of getting the blood itself. If you get it, you'll need to carry it. I remember this one fellow …"

Rose watched as the man continued his tales, talking of the different ranges of ignorance and poor preparation his clients had displayed.

"Why do you still take people, if you've never had anyone get the blood?" Theo asked Nikolai. "Especially when you don't seem to believe anyone ever will?"

"There's good money to be made in doing what you can for what you love," Nikolai replied. "Speaking of which, you'll be paying me now."

"You'll take us then?" Rose asked.

"Of course." He grinned down at her. "I'm not a believer in destiny perhaps, or much else, but I am a believer in good business."

"I can't argue with that," Rose agreed. "Philip, pay the man."

22

Philip leaned down close to Rose as they took another break. "I didn't think we would be leaving right away," he admitted.

"It's better if we keep going," Rose told him. "After all, we had plenty of time to rest while we were sailing over here."

"Not that you took the time actually to rest," Philip reminded her.

She glared at him. "I had enough," she said. "And if we don't keep going, I might get even more after my birthday."

"Enough for a lifetime, I'd imagine," Philip replied with a laugh.

Rose punched his arm. "You wouldn't like it if you were in my position," she snapped.

"I am not in your position, Rose," Philip agreed. "But humor is a good way to defend yourself from despair. I'm not trying to make you feel bad."

Rose decided it was best to ignore him. She turned away from him as Ethan and Theo finally came back into sight, and Sophia plunked her bag down on the ground next to her.

"Whew!" Sophia murmured. "I never thought I would say this, but I almost envy the guards we left behind."

"They'll be fine in Poiyana for the next week or so," Rose said, brushing the issue aside. She'd left Roderick, Lannister, and Captain Locke behind, under orders to look for Virtue, and to gather information and make plans for the return trip to Rhone.

It would not be easy getting back to Rhone, Rose thought. Even though she had not needed to spend the winnings they'd earned on Maltia to get to the Romani territory, the cost of lodgings for several days, supplies, and Nikolai's services were going to be hard on them.

And while Rose knew traveling by boat would be quickest, she was more than determined to find a trade route over the land. Battling the elements on the road was easier than getting tossed around on the turbulence of the sea.

"Maybe Ethan was onto something earlier. I could have used a day to get my land legs back, especially if I'd known I'd be scaling up a mountain today," Sophia said, nodding over to where her brother was, as Theo took Ethan's pack and fastened it around his own waist.

"The mountains only get higher, too," Nikolai called back. "We'll walk up and down them for three days, before we arrive at the mountain spine. And there, tucked into a small valley, will be the garden."

"Three days doesn't sound like a long time," Rose said. "So that's some good news."

"It'll be the longest three days of your life," Nikolai promised her.

"It won't be my hardest," Rose shot back, standing up tall. "I can guarantee you that."

Nikolai gazed at her. "You've known heartbreak before, then, haven't you?"

"What?" Rose narrowed her eyes quizzically. "What do you mean?"

"Your heart has been broken," Nikolai said, stating it rather than asking. "I can tell. It's a rare one who has the ability to suffer greatly without having been tried before."

"I have no heart to break anymore," Rose answered. "Now, let's get on with the journey, shall we?" She eyed him pointedly. "If these are going to be the longest three days of my life, then let's at least get on with it already."

Nikolai nodded and directed them toward the next part of the journey. "We've got several hours yet till sundown," he said. "Hopefully they, and we, will go fast."

As Rose continued to press on, Theo managed to catch up to Rose and Nikolai at the front of the group.

"What are you doing up here?" Rose asked. "I thought you were helping Ethan."

ONCE UPON A PRINCESS

"He's tired of my company," Theo told her. "Sophia's taking a turn watching him. Although I do still have his baggage."

"Not feeling rejected, are you?" Rose asked with a half-smile. "Or used, maybe?"

"Not at all," Theo assured her. "He's mooning over Penelope still, and while working through some of the song lyrics he has planned was a novel experience, I'm more than happy to hand the task over to Sophia for a bit."

Nikolai laughed. "You must have had your own heart broken, too."

"All hearts are broken," Theo replied.

"Spoken like a man of the cloth," Nikolai snorted.

"I grew up in the care of the church and I have been educated in various creeds and catechisms, and found them to be true. My brother is going to be taking his priestly vows soon as well." Theo shrugged. "So you would not be far off."

"But your heart hasn't merely been broken," Nikolai said. "It's been smashed."

Rose glanced over at Theo, watching him as he went into silence. There was the matter of his parents, she thought. And the hardship of being away from his only brother while he was with her.

"God seems to like working with broken people best," Theo finally remarked, although Rose wondered if it was somewhat forced.

Before she could examine her claim more clearly, Theo changed the subject. "You seem to know a lot about broken hearts. Has yours been shattered, too?"

"Yes." Nikolai nodded. "And mine is destined to keep breaking."

"Is that why you've given up on the fur trade?" Rose asked. "And that's why you only take people up to see the garden now?"

"Heard about that, have you? It seems like you've done your research on me."

"We had to," Rose assured him.

"I'll take it as a compliment, then." He turned his face into the fading sunlight. "But no. I stopped trading a long time ago. There's no need for me to do any more than I have to. Traveling to the Serpent's Garden earns me enough of a living. If you don't need something, you don't need it. Pure and simple."

"Is that why you don't believe in God?" Theo asked. "You feel like you don't need him?"

Rose was a bit surprised by Theo's forwardness, but after a moment she reconsidered. Nikolai had a forthright personality, and he seemed to like discussing the darker sides of life. As soon as she saw his face light up with the challenge, she knew Theo's instincts had been spot on.

That is just like him, though. Rose recalled other times when she had relied on Theo's skill for reading others. It was not just useful in battles, but in everyday life, it seemed.

"Oh, I'm sure that he's real enough," Nikolai said. "I even admire him, from time to time. But I have no loyalty to him."

"Why?" Theo asked. "That's a more uncommon position to take on the matter."

Nikolai frowned. "He is the one who broke my heart, and he is the one who keeps breaking it."

Theo went silent for a moment, while Rose almost laughed. "That explains the obsession with that particular topic," Rose muttered under her breath.

But, as much as she hated the scraggly guide's intruding questions, she sympathized with him. Was she not in the same category as he, when it came to belief in a higher power?

She had grown up, before learning of her curse, in the church. Rose could remember being enthralled with the story of God, and how he loved his children even though they were rebellious and proud and stubborn; how he'd loved them so much he'd sent his son to die for them all, even after all the terrible things they'd done.

But then she'd grown up. It was one thing to die for someone, Rose thought. But she had little evidence that he was still alive and still cared. After all, if dying for the sins of the world was so easy for him, why was it so hard to remove a vengeful sorceress' curse? What kind of loving god would allow her curse to remain?

Yes, Rose thought, *I can definitely see where Nikolai is coming from on that matter.*

She only half-listened to the rest of Theo and Nikolai's conversation, as she wondered what kind of curse Nikolai had on his heart that made him declare his own form of sovereignty from God and society.

Rose allowed her curiosity about her new guide to drift to the back of her mind as they continued on their journey to see Amalia, the Dragonkeeper guardian.

Nikolai was patient enough with them as they made their way up and down the mountain trail, but at the end of their days, he would look off into the distance with impatience in his eyes.

Rose wondered at his stamina, and began to envy him more and more as they continued. The mountain weather was cold and impassive during the day, and even more frigid at night. Tempers were hot and short, and more than one yelling battle ensued. Rest became an elusive end, and Rose had, more often than not, to shut out her thoughts by focusing on her plans.

Over and over she repeated them to herself: Slay the dragon, get its blood, go back to Rhone. Free her mother, and then herself.

On the morning of the third day, she woke up while it was still dark. The eerie silence of the night just before it turned to morning unnerved her. The stillness was just as disconcerting.

Rose found comfort at once, as she found Nikolai looking off into the distance once more. It was then she recalled her initial question. *What is Nikolai's curse?*

Before she could move to ask, he glanced in her direction. His large eyes were expressive and joyous, even though the bags under his eyes hinted at a lack of sleep.

"She's here."

ONCE UPON A PRINCESS

At those two simple words, spoken in such lovely expression and vivid voice, Rose knew all at once why Nikolai suffered so.

He was in love with Amalia.

Rose was almost tempted to watch Nikolai's face as the dawn brought forth the cherub who guarded the Serpent's Garden. His beard seemed to still along with his breathing, and his gaze never wavered despite the brilliant light.

But as the light sparking and pouring into her vision from the deepest part of darkness caught her intrigue, once Rose saw Amalia, she could no longer look anywhere else.

Amalia was a dazzling beauty; she wielded power without moving a finger, even as she tamed the world around her. Her long hair was dark at the top, its long length flowing easily into gold, crowned by a tiara of wings and light.

As Rose adjusted to seeing the bright light around Amalia, she saw the angel's gaze drift to Nikolai. Rose had a feeling they were having their own silent conversation, much like the ones she shared with Theo.

Rose took advantage of the moment to study the Dragonkeeper. She was tall and stood at ease; there was nothing to suggest she would engage Rose in battle. While power and light seemed to swivel around her, Rose felt no threat coming from her. And she had no weapon, or at least none that Rose could see. Like Nikolai, she carried a staff with her. Seeing the similar designs in Amalia and Nikolai's staffs, Rose had to wonder if it had been a gift from Nikolai.

"My Lady," Nikolai finally murmured, his voice warmer and softer than Rose ever believed possible. *Especially after three days of having him yell at me and the others,* Rose thought with a smile.

"I've been waiting for you, Princess Aurora of Rhone."

Even Amalia's smile was perfect, Rose noticed, as she turned to meet Amalia's gaze. "I hope I haven't been keeping you long."

"Not at all," Amalia assured her. "Indeed, I have been stationed here for many lifetimes by My Lord. I serve as a guard, keeping the serpent dragons inside, should they be tempted to escape the thorny, fiery gates of their home."

Rose felt her hand on her sword tighten instinctively. "I would hope that, given your expectation of my arrival, you would allow me access to see them."

"There are other gardens which are blocked from human passage," Amalia said. "But this one is only for keeping the dragons inside. Many men and women have come to seek the power dragon's blood has to offer."

"Nikolai told me no one has succeeded in slaying the dragon."

"Should it matter?" Amalia asked. "You will not be deterred with that knowledge. You learned at a young age not to listen to the crowds, instead choosing to take your own path and seek out counsel from those closest to you."

"When you put it that way," Rose muttered, "I guess you're right."

"In here, as a condition of your entrance, you will face your greatest challenge, which, for you, is also your greatest weakness." Amalia glanced down at Rose's hand, still clenched tightly around her sword. "I see you are more than ready to go in."

Rose nodded.

"I'm prepared to go as well," Philip spoke up from behind.

Rose nearly jumped. She'd forgotten about her friends; Amalia's presence had overwhelmed her senses.

"Me, too." Theo's sword clanged by his side.

Amalia looked amused. "You are all allowed to pass," she said. "But the promise applies to you as well: You will face your greatest challenge, and greatest weakness."

"I accept," Theo said, taking his place beside Rose.

"I do as well," Philip said.

"I must inform you, Sir Theo," Amalia warned, "if you go, you will not be able to kill the dragon."

"What do you mean?" Theo asked.

"While revenge hides in your heart, fear still plays a deeper game." Before he could ask another question, she turned to

ONCE UPON A PRINCESS

Philip. "You, Prince Philip, are also allowed the right to go, even though your biggest fear is misplaced in this instance. You can still help, of course, and your virtue in this matter commends you."

Philip glanced over at Rose, who shrugged and stepped forward. "We're ready."

Fear gripped her briefly, but years of battling had taught Rose to use it to sharpen her senses. "I'm ready to slay the dragon."

"It remains to be seen if that will be necessary." Amalia stepped to the side. A gate, with doors of iron and fire, covered in thorns creeping around in through the small crevices, appeared behind her.

"We'll be waiting for you out here," Amalia said as the gate opened, revealing the realm of woodlands beyond. "You have until nightfall to secure your prize. While I am not adverse to fighting them," she said with a cool gaze, "I prefer not to make my life difficult."

Rose, Theo, and Philip all started forward.

"Go, Rose!" Sophia cheered.

"You can do it!" Ethan called, as Mary waved as she perched on his shoulder. "We'll all be here for you when you get back."

"We believe in you," Theo whispered to Rose, as they headed in.

"Did you say your prayers?" Rose asked, giving him a secret smirk.

"You know I always do where you're concerned, Rosary."

The three of them walked through the gate. It shut loudly behind them and disappeared from sight, sealing off the rest of the world as Rose finally felt her restlessness leave her. Everything was going to plan at last.

23

The Serpent's Garden was full of trees and fields, with plenty of foliage both familiar and exotic, all encircled with thorn-covered gates. Rose felt the humidity of the atmosphere wash over her as she examined the ground for tracks and other signs of movement.

I almost wish Ethan had come with us. He was the better tracker. Rose sighed. She couldn't see him being quite that brave, especially since he was hesitant to learn how to fight.

"So … which way do you want to try first?" Philip asked after a few moments had passed.

"Shh … We'll be able to hear better if we're quiet," Rose said. Her ears strained to hear the faintest sound from around the forest-like surroundings.

"I'm not so sure," Theo whispered. "If this is the garden where the serpent was banished, and these dragons are his descendants, they might have supernatural capabilities."

"What do you mean?" Philip asked.

Rose smothered a sigh. "Maybe I should just call out to them?" she asked, her tone scathing and impatient. "Maybe they'll come running?"

Immediately, Philip and Theo both quieted.

It's about time those two stopped chatting, Rose thought, bristling. She had to push down her momentary frustration, but it was hard not to think about how they were not helping. Were they even taking this seriously? Rose wondered.

A moment later, there was a rustling sound in the bushes to her right.

"Over there." Rose pointed.

"It was just a small sound," Theo said. "It's possible that it was just the wind."

"I heard something. I'm going to go investigate," Rose insisted. "We need to work together, Theo."

"I'm trying to help you," he reasoned. "The dragons are rumored to be quite ruthless and cunning. There's a reason that no one has managed to leave here with their blood."

"Fine. Stay here. I'll go and see," Rose snapped. She held her sword up and headed out to see what she could.

"You might want to calm down a bit," Philip said lightly, as he followed behind her. "We have time."

"Time has *never* been an ally of mine. Theo knows that more than anyone else."

"He also knows more about you than anyone else."

"Then he should know we're not leaving here until we get the dragon's blood." Rose turned her attention back to the bushes, using her sword to push against the tangled foliage. "The sooner we get it, the better."

Another sound, rushing from her other side, made her whip around. "Over there," she said, hurrying back over to the left.

For the next several moments, Rose found herself barreling around the garden, with no serpents in sight.

Whoosh.

"Check it out. I heard it, from right there," she called.

Crackle.

"Here."

She ran back and forth, narrowing her gaze at Theo, as he continued to stand before the gate, in the middle of the clearing.

Finally, she slowed down and came up beside him. "Just stop it," she snapped.

"I'm not doing anything," Theo replied easily.

"I can tell what you're thinking."

He arched his brow at her. "Is that so?" he asked mildly. "I suppose it's not so hard to imagine, considering I can tell you're frustrated and unsure."

"Shut up." Rose stuck her tongue out at him before turning around. She called out, "Where are you, dragons? Come out and fight with me!"

"Rose," Philip said, "Are you sure—"

"I've learned so much about the Thornebacks," Rose called out. "A proud dragon race, descending from the serpent of Eden itself. Come out and prove your worth."

Theo and Philip glanced around as hissing sounds began to resound around them.

Rose smirked. "You couldn't resist a challenge like that, could you?"

A heckling laughter was the only answer given to her.

Rose stiffened but reaffirmed her resolve. "I'm not afraid of you!"

"What a shame," a voice replied from behind her.

Rose whirled around to see a long, scaly dragon latched onto the back of the garden gate that they had come through.

The dragon was unlike anything Rose had expected; he was more like an overgrown lizard than a snake, with stringy legs and feet crowned with long, sharp claws. There were small wings folded against his back, reminding Rose of the bats she and Isra had found hiding under one of the arched passageways of Havilah's castle.

"So," Theo spoke up. "You can talk."

"It doesn't matter if he could sing and dance," Rose argued. "I'm still not afraid."

"It is really too bad, you know," the dragon told her, as he slithered down the gate with his claws, landing on the ground. "For you would have found me more quickly, in that case."

"What do you mean?" Rose asked, her cheeks burning. Was the dragon trying to make her feel like a fool? "You should be more afraid of me than I am of you."

The dragon laughed again. "We have nothing to fear from you, Princess, especially when you are like that. You don't seem to know much about dragons, do you?"

"If I didn't know about you, I'd likely be afraid," Rose told him. "But I know plenty about you, including the fact your blood can kill the wicked half-fairy who cursed me."

"If that is true, you must not know about yourself then," the dragon told her. "For in here, you need only face your biggest challenge and fear."

"What do you mean?" Rose asked again. "I already told you, I'm not afraid of you."

"Ah, but you are afraid of something, aren't you?"

"Careful, Rose," Theo warned. "The serpent dragons are known to be crafty liars."

The dragon gave a mocking bow. "We have such a poor reputation from our ancestor, the one who had to give up his wings and legs after he tricked the humans," the dragon replied. "It is unfortunate."

"You're saying that your ancestor was not the one who tricked Adam and Eve in the garden of Eden?" Theo asked.

"No, no. Of course he did that. How else do you think we wound up here? But we are his family, not the snake himself." The dragon sniffed. "Even though we do love a good bit of trickery once in a while, of course."

"Then I will do what Adam couldn't," Rose told him. "I will kill you." With that, she swung her sword at him, frustrated rage spewing out as she twisted and turned, trying to get a good shot at him.

The dragon anticipated her move, easily side-stepping it. He laughed again. "If it is your wish, Princess, I will fight you."

"Don't laugh at me!"

"It is better than feeling sorry for you," the dragon hissed.

Rose struck him near the tail, making him roar in agony. "There's no need to feel sorry for me!"

His tail lashed back, whipping her across her body. Rose cried out as she was thrown backward. Her back pounded against a tree.

"Rose!" Theo called, running to cover. He ducked under one of the dragon's wings as it opened, using his own sword to block a swipe from one of the dragon's claws.

"And so the little defender of the church decides to jump into the fray," the dragon murmured. "I'm not surprised, considering your biggest fear."

Theo fought his way over to Rose, planting himself in front of her. "Are you okay?" he asked, as he kept one eye on their enemy.

ONCE UPON A PRINCESS

"Yes," Rose assured him as she steadied herself. "More of a jolt than anything."

Theo didn't respond, as the dragon lashed out another attack. Theo dug in and pressed back, catching the dragon's claws on his blade.

"Lady Amalia already told you that you will not be able to kill me, young warrior," the dragon's voice was calmer, as he slinked in a soft retreat. "You will not find your greatest fear from me."

"I came with Rose for dragon's blood myself," Theo said. "I have as much to lose as she does in this."

"No, she has the more to lose," the dragon assured him. "But she is not as aware of it as you are."

"I'm perfectly aware that I'm being ignored, if you're worried about that," Rose snipped. "But it doesn't matter if Theo can't kill you."

The dragon laughed. "Why do you say that?"

"Because Amalia didn't say anything about me," Philip called from behind, as he jumped on the dragon's back.

He landed hard on his feet, but used his free hand to latch onto one of the dragon's wings.

"Here," Rose called, ducking underneath Theo and hurrying under the dragon. She thrust her sword into its underbelly.

The dragon reared at the attack, but Rose found her sword had just scraped him; no blood came free from the beast. Before she could try again, Theo tackled her, rolling her out from under the dragon's trampling paws.

"Theo, stop!" Rose struggled against him. "I almost had him."

"*He* almost had *you*," Theo corrected, grabbing her arm and hauling her up. He tugged her to the side as the dragon's tail came flailing.

Rose was about to argue when a stream of fire, flashing green and purple, unleased from the dragon's mouth.

"Watch out!" Philip called.

The dragon roared angrily, as his wings flapped open. He jumped as Philip managed to jump down off his back, twisting into an awkward landing.

"This isn't working," Rose said, as her friends pulled back together.

"You have to admit, it's better than *not* having a dragon to fight," Philip said.

"It wants us to face our greatest fears and challenges," Theo said. "And mine won't be settled by killing him."

"So why are you here?" Philip asked.

"To stand by Rose."

"My biggest fear," Rose said quietly, "would be to fail."

"So the way you can win is by winning?" Philip asked. "That seems logical."

"Shh!" Theo murmured. "He's coming back."

The dragon fell out of the sky once more, circling and whirling around, whipping turbulence all throughout the landscape.

Rose held her ground as the wind pushed her back, while Theo and Philip dropped to the ground.

"Rose!" Philip cried. "Look out!"

The dragon snarled, his snout expelling ghastly smoke as he charged.

It was now or never, Rose decided. Rose held her sword firmly. "*I will not fail!*" she cried, charging forward.

She didn't have to see Theo getting to his feet to know he was determined to catch up to her. "Rose—"

"Not now, Theo!" Rose yelled back. "Stand down!"

"It's too dangerous," Philip called out, running after her.

Rose ignored him. *I can't fail. I just can't.*

With her sword out and ready for impact, carefully aimed for the center of the dragon's skull, Rose breathed out a quick, unspoken, barely acknowledged prayer.

Instantly, she was wrapped in a warm embrace as the world around her blurred. Her eyes squeezed shut as the world shook and she lost her balance; her sword went flying out of her hand as she hit the ground hard. A second later, she

ONCE UPON A PRINCESS

heard Philip cry out and she could hear Theo's sharp gasp of pain.

"Theo!"

He had reached her just in time to move her out of the dragon's way, pushing her down as the dragon flew overhead. On his back and arm, blood blossomed in three thick stripes from where he had been hit by the dragon's tail.

He cried out in pain as she tried to move him. "Just sit down," Rose screamed, trying to drown out his voice with hers. "It'll be okay."

Theo gritted his teeth together as he slumped over. "I'm not so sure," he grumbled.

"Let me find Philip," Rose said, just as the dragon roared angrily.

Rose's gaze shot to find the dragon. She reached over and grasped for her sword. "Stay here," she ordered Theo. She paused for a moment before adding, "And this time, I mean it."

"Okay." Theo nodded, his gaze tired and sad, submissive only out of necessity.

Rose touched his cheek briefly before leaving him. Much as he had on Maltia, he leaned into her hand. The intimacy, peeking out from behind the clouded pain in his startling green eyes, shuddered through Rose as she felt his tears on her palm. Before she could pull back, he slumped over, unconscious.

"Rose!" Philip called out for her. "Come quickly!"

Rose was torn for a moment, between guilt and fear and self-disgust. Another thought spurred her back to the battle. *If we can win and get out of here quickly, we can make take care of Theo more quickly.*

"Coming," she called back. Her eyes squeezed shut for one small, brief second as she pushed back the threat of her own tears.

Concern for her best friend, and anger at her recklessness, quickly dissolved as she saw Philip's predicament.

ONCE UPON A PRINCESS

Tree branches snapped as the dragon wriggled around, trying to dislodge Philip as he held onto its long neck.

"Try to get its eye," Rose called, as she hurried to help. "Or its snout! The scales on his body are too much for our swords."

The dragon roared, and began shooting out fire. Philip twisted around, but he was unable to make a dent in the dragon's exterior.

"No good, Rose," Philip called back. "I'm using both hands just to hang on."

"Well, just hang on, then," Rose ordered. She hurried over, slanting to the right and left as the dragon's tale shot from side to side. "I'll try to get it."

The dragon spewed out the flames again and again.

"Augh!" Philip hollered as he was finally flung to the ground.

"Move," Rose cried.

The dragon, free once more, blasted a long shot of fire against the ground. Smoke flew up as the earth was scorched. The dragon took off at once, the wind blowing dust and debris across their vision.

Rose and Philip coughed until they escaped the reach of the flames.

"Where did my sword get to?" Philip asked.

"I don't know," Rose admitted. "But let's go after him. He couldn't have gotten far."

"I think he could have, actually," Philip countered. "His wings were pretty strong and fairly proportional to his body. His flying skills were well-honed." When he saw the look on her face, he sighed. "I managed to get caught on them just a little while ago, Rose. I would know if that was the truth or not."

"I still say we should go after him," Rose murmured.

"What happened to Theo?"

"He's back there. Which is all the more reason we need to hurry if we're going to find a dragon."

ONCE UPON A PRINCESS

"What do you mean by that?" Philip asked, suddenly alarmed and suspicious.

"He's been hurt pretty badly. He's bleeding and unconscious."

"Then we need to leave."

"He would want us to keep fighting, Philip."

"Let's get him back to Mary and the others, and then we'll see what he thinks," Philip insisted. "I'm not going to have one of our group perish when there's something we could have done about it."

Rose bit her lip. "I don't know."

"What?" Philip rounded on her.

"I mean, he's bleeding but—"

"He's bleeding? What else would stop us from taking him back?"

"This is our only chance, Philip!" Rose shouted back. "This is our only chance to get the dragon's blood. What's the point of living if we're not going to be free to actually live?"

"You *do* get to live!" Philip cried. "You have had nearly eighteen years, Rose. Not everyone even gets that! And before you try to make this about Theo, too, you need to remember that not everyone gets their parents, either."

"I don't need to be guilted into going!" Rose gritted her teeth, rage and truth battling inside of her. Both sides were angry and bitter, both sides were demanding and fierce.

But then Philip took her arm. "You know I have fought for you, and Theo has too. We would do anything for you, Rose. But please don't let your fear take charge of you."

My greatest fear—failure. That's it, isn't it? Looking down at Theo, she suddenly wasn't so sure.

"All right. Fine! You're right."

"You don't need to sound so hostile about it."

"This is not easy," Rose yelled. "This is not easy for me at all!" She put her head in her hands. "I needed the dragon's blood. I can't fail."

"We *will* find a way to make it better," he promised.

"Don't try to placate me!"

ONCE UPON A PRINCESS

"Let's go for now."

"Okay. Okay, fine. Just fine." Rose felt anxiety rise up in her throat as they picked up Theo and shared his weight.

She knew Philip was right. But she still reeled from the blow. There was no way to win, she realized. There was no way to get free of her situation.

She had failed.

24

"Back already, are we?" Amalia asked.

Rose shot her a hateful glare. "You know the answer to that."

"I don't mean to celebrate," Amalia told her gently. "I wanted to congratulate you."

"It'll have to wait," Rose said, pushing past the Dragonkeeper. "Mary! Sophia! Ethan! Come quickly, and bring the medical supplies. Theo's been hurt, badly."

Mary fluttered over quickly, fretfully. "I was worried about this," she murmured.

"I know," Rose said. "But it was a risk we all knew to be possible. Can you check him over?"

"I will, of course," Mary said. "But I'm not sure there's much I'll be able to do. Dragons can have a numbing effect on fairy magic, even when they're this close."

"I've got the herbs and healing potions," Sophia spoke up. "Which ones do you think we'll need?"

"Philip, go see about setting up a tent. Use some of my blankets," Rose ordered. "Sophia, you and Mary will need to find items needed for burns, possibly, and spirits for open wounds."

"I can see the slashes through his back," Sophia said.

Rose flinched at the frightened quality of her voice. "Move him over to his pad. Get him as comfortable as possible. Philip, where's that stuff for the tent, so we can keep him warmer?"

The group scuttled around, bustling with their various duties as Rose gently arranged Theo's silent form. She cupped his face and spoke to him.

"Theo? Can you hear me?"

"Yes," he mumbled back, without opening his eyes. "Ugh."

"We're back out at the campsite," Rose told him. "We're going to patch you back together."

He opened his eyes. "Are you all right, Rose?" His question, honest and concerned, made her guilt come rushing back.

She ducked her face from his gaze. "There's no need to worry about me when you're in this condition," she told him. "I'm going to leave you to Mary for a bit."

Before he could object, she hurried off, calling for Ethan, who was nowhere to be seen.

Nikolai stepped forward. "Your boy's been off this morning, foraging a bit," he told her. "He's gone off on his own."

"Oh." Rose said. "I guess It's always good to make sure we have food stocked, right?"

"I doubt he'll bring back much."

"He's a good tracker and hunter, even though he's young."

"I've no problem with his youth," Nikolai said. "But he took his harp with him."

"I see." Rose gave him a small smile. "Broken hearts again, right?"

"Yes." Nikolai shrugged. "But he's young, and only the young can love so quickly."

"Those things have a way of staying with us sometimes."

"Yes, but it's a fallacy to assume it will." Nikolai leaned back, his eyes returning to the gate, where Amalia waited patiently, as the activity around their camp continued.

"She's the one who broke your heart, isn't she?" Rose asked.

"No," Nikolai said. "It was God who did the breaking, as I said before."

"What do you mean?" Rose asked.

Nikolai nodded down to Theo's camp, where Mary was hovering around him like an anxious mother, while Sophia and Philip were arranging Rose's blankets to protect him from the coolness of oncoming night.

ONCE UPON A PRINCESS

"I found this trail largely by accident, the first several times," Nikolai began. "But I met Amalia, I knew it had been worth it. I knew I would be content with no other bride."

Rose said nothing as he continued.

"But she's a guardian angel, a cherub. In a sense, she's not even alive as you and I are. We formed a friendship, but she is unable to love me the way I love her."

"I imagine that's hard," Rose said, trying not to sound too sympathetic.

"She has told me of God, and his kingdom," Nikolai continued. "But I can't believe he is good after finding her. What kind of God gives a man a love for someone he will never marry, or who will never know the fullness of that love?" He shook his head. "Sure, he may exist, as much as it would be better for him not to. But I don't believe in him. I can't, while my heart is broken, and still so much in love it is worth coming here time and time and time again, to see her. To be near her, to talk with her. To watch her remain perfect and unchanged, even as I grow older and the world moves on."

Rose said nothing. She felt a kinship with Nikolai in his pain, even though she had a feeling he wouldn't return the gesture.

But there was something different, Rose mused. After all, she had her friends. She had been able to save Sophia and Ethan from their father. She had made peace between peoples and nations, traveling between the fairy realms and distance lands. And there was Theo, with his patient composure hiding his compassion as well as his passion; Mary, with her bubbly and caring nature, so creative and eager to help; and even Philip now, with his honorable heart and his practiced nobility, which had been bred so deeply inside his bones it came out in his flesh.

There were others, too; she wasn't sure how Isra would take the news she had failed to retrieve the dragon's blood, but Rose knew her younger sister would be appalled at the thought of her earning it at the expense of Theo's life.

Despite her curse, Rose thought, she had lived a good life, with good people who loved her.

Wasn't that enough? More than enough, in many ways? Maybe it was a question of whether or not it *could be*, rather than *would be*, Rose thought bitterly. Redemption was still a far-off reality in many ways.

"I'm going to see if I can find Ethan," she told Nikolai. It would put some distance between her and the Serpent's Garden, and it would give her some peace of mind to tend to her youngest charge.

"He headed down that way," Nikolai told her, pointing to a wooded path. "Listen for the harp."

"I will. Thank you." She paused. "And thank you for telling me … your story. I'm not sure how, but maybe it could all still work out in the end."

Nikolai shrugged. Rose doubted her opinion mattered at all to him, but she was grateful for what he'd given her—a better perspective on her own life. Rose knew was not the only one who needed that occasionally; she'd even done that herself, several times, with Ethan and Sophia.

From the few stories she had been able to piece together from their time with their father, Sophia and Ethan had tried to run away and survive several times. While Sophia made the better hunter, Ethan excelled at the traps and snares. He also had better luck foraging and tracking, while Sophia fine-tuned her haggling skills.

She wasn't surprised when it took some time to find him. Rose might have missed him entirely if it hadn't been for the harp.

Just as Nikolai predicted, Rose thought with a small grin, as she watched the small figure on a lower branch—he was leaning into the tree, staring off into space while humming along as he played his music.

Ethan was going to turn into quite the romantic, Rose decided. He was growing up quickly.

"Hello, Rose," Ethan said in greeting. "Back already?"

"Hi, Ethan. Yes, we're back." She climbed up beside him, sitting further out along the branch. Her gaze lowered to the ground as she added, "We didn't get the dragon's blood."

He frowned. "I'm sorry to hear that."

"You can say that again," Rose murmured. Her failure and her shame paralyzed her as she relived the events.

"Are you okay?"

She shook her head, trying to regain focus. "Never mind me. How are you? Do you still miss Penelope?"

"I do miss her," Ethan admitted. "I had a lot of fun with her. I felt like a normal person for once." He glanced over at her quickly, suddenly flustered. "Not to say I don't like our journeying, Rose, but it gets old sometimes. You know what I mean."

"I do. I know more than most people what it is like to long for a normal life. Even if Magdalina's curse is broken, I won't have a normal life, exactly."

"You'll have us," Ethan said. "You'll have me and Theo and Mary and Sophie and maybe even Philip."

"Yes." Rose nodded. "I was just thinking about that myself."

"Something's wrong, isn't it?"

Time to admit it, Rose thought to herself. "Theo got hurt."

She was expecting a harsh rebuke or a plead to tell him everything would be okay. Rose was surprised when he reached out, patted her arm, and said, "He'll be okay."

"I'm not so sure," Rose admitted before she could stop herself. A renewed sense of sadness washed over her. Even though he was the one who had gotten hurt, Rose couldn't help but wonder if *she* would be okay again.

"You know, Theo's right. You worry too much."

"What?" Rose laughed. "That's not true."

"Yes it is," Ethan insisted. He sighed a moment later. "He's right about other things, too."

"Like what?"

"I talked to him before about how I was afraid to fight. He said I should learn, even if I don't want to." Ethan lowered his eyes. "If I had, I might have been brave enough to go into the garden with you."

"You don't have to worry about fighting," Rose scoffed, suddenly angry at Theo for his impertinence and Ethan for his dangerous ideas. "We're here to protect you, and you don't need to worry about the garden. We'll figure something out."

"I hate being afraid."

"I can understand that," Rose assured him. "But being able to fight doesn't mean you'll stop being afraid."

"You know what I think? I know how much my father would be disappointed in me. Part of me likes that I don't fight like he wanted me to." He strummed his harp absentmindedly. "I don't want to be reminded of my pain and suffering."

"You've found better ways to handle difficulties than fighting," Rose told him. "Your father might not have seen the need for that, but I rely on it." She took his hand and squeezed it reassuringly.

"Thank you." Ethan nodded. He looked down at the ground, his fingers dropping from the harp's strings. "But I still need to be brave."

"If that's what you want," Rose said, "we'll help you learn how to fight."

"Thanks. I hope I can help you with your fear, too."

She jerked away from him. "I'm not afraid to fight."

"I mean, you're afraid to *live*."

Rose blanched. "Excuse me?"

"Well, aren't you?" Ethan looked up at her thoughtfully.

"No, of course not," Rose snapped. "I just don't want—" She stopped as the question bore into her. *Is it true? Am I afraid to truly live?*

Ethan looked up at her. "You are the one who told me before that there are different ways to be brave. It's easy for you to fight because you don't fear death. But I've seen you. You seem to be afraid to be happy, to have fun. You're afraid

ONCE UPON A PRINCESS

of things you can't control. In other words, you're afraid to *live*."

Rose was silent for a long moment.

"Amalia and the dragon did say that I was supposed to face my biggest fear if I wanted the dragon's blood," Rose said, suddenly more miserable than ever.

"You only had to face your biggest fear?" Ethan furrowed his brow thoughtfully.

"I'd hardly say 'only.'" Rose snorted. "Maybe that was her way of saying I was going to fail." She didn't like to play the fool or the loser, but the thought of ending up both seemed too much to contemplate.

"You're afraid of more than failure. You're afraid of hoping for a future that won't come true," Ethan told her.

"You can't exactly blame me for that," Rose huffed indignantly.

"And you can't blame me from shirking a warrior's duty, based on my father's neglect."

"I wish I had your fears," Rose murmured. "Fighting is easy for me. Just like music is for you, apparently."

A curious expression flickered onto his face. "Theo told me you won't sing. Are you afraid to?"

"No," Rose snapped.

He raised his eyebrows at her temper. "Are you sure?"

Rose relented. "No," she admitted.

"Why?"

"I was only seven," Rose began, "when I found out I was cursed. Everyone had always seemed to love me. When I realized the truth, that it was pity, part of me died." She thought about how she'd felt after Theo had inadvertently informed her that she was destined to everlasting sleep on her eighteenth birthday—angry, betrayed, undignified, hopeless, full of despair. Every happiness seemed out of reach, including the joy of being loved. "I stopped singing after that. It was too painful to have hope."

"Maybe you should reconsider that."

She shrugged noncommittedly. "Maybe."

ONCE UPON A PRINCESS

Ethan straightened. "Is there still time for that Dragonkeeper lady to let people back into the garden?"

"I don't know if she'll let me go back." Rose slumped over, feeling defeated.

"Let's go see her. I have an idea. Maybe there's something else we can try with the dragon."

"We?" Rose asked as he hopped down from the tree and started heading back up the hill. "What do you mean, 'we'? What are you doing?"

25

Ethan's quiet voice, usually so youthful and innocent, seemed to change as he spoke with Amalia. And not just because he was getting older, Rose thought with a burst of parental pride.

She turned her attention to Amalia as Ethan presented his plan. She was certain that Amalia, in seeing Ethan's age and naivety, would tell him he had a good idea, but it was too dangerous by far. Especially for him, being so young.

Her thoughts wandered along with her gaze, and she found herself staring at Theo. He was lying chest down on his pallet, with his shirt off, the claw marks on his back red and raw against the hard muscles of his back. While Rose was glad he remained unconscious, she almost wished he would wake up and smile at her.

Rose felt disgusted with herself again. *How could I have ever risked his life?*

"So, Lady Amalia … what do you think?" She turned back as Ethan finished talking. He was holding up his harp, almost as an offering to the lovely guardian.

Amalia's full lips curved into a small, proud smile. She turned to Rose. "Did you agree to your ward's plan, Princess? For it would only work with your cooperation."

Fear in its purest form took Rose by surprise. She didn't want to endanger Ethan's life—but she knew she couldn't ruin his chance to be brave. She nodded.

"Well then," Amalia said, "I have a gift for you."

She held out her hands, gracefully folding her fingers over her palms. When she opened her hands a moment later, she revealed a bright, gleaming ruby.

Ethan's eyes widened.

"Is that the Rose Ruby?" Rose asked.

Amalia shook her head. "No, but it is a special jewel. It always amazes me—and amuses Nikolai—how many people want to believe they can slay a dragon and take its blood. The serpent dragon is cursed himself, and much like your own curse, Princess, it protects him from complete destruction."

"So you can't slay a dragon," Rose realized, "in order to get the blood."

Amalia nodded. "Dragon blood is a powerful form of magic. It needs to be contained carefully. Rubies, blood-colored diamonds such as this, are able to hold back the forces of great power."

Is that why my grandfather wanted the Rose Ruby? Rose wondered. Because it contained great power inside of it?

She supposed, after another moment of thought, that her theory made sense; ambition seemed to suffocate the bloodlines of both sides of her heritage.

Rose reached out and took the ruby, surprised to feel the cool sharpness of it in her palm.

"When you are close enough, put it up the heart of the dragon," Amalia instructed. "As you face your biggest fear, it will pull the blood out of its heart and into the ruby's center."

Rose closed her fingers around it tightly. "Thank you," she said.

Amalia met her gaze firmly. "You have proven to be a tenacious warrior, Princess of Rhone," she said. "But strength can fade, desires can change, and inspiration can be dulled. There are few things which can last throughout all the ravages of time. You must make an effort to cling to them once you find them." Rose watched as her gaze went to Nikolai behind her, and Rose suddenly wondered if Amalia loved Nikolai just as much as he did her.

"Thanks to your ward's loyalty, you have been given another chance, though you will have less time. It is almost sundown," Amalia said, turning her attention to the gate behind her once more. "Go now."

Ethan gripped his harp in his arms. Rose touched his shoulder. "I'll be ready in a moment," she told him. "I just need to do something."

She turned and hurried over to see Theo.

"Be careful," Mary spoke up, as she approached. "He's had some of my concoctions, but don't let him move just yet." Her face pinched. "Dragon wounds are harder to heal than most."

"I will," Rose promised. "I just wanted to see how he was doing before Ethan and I head into the garden."

"Why are you going back into the Serpent's Garden?" Mary asked, bewildered.

"Ethan and I have a plan," she said. "I know I failed last time. I thought I would just be fighting with the dragon itself; I didn't realize I would have to fight myself, too." She glanced down at her hands. "You can't win against your opponent if he's not the real enemy."

Mary came over to her and sat down on her shoulder. "I'll watch over Theo for you while you're gone."

Rose smirked. "I hope so; I'd hate to ask Philip to knock him out if he wakes up before I get back and realizes what I've done."

Mary smiled. "I'll put an extra spell of relaxation on him," she told Rose. She laughed lightly a moment later. "Although he'll probably wake up ready to fight you after he finds out."

"I think it'll be all right." Rose nodded as Mary went back to work, tending to Theo's wounds. "I'd appreciate that."

She allowed herself a long moment to look at him. Even though his back bore the marks of his determination to protect her, and the resulting injury, he seemed to be in a peaceful slumber. Some part of me, Rose acknowledged with chagrin, just can't handle this.

Quickly, she leaned down and pressed her lips against his forehead.

At her touch, he stirred slightly. Rose felt her breath leave her, and at her uncertainty, some part of her resolve returned.

ONCE UPON A PRINCESS

If there was one thing she knew how to face, she thought as she turned away, it was a battle. And if there was one thing she knew how to avoid, it was her fear. She just hadn't realized how good she'd been at it until now.

"I was beginning to wonder if you were going to change your mind," Ethan told her.

"I just wanted to make sure he was okay," Rose muttered, brushing her hair out of her face in order to hide from Ethan's scrutiny as the gate shut behind them.

Rose felt her heart begin to race. The forest of the Thorneback dragons welcomed her back with an unpleasant set of chills. She tried to calm down, recalling her previous failure to control herself. "Let's go looking, shall we?"

Ethan nodded and they went on their way.

"This doesn't look too scary," Ethan said after several long moments of silence. "Seems kind of nice, actually."

"Nice?"

"Sure. I mean, the serpent was supposed to be punished, right?" Ethan looked around. "It seems like these woods are pretty open and prosperous."

Rose shrugged. "I suppose the devil has only the flames of hell to warm the emptiness of his soul."

"The devil's right to envy me," the serpent dragon's voice called out to her. "Especially since I am allowed to have outside company."

Rose tensed, while Ethan dropped his harp. "You can talk?" he exclaimed.

"Yes."

The dragon nodded, shaking his long face. His tongue slithered out in a snakish grin. "You're not the same boy from before."

"No," Rose said, stepping in front of Ethan. "He's not."

"There's no reason to be so protective," the dragon told her. "You've given me no reason to strike you down … yet."

Rose gripped the ruby, tightening it against her palm as she forced herself onward. "I've come to try again. To face my fear and make peace with you."

ONCE UPON A PRINCESS

The dragon sniffed indignantly. "There was never a real reason to make war with me, was there?"

"What do you mean?"

"I should not be so surprised," the dragon told her. "Fear is a powerful enemy, because it is not evil in itself. But it is often used that way."

"I guess a lot of people try to kill you because they are afraid of you," Ethan spoke up, surprising Rose.

The serpent dragon nodded. "The Thorneback dragons are not our ancestor, but we do share similar traits to the Serpent and his Creator as well. We're more than willing to discuss terms." He sent her another wry look. "Many people just want to fight."

"You're open to negotiation?" Rose asked, surprised.

"Yes, and you'd think many people would be better for it. Even the devil has always tried to use reason and negotiation with God, before the last resort of engaging in bloody battles."

"Or," Rose said, "in my case, the first resort."

"Yes." The dragon nodded again. "My price is always the same." The dragon crept around them, closing in. "You must pass my challenge. You must face your biggest fear."

"I'm here to do just that," Rose whispered. She gripped Ethan's hand as he backed into her, comforted and strengthened to know he was scared, too. The dragon surrounded them, curling his long tail around them.

"Prove it," the dragon hissed, blowing his smoke in her face.

She coughed. "It would be easier if you didn't do that."

The rumble of his laughter echoed loudly next to her, as it chortled through his large stomach.

Rose clenched Ethan's hand tightly before releasing it. "It's time. Are you ready to help me?"

Ethan hurriedly pulled out his harp and began to pluck at the strings. "I'll follow you," he told Rose quietly. "Just go, and I'll improvise and adapt as needed."

ONCE UPON A PRINCESS

Rose nodded. She looked up at the dragon, noticing for the first time the crystalline swirls of yellow and green. And then, willingly and intentionally, for the first time since she was seven, she opened her mouth and began to sing.

Who alone can be worthy of great love?
Our worlds are full of fools with dreams
Of tender kisses, melting looks, of
Magic underneath the moonbeams.

Queen Lucia sought to love a special one
Sir Benedict, his heart became the prize;
He who was worthy of her love alone
She saw as worthy in her own eyes.

It had been more than ten years since she'd sung for anyone, but Rose's voice rang with clarity, gradually getting stronger as she continued on. All her hopes and dreams, all bottled up inside of her, broke free rushed out as she sang.

The dragon's heartbeat settled around her, adding a tempo to Ethan's strumming. Rose glanced up to see what she imagined to be a pleased look on his face. She pulled out the ruby and placed it over his heart, leaving the extra warmth of her palm to rest against the hardened scales protecting his heart.

Rose closed her eyes for a moment, allowing the moment to sweep her away into a world past her own. One where she was free of her curse, one where she was free to love. There was the throne, her family, her crown. There were talks until midnight, of policies, reforms, and people. Celebrations and commendations, weddings and birthdays. Her kingdom, alive and hopeful once more. Her husband, loving and happy. Her children, carefree and loved. Her life, fully realized. Before

ONCE UPON A PRINCESS

she could examine the dark locks of her daughter's hair, or the familiar twinkle in her son's eyes, Rose felt her own tears running down her cheeks.

It might have been her dream, but it was far from a dream come true. The possibility she would not be worthy of attaining it was poison to the core of who she was.

Opening her eyes, Rose watched the ruby's color turn from red to black as she drew the song to its close. Ethan's music slowed, and time resumed.

Rose was surprised at how easily she had slipped into the scenes, hidden deep inside of her heart. She knew at once they had always been there, calling out for her to fight for them as much as she fought for herself. She had not wanted to answer them before, fearful of pain, of disappointment. She felt laughter bubbling up insider of her as the fear of losing her innocent hope dissolved and from its death, virtuous hope was born.

While she remained awed by the sudden powerlessness of her fear, the dragon underneath her hand trembled. Rose quickly removed the ruby from his heart and placed it back inside her tunic.

What kind of dreams would a dragon have? Rose wondered. Or did he even allow himself to dream at all?

As if he'd heard her thoughts, the serpent sighed. "It is nothing to slay a dragon that has already been tamed." He nodded toward the gate, glowing brightly in the waxing moonlight. "Now, return to your friends. They are waiting for you."

"Thank you," Rose whispered.

"Don't thank me," the dragon told her. "I am allowed to protect myself, and bargain as I see fit. But I am constrained

ONCE UPON A PRINCESS

in many ways, and chief among them is to be still where I would rage."

"I don't understand," Rose told him.

"I am cursed, too," the dragon replied. "But one day, it will be broken, and I will be restored. Until then, thank you, Princess Rose of Rhone, for entertaining me today, and you as well, young man," he said, turning his attention to Ethan, who nodded. "Your song speaks of great bravery."

The dragon paused for a moment, and then sniffed indignantly. "But you can give that other friend of yours a kick, for jumping on my face earlier, trying to gouge out my eyes and cut out my tongue. I did not enjoy *that*."

Rose laughed. "I'll be sure to tell Philip he did quite the job of subduing you," she promised. "When Theo writes up the legend, Philip will have his place as a conqueror of dragons."

ONCE UPON A PRINCESS

26

Amalia's smile was much brighter and more bearable this time, Rose thought, as she walked out of the gates. Ethan was fast on her heels behind her.

"I see you have gotten what you came for," Amalia said.

"Yes," Rose said. "Thank you for the ruby."

"It is yours," Amalia told her. "Not everyone will face what they fear, or even recognize what it is exactly that they do fear."

"I couldn't have done that without Ethan," Rose insisted, wrapping her arm around Ethan's shoulders and hugging him toward her. "He's pretty smart. And brave."

"Come on, Rose," Ethan murmured in reply, before twisting out of her reach.

Amalia leaned on her staff. "To use its power, place the jewel in the hilt of your sword. When you go to slay your enemy, its power will activate."

Rose turned to Sophia, whose eyes lit up at the new challenge. "I know just the person who can take care of that for me."

"May I see it?" Nikolai asked. "I've never seen anyone actually manage to acquire the dragon's blood." Rose handed it to him and watched him, as he examined it. He held it up to the moonlight, awed by it.

As he handed it back to her, he gave her a small, genuine smile.

Two miracles today. Rose grinned back.

Together, they turned toward Amalia as she held up a hand in farewell. "Until we meet again," she whispered, before disappearing inside a flash of light.

"Goodbye," Rose murmured in reply, ducking away from the powerful light.

"So, Rose," Philip began, "what are we going to do now that you've gotten the dragon's blood?"

"We still have a plan to follow. We'll head back to Poiyana. And then, if we have enough money left, we can stay and rest for a few days as we put together a detailed plan to face Magdalina."

"Passage to Rhone by sea would be expensive," Nikolai spoke up. "But if you'd like, I'll recommend you to my sister, who lives in Poiyana."

"You have a sister?" Rose asked.

"Yes. She does traveling tours, the same as I do. But she'll go over the Apylian Mountains, over to Greece, and onto places such as the Crystal Lake Kingdom and Gaullian territories."

"You said the Crystal Lake Kingdom? That would be best, Rose, if we could go that way."

"I know it will be longer of a trip on land," Ethan said, as he pulled up one of his maps for Rose. "If we could afford passage on a ship, we would get back to Rhone faster. Assuming the weather cooperates this time, of course."

"Why do you want to go to the Crystal Lake Kingdom, Philip?" Rose asked.

"It's a small kingdom," Mary said. "There are some other fairies and pixies who live there that are friendly with humans."

"It's also the kingdom of my sister-in-law, Juliette," Philip said. "They'll be able to help us with supplies, and get us safe

ONCE UPON A PRINCESS

travel to Einish. We have a great university and hospital there, too."

"It would be a great help, Rose," Mary agreed. "My magic won't be able to heal Theo's scars completely."

"I'm okay with going by land, if that's what you want, Rose," Ethan said. "Especially if it would help us in the long term."

"I agree." Rose nodded. She turned to Nikolai. "We would be honored to have your assistance in our endeavors once more, good sir."

"Sounds like a good plan then," Nikolai declared. "Let's get packed up and head out."

The journey back to Poiyana was much longer, but it was more enjoyable. Even with Theo's injuries making slow recovery, once Rose showed him the ruby encasing the dragon's blood, he was much more optimistic and forgiving.

"This is wonderful," Theo told her, examining the small jewel as Mary once more set about changing his bandages for the night.

Rose glanced back at Theo as he sat, legs crossed and shirtless. Behind him, Mary dabbled around behind him, giving him alternating warnings and empathic ramblings as she tended to his back.

As Mary finished up and went looking for some more medicine, Theo gave Rose a half-smile. As the familiar warmth flooded over her, Rose once more faced a round of self-disgust. She realized once more how foolish she'd been to risk his life for dragon's blood. She shivered at the memory.

ONCE UPON A PRINCESS

"Are you okay?" he asked. "I know it's a small inn that Lannister, Roderick, and Captain Locke managed to find for us, but it's warmer than being outside."

"That's not it."

"Are you worried about the trip home?"

"Yes, a bit," Rose told him. "But I … wanted to apologize to you first."

"For what?"

"The dragon."

Theo shook his head. "You know I made that choice to defend you on my own, Rose."

"No. Not for that." She squatted down in front of him and reached up, brushing some hair out of his face. There was no one like Theo, she thought. He was unique. Someone she trusted. Someone who knew her, someone who was there for her even when she didn't want him to be. She owed him so much.

Rose sighed. "Not for just that, anyway."

He gripped her hands in his. "There is nothing for me to forgive. We have the dragon's blood, right? And you did face your biggest fear. Ethan was telling me all about it yesterday as we came down the mountain into Poiyana."

"I almost let you die," Rose told him. "Philip had to talk me into leaving."

Theo was silent for a moment after her admission. "I understand," he finally said. "And I will forgive you, of course, Rose."

"How?" Rose asked. "How can you do that?"

"Because you likely didn't think I would die, to begin with," Theo said. "I know we don't generally think that of each other."

"But I wanted to chase the dragon into the forest. It could have been hours before I'd given up, if at all. It was only when Philip pressed me into leaving that I agreed."

"I have my own revenge to fulfill, Rose," he reminded her. "I can understand why, especially in the heat of the battle, you would choose to pursue an enemy over retreating."

"You almost died!"

"But I didn't," he pointed out.

Rose groaned. "How can I get you to hate me? I hate myself for it."

"Do you want me to hate you, Rose?"

"No, of course not," Rose argued. "But I want you to realize how much of a risk it is for you to stay with me. Don't you see how horrible of a person I am?"

"What do you want of me, Rose?"

"To protect yourself from me. You have always been there for me, yet I gambled with your life carelessly." She shook her head. "I don't want you to think I hate you. You are more important to me than my revenge."

"The feeling is mutual." There was a small pause, and Theo smiled. "Will you sing the *Ballad of Queen Lucia* for me, like you did for the dragon?"

"What?" Rose looked at him quizzically, as though she hadn't heard him correctly.

"I'll call us even if you do."

"Is that really what you want?" Rose wrinkled her nose. "Hardly seems like enough."

"Of all things, love is a worthy pursuit," Theo told her softly. "And that's the song I want you to sing when your curse is broken and you are free to fall in love."

She felt her cheeks flush over. She wanted something from him, and it was impossible for her to name it, but when she

ONCE UPON A PRINCESS

allowed herself to fall into his gaze, she could almost hear it, crying out from the center of herself.

A hardness crept back inside her heart as he added, "And I want you to promise me you'll be careful. No more charging into battles, especially with dragons."

"If I sing for you, Theo," Rose asked, "can we forgo the other part?"

Another moment of silence passed between them, before Theo let go of her hands. "I guess it was a long shot to begin with. I better say my prayers for you, Rosary."

"You need to start praying for yourself more." Rose nodded toward his back. "That seems pretty bad."

"I've always prayed for you," he told her, tugging at a lock of her hair.

For a second, she felt herself hesitate. But then his hands cradled her face, and he locked eyes with her. "I've always prayed *for you*," he repeated gently.

Rose felt her breath catch and her face grow warm. As his gaze moved down to her mouth, she could no longer hold back. She'd faced down bigger fears already, she mused. Her eyes closed in silent permission as he moved in closer to her.

The door opened behind them. Rose sighed and pulled back, catching Theo's eyes long enough to see the mirrored disappointment in them.

They looked over to see Philip examining a stack of letters in his hand.

"Hey, Rose," he said, "I thought you'd like to know that Virtue is back, and he has some letters."

"Oh?" Rose felt like her tongue was suddenly too thick for her mouth. "Did he bring letters from Isra?"

Philip glanced up at her and smiled. "Yes, he did," he said. "I got one, and so did Theo." He handed her the letters.

ONCE UPON A PRINCESS

"That one's not from Isra," Theo said, pointing to the one Philip had been reading when he'd come through the door. "I don't recognize the crest."

"This one?" Philip asked. "Well, this one is from my mother. I'm actually trying to make sense of it."

"What do you mean?" Rose asked.

"She begins with the usual pleasantries, but she ends up admonishing me for neglecting to tell her I was getting married."

"Well, wasn't that why you were headed to Rhone?" Rose asked. "I mean, I know it's been a few months, but still, wouldn't that just tell her that you've been busy with your life?"

"It's more her words," Philip said. "Here, listen to this: 'When one's betrothed shows up at the palace in the middle of the night, one expects to have some kind of warning from her once-dutiful son.'" He folded the paper. "I don't know what she's talking about."

"Let me see." Rose grabbed the paper, tossing the others to Theo.

Theo looked through the letters, wondering if Isra had sent him anything as well. He saw her familiar scrawl, and hurried to open it.

He stopped halfway through breaking the wax seal. "Isra."

"What was that?" Rose and Philip both looked over at him.

"Isra. She went to Einish," Theo said, smiling brightly. "She's clever. That was the perfect thing to do."

"You mean she told my mother she was going to marry me, and—" Philip suddenly stopped. "You're right. That was clever of her."

"What do you mean?" Rose asked.

"It makes sense," Theo told her. He resumed opening his letter. "She can't go to anyone in Rhone, and she's never been outside your borders. The best thing to do was go where she knew she would have an ally. And that leaves Einish, among a few others."

He pulled out the letter from her and scanned it.

Dear Theo, Adopted Brother of my Heart,

Come and see me. I have much to confess to you, I'm afraid, as much as I wish to discuss our other favorite personal matters with you. Have you managed to admit the truth to Rose yet?

Ever Yours,
Isra

"Even the paper's the same as the one from my mother," Philip confirmed.

"I would call that substantial evidence," Theo agreed.

"'Personal matters?'" Rose read, grabbing the page out of his hand. "What does she mean by that?"

"Hey, you're not supposed to read her letters to me," Theo reminded her. "Give it back."

"So she really is in Einish?" Philip asked. He slowly smiled. "I guess I understand her other letters a bit more now."

"You're not upset with her, are you?" Rose asked.

"No, of course not," Philip said. "My mother, while she's a bit excitable, is a gracious host. Isra will be safe with her, especially with diplomatic matters such as this."

"That's good to hear," Theo said.

Mary appeared back in the doorway. "Rose, Nikolai is calling for you. His sister is here to talk business."

"All right. Thank you, Mary," Rose said. "Please tell him I'll be there in a few moments."

She turned back to Theo, reluctant to leave. But one look at his face, so content with her sister's letters, she decided it was for the best. She wasn't sure how well she would fare in a conversation about what nearly happened before Philip had shown up. "I'll be back later," she said, already aware she was lying. "Get some rest. Hopefully, we'll head out in the morning."

"As you wish, Rosary," Theo murmured.

Philip took her elbow. "I'll go with you," he offered. "I'm sure Nikolai's sister will want as much as her brother did."

Rose grinned. "I'm sure of it. It would be nice to have a partner to help me with the pricing. Especially if you can talk her down with your charm."

"Are you saying I have a way with women?" Philip asked.

"I'm saying you can use it for our good here."

"Rose."

Rose turned around as Theo called out to her. "Yes? Do you need something?"

"Don't forget," he said. "You promised. I get to hear you sing later."

"I won't forget." Then she smiled, tucked her letters under her arm, and headed out.

Theo watched the door close behind her. "Someday," he muttered, trying not to be too disappointed at Rose's departure.

There would be a day, Theo vowed to himself, when he would tell her his real greatest fear—that he would confess his love for her, and she would do nothing in return. Dying

ONCE UPON A PRINCESS

for her had been no trouble, he thought, recalling the moment he knew when the charging dragon might trample her. It would be living without her that would prove to be his greatest challenge.

Mary poked her head inside the room again. "Ethan and Sophia just got back from the market," she said. "Would you like something to eat? I found the medicine, too, if you'd like some more."

"Sure," Theo said. "But first, I'd like it if you could try another round of healing spells on me again."

"Are you sure?" Mary asked. "I already did more than enough for today."

"I'm sure," Theo affirmed. He glanced out the window, where he could see the thick clouds rolling in behind Poiyana's mountains. "We have a long road ahead of us."

C. S. Johnson is the author of several young adult sci-fi and fantasy novels, including *The Starlight Chronicles* series, the *Once Upon a Princess* saga, and the *Divine Space Pirates* trilogy. She currently lives in Atlanta with her family.

THEO
By Julia Mae Busko

AUTHOR'S NOTE AND ACKNOWLEDGEMENTS

Dear Reader,

There's nothing like an adventure and a plan to encourage one to have hope. And if you're anything like my mother, departing from the plan is painful, and often excruciatingly so. I know it sounds silly, but I often feel this way about my writing. I'd originally planned out all of Rose's adventures early on, and was astounded by the tweaks and twists I added—and encountered—along the way. Even now, as I write this part, I dread going through my notes and making new plans for Part III. And it's mostly because of fear.

There is so much fear in today's world; it's not just there as I work on my writing. As I get older, I really do learn more about facing it and putting it in its proper place—which is in prayer. There is a lot more freedom in choosing to be brave, even in—*especially* in—the face of great evil or uncertainty. I do believe stories are inseparable from the human soul for this very reason.

In many ways, stories exist that we might lose ourselves but also find ourselves. That's also why several of my own struggles often show up in my characters' lives. If friendship and commitment were main themes of *Beauty's Curse*, then I would say *Beauty's Quest* has to do more with fear, doubt, and hope—how who we are and who we choose to be can be shaped by them, even if we don't always recognize it.

When I was growing up, I never thought I would have what Rose also wants: A true love, a husband who adores me, a family to love, and a future to be excited about. How very wrong I was, thank God! It took a long time to recognize that a large part of my pain came from my own imagination and fear.

Thinking about it now, it makes perfect sense: If you do not have people in your life God can use to sharpen you, to shape you into a better person, the devil will be content to use your own mind to destroy you. It's never easy living through it.

I hope you've enjoyed this part of Rose's journey; please leave a review for the book, if you'd be so kind, so I will have some comfort while I piece together the next book in the saga, *Beauty's Kiss (Once Upon a Princess,* Part III*)*.

I'm looking forward to seeing you there!

Until We Meet Again,

C. S. Johnson

BEAUTY'S KISS

PART III OF THE *ONCE UPON A PRINCESS* SAGA

⁎ ⁎ ⁎ ⁎

C. S. Johnson

Library of Congress Control Number: 2017909187

ISBN-13 eBook: 9781943934-287

ISBN-10 eBook: 1-943934-28-2

ISBN-13 Book: 9781943934-294

ISBN-10 Book: 1-943934-29-0

For Sam. The heart has its reasons, whereas reason has lost
its mind.

This is also for my own darling prince and princess—may you
never once believe you are alone in this world, so long as you know
the truth and the truth of my love for you.

This book is published courtesy of

www.direwolfbooks.com

ONCE UPON A PRINCESS

ONCE UPON A PRINCESS

$\cdot$

PART III

"Everything in the world has a hidden meaning.
Men, animals, trees, stars, they are all hieroglyphics.
When you see them you do not understand them.
You think they are really men, animals, trees, stars.
It is only years later that you understand."

~ Nikos Kazantzakis

1

The small, persistent beam of sunlight crept through the narrow crevices of the distant mountains, its determined line breaking out from behind the clouds, cutting through the pockets of night and the early morning fog. Rose was transfixed by the sight before her, enraptured by the staggering amount of simple delight it gave her. The edge of Crystal Lake, for which the kingdom of Philip's sister-in-law was named, was in sight at last.

Now, Rose thought, *all I have to do is get back to Rhone, and Magdalina's reign will end.*

Rose glanced down at the ruby shining in the hilt of her sword. The slim beam of sunlight teased out its darkened red heart, where the dragon's blood resided.

A small burst of pride soared inside of her; Rose knew what the deadly jewel had cost her, but it was well worth the price she'd paid. Since leaving Poiyana, the city in the heart of the Romani territory, she had the power she knew she would need to destroy her greatest foe.

Rose continued to stare at the scene before her, as she folded her arms and leaned back against the sturdy tree behind her. *Good. We're here. That means we can* finally *say goodbye to Natala.*

Rose wasn't sure if she was happy to see the Crystal Lake Kingdom more for its beauty, or because it meant she would be free of Natala; the middle-aged woman traveled across the continent for her living, but it seemed more like she drew her sustenance from sucking the life out of her clients' souls.

ONCE UPON A PRINCESS

Not even the prickly bark grabbing the growing hair at her shoulders could dampen Rose's spirits at the thought of leaving Natala behind.

As he had promised, Nikolai, their guide through the Romani mountains, had introduced them to his sister, Natala. He had told them she was more than willing to lead them back through the worlds between the Romani territory and the small kingdom of Crystal Lake.

Much to Rose's dismay, it turned out Natala's temperament was far from the gruff, philosophizing manner of her brother's. Rose was certain she'd never known a woman more capable at setting her temper ablaze with her constant criticizing and perpetual moaning.

Rose sighed and bowed her head, squirming only a little as her hair pulled free from the bark. On some level, she had to wonder if she deserved the small twinge of pain. She knew it was a very practical thing, to have a skilled guide along for the ride. It was also a very fortunate thing, since they were navigating across the Romani plains, traveling through the northern passages of Greek territories, walking through the Apylian Mountains, and drifting down the Gaullian riverways. Natala had promised, for half the price upfront, to take them to Crystal Lake, where Prince Derick, Philp's older brother, would be holding court.

She knew she should be grateful.

But if she had to do it all over again, Rose would any other way to go; she would even choose to go by boat, a shocking revelation in itself, since they had been shipwrecked on an island and blown off course for days in their latest attempts to cross the great seas. Rose never thought she would be content to set sail again.

ONCE UPON A PRINCESS

She felt better knowing that she was not the only one who had trouble with the bad-tempered guide. Over the past several weeks, she had a wide range of small talks with her traveling companions, whether to talk them down from their irritation or to have them chastise her for her own disgust.

Even Theo has had a hard time dealing with Natala.

Rose felt surprised, as she smiled her first fully genuine smile in weeks. The thought of her best friend struggling to hold back his temper was amusing in the worst sort of way.

"You seem happy this morning. I hope you're not thinking of drowning Natala in the lake," Theo said. He appeared beside her suddenly, and Rose nearly jumped at his voice; she wondered if she had been that distracted by the scenery not to notice his approach.

"I wasn't," she promised.

"That's good to hear. It would have been unpleasant to fight you for the privilege."

Rose laughed before she quickly covered her mouth with her hand. She knew she had to be careful not to wake anyone, especially Natala.

"I wouldn't worry about waking her," Theo said, as if he had known what she was thinking. "Philip managed to get her some more wine last night, and she'll sleep longer thanks to that."

"Well, thank God for Philip," Rose whispered back, still trying to stifle her giggles. "We should have figured out her weakness weeks ago."

"I'm in complete agreement," Theo said, "even if I would have to repent for it later."

"I don't think God should hold it against you." Rose rolled her eyes. "Surely he would not be adverse to us putting her to sleep, especially if it means we don't actually kill her."

ONCE UPON A PRINCESS

"There is no sin greater than another."

"Come on, Theo, let me rationalize any possible guilt away."

He smiled at her. "If we could only rationalize away the things we feel all the time."

Despite the simple, seemingly harmless reply, Rose felt the heat rise in her cheeks as she experienced a mix of guilt and mortification. There were some feelings she did wish that she could rationalize away, banishing them at the mere thought. She had spent a good portion of the trip trying to do just that, but there were plenty of reasons to keep that from Theo.

She glanced over at him now, seeing the warmth in his emerald eyes, and she decided it was best to change the subject. "I guess we are getting closer to Rhone. You should probably be practicing all that priestly stuff again, if you are going to visit with your grandfather and Thad at the church in Havilah."

"I might have been raised in the church, but I would have thought all this time traveling would have shown you I don't intend to stay there."

His words were measured and calm, but Rose could have sworn there was a bite underneath them. She could not resist replying spitefully. "Well, all this time we've been traveling should have done a better job of drumming it out of you."

He shrugged as she huffed. He turned back to face the lake water, allowing her a moment to stare at him openly without fear or hesitation.

Certain he was not able to see her expression, Rose allowed herself to blush without restraint. Over the past month since they had left Poiyana, Rose had been unable to forget that moment in the inn.

ONCE UPON A PRINCESS

Theo had been sitting across from her, his shirt was off since Mary had just finished applying a new layer of healing ointment to the wounds he had sustained in their fight against the Thorneback dragon. And while she was confessing the worst of who she was, he had only placed his hands around her face, and drawn her close to him. Rose was convinced if they hadn't been interrupted, he would have kissed her.

And she would have let him.

Nothing about that moment had left her memory. She could close her eyes and slip into it all over again. Sometimes her dreams let her do more than remember it.

Rose felt that tension inside of her return in vengeful force as she peeked over at him, as he stood next to her, looking out into the distance at Crystal Lake.

Neither of them had said anything about it.

But Rose knew she was thinking about it. And she had a feeling he was, too. For all their trouble with Natala and dealing with the harsh elements of traveling on the road, there were times when she would look up to see him watching her, or she would catch herself staring at him, and something would rise inside of her, and she would have to force it down again.

She cleared her throat, trying to rid herself of any remaining wonderings. Rose had closed the door on romance and true love a long time ago, and she was not about to let anyone change her mind—not even Theo.

"So," she said, "how long do you think it will be until everyone else is up and ready to go?"

"If you can convince them there will be a comfortable bed and a warm dinner, I'm sure it won't take long."

"I'll make that Philip's first job this morning then," Rose decided. "He should have a better idea of what kind of hospitality we should expect here."

"From everything he's told me so far, we should be quite welcome."

"He would be; it remains to be seen about the rest of us."

"Crystal Lake has a good reputation for taking in strangers," Theo said. He reached over and pulled a lock of her hair free from the clinging crevices of the tree bark behind her. "And I have yet to see someone who wasn't charmed by you."

Rose stiffened, paralyzed with fear and, to her self-horror, longing as well. Forcing herself to breathe normally, she stepped forward. She gripped her sword with renewed determination. "I guess I can always evoke Isra's name," she said, thinking of her younger sister. "Since she's pretending to be engaged to Philip."

"I forgot about that. That would work, too. If the news has reached to this part of the kingdom, that is."

He was so infuriating, Rose thought. Theo was acting so … so normal! She was standing only a foot away from him, suffering even while she enjoyed his company, as she had done an uncountable number of times before. Why was it different now?

Or, she admitted very, very softly to herself, was it just harder for her to ignore how much she wanted him, now that she had admitted it?

That moment of surrender, of submission, sank into her once more, and inside she reeled at its force.

She needed to find another distraction, she thought. "How are your injuries?" Rose asked.

ONCE UPON A PRINCESS

"They seem to be getting better. Mary said the scars will still be visible across my back, but that doesn't bother me." He ran a hand through his black hair, pushing it back from his face. "I remember my dad and my uncle had plenty of battle scars."

"I guess it is a sign of accomplishment," Rose said. She almost reached out for him, knowing it was hard for him to talk about his family even after so many years had passed. But this time, her pervasive and unpredictable thoughts kept her from offering him comfort.

"Not everyone can boast of an encounter with a dragon," Theo said.

Rose nodded. "That alone should make it easy to promote you to the royal counsel."

His eyes gleamed appreciatively. "When you are Queen of Rhone, I will remind you of that."

You won't have to remind me, Rose felt like telling him. But she only nodded again.

Weighed silence passed between them again, as they looked at each other. Theo took a step closer to her. "Rose—"

They were swiftly interrupted as Natala's voice screeched out in angry tones, crying out from their camp. "Oh, my head!"

Rose and Theo both looked back.

"Where's my wine?" she cried. "Why didn't someone get me up sooner? Why aren't the rest of you up? We're almost there. Get up. Get up!"

"Great," Rose muttered. "She's awake."

"And she's moving," Theo said, cringing as various clanks and clashes rang out in the background as Natala began scrounging around, dumping out supplies and tripping over the others.

"Let's just hope she doesn't get into Sophie's tools again," Rose muttered. "Sophie was not happy about all the iron filings in Natala's hands, and Mary wasn't able to help her remove them any."

"I'm more worried she'll step on Ethan's harp again. When she stepped on it last week, I was pretty sure Ethan was going to cry."

"On the upside, he has been doing better at his training, since his harp needs repairs," Rose said. "I've noticed you've been teaching him more advanced techniques lately."

"I'd still hate for his motivation to be compromised—or inspired—by Natala," Theo replied. "We'd better get over there before everyone's in a bad mood."

"I guess I better get Philip up." Rose pursed her lips. "Natala is making this unpleasant."

Theo laughed. "We'll make it through, Rosary," he promised. "I said my prayers this morning."

ONCE UPON A PRINCESS

2

"And this is where you'll be sleeping," Philip said, as he gallantly pushed open the door to an unoccupied bedroom. "As you can see, it'll be much more comfortable than camping on the ground."

"Humph! I wouldn't have come up this far if I didn't think it was worth it," Natala grumbled. Her long hair, tucked back into a bun mixed with gray and brown, pulled free as she pushed past the others to enter her room.

Theo watched with sympathy as Philip's polite smile tightened with underlying irritation. The Prince of Einish was among the most even-tempered men he knew, but after weeks of Natala's complaints, even he was clearly glad she would be leaving soon.

Of course, not soon enough for Philip, by the looks of it, Theo thought. But it was safe to say that was probably true for the rest of their company, too.

"Well," Philip said, "please feel free to ring for anything that you need."

"I can just tell you what I need now," Natala said. "I'll need some extra blankets, and I'll need some laundry done, and something finer to wear while my laundry is getting done, and then I'll need some spirits to drink so my poor knees and back will have some relief, and then … "

"Just close the door on her," Rose ordered in a fierce whisper. "She's not looking. We can say you didn't hear her."

Philip, without hesitation, shut the door behind him. "I'll be happy to tell her that I heard her, I just didn't listen. I am a prince, after all. That stuff doesn't fall to me. But I will be

ONCE UPON A PRINCESS

making sure that whoever it does fall to will be amply
rewarded."

"Does Crystal Lake have any prisoners who might be up
for the job?" Ethan scoffed.

"They have a rule about cruel and unusual punishment
here," Philip said.

"Too bad." Ethan frowned. "After what she did to my
harp, she deserves to be punished."

"I think Philip was saying that serving her would be too
cruel a punishment, little brother," Sophia said, as she came
up and laid a comforting hand on his shoulder. "But either
way, I'm sure someone will take care of her."

"We do have several craftsmen on staff, Ethan," Philip
said. "Derick is always hunting, so he makes sure he has
plenty of repairmen around, too. I'll be happy to take your
harp down to the shops and see about getting it fixed up
properly."

"I'd rather do it myself." Ethan scrunched up his face. "It'll
give me something to do other than think about hitting her."

Rose cleared her throat, trying not to laugh. She knew
Ethan still missed his harp instructor, Penelope. He worked
hard to make sure that he kept up with his music, even
though it had been some time since he had heard from her.
While Ethan was able to send her a few letters over the last
month, he knew it would be a long time before he was able to
see her again. Rose did not want to see his innocent dreams
of true love to be lost, and she did not want someone like
Natala to cause him to lose hope.

"Alright, everyone," Rose said. "Let's not worry about
Natala anymore. She is an older lady, and there's plenty in her
life I'm sure none of us have ever had to deal with. She'll be

gone from Crystal Lake before too long, and in the meantime, we need not bother with her ourselves."

"Thank the good Lord," Sophia muttered.

Rose turned her attention to Philip. "Alright, *that's* taken care of," she said. "Now, show the rest of us where we'll be sleeping. Mary's still tired. I'm sure a proper mattress will make her sublimely happy." She glanced at the small fairy, who was sound asleep in the hood of her cloak.

Philip returned Rose's smile, and Theo couldn't help feeling a twinge of jealousy as Philip took Rose's arm and led her down the hall.

I need to stop that, he thought to himself. There was no point getting jealous over Philip's relationship with Rose. Not at the moment, anyway, when Philip was maintaining the pretense of an engagement with Isra, Rose's younger sister. When Philip and Isra admitted the whole thing was a joke, or even a necessary falsehood to protect Isra and Ronan from King Stefanos, *that* would be the time for Theo to worry.

Not that he would worry. Philip was a good man, and a good friend. He would treat Rose well.

Theo frowned at his own thoughts. He should have been more concerned over the situation in Rhone rather than his jealousy.

Since the assassination attempt on King Stefanos' life a few months before, Rose's mother, Queen Leea, had been imprisoned as the prime suspect. Isra and Ronan, also considered a threat, had been able to sneak out of the kingdom safely. They had no place to go—that was, until Isra was inspired to go to Einish and introduce herself as Philip's soon-to-be bride. They were going to meet with Isra and Ronan in a few days in Einish's port city, O'Lin.

ONCE UPON A PRINCESS

"What's wrong?" Ethan asked, as he fell into step with Theo. "Aren't you happy Natala is finally no longer our problem?"

"Oh, I'm happy about that," Theo said. "I was just wondering how Isra and Ronan are doing. I'm glad we are getting closer to seeing them again. Things have not been easy lately."

"When are we going to see them?" Ethan asked. "I'd love to show Isra my skills on the harp. Rose says she's the better musician between them."

"She is," Theo agreed, remembering when they were younger, Isra would delicately pluck at her harp while he bungled about on his. Rose would sit and compare notes with Ronan on how to turn it in a bow before managing a poor rendition of her scales. He smiled; over ten years had passed since then, but he had never forgotten how graceful Rose looked as she played, while she concentrated on her notes.

Ethan rubbed his shoulders, where he had tied his bag back earlier. "My shoulders hurt. I'm glad we can rest here for a few days."

"How are you feeling?" Theo asked. "We'll likely have some time later to train. Would you want to work on your sword skills some more?"

"No," Ethan scoffed. "But I will, because it's training. And this is not vacation."

Theo smirked. "Did you hear Rose say that as we can into the palace?"

"Yes." Ethan grinned.

"I thought as much. You might want to try to make it sound more innocent next time you imitate her. That way she will not realize you're making fun of her."

"Noted."

Theo glanced back up at Rose, just as she glanced back at him.

She hurriedly turned back to Philip. He could hear her asking about supplies, and paid attention to Philip's response long enough to know it was a needless question.

Rose was still avoiding him.

Weeks on the road had not let her forget that moment they shared. Theo felt a rush of satisfaction; it was good to know if he was suffering, he was at least not suffering alone.

Now, he thought, the trick was just to make her suffer enough that she admitted it.

A new voice called from down the hall. "So I hear my younger brother has come to visit, and he didn't feel the need to let me know he had arrived properly."

"Derick!" Philip cried.

Theo watched as Philip turned and hurried to rush over to his brother. It made him miss his own brother, Thad, who was helping their grandfather tend to religious matters back in Rhone's capital city, Havilah.

Philip's blatant devotion to his brother was heartwarming, Theo thought, as he watched his friend embrace the King of Einish and Crystal Lake. The feeling of trust and affection between them was mutual.

"I didn't know you were here," Philip said. "I thought you were with Mother back in Einish."

"I was, for a little while," Derick said. "You've been gone for over half a year, little brother. There are reasons that demand I travel."

"I'm sure Mother is one of the reasons," Philip remarked, his voice jovial.

"Yes, but there are other reasons as well, and, seeing as how they are kingdom business, I will be sure to fill you in on them later." Derick laughed, a full-throated laugh that reminded Theo of Philip.

It was not the only thing about them that was similar. Like Philip, Derick had copper-colored hair, even though it was a slightly darker shade. There were similar lines in their faces, with sharp eyes, and a round boyishness that, without a beard like his brother's, made Derick seem younger.

As the two of them exchanged affectionate barbs, both defending and deriding their mother's habits, Theo remembered Philip telling him that his father had died when he was very young. As he watched the two of them, he had a feeling Derick served as a father figure for Philip as well.

"Is Juliette here with you?" Philip asked. "I'd love for the two of you to meet my new friends."

Derick glanced over Philip's shoulder. "I'd love to meet them now," he said, waving them over. "Juliette is preoccupied, relaxing in one of the natural hot springs."

"I'd forgotten about the Crystal Lake springs," Philip said. He looked up at Derick with a quizzical expression. "Is she well? I know the springs are said to have healing powers."

"Plenty use the hot springs just to relax. But she's more than well," Derick said. "We just found out she's pregnant."

"That's wonderful!" Philip gave Derick another hug. "Congratulations."

"Thank you." Derick gave him a sheepish smile. "We had to try to beat you for good news, I guess. I heard of your own engagement only last week."

"Oh, yes," Philip said. "She's just lovely, Derick. I can't wait for you to meet her."

Derick turned to Rose. "Well, she certainly is beautiful." He graciously bowed to Rose.

ONCE UPON A PRINCESS

Theo might have laughed at the disgust on Rose's face—he knew better than anyone that she hated it when people complimented her on her beauty—if he didn't secretly want to punch Derick himself.

Philip shook his head. "Not this one," he said. "But Princess Rose is the older sister to Princess Isra, my betrothed."

"Oh, well, my apologies, Your Highness," Derick said.

Rose gave him a cool look. "Rose, please," she replied, keeping her tone light. "We are very grateful to be guests in your kingdom, Majesty."

"You are very welcome. Any friends of Phil's are friends of mine," Derick assured her. "Please, feel free to use the castle for whatever you need."

"Thank you," Rose said. "I will."

Theo heard the prim tone in her voice, and he knew Rose would make good on that promise. She would likely be raiding the stables for horses and supplies before the evening came, he thought.

Philip quickly introduced the rest of them to the King. When Theo's turn came, he was surprised when Derick reached out for his hand.

"I've heard about you," he said as Theo shook his hand, accepting the greeting of one solider to another. "I have some traders out in the Romani territory. They've told me about a man who fought the dragon of the Serpent's Garden and lived to tell the tale."

"Hey, that could have been me," Philip stepped in. "I was there, too."

"I was the one who was actually with Rose when she got the dragon's blood," Ethan insisted.

"I almost gouged out his eyes," Philip said.

ONCE UPON A PRINCESS

"That reminds me," Ethan said. "The dragon told me to hit you for that."

"Enough," Rose cut in. "Derick is the one who is talking to Theo. You really shouldn't interrupt, especially when he was the one who saved me from the dragon in the first place."

Theo felt proud, hearing her words.

"I'm sure it wasn't Phil," Derick said. "I would've heard his name for sure if it had been him. They said it was a knight of the highest order."

"Well, thank you," Theo murmured politely. "But I am not officially a knight for the kingdom of Rhone."

"Then you should be knighted here, as a solider for my kingdom," Deric said. "Of course, that's assuming the rumors were true."

Rose stepped forward to stand beside Theo. "Of course it's true. I just said he saved my life. He has the marks on his back to prove it."

"Well, that's settled then," Derick said as he stated retreating down the hall. "I have some meetings to get to, brother, so please excuse me. But come to dinner tonight, and we will feast at my brother's return, and the arrival of the kingdom's newest knight and champion. I'll send out the servants to get you new clothes and anything else you might need."

Derick continued to ramble on for some time, and ended up talking to himself more as he turned the corner.

"Well," Sophia said, "he's nice. But he seems distracted."

"He should be," Philip said. "He's going to be a father soon. And he hasn't been the King of Einish for that long. My mother was regent for several years, before he married Juliette last year."

ONCE UPON A PRINCESS

"Maybe it's Rose's fault," Mary said with a yawn, groggy from a lack of restful sleep and long hours of travel. "He probably got distracted when he saw her."

"That reminds me, I do apologize about his remark," Philip said to Rose. "He has heard more of your legend than anything about Isra. Many people don't realize there are two princesses of Rhone."

"I know." Rose snorted. "Not many people in Rhone know there are two princesses, thanks to the King and Queen. I can hardly blame your brother for not realizing it."

Theo knew from her tone she was still irritated by it, however nicely she tried to hide it. He almost reached for her, but decided against it as Philip came up and placed his arm around Rose's shoulders.

"The world will know the truth soon enough," Philip promised. "And anyway, Isra will still be a princess once you are Queen. So that should be an easy transition for you and Isra."

Rose rolled her eyes. "Let's just get to our rooms," she said. "I'm sure we're all ready to relax for a few hours."

"Just for a few hours," Sophia said with a giggle. "I'm going to see about finding those hot springs he was talking about."

Theo allowed his attention to turn to their surroundings as Philip began answering the questions that came his way. The castle of Crystal Lake strongly reminded him of Rhone's. It was in the classic style, with towers and winding steps. As they were currently walking through the keep, he saw it was furnished with various luxuries and even some fine art from around the world.

They had arrived at the castle just before the midmorning hour, and the fog of the mountains had cleared to reveal a small, but durable castle. It must have undergone quite a few

ONCE UPON A PRINCESS

repairs and updates over the years, Theo thought as he allowed himself to reach out and touch one of the hanging tapestries.

His hand stilled and he stepped back, looking up at the full picture.

His eyes widened in shock, and he stopped in his tracks.

"Queen Lucia," he said, awed by the picture before him.

The tapestry was very similar to the one his mother had hung so proudly in their house; the fairy queen looked outward, and he felt as though her eyes, such a pretty mix of green and blue, seemed to stare back at him—seemed to haunt him, the same way his past did.

Theo felt his chest tighten. He remembered that night, when his Uncle Thom had hurried to burn his mother's tapestry. When he had learned his parents were dead and someone had attacked his uncle.

Does this one carry Magdust between its threads, too? Theo wondered as he studied it. He pressed into the fabric, but it was too finely woven for him to detect any Magdust.

"Where's Mary when you need her?" he muttered to himself, sighing as he stepped back. The others were already out of sight. He supposed it was just as well, since Rose was carrying Mary in her traveling cloak's hood.

Theo decided he would have to ask about the tapestry later. It was not only unusual that it was here—the legend of Queen Lucia and her gallant knight, Sir Benedict, who would become the first knight in Rhone, and eventually king as well, was more history of Rhone than it was of either Einish or the kingdom of Crystal Lake—but the idea that it was connected to his past, connected to the illegal Magdust trade, gave him cause for concern.

3

Rose knew she should not let Derick's greeting make her feel alienated, but even if she could disregard that entirely, divorcing it from her memory completely, she knew soon enough that she would have still felt like an outcast.

Dinner was proof enough of that, she thought bitterly. She picked sparingly at her plate, full of foods she didn't recognize. Rose didn't even have time to learn the new foods by their names before some server came around, whipped her plate away, and handed her a new one.

Beside her, Derick and Philip were talking and chatting uproariously, and seeing how much they genuinely adored each other's company, Rose decided it would be unkind to blame that for her loneliness.

The others were eating without complaint—even Natala, Rose noticed, hiding her smile in her cup as she peeked a glance over at the surly guide. Sophia and Ethan were comparing different dishes, while even Mary seemed overly delighted by the pastries.

I should have sat next to Theo. She glanced across the wide table at her best friend, as he sat at Derick's left hand. Theo met her gaze and gave her a look she knew meant he was counting down the time to when he could escape, the same as she was.

There was something else, too, she noticed. There was a distracted quality to him. Something was on his mind.

She caught his eye. "Are you okay?" she mouthed to him.

He nodded, and the he titled his head in Ethan's direction. Rose glanced over just in time to see the younger boy grab a

ONCE UPON A PRINCESS

chunk of meat and stuff it into his mouth, before gnawing on it hungrily.

Theo's eyes widened, and then he gave her a half-smile, silently letting her know Ethan seemed to be willing to eat for two of them, or even more, so there was no need for him to be overly excited about dinner.

Rose shrugged back as she smiled, glad she could still talk to Theo, even if with a table between them.

Really the only one who was supposed to be eating for two was Derick's wife, the Queen of Einish and Crystal Lake, who was sitting at the other end of the table. Rose noticed that Juliette didn't seem as interested in food as Ethan.

If anything, Rose thought, the Queen was content to pick at her food as much as Rose was. Rose watched her for a long moment, and then realized that Juliette was probably as lonely as she was, given that Derick was preoccupied with Philip, and she didn't know anyone else.

At least I have Theo to exchange silent half-conversations, Rose thought.

It was then that Rose realized Philip and Derick's conversation had grown softer.

She leaned over carefully, under the guise of reaching for her cup, straining her ears to hear.

" … there are some issues that the people wanted addressed, so that's why I came here." Derick's voice seemed to grow even softer as he added, "I didn't want Juliette's people to worry, and I didn't want her to worry, either."

"I can understand," Philip replied. "We can check things out for you. We'll be headed in that direction before too long."

"I'm hoping that even though I know you are in a hurry to get back to Rhone, you'll be able to get some idea of how to

ONCE UPON A PRINCESS

solve it. I can send some troops with you, if you are willing to lead them."

"I'll ask Rose about it. She might prefer them to come after us, just to make sure we didn't miss anything."

"I don't want to impose on Her Highness."

Rose could not stand it any longer. "What's happening?" she asked.

Philip jerked around awkwardly, before clearing his throat. "Well, Derick, you do know of Rose's reputation. She might be able to do something."

Derick hesitated. "Okay. I guess it's okay to talk business over dinner."

"It's really alright," Philip insisted. "You know our mother is not here to object."

Derick nodded. "More true words were never spoken," he said. "If you say so, little brother."

"There's no one more reliable than Rose," Philip declared. "You can count on that."

Rose shifted in her seating, trying to keep the annoyance out of her face as much as she tried to keep her long skirts from keeping her in her chair. "Tell me."

"I mentioned earlier that there was some kingdom business that had called me to Crystal Lake Palace," Derick said. "It seems that there has been a surge in the illegal Magdust trade, between the border of Crystal Lake and Einish."

Rose felt her heart sink. "The small area of the border you share with Rhone?"

Derick nodded. "I intended to take this up with King Stefanos," he admitted. "But seeing as you are here, and you are the heir to the kingdom, I guess there's no harm in informing you."

ONCE UPON A PRINCESS

"I know there has been an increase in the trade since last year," Rose said. "That was part of the reason my father wanted me to come home from my travels before. He says Magdalina's fairies are getting bolder; I know there has been trouble since the fairyfolk in Rhone had fallen under Magdalina's rule many years ago."

She did not want to mention that the rise in crime was likely due to her eighteenth birthday approaching, the recent attempt on King Stefanos' life, and the resulting imprisonment of her mother. The kingdom morale had to be significantly low lately, Rose thought.

She was still determined to get back to her mother and find the villain who tried to poison her father, but she knew that Magdalina's curse still remained her first priority.

It had to, she told herself. Once the curse was broken, , Rose knew her kingdom would once more have the confidence they needed.

It was hard not to think that it might be better to go and settle the kingdom issues first, especially since she was so close to seeing her brother and sister again. There was no point in being free of her curse if she had no kingdom to rule when she got back from Magdalina's castle in the Darkwood Forest.

Everything took time, Rose thought bitterly.

"That must be why they have expanded their trade alliance into my kingdom," Derick said, making Rose return her full attention to their conversation.

"Rhone has long made the trade illegal," Rose assured him. "We have done what we could to stop the spread of it. The Magdust trade is such a horrendous topic in itself. The idea that it might be spreading is dreadful."

ONCE UPON A PRINCESS

"I agree. I was going to go and inspect the forest once more later on this week," he said. "I've had several scouting reports come in on the location of the trade alliance. So far I know there is a smaller group of traders who are using the Wandering Caverns as a base; it is a larger cave near the border, only a few hours from O'Lin."

"If you can get us a map," Rose said, "I'm sure we can take care of it. Ethan is our map reader, and I have yet to find a fairy that can defeat me as long as I have Queen Lucia's sword." She brightened at the thought of getting a chance to use her newly acquired ruby, the one that held the dragon's blood.

"I would be in your debt for taking care of this for me." Derick leaned back in his chair.

"Consider it a dowry of sorts," Rose said, giving Philip a smirk.

"We have a deal then," Derick said. He called over a servant and began whispering to him, calling for a written agreement to be drawn up, while Philip turned to her.

"Maybe you should have offered our services as a form of payment rather than a gift," Philip said.

"Nonsense," Rose said. "We have done more for less."

"I meant for Natala's room and board," Philip told her, nudging her shoulder.

Rose smothered her own laughter as she saw the woman, half-asleep, as she used her plate as a pillow. "I don't think your brother has enough problems for me to work off her debt."

"You don't have to work off any debt at all," Philip said. "I was just teasing. Or maybe pointing out that he would do better for a promise of a real and likely high debt, rather than

ONCE UPON A PRINCESS

a dowry he won't be able to use. My mother would be the one you should discuss the dowry with anyway."

Rose arched her brow. "We'll see," she said. "In the meantime, you should finish your dinner. We're going to start getting ready to leave. I don't want to stay here for longer than another day or two. If the Magdust trade in on the rise, I don't think I'll have time to bring it down and save my mother."

"I'll have the servants start working on preparing for our journey to Einish," Philip promised. "But maybe you should take your own advice. You've barely touched your food, and this is truly Einish's finest. My brother likes to eat well, and he's no doubt doubled down since Juliette is pregnant. Take some time to eat, drink, and refresh yourself, Rose."

Rose sighed. She did not want to explain to Philip why she was unable to eat. She just shrugged. "I think I'm tired," she finally said.

"While the servants get our stuff together, you should rest," Philip said. "Crystal Lakes is a great place to unwind. People come here from all over the continent to enjoy the nearby hot springs. There are some that are connected to the castle, just for the people here."

"Sure, sure. I'll consider it." Rose nodded, before as her attention turned to Theo once more. That brooding, contemplative look was on his face once more.

She wanted to find out what he was worried about. It was no good for them to be worried about different things, and she had more than enough problems to deal with.

But everything takes time, Rose reminded herself, as she headed off to her own rooms. She needed some of that time to herself.

ONCE UPON A PRINCESS

4

It was two days later when Theo paced around the small chapel, trying to find his focus. He had risen early—easy enough to do, after only a few hours of troubled sleep.

After considering his options, he had made his way down to the chapel, hoping God would answer his prayers more quickly if he went out to meet him.

The palace was nearly still, as most of the servants were still asleep, or they were sentries tending to the night watch. There was only one monk in the chapel beside him, who had taken one look at Theo, no doubt noticing his plain tunic and commoner's pants, before he dismissed him.

It is not like I am a threat to this place, Theo thought, as he sat down in one of the benches and bowed his head.

His prayers were silent and private, some of his own inner musings insisting on staying a secret even from himself.

Despite his desire for revenge against Everon, Magdalina's son, for slaying his parents, Theo knew that he had cause to be thankful for all the good things in his life. He might have been torn from another life—one where he had a mother and a father, and a home of their own. He knew his path to knighthood was unconventional, but he was grateful for Philip's brother to grant him such a high recognition.

Maybe even King Stefanos, who had always seemed at odds with Theo, would grant him the same privilege when they arrived back in Rhone.

Theo let out a small sigh. There were so many questions he had about the King, about Rose, about his family, and about his future. Their answers never seemed to come to him.

He opened his eyes as the monk came up next to him. "What troubles your soul?"

Theo hesitated. "Too much," he replied. "Too much worry and despair."

"Have you confessed your sins?"

Theo nodded, deciding not to let the man know he had yet to repent of all of them.

The monk nodded. "Our Heavenly Father hears your prayers. As your sins have been washed away, so may your worries. Let not your heart be troubled by your concerns, but continue to trust and have faith in that which sustains us all." He rested his hand on Theo's shoulder for a moment, before he began walking away.

"Thank you, Brother," Theo murmured. He crossed his arms and leaned back against the wooden pew. At the sudden pressure, he felt his back ache, the wounds from the dragon suddenly tender. He groaned and sat up.

"If you would like, sir," the monk spoke up, "the Crystal Lake hot springs are available for your use. A special room in the bottom of the castle leads out to a nearby pool. You might want to consider it if you are searching for peace. Even our Lord knew when to rest."

Theo nodded. From the monk's tone, he had to wonder if he was being told to leave. When the monk started to rearrange the ornaments on the altar, Theo decided it was best to slip out. Having been forced to clean and keep the sanctuary back in Rhone's capital city, Theo knew that it was always easier to care for the church when it was empty, and considering the early hour of the morning, he would not be surprised to find he had disrupted the monk with his company.

Besides, the hot springs actually sound like a good idea. Theo wondered if the rumors about the waters and their healing powers were true, and if the waters would do anything for his wounds.

With the help of some of the palace guards, Theo was able to find the stairway leading beneath the castle. The winding hallway ended with a grand door, with only one guard on duty. Theo nodded to the man, who remained silent as he stepped to the side and allowed him to pass.

Once he opened the door, and found himself alone on the other side of it, Theo felt his mouth drop open at the stunning surroundings. The room opened up into a tall, well-lit atrium, where the sky was hidden by the high ceiling of a cave. The floor gradually transformed into sand, and then gradually gave way to ashen waters, while the soft reflection of the lantern light danced on the surface ripples.

He knew the hot springs were a natural phenomenon in some countries, where heat escaped from underground volcanic pockets.

He breathed in deeply, tasting the moist air, as it intermingled with sulfur and other minerals. He coughed at the unusual taste, and smiled as the sound of it echoed across the large room.

Grateful to be alone, Theo stripped down to his linens, tossing the rest of his garments on one of the cave's proud stalagmites, before he slowly sank into the waters.

Immediately, the wounds on his back ached with pained pleasure. The warmth of the water seeped into each scar, tearing at the sensitive skin even while soothing it.

Sweat collected on his forehead as he moved slowly through the waters, Theo had to admit he was glad the monk had suggested going to the hot springs.

ONCE UPON A PRINCESS

The water grew deeper as he moved away from the pool's entrance. His feet dug into the gritty mud as he made his way to the far edge of the pool, toward a small niche, where the cave wall rounded against the shadows.

The other day, Ethan had told him that when they went down to the springs, Sophia and Mary had found some natural deposits, where there were piles of cream-like substance in some of the alcoves. It was supposed to be good for scars, and while Theo was not concerned with how his back looked, he did not want Rose to be upset at the sight of it.

Not that Rose would be upset because of how they looked, Theo thought, recalling how she had helped bandage him up several times on the road from the Romani territory.

But he knew she felt responsible for his pain, even though he had willingly protected her; he could see the guilt in her eyes each time, and he was getting less of a chance to displace her shame as she avoided him. Anything he could do to remove her guilt seemed like a worthwhile pursuit.

Just as he found a small pile of cream tucked just underneath the water, he heard the door to the hot springs open and slam shut.

He glanced over, ready to call out his welcome to whoever it was. He immediately faltered, stunned by what he saw.

Rose had pushed off her leggings and pulled off her tunic when he had caught sight of her. She was wearing only her undergarments, the white linen hanging delicately over her toned body. He could see her soft curves, usually hidden by her knight's armor; his eyes followed the flare of her hips. The lantern light landed on the delicate skin of her legs, touching her in places he could only envy. As if his thoughts had finally shocked him enough to return to reality, Theo turned away and ducked further into the alcove. He did not need to look at his reflection in the water to know his face was flushed over, colored a deep scarlet.

What is she doing here? Theo wondered. *Why would she come in this place, and why now?*

The heat of the waters seemed to increase drastically, as he heard Rose slip into the water. When he heard her release a small sigh of pleasure at the water's embrace, Theo had to squeeze his eyes shut and bury his face in his hands. He shook his head and hurriedly wiped it off; it was the absolute worst time to get anything in his eyes, if he was going to try to sneak past Rose before she discovered him.

If that's the only option I have, he thought to himself.

He glanced back toward her, relieved to see Rose had found a place to sit and stew, close to the water's edge. He was supremely grateful to see that her eyes were closed. Theo began to move slowly, not wanting to rouse her from her meditative position.

But once he realized he was safely out of her sight, for the moment, Theo gave into temptation to look at her. She was sitting with the water up to her neck, with her hair bound up in a high bun; several tendrils of shortened length escaped the tie and curled at the heat. He could see the porcelain skin of her shoulders peeking out of the gentle waters. He could see the linen of her undergarments, as they bubbled up from the pressure of the underwater springs.

Theo took another few steps forward. He was careful to slip off to the side, standing far off to the side of Rose. As he neared the edge of the water near the door, he realized that he might be able to get out of the pool without Rose's notice, but he would have a harder time leaving the room. She was

ONCE UPON A PRINCESS

relaxing right beside the stalagmite where he'd thrown his things earlier.

He was no longer able to move without possibly disturbing her. He tried to think of a way not to terrify her when he stepped on a sharp rock and lost his balance. He stumbled around in the pool as he quickly regained his balance.

Theo felt his breath suck in as the water rippled stridently across the pool. He hoped beyond all hope Rose did not hear the noise.

When Rose's eyes snapped opened, and she whirled around, he knew he was in trouble.

For a split second, all they did was stare at each other. And then Rose screamed and began scrambling to get away.

"Theo!" she yelled, sending the hot water flying as she hurriedly moved away from him. "What do you think are you doing here?!"

"I'm sorry," he called back, trying to shield himself from her splashing. "I was just relaxing, I swear. I promise didn't see anything."

"I don't believe you," Rose yelled, as she shoved another wave of water at him.

"Rose, please stop," he shouted. "It was an accident."

She crossed her arms, sinking all the way into the water. There was a look of unmatched fury on her face as she glared at him from just above the water's surface. "What … are … you … doing … here?" she repeated, her teeth grinding out each word, letting him know she was more than livid.

"I couldn't sleep," he said. "So I came here. I thought it would be good on my back."

"Why didn't you tell me you were here when I came in?" she grumbled.

"I didn't hear you until … " Theo let his voice trail off as he thought of seeing her bared flesh, the fair ivory of her legs and the strong muscles of her arms.

Rose sent another splash flying at him, this time striking his face.

"Ouch!" His eyes burned at the mixture of the hot water and natural minerals. "What was that for?"

"For lying," Rose snapped.

He could tell from the direction of her voice and the streaming water sounds she had stepped out of the water. Theo glared in her direction. "I wasn't lying."

"I can tell by looking at you!" she yelled. "Your face is all red."

"It's really warm in here, if you haven't noticed," Theo argued back. But he didn't want to admit that she was right; he had seen more than enough to make her feel uncomfortable. "It's just the temperature in here, that's all."

"I still don't believe you."

"Come on, Rose, you can trust me."

"I don't know about that anymore," Rose said angrily.

"If I wanted to look," Theo said, his own temper getting the better of him, "I wouldn't have come forward. I wouldn't have said anything."

He stopped trying to brush away the burning in his eyes, as he realized how cruel he sounded. He heard her inhale sharply, and instantly he regretted his words. "Rose … "

She went quiet, and he could tell she was distracted.

"You know what? It doesn't matter," Rose said. "I'm sorry for splashing you, I suppose, but at least this way I know you can't see me now."

ONCE UPON A PRINCESS

Theo groaned. "Didn't you ask the guard if there was anyone here before you came in?" he asked. "What if there were others?"

"I didn't see a guard," Rose shot back, her tone sharp, even if her voice was muffled. "And I didn't think anyone would be here. This is really early in the morning, you know."

"Yes," he said. "I know. Did you have trouble sleeping?"

"There are so many things to do," Rose replied in a noncommittal tone. "I don't have time to answer all your questions. I'm leaving."

He finished wiping the water from his eyes. He was still blinking furiously when he saw she had her shirt on once more.

For all the good it did, he thought. The hot springs had added a flush to her legs, and the wetness of her skin ensured that her shirt clung to her body. He had a hard time ignoring how short her shirt was. How one sleeve hung off one of her shoulders.

How much he wanted her to be his.

He stopped moving toward her, his body still half-sunk in the hot springs.

Rose held her tunic and her other clothes against her tightly, still having trouble looking him in the eye. "I'm leaving," she repeated. "You can stay. You're probably right that the water would be good for your injuries. I don't need it as much as you do."

"Rose," he said, as she headed toward the door. "It *was* an accident."

"It doesn't matter," she murmured, but he knew she was lying. She gripped handle on the door, and hurriedly disappeared on the other side.

ONCE UPON A PRINCESS

Theo felt awful as she left. They were already having problems when it came to communicating. *This isn't going to make it any better,* he thought.

He sank back into the water, alone once more, letting the hot springs massage their comfort into his back. Time passed, slowly and quietly.

Despite the physical comfort, Theo could only grimace.

But on the very small bright side, he thought reluctantly, he certainty had something else to occupy his thoughts.

5

Rose hurried down the hall, tugging her tunic over her head while trying to juggle her boots. She had wriggled into the rest of her clothes as soon as the door to the underground springs had closed, but the moment she could leave, she did.

How dare he! How dare he sit there and act like nothing had happened.

Her heart was still racing, as her mind screamed with humiliation and, she cursed herself, excitement. The thought of what had just happened angered her as much as it embarrassed her.

The rough texture of her shirt rubbed against her wet skin, as she nimbly finished tying her belt. Her feet, still bare, flinched at the uneven flooring of the castle, but she did not slow her pace.

She vowed that she would not think of seeing Theo, seeing him in his wet undergarments, fighting off her watery blows as he tried to calm her.

It was not the first time she had seen his chest or his back, but something about the way he had been covered with the steam of the hot springs, and the way the light had flickered off his chest....

"No!" she admonished herself. "No, stop thinking about it! This is *exactly* what you know you cannot do!"

Rose was relieved that she was still alone as she hurried through the castle. She knew they had guards keeping watch, but she had been lucky enough to avoid them.

In fact, she suddenly realized as she looked around, she was lost.

433

"How stupid can you be?" she asked, chastising herself. Rose looked around the unfamiliar halls of the palace, uncertain of where she had made a wrong turn. "Great."

She took a few moments to put her boots on, and then tried to recall her steps. Invariably, she had to stop herself from thinking of everything that happened before she left the hot springs.

Finally, she saw a familiar marker.

The tapestry of Queen Lucia hung proudly against the cold stone of the castle walls. The penetrating eyes seemed harrowing as they gazed down at her. Rose watched as the first gleam early morning light—or maybe the last of the moonlight—as it illuminated the Queen's gaze.

From where Rose stood, she saw a look of quiet judgment, almost a motherly look of sorts. It was as if Lucia knew of the dark secrets of her heart, the ones that she might have sung to the dragon, but still tried to silence inside her own heart.

"It's a lovely tapestry, don't you think?"

Rose didn't move as Juliette came and stood beside her. "It was a wedding gift from one of our ambassadors who lives in Einish."

"It is beautiful," Rose said, as she stared at it. She didn't feel the need to admit it made her unnerved.

"There aren't many of these tapestries in the world anymore," Juliette said. "The lady who made them died several years ago. She was a very skilled weaver. She used to work at some of the tournaments around the Einish border near Rhone."

"What happened to her?" Rose asked, more concerned with establishing rapport with the new Queen than finding out more about the weaver's fate.

"She fell in love with one of Rhone's knights, from what I heard, much to her father's dismay. It wasn't too long before they married and had children."

Rose felt an uncomfortable amount of jealousy at the woman's happiness.

"The tapestries of Lucia are thought to have magical powers," Juliette continued. "Of course, I don't believe that. But when you see it, there are moments when you have to wonder if it's not true."

Rose nodded. "I will agree with that," she said. "I've met Titania, Lucia's daughter who lives out in the Greek territories, near the Aegean. This picture reminds me of her."

"Lucia was known for her charms, before they ended up costing her."

"Titania told me that she made Benedict, one of King Arthur's wandering knights, a knight of Rhone. He became King after he managed to dispose of her."

Juliette giggled. "There's always more to the story," she said. "In the version of their story I have heard, Benedict and Lucia, coming from their different worlds, had trouble deciding how to rule the people of Rhone. Benedict had the advantage in war; Lucia had her fairy power. He wanted to rule through force, and she wanted to rule by magic. He went along with pleasing her for a long time, but as it grew harder not to feel like her equal, her partner, and even her king, he used Magdust to gain power."

"And that's why he imprisoned her?" Rose asked. "Because she wouldn't bow down to his wishes?"

Juliette smiled. "Have you ever been in love, Princess?"

Rose felt the familiar fury at the question, but she knew Juliette was asking it out of ignorance, not to make her feel bad.

ONCE UPON A PRINCESS

"No," she answered. "And please, call me Rose."

"It might be hard for you understand. Love between two people almost has a life of its own. Some poets have compared it to dancing, where there is a give and take, a leader and a follower. Other philosophers have said that it's more like a sword fight."

"I'll take that one over the dancing," Rose said. She grinned. "I'm better at fighting."

"With all the fighting you've done, from the tales I've heard, you should know that there is a time for peace."

"Of course." Rose nodded.

"It is the same in marriage, when two people are in love. Sometimes one person leads, and the other must submit." Juliette sighed. "I don't think either Lucia or Benedict were able to handle the submission part that comes with love."

"I don't blame them," Rose scoffed. "It's a sign of losing."

"When you truly love someone, it is more a sign of trust." Juliette smiled. "When Benedict had to earn her love, I imagine it was very hard for him to trust her. What if he wasn't able to keep hold of her affection? That was why it was easier to dispose of her in the end. If it wasn't for the matter of the kingdom, he likely would have just left her."

Rose looked back up at the Queen, and suddenly she saw her sad, judgmental eyes in a new light; Lucia suddenly came across as too proud, too stubborn, and too aloof. She never had to earn Benedict's love, but she was free to be the judge of whether or not he was worthy of her.

"Well," Rose said, after a few long moments of silence, "I guess either way you look at it, at least the tapestry is beautiful."

"Beautiful things can hide ugly secrets," Juliette said. Rose cringed, thinking of her own heart, hidden by her outward charms. "But you're right about the tapestry."

"Do you come down here to look at it a lot, or did you just happen to be passing by when you found me?" Rose asked, happy to find a way to change the subject. She did not want to think about true love and marriage, real or legendary.

"I usually wake up early to say goodbye to the moonlight," Juliette admitted. "Even though it has been over a year since the sorcerer who enchanted me was killed, I fear I will wake up to find this has all been a dream, and I will turn back into a swan at moonset."

"I can tell you it's not a dream," Rose told her. "If that makes you feel better."

Juliette giggled again, making Rose wonder how young she was. She seemed very innocent. Derick was a few years older than Philip, but Rose had a hard time imagining that Juliette was much older than she was, if Juliette was older at all.

"There's just so much in my life I couldn't believe before," Juliette said. "I mean, not too many people end up cursed."

"Tell me about it," Rose muttered.

"And now, here I am," Juliette continued, oblivious to Rose's increasing discomfort, "pregnant, with a husband who loves me, and a stronger kingdom coming out of our two lands. It is a miracle."

"See?" Rose said. She gave the Queen a kind and sad smile. "If it's a miracle, then it's not a dream."

"I'll take comfort in your observation, Rose," Juliette said, her eyes lit up with happiness. "And I thank you for it."

"You're welcome."

ONCE UPON A PRINCESS

Rose shifted her feet uncomfortably as Juliette put a hand on her belly, where, inside of her, her child grew. Rose did not want to think about how much she envied Juliette.

"Speaking of observations, Juliette," Rose said, deciding it was time to change the subject once more, "I was wondering if you would be able to point me in the direction of my room? I seem to be a bit lost."

"Sure," Juliette replied.

Despite Juliette's kindness, Rose was glad, moments later, to be free from the Queen's presence. *And that,* she told herself, *is why I don't want to get married.*

Juliette was a very lovely lady, and Rose was sure she was a nice person. But what did she really know of the world? Of another's suffering? Juliette was just a pretty queen who could empower the nation by having children. Rose doubted Juliette would ever play a real, decisive role in her nation's future again, and she even suspected that Juliette would not mind if that were the case.

Rose tried not to sigh. It was also possible Juliette would not even notice her secondary role. Juliette would just do what she had been talking about earlier; she would see it as part of a loving marriage, and submit.

Rose frowned. She knew she certainty had no desire to do that.

But as she approached the door to her room, she knew she was not being completely honest with herself.

Theo was standing outside her door.

The sight of him, fully dressed, with his hair still sticky with steam and sweat, caused a pool of heat to settle into her belly. Her mind was flooded with that moment back in Poiyana, when she *had* surrendered, when she *had* submitted—when she had closed her eyes and waited for Theo to kiss her.

ONCE UPON A PRINCESS

Not only had she wanted it, she had willingly hoped for it.

Rose watched as Theo raised his hand to knock on her door, and waited again. She realized he did not see her in the shadows of the hall behind him. He thought she was already back in her room.

He faltered just as his hand poised to knock.

Rose held her breath. Her whole body went rigid as she watched him, wondering if he was going to knock on her door.

She wondered, if she were on the other side of the door, if she would open it.

Slowly, eventually, Theo dropped his hand.

He ran his hand through his ebony hair and then shook his head. He slowly backed away, before he headed down the hall in the other direction. He never saw her.

The instant he was out of sight, Rose hurried into her room, suddenly distraught. The heat in her belly cooled into nausea, and she felt dizzy.

Rose was not fooled; she knew the answer to her question. She had wanted him to knock, and she wanted to believe that she would have answered. Part of her wanted to go find him again and tell him what she was thinking.

Rose fell back against the door, the rough wood. "No, no. That's stupid. I'm not going to say anything."

"Not going to say anything about what?"

Mary's voice, rested and relaxed, so much at odds with her own reality, jarred against Rose's exasperation.

Rose looked over toward the small fairy, who was lying down on one of the bigger pillows on her bed.

"What's wrong, Rose?" Mary asked, sitting up.

Rose shook her head. "Nothing," she insisted. "How are you feeling? Did you get enough rest?"

ONCE UPON A PRINCESS

Mary glowered at her. "I'd be better," she said, "if I knew you weren't lying. Tell me what's wrong."

Rose felt the heat in the back of her neck. "I don't want to talk about it, Mary. It's too embarrassing."

"I could always do a truth spell," Mary mused.

"Now I know you're teasing me." Rose gave her a small smile. "I know you would never betray me."

"Rose." Mary sat up against the fluffy pillows. "I'm worried for you."

"Please, don't worry about me right now. We have a lot prepping to do before we leave tomorrow."

"Rose," Mary said. "Come and lie down. Your cheeks are flushed and your eyes are glassy. You're feverish." Her wings, thin and delicate against the last shadow of night, fluttered. She held up her hand against Rose's forehead.

"Little mother," Rose murmured, giving Mary a pat on the head, ruffling the short ginger locks affectionately.

"Let me help you sleep, Rose," Mary said. "You'll feel better. After all the weeks on the road, you need to get some quality sleep. I can attest to the comfort King Derick has been kind enough to offer us. I've barely wanted to move since we've come."

"I know you needed it," Rose said. "After all the healing you've done for Theo, I'm well aware you needed it. I know it took a lot out of you, fighting against the dragon magic."

Saying his name was a mistake. Rose took another deep breath to steady herself.

"I might be rested, but you're the one who needs it now, Rose."

"No. I'm too afraid of what I might dream of," Rose told her.

ONCE UPON A PRINCESS

"You know, you never did tell me the full story what happened back in the Serpent's Garden," Mary said. "But I never thought it was that terrifying to you.

"I sang to the dragon," Rose reminded her. "I told you that."

"It wasn't just singing," Mary pushed. "I know you, Rose. I've watched over you since the day you were born. Something has changed, and you won't tell me what it is."

"It's awful." Rose pressed against the door, allowing herself to slide down to the floor, her head falling to her chest. More of her hair escaped the quick bun she had tied back earlier.

"I know you have had a hard life, but I have been there more often than not," Mary said. "Let me help you, Rose."

"You can't," Rose told her. "It's me. I'm the problem."

Mary looked at her with an expectant look.

"It's less than six months until my birthday. I don't have much longer."

"We're getting there, Rose."

"I still want so much more out of life." Rose sighed. "I am grateful for you, and the others. I just want … more." She felt the lump in her throat tighten again. "When I went to go see the dragon, and I sang, I sang Queen Lucia's song. About how she wanted love, someone who would be worthy of her love."

"Is that what you want?" Mary asked.

It was harder to answer, now that she knew more about Queen Lucia and her complicated relationship with Benedict.

"Yes. No. I don't know." Rose shook her head. "I'm not worthy of love, Mary. Not really. I'm cursed. I can't offer someone a future, or a family. Not until the curse is broken. I just want the curse broken, so I can be free."

ONCE UPON A PRINCESS

"I think someone will love you even if your curse can't be broken," Mary told her softly.

"I don't want someone to love me like that. Like this," Rose said. "I do have to kill Magdalina if she refuses to free me from her curse, remember? I have to destroy her, to save myself."

"You will be protecting the rest of your family, and likely others, from her wrath," Mary said.

"Even though that's likely true, there is the matter that if I don't make it, anyone who loves me will be devastated." Rose sniffed. "Magdalina has to be the cruelest person who ever lived, to make me suffer like this."

"She was very adamant about making your father pay," Mary remarked. "It seems she did a good job of that."

"Why? What did she want the King to pay for?" Rose asked. "She couldn't have been that upset, just because she was not invited to my party."

"It wasn't just that she was not invited," Mary said. "Everything that could have been done to shield you from her was done. The King didn't even want her to know of your birth."

"Why?" Rose asked. "Why was he afraid of her?"

"I don't know for sure," Mary said. "I heard him talk about breaking a deal with her once. That was it. I didn't hear any details. And that might not even be why she's so upset with him, really."

Rose thought of Theo again. "He hates Theo, too, doesn't he?"

"The King never liked him, precisely because you did," Mary said. "He was upset with him for telling you the truth about your curse, and all the resulting grievances you gave

ONCE UPON A PRINCESS

him. You were a perfect child, Rose, before you found out about everything. Once you knew the truth—"

"I was never the same." Rose put her head in her hands. "And the King blames Theo for that."

Mary nodded. "He didn't like that you demanded that Theo would join you and your siblings for classes, either. He felt he should have stayed in the church and let his family take care of educating him. You were lucky you insisted, Rose, or you might not have Theo by your side today."

"I'm the one who's letting him pursue his revenge," Rose said. "Theo might be more lucky if I hadn't."

"Life is never free of pain, Rose," Mary said softy. "But we each get to choose what kind of pain we experience."

"Sometimes it's not a choice," Rose said, thinking how Theo just stood there, in the hot springs, as he looked at her with that strange expression on his face. She wanted to go back to that moment and reach for him instead of run from him, back to that moment when her heart had fluttered so dangerously. "I would never choose this."

"No one would choose to be cursed as you, Rose," Mary said, patting her hand.

Rose nearly jumped. "Yeah," she agreed, her voice listless.

She decided not to correct Mary. She could not imagine confessing her dreams of letting herself fall in love, without fear that the fall would lead to only despair.

There was nothing to be done, Rose thought, desolate once more. She would just go on, as she had always gone on.

"Mary?" Rose looked over at her longtime friend. "It's morning. Let's go over what we need to take care of before we leave here tomorrow. Derick and Philip wanted us to take care of some trouble while we travel through the forest."

ONCE UPON A PRINCESS

"Rose," Mary said, "please, go to bed. You need to rest. You're exhausted. I'll see to everything today."

"No. There's so much to do still. There are so many questions to answer." Rose shook her head, but as soon as she stood up, the room began to spin.

She barely realized she was still awake as Mary whisked her off her feet. The last thing she heard herself say was, "Please don't let me dream, Mary," before there was nothing but darkness.

6

It was hours later when Rose finally stirred from her slumber. The call to wake up came as she felt the easy pressure of a wet rag on her forehead.

"Stop it, Theo," she murmured, waving him away. "I'm fine. See? I'm awake."

"You might be fine, but you're definitely not awake," Philip said, "if you can't see that it's me, instead of Theo."

Rose opened her eyes and rubbed them. "He's the one who usually takes care of me," she heard herself say.

"He passed that duty along to me today, then," Philip assured her as he dabbed her forehead with a dry cloth this time. "He said that you would want to leave the moment you got up, so it would be best if he took care to get everything ready."

Rose stiffened, wondering if Theo had told Philip about what had happened down in the hot springs. She studied Philip's face carefully, trying to see if he was hiding anything from her.

"What?" he asked. "What is it?"

When she decided that Philip's handsome face was innocent enough, she sat up against her pillows.

"I told you sleep would help you, Rose," Mary said. Rose looked over to see Mary was sitting by the window. The thick curtains were drawn back some, allowing the full light of the afternoon to pour into the room.

"So we're going to leave today?" Rose asked, as she pushed past Philip and her covers. She hurried to look outside.

Mary chuckled. "Not as soon as Natala is."

Rose breathed a sigh of relief as she looked down at the courtyard below, where Theo was indeed giving a cranky Natala some assistance as she climbed up onto a horse. Even from where she was, she could hear Natala's groaning complaints and screechy interrogations.

"It's too hot to travel today. I'll be dead by nightfall. Did you make sure to pack me plenty of blankets? I'll need them when it gets cold. I can tell it's going to get cold tonight. I'll probably die freezing. I can't believe this is the best horse you were able to get for me. I thought this was a king's palace?"

Natala whirled around as she sat on the horse, making sure the ropes holding up her packs, many of which clearly had blankets inside, before pinching her mouth into her favorite frown.

Theo took her hand, giving her a gallant bow, a farewell worthy of a true lady. Rose smiled at his kindness. There was no way Natala was even close to being a lady.

"I hope your brother doesn't mind she's taking a horse," Rose said, turning back to Philip.

"Believe me, Derick was fine parting with it, once he knew it would get rid of her more quickly," Philip said. "When I told him of her temper and her shrewish ways, he didn't hesitate to give into most of her demands."

"Most?" Rose asked. She grinned. "What did he deny her?"

"A lot of money," Philip replied.

Rose laughed as the door opened, and Sophia came inside. "Figures," she said.

"What's funny?" Sophia was carrying a large bundle in her arms. She carried it over to Rose's bed and set it down, her nimble fingers already unraveling the bundle's ties.

"Natala's leaving," Philip said. "I was just telling Mary and Rose about all the money she'd tried to get out of my brother."

Sophia shook her head. "She would have been smarter to ask for a guard," she said. "If she's not taking anyone back, all of her bags will just make her an easier target for thieves."

"Maybe I should send Lannister back with her," Rose said. Of all the members of the group, Lannister, one of the royal guards assigned to protect her, was the only one who had been able to get along with Natala on the way to Crystal Lake. "They did have similar tastes when it came to their choice of beverage."

"Roderick and Captain Locke would probably be okay with that," Mary said. "I've overheard them complaining about how he has not been carrying his weight lately."

Rose was tempted to say she was okay with all of them escorting Natala back to Poiyana, but she had grown more fond of Roderick since their adventures on the island of Maltia. He had proven himself to be her mother's champion while they were there.

He was also mostly quiet and kept to himself the majority of the time, so it wasn't like she had to worry about ordering him around. Captain Locke was content with his duties and his silence as well. Rose knew she had an honorable captain for her guard.

"We could do without Lannister," Rose said. "I would prefer it, as much trouble as she is, that she doesn't go back alone."

"Ethan told me that she had a few people ready to leave for Greece," Philip said. "She's meeting them in the town square today. So I wouldn't worry about her. She seems pretty smart. I suspect if she hides it only if she knows she'll be able to

ONCE UPON A PRINCESS

swindle more out of people by playing the victim or the shrew.”

“Or both,” Rose mused.

“If she’s made it this long without one of her passengers letting her get too drunk to avoid walking off a cliff, I suppose I’m not giving her enough credit,” Sophia replied.

“Or throwing her off the cliff,” Rose muttered.

“Rose,” Mary said.

“Hey, you were asleep way more than I was,” Rose defended herself. “She was a terror, Mary. While you slept she was constantly on our nerves.”

“Speaking of which,” Philip said, “you need to make sure you are getting enough rest, Rose. Mary was terrified when you collapsed earlier.”

“I did not collapse.” Rose willed herself to believe it as much as she wanted the rest of them to believe it.

Sophia rolled her eyes, regardless of the confidence of Rose’s assertion. “Come here and check your sword, Rose. Let me make sure it’s ready for you before we leave.”

“Seriously,” Philip said, “you do need to take care of yourself, Rose, and that includes sleep. I don’t want to go and meet your brother and sister in Einish only to have to explain to them why you keep falling asleep at the most random times.”

“Do you seriously care more about what Isra and Ronan think than what I do?” Rose put her hands on her hips while Sophia ran a rag over the ruby at the hilt of Rose’s sword.

“Of course,” Philip said. “I promised Isra I would watch out for you while we were away. I don’t want to fail her.”

“I’m curious,” Rose said. “Did she *make* you promise that, or did you gallantly offer to be my babysitter?”

Philip seemed to realize that he might have said too much. "Come on," he said. "That's being unfair, Rose."

"Here," Sophia said, handing Rose her sword. "Check its balance for me, please."

Rose held out the sword straight ahead, teasing Philip enough by leveling it at him while he stood by her bed. "I have a right to ask you about the relationship you have with Isra," she insisted. "After all, she's your betrothed now."

"Not officially," Mary said. "Even if Rose signs the contract, King Stefanos still has to approve it. We haven't heard anything from Rhone for weeks now. Besides, Isra is too young to get married at only sixteen."

"Let's hope the King's still holed up in his room, paranoid and sick," Sophia said. "If Rose can take over the duties of the crown, it'll be easier to convince Magdalina we're not to be trifled with."

"I won't argue with you there," Rose said, "but I don't want to mutiny against my father. It would set a poor precedent for future generations."

"Rose, give the sword a few practice swings," Sophia instructed, interrupting Rose's conversation with Philip again.

"But at least you could okay things of that nature, such as your sister's marriage," Philip said. "That would be easier."

"Is that what you want?" Rose asked.

Before he could answer, there was a knock at the door. Rose's heart beat wildly, remembering how she had felt earlier, seeing Theo outside her door.

"Who is it?" Mary called.

Rose instantly recognized the voice on the other side of the door as one of the many guards. "His Majesty has called for Prince Philip."

"Well, I will go and see him at once, then," Philip replied. "I will have to take my leave. I'm glad to see you're feeling better, Rose, and I will make it my duty to make sure you get more sleep, more consistently, from now on."

Rose frowned at Philip as he sauntered over to the door. "Don't think that we're not going to finish this conversation later," she told him.

"I wouldn't dream of it," Philip assured her, before giving her a quick, teasing smile, and then heading out with the guard. "I know you will fight me on the matter of your health."

"I was talking about Isra," Rose called after him. She closed the door behind him.

"I wonder what the King wanted," Mary said.

"Well, we are heading to Einish soon," Rose said. "I imagine, from what I've seen of those two, he just wanted to spend more time with him. Maybe they are reviewing over their plans for helping us take care of any Magdust traders we find."

"They are good people," Mary said. "And good brothers."

"Speaking of good brothers," Sophia said, "I wonder where mine has gotten off to. He's supposed to help me load up my tools."

"He's probably already doing that with Theo," Rose said. "Either that, or he's training with him again. We should do more training too, come to think of it, Sophie. It's been a few days since we went over fighting techniques."

"I think it's better we've slowed down some. If I can let Ethan catch up with me, he'll make a good sparring partner. Plus, I can try a few more things I learned from King Derick's blacksmiths. They have some interesting tricks about melting metals and controlling the heat."

ONCE UPON A PRINCESS

Rose felt a small feeling of dismay at Sophia's admission. As much as she had wanted to train Sophia to be a knight, Sophia was more interested in her smithing, as she had always been. As frustrated as it made Rose feel, it was nice Sophia was interested enough that she could help Ethan develop his skills.

One day, Rose thought, they both might need it, especially if she was not able to break her curse.

"How's the sword?" Sophia asked.

"Perfect, as usual." Rose smiled at her, before sheathing the sword in the scabbard at her belt. "Thanks, Sophie."

There was a bright gleam in Sophia's mismatched brown and blue-green eyes. "You know you're always welcome, Rose."

"It'll be ready when we find those Magdust traders. If we leave now, we can arrive at O'Lin before nightfall tomorrow."

"I wish you wouldn't push so much, Rose. You do need to take better care of yourself," Sophia replied. "We love you, you know. All of us."

"You know," Mary said, "it wouldn't hurt us much if we were to leave tomorrow morning, Rose, instead of heading out tonight. You really should rest more."

"It would make the rest of us feel better," Sophia agreed. "Besides, Mary sure likes the mattresses here better than the ones we use on the road."

Rose knew when she was cornered. "Philip is trying to get me to agree with him by using tricks and humor, while you're content to pour on the guilt. Is that it, Sophie?"

"Is it working?"

Rose grimaced. "If it is, I'll never admit to it."

"I thought as much." Sophia laughed. "Here, let me go ahead and have you check the other weapons I brought you. I have your knife here, Rose. And I have Theo and Philip's as well for you to approve."

"Shouldn't they be the ones to approve?"

"They're busy with other stuff, and this is easy. Come on, we'll get some food right after. You're likely hungry, so it's something important you can do, and then you can go eat and feel like you've had a productive morning even though you slept through all of it."

Not all of it, Rose thought. But seeing Sophia's eagerness and feeling the groaning hunger in her own stomach, she conceded to Sophia's direction. "Alright. If you are all so worried about my health, then I will agree we can leave tomorrow morning, rather than tonight. But it's early bedtime for everyone, and there will be no exceptions."

Despite her reluctance to delay their departure, Rose felt better about her decision when Sophia and Mary both cheered.

ONCE UPON A PRINCESS

7

As the morning dawned, Theo congratulated himself on having avoided Rose successfully since the embarrassing incident down in the hot springs. He told himself to take comfort in the time he'd had to reflect on what he would say to her, and how she would react, because there was no avoiding her on this day.

Theo prayed for extra mercy that morning.

He heard a knock at the door to his and answered it, fearing the devil was already going to give him grief.

When he saw Roderick's rust-colored beard and large girth in the doorway, he almost sank to his knees in gratitude.

"Sir," Roderick greeted. "Captain Locke and Lannister are getting the horses ready now. We will be ready to depart as soon as everyone is ready."

"Excellent," Theo said. "That's good news."

"Good news for the Princess," Roderick said. "But I for one will miss the comforts of the castle. Crystal Lake is a beautiful place."

"Your accommodations were to your liking?"

"Oh, yes," Roderick nodded. "It was much easier to slip out to the town at night than I thought it would be."

"Did you and the others learn anything interesting about what's going on in the woods?" Theo asked. "I know King Derick has been looking into it, but he has a lot of other concerns."

"He has quite a few loyal men to delegate the task to," Roderick said. "I talked with many of them while I was in town."

ONCE UPON A PRINCESS

"What about the city residents? I know there are places you can get into that he couldn't. At least, not without a good disguise."

"True enough. The King does have some subjects who are more than reluctant to face the unification of Einish and Crystal Lake. He will likely have to deal with later." Roderick chuckled. "But besides that, there's not much I did find out about the trouble between the countries at their borders. All I have been able to discover for sure is that it is connected with the Magdust trade."

"That's what Philip told me and Rose," Theo said.

"I've heard some other rumors, but I could not verify them. I have to admit I'm a little hesitant to share them with you."

"What? Why?"

"There are rumors that Magdalina herself has been spotted in the forest between Einish and Rhone, close to where Crystal Lake also borders the two."

"We will be going right through that area," Theo said. "At least, according to Ethan, that is."

"Yes. I don't want you or the Princess to get your hopes up."

"What about Everon?" Theo asked, thinking of the large, brutish fairy who had killed his parents. Despite his upbringing, Theo felt his blood hum with vengeful anticipation.

"He has not been spotted, just Magdalina," Roderick said. "Again, that was just a rumor, and I have no solid consensus on it."

Theo's optimism plummeted. "Oh."

"I'm curious," Roderick mused, "how she would have been able to come into this place at all, though."

"What do you mean?" Theo asked.

ONCE UPON A PRINCESS

"From what the people I talked to told me, the pixies who reside in Crystal Lake have no love of fairies, that's for sure, but they have had a peaceful coexistence for years."

"I remember Mary saying something about the pixies," Theo said. "She said they were friendly."

"Not a lot of them, really. I was able to learn more about them when I was in town. Pixies have, in the past, used their own spells and power to keep fairies, even those such as Magdalina, from moving onto their territory. So it is interesting that the Magdust trade has expanded to the Wandering Caverns."

"What do you think it means? Based on what you've heard?"

"As I see it, there are only a few things it could be." Roderick sighed. "It's possible the pixies are working with the traders, or they have been ambushed by the traders themselves."

Theo frowned. "But how would the traders overpower them?"

"Magic has rules, remember?" Roderick stroked his beard thoughtfully. "Pixies have their own rules, different from the fairies; it's part of the reason they don't live together very often. If a human was able to control a pixie, it would be easy for them to attack the fairies and also move in on the pixies' territory. It also makes it easier to make Magdust when you already have magic, from what I heard down by the prison."

"I've never thought about what it takes to make Magdust," Theo admitted. "I just knew the fairies are killed for their power. I know there are ways to kill fairies, but butchering them for their power is a whole different thing. I didn't think about that before."

ONCE UPON A PRINCESS

Roderick snorted. "Well, you wouldn't, would you? The idea of Magdust is already unpleasant enough."

"The Magdust trade goes back many years," Roderick said. "I've listened to a lot of people's stories, and most of them agree that the fairies have become endangered because of Rhone's first leader. He was the one, they tell me, that first used it to gain power."

"That's true. Titania, Queen Lucia's daughter, told us as much when the rest of us were looking for her," Theo said. "She said Benedict used the Magdust to gain power over Lucia. Once she was out of the way, he was able to establish himself as the ruler of Rhone, rather than just a knight."

"Yes, but he was far from the only person who knew how to make the Magdust," Roderick said. "So other people knew about it and how to make it."

Theo thought of his mother, whose face seemed blurry in his memory after more than decade without her. He thought of his father, too, who was more knight than father in his memory. "I can agree to that," he said.

Roderick sighed. "It can be profitable. Even if you are not a king, you could live like one if you were able to sell enough."

"I think that's why my father was in it," Theo admitted quietly.

He thought back to the unpleasant conversation he'd had with his older brother the last time he had been in Rhone. Thad had told him the truth of what he'd found from their Uncle Thom, who had also been killed by Everon and his cronies.

Of all the people from his past, it was his uncle that remained completely real against the passage of time. The breadth of his shoulders, the warmth of his laugh, the blood splattered on his beard and hands and back as he tried to get

ONCE UPON A PRINCESS

Theo and Thad out of their home the night his parents died. All of Uncle Thom still seemed very vivid in comparison to the memories of his parents.

They walked down the hall some, when Theo stopped by the tapestry of Queen Lucia. The wall drapery, with all its advanced weaving and skill, made him wonder. He reached out and grabbed Roderick's arm. "Do you know someone managed to weave the Magdust into fabric?"

"I've heard some tales. Magdust was used by some sorcerers for any number of things." Roderick looked up at the tapestry alongside Theo. "Why? Do you think this one has some in it?"

"It looks a lot like one my mother had hanging in our house," Theo said. "I'd love to know if it does."

"How did you destroy it?"

"My uncle burned it," Theo said.

"Makes sense," Roderick said with a nod.

"What do you mean?" Theo asked. "Why would that work?"

"Fairies are very, very cautious around fire," Roderick said. "They are creatures of creation, you know. Mary is proof of that, isn't she? You can see that they have no trouble creating something new, or even making something different, but they do not use the power to destroy. When they need light, they usually collect sunlight or even moonlight."

"That's true." Theo nodded. It would explain why fairy magic would not work around dragons and their blood.

"Fire, on the other hand, is a natural destroyer." Roderick shrugged. "But I'm not sure King Derick would be happy if you burned up his tapestry and there was nothing wrong with it."

ONCE UPON A PRINCESS

Theo did not like to think about it, but he had an idea. "Maybe Rose can use her sword to find out if there's Magdust in it somehow."

"No harm in trying," Roderick agreed. "We'd likely get better results than trying to burn it, if nothing else."

"There might be no harm in trying," Theo said, "but I'm hoping there is no harm in asking. I wouldn't want to inconvenience Rose."

"She does have a temper," Roderick agreed. "I properly pity anyone who has the gall to make her upset."

"Me, too," Theo muttered. "Me, too."

Rose already had a list of reasons to argue with Theo over something, so she was even more unhappy when she opened her door in the morning and there was Roderick, who Theo had sent to her room in order to summon her to his side.

"I'm in charge," Rose reminded Roderick. "Theo doesn't have the right to order me to come see him."

"It was a poor choice of words on my part, My Lady."

Rose scoffed. "Rose, please. You know I hate formality between friends."

"We are friends then?"

"I guess so," Rose told him, giving him one of her smiles. She appreciated that his cheeks dulled with a pleasing flush; Roderick was smart enough to know that her trust was hard won.

Now, it is time to remind Theo of that as well.

But despite her anger, Rose forced herself to act normally when she saw him. "What did you want, Theo, that was so important that you ordered me away from breakfast?"

ONCE UPON A PRINCESS

"You haven't eaten yet," Theo told her easily enough. "I know you well, Rose. You pack your breakfast to go and eat it while we're on the road."

"For your information, I was going to go to the dining hall before you sent for me."

"But not to eat. Just to get food. It's still different."

She glared at him, no doubt angry because he was right. "Well, now that you've ruined my appetite, what do you need me for?"

Theo nodded toward the tapestry. "I wanted to see if there was any Magdust in this design," he said.

"Why would you think it does?" Rose scowled. She glanced up at the tapestry once more, where Queen Lucia's gaze was just as imposing as it had been the day before.

"My mother had one that carried Magdust," Theo told her quietly. "It was very similar to this one."

Rose raised her eyebrows at that. She sighed, and some part of her had to admit she could not keeping looking for a fight to pick with him.

They had work to do, both of them, and bickering every step of the way there was not going to help. And Theo did not talk much about his parents or his past before he came to Rhone's capital. If he thought this was important, she had a duty to comply.

"What do you think we can do?" Rose asked. "I talked with Juliette about this tapestry yesterday. She said it was a gift from one of the Einish court ambassadors."

"I was thinking your sword might be able to do something," Theo said. "Remember when you were jousting with Marsor on Maltia? You were able to shatter his sword and find the stash of Magdust the hilt had."

ONCE UPON A PRINCESS

Rose pulled out her sword. "I'd hate to cut this," she said. "I mean, if it's just a normal tapestry."

"Well, the fairy magic should still respond to it, right?" Roderick asked. "Just use your sword to touch it gently."

Feeling silly, Rose pressed the tip of her sword against the tapestry.

For a moment, nothing happened. All of them seemed to be holding their breaths, waiting for something to happen.

Then, slowly, a small pink-and-green glow emitted from the point where the sword and the fabric came together.

"I was right." Theo's expression was grim and glad at the same time. "There is Magdust in it."

"We'd better tell the King," Rose said. She pulled her sword away from the tapestry. Immediately, the shimmering cloud of dust disappeared back into the folds of the fabric. "He needs to get rid of this, before he's accused of helping the Magdust trade flourish."

"I'll go and get him," Roderick offered. "You two can stay here." He was already sprinting down the hallway when Rose started to object.

"No, that's alright—" Rose tried to stop him, wanting to insist that she would go and get the King, that it would be her great pleasure, that she should be the one to break the bad news. But it was too late.

She was forced to be alone with Theo.

I hate this. This situation would have never bothered me before.

"So, did you get enough sleep last night?" Theo asked. His tone, inquiring and calm, was the same as it had always been, as he asked her the question he must have asked her a million times or more.

ONCE UPON A PRINCESS

It irritated Rose to no end. "Yes," she replied, determined to show him that two could play the normal game. "How about you? How is your back?"

"It is getting better."

His tone was the same, Rose noticed, but he wasn't looking at her.

"You said your mother had one of these?" Rose asked, gesturing to the tapestry.

"She said that my father won it at a tournament," Theo said. "She had a gift for weaving herself though. I remember she used to spent a lot of time at her spinning wheel, before the King outlawed and destroyed them."

Rose only nodded. "Juliette told me that there was a famous weaver who made these and sold them at tournaments, so it fits."

"Is the weaver still alive, do you think?" Theo asked. "We might be able to find out more about it from her."

"Well, Juliette said she died. But she had children. And there's always the possibility she had an apprentice or her teacher could still be alive. Tradesmen and artisans of all kinds would have apprentices. Even Sophie gets excited when we're at a place where she can learn about a new tool or technique." Rose sighed. "I'm actually worried she might not want to be a knight at all, considering her interest still lies in blacksmithing."

"She's still a good fighter. And a good squire. Not all squires make it to knighthood," Theo reminded her gently. "Even though I know you wanted her to succeed as a lady knight."

"It's fine," Rose said, waving the issue aside. "I guess we need to be more concerned with the weaver right now than

Sophia's trade. Juliette said she got this from someone at the Einish court. We can ask around when we get there."

"Maybe Isra will be able to tell us something, too."

Rose nodded. "Maybe. She hasn't sent any letters back lately."

"She knows we're close."

"True." Rose glanced out the nearby window, looking up at the clouds. "But I miss Virtue."

Her gyrfalcon, with his large wings and his soulful eyes, acted as a messenger between her worlds. She decided to herself that when she saw him again, she would take a few hours and go hawking with him.

"Rose."

She flinched; the past few moments had been nice, almost normal. Hearing Theo say her name ruined it.

"What?" she bit back.

"I talked with Roderick some," he said. "He and the others were able to find some information for us."

"Oh?" Rose lost her defensiveness immediately. "Anything interesting?"

"There are rumors—just rumors—that Magdalina has been spotted in the Einish forest."

Rose's hand tightened around her sword hilt. "That means that we might … "

"We might get a chance to fight her," Theo concluded.

"I'm ready." "I'm more than willing to engage Magdalina in battle. She might have caught me by surprised at my birthday party this past year, but she's no match for me with a sword."

"Especially one with dragon's blood," Theo agreed. "She won't be able to stand up to that."

Rose nodded. "I could finally be free," she whispered.

ONCE UPON A PRINCESS

"That's right." Theo gave her a grin, meeting her eyes for the first time. "And then you'll be able to sing again."

Rose flushed.

"You never did sing for me," Theo reminded her. "You still have to do that."

Rose scowled. *Just when I thought things were starting to go alright,* she thought bitterly. She crossed her arms, folding her sword underneath her arm. "Can you just forget about that? I mean, after yesterday's incident, we should be even."

Pure hatred, mostly for herself, throbbed through her, drowning her in self-inflicted rage. She saw the change in Theo's expression immediately, and she knew he was not happy with her remark, either.

"Fine," he said. "We'll call it even."

"Good," Rose snapped back. "And I don't want to talk about it anymore."

"Fine."

"*Fine.*"

"There's no need for you to be a brat about it," Theo told her. "Your behavior is hardly mature."

Rose stuck her tongue out at him.

Before Theo could reply, Roderick and Derick came into sight. Juliette was not far behind the two of them.

Rose greeted her with a smile, but it was not enough to ease the worry she saw on Juliette's expression.

"Rose," Derick said. "Good morning. Starting the day's adventures early, are you?"

"Apparently," Rose said, trying to match the chipper tone of the King's, even though her mood was far from cheerful, and the news she had for them even less so.

When Rose placed the tip of her sword back against the tapestry, Juliette gasped in horror.

ONCE UPON A PRINCESS

"What do we do?" Derick asked.

"Burn it," Theo said. "I know from experience it's the easiest way of getting rid of it."

"What about the baby?" Juliette asked. "Will the baby be alright?"

"What about it?" Rose looked over at her. Juliette reached out and took Derick's hand for support.

"If we get rid of the tapestry, it wouldn't hurt the baby, will it?" Juliette looked distressed. "Ambassador Rolez told me that it was supposed to bring good luck for babies and their health. He said it was supposed to protect our children."

"That's likely just superstition," Rose said, watching as Juliette put her arms protectively over her tummy again. Rose struggled to feel sympathy for Juliette, but she was unable to muster much. The Queen's reaction seemed too much like an overreaction. Wasn't Juliette the one, after all, who had told her before she didn't believe the tapestry was actually magic? Why would she worry that getting rid of it would somehow harm her child?

Rose knew she was not the one to handle this anymore. She immediately looked to Theo. He was better with this sort of thing, she thought. "Theo?"

Theo immediately jumped forward and began comforting Juliette, while Roderick and Derick began to take the tapestry down from the wall.

It wasn't long before Theo sent Juliette down to the chapel, along with Derick to support her, and the tapestry was burning in a nearby fireplace.

Rose watched it burn, her eyes following the ballooning puffs of pink and green shimmers. "I guess the Magdust trade is more complicated than just transporting it in its powder form."

ONCE UPON A PRINCESS

Theo stoked the fire with a poker. "If it makes you feel better," he said, "it has been going on for decades now. It won't be an easy fix."

"If it's been going on for decades, why hasn't Rhone been able to do much about it?" Rose asked. "Isn't that why Magdalina and her forces are so angry with the people of Rhone?"

"Wars like this are cyclical," Theo replied. "They come and go, almost like the tides. Where there is the opportunity to engage in profitable activity, there are people who indulge it in. And then there are people who educate themselves and others on how to stay away from it. It is a war on the individual that has consequences for the whole community."

"Do you think once Magdalina is no longer a concern, we will still face this problem?" Rose asked.

"There will be years of repair that we will need to do with the fairyfolk who are upset with us," Theo said. "Magdalina is only one symptom of a larger problem."

Rose smiled sadly. "So, yes then?"

He nodded.

She sighed. "It seems too big of a problem."

"Not when we can face it together, Rosary," Theo said. "And *that* is something you don't have to worry about."

He stuffed the poker back in its place and stood up. Rose was about to thank him for his kindness when he added, "Even if I did happen to see you soaking wet, half-clothed in your undergarments."

"What's that about seeing Rose in her undergarments?" Philip asked as he came into the room.

Rose scowled at Theo. "You're the worst," she hissed, angry at him all over again. If he was getting back at her for her earlier remarks, he could not have done a better job, she thought bitterly.

Philip looked surprised. "So something actually happened? What's the story?" he asked. "Tell me."

"No," Rose snapped. "It's none of your concern."

"Come on, Rose—"

"No." She huffed and then stormed toward the door. "Now that the Magdust has been taken care of, let's go say our final goodbyes to your brother, Philip. If we want to get to Einish sooner rather than later, we better get going."

She didn't wait around for their reactions; she felt their lingering stares as she headed out of the room and down the hall.

Rose briefly glanced back at the blank wall, where Queen Lucia's tapestry had hung only moments before. The brocade of the Queen's portrait was gone, but she still felt the shadow of Lucia's soft and condemning judgment as she made her way out of the palace.

ONCE UPON A PRINCESS

8

"So," Philip goaded as he galloped up next to her, "Tell me about what happened."

"No." Rose gripped her horse's bridle in her hands, glad to be riding again, even if it was as much a pain on her bottom as walking was on her feet. She prepared herself for the worst; they had already been on the road for a full day, and Philip had tried several different times to get her to explain Theo's remarks about seeing her in her undergarments.

"Do you want me to get the details out of him?" Philip asked.

"No!" Rose glared at him. "Stop. I'm not talking about it, he's not going to talk about it, and you need to stop worrying about it."

"You *do* want to talk about it, though," Philip said with a teasing laugh. "I can tell by the look on your face."

"What look?"

"The one that says you have something on your mind, and you're more than cross about it. Come on, Rose, tell me. You might feel better. After all, I'm your babysitter, remember?"

"Is that actually the word Isra used?" Rose shook the sweat out of her eyes, taking the moment to glance over their caravan.

"Well, it was the one you used."

Mary was riding with Sophia and Ethan, jumping from one horse to another as they talked about the history of the Magdust trade. Theo was right behind them, probably lost in some prayer or some other deep kind of thoughts. The guards, led by Captain Locke, were at the rear, with Roderick's ruddy beard served as a marker, one Rose could

ONCE UPON A PRINCESS

easily use to see the end of her traveling company. Beside her, Philip took the lead in guiding them to his home.

Rose turned back to Philip. "Did she use it too?"

"No," he said. "But Isra did make me promise to see to your care. This would include discussing what troubles you."

Rose rolled her eyes. Her sister, not even two years younger than her, had an insurmountable amount of charm. It was not hard for Rose to see that Philip had fallen into Isra's close counsel. If the situation was any different, and if Philip were more ruthless, Rose knew she might have suspected Philip of using Isra to gain her trust.

Maybe he would even use my sister to secure an offer of marriage from me, Rose thought, momentarily cynical.

But she doubted that he would do that. He had been her friend, and that was all. She respected him and she admired him, but that was all. Philip was her friend.

"I'd rather talk about the Magdust trade here in the Einish forest," Rose finally told him. "Did Derick give you any new information since he discussed it with us that night at dinner?"

"No," Philip said. "In all fairness, he was more concerned with consoling Juliette after this morning to give me any last minute details."

"I don't understand her reaction to burning the tapestry," Rose admitted.

"I know that there are some concerns over destroying artifacts that are embedded with magic. Like you said, it is more superstition than truth. But where children are concerned, including the future ruler of Einish and Crystal Lake, mothers worry about their children quite desperately."

"But Juliette had told me before that she didn't think the tapestry was magic, as some people have maintained."

ONCE UPON A PRINCESS

"I don't see her reactions as that unusual. People are more likely to believe in bad luck than good luck." Philip straightened in his saddle, taking them down the left side of a split trail.

Rose shrugged. "I guess so. I'm sure my mother would agree with you."

Philip nodded and said nothing. They both knew that Rose's mother had faced the terrifying reality of Rose's curse.

Rose had to wonder if Philip pitied her, because his hazel eyes seemed sad when he looked back at her.

Maybe that is why he wants to know so much about what happened with Theo, Rose thought. He wanted to distract her with one set of problems while they faced another.

Before she could tell Philip not to waste his time worrying about her, Mary appeared at her side.

"We're about to go through the Crystal Lake's Wandering Caverns," she said. "This is where a lot of the trade activity has been rumored to take place."

"Stay with me," Rose told her. "I don't want anything happening to you. I can protect you better with Queen Lucia's sword if something goes wrong."

Mary nodded. "Thank you, Rose," she said, as she climbed into the hood of Rose's cloak. "I'm not surprised that this is the area where a lot trouble has been brewing. The pixies who lived here have retracted their protective spells."

"Pixies live here?" Rose asked.

"Pixies are able to withstand more extreme environments," Mary explained. "They are not as afraid of fire and volcanic activity as fairies are. They have made the caverns their home for many centuries."

"I didn't know you were afraid of volcanoes."

ONCE UPON A PRINCESS

"Not exactly. Iron and other minerals can harm us just as badly as more powerful magic or if we are injured enough by other weapons," Mary said. "It occurs naturally in volcanoes, which is why you are more likely to find fairies in the woods or by the sea. There are some fairies that have the power to stand up to the elements, but the majority of us cannot."

"Good to know," Rose whispered. "In the meantime, I'll keep you safe as we go the caverns."

"We likely won't have to worry," Mary said, even though she shivered. "But it's best not to tempt fate."

"That's true."

"The path leads through the caverns," Philip said. "We'll need to stick together while we're in there."

"There are still some enchantments in place from pixies," Mary warned. "So we need to watch out for them as much as we need to watch out for Magdust traders."

"Pixie magic, huh?" Philip grinned. "I'd forgotten about that. But then, this is the Wandering Caverns, isn't it?"

"What are you worried about?" Rose asked.

Mary tugged on her dress, nervous and distressed. "This place is one of the places where the pixies made the tunnels shift as you walk through them," she said. "It might be hard to navigate. I can't read pixie magic the way I can fairy magic."

Ethan came up beside Rose. "Are we really going to go in there?"

"Yes, Ethan," Philip answered. "Yes, we'll need to go into the caves. It's only for a little while."

"I don't have anything on the map for it," Ethan said, brandishing one of the many scrolls he carried in his pack.

"The forest has a trail," Philip replied. "The map just doesn't show that the main path leads through a cave. We're still going in the right direction."

"If it's enchanted I don't like the idea of going in," Ethan said. "Especially without a solid map of the place and rumors of the illegal traders."

"We'll just have to be careful about it," Rose said. She halted her mare and dismounted. "We've had similar situations before."

"Yeah, which is why I'm nervous about it," Ethan told her.

Rose pretended she didn't hear his remark. "Let's go ahead and partner up as we go into the cave. I'll lead."

"But what if you don't know which way to go?" Philip asked. "I should lead on this one, Rose."

"You can stay behind me," Rose told him. "And anyway, you just said that the main trail just went through the cavern. How hard could it be to follow the map while we're in the cave?"

Mary chimed in. "If Rose leads," she said, "I'll be able to light the way for everyone better. And Philip can be on the lookout for the traders, since he is more familiar with the cave."

"I'm not familiar with the cave. I'm only familiar with the path on the map," Philip insisted, but he was largely ignored as Rose and Ethan studied the map together.

"What's wrong?" Theo asked, coming up beside them.

"Nothing," Rose told him. "We're checking the map."

"We need to get in pairs," Ethan said. "Mary and Rose can go in front, since that will help with lighting. And Mary can sense some magic, so it might be good to have her out in front."

ONCE UPON A PRINCESS

Philip looked over at Theo. "We can follow them," he said. "You take one side, I'll take the other, and we'll be able to anticipate any trouble for Rose or for Ethan and Sophia."

"Why do I have to be paired up with Ethan?" Sophia asked. She had already dismounted from her horse, and she was tapping her foot impatiently.

"Just do it," Rose said. "If Ronan were here, I would protect him."

"Easy for you to say since he's not," Sophia accused, but she took her place beside Ethan without further protest.

"The guards will be able to protect the rear," Rose said. "Swords out and ready, but be sure before you strike. The pixies who might be in here have never been a threat to Rhone."

Rose was glad to see there were no objections as they headed in.

Once she was in the cave, Rose couldn't help slowing her steps. She found her eyes lingering on some of the crystalline rocks; they were colored and bright, cheery enough to dispel any forethought of danger.

"This place is beautiful," she whispered to Mary.

"The pixies are a studious lot," Mary said. "They value beauty above nature. I wouldn't be surprised to find several of these crystals have been curated specifically for their magic."

"The crystals hold magic in them?" Rose asked.

"Not all of them. But some of them, I'm sure. These are likely fake, to distract any marauders from finding the real treasure."

"Distraction," Rose murmured thoughtfully.

"Yes," Mary agreed.

They walked slowly through the cave. Time passed by at an unknowing pace, as they made their way deeper into the heart of the cave.

Eventually, Rose started to notice the hard ground beneath her boots. She blinked and realized she had to have been walking for at least an hour.

Philip further interrupted the spell that had fallen on them when he announced, "We're almost halfway through the cave."

Rose glanced back. "Everyone doing okay?"

A small round of murmurs, replying in the affirmative with their words and in the negative with their tone, answered her query. The roof of the cave began to curl back, opening up into a larger room, where light poked through the roof and fell on the shimmering crystal-lined walls. They glowed with a brilliant light. Rose faltered as she watched the twinkling colors blink at her. She called back to her crew. "We can take a break up here for a little while."

"That's a relief," Mary murmured, as she settled onto Rose's mare.

Rose giggled. "You seem rather comfy," she said.

"It does not mean I wouldn't like a break."

The rest of her friends and traveling companions agreed with more cheerfulness. The thought of water, food, and sitting down stopped several of their echoed grumblings.

Rose was glancing up at the ceiling as it opened up into an even larger cavern when she heard Philip call, "Watch out, Rose!"

"What? What is it?"

He never had to answer her. Rose saw a pair of big, burly shadows detach from the side of the cave and step out in front of her. "Traders!" Rose brandished her sword.

ONCE UPON A PRINCESS

A small band appeared behind the men, their own weapons held aloft and ready to strike.

Time to fight! Rose stepped forward.

Everything seemed to happen at once. The band of traders rushed at them, but Rose ducked and rolled, sending some of them falling fast. Theo and Philip teamed up to take down several of the men surrounding Rose, while Sophia, Ethan, and the rest of the guards alternatively protected the supplies and attacked the traders who came too close to their camp.

Rose heard her horse jitter nervously, and she hurried to calm her. Before she could tighten her grip on her bridle, the horse reared and headed off, further into the cave, while Mary screamed in fear.

"Mary!" Rose cried, watching as her fairy clung to the horse's mane.

"Go get her, Rose," Theo yelled, charging toward the men. He pushed Rose forward, sending her running. "We can cover for you."

"But—"

"Just go, Rose," Philip called out. He blocked another opponent, fighting with a new bandit who appeared behind them.

Rose sighed as her horse neighed again, the terror in the beast's cry echoing back into the atrium. "I'll be back as soon as I can!" Rose turned and headed after her horse.

It didn't take her long to catch up with the wayward horse; she caught up with them to find Mary had cast a spell on the horse, rendering the horse motionless.

"Mary!" Rose called. "I'm glad you're safe."

"I forgot I can do magic," Mary admitted sheepishly. "I know, I know. But I was taken off guard when she started running."

Rose gave her a nervous laugh. "I understand. I'm just glad you're okay. You can unfreeze her now."

As the mare became animated once more, Rose's hands tightened around the reins. The horse skittered around fretfully, still in mid-motion. Rose fought to keep her footing, while Mary continued to cling onto the horse tightly.

As Rose managed to stop her frightened mare, she noticed the fighting behind her had gone quiet.

Rose turned around and saw she was suddenly alone with Mary and her horse. She ran back in the direction she had come, only to find the blackened walls of the cavern wall had closed in on her.

"Rose," Mary said. "We must have stepped into a trap." She jumped from the mare's back into the hood of Rose's cloak.

"We need to step out of it then," Rose said, circling the small, circular cave. "Stay down in case this was a trap set by the Magdust traders."

A familiar voice spoke out of the shadows. "I wouldn't worry about the Magdust traders. Your friends are fighting them as we speak. They're winning, too, which is really no surprise. Not after the Eastern Warlords you battled two years ago."

Rose gasped, hurriedly raising her sword into a fighting position as Magdalina's bright face appeared out of the darkness.

Rose's hands held fast to her hilt, and she was determined to fight the ruler of the fairies who had cursed her.

This is it! I can be free, if I can defeat her.

"What are you doing here, Magdalina?" Rose asked. "Have you come to punish the traders?"

ONCE UPON A PRINCESS

"Why, no," Magdalina said. "The fairyfolk have largely rejected me as a member of their community, even though I am their leader. It doesn't actually bother me if they are killed. But I thought that it would be a good reason to have you come this way."

Rose faltered only slightly. "Why did you want us to come here, if not to punish the traders?"

"Well, your friends are taking care of them for me now," Magdalina said. "Just take a look, if you want."

A white hand wafted gracefully out of the darkness, and pointed to the wall to Rose's side. Rose glanced over to see the rock turn transparent. She watched as several bandits attacked her friends. She could hear their shouts and the clash of their swords against the enemy's blades.

She could only allow it a second of her time before she turned her full attention back to Magdalina. To her credit, Magdalina had not moved, so far as Rose could see. Her eyes adjusted to the dark, and she thought she could make out the edges of Magdalina's black robes and the high atora on her head. Her magical staff appeared in her hands as she began to walk toward Rose.

Rose saw the small gleam of her sword's ruby. The dragon's blood was reacting to Magdalina's presence.

Rose took a strong step forward, her sword ready to strike. She let it swipe down hard, but the second before it touched her, Magdalina disappeared.

"Come out and fight," Rose called. "You coward!"

"I hardly call being smart enough to avoid death being a coward."

"You dodge battles and place curses on innocent children," Rose scoffed. "I'd say that's pretty cowardly. You punished me when I was just a baby. I didn't do anything to you."

ONCE UPON A PRINCESS

"I know."

Rose gritted her teeth together. "How is that not being a coward?"

"I told you before, I was punishing your father," Magdalina said.

"Why?" Rose blurted out, as she dropped her sword ever so slightly. She hoped Magdalina would see it as exhaustion. Beside her, she could still see through the rock wall, where Philip, Theo, and the guards were leading the attack against a large band of men.

She knew she had to defeat Magdalina, and the quicker she was able to take care of her, the sooner she could join her friends.

"Even if you cursed me to punish my father, you know I have a right to fight you for what you've done."

"I agree. Still, I'd rather not die," Magdalina said. "I know you have acquired the dragon's blood. No easy feat, and you are so young and naïve besides. You are a formidable opponent. But I don't want to fight you."

"Then remove the curse from me!" Rose cried, lunging out with her sword once more, searching for any target to strike. Her sword scrapped into the other side of the cave.

Magdalina appeared behind her. "I might not want to fight you, but I have something else I wish to discuss with you. I have given this a great deal of thought," she said. "So much so that I have traveled a great distance to get here. I have decided to offer you a deal."

Rose stopped moving, shocked. Her grip on her sword went limp, and immediately she felt Mary's small hands grabbing onto her cloak's collar, as if to remind her to keep her guard strong.

ONCE UPON A PRINCESS

Rose adjusted her stance and tightened her grip. "What kind of deal?"

Magdalina's red lips parted as she smiled. "Do you want to know what your father did to me, that I placed such a curse on you?"

"I thought we were making a deal," Rose huffed.

"We are. I want to make the same deal with you that I made with your father."

Rose had a hard time keeping her fighting stance strong. "What was the deal?" she finally asked, standing up straight once more. She decided that she still had plenty of time to protect herself from a possible attack. .

She kept her fingers tight against the hilt of her sword as she asked once more, "What was the deal?"

"You know enough about Rhone's history to know that my mother was supposed to be the nation's first queen," Magdalina said. "When Benedict betrayed her and sealed her away, he eventually married another, a lady who was already a queen in her own land, as small as it was. Together, their rule made up the present-day borders of the kingdom."

"So what?" Rose asked.

"So," Magdalina said, "I could have been queen myself, once. I am Lucia's daughter, after all."

Rose frowned. She doubted that would have worked, considering Benedict had been the first king. He would have wanted his own offspring to rule, not Lucia's other children.

"Since then, the fairyfolk have harbored a great deal of mistrust of the crown. Occasionally, they would try to work together. Your little friend there is proof that some within the fairy community have managed to ingratiate themselves to the monarchy."

ONCE UPON A PRINCESS

Rose raised her sword, protecting Mary from Magdalina's gaze.

"I am already going to do what I can to get rid of the Magdust trade, if that was the deal," Rose said.

The instant she heard herself say the words, she knew that was not the deal Magdalina was talking about. Magdalina had just admitted moments before that she didn't care if the fairies were killed. They had rejected her, and only served her out of fear of her power or out of hatred for Rhone's rulers.

"They could have had their own ruler on the throne," Magdalina said. "So when your father came to me, I promised to give him what he wanted, in exchange for the promise that his firstborn would marry a fairy of my choice."

"What did my father want?" Rose asked, not certain she wanted to hear.

"A child. What else?" Magdalina laughed. "He desperately wanted children. He is getting old, haven't you noticed? He was married to Leea for many years before they had you and your half-siblings."

"The King told me that he'd received word from a prophet of the church that I was going to be born and I would save the crown," Rose said, feeling foolish for even saying it.

Magdalina waved her arm dismissively. "So?" she said. "If that's true, it still does not make a difference. I don't care if you save the crown. In fact, I hope you do."

She took another step toward Rose. "Here is my deal: I want you to marry my son, and make him King of Rhone."

"What?" Rose tasted the bile at the thought. "Never. That's a terrible deal. And it's annoying. Why are so many people so concerned about me getting married? Haven't I proven that I'm more than some marriage prize?"

ONCE UPON A PRINCESS

"You should consider it an honor," Magdalina said. "Men might be seen as the great conquerors of the world, but look at all the destruction they leave in their wake. Men destroy things, men shape things. But they cannot create new life. Only a woman has the power to create life, to create a new path for an old world to walk."

Rose felt her mouth drop open, unsure of her complete reaction. Magdalina had a point. "It still seems unfair."

"Oh, do stop worrying so much about what is unfair with this world," Magdalina muttered. "Life isn't fair, Princess, and you and I are prime examples. But the fact remains, if you want me to remove the curse I placed on you, I will, but only if you agree to marry my son, Everon, and make him the next ruler of Rhone. Whole civilizations depend on their women, and you have the chance to end the decades of distrust between my family and my subjects."

Pure rage ate at Rose's insides.

"So there you have it. All you have to do is marry my son, and I will free you from my curse, even at the cost of my own life."

Rose glanced down as Magdalina held up her wrist. She said before she had put a blood seal on the spell, Rose recalled.

Rose turned her attention back to her sword.

As if she knew what Rose was thinking, Magdalina laughed. "Please. You won't kill me. All I have to do is avoid you."

"You can't avoid me forever!" Rose yelled back.

"I don't have to avoid you forever," Magdalina said. "I only have to wait until your eighteenth birthday. It's less than a year away now, isn't it? How much longer do I have to wait? Only about five months, right?"

Rose said nothing at her taunting; she only took another step forward, securing the hilt of her sword in both hands.

"Maybe as you get closer to the date, you'll reconsider my offer. I'll give you until then for you to decide. That seems fair, doesn't it? I should give you everything up until the moment when you have to choose between marriage to my son and fateful sleep." Magdalina's voice was smooth with confidence and power. Her elegance made Rose feel even more helpless when it came to her fate.

"I'll never succumb to the curse," Rose declared. "I'll never choose either. Never!"

"We will see," Magdalina replied, before she disappeared in a ball of greenish flames. A flurry of stormy wind blew out from the center of her power, pushing Rose back up against her horse.

They were once more alone; Rose could hear her friends fighting in the distance once more.

"Rose," Mary gasped. "Are you alright?"

Rose felt her body shake, as she struggled to maintain her posture. Her legs felt weak. "I'm fine," she lied, trying to steady herself.

"I'm here for you," Mary whispered.

"I wish it were so easy," Rose said, her voice cracking. She put a hand to her throat, forcing herself not to cry, no matter how angry or sad she was.

Mary's tiny caress of her hair made her feel better as she slumped against the floor. "How do we get out of here?" Rose asked. "We have to go and help the others."

"I can try a spell," Mary offered. "I wasn't able to work my magic while I was so close to Magdalina. She is much more powerful than I am."

"I was hoping so much, that I would be able to defeat her."

ONCE UPON A PRINCESS

"I know." Mary wrapped her arms around Rose's wrist. "She has always been a formidable opponent. We can learn from this."

"I already have," Rose assured her. "Dragon's blood won't be enough to kill her. I'll need help fighting her, too."

Mary only nodded.

A few moments passed, as Rose rested and tried to regain her focus. She eventually stood up and went back to her horse.

"Rose?" Mary whispered.

"What is it?"

"What do you think of her deal?" Mary asked. "Do you think you will accept it?"

"I might be cursed to sleep forever after I turn eighteen," Rose said, "but it would still be better than being married to Magdalina's son. Theo wants his own revenge against Everon, too, don't forget."

"You said you'd never choose to let your curse be fulfilled," Mary pointed out.

"And I never will," Rose said. "I'm going to defeat her, no matter what, Mary. I have to."

Mary patted her shoulder reassuringly. "Maybe her deal is still something we can work with."

Rose shook her head. "I'm not even going to consider it," she said. "I don't want you to tell anyone what she told me."

"But, Rose, we might—"

"No." Rose shook her head. "No, Mary. Do not tell anyone about this. Especially Theo. Do you hear me?"

"But it's your life."

"And it would be my life that would be ruined," Rose argued. She sighed. "You know what my greatest fear was,

Mary? The one I confronted when I battled the dragon for his blood?"

Mary was silent.

"I want a family. My own family, with my own husband and my own children," Rose said. "Children, who know they are loved and treasured. I want to rule Rhone one day and I will never forgive myself if I cannot free myself from my curse. The idea that I will never be loved, the idea that no one will be able to marry me and start a family with me—it's too much to bear. It's too hard to even admit to myself!"

"But Rose...."

"The very idea that I would marry a fairy like Everon, who is little more than Magdalina's glorified bodyguard or her main stooge, is not only sickening, it is unforgivably vile." Rose shook her head. "I guess at least, if my curse is fulfilled, Isra will be able to inherit the throne."

Another realization struck her, and left her feeling dazed. *Isra ... my half-sister, from what Magdalina just told me.*

"Mary, what did Magdalina mean when she said that Isra and Ronan were my half-siblings?" Rose asked. "They will still be able to inherit the throne, won't they?"

Mary shook her head. "I don't know, Rose. I don't know."

"Was she telling the truth?"

"I don't know," Mary insisted. "That's something we will have to ask your mother when we get back to Rhone."

"Well, let's round up these Magdust traders," Rose said, "and then get back on the road. If our answers are in Rhone, I want to get there as quickly as I can."

9

"How are you doing?" Philip asked Theo, giving him a grin as he lowered his sword, finishing off his adversaries. "I've taken care of these three."

Theo watched as Philip lunged his sword forward, just barely missing the large man who had stepped out and blocked his path moments earlier. "Good shot," he said, as he clashed with another trader.

Theo shuffled low and managed to elbow his opponent in the gut, sending him to the ground, knocked out. "I've got two of them knocked out now," Theo replied.

"Where's the leader?"

"Ethan and Sophia are working on him." Theo nodded toward the pair of siblings as Sophia climbed on his back and Ethan punched him in his gut.

"There are a couple of younger traders that ran away down the tunnel," Philip said.

"You want us to follow them?"

"Not now," Philip said as he shook his head. "If they really were younger, there's little chance they are the ringleaders."

"Where's Rose?" Theo glanced around. "I don't see her."

Roderick came barreling through, helping Sophia and Ethan finish off the last attacker. "She ran ahead after her horse to get Mary," he said. "And I haven't seen her since."

Theo glanced over at their attackers. Bruises were beginning to form on their faces, and many of them looked well beaten. "Captain," he called. "Watch over these traders. Bind them up and take them back out of the cave. King Derick's men should be able to come and gather them."

"What are we going to do?" Ethan asked.

"Find Rose." Theo wiped the sweat off his face, hiding his concern.

"I'm here," Rose called.

Together, all of them turned around to look at her. Mary was on her shoulder, her wings giving off a soft bubble of growing light.

He nearly ran to her in relief. But he stopped the moment he saw her face. "What's wrong?"

Sophia came up to her, pushing past Theo, and gave her a hug. "Rose," she said. "What happened?"

"I got lost."

"I saw you disappear," Roderick said. "Was it the Wandering Caverns?"

"Must've been," Rose said, brushing off their concerns in an easy tone. "I apologize if I've worried you."

Theo saw her wring her hands, and he was only slightly comforted when she reached for the rosary beads he knew she wore under her sleeve. He had given her his rosary beads when they had returned to Rhone for her seventeenth birthday. While Theo doubted she used them for prayer, he took comfort in knowing that she carried them with her.

As the others began to talk with her, Theo noticed the expression Mary wore on her face. The small fairy was silent as her wings fluttered, and she took off from Rose's shoulder.

"Tell me about the attack," Rose said. "Did we get everyone?"

"Not everyone," Philip told her. "But the ones who ran away were the smart ones. They seemed young. I think Derick's forces can take over from this point. They were not too far behind us when we left."

"You managed to fight off a group of Magdust traders," Rose said. "There might be more. We should continue onward and keep looking."

"True," Philip said. "We didn't see any sign of Magdalina, anyway. It's possible we could still see her."

In the soft, colorful light of the cavern's atrium, Theo saw Rose's face pale. He was willing to bet that Rose was not telling them the whole story. He watched her as she began asking Philip and Ethan more questions, while Sophia tended to the horses, and Roderick and the other guards were binding up their newly-bound prisoners, preparing to take them out of the caverns.

Something is not right, Theo thought.

"Send Lannister back to the King," Rose said. "He's the lightest man we have. He'll be able to ride to the palace quickly. Captain, you and Roderick can stay with the men until they are arrested."

"Yes, my lady," Captain Locke replied. He bowed his head. "But please be careful as you make your way through the rest of the countryside. Bandits and traders are often reluctant allies in places such as this."

"I will be careful, Captain. You do the same."

Theo watched as the captain nodded and set out to do his assigned work. The older man never had a problem following Rose's orders, he thought. It was gratifying to know he was as reliable as he was.

As soon as the captain took his leave, while the others were getting themselves together, Theo took Rose's arm. "You're lying," he told her softly.

"And you're bothering me," Rose snapped.

"Something happened while you were gone. Tell me."

"You're paranoid." Rose tugged her arm free and stomped away from him. "And I have work to do."

"Rose."

She shook her head. "We have to get to Einish. We can still make it to O'Lin before too long if we hurry."

He sighed.

"Come on, Theo," Rose said. "Isra is waiting for us. I'm sure you'd love to see her."

"What's that supposed to mean?" Theo asked, surprised by her accusing tone.

Rose glanced over her shoulder at him, frowning. "Never mind. Now, let's go."

"I've never accused you of being ugly before, Rose," Theo said. "And no one in his right mind would. But this is coming awfully close."

"Well, it's good that I'm tired of hearing how beautiful I am, then," Rose retorted.

Theo said nothing else. He looked at Mary, who gave him a sympathetic look. He felt like following Rose, fighting with her until she admitted what it was she was keeping from him. But he knew it would only cause his relationship with Rose to be further fractured in the end.

Sophia called out to him from further down the trail.

"Theo?" Sophia called. "Can you help me?"

"What is it?" he asked, coming over beside her.

"This." Sophia held up a small object in her hands. It took Theo a moment to realize it was a pixie.

He had never seen a pixie before in his life, outside of drawings. He knew the pixies were a diverse race, with different languages and different physical traits. The one Sophia carried had a twiggish face, twisted and hard, almost as if he had grown out of a tree like a branch. The pixie's

ONCE UPON A PRINCESS

large eyes were closed and his body was limp as Theo looked him over.

"Is he … okay?" Theo asked softly.

"I don't know," Sophia said. "I was hoping you could check."

Theo nodded and began looking for any sign of a pulse, hoping he would find any sign of life. The instant his finger touched the creature's neck, he felt a small amount of breath inhaling and exhaling from the body. It wasn't a pulse, he thought, but it was enough for him. "He's alive."

"Is he hurt?"

"Likely. We better tend to him. Are there anymore pixies around that you've seen?"

"No." Sophia shook her head. "Not yet, anyway. Ethan and I saw him crawl out of one of the caverns while we were fighting. I think he was hit with something while we were distracted with the traders. Ethan went down the side path some, to check for more."

"I'll go and get Ethan. He shouldn't wander off on his own. In the meantime, take extra good care of him, then," Theo instructed, pointing to the pixie in her hands. "We'll need to see if he can answer some questions for us."

"What if he was working with the Magdust traders?" Sophia still cuddled the small creature like a baby, but Theo knew for all her compassion, she had a right to question the pixie's motives.

"Go and get Mary," Theo said, brightening at the idea. A distraction for Mary could mean that he would get some time to see if Rose would tell him what happened while he had been fighting off the traders with the others. And, he added, trying to justify it, Mary would be able to make sure that the pixie did not cause them any trouble. "See if she can help

ONCE UPON A PRINCESS

with him. She might be able to use some of her healing magic."

Sophia nodded and hurried off, while Theo went off in search of Ethan.

He walked into the side tunnel and felt a strong presence of magic. Theo's fingertips brushed against the wall, and he felt the tingle of magic.

Magdust.

"Ethan," he called. "Ethan, come back this way." A sense of foreboding came over him.

He breathed a sigh of relief when he saw his young companion appear only a few yards ahead of him.

"Theo," Ethan said. "You won't believe what I found here."

"I don't know about that," Theo said as he went over to stand next to Ethan.

There was a small crevice in the rock. Glancing through it, Theo saw a blueish glow. He looked through it and immediately felt a rush of sorrow.

The cave reeked of painful death. Theo was already praying for peace as he pushed through the small opening in the rock, and stepped into the cave opening.

Blue light washed over him instantly. It felt cool on his skin, and even through his armor, he could tell some time had passed since the death of the fairies.

Ethan stepped in behind him. "What is this?" he asked. "I don't like it."

"It's a death chamber," Theo told him. "The blue residue you see is from fairy blood."

"Fairies? Not pixies?"

Theo nodded. He looked around, careful to watch his step. He saw the old, dusty footsteps in the rocky dirt. "The traders must have brought them here after they captured them." He saw a cage in the corner, smashed in. He examined it closely.

Fairies were not supposed to like iron, he knew; that was part of the reason that almost all the steel used in making swords contained iron. The cage gleamed dark silver against the blueish glow.

"Theo, look."

At Ethan's startled gasp, Theo came over to stand beside Ethan.

"It's a spinning wheel," he said. "To make thread."

"Well, we have to keep Rose away from here for sure now," Ethan joked, his voice humorless. "The spindle is still on it."

"They were using the Magdust," Theo said examining the spinning wheel more closely. "Spinning it right into the yarn."

"Why?" Ethan asked. "Why not just consume it?"

"I don't know," Theo replied. "It's probably a mystery to people like you and me because we would never do this sort of thing in the first place. But that's a good question."

His thoughts went back to his own upbringing, where his mother had hung that tapestry in his house. Thad had mentioned that their mother might have found a way to force his father's hand in marriage, but things were starting to wear off by the time they had to leave their home. Was she able to use the Magdust in the tapestry to convince her father to stay? "Maybe it is easier to use by a human when it comes to granting wishes for things other than power."

Ethan did not seem to hear his speculation. "We should go back," he said. "Before someone gets worried about us."

Theo nodded slowly. "I'll leave a message for King Derick with Captain Locke," he said. "So he knows about this place."

The two of them made their way back to the main trail. Ethan was quiet and sober, while Theo was contemplative. His heart ached for the fairies and their losses. How was it that humans were able to capture and kill them so easily? Theo wondered. It did not seem like the men they had fought were that powerful. They were missing something. But what? Mary could have told them easily if it was something she knew.

Theo knew the church's teachings on the fallen state of human beings and the rest of the world. It was not hard to imagine why people would do something as terrible, something that required the reality of the scene he had just left. Desire, power, magic … all of it held an allure to the fallen soul, and some souls could not help but search after such things.

"There you are."

Rose's voice might have been edged with impatience, but it still carried the same graceful song. Theo couldn't stop himself from smiling at her, even if it made her frown even more.

"Ethan," Rose said, "you shouldn't have gone off on your own. You're lucky we didn't end up losing you."

"Sorry," he said. "I was just doing a quick check for other pixies. How is the one Sophia and I found earlier?"

"Still unconscious," Rose said. "We'll have to see about getting him help once we arrive in Einish."

"I'll rig up a pallet for him," Ethan offered.

"Sophia said she could carry him. Mary's watching with her."

Ethan rolled his eyes. "Trust Sophia to find a way to have all the fun."

ONCE UPON A PRINCESS

Theo came up beside Rose as Ethan sauntered back over toward his horse.

"I need to leave some notes for the King," Theo told Rose. "There's a cave back there with a multitude of dead fairies inside."

Rose's eyes watered. "So we were too late."

"Considerably," Theo agreed sadly. "But the cave has been in use for some time."

"Did you find anything else?" Rose asked. "No more guards or traders or anything else?"

Theo shook his head, deciding not to mention the spinning wheel. "There might be more throughout the caverns," he said. "Tucked off to the side."

"Or just hid with other magic," Rose murmured. "What do you think? What should we do?"

"We have removed one band of Magdust traders," Theo said. "Let's keep an eye out for more, and take care of them if we see it."

"And if we don't find any more?"

"There's no need to go looking for more trouble, Rose," Theo replied with a smirk. "We always find enough of it on our own."

"So we should just keep going through the cave?"

"I think we can head out for Einish without worry. Didn't the king say he was going to send some of his own men to take care of this matter anyway?"

"Yes, he did."

"Then he will. So we can move onward." It was so tempting to tug on a lock of her hair as he had done many times before. It was something that always seemed to cheer her up. But Theo knew Rose was still upset with him, and it

ONCE UPON A PRINCESS

would be better if he kept their conversation focused on business. "Philip needs to get to his betrothed, after all."

Rose gave him the smallest hint of a smile. "You're right," she said. "Thank you."

Her hand reached out and gripped his for a brief moment. Theo did not allow himself to be happy over it; he knew Rose was only allowing them to reestablish their normal boundaries.

And if there was one thing he knew, it was that he did not want their normal relationship any longer. He wanted more.

ONCE UPON A PRINCESS

10

The first glimpse of Einish's grand palace in their port city was nothing short of breathtaking.

Literally breathtaking, Rose thought, as she finally came to the top of the mountain trail. Over the last day, from climbing out of the Wandering Caverns to climbing up a mountain, she was already tired. But the high mountain air seemed to slow her breathing.

She was not the only one who suffered from the high altitudes. The terrain had been hard on her horse, so she had dismounted several hours before, leading her mare and her company on foot. With the others following her example, their pace had slowed, but they were still making good time.

The view of the city, lingering in the distance, brightened her mood. "We're almost there," she called back. "I can see it from here."

Philip came up beside her, his horse nearly bumping into hers as he gazed at his home. "It'll be only another hour," he said. "The mountains around this part of the city are the last real challenge, and now that we're at the top, it's all downhill from now on."

Rose grinned. "And then we'll see Isra and my brother again."

"Oh, yes, I'd forgotten your brother will be there." Philip gave her an amused look. "I shouldn't have to worry about him, right?"

"He's here as your guest," Rose said. "I'm sure he will be the one who is worried."

"Is he the sort who gets overprotective of his sisters?" Philip asked. "Do you think he's anxious to meet me? I know

ONCE UPON A PRINCESS

I wasn't able to meet him when we were back in Rhone for your birthday."

"I think he'll only be worried for when you come," Rose said, "because it will be harder to get everything that he wants."

Philip laughed. "Oh, I get it. He's probably making himself right at home then?"

"More than right," Rose assured him. "He's into his creature comforts, but he can be very charming. So your servants will be running around all night, but he will be running them around with a smile. Even your notorious mother I've heard so much about might have a hard time telling him no."

"My only hope in this matter is that I have you with me, isn't it?"

Rose grinned. "Well, that and that Isra is there. But she might let him do what he wants, under the pretext of keeping up appearances."

"Well, then let's hope I have a full castle and staff to get back to."

"You mean your mother wouldn't order them to stay?"

"True enough." Philip kept in step with Rose as they continued on the path. He asked her more questions about Ronan and even some more about Isra, and that was when Rose confronted him.

"Why do you want to know so much about them so badly?" she asked. "You've met Isra, and you seem to know her better than I do some days. Ronan is not much like either of us, but there's no reason to think he wouldn't come to like you. You are a very likeable person."

ONCE UPON A PRINCESS

"Thank you," Philip said. He smiled, and despite his thick beard, Rose was able to see the small dimple at the side of his cheek. "I'm glad you find me likable."

"Of course. We have always been able to get along."

"Not always. You didn't like me much after I beat you in the joust back in Rhone."

Rose rolled her eyes. "You should know by now I'm used to winning. I haven't learned to be a good loser, and if that's the one thing I'm never going to learn, I'm okay with that."

Philip laughed. "Well, for what it counts, the feeling is mutual. I think you're very likable, too."

Rose felt her face turn red with embarrassment. "I do like you," she said, "and I hope you know I consider us friends."

"Of course." He gave her a wink. "The best of friends."

"Well, sort of. I don't think as a future monarch we can have a lot of friends like our subjects can, but—"

"You know I don't mean that," Philip said. He took her free hand in his. "You know I mean that we are more than just friends."

"What?" Rose stepped back. "No, we're not."

"Come on, Rose," Philip said. "We're going to be a part of each other's lives for a long time. You might as well just admit what's in your heart."

"What's in my heart?" Rose repeated.

"We're going to be a big, happy family one day."

Rose felt her embarrassment transform into fear. "No, we're not."

"Why not?" Philip asked. "You just said that we were friends, and I know for a fact we are more than friends."

"If you were really my friend, you would stop prattling on as if we were going to get married one day."

"Well, aren't we?" Philip asked.

"No!"

"Why not?"

"Because I'm not in love with you!" Rose glared at him. "And despite what you might think, you're not in love with me, either."

"Why aren't you in love with me?" Philip asked, looking wounded. "Is there someone else?"

"No!" Rose asserted, as her cheeks turned hot.

Philip gave her a teasing smile. "I think there's someone else."

"No," Rose reiterated desperately. "No there's not, because he shouldn't love someone like me, and I won't let him."

As soon as the words left her mouth, and she heard herself say them, Rose stilled. Anger, with fear, with sadness—all of it unleashed inside of her, as she realized she had revealed herself. She ducked behind her horse's face as she continued walking, her steps suddenly much stiffer.

"Are you alright?"

"Please," she said, loud enough Philip could hear her, "don't talk to me about this anymore."

"It wasn't really that hard to admit, was it?" Philip asked gently. "I've known about it since we met in Rhone."

She glanced back over at Philip, who was looking at her with a kind patience.

"Rose," he said, "you know that there is a tradition in Rhone that a suitor must complete an assigned task to grant the right to marry into the crown's family, right?"

Rose slowly nodded. "I hope you don't think that coming with me to the Serpent's Garden counts as a task," she said. "The ruler is the one who is supposed to assign the task in question."

ONCE UPON A PRINCESS

"Well, Isra was the one who assured me that the task she gave me would count."

Rose narrowed her eyes at him suspiciously. "What makes you think I would give you my hand in marriage just because you came along with me and the rest of my crew? Isra can say what she pleases, but I won't consent to marry you for embarking on this task."

"I wasn't really concerned about your hand," Philip said.

"But why were you just—"

"My assigned task wasn't specifically to come along with you, even though I ended up doing so," Philip said. "I appreciated that Isra was happy to let me come, because I did want to have grand adventures on my own. It was hard to do that, you know, until my brother got married. When you meet my mother, I think you'll find out why."

"So you didn't want to marry me," Rose realized. "But why did you just do all that right now? With all the 'we are more than friends' speech, and how we're going to be 'one big, happy family' one day?"

"Why do you think, Rose?" Philip asked. "It's the same reason I've been provoking you and Theo since we left Rhone. My task was to get you to admit you were in love with him."

"What?" Rose stopped short in her tracks. Immediately, she glanced around to make sure that they were still far enough ahead of the others that they couldn't hear her panicked shrieking.

Philip nudged her along. "Come on, keep moving. This is just as awkward for me as it is for you. Theo's already looking like he's trying to find an excuse to get up here so he can cut in on my flirting. Of course, he never does, if he doesn't think you'll find his excuse believable."

Rose glanced back at Theo, only to see Philip was right. When Theo saw her look at him, he turned away, but not before she saw the frustration on his face.

"Next thing you know, he'll look for an excuse to throw me off the mountainside." Philip tugged on his horse's reins again. "I can't say I blame him. I'd probably do the same, if you were mine."

"I'm not his." Rose looked down her nose at Philip. "I don't belong to anyone."

"Well, he's certainly yours," Philip said. "I'd hate to think what he would do to me if he wasn't my friend, too."

"You're crazy," Rose said. "He knows, of all people, how I feel about love."

"And he is the one person, of all people, who is determined to get past the barriers you have in your heart."

Rose shook her head. "He won't."

"Well, I did get you to admit that you didn't have someone because you would never let him love you," Philip reminded her. "So there's that."

"Don't you see?" Rose asked. "I'm not going to marry anyone."

"Don't *you* see?" Philip countered. "If it wasn't for the curse, you would be free to do what your heart wants. And that includes admitting you love him."

"You said this was supposed to be awkward for you, too," Rose said, trying to ease out of the topic. "Tell me this. If you didn't come with me as your task, and if your task was in fact to get me to admit I was in love with … someone else … then why did you do it?"

"Why else?" Philip asked. "I'm in love with a princess of Rhone, indeed, Rose, even if it's not you, and I will happily set to accomplish what I can to make her happy."

"Isra." Rose rubbed her forehead. "Really? Didn't you *just* meet her what, nearly seven months ago? And weren't you only with her for *two days*? Who falls in love after only two days?"

"I can't explain it," Philip said. "I met her, and then … then everything just came together. We knew each other so well, and we'd only just met. It was like a dream."

"If it was a dream, how do you know it's real?" Rose retorted.

"That's how I know you've yet to let yourself fall," Philip said. "When it comes to love, you don't always know it's real outside how you feel. But sometimes you have to have faith in something before you see it. And then, all of sudden, you can see it."

"So you really do love her?"

"She stole my heart the first time we danced," Philip said. "Sometimes, when I have trouble sleeping, I relive that moment. I felt my heart slip out of my chest and fall right into her hands."

Rose briefly recalled how talented Philip was as a poet and, despite her concern, smiled. "And Isra loves you, too? So much that she sent you out on a special task to earn her hand?"

"Well, she was more like you about that," Philip admitted. "She told me about the tradition of the task, and told me if I wanted to prove myself true to her, she would give me a task to carry out."

"So she gave you the task of humiliating me," Rose muttered. "Nice."

"She loves you, Rose, for all she doesn't understand you." Philip reached out and patted Rose's shoulder. "I have no

ONCE UPON A PRINCESS

doubt that she wanted me to succeed, but it would also give me some time to prove myself worthy of her in other ways."

"Your letters." Rose shook her head again. "I thought you were pushing me to write to her more often just to annoy me and gain support from her. But you actually set out to please her."

"Yes. I want to make the engagement official."

"You might have to talk to King Stefanos about that," Rose said. "He's still the ruler of Rhone."

"It was your blessing I wanted," Philip said. "Despite all the trouble I have given you."

"Well, you have my blessing," Rose told him. "Really, you *are* my blessing. You had my respect early on. I think if you can earn that, you have a good chance of winning Isra's heart. She's the only one who should be free to give it to you. So if you are sure—"

"I am." There was no hesitation in Philip's voice. Rose felt the hard reality of jealousy, though more for Philip's certainty than for his constancy.

She smiled. "Well, if she is sure, I will sign the official engagement papers while I am here."

"Really?"

"Yes. But you will have to wait until she is older. She's only sixteen yet."

"I'm so grateful, Rose."

Rose laughed. "Don't look so surprised. I want someone who will be able to protect Isra from Magdalina and any other trouble, and someone who will love her more than anything else in the world. If what you say is true, and I have no reason to doubt you, then I should be fortunate you want to marry her."

ONCE UPON A PRINCESS

"Thank you, Rose." Philip reached out and kissed her hand. "You are a wonderful sister."

"Only if my wonderful sister is eager to make it so," Rose reminded him.

"You said it yourself; if I can earn your respect, I can win her heart." He glanced behind him. "What about you? Are you going to tell Theo?"

"We're talking about you right now," Rose said, determined to keep away from that topic. "After all, we're almost to the castle. You should have some kind of speech or poem ready for Isra when you see her. I'll be happy to help you with that."

"Come on, Rose."

"Come on, Philip." Rose smirked. "I'm not that terrible at poetry, and hearing you put all my sister's charms into stanzas might let me see just how much you know her, and just how much you love her."

"You're a tough opponent, Rose," Philip said. "I don't envy you. You have to fight yourself a lot, don't you?"

It was a light jab, but Rose felt the sting of truth inside of it. Rose frowned at him. "Stick to poetry for now, Philip. Consider that your first piece of advice from your new sister."

504

11

Theo watched as Rose and Philip chatted together in front of the castle as several grooms approached and began taking their baggage and their horses to the royal stables. He had watched them as they made their way down the mountain, and he had felt the pain of Rose's rejection as she turned away from him once more.

I should be used to it by now.

But, he added to himself, it at least looked like Rose was doing better than she was when they were in the cavern. She had not had an easy night, as they camped once they arrived at the base of the mountain. Earlier that morning, he had woken up to find her restless and distressed. But when he approached her, she had gone back to her pallet, immediately convinced she wanted to try to sleep more than she wanted to talk with him.

From where he was, he could see she was happy.

And he was happy for her.

Or so he told himself.

"Rose!"

Theo glanced up to see Isra, running down from the castle steps. She held her skirts high in one hand, and he could see her black hair was tumbling free from its pins as she waved hi.

"Hi, Isra!" Rose called.

"Isra!" Philip bellowed, cupping his hands around his mouth as he greeted her. "My belovéd!"

Theo watched, confused, as Philip ran out to meet Isra.

Ethan came up beside him, his eyes bright as he held onto his satchel. "Do you think Isra will want to listen to me play

505

ONCE UPON A PRINCESS

my harp tonight?" he asked. "I might have to tune it, but it shouldn't take me long to play a song or two for her."

"Probably not tonight," Theo said.

"Aw." Ethan pouted. "I was able to fix it up really nice at the other palace. And I figured Isra would be able to help me out with some of the more complicated chords. It's been a long time since Penelope taught me. I don't want to forget before I see her again."

"I'm sure you'll find some time to let Isra help you," Theo assured him. "But it's late enough as it is. The sun is going down, and Philip still has to meet with his mother. She's the one who is really in control of this castle. We'll need to be on her good side if we're going to be able to take care of our work while we're here."

"I know Isra and Philip are supposed to be engaged," Ethan said. "I didn't know there were other things we have to watch for."

"While we're here, I'd like to see about arranging a meeting with Ambassador Rolez," Theo said, forcing himself to stop watching Rose as she watched Philip catch Isra by the waist and circle her around.

He could not forget that he had a mission. They all had a mission. Even though they had fulfilled their promise to Derick, they still had to find Magdalina and Everon, and Theo knew the Magdust trade was somehow connected to everything. He needed more information, and the man who had been so insistent on the good fortune the tapestry would bring to Queen Juliette's children was a logical priority.

"Who's he?" Ethan asked.

"The man who gave that tapestry to Juliette," Theo replied. "I want to know where he got it, and if he knows anything else about it."

ONCE UPON A PRINCESS

"Because of the spinning wheel we found?" Ethan asked quietly.

"Partially. But I have other reasons as well." Theo did not want to elaborate on his family history to Ethan. Both Ethan and Sophia had enough experience of their own when it came to family concerns. They had been neglected and abused by their father, and ever since Rose and Theo had rescued them, Theo had tried to keep his own dark past from them. He was glad when Sophia called out to him.

"What is it?" he asked, coming up to her.

"The pixie," Sophia replied. "He's starting to wake up."

Theo came over to the small bundle strapped to Sophia's saddle. He watched as the large eyes of the pixie blinked open.

Instantly, the pert little face twisted into a painful, bitter scowl. "Who are you?" the creature demanded. "Where am I?" He sat up and grabbed at his left leg. "And why is my leg aching like the devil?"

Theo stepped up. "You were injured when we found you in the cavern in the forest of Einish. We have brought you to the city so we could see to your wounds."

"I am free?" The pixie's large eyes were suddenly very wet with emotion instead of pain.

"Free from what?" Sophia asked.

"Where is my master?" The pixie asked. "I need to find my master." He sank back into despair.

"We're not sure," Theo replied. "What is your master's name?"

"Master Mick," the pixie answered. He tried to sit up, but Sophia held him down. As he protested against her concern, Theo looked back over to see Rose was now talking with

ONCE UPON A PRINCESS

Philip and Isra. She was probably going over the story, he thought.

Mary came up beside him. "I can see if his master is alive," she said. "He's obviously too weak to use his magic, but I can check for it."

"Check for what?" Ethan asked.

"When a pixie has a master, there's a mark on his palm," Mary said. "You can see it with revealing magic."

"Let's see if he'll let you," Theo said. He faced the pixie. "What is your name?"

"Bachas," the creature replied. "I am a native of Crystal Lake. My master saved my life, and I was bound to him through a life debt."

"That's how it usually happens," Mary muttered. "You know that can be faked, right?"

Bachas blinked at Mary, before his face contorted with disgust. "You're a fairy," he spat. "Your kind was the reason I was in danger in the first place."

"Still, she has nothing to do with your personal situation. And she can see if you are still bound by your oath," Theo said. "Mary, check his palm."

"No!" Bachas twisted away from her. "I won't let a dirty fairy touch me."

Mary shot Theo a hard look. He glanced at Ethan and Sophia and gave them a quick signal. Together the three of them grabbed one of the pixie's small limbs.

"Go, Mary," Theo said, torn between feeling sympathetic for Bachas and angry at him, as the small creature kicked at his face relentlessly. "We got him."

"Stop twitching!" Mary shouted. She grabbed his hand and he cried out in pure, angry terror. A flash of light sparked,

ONCE UPON A PRINCESS

followed by a rush of energy. Mary backed up and grabbed her hand. "You stung me!"

Bachas grimaced. "Small reward for my trouble."

"Are you okay, Mary?" Ethan asked.

Sophia turned on Bachas. "You've got some nerve hurting our friend! If we hadn't taken care of you, you could have died."

"I wouldn't have died," Bachas insisted, but Theo was certain he saw a small amount of remorse at Sophia's chiding.

Or maybe fear, he thought. Bachas had to realize he was still too weak to get too far away if he tried to run. And with a fairy and weapons nearby, Theo had a feeling Bachas knew he could easily get in further trouble.

Mary fluttered up beside him. "I didn't see any seal," she said. "But if he's powerful enough to burn me, he'll be able to see it himself."

Bachas stuck his tongue out at her, but he did check his right hand. A moment later, he was struggling not to cry.

"So it's gone?" Sophia asked. "You're free?"

"Yes." Bachas blinked his large eyes up at her. "I am free now. My awful master is dead."

No one said anything for a long moment, with Bachas only letting his tears fall. "I can return to my family," he said happily, and then he stopped. "Assuming they are still alive."

"Can you tell us what happened to you?" Theo asked. "We have a few questions about what was going on in the caverns as well."

Bachas hesitated. "I don't want to help any fairies," he said. He added, "Or anyone who is working with them."

"We might be able to help you get back to your family," Theo said. "We have friends here. Someone can take you back. We can also get some medicine for you, to help you grow stronger. We can also provide supplies to you, if you need it. Believe me, we face a bigger foe than a fairy."

"Who is that?" Bachas snorted. "That wicked fairy ruler, Magdalina?"

"Yes."

Bachas stared at him for a long moment before he laughed. "Well, you're on the losing side," he said. "She's managed to hang onto her power for years, even after she was kicked out of the fairy realm by Oberan."

"The King of the Aragonian Fairies?" Mary asked.

"Who else? Stupid fairy." Bachas scowled at her.

"Hey," Mary snapped, "I don't know much about him for good reason. He's not *my* ruler!"

"Doesn't matter. If Magdalina was able to find a place to take refuge in your world, it's your own fault for letting her."

"We want to stop her," Theo said. "After all the help we've given you, by setting you free and offering to get you back home, won't you help us some? All we need are some answers."

"I'm tired, and my leg aches," Bachas said, yawning. "Maybe in the morning. If I'm alive. I don't see any reason to trust any of you."

"You can trust me," Theo said. "I was raised in the church and I know the demands of the priesthood."

"But you're not a real one," Bachas pointed out. "God's power won't protect you like it would protect a real priest."

"Priests are protected from your magic?" Ethan asked. "I didn't know that."

"There's a reason we stay away from the churches," Bachas said. "It's harder to make mischief there."

"We still protected you," Sophia said. "I carried you in my arms as we walked over the mountain. Ethan was the one

ONCE UPON A PRINCESS

who made up a sling for you so you would be comfortable when I got tired."

In the darkening light, Theo thought he saw Bachas' cheeks turn a dull shade of gray. Sophia was making him uncomfortable, he realized. Maybe the pixie had a soft spot for ladies.

"Fine." Bachas eventually gave up. "But I want to eat first."

Theo smiled. "I think we can arrange that. Let me go and speak to Isra."

"She is waiting for you, by the look of it," Ethan said. "She keeps looking over this way."

Theo craned his neck, looking over at where Philip and Isra were talking with Rose. He watched as Rose hugged her sister, obviously glad to see her safe.

As she held onto Rose, Isra caught his eye. She waved at him, beckoning him to come over.

"Well, I guess you're right, Ethan," Theo said. "I'm being summoned. Stay here and keep watch over Bachas. Make sure he doesn't try to hurt Mary or run away."

"I will," Ethan promised. He lowered his voice, "Will you ask Isra about letting me play the harp for her?"

"You have my word," Theo promised, before he made his way over toward Isra.

Rose's younger sister sometimes made him wonder what Rose might have been like if not for Magdalina's curse. She was smart and insightful, and she knew how to wield her wit as sharp as a weapon. She was also much more cheerful—or at least she was when she was around him.

He noticed that, as she stood next to Philip, she looked like she was having the time of her life.

"Theo!" she cheered. "I'm so glad to see you. I've saved all your letters since we last met."

ONCE UPON A PRINCESS

Rose rolled her eyes. "It wasn't that long ago, Isra."

"My life might as well have begun again, Rose," Isra told her in her most demure tones, while she leapt into Theo's arms. "It's nice to see you again, brother," she whispered into his ear. "I have missed you."

"It's nice to see you again, too," Theo said.

"I am really happy everyone is here," Isra told him. "I worry about you, you know."

Theo let her go, carefully setting her back down on her feet. "There's no need to do that."

Isra's kind eyes blinked up at him, the dying sunlight transforming the amber to gold. "Rose makes everything more difficult," she said, loudly enough to let Rose hear. "That's why I wanted you to write to me. So I could interrupt her monopoly on your time."

"Is that why?" Rose crossed her arms. "I thought it was just to annoy me and make me feel like someone else was trying to keep tabs on my every movement, just like they did when we were younger."

Isra gave her a brilliant smile before she turned back to Theo. "Come and walk with me," she said. In a lower voice, she added, "It'll make Rose upset."

Theo did not argue with Isra, but he did ask, "Why do you think it would be good to upset her?"

"So she will be less angry about the party Philip's mother is planning for us at the end of the week."

"Oh, I see." Theo smiled. "She won't like to hear that."

"No, she won't," Isra agreed. "I know she wants to get home quickly, but Philip's doing so much for our group of friends. I feel like we should try to make his mother happy. She is an older lady and suffers from the vapors a lot."

"A lot?"

ONCE UPON A PRINCESS

"Let's just put it like this. If I ever suffer from the vapors, please kindly don't take me seriously unless I am dying."

Theo chuckled. "So how many false alarms has there been since you arrived?"

"Plenty," Isra said through gritted teeth. "The Dowager Queen, Utopa, is quite dramatic."

"You think Rose will like her?"

"Tolerably."

"That's all?"

Isra shrugged. "That's all I need, right?"

Theo paused. "Are you actually going to go through with the wedding?" he asked. "I thought you were lying about it. You said you needed to confess some terrible things in your letter."

"I know. I think I forced Philip's hand," Isra said. "I mean, we talked about marriage when we first met—"

"What?" Theo's eyes widened. "Why?"

"Because. We just … fell in love." Isra blushed, but she held her ground as he stared at her. "Come on, Theo. I expect this sort of response from Rose, but not you."

"He didn't tell me."

"I told him not to." Isra tightened her grip on his arm. "I didn't want Rose to punish him or try to scare him off. And I thought it was prudent when he went off with you guys, because I thought it was a very small way I could help protect you. I had no idea I would be off on my own adventure, if you would even call this an adventure." She nodded toward the high castle towers before her.

"You don't think this is very adventurous?" Theo asked.

"No. Dealing with actual dragons seems infinitely more stimulating than dealing with my future mother-in-law and her love for etiquette. You would think she and Ms. Winston,

ONCE UPON A PRINCESS

my old governess, were long-lost sisters! They chitter-chatter together every day for tea and it is appalling to watch them. Especially when they are criticizing me, and thinking themselves the better for it."

"I've got to admit, I'm looking forward to meeting the Dowager," Theo said. "Between delaying Rose, throwing fits and throwing parties, and being compared to dragons, I'm curious to see her."

"Her fangs are probably not as visible," Isra warned. "You might regret your enthusiasm."

Theo patted her arm. "There's no need to accustom me to disappointment, Isra. I'm well taught, from traveling so long with Rose."

12

"I don't see why you're so upset, Rose," Isra said as she sat down next to the open window in Rose's room. "At least we're safe for the moment. And it's just a week."

"In a week, we could make it to Rhone and back," Rose muttered as she threw her bag of clothes on the bed before her.

"Come on. This is a chance for you to relax. I know for a fact that you didn't enjoy yourself at Crystal Lake."

Rose's temper flared at the mention of Crystal Lake. Did Theo tell Isra what had happened at the hot springs, when he'd seen her at the pool? She struggled to keep her voice even as she asked, "Is that what you were talking about with Theo?"

"Does it bother you he'd rather talk to me about certain things?" Isra asked, her eyes wide and innocent.

"I just don't understand why you're so dependent on him," Rose scoffed. "That's all."

"You depend on him."

"He is my confidant and one of my knights," Rose said. "He's nothing important like that to you."

"He's my friend, and I consider him as another brother," Isra said. "And you're just horrible if you think that he is just some knight or counselor to you. He's the one who changed your life, Rose. He's the one who set you free."

"I'm not free," Rose snapped. "I'm still cursed."

"Cursed, yes, but at least you know about it," Isra pointed out. "Don't you ever wonder what would have happened if you never went crying into the chapel that day? You would have grown up as this naïve, innocent pawn doomed to a fate no one could tell you about. You would have been pampered and courted and married off, if the King could find someone. That's just the best case scenario, too. At worst, the King and Queen would have made up a tower where, once you pricked your finger on the spindle, they could loving lay you down and allow citizens to parade through the room once a year as if it were some kind of holy political pilgrimage."

"You certainly thought it all out, did you?" Rose laughed.

Isra shrugged. "It sounds like a story of some sort."

"The awful kind."

"I won't argue with you there." Isra turned to face the window, where the cool evening air carried the scent of the nearby bay.

"I don't want to argue with you, even if I think I still would have found out about my curse," Rose said. She sighed. "I thought about what you said to me last time we were together. And you were right. I pushed a lot of people away, including you. I would like us to be friends."

"We always were," Isra assured her. "But I want more communication before you make decisions."

"You mean like how you agreed we would all stay for your big fancy engagement party?" Rose asked.

"That one doesn't count," Isra replied proudly. "Utopa made that call. I didn't have a lot of room to disagree. I mean, I'm fearing for my life here, Rose. Don't tell me you wouldn't protect me from Utopa as much as you would from King Stefanos."

"The King would just imprison you. Utopa is insistent on throwing you a party."

"When you meet her tomorrow, you'll see what I mean when I say it's hard for me to disagree with her."

"My life is not dependent on following her orders," Rose said. "I'll have to see what she's made of."

"Theo told me that it would be best for you and your traveling companions to stay here for a while anyway," Isra said.

"Really?" Rose sat down on her bed. "What reason did he give for that? My poor health? My inability to rest? My endless irritation?"

"Well, he said he wanted to talk to some ambassador while we were here. Something about a tapestry?"

Rose immediately felt shamed. She had forgotten about all about the tapestry she had seen at Derick and Juliette's castle. "Oh, right," she said. "There is that matter we have to sort out."

"I want to help you while we're here," Isra said. "So get some rest. Tomorrow, you can tell me all about this investigation, and we can help the others with that pixie they brought."

"The pixie?" Rose briefly recalled what looked like a sleeping log on the back of Sophia's saddle.

"His name is Bachas, and he does not like fairies at all. Mary's placed a spell on him to protect us from any of his harmful magic. It's a good thing she was there when he woke up. Pixies can be tricky creatures from what I've learned from here."

"You learned about pixies here?"

"We don't have practically any in Rhone," Isra said. "The fairyfolk we do have seem to have a grudge against them or something. They're more territorial than we realized."

"Well, I guess it's no wonder Magdalina wants our kingdom so badly," Rose said. "She told me that Lucia was supposed to be our first Queen."

Isra frowned. "When did she say that? I don't remember her saying anything about Lucia's legend at your birthday party."

Mary fluttered into the room before Rose could answer. Behind her was Isra's fairy, Fiona, who was also Mary's cousin. "That's because she told her while we were in the cave in the forest," Mary said.

"I didn't want you to tell anyone," Rose reminded her.

"Fiona and I have been discussing it," Mary explained. "We have been trying to find some answers for you, Rose, and I can't do that on my own. I am a younger fairy, don't forget. I don't know as much as someone like Fiona or Juana might know."

Fiona tapped her wings together thoughtfully. "And I do need all the details to be able to offer my best advice, darling Princess," she said.

Rose rolled her eyes. *What sorts of things people say to themselves in order to feel like they are not gossiping!*

"You mean you've talked to Magdalina again?" Isra asked. "While you were out in the caverns on your way here?"

"It's nothing," Rose said. "She did tell me a few things."

"Like what?"

Like how you are my half-sister. Rose did not want to say anything. "I can't tell you now, Isra. I need to verify what she said. You know Magdalina. She's all curses and riddles, and she only cares for herself."

"I guess so." Isra shook her head. "But as soon as you verify things, I want to know."

"Believe me," Rose said, "you'll find out if what she said was the truth or not soon enough."

It might be the reason the King is more than happy to imprison you and Ronan along with our mother.

Rose sighed. "There are so many things we need to find out, I'm tired just thinking of them all."

"Well, let me let you get some rest." Isra smiled. "Philip and I are going to take a walk on the battlements before bed," Isra said. "And then Theo asked if I would go and visit Sophia and Ethan. Ethan has a surprise for me, apparently. How sweet is that?"

"What is the plan for tomorrow?"

"Reception's before breakfast," Isra said, "where you'll officially meet Utopa. And wear a dress, please, Rose! She will have a fainting spell if she sees you in your knight's clothing."

"Fine," Rose replied bitingly. "What else?"

"I know we're going to go on a tour throughout the city," Isra said. "I've already mentioned this to Theo, and he agreed we should all go together."

"What? Why?"

"So you can find that ambassador," Isra answered.

"You tell Theo next time you talk with him I'm the one who is in charge."

"Rose, please. He's allowed to have his say. And it's not like he would do something to displease you. I can't imagine he likes getting you to yell at him all the time. No wonder he has to pray so often. He'd been insane otherwise."

Rose sat back on her hands, silently reminding herself that it was frowned upon for someone to choke her sister. As her fingers curled into her palms, she felt the rosary beads Theo had given her rest on her wrist. She took a deep breath as Isra listed off the rest of the coming day's projected activities.

"Then, I figure Philip and I can do enough things together that we can provide you some cover, so you can ask your questions around town and see if there is anything you can do about the Magdust trade and find that ambassador."

ONCE UPON A PRINCESS

"I guess I have to wait for Lannister to return from Derick's palace with some news before we continue on to Rhone," Rose admitted.

"See? Why don't you just relax. For the moment, Magdalina can't hurt you. And I got a letter from the Queen Mother just last week, saying while she is still in prison, she is doing fine and things are mostly alright. So we have done what we can today."

Rose shifted onto the comfort of her mattress. It was nice to have Isra around, she thought, if for no other reason Isra could make her believe it was possible to forget about worrying. For some time, anyway.

"Okay," Rose said. "Alright. You win. We'll stay. I'll get some rest. We'll be fine."

"That's the spirit," Isra said. "Now, if you don't mind, I'm going to go and meet Philip."

"Take Juana and Mary," Rose ordered. "If you're really engaged, I'm going to treat it as such. So you need chaperones."

Isra giggled. "If it will help you sleep better, Rose. But there's really no need to worry about it. Ronan is going to join us. He wanted to make sure he could talk to Philip where, if he needed to throw him off something, he would have the opportunity to indulge himself."

Rose waited until she was alone in the room before she replied, "I doubt that will help me sleep better."

If anything, knowing Ronan will be there makes me even more nervous.

Still, she smiled. She was looking forward to seeing her brother again.

Half-brother.

ONCE UPON A PRINCESS

Rose shrugged off Magdalina's words, and settled into her covers.

While she was able to relax in the borrowed bed, and she was able to believe Isra was right about the castle's security, Rose knew there were still too many questions running around inside of her head for her to fall asleep.

What did Theo tell Isra about their time at Crystal Lake? Would they be able to find the ambassador who had given Juliette the tapestry, and what did he say that made her so anxious to get rid of it? What was she going to say to her father when she saw him again? How would she defend Isra and Ronan from him, especially if they were her half-siblings?

Was she really going to be able to defeat Magdalina?

Too many questions, Rose thought. Not enough answers. Or maybe too many possibilities.

It seemed like hours had passed before she finally fell into a fitful sleep.

13

Theo also found himself awake, trying to answer lingering questions. He kept wondering what Rose had seen in the caves. He was determined to find a way to get her alone, so he could coax the answer from her at last.

His chance to do just that came shortly after breakfast finished up. It had been a lively, cheery breakfast, where Utopa, the Dowager Queen of Einish, nearly had a fit of the vapors when Rose wanted to talk business.

Theo had to swallow a laugh at the sight of Philip's mother as she finally agreed to have the contract for their engagement drawn up that very day, on the condition that Rose meet with her later to discuss the details in private. It was clear she had been appalled by Rose's manners, but she was determined to secure an alliance with Rhone.

The rest of the kingdom already seemed to be in agreement, he thought, as he sat with Rose, Isra, and Philip in the royal carriage.

As the rumors and gossip began to flow from room to room, and room to courtyard, Isra and Philip were prepared to go out on their tour of the city.

Theo had the others stay behind, so he could have some time alone with Rose as they sneaked off to go looking for Ambassador Rolez.

"So, what do you think?" Rose asked him, as she settled into the seat of the high coach beside him. They were on a carriage ride throughout the city, and even though they had just set out, Rose was already eager to escape.

Theo looked down to where Rose was looking. Isra and Philip were below, still waving to the people of Einish who had come to see their Prince and his betrothed bride set off on their tour through O'Lin. There was a large crowd, but there were plenty of guards around, all of them working to keep back the crowd's enthusiasm.

"I think you managed to throw Utopa off quite a bit at breakfast," Theo replied. "The outfit was a nice touch."

"She didn't make me change," Rose said, glancing down at her new dress, which was much neater than the one she had been wearing earlier. "She 'strongly suggested' it, but I did this myself."

"I think it's safe to say she knows you are not going to follow her lead by now," Theo said. "Especially after breakfast and how you managed to run the negotiations."

"I think she's out of practice," Rose said. "She didn't do a very good job at the start. And she easily could have called me out on some of my own shortcomings or double standards. After all, I was the one who insisted on protocol at the end, but didn't care for it at all until then."

"She's smart enough to know Rhone is a good match for Philip. It helps because he sincerely seems to like her enough to want to marry her."

Rose wrinkled her nose. "They both admitted to me that they're in love. Can you believe that? After only two days of knowing each other, and then almost seven months apart?"

Theo smiled and nodded, but inwardly he thought of his brother. Thad had told him before he knew Theo was at least half in love with Rose when he'd first met her, the time she had punched him in the nose. Some part of him wondered if he knew the exact moment he had fallen in love with Rose, and the other part knew it was pointless to try figuring it out after so many years.

ONCE UPON A PRINCESS

"Love is mysterious to the people outside any relationship," he finally said.

"I guess so," Rose agreed.

Theo decided it was best to start distracting her. "Let's talk about how we're going to find Ambassador Rolez," he said.

Rose nodded. "Philip said he vaguely remembers him," she said. "If he sees him, he said he'll point him out to us as we go around to the different stops along the tour."

"Isra told me that they'll be stopping at many places, so I thought it might be better for us to slip away the first chance we get." Theo glanced back down at Isra and Philip, as they continued to wave at the people. "We might be able to save a lot of time by searching for him on our own."

"I'm okay with leaving once we get to the market," Rose said. "There are some dignitaries' houses they have to stop at first for some reason or another, but once we make to the market, we should be able to find out where the ambassador lives, or where he might be."

"I just hope he's in the country," Theo said. "I might want answers, but I don't want to travel all the way back to the Romani territory to get it. Or even further out."

"Agreed." Rose shook her head. "I hope this doesn't take too long."

"We have some time this week to find him," Theo reminded her.

"We have other problems to attend to," Rose said. "This is just one of the easier ones to solve."

It was an hour later when the carriage finally pulled up to the market, and Theo and Rose were able to slip out while Isra and Philip stepped out and started waving again.

ONCE UPON A PRINCESS

"This seems demeaning," Rose said, as she watched Isra and Philip from around the corner of a nearby building. "Not to mention it takes forever."

"Traditions here differ from those of Rhone," Theo replied in a neutral tone. Unlike Rose, he had been grateful for all the time in the carriage. Isra had been able to point out several of the nobles and their residencies, and when they had stopped, Isra had used her charm to smooth over their audience— which, much to Rose and Theo's chagrin, was sorely needed, because many of the nobles mistook Rose for Isra, and even the ones who did not were caught staring at Rose enough that it was extremely uncomfortable—while asking indirect questions about Ambassador Rolez.

Rose wrinkled her nose. "I still like Rhone's better."

"Yes," Theo mused, "because it's just more convenient for one person to complete a monumental task than it is for the engaged couple to go around and greet their people."

Rose gave him a reluctant smile. "I guess so," she said.

"Your father had to complete a task for your mother," Theo reminded her. "I'm sure he would have appreciated this much more."

Rose made a face at the mention of her father. "Maybe it's more of a matter of how you always want what you can't have."

Theo was tempted to ask her what she would want to do if she ever got engaged, but he decided he did not want to know the answer.

"Well, let's get moving," Rose said. "That last duchess lady or whoever she was said that Rolez was not a native of Einish. He was an ambassador to Einish from Aragon."

ONCE UPON A PRINCESS

"His townhouse is supposed to be around here," Theo said. "I'm trying to figure out which way is right of the town center. Her instructions were not the clearest."

"That's being kind," Rose said. "I'm amazed you were able to follow her at all, with all those stories she told in between her instructions."

"You get used to that, traveling around the world," Theo said, unable to stop him from tugging on a lock of her hair in play.

She didn't seem to remember she was supposed to hate it, so he took her arm. "Come on, let's go this way."

"I can walk myself," Rose grumbled.

"You look like a lady," Theo said. "And you're too pretty to be here by yourself. If you're with me, there's a smaller chance people will bother us."

"You're not so scary," Rose replied with a laugh. "I doubt you'll be able to scare off all the potential suitors."

"Then you'll just have to convince them all that you already belong to me."

He felt Rose stiffen as he said it, but when she laughed a moment later, he relaxed.

She batted her eyes up at him, pretending to flirt. "Is that so, darling?"

Theo grinned. "You have always valued an efficient plan, Rose."

"Don't you know me so well?" Her eyes lost their flirtatious edge as she looked up at him.

"I do," he told her, his tone much more husky than he had intended.

Rose shifted away from him, before she suddenly pointed at a building. "There's the city council building," she said.

ONCE UPON A PRINCESS

"That's the banner of Einish that the old lady was talking about. We're supposed to turn down this street."

She tugged him down the street, and they found themselves at a bazaar, a trader's outpost.

"There are so many things here," Rose said.

"After traveling through the mountains and countryside, I feel like this is a little surreal," Theo remarked. "Look over there. There's a shop from Maltia."

"I wonder if the shopkeeper knows Felise?" Rose pondered, craning her neck to see over the crowded alleyway.

Thinking of the older man who had overseen their care while they were stuck on the island, Theo shrugged. "Couldn't hurt to ask," Theo said. "Felise did tell us he often traded with any number of people in Maltia City."

"I see a shop with goods from Aragon," Rose said. "Maybe we should check there? To see if their ambassador found that tapestry from here?"

"That's a good idea," Theo said. "I didn't even think of it from that angle."

"Me either, until I saw it." Rose slipped through the various lines of people, still clinging to him, as she made her way over to the seller's table.

As they approached the shop, Theo had a hard time keeping his laughter to himself. The seller was an older man, with only a small streak of silver in his beard and at the edges of his hairline; it was clear he had been a seller for a long time, but while he had seen all manner of things before, Rose clearly managed to awe him considerably.

"Good morning," he called, heralding them with an excited energy. "What can I do for you, My Lady? Such a beauty as you deserves only the finest available. It is no coincidence that you have found your way to my shop."

ONCE UPON A PRINCESS

"Oh, I agree," Rose said, giving the owner a wide-eyed, innocent look. "I came here looking for something I've desperately wanted for ages now."

"Far be it from me to keep a lady from her desire," the man said, taking her free hand and gallantly kissing it. He was unable to take his eyes off of Rose. "My name is Enrique, and I am at your service, My Lady."

"Thank you," Rose said, trying to step back from the man's grip. She turned and patted Theo's arm. "My husband here is a good man and he has promised to buy me a very special tapestry."

"Your husband?"

Theo tried not to look too shocked as the older man sized him up. He could see the second the man resigned himself to Rose's claim; he had a feeling any prices that Enrique was going to offer before had just jumped significantly.

"Yes," Rose assured him. "My darling husband here promised me a grand tapestry of Queen Lucia. It was my favorite legend as a child, and after hearing Queen Juliette has one, I knew I just had to find one."

"You have excellent taste," Enrique said. "At least in goods." He glanced at Theo again, as if to condemn her choice in men.

Rose stayed focused on the tapestry. "I know Queen Juliette got her tapestry of Queen Lucia from Ambassador Rolez," she said. "I was hoping you would have one in stock, or you would be able to point me in the right direction."

"For a good price," Theo added, hoping to win some favor with the man.

Enrique arched a brow at him.

Okay, I did not win him over.

ONCE UPON A PRINCESS

Rose seemed to realize this too. She let go of Theo's arm and took Enrique's hand. "Please, sir, you have to help me."

Enrique only had to look into her large, cerulean eyes before he crumbled. "I'm so sorry, My Lady," he said. "I do not have any in stock. I do not carry any tapestries of Queen Lucia."

Rose pouted.

"But," he said, "I do know where Ambassador Rolez bought his. He had a sister who was a duchess in the Aragonian court. He bought the tapestry on the way home from her funeral."

"Oh, I'm sorry to hear of his loss," Rose said, truly compassionate.

"He was very close to his sister, and so he rightly was. She was a very dear lady, trapped in a political marriage," Enrique said.

"You knew her?" Rose asked.

"Of course. She practically lived here. He went to go and bury her in their ancestral home."

"And the tapestry?"

"Shh … there is a weaver who lives in Rhone," he said, whispering. "She is from a family of weavers. Her name is Annalora, and she is the last remaining weaver who will do special tapestries such as the one you seek."

"Annalora?" Theo repeated. He held his breath as he asked, "Did she have a sister named Eleanora?"

"So the rumors go," Enrique replied, clearly forgetting he was supposed to object to Theo in light of the glory of sharing gossip. "I know Eleanora is gone. She and her husband were ambushed by a pack of hostile fairies just as they were going to visit Annalora. She has been distraught since then. Now, she only takes on special commissions."

Theo said nothing. It was so strange, he thought, to hear his parents' deaths described in such a matter-of-fact tone. It was just as strange as hearing his aunt was not only still alive, but she was still apparently working in the Magdust trade.

Rose did not seem to realize Theo was in shock. "Maybe Ambassador Rolez picked up an extra one while he was passing through Rhone," she said. "Can you tell us where we might be able to find him?"

"His townhouse is not far. But he is not receiving visitors," Enrique said. "He has only just returned from his sister's funeral, not even a week ago."

"Please," Rose entreated. "Please tell me. I will be content to write to him."

"Oh, My Lady, I cannot say no to you," Enrique told her. He took a hold of her hand again and squeezed it as he gave her the directions to the ambassador's house.

"Thank you," Rose murmured politely. She extracted herself from his grip and gave him a smile. "You have been most helpful."

She grabbed onto Theo's arm once more, and hurried away.

"You can slow down some," Theo told her, stumbling a bit at the sudden lurch in his steps. "It's not like you're trying to lose me. After all, I am your husband." He shot her a teasing grin.

"Ugh, please," Rose said. "That guy was creepy. I'm going to have to wash my hands extra thoroughly."

"Even if he was enchanted with you, at least he was able to be of some help."

"So?" Rose said. "I don't like it when people like him fawn over me like I'm some horse at an auction. Flirting with people like that makes my skin crawl. From now on, I'm just going to use straight intimidation."

"I'd prefer it, too," Theo admitted. "I know it makes you uncomfortable."

"Well, you're right; at least we got the information we need, for now, anyway."

"Even if Enrique is right, and he's not receiving visitors? How will we find a way to ask him questions?"

"I guess we'll see him at Isra and Philip's party," Rose said. "Any good foreign diplomat would not dare to miss an event like that."

"So that inconvenient party might be good for something after all?"

"Stop teasing. You know I hate it when you do that."

"And I know you're lying when you say that," Theo told her. He hesitated briefly. He was tempted to say, "Just like I knew you were lying about what happened in the cavern," but he knew it was too soon.

And, he had to admit, he was not willing to risk her temper. He was enjoying the day with Rose. They were alone in a crowded city, where Rose was comfortable enough with him that she was pretending he was her husband.

That fantasy alone was enough to intoxicate him into staying silent.

For the moment, he tightened his arm as it wound around hers and led her down through the bustling streets. Soon, one of the shops caught his eye.

"Hey, come over here," he said, as he pulled her further down the streets of the bazaar.

"What is it?" Rose asked. "Is it food?"

"Why? Are you hungry?"

"I didn't bring food with me for once."

"Really?"

ONCE UPON A PRINCESS

"Come on, don't give me that look," Rose huffed. "I'm wearing a dress. It doesn't have pockets or anything."

"I could have carried something for you." Theo patted his own belt. "I have plenty of room to tie on traveling packets."

"Well, now you'll have to settle for buying me something," Rose told him.

"No need for subtlety, Rose," Theo said, drawing out some of the coins he'd tucked away. "We'll get some food for you in a moment. First, I want to check out this shop up here."

"Which one?"

Theo pointed to the small store where flowers and small, twinkling gems of all kind gleamed in the afternoon sunshine. "Here."

Rose pursed her lips. "You're not going to buy me a present, are you?"

"No," he said. "But that could be a pretense while I ask the lady some questions."

He could see Rose calculate a mental estimation of the shopkeeper. This one was a woman who had a large wart on her face, right between her eyes, and long, scruffy hair.

"Why do you want to ask her questions?" Rose asked.

"Because she has a pixie with her."

Rose glanced behind the voluminous folds of the woman's dress, trying not to notice how tightly the fabric was stretched across her impressive girth. Sitting down beside her, with wide, tired eyes, was another woodland pixie in a tattered dress.

"That one reminds me of the other pixie we came across in the Wandering Caverns," Rose whispered. "Bachas, right?"

"Exactly. I want to find out some information about the pixies, if we can. I'd also like to see if there is something they can do for Bachas. He has been very melancholy, and he told Ethan and Sophia this morning his leg is still bothering him.”

“We can ask Philip if there’s anything at the palace for him,” Rose said. “I know Mary has said he is nothing but rude to her.”

“Maybe if he feels better, he’ll be easier to deal with,” Theo suggested.

Rose relented at his reasoning, and the two of them made their way to the stand. The lady blinked up at them and brushed her hair out of her eyes, letting Theo and Rose have a much clearer view of the wart. It wiggled in greeting as they watched her.

“What’s your pleasure?” the lady asked, her voice as scraggly as her gown was tattered. “I am Madame Sageberry. Welcome to my shop.”

“I have heard about pixie magic,” Theo began inconspicuously, “and I wanted to see what kind of gems you had for sale here.”

The woman’s eyes lit up with a mercenary gleam. “I have plenty for sale. What kind of magic do you need? Protection from magic? Need to ward off fairies?”

“Do they actually work?” Rose asked. She glanced over at the pixie, who cowed at her look.

“Of course they do. Nothing but the best from Madame Sageberry.”

“I’m looking for some healing magic,” Theo said. “It’s for a pixie with a pained leg.”

“A special order.” Madame Sageberry grinned, showing off her brittle teeth. “Excellent. Mora, get to work.” She turned to the little pixie, who nodded and took a gem down from a nearby table. As she held it, the gem began to glow in different colors.

"Is this your pixie?" Rose asked. "She's beautiful."

The pixie looked up at her with a tepid smile, even though Theo thought he saw her tremble.

"Bah, there's no need to flatter her," Madame Sageberry snapped as Mora handed her the newly-minted gem. "She's bound to me by a life debt. She'll do the spell and the magic so it will work perfectly, or she'll be punished."

"There's no need for that," Theo said, as he handed off some coins to Madame Sageberry. She handed him the gem in return, and he quickly pocketed it.

"I agree. But if you have any trouble with the order, you can bet I'll hear about it and punish her for it."

The pixie nodded dutifully up at Rose, who suddenly had a determined look on her face. "How much for the pixie?" she asked.

Madame Sageberry scoffed at her. "You can't transfer a life debt," she said. "Mora here is mine until I die."

"Can't you set her free?" Rose asked. "I have plenty of money. We would be happy to compensate you for her."

"We don't have that much," Theo whispered softly.

"Theo," Rose murmured back. "We have to do something."

Before Theo could reply, Madame Sageberry drew herself up proudly. "I'll not be bought," she declared. "I saved this pixie's life, and it is her duty to serve me for the rest of mine. Now, take yourselves off before I charge you more."

"But—"

Madame Sageberry took a menacing step closer to Mora, who gave the barest hint of a flinch. "Don't bring more trouble to poor Mora, here, lady. I'd hate to punish her for your insolence."

"My insolence?" Rose huffed. "What about yours?"

Seeing that Mora was in danger of getting attacked by her mistress, Theo stepped in. "Thank you for your help today," he said, doing his best to keep his tone civil.

"Theo," Rose grumbled. "No."

"Rose." Theo tugged on her arm gently. "Come on."

"Be on your way!" Madame Sageberry hollered. "I'd hate to call the kingdom guards."

Theo stopped Rose from telling Madame Sageberry to go ahead and do just that by pulling her hand and leading her down the street. Theo managed to duck into a small alcove by a side street when Rose managed to free herself from his grip.

"What do you think you're doing?" Rose snarled. "She was abusing that pixie."

"And by the pixie's own laws, there's nothing to be done about it," Theo reminded her. "At least, nothing short of killing Madame Sageberry."

"Don't tempt me."

"That's exactly why I was trying to get you to leave," he told her. "This isn't Rhone. We're here for Isra, and at Philip and his family's pleasure. There wasn't anything we could do for Mora, and this isn't something where we can get involved in the kingdom politics. The pixies have their own governing rules."

"It's just so unfair," Rose said. She put her head in her hands, angry and sad.

"I know." He pulled her close, wrapping his arms around her while she put her head on his chest. Theo sensed she was not just thinking of Mora's fate, but her own as well.

Moments passed before Rose eased back from him. "I'm sorry," she muttered. "If I stand around here and mope at all the awful things in the world, I'll never do anything else."

"It's alright. I know how you feel about things like this," Theo told her. "And it's nice you still mourn for it. More cynical people would dismiss it. You bring beauty to the world, Rose, even when you cry over its ugliness."

"I know I can't solve every problem, but it makes me miserable to see other people in the same situation as I am."

"Mora's mistress seems old," Theo said, trying to find a way to comfort her. "Maybe it won't be too long before she's free."

Rose shrugged. "It's shameful she has to be bound to her in the first place."

"Bachas would probably agree," Theo said, thinking of the small pixie rooming with Sophia and Mary. He recalled the glorious joy on Bachas' face, as he realized he was no longer bound to serve his master. "I know that made you unhappy. Let's hope this gemstone we bought will heal him, so some good will come out of this."

Rose nodded. "I hope it helps."

"I know you're not used being unable to do something when it comes to tough situations like this."

Rose snorted. "That's my whole life."

"Even with just Magdalina's curse, you have done everything but nothing." Theo gave her a kind smile. "Just watch. You'll be able to overcome her yet."

He felt her tense. "Even with the dragon's blood," she said, "I'll have to find a way to fight her."

"*We* will find a way to fight her, Rose," he corrected her. "Magdalina does not have many friends the way you do."

"She still has magic she can use."

Theo dropped his hand into hers. "There are things besides magic we have at our disposal. We'll use it all to find a way to

ONCE UPON A PRINCESS

free you," he said, catching her eyes with his. "I promise you, Rosary."

Rose finally managed a smile. "I guess you'll just have to say your prayers, huh?"

At the subtle scorn in her voice, Theo sighed. "Later," he said. "For now, I'll settle for getting you that food you wanted."

"I don't know if I have an appetite anymore."

"I can't blame you for that," Theo agreed. "Still, let's keep moving. Maybe we'll find something else."

As they made their way through the town, Theo turned his thoughts to what Enrique had said earlier about his aunt.

His mother's sister was still alive. Why had he not been told? He barely remembered her at all; she had sent gifts for Christmas one year. Surely his grandfather would have let him know that his other daughter was still alive.

But then, Theo knew, the old reverend never seemed to share much with him, or even Thad, in all the years they had lived under the protection of the church.

ONCE UPON A PRINCESS

14

Rose sighed as she stared out the window of her room, watching as a parade of servants and guards all shuffled through the palace, putting the final touches on the palace as guests began to arrive for Philip and Isra's engagement ball. Part of her was keeping an ear out for Ambassador Rolez's name as announcements were made, but most of her mind was content to linger elsewhere.

"Enjoying the view?" Mary asked.

Rose glanced up to see Mary as she appeared inside her room. "Not really," Rose admitted. "This makes me think too much of my last birthday party." She grimaced at her accidental choice of words.

Mary came up to her. "You're not the only one who is down," she said. "I was finally able to sneak away from Bachas. Fiona's taking a turn helping your squire and her brother watch him."

"I take it he hasn't been any less obnoxious since Theo brought back that healing gem for him?"

"Not to me," Mary replied. "He's warmed up to Theo considerably, though."

Rose felt a small smile curl on her lips. "That's not hard to believe."

"Okay, I'm just going to say it." Mary sighed. "You know, you really should just tell Theo what Magdalina said to you. He asked me about it. He hasn't forgotten about it."

"Neither have I," Rose said curtly. "He's just been playing the waiting game, hasn't he?"

"As much as I'm surprised by it myself, I would say no. He's got something else on his mind. He has been distracted

ONCE UPON A PRINCESS

ever since you came back from your unofficial tour of O'Lin."

Rose frowned. "I wonder what he's worried about."

She thought of their time in town and around the castle. Between the meals where she often had Utopa in tears, the adventures in finding Ambassador Rolez, and the distractions that came along with Isra's party, Rose realized she had been distracted enough that she had failed to notice there was something on Theo's mind.

"What is he doing now?" she asked Mary.

"He and Ronan are playing a game of chess in one of the palace dens," Mary said. "But as more guests arrive, I imagine he'll meet us outside in the ballroom."

"I guess that's good. Let's hope he remains distracted, so he will forget about me and my secrets."

"I don't know why you don't just tell him and the others about Magdalina's deal."

"Because I don't need any more pity," Rose explained. "I love my friends, Mary. You are all so special to me. But I know you all worry for me, and you're all here for me. I can't ask anything else of you."

"Rose, you have always been so fiercely independent," Mary said. "I fear too much at times. We all need help at times. And you know we are all here willingly."

"That makes it worse," Rose argued. "If it were something I could pay for, I would pay for it in a heartbeat. Then I wouldn't have to worry about letting all of my friends down in addition to my kingdom."

Mary shook her head, making her wings shimmer. "Please, Rose—"

Rose shook her head. "It's too hard for me to explain, Mary."

ONCE UPON A PRINCESS

"It's not for me," Mary said. "You're too proud, Rose, and you're too afraid and angry."

"So?" Rose crossed her arms and looked down at the scene outside once more. "Don't I have a right to that?"

"You might not be able to stop how you feel, but you can choose how you respond to it. And that includes trusting us and having faith that we can make a difference together."

Mary cleared her throat. "You know, Magdalina is in a similar situation. She doesn't trust anyone, Rose. She has no friends, except for maybe Everon. All of her supporters have other, more personal or selfish reasons for serving her."

"What are you saying?" Rose asked. "That I'm just like her?"

"Don't twist my words, Rose," Mary chided. "I'm saying you can make different choices than what she's made, and you should. Especially if you want to beat her."

Rose went quiet once more. Theo had said something similar earlier; he had been adamant that they would defeat her together.

"Please, think about it," Mary said. "I'm going to go and help Isra get ready now. I'll see you downstairs soon, right?"

Rose only nodded, her gaze firm as she continued to watch as new guests arrived.

She waited until she was certain Mary was gone, and then she heaved a heavy sigh. As much as she hated to admit it, Mary had a good point. She let her fingers tangle around the prayer beads Theo had given her.

Rose hated how much both Mary and Theo were right. She knew, despite her fear, and in spite of her anger, she could trust them. She had no reason to doubt them with her secrets. They had both been with her since the beginning.

ONCE UPON A PRINCESS

Technically even before then, too. Rose rolled the rosary beads between her fingers, shocked to realize it had been over ten years since she had first met Theo.

He had been so precious, she thought, that first time she had seen him.

Devastated to realize she was pitied, rather than beloved by her nation, Rose had run to the comfort of the church, which she had always loved for its grand design and inspiring artwork.

She had come to cry at the altar, only to find a precocious altar boy cleaning as she came rushing in. He had been stubborn and matter of fact about the matter, telling her of Magdalina and her curse. He did not even realize she was the princess as he told her the truth; when she told him that she was, he told her, laughingly, that she couldn't be Princess Aurora, because the Princess of Rhone was supposed to be beautiful and kind.

She had punched him for that, causing his nose to bleed all over his wrinkled robes.

Rose smiled as she recalled that feeling of power. There was something inside of her, she'd realized, that could fight. She had been so shocked she did not even think about the boy until later. She decided she would keep him around her to remind her that she had the power inside of her to overcome her troubles.

Later, she thought, she had come to rely on him for much more than that.

Before Rose could sink further into her thoughts, she heard another announcement.

"Ambassador Alfonse Rolez!"

Rose peeked out the window. She watched as the ambassador, a short man, dressed in glided robes and tall boots, as he made his way through the receiving line.

"He's here!" Rose cheered. She knew she had a lot of problems to solve and decisions to make; this was likely her only chance to get to talk with the ambassador. Enrique had been right; he had closed his house off to all visitors, and if the snooty look on his high-mustached, tight-lipped expression was any indication, Rose had a feeling he was only attending the ball tonight at the compulsion of Utopa. She was going to make sure she took full advantage of his appearance.

She headed downstairs at once.

"Check."

Theo grimaced, aware he had been unable to concentrate on the game in front of him. He glanced up at Rose's younger brother, Ronan, with a look of tired sadness.

"Come on," Ronan insisted. "This is war. No sympathies, Theo."

Ronan, as Isra's twin, was just over sixteen, but in many ways, he seemed much younger than Isra, and especially much younger than Rose. He loved to play games, to go hunting and fishing, and he never had enough adventure. Theo was convinced that King Stefanos had sent him out on his Grand Tour of Rhone just to get him away from the castle at Havilah.

Theo chuckled. "It's still worth a try, isn't it?" he asked, as he moved his king out of danger. "Besides, it'll make the game last longer."

"Ha." Ronan smirked. "I can see why Rose is always warning me not to get into an argument with you. You're very convincing. Check."

"Not convincing enough, obviously," Theo said, "since you're still intent on defeating me." He moved his king once more, shuffling him toward the middle of the playing field, already feeling defeat.

"Checkmate!" Ronan jumped up and cheered, slamming his knight down on its final square. "Woo-hoo!"

Theo grinned. "Alright, you won," he said. "There's no need to make me feel old in addition to feeling vanquished."

Ronan continued to celebrate, and Theo eventually laughed. Ronan was still young, but even with taking his age into account, he seemed much happier than his father.

"Come on," Theo said, after another moment. "Didn't your father ever teach you to win with dignity?"

Ronan quickly sobered at the mention of the King. "When has my father done anything with dignity?" he asked. "You have not been around as much as I have in the last five years, Theo. The King is a mess."

"I know he's getting older," Theo said. "But from what I have seen, he seems to be keeping the kingdom together."

"Barely." Ronan sat back down. "That was part of the reason he sent for Rose, you know. He was content to groom me and Isra for the crown until the rumors about Magdalina started."

"What rumors?"

"She's been hanging around the castle at Havilah more," Ronan said. "Or at least, that's what he says. I talked with his physician a few times. I think he's going mad."

"Rose is having a hard time with her curse, too," Theo said, trying to keep his voice even.

"He's not worried about her. He's worried about himself." Ronan shook his head. "There's always more talk about what will happen if Rose does succumb to her curse. A lot of people are scared for her."

"Well, they're scared for themselves," Theo said. "I don't think any of them actually care too much about what she's had to go through."

"True, true." Ronan nodded. "But the King still hasn't told the majority of the country that he has Isra and me to fall back on. And then he went and imprisoned our mother? If it's one thing I saw on my trip, Theo, it's that people are angry and scared, and they're losing faith in the king."

"What do you think?"

"I think," Ronan said, "I'm going to enjoy watching Rose when she gets back. She's going to have a bit of a tangle to unravel. But even in the three days she was home, she managed to inspire plenty of our citizens. I think just getting her back there and back to work will make a lot of people much happier. I heard about her visit all the way across the country."

Theo was just about to ask him about Magdalina again when Rose entered the room.

"And there she is," Ronan said, jumping up. "I was just talking about you, Rose."

Rose scowled at Theo. "Why?" she asked.

Theo shrugged before he realized that she was probably worried he was telling Ronan about their serendipitous meeting at the hot springs.

"I was just commenting on how the King seems to be having a hard time," Ronan said. "When I passed through Rhone on my Grand Tour, there were plenty who were

ONCE UPON A PRINCESS

already worried enough. Now we have the Queen to worry about."

"How has she been?" Rose asked. "Did you hear anything from her lately?"

"She's fine. Virtue came with a pack of letters earlier today," Ronan told her.

"Virtue's here?" Rose grinned. "Wonderful! I will have to go and see him after we're finished with business tonight."

"I guess it is time to go," Theo said, standing up.

"Yes, it is," Rose agreed. "I saw the ambassador arrive. He's here. We need to make sure we can interview him before he leaves."

Ronan forced a yawn. "I guess that's my cue to go and give my proper greeting to Philip and Isra, before I sneak out and find more interesting things to do."

"More interesting things to do?" Rose repeated.

Ronan gave her a smirk. "Come on, Rose," he said. "You have to admit, town life is a lot more lively than the palace."

"You're going to go to the town and party?" Rose wrinkled her nose in disapproval. "Ronan."

"Get over it, Rose," Ronan said. "I'm going to be stuck in palaces all my life. Let me have some fun."

"You'd better not get into any trouble, or that palace will easily become your prison."

"It's not like it hasn't been before," Ronan scoffed. He turned to Theo. "Hey, you want to come with me? I could use someone with an honest face, especially when things get really wild."

"He's not going with you," Rose snapped.

"Let the man decide for himself, Rose," Ronan replied. "And lighten up. It's not like I don't like Philip. He's a nice guy. But I don't want to stay here and watch him stare at Isra all night. And you and Theo have your mysteries to solve and stuff to do. All I have to do is make nice with the people, and I can score better points here by hanging out with the locals."

Theo stepped in. "I'm going to stay with Rose," he said. "We'll see you down in the main hall."

Ronan grinned and waved as he stepped out of the room.

Rose huffed. "That brother of mine."

"He used to do the same thing when we were in Rhone," Theo said. "I remember him going out as early as twelve, Rose."

Rose shook her head. "Still," she said, "he doesn't seem to take anything seriously."

"That's why Isra was born before him," Theo joked. He cleared his throat. "In all seriousness, though, he's a good kid, Rose. But he's still a kid. And Roderick and Lannister are also ready to watch him for us."

Rose gave him a small smile. "I should have known there were contingency plans," she said. "And did you say Lannister was back from King Derick?"

"Yes, he is," Theo said. "The traders have been picked up and the rest of the caverns have been cleared. Lannister has an official report for you, but I left it upstairs with the mail."

"Good." Rose nodded. "This is a good night for news. Let's hope the honorable Ambassador Alfonse Rolez will give us some more." She put on a dazzling smile as she reached for his arm once more.

"Remember your promise."

"Promise? What promise?"

"No charm this time," Theo said with a smile. "Intimidation only."

Rose laughed as they headed down to meet with Isra and her guests.

15

Rose clutched onto Theo's arm more tightly as they maneuvered their way closer to where the ambassador was standing. There were people dancing and chatting in circles of friends, all while servants were ducking and sliding around them and each other.

She allowed herself a moment to take in the scene around her. The servants had cleaned up the room since they had arrived, and the room sparkled—although Rose had a feeling that was more due to Mary and Juana's magic at work. The music swelled as Theo guided her past the music pit.

At the front of the room, Rose could see Isra and Philip as they stood together, greeting their guests in small groups.

"Isra looks beautiful," Theo said, as they drifted along with the crowd.

"She has always been beautiful," Rose said. She watched as Isra took a step closer to Philip, who towered over her. She watched as he leaned down to hear Isra as she said something to him.

"They really do seem to like each other."

"She's so young," Rose said. "I worry for her."

"Philip's our friend," Theo said. "And they do have a lot in common."

"That doesn't mean much." Rose watched Philip take hold of Isra's hand, interlacing his fingers with hers.

"Of course you would think so," Theo said.

"What's that supposed to mean?" Rose snapped. "I'm not against their relationship, but there's nothing wrong with thinking things through carefully."

"I know that, and I agree with that," Theo replied, this time with some hesitation in his voice. "But you have to admit, you don't like to trust in things that you can't see or touch or prove."

Rose glared at him. Before she could roundly dismiss him, she caught a glimpse of shining gold out of the corner of her eye.

Theo followed her gaze. "That's the ambassador?"

Rose watched as the man she had seen earlier took a glass of wine from one of the servants. "Yes," Rose answered. "I'm certain that it's him."

Theo glanced around. "We should see if we can get him to go into another room," he said.

"There's a corridor leading to the kitchens over that way." Rose pulled him after her, as they hurried as politely and nonchalantly as possible through the crowd once more, this time with a destination in sight. "What do you think?"

"That will work."

Rose felt a rush of excitement as they slipped around to where the ambassador was standing. Their movements were coordinated over the past years of battles and sparring, and Rose knew they would get their prize.

Theo came up from Ambassador Rolez's right side, while she slipped in front of him.

"Ambassador," she said in greeting. "How very nice to make your acquaintance."

The man drew himself up proudly, flinching as Theo came into view. "I say, what do you think you're doing?" he sputtered.

"We would like to ask you a few questions," Rose said. "And this is exactly as charming as I'm going to be."

"Hmmph. Well, you don't appeal to me in the least," the man said. "I'd recognize you anywhere."

"That's right," Rose said, rolling her eyes. "I'm Princess Aurora of Rhone."

"I hardly need an introduction, Your Highness." Rolez narrowed his shifty eyes at her. "One doesn't even have to look closely to see you and your uncle have a similar cunning aspect to your face."

"My uncle?" Rose repeated. "That's a new one. Most people cite the beauty or the grace or something else when they recognize me."

"How do you know Rose's uncle?" Theo asked.

"Oh, you're going to ask questions, too, are you?" Rolez's face began to turn purple. "I think I've had enough of this conversation. Excuse me."

"Stop," Rose commanded. "We want to talk to you."

"Well, *I* don't want to talk to *you*."

"*You* don't want to make *us* mad," Rose insisted. "This is my sister's engagement party, remember? We just want some answers, and then we'll be on our way, and you don't have to deal with us again."

"Good. I wouldn't want to deal with anyone from Hebert's family. The man might have been my brother-in-law, but if I had my way, I would take him to court even *after* my sister's death just to get them divorced."

"So your sister was married to my uncle," Rose realized.

"We are sorry for your loss," Theo chimed in quickly.

"You should be," Rolez muttered. "All those years, and she has been absolutely miserable."

Rose thought about what Enrique said. "At least you were there for her," she said quietly. "You were able to make it better for her."

"For all the good it did in the end," Rolez muttered. "She had the best doctors looking after her. But she died because your uncle was horrible to her."

"What did he do?" Rose asked, appalled by the thought.

"He neglected her," Rolez snapped. "She wanted children and a family, and he locked her out of his side of their house in Aragon. She was cast away every day they were married."

"Why?"

"Why do you think?" Rolez scoffed. "He was in love with someone else. I don't know who, and neither did my beloved Isabel, but she knew. How could a wife not know when she is not wanted?"

Rolez teared up and pulled out a handkerchief. "See? See what you've made me do now? I'm going to be all flummoxed for this entire affair now."

"I'm sorry for your loss, sir," Rose said, trying to be kinder. She patted his arm gently, barely touching him. He slid away from her as she advanced, but Theo held him close. "But we still have to ask you some questions. Where did you buy that tapestry? The one you gave to Queen Juliette?"

Rolez's despair vanished as proud defiance took its place. "I'd forgotten about that!" he said. "Why do you want to know? It's not my fault if she's in danger."

Rose and Theo exchanged concerned glances.

Seeming to sense his mistake, Rolez waved it away. "Never mind about it. The tapestry was just a gift."

A quiet voice spoke up from behind them. "He's lying."

Rose and Theo whirled around to see Bachas as he came up the hall from behind them.

"Bachas," Theo said. "What are you doing here? You should be resting. Your leg—"

"Is much better now, thank you very much."

ONCE UPON A PRINCESS

Rose knew from Theo's expression he was just as shocked as she was by the genuine politeness in his tone.

"It's so good," Bachas said, "that I can now use my own magic."

Rose tensed. *Where are Mary and Fiona? Is he going to attack us?*

"Which means, Ambassador, you might want to think again before running off."

A snap crackled between them, and Rolez was suddenly whimpering. He was frozen in a half-jump, caught between sprints.

"What are you doing here?" Theo asked.

"I thought about your offer," Bachas said. "And I've decided to help you—if you'll help me in return."

"I will do what I can to help you if you need it," Theo said. "But I want specifics before entering into a deal with you."

"Later," Bachas said. "Right now, we need to get this guy to tell us where Annalora is."

Rolez struggled even harder. "I'm going to scream!" he yelled, before there was another snap of power, and his voice went mute.

"Scream all you like," Bachas muttered, as he guided Rolez's frozen, mid-air body further into the darkness of the hall. "In fact, I welcome it, if that means I'll be able to keep you from blubbering."

"I'm not sure of this," Rose whispered to Theo.

"Me, either," he admitted. "I know he was really happy to get the healing stone from me earlier, but I didn't think it would make him violent."

"Where's Mary or Fiona when you need them?" Rose asked.

"Probably with Isra," he said. "They are serving as the official chaperones tonight."

ONCE UPON A PRINCESS

"Oh, I forgot about that," Rose admitted.

Behind them, Bachas allowed Rolez to regain his voice, and Rolez was clearly not happy about the situation.

"Let me go," he said. "Or I'll have charges taken up against you."

"I can make you forget everything with a snap of my fingers," Bachas told him. "So I'm not worried about you at all."

"Bachas," Theo said. "Maybe we can ease up a little?"

"Only after he tells us where we can find Annalora," Bachas said. He rounded on Rolez. "Tell us!"

"Okay," he muttered. "I ordered a tapestry from her for the new queen."

"Why do you think Queen Juliette is in danger?" Rose asked.

"Because he knows Annalora makes the tapestries with Magdust," Bachas told her. "He went to go and meet with her precisely because of that."

"How do you know?" Theo asked.

"I know," Bachas snapped.

Rolez squirmed. "Fine. The pixie's right," he admitted. "I didn't want anything bad to happen to her or the King, per say. I just wanted to punish Rhone."

"So you endangered the lives of Einish's monarchs?" Rose asked. "Why?"

"Tell us." Theo's voice went dark and hard. "If she's in danger, you will tell us now."

"Did you think the Queen was in danger because of the Magdust?" Rose asked.

"Magdust in small doses is gradually supposed to affect people," Rolez muttered. "I didn't think anyone would notice. It hasn't been that long since she received it from me."

"What was the tapestry for?" Rose repeated.

When he did not answer, she grabbed Rolez by the ear and dragged him further down into the darkened alcove.

"Nothing," he shouted. "Nothing I swear!"

"That's a lie. Tell us!"

"Allow me to help with the persuasion," Bachas said, snapping his fingers. Rolez dropped to the floor from his frozen state. The diplomat easily crumbled over into a ball.

"Alright, fine," Rolez snapped. "But stop it. I'm not cut out for this. Or starting a war, apparently."

"You wanted to start a war?" Rose gave him a skeptical look. "How would that work?"

"Once it became known that the Queen of Einish had a special Magdust tapestry, the fairies would revolt, and Rhone would be upset with her for encouraging the enterprise that has weakened their whole national community," Rolez said. "The engagement between the Princess of Rhone and the Prince of Einish would be cancelled, and Crystal Lake would be weakened further by its inability to gain support. The people would be ripe for a rebellion."

Rose and Theo exchanged a quick glance. "Maybe we should get him to a guard," she said. "It sounds like there's enough there to get him arrested."

"I was just thinking the same thing," Theo said with a nod.

"No!" Bachas jumped up again. "No, he's not going anywhere, until he tells us how to find Annalora."

"Right." Rose turned to him. "Where can we find Annalora?"

Rolez looked terrified. "You aren't going to tell her I told you, are you? She knows how to get revenge on people."

ONCE UPON A PRINCESS

"We won't tell her," Rose said, but Bachas interrupted her.

"If you don't tell us where to find her, you won't have to worry about her coming for revenge," he said. "I'll take care of it myself."

Rose nearly choked. "Come on, Bachas," she said. "There's no need to put that kind of pressure on him."

"I'm a free pixie," he scoffed. "I'll do what I want."

"Bachas," Theo started to say, as Bachas snapped his fingers once more.

Rolez cried out in pain. "No!"

"Stop it," Rose insisted.

"Not until he agrees to tell us!" Bachas shouted back.

"Fine, fine," Rolez cried out. "I'll tell you. Just let me go."

Bachas folded his hands, and the flow of power halted.

"Annalora only takes on special commissions," Rolez said. "I heard about her and her tapestries as a child. I didn't think they were real. But when I was passing through Rhone, there was a tournament. She was there, trying to sell her work. When she caught sight of me, she approached me and began talking to me."

"She found you?" Theo asked.

"Yes. She told me she would have a tapestry ready for me by the time I went back to Einish with my sister. I was picking up Isabel from her manor, and taking her back with me. She had written to me, telling me that Hebert had been raging with her and arguing with her more often lately. She never stays home for long while he is there, but it was especially bad, so I went to go and secure her myself."

"I'm sorry for your sister's trouble," Rose said. "I don't know my uncle, but I can assure you he is nothing like me."

"I don't care," Rolez spat. "You're still his blood."

"But I'm not him!" Rose argued.

ONCE UPON A PRINCESS

"I don't care," Bachas said. "How did you find the tournament?"

"It was close to the Aragonian border, about a week's ride from Havilah," he said. "You follow the main trail to Aragon, and close to the border, there is a place where tournaments are held. Annalora lives close by, on the outskirts of a town called Urra."

"Urra," Theo repeated. "I've never heard of it."

"That's where she lives." Rolez nodded to Bachas. "You can even use your magic to see I am telling the truth."

Bachas did not stop to question him. He simply grabbed Rolez's hand. A moment later, as a light poured out from their hands, Bachas nodded. "I believe you."

"Can I go now?" Rolez groaned. "I don't want to be here any longer."

"Be gone!" Bachas clapped his hands, and Rolez disappeared.

Rose frowned. "I'm glad to see you're feeling better, but he had just confessed to ordering that tapestry for the Queen in order to start a trade war. I would have preferred to have Philip question him."

"Your friend can question him later," Bachas said. "I sent him to a cell in the dungeon here."

"We thank you for your consideration." Theo knelt down beside the small pixie. "And for your help in getting the information. But I have to wonder, why are you so concerned with our mission?"

"I need to know where Annalora is," Bachas said. "She's using pixie magic to hide herself from my seeing stone." He pulled out a small marble from his pocket and handed it to Theo.

ONCE UPON A PRINCESS

As Rose and Theo examined the small gemstone, it glowed with power, and a small, feminine pixie face came into its center.

"My beloved wife, Elva," Bachas explained. "Once I was bound in a life debt, I was unable to use my magic for anything except what my master said. Now I can see her again, and she is also in a life debt."

"To Annalora," Rose guessed.

Bachas nodded. "I have to go and free her. I know you are looking for Annalora too. I will need your help in finding her, so I can see Elva again."

"I don't know how we can help," Rose told him. "Annalora is a concern for us, but it is one we will have to address after we have dealt with Magdalina. But maybe King Derick will be able to help you. He is the one who should be the most upset at the issue with the tapestry, especially since it was given to Juliette."

"That won't work," Bachas said. He pointed at Theo. "He's the one who can get me back to Elva."

"Why's that?" Rose asked. "You already told him that he's not a priest, so he doesn't have the protection from your magic that they do."

"He's—"

Theo stepped forward and cut him off. "She's my aunt," he admitted quietly. "Annalora is my mother's sister."

Rose felt her mouth drop open in surprise.

16

The surprise on Rose's face was immediately washed away and replaced with suspicion. "Why didn't you tell me?" she asked Theo.

He watched her eyes narrow, and he suddenly felt irritated. He was entitled to his secrets, same as she was, and he told her so. "We all have secrets, Rose."

Instantly, Rose crossed her arms over her chest and prepared for battle.

He inwardly groaned. He did not want to fight her, especially now, when they were supposed to be having a good time, celebrating Isra's engagement.

"You still should have told me," Rose insisted.

"We have enough to do as it is," Theo replied. "You just said it yourself: Magdalina is our first priority."

"That doesn't mean that we just push everything off to the side," Rose said. "Especially when we're face to face with the issue like we are right now."

Bachas cleared his throat. "I think I'm going to take my leave," he said. "My leg is better, but still sore, and I don't think I want to get caught in the middle of a fight."

"We are not fighting," Rose snapped down at him.

Bachas smirked slyly. "Call it what you want, Princess," he said. "But I'm not stupid."

Before she could correct him, he snapped his fingers and disappeared.

"We are not fighting," Rose repeated, as if saying it again would make her believe it more.

ONCE UPON A PRINCESS

"I don't want to fight you," Theo told her. "But you are keeping secrets from me, too, and if I'm forced to tell you mine, I want to hear yours."

"You don't want to know my secrets," Rose told him, her voice suddenly so weary Theo almost wondered if he should sit her down somewhere.

Maybe I should leave her alone. This has been a long day, and we will be heading back to Rhone soon.

He decided to go. He did not want to have to tell her about his family history, and it was easier just to leave. "Excuse me," he said, before heading down the hall.

Theo was not surprised when she started following him. "Where are you going?" Rose asked, as she followed him. "We're not finished talking."

"I don't want to talk to you right now," he told her.

"Why?"

"I already told you." He pushed open a door at the end of the hall and found himself outside, on a small balcony overlooking the gardens. "I don't want to talk about Annalora, any more than you want to talk about what's bothering you."

Rose grabbed his arm and stepped in front of him. "Don't you trust me?"

Theo stopped. "That's an unfair question, Rose," he said.

"Why?" Rose put her hands on her hips.

"Because I know you were lying when I talked to you in the caverns," he said.

"I'm just trying to protect you," Rose snapped.

"I don't want your protection," Theo argued. "I want the truth."

"There's no need to get angry about it."

ONCE UPON A PRINCESS

"If that were true, why do you need to know about my family?" Theo asked.

"Are you worried I would judge you because of them?" Rose asked. "Because you know I wouldn't. You have never done that to me, even though the King has never warmed up to you."

"No," Theo said. "You know I don't talk about them much, and that's because I don't know a lot about them myself. When Enrique told me about my mother's death, I didn't know what to say."

"There isn't much you can say," Rose told him, as she stepped up beside him.

"It's still a shock," Theo told her. He made his way over to the edge of the balcony and gripped its wall. "After Thad told me he'd found my uncle's letter to our grandfather, and I learned more about them, I knew there were connections to the Magdust trade. But I never imagined it would go this far. I don't want to talk about it."

"According to Bachas," Rose said, "Annalora is using Elva's magic to protect herself. You might be the only one who can really help him, since you're related to her."

"I don't know what good that will do," Theo said. "My mother and father still died."

"By Everon's hand," Rose reminded him gently. "Not Annalora's."

"I guess so." Theo shrugged. "You know, I never thought about it much, but this is part of the reason Jesus said not to judge. I can't help but wonder if my parents deserved to die, for participating in the Magdust trade as they did. Especially after hearing all of this."

"You're the one who would tell me that we're all fallen," Rose said as she came up beside him. "You would also tell me that good things can still come from bad things."

Theo gave her a sad smile. "Is this your revenge for when I try to comfort you?"

"Maybe," she teased. "But not really. It's true, isn't it? If nothing had happened to your parents, I never would have met you."

"Just like if you hadn't been cursed, we might have never become friends." Theo sighed. "And I would have had to watch you grow up with all those suitors around, watching them fall over themselves as they charmed you, and you would have been charmed by them."

Rose made a face. "I would not," she insisted. "Some of them were terrible. Even without my curse, I wouldn't have liked them. They were still too focused on what I looked like, anyway."

"Are you saying that your beauty is more of a curse than the one Magdalina bestowed upon you?" Theo asked. He reached over and tugged on a lock of her hair, teasing her back. As Rose laughed, Theo found himself running his hand through her hair. It was soft and delicate and strangely enthralling.

Under the light of the moon and surrounded by the magic of night, she was more irresistible than ever.

Even when she stopped laughing, he had a hard time letting the last of her locks slip through his fingers, forcing himself to step back.

"Either way, I don't think it matters too much," Rose answered. "I know you're worried about your family, and wondering about them, too. But it's just like everything else

ONCE UPON A PRINCESS

we face. We'll work it out." Rose laid her head against his shoulder. "Together."

Theo let her comfort him for a long moment. "Do you really believe that?" he asked.

"I do." Rose nodded.

"Then why don't you tell me what happened in the caverns?" he asked.

Rose jerked away from him. "You just had to ruin it, didn't you?"

"Ruin what?" he asked, keeping his voice innocent.

"How nice it was, being out here, with you," Rose shot back. She pushed back her hair, and he thought he saw her blush. "I mean, it could've been so nice. I comfort you, we feel better, and then we go back into the ballroom, have a nice evening, and then everything's fine. But no, you had to bring up Magdalina."

"I didn't bring her up," Theo said. "Not exactly. I just wanted to know what happened in the cave—" He stopped as he realized what she said. "That's what happened. You saw her."

Rose turned away from him, crossing her arms.

"That's it," he said again. "You saw her, and you couldn't defeat her."

"There's no need to rub it in my face!" Rose yelled.

"What did she say?" Theo asked. "Tell me, Rose."

"She told me she would take off the curse," Rose said.

For a moment, he was only full of hope and happiness. But then Theo remembered the anger and sadness in Rose's eyes as she came back to them, following the attack by the traders in the Wandering Caverns. "But she didn't, did she?"

"She said she would."

Theo walked around and stood in front of Rose. "If you did what?" he pressed.

Rose sighed. "If I married her son and made him the next King of Rhone."

Theo did not know if he was more shocked or outraged by the thought of Rose marrying Everon. Either way, he was too distracted by Rose's further silence to decide properly.

"What did you tell her?" he asked.

"I told her I was tired of people wanting to marry me," Rose said.

He felt his breath leave him in a rush.

"She had some nerve to try to convince me it was a compliment of sorts, but I didn't believe her. She told me I had until my birthday to decide."

"But you told her no, right?"

"I tried to tell her no," Rose replied.

"Rose."

"Theo," she muttered back. "Come on. You don't know what it's like. When I hear things like what Rolez just told us, about how the Magdust trade has ruined my country's hope, then I worry. I want to know that everything will work out the way I want, but there's no guarantee."

"You're saying that you would marry Everon, in order to save yourself?"

"Myself *and* my kingdom," Rose insisted. "But only if that was the only way. And I mean, *only*."

"And you actually believe Magdalina will fulfill her promise?"

"Well, it's already something I don't want to worry about," Rose said. "So I haven't really thought about it much. But I guess you're right. I don't trust her, either."

Theo shook his head. "I can't believe you," he said.

ONCE UPON A PRINCESS

"I thought you would be more upset that I didn't manage to kill her," Rose admitted.

"No," Theo snapped. "No, I'm angry you didn't tell me about her deal, and I'm angry you didn't think it mattered enough to tell me, and then I'm angry you're not ruling it out entirely."

Rose huffed. "Well, can you blame me? My birthday is almost here, Theo. I only have four months left."

"Still, it's—"

"It's what?"

"It's not supposed to work that way between us. I have been beside you, suffering as you suffer, working as you work, for more than half our lives now. I'm not like Felise or Natala or even Sophia and Ethan and Philip. I'm not someone who just passes through your life, Rose. I'm not just going to leave you."

Theo took her by the shoulders, attempting to steady himself. He realized less than a second later that touching her was the wrong thing to do.

"What are you saying?" Rose asked. She seemed to sense the change between them at the same time. Her hands gripped onto his arms as her eyes found his.

"I'm saying there shouldn't be any secrets between us," he said, as he found himself under the spell of the moonlight once more, too swept up in the scent of the gardens, the warmth of the palace, the echo of music in the air.

"Theo?" His name came out as a whisper.

His eyes slipped down to her lips, and he heard her breath stop. "Rose."

Theo let himself take a step closer. She was not moving away; she was only watching him, waiting on him to move. He had to tell her. He had to tell her the truth.

"Rose, I—"

"Princess?" Lannister's voice called out from behind them, and the air between them suddenly turned cold.

"Remind me to retire him," Rose murmured, as they reluctantly stepped away from each other.

Theo caught her disappointment and hid a smile. He felt a little better, knowing she was as jarred by the interruption to their interlude as he was.

"Princess?" Lannister's voice called again.

"Over here," Rose responded. She stepped out from behind Theo, heading back toward the castle.

"Oh, there you are," Lannister said. "Good. I was looking for you. And you, too, actually," he added, gesturing toward Theo.

"Is something wrong?" Theo asked.

"Your brother and the Reverend Father have arrived."

"Thad's here?" Theo's eyes widened in surprise.

"Yes. They are both looking for you and the Princess. The King heard about Isra's engagement and sent them as envoys."

"That's wonderful," Rose said with a large smile on her face. "This means that the King is in agreement to the arrangement. I can sign the papers for Isra and Philip without worrying he could object."

Theo watched as Rose gave him an uncertain glance. He turned away; the moment between them had passed. And now his brother was here, waiting for them. "Let's go see them," he said.

"Yes," Rose agreed.

Together, they followed Lannister back into the castle and headed off to meet with Thad. Theo allowed himself one last look behind him, glancing back at the magic of the night,

ONCE UPON A PRINCESS

wishing he'd had the courage to confess his love for Rose when he had the chance.

17

"Theo!" Thad's enthusiastic welcome greeted them as they stepped into a small library in the castle. He raced forward and hugged his younger brother, and Rose had to envy Thad for his open affection.

Her heart was still racing as she stood there, watching as Thad and the Reverend Thorne met with Theo, greeting him alternatively with warmth and cool reserve.

She hated that Theo was right in some ways; he was a part of her life, and she had been wrong to conceal things from him. Once she saw the look on his face when she admitted the truth—that she was bound by her life and blood to do what she could for her kingdom, and that meant considering, for at least one span of a second, agreeing to Magdalina's deal—she knew it was a waste of a second to pretend she could.

Not while she was in love with Theo.

Oh, God, what have I done now?

Rose felt her heart lurch, sending the rest of her world spiraling, as the thought leaked out of her mind and into her heart before she could stop it. She wondered that the floor did not shake beneath her feet, that there was no lightning or thunder accompanying the crumbling walls inside of her.

As she stood there, watching the three men confer with each other about their travels, Rose reeled and reveled in the realization that she was in love, and it was beyond terrifying and exhilarating.

She was only interrupted from her inner freefall when Thad turned to her and knelt before her. "Your Highness," he said, his tone humble and gracious, just as welcoming as he had been to Theo.

"Brother Thad," she heard herself respond. Her eyes blinked slowly, as she looked from him to the Reverend Father, and then to Theo. She hurried to make her mind orientated for business, but she could not stop her heart from one last flutter as she looked on Theo's face.

She cleared her throat a moment later. "Please, rise," she said. "It is good to see you again. I am especially happy to see you, since Isra and Philip's engagement can be properly celebrated."

"His Majesty the King has sent us here to celebrate the engagement," Reverend Thorne said, "but he has also sent us in order to summon you home."

"I'm already on my way," Rose said. "Rhone is our next stop."

"He needs you home. He was relieved to hear that you were close by. He sent me and Brother Thad in hopes of getting you home faster."

"What's wrong?" Rose asked. "Is the Queen Mother ill? Or has there been another attempt on his life."

"A visitor has come to Rhone," Thad said. "Your Uncle Hebert has arrived, with a small legion of troops. He has come to the castle and there is a silent coup among the servants, since your uncle is demanding the release of the Queen."

Rose groaned. "Trust my family to mess everything up," she said. "And the King needs my help in fixing everything, I suppose?"

Thad nodded. "That's what we are facing right now. He sent us here as a pretext to find you and get you to leave at once for the capital."

ONCE UPON A PRINCESS

"I don't see why he needs my help," Rose muttered.

"Your father married into the throne," Reverend Thorne spoke up, his old and ancient voice hesitant. "As your eighteenth birthday draws near, and the Queen remains in prison, many see the King's actions as hostile to the nation."

"What about Isra? And Ronan?" Rose asked. "Surely his other heirs would put settle quite a few people's concerns."

Thad and the Reverend Father exchanged knowing glances, before Thad spoke up. "You might as well know," he said slowly, "that there are rumors circling that Isra and Ronan are illegitimate heirs."

Rose remembered what Magdalina had said before; she had called Isra and Ronan her half-siblings.

"I didn't think a lot of the kingdom even knew about Isra and Ronan," Rose said, confused and frustrated. "How would they know that they are illegitimate?"

"Because *we* know." Reverend Thorne frowned at Thad.

Rose was glad when Theo reached out and put his hand on her shoulder. Her legs went numb at the news. "What?" she asked.

"The Queen has confessed, and the church has long known of King Stefanos' impotency," Reverend Thorne said.

Rose slumped down into a chair. "I apologize," she said. "I had no idea."

"I would not confess this to you, Princess, as a man of the cloth, if the rumors were not already circulating," Revered Thorne said with a sigh. "And if my grandson here hadn't just told you."

"It's written testimony, located in some of our saved records," Thad insisted. He glanced over at Theo, and Rose had to wonder if he was letting him know he was the one who had discovered the truth. Rose knew Thad liked to read.

That was how they had learned so much about the dragon's blood and the Serpent's Garden.

"Yes, that too." The Reverend gave Thad a quick, stern look.

"Well," Rose murmured, "I guess that explains some of the secrets my father told me, the kind that all kings and queens keep to themselves."

"I know this must be shocking," Thad said.

"To put it mildly," Rose assured him, giving him a kind smile, before she thought of something else. "But wait," she said. "If the King was impotent, who is my father?"

"You were a miracle," Revered Thorne said. "The day the Queen told us she was pregnant with you, there was a prophecy spoken during chapel. The prophecy said you would save the crown's lineage and be a great leader. Everyone was thrilled."

"I can imagine." Rose shook her head as it all came together. Her father, knowing of his condition, went to Magdalina to see about an heir. He had agreed to her deal, that Rose would marry a fairy of Magdalina's choice. He had reneged on the deal when she was born, and that was why Magdalina had cursed her to die on her eighteenth birthday.

Her mother, grief-stricken, had flown into the arms of another man. Was it Roderick? Rose wondered, thinking of the close relationship she had witnessed between her guard and the Queen.

But he'd said he was just her friend, Rose recalled a moment later. He was her messenger to Aragon....

Where her father's brother lived, married to a woman he neglected.

Rose's eyes widened at the possibility. Was it her uncle who was Isra and Ronan's real father?

ONCE UPON A PRINCESS

"And you said Uncle Hebert has come to rescue my mother?" Rose asked.

"Yes," Thad answered with a nod.

"I see." Rose sank back into her chair. "Did you find out who was behind the attack on the King? The one who tried to poison him?"

"No one other than the Queen has come under investigation."

Rose rubbed her temples. "Well, I guess everything is a mess at home," she said.

"We believe you are under the protection of our Lord and Savior," Reverend Thorne told her. "We are prepared to follow you, Princess. Our nation has heard of your conquests and your trials. We know you have found the dragon's lair and secured its blood."

Rose looked at Theo. She saw the concern on his face, the fire in his eyes.

"I have never found myself to be under much protection from God," Rose said slowly, "but I do think you are right. I need to go home and make things right with Rhone."

She was tempted to tell them she would go home and fix her parents' mess, but she decided it was not what the representatives to her kingdom needed to hear. "Excuse me," she said, standing up. "I need to go and get ready."

Thad and Reverend Thorne bowed their heads, but Theo reached for her.

She shook her head at him. "We'll talk later," she said. "Not now."

He seemed to sense the sadness behind her words, and said nothing. He only nodded and watched her leave.

574

18

Theo waited until Rose was out of the room before he turned back to face his brother and grandfather. He kept one ear out for the softening of Rose's footsteps, as he did not want her to interrupt them.

Rose had family issues of her own to contend with; Theo did not want her to get in the middle of his.

"What is it?" Reverend Thorne sighed heavily as Theo came up beside him.

"I want to know about Annalora," he said.

Theo had to give his grandfather credit; the old man only blinked at him. Thad, on the other hand, gasped in surprise. "Annalora is alive?"

"Yes," Theo said. "I have some idea of where she is located, and I would like to know more about her."

"Why?" The Reverend's eyes narrowed. "She is nothing but trouble, Theophilus, and you would do well to forget about her entirely as I have."

"I doubt you really mean that," Thad said gently.

Theo did not indulge his grandfather as Thad did. "I need to know more about her," he said, "because she has been causing trouble for Rhone and other nations now."

"What have you heard?" Reverend Thorne asked, only slightly concerned.

"She's still working in the Magdust trade, for one."

"That's no surprise," his grandfather replied. "Her mother was a talented weaver, and she taught Annalora and Eleanora everything she knew."

"I also found out with the help of a friend she's using pixie magic to cover her tracks, but she's still active in the Magdust

ONCE UPON A PRINCESS

trade. She's using her weaving talent to make enchanted tapestries, just like the one we used to have in our home."

Thad met Theo's eyes. "I remember that one. The one of Queen Lucia?"

"Yes." Theo nodded. "That's the one. She recently made another one for the new Queen of Einish."

Reverend Thorne was increasingly still. "I see."

"Is that all you have to say?" Theo asked.

"I've known about the magic for a lot longer than you have," Reverend Thorne said. "Why do you think your uncle had to write me a letter? I barely had any idea of what kind of life Eleanora had lived. It had been so many years since your grandmother had died, and I had disowned them for their sin."

"You didn't report them?" Thad asked.

"No," Reverend Thorne's pale cheeks burned red. "I did not want to get caught up in all their trouble again."

"You didn't do anything to protect other people?" Theo shook his head. "Do you know how many fairies and other people have died because of your inaction?"

"It's not like I could have saved anyone for certain." The older man's eyebrows furrowed together in grave concern. "I told you, I lost track of them years ago. I doubt I would have heard from Eleanora again if she had lived. There is no way to change the past."

"No," Theo agreed, "but we can change the future. We need to find Annalora and bring her to justice. For all the fairies she's killed and all the people whose lives she's ruined. And for Rhone. The Princess wants to stop the Magdust trade, and it's up to us to do what we can to stop her."

"We cannot do anything that will stop her," the Reverend moaned.

ONCE UPON A PRINCESS

"I don't believe that," Theo said. "I'm more likely to believe that you just don't want to do anything."

"Well, I don't," the Reverend snapped. "Eleanora and Annalora died to me the day they decided to follow after my mother's profession. Weaving magic into fabric, all for the sake of silly wishes to be fulfilled. They didn't seem to think some that fairies would have a problem with that."

Thad frowned. "Would the love of our father be one of those wishes?"

Theo was wondering the same thing.

"I do not speak of it," Reverend Thorne snapped. "I do not like to do anything that is connected with them. I am ashamed of my daughters and their choices, but there is nothing I can do."

"If that's true, why did you take us in, then?" Theo asked.

"Because you are family, and you were innocent. God deal with me ever so harshly should I fail to protect innocent blood."

"I need to know what you know about Annalora," Theo insisted. "If you want to protect other people, you need to tell me what you know. She's already aided a man who was trying to start a war between Rhone and Einish."

"What a foolish man."

"Foolish, maybe, but he still managed to endanger the lives of Philip's brother and his wife. And possibly their new baby," Theo said. He told them of what had happened in the castle at Crystal Lake, citing Juliette's fear and distress for her unborn child.

There was a small shuffling noise behind them as Theo finished his tale. He glanced over to see Bachas had come into the room.

ONCE UPON A PRINCESS

"That's not all of it, either, by far," Bachas said. "She tricked my wife into a life debt. It was many years ago. Since then, she has used her to protect herself from any repercussions while she continues to oversee a majority of the Magdust trade."

Theo watched his grandfather's wrinkled face, usually as stoic as weathered leather, as it collapsed with despair. Theo and Thad each took an arm and guided him over to the chair where Rose had been sitting only moments before.

"Grandfather," Theo said, "you have to do something. All it takes for evil to prevail is that good people do nothing, remember?"

"I've already done nothing," the Reverend said. "It's too late. The kingdom is doomed. Annalora and Eleanora have already ruined it. They never should have made that Magdust tapestry for King Stefanos, even if he needed an heir."

Theo and Thad rounded on him.

"What are you talking about?" Thad asked. "You just told the Princess that she was a miracle baby."

The older man frowned. "I'm not saying anything else," he insisted.

"If you don't," Bachas spoke up, "I can make you change your mind."

"You can't use magic on me," the Reverend scoffed. "I'm a priest, remember?"

"I can still try," Bachas insisted. He stuck his tongue out at him. "And if nothing else, I feel no obligation to spare you any pain just using my fists."

"Ha! I'd love to see you try."

Theo stepped in between them. "There's no need for that. Just tell us the truth, Grandfather. Tell us what you know."

ONCE UPON A PRINCESS

"I've kept the secrets of the kingdom for many years," the Reverend said.

"And they destroying us now," Theo told him. "Now, you must tell us the truth. Only that will allow us to make things right."

"You can't make things like this right."

"We can at least try, instead of sitting there and doing nothing!" Theo insisted. "Tell us."

Bachas took a menacing step forward, and the Reverend noticeably winced.

"Fine," he said. "Magdalina made a deal with Stefanos. She gave him Magdust in order to be able to conceive a child."

"Rose."

"The Princess, yes." The Reverend sighed. "The church was delighted, even though I knew it was magic. I did not say anything. Stefanos found out I knew, and threatened to remove me from the church."

"And you didn't resign or quit or transfer in protest?" Thad asked. "That's terrible."

"I wanted protection from your mother and aunt," the Reverend reminded him. "I wasn't about to leave the most connected sacred plot of land in the whole nation if I could help it."

"Did you tell the church the prophecy?" Theo asked. "The one you just told Rose about?"

"No," Reverend Thorne scoffed. "I'm not stupid. The King would have seen that as a desperate ploy for me to stay on his good side. The former head priest was the one who received it."

"So Rose is really a miracle?" Theo asked.

"Does it matter?" Reverend Thorne sniffed.

"It matters if you lied."

ONCE UPON A PRINCESS

"Hardly."

"You say that, but it's your fault that Annalora is still on the loose, making tapestries full of Magdust."

"That's enough, Theo," Thad interrupted. "We have to get the facts first. Then judgment."

Theo scowled at him, but relented as Thad asked the Reverend about their mother's role.

"There's a problem with Magdust when you ingest too much of it. You can easily go insane. Magdalina poisoned the King with too much Magdust. He was slipping into madness. There was only one thing I could do, and … "

"So Mother and Annalora made a tapestry for him," Thad finished. "I see it now. You were the one who contacted them."

"Not directly," the Reverend said. "But Magdalina was determined to have the throne. She wanted Stefanos out of the way, no doubt, so she would be able to rule while the Princess was still a baby."

"And once Rose married Everon," Theo said, "everything she would finally have everything she wanted. She would have a kingdom of her own and a future for her son."

"That's about it," the Reverend said. "But when your mother and Annalora stepped in, and the King did not die, Magdalina was infuriated. She cursed Rose not only because he reneged on his promise that Rose would marry her son, but because he knew Magdalina had tried to kill him."

"If our mother saved the King's life," Thad asked, "why do you still avoid contact with Annalora?"

"Your aunt was very reluctant to help. She was upset and angry when Eleanora revealed what she was going to do with the tapestry. Annalora vowed never to work with her again, and she made certain threats at the time."

ONCE UPON A PRINCESS

"So when our parents died," Theo said, "Annalora didn't know what had happened to them?"

"I doubt anyone knows for sure," the Reverend told him. "All I knew was what your uncle told me. There is a chance she knows something, but I couldn't tell you for certain."

There was a long moment of silence, and then Theo spoke up.

"I'll go and get her," Theo said. "Once we stop her, the Magdust trade will be down one supplier, and she can be brought to Rhone's capital for justice. And maybe her testimony will remind people that we need to band together to fight the Magdust trade once and for all."

"It's still too late. I failed her," Reverend Thorne whispered, his voice catching in his throat. It seemed that he had forgotten how to cry, to weep, to mourn.

Theo felt his sadness, so strained and unable to be released, as it weighed down on his weak shoulders. "It is tragic what happened to our family," he agreed.

"So many lives lost, so many people buying into empty promises, so many others caught up in the collateral damage," Thad muttered. "It's just awful."

Reverend Thorne sank deeper into the cushions. "It has been too many years. I can't just go and see her, or summon her."

"You're not able to travel well, anyway, Grandfather," Thad said. He turned to Theo. "He had trouble on the way here. We would have been here earlier if he had been able to handle the terrain better."

"I'm almost eighty-three," the man reminded him. "There's nothing wrong with me."

"There's nothing wrong with admitting that traveling across Rhone to meet with a formidable Magdust dealer might not be in your best interest," Thad pointed out.

"I already said I would go and get her," Theo said.

Theo did not like the idea of getting Annalora. He was certain Rose would be unwilling to go and bring Annalora to justice. Facing Magdalina and Everon had been their goal since he had set off with Rose over five years ago, and the thought of leaving her crushed him.

But as he watched his grandfather's face, Theo knew he had to do something. His grandfather, while he obviously did not like the idea of Thad and Theo running around in his church, had taken them in and raised them as much as he could. He had given them a home, and Thad a future. Theo knew he would never have met Rose without his grandfather taking him in.

Before Theo could ask for more details about Annalora again, Bachas snorted behind him. "I'd rather just kill her," he said.

"Bachas, please," Theo said. "This is a member of my family we're talking about."

"And she has my wife as her slave," Bachas reminded him. "I'm allowed my say, or do pixies not have the same rights as humans?"

"You can have your say," Theo told him. "But it is more a question of manners, than rights, and kindness over legalities."

The small pixie rolled his large eyes, almost eliciting a smile from Theo, before Bachas crossed his arms and stuck his nose up in the air.

"This is my fault," Reverend Thorne said. "I have been running away from all this trouble since the day Annalora and

Eleanora decided to follow their mother into the weaving business."

"It was still their choice," Theo said. "You don't get all the blame or all the glory when it comes to your child's choices."

"Let's hear you say that, and have a child who turns out as mine did," his grandfather scoffed. "Theo, the church is protected by magic. Why do you think I turned to the priesthood after my wife died? I knew all her troublesome activities would catch up to me one day."

"You know you should not use the church as a refuge for your own sin," Thad chided him lightly.

"It doesn't matter now. Annalora is my only child still left alive, and she is causing nothing but destruction for everyone who crosses her path."

Theo watched as Thad comforted their grandfather. A moment later, Bachas came up beside him, tugging on his pantleg. "What is it, Bachas?"

"I will go with you," he said. "I'll get everything ready while you talk to your princess."

"What makes you think I'm going to go now?" Theo asked.

"My seeing crystal," Bachas told him, holding up the small marble. "Why do you think I came here tonight? What business does a pixie have with a pair of priests otherwise? Besides, you know you are the most qualified and able to go. And you will. I have seen your heart, Sir Theo, and I know you always step up to help family."

Theo stilled. "What about Rose?"

"What about her?" Bachas frowned. "She has her own family to attend to, doesn't she?"

"But I'm her family."

"No, you're not," Bachas told him. "You're her partner, her protector, and her trusted advisor—until she needs to keep her heart and secrets safe from you."

"That's not true," he said, balking at his words. But Theo had a harder time dismissing Bachas' claims than he would have liked to admit.

"You've thought of leaving her before," Bachas chided him.

"For revenge," Theo muttered. "But I know now that I … I just can't leave her. And you really need to stay out of my mind."

"Seeing crystal," Bachas reminded him, holding up the small marble once more.

"Stop using it on me, then." Theo shook his head. "You don't get to tell me what to do."

"Even though I know what you'll do," Bachas whispered, his voice just sly enough to make Theo grimace. "Go and talk to your princess. See if I'm not right in the end. I'll be waiting for you in the stables."

Theo did not like the look on Bachas' face as the pixie left. There was a grim certainty on his face that made Theo nervous.

He struggled to shrug it off. He had work to do, he told himself. Thad was still arguing with their grandfather when Theo stepped forward.

"That's enough," he said. "If Annalora is as dangerous as we think, it is only right that I go and get her." He glanced down at the pixie beside him. "Bachas can come with me, to show me the way and to get his wife back."

The Reverend Father sniffed. "What makes you think you will convince her to come to Havilah and face me?" he asked.

ONCE UPON A PRINCESS

"I don't know," Theo admitted. "But you're too old, and you need to be here for Isra anyway."

"That's right." Thad straightened. "We have been sent here by the King to be his representatives. We need to work through her marriage contract and discuss her dowry with the Dowager Queen."

"I'm sure Utopa will be more than happy to discuss those details," Theo said. He turned to his brother. "Thad, why don't you come with me? I can give you back the manuscripts you lent us."

"I'll be more than happy to do just that," Thad said, brightening up at the mention of his scrolls. "I think it would be best if you find a way to rest for now, Reverend."

Their grandfather turned away from them and said nothing as they left.

"Do you think he was telling us the truth?" Theo asked Thad.

"Unfortunately, yes," Thad replied. "I have been going through the written records we house at the church. We have several thousand scrolls and books dedicated to testimonies the church has collected over the last several decades. But King Stefanos has very few, and he never makes much of an effort to come to mass or confession."

"If those are his secrets, I can see why."

"Yes, well, I suppose you've got a point."

They walked up to Theo's room, where he kept the manuscripts Thad had let them borrow. Thad cheerfully talked about other things, from the party to how nice it was to see everyone again.

Theo barely listened, as he thought about what Bachas said. It was only as Thad eagerly pawed through his papers that he said something that caught Theo's attention.

ONCE UPON A PRINCESS

"What did you say?" Theo asked.

"I was wondering what Rose thought about what I told you before," Thad replied. "About true love's kiss. That has the power to break spells."

"I didn't tell her," Theo admitted.

"Why?" Thad grinned. "Too afraid she would look to Philip for deliverance?"

"No," Theo grunted, but he had to wonder if Thad was at least partially right.

"Oh, brother," Thad said. "You should really just tell her you love her. You said it yourself earlier: Truth will make things right."

"I don't know about that where Rose is concerned," Theo argued.

"Come on, Theo," Thad said. "Don't be such a hypocrite. You know it makes the rest of us look bad. And besides, sometimes you have to lead others by showing them the way."

"It was easier to tell that to the Reverend than it would be to tell her that." He did not want to tell Thad what Bachas had told him.

"Still, if true love's kiss would be enough to break her curse, she would want to know."

"Of all things, I know that's what she wants the most," Theo said. "Or at least, that's what she wants the most that she will admit to herself."

"Please," Thad said. "Just go and tell her."

"I should pack up and get ready to leave," Theo said, brushing his brother's concern aside. "After all, I have a lot more to think about right now, with everything we learned tonight about our family. Did you get your manuscripts?"

"Yes," Thad remarked. He gave Theo a hard look. "I'm going to get settled into my room," he said. "I'll talk with you again soon. I love you, brother."

"I love you, too." Theo gave him a smile as he left, glad that he did have family to support him, even when it was his own fear he found himself up against.

As soon as he was alone, he allowed himself to admit Thad was right.

If he wanted to know what was in Rose's heart, he would have to give her his first.

Long moments passed, as the music swelled from stories below. The night continued on, and the beauty of the night began to pass away into a quiet morning.

It was only then, after much thought and prayer, Theo made his way downstairs.

ONCE UPON A PRINCESS

19

Not for the first time, Rose had trouble sleeping. It made no difference that on the night of her sister's engagement party, not too many other people were sleeping.

In fact, as she changed into her knight's clothes, and packed her things, she was comforted by the large gathering of people below. After a few hours of preparing to leave, Rose made her way out to the balcony of the ballroom once more, this time staying back and off to the side, watching all the dancers and cheers and eager faces as they slowly waned and began to tire.

Everyone is having such a good time, she thought.

Mary and Fiona were staying close to Philip and Isra, following them around even on the ballroom dance floor. Rose could see Ethan as he brought out his harp, strumming out a tune a few times here and there; even Sophia was there, in a fancy new dress Rose recognized as Mary's work, dancing with several elegantly dressed men. Rose smiled. *My kids are growing up, I guess.*

Which made the idea of leaving seem even harder.

After the ball, none of her friends would be eager to get back on the road to Rhone.

She had a lot of business to take care of, and there would be no fun such as this once she got back to her home. The King was under attack, either by another's hand or his own mind; the Queen Mother was in prison, and there was Uncle Hebert, whom she had trouble remembering if she ever even met, who was bringing an army to her mother's defense. And then there was the kingdom itself. How was she going to convince them that she was able to take care of them? That they could trust her, and that their nation would be safe?

"I don't even know the answer to that," Rose muttered to herself.

She sighed and turned away, and headed outside.

Back under the waning moonlight, she felt the tranquility of the moment before Lannister had come barreling into the gardens, before she had been called to meet with Reverend Thorne and Thad.

Everything seemed more potent, she thought, looking up at the early morning skies as they waited for the sun to rise. The earth seemed to breathe more easily. The flowers gave off their scent more freely. The air seemed more crisp.

"Rose."

Rose nearly jumped at the sound of Theo calling her name. Even his voice seemed more full of magic this morning, she thought as she turned to face him.

"Theo," she said. "What are you doing out here?"

"Probably the same as you," he replied. "I know you want to leave soon."

"I'm ready to go," Rose admitted. "I just don't know how to break the news to the others. I'm not even sure if I should make them go. Isra and Philip seem so happy here."

He nodded. "We have been moving around a lot in the last several months. I'm sure Philip is glad to be home, for sure. He hasn't traveled around as much as the rest of us."

"And I can't imagine Sophia and Ethan really want to go back to their home," Rose added.

Theo nodded. "What about you? Will you be happy to be back in Rhone?"

ONCE UPON A PRINCESS

Rose bristled. "I doubt it. According to what your brother and the Reverend said, there are plenty of complications back home to keep me busy."

"I know how you feel." He came up next to her and held out his hand. "Why don't you walk with me for a while?"

"I don't need your arm," Rose told him.

"Come on, Rose," Theo said. "It's not that unusual. It's not like I'm asking you for your foot."

Rose smiled, even though she felt a rush of nerves. "Alright," she said, taking his hand.

She let him lead her down into the gardens. The music still played in the background, but the sounds of another world slipped away more and more with each step.

"This place seems magical," Rose said as they passed by several rose bushes. "Looking around, you could almost believe anything is possible. I feel like I could take on Magdalina herself in places like this."

Theo nodded. "I feel the same as you, but I'm curious as to how you would plan such a victory."

Rose had almost relaxed. She was glad they could talk about the upcoming battle, but she hated that he was going to ask her uncomfortable questions.

"After all," Theo said, "there's a chance the dragon's blood won't work."

"It's not like there is anything else that could," Rose replied, her tone hard.

She felt his hand tighten around hers. "Thad mentioned that there is something else that might work," he told her.

Rose stopped in her tracks. "What?"

"There's something else that might break Magdalina's spell," he said.

"If you're talking about marrying Everon—"

ONCE UPON A PRINCESS

"No, I'm not," Theo told her. "Never that."

"What is it then?" she asked, genuinely curious now.

"True love's kiss."

Rose would have let herself laugh, if it wasn't for the look on his face. It was too serious now, and she could not stop her body from giving an involuntary shudder. "I don't believe it," she whispered. "It's too easy, and too hard, to just believe."

"You said this place felt full of possibilities. What about falling in love?" Theo asked, his voice quiet. "Why not?"

"Are we ever really free to fall in love?" Rose asked. "Because it seems to me that it just happens, and then there's very little to be done about it."

"There's still a choice," Theo said. He came up beside her, and she realized he was standing too close to her. Rose could feel the heat of his body. She could smell the sweetness of his breath. Hear the beating of his heart.

Rose knew she could have moved, but she did not. She stayed where she was, allowing him to be this close to her.

"How do you know?" she whispered.

"Falling in love and taking a leap of faith aren't so different, Rose." He reached out and took her other hand.

She felt her response immediately, and she knew he did, too. The shape of his hands, the feeling of his palms, the quiet trembling—she memorized all of it, taking in the strength and softness he radiated. She felt the bite in the wind as she inhaled sharply.

There was no one around this time. There was no Philip to come bursting through the door, no Mary to poke her head in, no Sophia and Ethan to interrupt them.

There was no one who would prevent her from making a choice; there was no one to stop her from making the choice she wanted to make.

Her eyes lifted to meet his. His emerald eyes, shadowed by the morning light and the misty fog, captivated her.

Rose knew in that second she was lost. She felt her body sway into his in silent surrender. Her eyes closed as he leaned down. For the briefest second, just before his lips touched hers, Rose went very still. And then she pressed up on her toes, aching for him. She felt the foreign press of his mouth against hers melt into a familiar caress. His lips fumbled against hers, just as she'd known they would; his scent consumed her, just as she'd known it always had. The taste of him scorched through her, just as she'd known it would.

Suddenly, she was kissing him as ardently as she'd known she'd always wanted to.

Rose pulled her hands free, wrapping her arms around his neck, her fingers digging into his back. She felt the desperation fueling them, as they struggled to move closer to each other, and matched his passion with her own.
"Rose," he breathed, pulling away from her only long enough to take another breath.

There was nothing she could do to protect herself.

He pulled away from her again, as his hands tangled up in her hair, his body pressed against hers. "I love you," he told her. "You know that, don't you? I'm in love with you."

All at once, the mood shattered. Fear flooded through her, and she quickly pushed him away.

Nothing had happened, Rose realized. There was no spell that had broken as she kissed Theo, save for the one where she could believe true love's kiss could work. "No," she said, shaking her head. "No, we can't do this."

ONCE UPON A PRINCESS

"Why not?" Theo asked.

"Magdalina's curse … nothing happened. I'm still the same as I was before we kissed. Her curse is still there." She tried not to slump over. "You don't have to pretend."

"I'm not pretending," Theo insisted, and before she could stop him, he was kissing her again.

Rose was unable to resist him, and the gentle urgency of his mouth. She trusted him. She knew he was telling her the truth.

He *was* in love with her, and she was in love with him.

Was this how it felt for Isra and Philip? Rose briefly wondered, as her pulse raced. If it was, Rose decided, she could see why Philip seemed so certain, and Isra was so determined. Theo's kiss overwhelmed her.

But just as she reveled in feeling his love for her, she knew the agonizing pain she would cause him. He loved her, and she was only going to end up hurting him.

As desperate as she was for him, she knew she had to save him.

"Theo," she murmured, allowing herself one last lingering taste of him.

"What?" His voice was breathless, and Rose suddenly felt like crying.

"I can't do this." She squared her shoulders and bravely tried to meet his gaze. "I don't love you."

"Don't you?"

"No," Rose whispered, unable to stop her voice from shaking. "And you don't really love me. I mean, we're friends. We've always been friends. You came with me because it was convenient, so you could find a way to get your own revenge—"

"I have always followed you. And not because it was convenient," he said. "I followed you because I wanted—"

"Because you wanted to."

"No, because I wanted you!"

Rose quickly stepped away from him. She did not want to hurt Theo—her strong, caring, compassionate, and loving Theo—all because he was in love with her.

"I know you, Rose," he said, taking her hand. He put her palm on his cheek. "I know you. I know you're lying."

"No, I'm not," she insisted, but her voice cracked.

"You wouldn't kiss me like that if it meant nothing."

Rose blushed furiously.

"You think you're protecting me," Theo told her. "But I know you're just trying to protect yourself." He let her hand go.

Rose felt her trepidation transform into anger. "Why shouldn't I?" she asked. "Why shouldn't I protect myself? If I don't want to love you, that's my choice."

"Is it?"

"Yes!" Rose shouted. She forced herself to meet his eyes with her own. "I don't want to love you."

He stared at her for a long moment, and Rose hoped he would not see how hard she was trying not to squirm under his imposing gaze. Her eyes slipped down to his mouth once more, and she stepped back even further from him.

"Please," she said. "Please, just leave me. I don't want you."

Of all the times she had fought with Theo over the years, she had never seen him take a blow like that. As she dismissed him, he had a stricken expression on his face, a mix of disbelief and despair. Rose wondered if he would be in less pain if she had run her sword through his heart.

Finally, he gave her a slight nod. "If you won't let me love you, there is nothing more I can do here," he said. It was his turn to step away from her. "I have some family business to attend to in Rhone."

"You're leaving?" Rose asked incredulously.

"You want your space," Theo told her. "You'll have it. Please convey my regrets to the others."

"You're really leaving me?" Rose asked. "What about what you said earlier? About how you've always been a part of my life?"

"You also told me I need to protect myself from you," he said. "You've made your choice. I'm allowed to make mine, aren't I?"

Rose had to stop herself from wincing at his words.

He paused. "If you don't want me to go, all you have to do is tell me. You know I will do as you wish."

There was no way he was going to make her take full responsibility for this, she thought. Rose wondered if he was trying to make her admit it, to take back everything she had just gone through, in order to keep him by her side. Was it an ultimatum of sorts? Rose wondered.

She shook her head. "No," she said. "You're right. You should leave. Family matters, and I have my own family to deal with once we get to Rhone."

Theo looked crestfallen, but he nodded. "Alright, then. Goodbye … Rosary."

Rose watched as he turned away from her, surprised to feel a sharp pain inside her own heart, not relief. Rose curled her fingers into her palms, digging her nails deep into her skin, doing all she could to stop herself from calling him back.

As he disappeared back toward the castle, the tears finally slipped down her cheeks. She touched the rosary beads at her wrist, feeling the burning shame of her guilt.

20

Theo brushed against the rough wetness of his cheeks, letting their stinging saltiness sink into him as he entered the stables.

Bachas stepped out to meet him. "I told you we would be leaving," he said.

"I don't want to hear it," Theo said. "Please stop using your seeing crystal to see the future."

"I will tell you a secret," Bachas said. "I can see the future, but the future can still change. Everything I see is dependent on choices and circumstances."

"So you knew Rose would tell me to leave?" Theo asked.

"It was either that or give up the battle she has been fighting with her own heart for many years," Bachas replied. "And you know the Princess well enough to know she would never willingly give up a fight."

Theo nodded. "Well, let's head out then. Rhone is a good distance away from O'Lin by horse."

"Your brother is coming," Bachas said.

"Why?" Theo asked.

"I told him we were going to leave in the morning when he came to pester me with questions about pixie magic and their history."

Despite his sorrow, Theo smiled. "That's my brother for you," he said.

"Annoying."

"Sometimes." Theo shrugged. "But for the right reasons."

"If there are right reasons to be annoying."

"I'll remind you of that as we ride," Theo said. "I'm sure you'll have more of an argument for being annoying by the time you spend a whole day riding hard."

Bachas smirked playfully at him. "We'll see, Sir Knight," he said.

"I'm not a real knight. Not yet."

"Sure you are," Bachas said. "You've always wanted to follow in Benedict's footsteps, haven't you? Well, now that your lady has rejected you, your training is complete."

Theo's heart ached, and he struggled not to let Bachas see his pain. "I guess I wanted his success, but never his pain," he muttered.

"Theo?" Thad's voice called out from the far end of the stables.

"Over here," Theo replied, waving from his horse's stall. "We're about to head out, I guess."

"I'm glad I caught you," Thad said. "I'm so sorry we haven't had much time to catch up."

"We will have plenty of time," Theo promised, "as soon as I get back from Annalora's."

"Theo?"

"What?"

"You told her, didn't you?"

Theo cringed. "I don't want to talk about it," he said.

"But you did tell her?"

"For all the good it did," Theo replied. He sighed. "She wanted me to leave, so I am leaving."

"I will let her know why," Thad promised.

"If she cares at all," Theo grumbled.

"You know she does."

"She might, but she doesn't let herself do anything about it. Other than ignore it."

ONCE UPON A PRINCESS

Thad shook his head. "I'm sorry," he said.

"It's fine. But Bachas and I are heading out." Theo turned to see the pixie climb up behind the horse's saddle, already working on a way to secure himself so he could rest easy on the way to Rhone.

"The Grand Father and I will be back in Rhone within a few weeks," Thad said to Theo. "Once we settle everything for Princess Isra, we will return."

Theo nodded. "I'll likely need some time to ride. Annalora's last location was near Aragon."

"Send me a message when you get the chance."

"I will." Theo clasped his brother's arm in his firmly, before he climbed up onto his horse, carefully avoiding Bachas as he swung his leg over. "Please take care of Rose for me."

"If she will let me," Thad replied. "Other than that, I'll do the best I can."

With that, Theo urged his horse forward, and he set off for Rhone. The moonlight has passed into sunrise, and the misty morning fog was already clearing itself from his path. The music of the ballroom had gone quiet, and the dew on the flowers was already starting to evaporate.

Behind him, Bachas sighed contentedly, relaxing as he settled behind Theo's saddle.

Theo tried not to think of all his friends as he left. He knew that he had to take care of his family, and he knew that Rose wanted the break between them. His heart was already in pain, and he needed to focus on the road as he headed toward Rhone.

As he passed through the last of the castle grounds, Theo reined in his horse, slowing down. He thought he could hear the music rising up from behind him again.

But once he could hear it, he knew what it was.

Who alone can be worthy of great love?
Our worlds are full of fools with dreams
Of tender kisses, melting looks, of
Magic underneath the moonbeams.

Queen Lucia sought to love a special one
Sir Benedict, his heart became the prize;
He who was worthy of her love alone
She saw as worthy in her own eyes.

He embraced her love and held her close
He fought for her hand and heart—
Only when he won did she choose
A life where they would never part.

Rose was singing to him.

"Goodbye, Rosary," he whispered once more, before he pushed his horse back into a trot. Theo knew he would be haunted by every moment over the past years that he was close to Rose; he already felt his heart breaking all over again, and it was more painful to know he would let it break forever if it meant he could kiss her again, if he could have her respond to him once more.

Theo knew he was free from her presence, but there was nowhere he could go where he would be free of her.

Of course, he thought to himself, that wouldn't mean he wasn't going to try.

"Hold on, Bachas," he called back, as he urged his horse into a full gallop. "It might get bumpy back there."

Bachas groaned as they sped up, heading out on a new adventure.

C. S. Johnson is the author of several young adult sci-fi and fantasy novels, including *The Starlight Chronicles* series, the *Once Upon a Princess* saga, and the *Divine Space Pirates* trilogy. She currently lives in Atlanta with her family.

PRINCE PHILIPPOS

By Julia Mae Busko

603
ONCE UPON A PRINCESS

AUTHOR'S NOTE AND ACKNOWLEDGEMENTS

Dear Reader,

Over the many years I've had the privilege of traveling, I've noticed that the hardest part always seems to come in the middle of it—that part where you are not quite home, but the terrain begins to bend in that familiar way. It is frustrating, since you are so glad to be so close, but wearying, to know you are not quite there yet. I think this is what I most tried to capture in this book. Despite the progress, despite the encouragement, the human heart is always somewhat restless until it is secure in the knowledge that it has arrived to where it needs to be.

In the last book, I focused on the quest Rose faced, as she journeyed across the world. For this one, I wanted a more introspective journey, one that would force her to confront her own heart. Julius Caesar's famous assertion, courtesy of Shakespeare, that the courageous die only once is admirable, but when it comes to living, I am certain that introspective people (people who tend to be writers, unsurprisingly) live several, possibly innumerable, lives. The physical journey is often just as important as the inner journey, but life becomes even more than we thought it was, as we reflect on the different parts of what makes us who we are. Rose's journey here, to not only recognizing what is in her heart, but also making her choice to act on it, reveals the tension between idealism and realism, hope and hopelessness, and the fear of the choice and the choice itself.

It's all of life's little complications and all of the possible repercussions that make me excited to see what happens next.

As always, I am so grateful you took the time to read my work, and I hope you have enjoyed it. Please leave a review of it somewhere on the vast sea of the Internet, so I can see what you think—good or bad, I'm always interested to see what others think of my work. It's hard to see your work objectively as an author.

It shouldn't be a long wait until I finish the conclusion of this saga, *Beauty's Gift (Once Upon a Princess*, Part IV). I'm looking forward to seeing you again soon!

Until We Meet Again,

C. S. Johnson

ONCE UPON A PRINCESS

BEAUTY'S GIFT

PART IV OF THE *ONCE UPON A PRINCESS* SAGA

C. S. Johnson

Library of Congress Control Number: 2017912444

ISBN-13 eBook: 9781943934300
ISBN-13 Book: 9781943934317

ONCE UPON A PRINCESS

For my mother, with much love. It always stuns and amuses me that as a writer that I have trouble putting into words just what you and your support mean to me.

And again, this is also for Sam. God doesn't give people to me randomly or haphazardly. I've seen some of the reasons for you and look forward to seeing more.

This book is published courtesy of

www.direwolfbooks.com

ONCE UPON A PRINCESS

611
ONCE UPON A PRINCESS

PART IV

"… Love is not love
    Which alters when it alteration finds,
Or bends with the remover to remove.
    O no! it is an ever-fixed mark
That looks on tempests and is never shaken;
    It is the star to every wand'ring bark,
Whose worth's unknown, although his height be taken.
    Love's not Time's fool, though rosy lips and cheeks
Within his bending sickle's compass come;
    Love alters not with his brief hours and weeks,
But bears it out even to the edge of doom."

~ "Sonnet 116," William Shakespeare

"Greater love has no one than this: To lay down one's life for one's friends."

~ John 15:13, NIV

613
ONCE UPON A PRINCESS

1

It was an unescapable observation that, after years traveling across the world, seeing distant lands, meeting new people, fighting battles, and forging peace between fighters, Rose, the Princess of Rhone, found the day to day business of the king's council room seemed unforgivably dull by comparison.

Especially when her father used it as an excuse to herald his "brilliant" discoveries and decisions over the course of his reign, she thought, irritated as King Stefanos, as he continued droning on about some unrelated matter or another with one of his advisors.

Inside her father's council room, it seemed that it was business as usual, and that meant the king was intent on ignoring actual business.

She tried not to sigh in exasperation—again.

Even a princess has to learn how to deal with politics.

Moments, seemingly hours has passed as the knights of her father's council chatted, often getting off topic. Which would have been bad enough, but the topics were hardly relevant to the kingdom in the first place, Rose thought.

Finally, Rose had enough. She cleared her throat, cutting into the conversation. "Excuse me."

"What's wrong this time, Princess Aurora?" Stefanos asked, glaring down his nose at her.

Rose almost rolled her eyes. There was no need for him to look so repugnant. It was clear from his tone and his use of her proper first name he did not appreciate her interruption as he was describing the cuisine of the Orlo Empire.

"I was hoping we could move onto the next topic of the kingdom agenda, Your Majesty," Rose said, her own voice clipped. After several days of similar meetings, she could tell the King did not care she was getting impatient with him.

"We'll get there in a few moments. If you are feeling tired, you may be excused," Stefanos told her, chiding her as if she was a child. "I know this cannot be easy for an active young lady such as yourself."

Rose gave him a bitter smile. "I'm perfectly capable of sitting through a meeting, Majesty, but our subjects are more concerned with our decisions for the future, not stories of the past."

Stefanos' face reddened. He caught several looks around the table and suddenly laughed. "My daughter certainly has a bleeding heart for the people," he said. "No doubt they are much relieved to have her back in Rhone after all the years she has been abroad. Let us hope she will be able to learn how things are done here quickly, so we might truly be a force for good."

There were many nods and small voices of agreement around the table, before Stefanos once more turned the conversation back to himself.

Indignation simmered inside of her, but Rose held still. Since she had returned to Rhone several days prior, Rose had learned quickly that there was no stickier and messier battlefield to navigate than politics.

She breathed out a silent sigh as the King and his knights continued to laugh and joke as they half-discussed border security policies and taxation.

She was the heir to the kingdom's throne, and she had a right to be there as much as the King or any other of his knights—not that all of them would agree with that. As Rose looked around the table for support, she was not surprised to find many knights who avoided her gaze; of the ones who did

ONCE UPON A PRINCESS

look her way, most of them were glaring at her, suspicious. It did not help that several of the knights were older than her father, and years had passed since many of them had been sent out on assignment or they had fought in battles. Rose had her own ideas of who would be demoted the moment she took over the kingdom.

If I ever take over the kingdom.

As King Stefanos started telling another one of his stories, arguing for this or that, and the room resumed its informal, unserious atmosphere, Rose groaned.

If I ever get through this meeting.

Rose felt her eyes slip to the wall behind the King, wishing there was a window in the room. The room would have felt less like a prison.

A small amount of color in the council room would have brightened up the room considerably. After several days' worth of meetings where their subjects' concerns were either dismissed or endlessly debated, it would have been nice to have a reminder that they were responsible to their nation and its people.

Rose sighed as she thought about her trip home. It had taken her several days to ride through the countryside, going from one small village to the next, before crossing forests and open plains. Rhone was a smaller country, surrounded by others with a few port cities, where traders hustled and sellers would bring their goods out to market every day. Rose had seen it on her own grand tour, and she knew that her nation was as indebted to the sea as it was to the forest.

Thinking of the trip back to Rhone, one she had made with only the company of Mary, her fairy and friend, only made her think of the morning sky of Einish, and why she had been so desperate to get away.

ONCE UPON A PRINCESS

She could see the sky as it glittered with early morning stars, the night of Isra's engagement ball. That was the night she had discovered her father's secrets, the night she had learned of her uncle's heavy-handedness, the night she had allowed herself to revel in a lover's kiss.

Theo's kiss. Rose could not resist reliving that moment, when his lips pressed against hers, and her heart ached with sudden pleasure.

At that thought, Rose quickly jolted out of her reverie. She gripped her hands together tightly, letting her fingernails dig into her knuckles. Pain wrecked through her, vivid and devastating, compounded by the weeks of carrying around her hidden longing and silent suffering.

That was the night she had last seen him. The early morning dawn had come just as she watched him vanish out of Einish's palace, and out of her life as well.

No.

Her hand slowly covered her heart, as if to steady its sudden, erratic beating. She almost cursed at herself. Several weeks had passed since she had seen him, and she still felt the same tumultuous rush of shame and regret. It was too much to bear, the thought that she would never see him again.

No, Rose thought. *I know him. He will come back.*

He had been her best friend for years. He had family matters to attend to, and then he would come back to Havilah.

But would he really come back? The voice at the back of her mind whispered. *You sent him away. You let him leave. You hurt him.*

Her head suddenly ached as much as her heart. Rose pretended to brush her hair out of her face as the prickly feeling behind her nose warned of unshed tears.

ONCE UPON A PRINCESS

Her attempts to feel better were always half-hearted and nearly useless, but Rose just could not make herself stop. She tried to console herself with the knowledge that he had family issues of his own to take care of, as he was going to find his aunt.

Surely, Rose told herself, she could understand that. She had her own family problems.

"That reminds me," she said, raising her voice as she glanced back up at the King. "Have you worked out any resolution with Uncle Hebert?"

At her words, the room finally went silent.

The king crossed his arms. "What are you talking about, Aurora?"

"I asked what you and others have decided to do about Uncle Hebert," Rose repeated. "He has been here for a little over a month now, hasn't he? What are you going to do about him?"

"Why do anything about him?" One of the other councilors asked. "He has not done anything wrong."

"You mean other than bringing in his own troops to patrol castle?" Rose crossed her arms over her chest. "Not to mention he has blocked off a number of visitors to the Queen since my return?"

Stefanos dismissed that matter with a wave of his hand. "Hebert is my brother," he said in even tones. "There is no cause for concern."

Before Rose could say anything else, Stefanos turned back to his friends. "Councilors," he said, "I'd like to adjourn our meeting for now. It's been a long day, and we have done much for the betterment of our people. You're dismissed. All of you may leave—except for you, Princess Aurora. Stay where you are."

ONCE UPON A PRINCESS

Rose was surprised the king was going to hold her back. He had ignored her throughout the last several meetings, unless it was to chastise her or challenge her. But she knew Hebert was an important issue, despite what the king might have told his advisors.

She was almost concerned when the doors shut, the rest of the council members on the other side, and she found herself face to face with the King.

It was almost like last time, Rose thought, suddenly infuriated. Before she had left Rhone for the Serpent's Garden, she had talked with the King about her abdication, and he had not been happy with her decision to continue fighting for her freedom.

She was not surprised to see he looked even more upset with her this time.

"You need to stop this, Aurora," he said. "You can't keep coming to these meetings and expecting my men to support you when all you want to do is tear down my legacy."

"What legacy?" Rose huffed. "*I* am your legacy."

"I've done other things."

"Most of them more than thirty years ago."

"I am your father, and I am still your king. You need to show respect."

"I have," Rose insisted. "I've allowed you to sit here and waste time while we have real problems to deal with. There's our new treaty with Einish to finalize—"

"Isra's engagement *is* finalized."

"No, not that one. There's the new one, where we're pledging to help stop the Magdust trade from crossing our borders," Rose said. "We need to solidify our relationship with them if we're going to take on the traders."

"Isra's engagement—"

ONCE UPON A PRINCESS

"Is finalized, I know," Rose interrupted. "But we still have plenty of time before she actually gets married. She's not even seventeen yet."

"You could have gotten married at sixteen, or even younger," Stefanos said. "Isra does not need to wait so long for that."

"She's still a child."

"A child of the crown, and therefore she must make certain sacrifices. It shames me that she knows this, and you don't, Aurora."

Privately, Rose knew that Isra had much more of a reason to be eager for marriage. Her younger sister had fallen in love with her betrothed, and Rose was even glad she would soon be able to count him as a brother. He was a good man, with a good family, and an even better friend.

"I know that just fine," Rose insisted. "But you know I am determined to make my own choices in the matter. After all, it wasn't my choice to be cursed by Magdalina, was it? It was hers, after you went to her to get some Magdust."

Stefanos' face instantly purpled with flustered rage. "You wouldn't be here if I didn't," he pointed out.

"But I *am* here," Rose argued. "There's no point in arguing out possibilities, Majesty. Not that you seem to be willing to discuss other, real problems we face. Including Uncle Hebert's presence here in Rhone."

"You need to stop talking about him," Stefanos hissed. "Aurora, these are my councilors. I'm not blind to the reality that they serve me at their leisure more than my command. Their armies and the people on their lands help protect us."

"I know that."

"But what you're forgetting is that Hebert used to live here, before I arranged his marriage to that Duchess of Aragon. He

ONCE UPON A PRINCESS

has his friends as much as I have mine on the council. They've remained loyal to him as well as to me. Don't ask me to make them choose, especially needlessly. They might choose him."

She was astounded to realize her father was afraid. He was afraid, she thought, and alone. Rose softened. She wanted to ask him if he thought the queen would choose Hebert, too.

"Maybe I can help you with Uncle Hebert," she said. "I can go and talk to him. And the queen, too."

Stefanos shook his head. "I don't want to make him upset," he said. "He was angry when I was the one who managed to bring the Rose Ruby back to Leea's father."

He began to pace the floor, wringing his hands nervously, as Rose reached over to her own wrist, feeling the rosary beads Theo had given her. She felt another wave of sadness.

"I can understand the fear of not being loved," Rose told her father quietly. "But I would not choose to sit around and do nothing."

He stopped at her words. "Aurora," he said. "That's all well and good, but sometimes you just don't know what to do as a leader."

I would at least stop all the meaningless chatter at our meetings, Rose thought, but she kept that to herself.

Stefanos shook his head. "My councilors are reluctant to face Hebert. And I am, too. You might not believe it, but he is doing me a favor by staying here."

"What?" Rose gaped at him. "What are you talking about?"

"He said he was here to protect Leea and oversee that she had a fair trial."

"Okay, well, the queen's trial is coming soon," Rose said. "Right?"

ONCE UPON A PRINCESS

"Once we get through the rest of the kingdom's problems," Stefanos told her.

"You've delayed it plenty of months," Rose argued. "Can't we just go through with the trial, now that I'm home?"

"No, Aurora, that's not how that works."

"How that works is wasting time!"

"It is not wasting time if it is in accordance with the kingdom," Stefanos snapped back.

"I don't understand why you just don't change it," Rose said.

"I have my reasons, just like I have my secrets," he told her firmly.

What's that supposed to mean? Rose wondered. She had discovered some of his secrets, and she knew that they were more shocking than she would have liked. She hated to think that his reasons for his actions could somehow be worse.

"In the meantime, you're better off worrying about your own problems, Aurora. You've been here for the past several weeks, interfering with my work and trying to usurp my meetings."

"This is my kingdom, too."

"But it is under my rule right now, and you should respect that." Stefanos shook his head. "For now, just stay away from Hebert and his guards. And stay out of my council room, too. I have too much to do, and you're getting in the way of my work."

Rose felt insulted.

"Besides," Stefanos said, "your siblings are due to arrive from Einish with Prince Philippos any day now. You might as well see to the castle, especially since your mother is occupied otherwise."

ONCE UPON A PRINCESS

It took more willpower than Rose would have liked to admit to grit her teeth together and say, "Yes, Your Majesty," before she stomped out of the room.

2

"Well," Rose said, as she made her way up to her tower room, "I can see why nothing has gotten settled since I left."

"You really should be grateful for it," Mary told her, as Mary fluttered a few feet in front of her.

"What? Why?" Rose faltered, taking a moment to glare at her small fairy friend.

"Because," Mary said, "now that you've come back, you have more power to control the outcome."

"For all the good it does me, dealing with my father," Rose said, as she finally made it to the top of the princess tower.

"From what Juana has told me, he's been much better since you've come back," Mary said, referring to her fairy cousin who tended to the queen.

"Probably because it's a good distraction for the kingdom," Rose said.

Mary giggled. "I did happen to find a couple of newsletters telling about some of your adventures," she said. "There's a rumor mill somewhere in town. Apparently one who wants to put you and Philip together."

"Great." Rose shook her head. "Isra will love that."

"Your sister will be fine," Mary said. "She was really grateful that you let her stay in Einish with the rest of our friends."

"Sophia and Ethan, along with Ronan and Fiona, are more than capable of keeping tabs on her," Rose said. "I appreciate you coming with me, even though it was an early morning ride. I know how much you barely tolerate them."

ONCE UPON A PRINCESS

"I have never felt comfortable leaving you alone," Mary admitted quietly. "And after Theo left, I knew I would have to watch you."

Rose leaned down against a nearby windowsill. A long moment of silence passed between them, and Rose spent most of it hoping Mary would not press the issue, especially since Rose had been unable to admit to anyone else the real reason Theo left.

She knew that did not mean that the others did not suspect something.

In the days following their return to Rhone, Mary had asked several uncomfortable questions, and Rose had carefully answered each of them to avoid suspicion.

"Rose?" Mary asked.

No such luck. Rose grimaced. "What is it?"

"Why don't you tell me what's bothering you?"

Rose bristled. "You know what's bothering me," she said. "I've complained about my father and the kingdom's politics plenty, haven't I?"

"As detestable as I know you find them, I doubt politics would make you act the way you've been acting since we left Einish," Mary said. "You barely eat. You have trouble sleeping. You've been training when you're not otherwise occupied with something, but I've watched you enough to know you're distracted."

"There's still the matter of Magdalina's curse," Rose said. "We don't have much longer, Mary. My birthday is less than two months away."

"I know that's not what is bothering you," Mary said. "Something has changed."

"What do you mean?" Rose asked. "I'm still the same person."

ONCE UPON A PRINCESS

"Something happened, didn't it?" Mary asked. "Between you and Theo."

Rose felt her face flush over. She looked away. "No," she lied.

"Rose." The admonishment in Mary's voice was soft, but Rose suddenly felt terrified.

"I don't want to talk about it, Mary." She measured her words out carefully, keeping her tone light. "I told you, he had to go and take care of something for his grandfather. It was important."

"It was more than that."

"It doesn't matter."

"Obviously, it does, or you wouldn't be acting like this." Mary came up beside her. "He told you that he loved you, didn't he?"

The blush on her cheeks burned hotter. "Please stop, Mary," she said. "Isn't it bad enough that he said it?"

"But Rose, you love him, too." Mary arched her brow at Rose's silence. "Don't you?"

"Of course I do," Rose snapped. "But he doesn't deserve to be stuck with me and my curse. That's why it's better that he left."

"Oh, Rose." Mary came up and leaned against her, stroking her hair in a motherly manner. "I'm so sorry."

"Don't be." Rose tightened her grip on the windowsill as she repeated the same lie she had been telling herself. "It's better that he left."

"But you're not happy." Mary shook her head. "Don't pretend that you're fine when you aren't. I know you miss him."

Rose shrugged.

ONCE UPON A PRINCESS

Mary suddenly narrowed her eyes. "Oh, Rose. Don't tell me he told you he was in love with you, and then you sent him away?"

"He decided to leave of his own accord," Rose insisted, blushing once more.

"He told you he loved you and then he was going to leave you?" Mary frowned. "That doesn't seem like Theo."

"He does have to take care of his family, from what Thad told me. He told me he was going to leave, and I … I just didn't stop him."

"Rose." The disappointment in her voice was clear.

"What, Mary? What else would you have me do?" Rose asked. "I didn't know what else to do."

"I would have rather you told him you loved him, too."

"What about his family? His own plans for his life?"

"You could have gone with him."

"And then what of my own family?" Rose asked. "I've been eager to get back here for so long, so I could help my mother."

"It doesn't seem like you've been able to do anything about that anyway," Mary pointed out. "Your mother is still being tended to in the dungeons, and the king is unwilling to move up her trial."

"Which keeps getting further moved back," Rose admitted bitterly.

"And your plans for attacking Darkwood have also been delayed," Mary said. "I know we're waiting to hear from King Derick."

"He said he would send aid," Rose said, briefly wondering if her gyrfalcon, Virtue, was close to returning to Havilah. He would have the latest letter from Philip's older brother, the King of Einish and Crystal Lake.

ONCE UPON A PRINCESS

"Your birthday is still weeks away," Mary said.

"It's getting closer every day," Rose said. "That's why I want to go and attack Darkwood soon."

"You know that there are plenty of things that we need to plan for with that."

"I know, and I have done everything I can think of to do for it. I need Philip here to plan more," Rose admitted. "He'll be more familiar with his country's soldiers than I am."

"So what would have really prevented you from going off with Theo to help him take care of his family's business?"

Rose frowned. Mary had managed to set her trap well, she realized. She tried to shrug it off. "I told you, I didn't know what else to do," she said. "And I'm not about to go after him. Not after I hurt him like that."

Mary sighed. "You're only hurting yourself in the meantime."

"It's better this way," Rose insisted.

"Rose, come on. That's terrible to say," Mary said. "You want to be the queen one day, right? What of mercy?"

"I hurt him, Mary." Rose gave up and looked at her. "I *hurt* him. He kissed me and told me he was in love with me, and I told him I didn't want to love him, that I didn't want him around."

"He kissed you?"

"Yes." The heat of his kiss washed through her again, as Rose looked down at her hands, where the rosary beads of her bracelet glittered.

She thought of another time, when they had fallen asleep just outside the inn on Maltia. He had been telling her the stories of the different beads when she had fallen asleep, allowing herself to drift off to the sound of his voice. Rose thought about how he looked in the moonlight, remembering every twinkle in his eye, every line on his suntanned face, the shy stubble on his cheeks.

Rose looked down at her hands, no longer wondering which finger would betray her to sleeping death, instead recalling the feeling of his hands in hers as he held her close to him.

Before her mind could wonder further, Mary sighed, breaking her concentration. "I have to admit," Mary murmured, "I thought you were lovesick. I didn't realize you were heartbroken."

"I didn't want you to know," Rose replied wearily, as she once more turned her attention out to the far-off distance. From her vantage point, she could see far out into the mountains and forests of Rhone. She glanced down toward the town, looking down at the road that led to the castle, wondering if Theo would come back soon. She shook her head, trying to brush aside that hope.

"It's better this way," she repeated, more to herself than to Mary. "He's probably doing much better without me there."

3

The village near the border between Aragon and Rhone was just up ahead. Despite the sun sinking down below the horizon, Theo could see the small outlines of houses and shops set around in blocks, all making up the bustling town.

"Look, Bachas," he said, looking over his shoulder at the small pixie who lounged on the back of their horse. "We're here."

The small town of Urra was at the western edge of Rhone, close to the Aragonian border. It was the rumored home of his aunt, Annalora, who he was tasked with bringing home to his grandfather. Looking around, Theo was relieved to see that it would likely be easy to locate her. While the village was surrounded by farming land and tournament grounds, he could see the edge of another forest in the distance.

"It took us long enough," Bachas grumbled.

"You should have known it would take this long," Theo replied. "After all, you're the one with the seeing crystal, not me."

Bachas grunted and began muttering under his breath, while Theo allowed himself to smile. Over the past weeks of riding, he had gotten to know the small pixie well enough to know he had very little sense of humor, unless he was the one who was making the joke--or, Theo thought with a grimace, he was watching someone else get hurt.

He often let it go. He knew Bachas had his own pain. A human had tricked him into a life debt, separating him from his wife for many years and forcing him to work his magic in the Magdust trade. Bachas' master died after attacking Theo and his company in the Wandering Caverns, while Bachas had not escaped without getting hurt. Theo knew it was because of how he and the others had helped nurse him back together that Bachas was with him at all.

Well, that and my aunt is the one who has his wife, Theo added silently. For all Bachas was less than pleasant company, it was nice to have some company on the road.

Traveling with Rose and her small troupe of guards, in addition to Mary, Sophia, Ethan, and Philip, Theo had gotten used to having other people to look after, and people who would help look after him. It had been a long time since he had to worry only about himself.

Theo grimaced. It had not taken long to realize he did not like himself as much without his friends. He only thought of finding Annalora, taking his revenge upon Everon, and wondering what to do about Rose. Between the frustration with his family, the delay in his revenge, and the unrequited longing in his heart, he was beginning to wonder how he managed to think of himself so well for so long.

It was probably Rose's fault, he thought. When he was with her, he could see plenty of beauty in the world, and that allowed him to overlook the ugliness inside of him more easily.

Thinking of Rose was still painful, he realized grimly. He shoved at his inner turmoil, trying, as he had the last several days, to forget about her.

But there was no forgetting the fire in her fighting, the comfort in her calm, and the strength in her spirit. There was no hope for him, as he tried to remove all thought of the light in her eyes, the softness of her sunshine-colored hair, and the purity of her voice in those moments when she had wept and sung to him.

There was no forgetting the taste of her lips under his.

ONCE UPON A PRINCESS

Theo groaned. *I might as well tell myself to stop breathing or for time to stop moving forward.*

He knew he was not fooling himself; he knew it was still more painful *not* to think of her than it was to think of her and miss her.

"Come on. Move it," Bachas snapped. "We're getting closer to Elva. I want to see her."

"I know," Theo said impatiently.

"I don't know why you're moving so slowly, now. The sooner we're done getting your aunt, the sooner you can see your princess again."

Theo hastily tied his horse's bridle to a nearby tree. "Maybe I'm just trying to get used to the ground again. You do realize that riding on a horse for nearly two weeks is uncomfortable, don't you?"

"Can't be any easier for the horse."

"It's certainly easier for the pixie riding behind the saddle."

"Hardly." Bachas rolled his eyes as he peeked through a pack of bushes. "Come on, let's go. Urra's night life is starting to come out from the fields."

"Not yet," Theo said. "We need to be careful."

"Why?" Bachas asked. "You do know I can use magic, right?"

"I'm used to that," Theo replied. "Remember? I traveled with a fairy before."

"You didn't like me using my seeing crystal. And you really didn't like me using magic to get information out of those other people from the last town."

"That's because you were hurting them," Theo retorted. "You didn't need to hurt them just because they threatened us."

ONCE UPON A PRINCESS

"They don't remember anything," Bachas said, a malicious glint in his eyes. "I made sure they didn't."

"That doesn't make me feel better."

"Having my wife in a life debt with a whole country between us doesn't make *me* feel any better," Bachas reminded him.

"We'll get her when we find my aunt." Theo studied the town further down the road.

"That doesn't make me feel any better, either," Bachas muttered.

Theo silently agreed. From what his grandfather had told him, his aunt, Annalora, was heavily involved with the Magdust trade. It was likely she was using Elva's pixie magic to spin Magdust in her specially woven tapestries.

"Why are we over here on the other side of town?" Bachas asked. "That solider at the inn last night said she lived on the far end of town."

"I don't want her to find our horse," Theo reminded him. "You might be able to use magic to get yourself into different places—"

"And different realms," Bachas said with pride.

"But I do not have that skill," Theo said tartly, irritated at his interruption. "Nor does Thunder here."

"I don't know why you insisted on naming the horse that," Bachas grumbled. "It's silly."

Theo was getting annoyed with Bachas' interruptions, but he had to admit, he was genuinely curious. "Why is it silly?"

"The horse told me his name is Charlie."

"Fine. I'll call him Charlie then. Either way, I don't want my aunt to find him and hurt him or anything."

"I suppose that's fair."

ONCE UPON A PRINCESS

"I thought pixies were supposed to like nature and animals," Theo grumbled, disturbed at Bachas' apathy.

"And I thought humans were all about asserting their power over others." Bachas gave him a sour look. "We all have to realize there are exceptions, don't we?"

Theo sighed. "Never mind. I guess it will be dark enough to give us extra cover by the time we make it to the other side of town."

"Great." Bachas rolled his eyes again.

"I'd think you would like to walk through the woods," Theo said, gesturing at all the trees around them. "Unless your leg is still bothering you some?"

"My leg is fine, along with the rest of me. I don't see why we can't just use magic to get there."

"We need to be careful," Theo said. "I don't know what kind of magic Annalora has in place, and I don't know if your magic would alert her to our presence at all. It's best to be careful about things like that."

"Elva would never turn me in."

"I thought it was part of the life-debt that she has to protect her mistress?"

"What harm would her mistress expect from me?" Bachas asked, giving Theo as innocent of an expression as possible.

"What harm indeed?" Theo shook his head.

The two of them walked through the forest and headed toward the small town.

"There sure are a lot of Aragonian soldiers here," Bachas grumbled, as he crawled up onto Theo's shoulder.

"Worried?" Theo asked, grunting as Bachas' legs dug into his back. "I'm trained as a knight."

"Trained as a priest, too, but I'm not saying my prayers."

ONCE UPON A PRINCESS

"You are about to go into battle, not church. Doesn't that make you feel somewhat better?"

"Given your skill levels? No."

Theo frowned. "I grew up in the church, and I've been studying for years to be a knight."

"So?" Bachas stuck his tongue out at him. "You're not really either one or the other, are you?"

Anger rushed through him. Theo knew that Bachas had a point, but it was a sore one with him. "Never mind," he said. "I don't see why you're so worried. I know my aunt is likely to be a problem, but you're the one who insisted I would be able to handle her because we're related."

As Bachas grumbled to himself again, Theo thought about that night in Einish, when his grandfather and brother had come to talk with him. Hearing that Annalora, his aunt, was still alive and part of the Magdust trade, he was more than ready to confront her.

Especially, Theo thought, after he realized her tapestries were affecting the lives of his friends as much as his grandfather's conscience.

"Maybe I'm worried because there's a general over there," Bachas said, "and he seems to be preparing them for battle."

"What are you talking about?" Theo asked, before he saw the growing circle of soldiers near the town center. He watched as a solider on horseback called out to the crowd before him, calling for order while others called out questions.

As they came closer, Theo was able to listen to part of the general's answer.

"We have our orders," the general called. "We are to wait here until the witch is ready. And then we will march!"

ONCE UPON A PRINCESS

The crowd roared various responses, as Theo realized who the "witch" was they were talking about.

Aunt Annalora.

Theo changed his direction, heading away from the crowd, as the men called out more cheers and jeers. As he walked by various shops and stands, he noticed some of the vendors would shrink back from him.

"Looks like they're hired mercenaries," Bachas said.

"I agree." Theo tightened his grip on his own sword. "Stay down under my hood," he said. "I don't want other people paying attention to you."

"Good idea," Bachas said, agreeing with him in a rare moment, ducking under the hood of Theo's cloak. "I wouldn't want the attention of men like these. They're ready for battle."

"And they are suspicious of the witch," Theo said. "I doubt it would take much for them to mistrust all magical creatures such as yourself."

Bachas said nothing in reply, but Theo felt the pixie's stubby fingers dig further into the folds of his cloak. As they headed out of the town center, Theo watched as some of the soldiers began picking fights with each other, some of them laughing, and others growling back.

When they began walking down less crowded streets, Bachas peered out. "You know, I'm surprised you aren't."

"Aren't what?"

"Suspicious of magical creatures. Especially being with me for so long now."

"I had a good mentor tell me once that while humans are commanded to stay away from magic, it seems only right for you to use the gifts granted to you." Theo grimaced. "Of course, I would appreciate it if you were a bit more ethical in your usage of them."

"Maybe one day your hesitation will rub off on me," Bachas muttered noncommittedly.

Theo said nothing, keeping his focus in front of him. He took note of the people as they hurried to their homes, the near-empty market, and the sense of frustration running through the town.

"Something is wrong here," Theo said quietly.

"The soldiers are no doubt making people nervous," Bachas replied. "This is a tournament town, right? They probably only come for a few days at a time. My guess from looking around is that they've been here for at least a month, if not longer."

"They are supposed to march as soon as my aunt is done with her part of some deal," Theo said.

He had to wonder if Ambassador Rolez, the man who had given one of Annalora's tapestries to Philip's brother, had something to do with this.

"We could ask some of the soldiers for specific details," Bachas suggested, as if he was reading Theo's mind.

"I don't want you hurting them for answers. We need to stay hidden."

"I've already told you before, when I'm done with them, they don't remember anything."

"*I* do."

"I could make you forget things, too, if you really wanted." Theo could hear the slyness in his voice as he added, "If I haven't already."

"I don't believe you would do that to me," Theo assured him.

ONCE UPON A PRINCESS

"Good. It makes me feel better about doing it, then, knowing there's little chance I'll get caught."

Theo glanced back at him with a prudent look. "I have my reasons for doubting you'd do it, you know."

"Really?" Bachas sounded intrigued. "May I ask why?"

"Sure you can ask. But that doesn't mean I'll tell you."

Theo ignored Bachas' grumbling reply as he caught sight of a small girl selling flowers up ahead.

Seeing her tussle of dark hair reminded him of Isra as a younger girl, and his heart softened considerably at the thought of his other friend.

"What do you want?" the girl snapped at him.

She could not have been more than ten years old, but she was obviously a seasoned vendor. "I, uh, just wanted to buy some flowers," he replied, taken aback by her sharp tone.

The girl's eyes narrowed in suspicion. "Is that all?"

"Yes." Theo waited a long moment as she scrutinized him. He almost breathed a sigh of relief when she turned her attention back to her flowers.

"You're a soldier," she said, as she bundled a small bouquet together.

"Is there something wrong with that?"

"Not if you pay me," the little girl said.

"Of course I'll pay you," Theo promised, already reaching for some coins. "Are there other soldiers who haven't paid you?"

"A lot of them kick dirt in my face," the girl replied. "Some of them steal my flowers when I'm not looking."

Theo gave her some more coins. "Keep the change," he said warmly.

"I don't want your pity," the little girl snarled.

ONCE UPON A PRINCESS

"Well, consider it another payment," Theo said. "I'd like some information."

"What do you want to know?" The girl's dark eyes narrowed once more.

"I was hoping you could tell me about the soldiers here," Theo said.

"Aren't you here to join them?"

"No," he said. "I'm just passing through, really." Which, he told himself, was more or less the truth. Once he found his aunt in tow, he would head back to Havilah, where his grandfather was waiting for their return.

When the girl said nothing, he asked, "What is your name?"

She still hesitated. Theo wondered if she was still unsure of him. He was just about to repeat his question when she finally replied. "Iris," she said.

"Iris. That's a pretty name."

"My father liked flowers," Iris told him. "My mother used to sell them."

"Where is she?" Theo asked, looking around.

"She's at home, caring for my new brother," Iris said. "He's just a baby."

"Oh, I see." Theo nodded. "Well, that's a big job for a girl like you."

"I can handle it," Iris insisted. At the look on her face, Theo faltered as he remembered the time when Rose, at ten years old, demanded that the King allow her to train as a knight. She'd had the same look on her face—the pouting lips, the fierce eyes, and the wayward hair.

"I believe you can," Theo told Iris quietly, struggling for a moment to clear his mind of Rose. "Surely you have the strength to do just that, especially if you've managed to stand up to the other soldiers here."

ONCE UPON A PRINCESS

"They're here from Aragon," Iris said. "Some of them come for the tournaments a lot. But they're here, waiting for the witch to finish something. Then they are supposed to go and meet with their leader."

"Who is the leader?"

"Some duke from Aragon, but he's not here right now. He's already moved on to the capital. Some of the troops say he's ordered something from the witch who lives in the woods, and then the rest of them will be off, too."

At the mention of the duke, everything fell instantly into place. Theo could picture it as Iris continued to give him the details. He could see Rose's uncle, an imposing if unclear figure in his mind, calling for troops to fight for Queen Leea. He could see Hebert as he commissioned his aunt to make something to protect him or to hurt his brother. He could see the impending doom headed for his home.

I have to protect Rose. Despite the pain and the distance between them, nothing had dulled his instinct to protect her.

"We have to go," Theo said, cutting Iris off in mid-sentence. "But thank you, Iris, for all you have given me. The flowers are lovely." He dumped another handful of coins in her lap before he continued onward, heading toward the forest on the far end of town.

Iris gave him a kind smile, despite his brusque departure. "You're welcome," she called after him, waving after him.

Theo was gratified by her sudden cheerfulness.

"You didn't have to do that," Bachas said. "She's actually making good profits, despite her earlier trouble with other soldiers."

"You never *have* to be kind to someone," Theo insisted. "Besides, what she said makes a difference. I know who we are dealing with now, and why it is a problem."

ONCE UPON A PRINCESS

"More of a problem than your aunt?" Bachas snorted. "Unlikely."

"You're probably right," Theo agreed. "But still, if what Iris said is true—and I have no reason to doubt her—Annalora is only going to be the first problem we deal with."

"I don't know if she will be the first," Bachas said, pointing toward the edge of the woods. "Look, there's someone else ahead of us."

Theo glanced in the direction where Bachas was looking and saw a tall figure on their far right. In the last moments of daylight, Theo was able to see that the walking shadow was not fully human.

He was a man, but there were shadows of hidden wings protruding out of his back, and as the daylight folded into the clouds, a spectral quality took hold of the figure.

Theo frowned. *Who is that?*

His question was answered as a young lady's voice called out into the darkness.

"Everon!"

Theo stopped short in his tracks. He watched, transfixed with confusion and anger, as he realized the creature in front of them was none other than Everon, Magdalina's son, and his parents' murderer, heading into the heart of the forest ahead of them.

ONCE UPON A PRINCESS

4

It took a long moment for Theo to react to the reality before him. Then, suddenly, something inside of him broke. After all the years he had traveled the world, looking for answers to his family's killer, he knew the truth—and now, at last, he was able to take matters into his own hands.

As he stood there, watching Everon, Theo remembered that night, the night his uncle had roused him from his bed, before being sent off to a new world, one without his parents and his childhood home. He saw the tapestry hanging in his mother's house, the one that allowed Queen Lucia to watch over him and weave herself into his dreams. He saw her eyes burn in a fire of pink and green dust.

Theo had felt his heart break in despair and rage, saving that feeling for the moment when he could finally demand someone pay for causing him pain. All the goodness of his innocence, all the truth of his training, and all the beauty of love in his heart disappeared as only his young anger returned in a flash of pain and heartache.

Quickly, he drew his sword, grappling with the hilt as he began to hurry forward.

"What are you doing?" Bachas hissed. "Stop!" At his command, Theo felt his legs stick to the ground.

"What am *I* doing? What about *you*?" Theo snapped angrily, trying his hardest to fight against the magic holding him back from moving forward. "That's the fairy who killed my family."

"Yeah, but he'll kill us too, if we walk in on him and his lady love."

"Lady love?" Theo saw the woman running out to greet Everon and stopped fighting against Bachas' hold.

The woman reached out to Everon, wrapping her arms around him. Theo blinked, suddenly dazzled by her. She had the same color of hair as Theo, only it was long and loose; from where he stood, Theo could just make out the familiar, simple lines of her face.

"Mother?" His voice was barely a whisper. After so many years, it was hard to believe that it could be anyone else besides his mother.

He watched as Everon, with his fierce features, pressed himself into the woman's embrace, clutching at her as he leaned down and kissed her. "Annalora."

Theo understood at once. He straightened, relieved and depressed all at the same time. *It isn't my mother.*

He shook his head. He knew he should have realized it before. He knew his mother was dead; the vicar of his home village had confirmed both his parents' deaths and then buried them. It had been over ten years since Theo had last seen her.

"Well," Bachas whispered. "Looks like we found your aunt."

"Yes." Theo barely felt himself speak. He was still stunned, not only at how much his aunt looked like his mother, but because she held Everon in her arms.

It took a long moment, but Theo was glad, finally, that Bachas had stopped him. He breathed out quietly.

"I'll bet anything that Elva's magic is the reason she looks so young," Bachas said. "Typical human. Using magic to keep outward appearances up."

Theo nodded glumly. He had to agree; his mother had been the youngest sibling of their family. There was no way

ONCE UPON A PRINCESS

Annalora would have managed to look so young without magic. From what he could see, she looked no older than he was.

Although she could have had Everon's help with that, rather than Elva's, he thought to himself.

As Annalora and Everon began making their way to a small cottage, Theo felt Bachas' magic hold on him disappear. He still stayed where he was, his fury simmering as bitter betrayal took its place, and memories, memories he had buried for years, came rushing forward.

He thought of his mother, her vivid cheerfulness, and his father, with his purposeful movements. His childhood was dotted with happy times, as his mother worked on her weaving and sewing, and his father would travel for the kingdom as a knight, with his brother, Theo's Uncle Thom, often at his side.

Only a few times did he remember his parents arguing. He frowned as he thought about what Thad had said before, about how close his father and mother were to fighting all the time, and their trust in each other was quickly breaking down, closer to the end.

Queen Lucia's threaded eyes gleamed at him from her tapestry, and he forced himself back into the present.

From what his grandfather had told him, his parents had worked to save King Stefanos from madness before, after Magdalina had tried to poison him with Magdust. His Uncle Thom had been able to write down the name of their killer before he succumbed to his own deadly wounds.

Annalora was still working against the King of Rhone. She was still making tapestries that would charm or poison people.

The soldiers in town were waiting for her to finish her latest project, commissioned by Rose's uncle, before they were going to march on Havilah.

At the thought of her, Theo suddenly wished Rose were there with him. She would know what to do. She would reach out and squeeze his hand in comfort, and he would be able to face whatever challenge came next.

Theo watched the last glimpse of his aunt disappear behind the cottage door.

Was he ready to take his revenge? What if his aunt was just as responsible for the death of his family as Everon was?

"It doesn't matter," he told himself. "It doesn't matter. They're still dead."

His parents and his uncle were still dead—and all their happy memories were just memories.

"What doesn't matter?" Bachas asked.

Theo sighed. "Nothing."

Having fought on the battlefield, he was no stranger to killing and death. But it had been a long time, he knew, since he had allowed himself to feel the personal side of it. Despite all the years of planning for this day, Theo suddenly felt uncertain.

"A whole lot of nothing is keeping you from moving."

"You were the one who used magic to stop me before."

"Magic is nothing compared to the power inside your own heart," Bachas said gruffly. "I might have used magic to stop you before, but there's nothing keeping you there now. Come on, we're here to get Elva first, remember?"

"You're right." Theo took a deep breath, trying to center himself, angry that he was unable to find peace. Then he began to move forward again, his steps calculated and slow. He held his sword by his side, gradually stepping out of the

ONCE UPON A PRINCESS

shadows. Before he could get too far, Bachas climbed down from his back.

The moment he did, Theo heard a quiet gasp.

"Bachas?" The small cry was as hesitant as it was hopeful. Theo momentarily forgot his own inner struggle as it was Bachas' turn to go still. He watched the hard look on his pixie companion's face melt into a mixture of shock and overwhelming gratitude.

"Elva!" Bachas ran toward the cottage, and Theo was just about to call out to him when he saw the air ripple with power. The call caught in his throat when he saw a new pixie emerging from the center of the aura.

Elva was just like the image he'd seen before the Bachas' seeing crystal, Theo realized. She had eyes that shimmered with green and blue speckles, while her skin was a soft blue-gray, close to what Bachas had. She was wearing a simple dress and an apron that seemed very well worn.

Theo watched as the pixies hugged, and while he was happy for the two of them, to have found each other again after so long, he couldn't help wondering if Rose would welcome him back in such a loving manner. He turned away as the two pixies celebrated together, both of them talking quickly in hushed tones.

Theo glanced back over at the cottage, surprised to see Elva had managed to tear through some of the protective barrier around it. Theo could see the familiar blue aura of fairy blood coming out from the chimney like smoke.

Theo thought of Mary, of how good and beautiful she made the world, just by being a friend. *How many other fairies has the world lost to such treachery?* Theo wondered sadly.

ONCE UPON A PRINCESS

"It's awful, isn't it?" Elva said as she stepped up next to him, with Bachas' arm tight around her waist. "She's killed so many using my power."

Theo glanced down at Elva. He had not seen too many pixies other than Bachas. As Bachas quickly introduced them, her blue-green eyes glisten with tears as she dropped her pointed chin in resignation.

"I've come to stop her," Theo said, "at the request of my grandfather."

Elva sighed wistfully. "If only you could."

"Why can't we?" Bachas asked her, his twig-like fingers tightening around her.

"No human can enter into the cottage," she said. "Except for her, of course. Even with Everon's power, she's still a human."

"We're in luck," Bachas said. "Elva, this is Annalora's nephew."

"Oh, my." Elva gasped and tried to take a step back, as she looked up at Theo in horror. She did not get very far, as Bachas was still holding onto her.

"What's wrong?" Theo asked. "It's okay. I'm not going to hurt you."

"You have to understand," Elva said. "My mistress has been around for many years, even before she managed to find me. She has put every last bit of her power into making sure she gets exactly what she wants. She will turn deadly if she feels threatened."

"I already know she is dangerous," Theo assured her. "She was the one who recently tried to enchant one of my friends' relatives."

"It's not just her you have to worry about," Elva whispered fearfully, as her eyes darted to the window.

ONCE UPON A PRINCESS

Theo followed her gaze, able to catch a glimpse of Everon's dark hair and powerful wings through the wooden shutters. Recalling their intimate greeting, he said, "She works with Everon."

"Yes." Elva sighed.

"Tell us," Bachas implored, surprising Theo with a kind and gentle tone, one he'd never heard his pixie companion use before.

Elva hesitated.

"We're here to take her back to my grandfather," Theo told her. "By force, if necessary. She will be arrested for conspiracy against the crown and for her participation in the Magdust trade. Please, help us. We will do all we can to help you get free from her."

At Bachas' prodding, Elva finally nodded. "Alright. Annalora is not just conspiring against the crown. She wants it for herself. Well, for herself and Everon. The two of them have been together for almost twenty years. He brings her the fairies—the ones that try to set up a rebellion against his mother, Magdalina, and I … I have to … subdue them."

Theo gave her a sympathetic look, while Bachas began muttering about humans and sorcery all over again.

Before he could stop Bachas, a loud *bang!* echoed from the cottage.

"Don't worry," Elva said. "It's just part of the spell she uses to spin the Magdust into her thread. She had a good supply before Everon came. I am not sure if he has another shipment of fairies for her or not today. Sometimes he just comes and visits."

"How terrible for you," Theo said sympathetically.

"I actually like it when he visits. Annalora does terrible things, but she is not too bad of a mistress. She allows me to

ONCE UPON A PRINCESS

have more free time when he comes, which is why I was able to see you today. I was out gathering food." She jiggled her apron, and for the first time, Theo noticed that Elva had several pockets full of truffles.

"How long does he usually stay?" Theo asked. He thought about the soldiers in the village. His plan had been simple enough, just minutes before. He knew he would need to stop his aunt from finishing the duke's order. He could take her, along with Elva, to his grandfather, before turning her over to King Stefanos.

Assuming Annalora would testify against Hebert, the duke's plans would fall through, and his aunt would never participate in the Magdust trade ever again.

It was a plan entirely too neat and tidy for reality, Theo thought bitterly. Now, in addition to a coup from Hebert, he had to deal with his aunt's attempt to take the crown, and he would finally face Everon.

He nodded to Elva politely. "Excuse me." Slowly, Theo turned around and headed back toward town.

"What are you doing?" Bachas asked, hurrying after him.

"I need some time," Theo said. "We have to think of a better plan, or we're not going to be able to do anything, like Elva said."

"How long do you need?"

"I don't know." Theo glanced back at the cottage again, watching as Everon's shadow disappeared from the window. Despite everything, some part of him felt glad. At least, Theo thought, Everon did not seem to want to marry Rose as much as Magdalina wanted him to. "But see what you can find out about the cottage and its barriers. I don't know the specifics, but when we go in, it'll be a fight, one way or another."

ONCE UPON A PRINCESS

"I can tell you the specifics if you want," Bachas said, patting his pocket, where he had placed his seeing crystal.

Theo almost smiled. "I guess I should know that by now."

651
ONCE UPON A PRINCESS

5

Rose frowned as she finally faced her mother. "What do you mean, you don't mind being stuck down here?" she asked incredulously.

Frustrated, Rose barely listened to the queen as she began rattling off assurances that Juana and her needlework were keeping her busy, among other things.

This is not what I expected at all. Rose glanced around the small dungeon room. It looked almost like a miniature throne room, with plenty of ornate furnishings and royal luxuries, including several large chairs and tables. She was sitting at one of them, drinking tea with the queen and Juana.

From what Rose knew of prisons, and what she had seen on her travels abroad, this was a dream for any regular convict. It irritated her that her mother was acting completely fine with her situation.

Leea gestured to a small plate of pastries. "Here, darling," she said. "Take one. I know you like them."

"I'm not hungry," Rose told her.

"Juana's told me that you haven't been feeling well lately," Leea said. "She said you have barely eaten since you've come back. You are looking much thinner, Aurora. Is something wrong?"

Rose shot Mary's cousin a quick glare and then reluctantly grabbed a pastry.

Leea nodded approvingly before sipping from her teacup once again. "So, how are things? I feel like we haven't talked in years."

"We haven't." Rose pursed her lips together.

"Haven't what?"

ONCE UPON A PRINCESS

"Talked in years."

"Well, after you dismissed the idea for a wedding, I had really nothing to discuss with you." Leea sighed. "What does someone like me know about knighthood, after all? But I thought you would at least appreciate my efforts for the tournament at your last birthday."

"Why would I appreciate that?" Rose asked. "I have a curse to break. I don't need suitors coming here for a short engagement and an even shorter marriage."

"What else could I do?" Leea asked. "Besides, marriage is not so bad. Once you get it out of the way, you have a lot more say in your life."

Rose looked skeptical. "What about the kingdom?"

Leea shrugged. "What about it? As long as our alliances are strong, our officials are working diligently, and trade is good, there's very little that leaders do, especially in the day to day lives of their people."

Rose suddenly wondered if being in a dungeon was so very different from her mother's usual routine. But, recalling the meetings she had with her the king and his council, she had to admit her mother might have had a good point. She picked at her pastry as she watched her mother take another sip of tea.

"Well, what are your plans for breaking your curse then?" Leea asked.

By her tone, Rose could tell her mother was struggling to feign interest. "Once things are settled here, I'm going to take a legion of soldiers up to Darkwood Forest, where Magdalina lives. And then we're going to fight her."

"Sounds unpleasant." Leea sighed. "If only there was a way to break your curse without worrying about going to battle."

ONCE UPON A PRINCESS

Rose looked down at her pastry again, her stomach twisting with sudden hollowness. She bit her lip, thinking of what Theo had told her before, that night. *True love's kiss.*

It hadn't worked, she reminded herself. There was no flash of light, there was no inner revelation; there was nothing that happened when Theo had kissed her, other than she had allowed herself to kiss him back.

"Aurora?"

Rose blushed, embarrassed her mother caught her daydreaming about Theo. "What?"

"I was just asking you how things were here at the castle. I know you could not have had such accommodations while you were abroad."

"Everything is wonderful," Rose assured her. "I just wish things were a little less intense."

"What do you mean?"

Finally, we've arrived at what I wanted to talk about. Rose swirled her teaspoon in her cup. "Well, I've been home for several weeks, and this is the first time I've been *allowed* to come and see you," she said, carefully emphasizing her words to show only some of her frustration. Rose was hoping her mother would be appalled by the fact that she had to be cleared to see her by both the king and her uncle.

To Rose's dismay, Leea waved the matter aside. "You know how these things go," she said. "When one is being held in prison, things do not go as easily as they used to."

"But it's *me*," Rose said, this time with more anger. "I shouldn't have to ask if I can go and see my mother."

"It's for the best," Leea assured her.

Rose slammed her teacup down on the table. "What? What are you talking about? That's ridiculous, and you and I both

ONCE UPON A PRINCESS

know it. I am the heir to the throne, and I have a right to see my mother while she's being held captive."

"Rose, sit down," Leea hissed.

Rose reluctantly sat down again, before Leea turned to Juana. "Can we have some music, please, Juana dear?"

Rose glanced over at Juana. She had barely paid any notice to her mother's fairy companion. But, Rose thought, in all fairness, she would often ignore Juana if she had the choice. It was a rare occurrence that Juana left people that option; she was always full of gossip and tales, and after a while, it was hard to tell what was true, and what was her opinion— especially since she presented them as the same thing.

But as Juana snapped her fingers, and music began to play, Rose realized that the music was not just music; there was a spell woven within the notes.

"What is this?" she asked.

"It's a spell to keep out eavesdroppers," Leea said. "So we can talk more freely."

"More freely?" Rose arched a brow at her.

"Rose, please," Leea said, surprising Rose with the use of her preferred name. "Give me some credit, would you? If you had grown up as I had under my father, you would know the pitfalls of all sorts of politics."

Rose just stared at her.

"What?" Leea asked. "You think I've been kept out of the dark here?"

"Well, considering you have Juana with you, I wouldn't say completely."

Leea gave Rose a sharp smile. "I'm sure she would agree with that. Juana has been my closest friend all of these years, and she has been a big help in allowing me to protect myself. And you, too."

ONCE UPON A PRINCESS

"What do you mean?" Rose asked.

"Rose, you are old enough and you have seen enough of this world to know what people do and what people think are often very different things." Leea sighed. "It is time you learn the truth about my situation, and why I am in this place."

Rose felt a growing suspicion inside of her. "Did you actually poison the king?"

Leea seemed shocked by the question, but she did not back down from it. "Yes," she admitted. "It was me."

"What? Why?" Rose asked, jumping out of her seat in outrage again.

"He's not well, Rose," Leea said. "Ever since he made that deal with Magdalina, he has been deteriorating."

"You know about the deal?" Rose asked. "The one where he agreed I would marry a fairy of Magdalina's choice if she gave you the power to conceive a child?"

"Of course," Leea said. There was a sour look on her face. "Forgive me, Rose. The very sound of Magdalina's name is very unappealing."

"Understandable." Rose glanced over at Juana. "Who else knows?"

"To be honest, I'm not sure," Leea said. "I didn't even know you knew, until you came back here, and Mary was able to inform Juana of your situation."

"Mary." Rose shook her head.

"She keeps me updated on some things," Juana said. "And I supply her with more information. So you should not hold it against her. And you can rest assured that she has not told me all your secrets."

Probably much to your dismay, Rose thought angrily as she blushed again. She was unable to stop herself from wondering just which secrets Mary had revealed.

"He reneged on that deal," Leea said, returning her attention to the story. "Stefanos broke his deal with Magdalina."

"I know," Rose said, hoping that Mary had not revealed that Magdalina had offered her the very same deal recently.

"He wasn't particularly happy with Magdalina, after she tried to poison him with the Magdust," Leea continued. "He doesn't consider it an unfair move, breaking the deal, because of that."

"Why didn't he die?" Rose asked.

"The Reverend Father was able to do something for him," Leea said. "He had connections to a lady who, after he implored her, made a strange tapestry for him."

Rose thought of the tapestry she'd seen in the Crystal Lake Kingdom. "I thought they were supposed to curse people," she said.

"It depends on the weaver," Juana spoke up. "Magdust can do any amount of things, which is why it is so dangerous."

"But too much of it can kill."

"Yes." Juana shook her head. "Just like anything, Rose. Too much of it is too much for many people to handle. Your father ingested too much. We were able to keep him in stasis here at the castle while the Reverend Father went searching for a way to save him."

"When he came back with the tapestry, the king stabilized. Eventually, as I became pregnant and you were born, he was able to get rid of the tapestry entirely," the queen said.

"He burned it?" Rose asked.

Leea nodded. "Yes. And he has been healthy for many years since then. But now, he's getting desperate."

"Why?"

"Why do you think?" Leea sighed. "Your eighteenth birthday is less than barely two months away, and we have nothing. We are going to lose everything when you fall asleep, Rose."

Rose ignored her selfish slant to the curse she bore. "Isra can still rule," Rose insisted.

"She is not a legitimate heir." It was Leea's turn to blush.

Rose wanted to talk about Hebert some, too, but she pressed on for her sister's sake. "She is still *your* heir. You spent all those years hiding her from the public. Why can't you hide the circumstances of her birth?"

"Don't you think I tried?" Leea sighed. "It is a dark secret, Rose, and not one of our happier ones."

"What happened? Tell me."

From the look on her mother's face, she was not sure if Leea would grant her request. But after a long moment, Leea sighed, and nodded.

"Hebert was the one who originally wanted to find the Rose Ruby for me," Leea began. "He was young and strong and the three of us—your father, myself, and Hebert—had grown up about the same time. They knew of my father's ridiculous demands and his various problems."

"I've heard he was a harsh ruler," Rose murmured.

"He was, and more," Leea assured her. "He was frugal with everything, unless he wanted it, especially after my mother died. He was cruel and heartless, and he only wanted more power."

"That's why he wanted the Rose Ruby, I assume?"

"Yes," Leea agreed. "The Rose Ruby is a special jewel. It has a unique power, even among the other enchanted rubies of the world. It has a power inside of it that cancels out other creatures' magic. With that sort of power, my father knew he

ONCE UPON A PRINCESS

would be able to stand up to Magdalina, who had caused him quite a bit of trouble, too."

Rose recalled what Felise, the charming innkeeper on Maltia, had told her before. *The Rose Ruby had the power to bring down great men and great kingdoms.*

"When Stefanos managed to bring it to him," Leea said, "my father was more than happy to get rid of me."

"Why didn't you use the Rose Ruby on my father when he was sick from the Magdust?" Rose asked.

"There was no way to know if it would affect me—and you," Leea admitted. "When my father died, it fell to my care, and I largely forgot about it, until after you were cursed and I fell into a deep depression."

"I was wondering where it went," Rose admitted.

"Well, I don't have it anymore," Leea said. "Before you get too excited."

"Why?" Rose asked. "What did you do with it?"

Leea blushed. "While I was pregnant with you," she said quietly, "your father was ill. Hebert kept me company. He was good to me. I knew he had been in love with me since we were younger, and … " She shook her head.

"So that's how Isra and Ronan were born eventually," Rose finished.

Leea nodded. "When your father recovered," Leea said, "he was upset about everything. He arranged Hebert to marry one of our more volatile alliances, in an effort to stabilize relations as well as send his brother away with a legitimate reason."

Rose thought about Ambassador Rolez, the brother of her uncle's wife. "He probably made things worse, from what I've heard," she said.

"We've all had rough lives, Rose. He fell in love with me, and I was to marry his brother, who wanted to marry me for

ONCE UPON A PRINCESS

the crown. He went mad from taking the Magdust, and I was depressed at losing you and him and everything seemed too much. Hebert was there for me, and I was unable to stop him from his obsession with me." Leea shook her head. "Admittedly, after you were cursed, it was the only thing that seemed constant in my life."

Rose knew she had never pitied her mother's loss as much as she could have. In that moment, having felt the loss of Theo's presence and her friends' companionship, she understood more of what it was to be trapped by the darkness inside.

"When I felt better, and Stefanos was better, we worked out our problems. I lied to Hebert, telling him that Isra and Ronan were not his," she admitted. "I feel terrible about it, but I know if he knew the truth, he would never accept you, Rose. He would try to take the throne away from Stefanos."

"What about you?" Rose asked. "Didn't you love him?"

"I might have, once, but I also loved you, Rose," Leea said. "I knew enough about Hebert that I knew he would not accept you as his own, as your father accepted Isra and Ronan."

"The king knows?" Rose was surprised. "Well, I guess that's why he seems more reluctant to give Isra the throne."

"You must forgive him. We are all under a lot of stress, even though we hide it. His madness has started to return," the queen said, "and it gets worse as your birthday approaches."

"He seems mostly normal to me," Rose said.

"He is very careful to hide it around you, especially," Leea said. She frowned. "And you should be grateful for it, too. Once he married me, he never had a problem being himself

ONCE UPON A PRINCESS

with me. There's very little I did, and very little that I would ever do, to stop him."

"Except try to poison him," Rose pointed out.

"Once more, despite everything," Leea said, "he understands."

"He knows about this, too?" Rose asked, angry and more frustrated. "What is wrong with you two? Don't you know how to have a normal marriage?"

"Rose," Leea muttered through tight lips. "You're young. You don't understand. Love is complicated and marriage is even more complicated—especially if there is not enough love."

"Knowing this, I can't believe you wanted me to get married."

"When it comes down to it, it's part of the royal politics." Leea sighed. "You know, I was actually hoping you would find someone while you were off on your journey, especially when you set out last year with Prince Philip."

Rose briefly thought of Theo again. "Philip and I are just friends. And he has Isra now."

"Yes, I've heard. I think it's a good match." Leea's eyes twinkled. "I've heard of the Dowager's love for parade, too, so I hope I will be able to see the wedding when it happens."

"So what about Hebert?" Rose asked. "Why is he here?"

"I sent for him," Leea admitted. "I had Roderick send him a message when I was imprisoned."

When you tried to poison my father, Rose mentally corrected her.

"Why did you poison him?" Rose whispered. "I don't understand why you would do something so terrible."

"I told you, I was trying to protect you," Leea said. "I thought if you had the crown, you and the kingdom would both be better off. The king is slipping into madness again,

ONCE UPON A PRINCESS

Rose. He's just as bad as you. He barely eats, he hardly sleeps, he doesn't try to do anything to better the kingdom. Rhone is ready for a new ruler."

"How do you know he's actually mad?" Rose asked. "Maybe he's just getting old."

"Either way, Rhone would benefit from a new ruler."

"There's still no reason to kill him," Rose insisted.

"Oh, so he would just abdicate, and we would place you as a ruler, before the fulfillment of your curse?" Leea shook her head. "The kingdom would revolt. I needed a more dire reason for you to take the throne. It just seemed more merciful."

"So then you sent for Hebert? Why?"

"I thought he would be able to help," Leea admitted. "I see now that it was a mistake bringing him here. I thought maybe he would be able to protect Isra and Ronan, but when Isra was able to go to Einish, I realized I didn't need him to protect them."

"That was terrible idea," Rose said.

"Rose, please. I was desperate. And there's also the matter of the Rose Ruby."

"What about it?"

"Hebert is the one who has it now." Leea's cheeks flushed with shame. "When he left for Aragon, I gave it to him as a parting gift."

Rose felt her mouth drop open. "He has the Rose Ruby?"

"Yes." Leea sighed. "I thought maybe we could use it against Magdalina. I wanted him to come and bring it. I thought if he had me, that would be enough. I thought it might be able to save you, and the throne would be secure at last."

Rose said nothing for a long moment. She realized her head was starting to hurt, as if all of this terrible information was actually hurting her.

"Be careful around him, Rose. He doesn't know the truth about Isra and Ronan, but even if he did, that wouldn't stop him from hurting anyone who got in his way."

"And he just wants you?" Rose asked.

"Me and the crown." Leea gave her a sad smile. "It's terrifying to think that a throne is all the reason men want to love me."

Juana huffed. "You are beautiful, Leea. You have much to offer anyone who would be so lucky as to love you."

Rose stood up, rubbing her temples. "Well, thank you for your time today, Mother. I need some time to process this properly. Please excuse me."

"Fine." Leea stood up from her chair as well. "But see that you take care of yourself, too, Rose."

"Why?" Rose frowned at her. "Are you going to try to poison me if I don't eat enough or get enough sleep?"

At the shocked look on her mother's face, Rose stopped. She was about to apologize when Leea took a deep breath and said, "I suppose I deserve that. But please, Rose, don't tell anyone what I told you," she said. "The king knows, as I told you, but we are trying to hold off the trial as long as we can."

"I see." Rose headed out of the prison, closing the door behind her. There were several guards—two of Hebert's, and two of the king's—waiting on the other side. Rose heard Juana's music fade into nothing as she began to head up to the castle's keep.

6

Rose decided she would never understand her parents. *Never.*

From her father's fears and anxiety, to her mother's deception and idiocy, she was confounded as to how they had survived as long as they had. Especially together, Rose thought, shaking her head at the scandals that her parents had engaged in over the years.

Rose was nearly to the king's council room when she saw her uncle stepping out into the hallway.

And then there is the matter of my uncle, Rose thought.

"Princess Aurora," he greeted.

There was something about him that she just did not like.

"Uncle Hebert, Your Grace," she replied, hoping her headache would be able to let her get through this conversation.

"I was heartened to learn you went to go and see your mother today," he said. "Leea has been very lonely."

Rose nodded, deciding it was not the best time to unleash a tirade on how he did not have the right to keep her from her mother.

"I have not seen you at dinner much," Hebert said. "I was hoping to get to know you better. There is so much to catch up on. After all, we have not seen each other since you were a little baby."

"You're right," Rose said. "There is much to discuss, such as when you and your troops are going to leave. My father has neglected to inform me of how long to expect you."

She saw the flicker of anger on his face before he could disguise it properly.

Her mother was right; she would have to be careful.

"I have neglected in setting a timeframe myself," he said. "I have not been home in Rhone for many years, due to the sickness of my late wife."

"My condolences on her loss," Rose murmured. "When I join my father in our next council session, we can set a date for your departure, so we might be able to celebrate your visit appropriately. Surely with the loss of your beloved wife, there is much to settle back in Aragon."

She turned away, entering into the council room, before he could say anything else.

Rose knew he was fuming. She could hear the angry huff of his nostrils; she was amused to wonder if Hebert shared some of her father's angry faces.

Speaking of which, Rose thought, *now I have to deal with my father.*

She glanced around the council table to see that her father was alone in the room, save for one of his valets, and he was sleeping in his chair.

"Disgraceful," she muttered to herself, as she came up beside him and cleared her throat. "Majesty!"

Stefanos' eyes blinked open. "Aurora, please. It's the middle of the day."

"Exactly," Rose said. "You should be working."

"I'm not a young king anymore," he complained. "I'm allowed to have my naps. It's for the good of the kingdom."

"I shudder to think that you mean it's best for the kingdom that you're asleep, rather than helping your countrymen."

"You will only be able to hope for that," Stefanos snapped back, clearly upset she was deriding him. "Especially since we only have what? Two month, is it? And then Magdalina's curse will be fulfilled, and you'll be asleep more than I am."

Rose frowned at the insult. "Well," she said, "I'm not asleep now, so that's something."

"What are you doing for the kingdom that's so great then?" Stefanos scoffed. "Besides robbing me of my slumber?"

"I want to talk to you about Hebert," Rose said. "I want you to order him from the castle. I'm here now. You don't need to worry about Mother, or Isra, or Ronan. I'm here to protect them."

"For how long?" Stefanos asked.

"Long enough," Rose snapped.

"You foolish girl," Stefanos said, rising from his chair. "You disobey and dishonor me at every turn you can, don't you? You think it's so easy to defy a king, no wonder you think you can overcome a fairy like Magdalina."

"Half-fairy," Rose corrected.

"This is all that boy's fault, isn't it?" Stefanos grumbled. "Some paragon at the church befriends you, and you think you can outsmart me, like God is on your side or something like that."

"Leave Theo out of this," Rose hissed. "He's not the one who lied to me. He's the one who told me the truth."

"Oh, really? He was so quick to tell you about our family. What did he tell you of his own?"

Rose shook her head. "This has nothing to do with them," she insisted.

"They were part of the Magdust trade, you know," Stefanos said. "The Reverend has been keeping his own secrets for years along with mine, but we are at last on even footing."

"I know what happened," Rose suddenly shouted, as her patience broke. "I know everything. I know about the Magdust, I know about the tapestry, I know about Mother and the twins."

ONCE UPON A PRINCESS

Stefanos blinked, and suddenly his whole demeanor changed. "Aurora," he said. "Help me."

"Help you what?" Rose frowned. "I'm trying, but I can only do so much."

"I need to lie down," he said.

Rose sighed. She then took his arm, and helped him around the table. She thought of the kingdom, and all the people in it who looked to him to lead, and she wondered if this was something that she would struggle with when she was older.

If I can break my curse at all.

After she and the king's valet escorted Stefanos back to his room, Rose headed back to her tower to consider everything that she had learned from her parents.

Her father had a lot of secrets, as he'd said before. And none of the ones she had discovered seemed anywhere close to pleasant. He had married her mother for the crown, and he had made a deal with Magdalina to secure the thrown with an heir. After she betrayed him, he was lulled back to sanity by a tapestry weaver the Reverend Father knew. Hebert had romanced her mother, but in the end, her mother had decided to choose Rose's wellbeing over him. Hebert, rejected, went to marry and live in Aragon as a duke, taking the Rose Ruby with him as a parting gift from her mother.

Now, Hebert was back, to try to free her mother and get the crown, and he was using his remaining goodwill to leverage a better position.

With Leea in prison, and her father indisposed, Rose knew it would be up to her to get rid of him. But it would not be an easy task.

She thought of her father's warning. She needed the support of the country and his nobles behind her in order to get rid of him without losing loyalty.

Rose shook her head. She had spent the majority of the last years out of the country, trying to break her curse. Her people had pitied her, and while she had come to understand their position, she still did not enjoy their confidence as a warrior or as a leader.

There was no time to do another grand tour of the kingdom, Rose thought wistfully, wishing she did have more time to travel.

"If only," she thought aloud, "there was some way to bring the whole kingdom to me."

"Rose!" Mary called.

Rose glanced down at the castle's courtyard, watching as her faithful fairy friend came fluttering up beside her.

Mary greeted her with a smile. "I've been looking for you."

"Sorry," Rose said. "I was with my mother for a while."

"Oh." Mary stopped. "I suppose she told you I'd mentioned I was worried about you?"

"In more specific ways," Rose said. "But I'm not concerned about that right now. I'm more concerned about the king."

"Well, he will have to wait for a while," Mary said. She gave Rose a big smile. "Philip and Isra and all the others are close. I just heard the announcement that they are heading into town!"

"Really?" Rose glanced out over the balcony, eagerly looking for her friends. She saw the colorful banner of Einish as it came closer to the castle. "That's wonderful! I could really use some allies right now. And I'm eager to plan out our attack on Darkwood Forest."

"I know it's been several weeks since we've seen them," Mary agreed. "Go out and greet them. I'll alert the staff and start getting their rooms ready."

ONCE UPON A PRINCESS

"Thanks, Mary," Rose cheered as she headed out to reunite with her friends, already feeling less alone. Despite all her troubles, she knew that she could face them as long as she had her friends at her side.

7

"I don't see why you had to wait, if all you're going to do is walk up and knock on the door," Bachas grumbled, shoveling a handful of food into his mouth as they walked along the edge of the forest once more. "We would probably get farther if we did this in the middle of the night instead of in the middle of the day."

"I thought about it carefully," Theo said. "And as much as I'm certain it won't be easy, I need to try to gain my aunt's trust before we do anything else. I am hoping you won't be opposed to helping me."

"I'm helping myself first," Bachas asserted. "But I don't want to be the one your princess comes hunting down if I don't save you."

Theo stopped in his tracks. "I don't think you would have to worry about that."

Bachas smirked. "Don't I?" he asked. He took the seeing crystal out of his pocket. "Show me the princess."

"Hey, come on, Bachas," Theo said, before a quick flash of light sputtered out the small crystal.

"Look, there she is," Bachas said. "She's in her tower again."

Before Theo could tell Bachas it was too painful, and he did not want to see Rose, the pixie had clawed his way up his back and shoved the crystal under his nose.

And there she was. Theo watched as Rose leaned against the battlements of her tower. He was surprised to see that, for all her beauty, her face was careworn and tired as she looked out into the distance.

"She's waiting for you," Bachas said.

"How do you know?" Theo asked.

"Who else would she be waiting for?" Bachas scoffed.

Theo looked back at the crystal, wishing he could just fall into the small orb and find himself beside her, as he had done countless times while they traveled together. He would walk up to her and tug at her hair, standing close enough to her that it was just natural that she would lean against him, or they would find a way to reach for each other.

She was wearing a dress. Immediately he had to wonder if she had an audience with her father. He knew King Stefanos did not appreciate Rose's affection for her knight's attire.

Theo continued to stare at the crystal's light, watching as Mary came up beside Rose. He was glad she had the company, even if she still looked weary.

He was about to push the crystal out of his face when he saw her smile.

"Rose." Theo felt his heart race as she grinned. Could she see him? Did she know he was watching her?

And then he saw the trail of horses and carriages arriving below, with the banners bearing the colors of Einish. *Philip and Isra must be arriving from O'Lin. Or maybe King Derick is sending her the troops to help attack Darkwood.*

He sighed and gave the crystal back to Bachas. "Like I said," he remarked, "I don't think you have to worry about Rose coming to hunt you down. She has other things on her mind right now besides me."

Bachas laughed, making Theo even more irritated. He ignored him as they made their way back toward Annalora's cottage.

"If you're going to use your crystal, why don't you make sure Everon is no longer here?" Theo asked.

ONCE UPON A PRINCESS

"He's not here." Elva's voice was hushed as she slid down the tree beside them. "He headed out early this morning. He said that his mother has been bothering him more and more these days, so there's always a lot for him to do."

"Elva," Bachas hopped from Theo's back to the tree in one large leap. He curled his arm around his wife's neck.

Theo stepped forward, heading out of the shadows and into plain sight as the two of them snuggled together. After seeing Rose, he did not want to think about anything besides the task before him.

The barrier was still there, a small bubble of power around the cottage. As Theo pressed into it, a sloppy feeling glommed onto him, almost as though he were walking underwater, pressed around on all sides by immersive magic.

But he was still able to move, and he was still able to see the cottage. Theo took that as a good sign.

He reached the door and knocked.

An instant stillness came over the atmosphere as a voice croaked, "Who is it?"

Theo was surprised at the scratchy sound. It did not belong to a young woman.

The door snapped open before he could give his answer. He instantly found himself staring at the young woman, watching as wrinkles on her skin disappeared and the gray in her hair transformed into a shining ebony. His eyes found hers again, and he was surprised to see a shade of green that nearly matched his own.

"Aunt Annalora," he said.

The now-young lady frowned. "Who are you?"

"Pardon me," Theo said, feeling rude for staring. "My name is Theo. I'm Eleanora's son."

ONCE UPON A PRINCESS

Something darkened in her eyes, and she shifted in demeanor. "What do you want, *Theo?*" she asked, emphasizing his name carefully, as if she were still weighing whether or not she believed him. "My sister is dead."

At her blunt rudeness, Theo gripped the hilt of his sword in irritation. "Your sister is dead," he agreed, "but your father is not. He sent me to find you."

"The old man is still alive?" Annalora's eyes narrowed. "Considering his age, I should be surprised. But I am not really that shocked. He always did everything he could to make sure he had a good life, and he kept it that way."

"He's the Reverend Father at a church," Theo said.

Annalora suddenly laughed, her chortling tart and brisk. "Now, *that* is surprising," she said as she turned around and headed back inside. She waved him in behind her, as she pulled a pair of teacups down from her cupboard. "I guess my threats worked."

"Threats?" Theo tentatively followed her into the cottage, feeling tall as his hair brushed against the ceiling rafters. He glanced around, taking in the different features of his aunt's house. She had a largely open house, with a fire in the chimney that still glowed with an ominous blue color. He followed the blue residue's shadow and saw that it came crawling out of the back room.

"I told him to stay away, or I would curse him," Annalora said. "He was always afraid of my mother, after he found out about her skills. It didn't take much to convince him I was a threat, too."

"I can well imagine it would have been easy for him to believe," Theo said. "Especially after my mother and father were killed."

ONCE UPON A PRINCESS

Theo moved toward a corner of the room, trying to angle himself to where he could see back into the other rooms. He wondered if any fairies were still alive in the house.

"I'm surprised you're so calm about it," Annalora remarked, still carefully watching him as she boiled water for the tea.

She was curious, Theo realized. She wanted to know more about him. *Probably just to make sure I am her relative. She wants to make sure that was the only reason I was able to get past her barrier.*

"It's been many years," Theo told her simply, hoping she was satisfied with his vague answer.

He caught sight of Bachas and Elva in the window. They were both waving their hands erratically. As Theo locked eyes with Bachas, he heard a small whisper in his mind.

Don't drink the tea.

Theo sighed, moving around some as Annalora poured some tea for him. "You look a lot like my mother, but I know she was younger than you."

"Wondering about my beauty?" Annalora smirked. "You know that I'm a witch. It's a simple trick to look young again."

"Just like spinning Magdust into tapestries?" Theo asked.

Annalora did not blink at his question. "That's a little harder," she said. "But I thrive on the challenge. If you're like me, you'll understand that."

"The Reverend Father said that you did not want to make one for King Stefanos," Theo said. "My mother did."

"What do you care for the crown?" Annalora scoffed. "Eleanora's downfall came after she saved the crown, too, thanks to her wretched husband."

"He was a good man," Theo insisted, struggling to keep his voice neutral.

ONCE UPON A PRINCESS

"Yes, and that was the problem. Good people always want you to help them get rid of other peoples' problems. I warned Eleanora not to fall in love with him. She was beautiful; surely you remember that. But no, instead of finding someone who had power, she didn't listen. She tricked him into marrying her, and look where it got her. Nothing good came from that."

"I was born," Theo reminded her.

"So what? Even when Henry did come eventually to love my sister on his own, do you honestly think it was good for them?"

Theo felt a rush of shock, hearing that his father really did love his mother. He felt a small prickle behind his nose at the news, grateful to know the truth. His mother and father had their problems, but their love had been real.

He made a mental note to tell Thad what he knew when he returned to Havilah.

"Eleanora was a fool," Annalora continued. "She fell in love with Henry, that knight, and he was a fool, too. She used her magic to get him to agree to marry her and gave up her craft. She was running out of her supply of Magdust when she finally was killed."

Theo told himself to keep calm, but his anger continued to burn. "How do you know that? Did Everon tell you that?"

"So, you know about Everon. It seems I underestimated you."

"I know he killed them, and Uncle Thom as well," Theo told her. "Uncle Thom went to defend them that night. Did you know?"

"I knew," Annalora said. "Eleanora and her precious knight had protection until her power and the Magdust were gone.

The instant they tried to get more, Everon found them and killed them. And I was glad for it."

"Why? She was your sister!" Theo shifted his weight carefully. He knew that he had promised the Grand Father to bring her back, but he knew if he was going to keep his word, he would likely have to fight her—and he would have to make sure he would not allow himself to hurt her any more than he needed to.

Temptation is not sin, he reminded himself carefully.

"She might have been my sister by blood, but once she married that man, she was no longer the same. She no longer cared about power," Annalora said.

"And that is all you care about," Theo accused. "Isn't it? That is why you helped ambassador Rolez; you didn't care if people got hurt, so long as you could disrupt their kingdom. And that's why you accepted Hebert's commission."

Annalora laughed. "My, my," she said. "You have been busy."

Theo glared at her, but she only smirked in return.

"Well, you're almost right. I accepted Hebert's commission because of his payment."

Before he could ask her what Hebert had paid her, his aunt said, "Everon's mother is after the throne of Rhone. I would be more foolish than you to stand up against her."

"Did you know she's trying to force Rose to marry Everon for the throne?" Theo asked.

"Rose?"

"Princess Aurora," Theo corrected himself.

"I didn't know about that," Annalora said. "But I do know it doesn't matter. One day, Everon will be king and I will be his queen, no matter what his mother says."

ONCE UPON A PRINCESS

Theo felt a new rush of fear for Rose. Not only was she in danger from Hebert, she was in trouble from his aunt. "I won't let you hurt her," he declared.

Annalora cackled. "You won't need to worry about it. You'll be dead before too long yourself, especially if you are still adamant about taking me to see my father."

"He wants to see you again," Theo said. "Doesn't that mean anything to you?"

"Why would I need to see him? I have no need for his forgiveness."

"What of God's?" Theo asked. "Given all the destruction you've caused, it wouldn't be inappropriate to feel sorry for it."

"I have done nothing wrong," Annalora said. "Sure, I make magical tapestries. So what? It was Everon who killed your parents, after finding out they saved King Stefanos. And what about all the people who commission me to make my tapestries and charms? It seems to me that they're the ones who should pay in the end. I'm just a means to their ends, and they pay me well enough to assuage any conceivable guilt. I make a living this way, and even more. You're the one who has killed people, right? As a knight for the king?"

Theo frowned. "Going to war for your home is different from selling things that destroy lives."

"Hardly." Annalora laughed.

Theo followed her gaze as she gestured toward the back room. He watched as the blue aura of fairy blood continued to leak freely from the doorway.

As if Annalora sensed his discomfort, she pushed the cup of tea closer to him. "Here."

"No thank you," Theo said politely.

ONCE UPON A PRINCESS

"Shame," Annalora told him, as she picked the cup back up. "I've been told there's no tea in the world like mine."

"I'm sure." Theo kept her eyes on her, watching as she took a sip of the tea from the cup that she had offered him. Her lips, red and youthful, curved into a smile. Theo was just wondering if he had made a mistake, listening to Bachas, when she flung the cup at him.

Theo ducked and slid behind her small table, as the hot liquid burned into the wall behind him. Smoke came up from the point of impact, leaving an acrid taste in the air.

Annalora grabbed her own cup and threw it down at him. Theo rolled away, barely managing to escape her second attack. "You fool," she hissed. "You didn't really think it would be so easy to get me to leave this place, did you?"

Theo stood up and used his sword to block the teapot's assault. As she reached for her herbs, Theo dashed out of the kitchen, heading down the hall. He heard Annalora call for Elva as he headed for her backroom.

"You can tell my father that I have no need to atone for my sins anymore," Annalora called. "I have no need for forgiveness, now that mortality no longer has any power over me."

"You sound pretty certain of that," Theo called back. "But even your blood seal wasn't enough to keep me out."

"I wondered if you noticed that," Annalora replied coyly. "It is good to know you are reckless, then, rather than just a blundering half-wit. Just like your simpleton parents, no doubt."

"Leave them out of this," Theo shouted back. "I came to retrieve you for your father, nothing else."

"I'm not going to see him."

"Even though he wants to see you? What if he dies without seeing you again, without making peace with you?"

"Let him die," Annalora said. "Let it be quick, too, and if he has regrets about our relationship, all the better."

She jumped forward, throwing a handful of dust at him; it scattered around him, landing on him and burning his eyes. He shielded his face and ducked into the room beside him as Annalora cursed and called out for Elva again.

The blue aura encompassed his body the moment he stepped into the small room. Theo saw the area was full of Magdust and felt his breath catch at the terrible pressure in the room.

He made his way toward the spinning wheel in front of the fireplace, where another magical barrier pushed back the aura. Stepping into the small bubble, Theo immediately felt the magical effects recede and he was able to breathe correctly.

Just then, Annalora appeared in the door with Elva by her side. "Elva, get rid of him!" she ordered.

Theo felt his first shot of doubt as he looked at the nervous pixie. He saw the anguish on Elva's face as she lifted up her hands and began to work her magic. Little streams of blood-red power leaked from her hands.

Glancing around, Theo realized with a sinking feeling that he was trapped. His eyes squeezed shut as Elva unleashed her power at him.

8

Theo was prepared for pain. He was even prepared to feel nothing, as death came and took him to his spirit's final resting place.

But none of that happened.

Nothing happened.

He opened his eyes to see Elva's power still lashing out at him, but the barrier around the spinning wheel rendered her power null.

Behind Elva, Annalora was shouting at her to do even more, while Elva was trying to tell her that it was not her fault that she was unable to do any damage.

Theo brandished his sword when Annalora came up to Elva and began shaking her. "Stop!" he yelled, watching Elva's eyes widen in fear.

"Fool." Annalora shoved Elva down on the floor, hard. Elva crumpled and curled into a ball, shielding her eyes with her arms.

Theo held his sword out in defense as he hurried toward Elva.

At that moment, Bachas came up behind Annalora and pushed her, using his own magic.

Annalora flew toward Theo. He watched as she passed through the magic barrier by the fireplace. Instantly, her skin turned dull and wrinkled, and her eyes dimmed with her true age.

His sword struck her at the hip as she fell against him. Blood dripped out from between the folds of her dress. Theo pushed her away from him as another cloud of her magic

ONCE UPON A PRINCESS

herbs went flying, but this time, he noticed, there was no sting in his eyes or in his nose.

Before Theo could check on his aunt, he heard Bachas cry out. "Elva!"

Bachas hurried over to his wife and cradled her head. "Are you alright?" he asked her, his voice tender as he held her.

Elva nodded shakily. "My mistress always gets violent when she is unhappy."

Theo looked down at his aunt, who had also gone still. The blood was still dripping from her torso. He put his sword down and reached for her pulse.

"She's old," Bachas snorted behind him.

"She's not that old," Theo said, even though Annalora's face looked even older than his grandfather's.

"Stripped of her magic, she's unable to maintain a regular body like ordinary humans," Bachas explained. "And injured besides? She's not going to last."

"She will," Theo insisted, as he found her injury. He grimaced at the blood; his sword had cut into her more deeply than he had thought. "Help me move her."

Bachas stilled, and shook his head. "No," he said. "I will not help you this time."

Theo scowled at him. "She'll die if you don't help me."

"Exactly." Bachas gave him a hard look. "Elva will be free. And the tapestry will be only half-finished. Your princess will be safe from her and those soldiers."

"That still doesn't mean I should allow her to die," Theo shouted.

He carefully pulled his aunt's body out from behind the spinning wheel. Instantly, the blue aura of fairy blood choked him further, but Theo forced himself to breathe through it as he grabbed some cloth and tried to bandage his aunt up.

ONCE UPON A PRINCESS

Before he could do anything else, a flash of light exploded behind him, and Theo briefly felt pain in the back of his head and shoulder before the darkness took him.

There was no way to tell how much time passed before Theo heard whispers as he began to stir, but he had a feeling it was not very long.

"I think he's waking up now," Elva said. "Do you think we should let him?"

"It's fine," Bachas replied. "He can't do anything else. And despite the less than appealing way I knocked him out, he's a good man."

The words were soft, but Theo heard them and almost smiled. After all their time together, he was glad he had won Bachas' admiration.

Even if Bachas had been the one who had stopped him from saving Annalora.

At that thought, Theo blinked his eyes open. Immediately, the smell of blood wafted over him, and he looked to see he was still in the corner of Annalora's workroom. Her body was sprawled across the bloodstained floor.

As Theo sat up, the small pixie suddenly stood before him, the same hardness on his face.

"So," Bachas said, "Elva was right. You are awake."

Theo nodded, feeling dizzy from the pain in his head. "You hit me." He reached up and felt a small bump on his head.

"You're welcome," Bachas said.

"I didn't want you to let her die," Theo said. "Why did you do that?"

"The same reason you go off and fight in war and battles," Bachas said. "To protect the one I love."

He glanced over at Elva, who was sitting in the far corner, wrapped in a blanket.

ONCE UPON A PRINCESS

Theo sighed. "She is okay, then?"

"She's a little sore, but overall, yes, she is fine. And she is free, too."

The wonder and joy in Bachas' gaze made Theo's heart warm. He was glad for the pixie's happiness, even if he was upset at the cost.

"She was my mother's sister," Theo said quietly. "I was hoping she would tell me more about her."

"Well, your aunt was a terrible person, from what I saw," Bachas said. "You wouldn't have been able to trust her information anyway."

"True.," Theo said, trying not to think of how much he missed his mother. "I remember my mother used to tell me bedtime stories of Queen Lucia and Benedict, who became the first knight of Rhone, and eventually its king."

"If it's any consolation," Bachas said, "I don't remember my parents. They were killed by some fairies themselves. So I do have some understanding of your feelings toward Everon, if not any sympathy for your aunt's loss."

Theo glanced over at his aunt's body once more. All of her magic was gone. The young woman who had greeted him warily at her cottage door was gone, and an old woman had replaced her.

Theo nodded slowly. "I understand," he said, "even if we still disagree."

"You've seen death before. I don't know why you're upset."

"Death was not originally part of God's plan," Theo said quietly. "I know why it happens, and I know that there is no stopping it sometimes. But I also know that life is precious, and my aunt might have had a chance at a better life if she was still alive."

ONCE UPON A PRINCESS

"*Might have.*" Bachas rolled his eyes. "I think you're being difficult about this on purpose. In fact, you are being a complete hypocrite about it."

"How?" Theo asked, narrowing his eyes at him.

"Listen to yourself. If it had been Everon who was maimed, you wouldn't have had any trouble letting him die," Bachas pointed out. He snickered deviously. "Besides, you don't have to worry about it. I'm the one who stopped you from saving her. I'm the one who let her die."

"It's not an easy thing to bear."

"It's easier for me to bear than it is for you, then," Bachas said. "I have no qualms about the fate of a lady who tricked my wife into a life debt."

Theo watched as Bachas looked over at Elva. The softness in the pixie's eyes was clear, and Theo felt a small amount of envy. Bachas had told him before that he had not seen Elva in many, many years. Even after all their time apart, he was still very much in love with her.

Theo stood up and rubbed his head. "What do we do now?"

"I say we destroy this place," Bachas said.

"So many fairies lost their lives here," Elva said. "It is a graveyard of the worst sorts."

Theo agreed with her assessment. "Alright. But I still want to bury my aunt. Will you help me?"

Elva nodded. "I'll start a fire."

Theo, Bachas, and Elva all worked diligently as the moon began to climb into the sky. No one talked too much, until Bachas and Theo moved Annalora's body outside of her cottage.

"Let's bury her here," Theo said. "It's close to her garden."

ONCE UPON A PRINCESS

"Fine." Bachas snapped his fingers, and a shovel appeared. "I'll let you do the honors."

"Thanks," Theo muttered grimly, as he began to work.

Several more moments passed in silence, and Theo finally asked Bachas a question that he'd had on his mind for some time. "Why do pixies have life debts, Bachas? Especially if you know some are tricked into it? Wouldn't it be better just to stop the practice?"

"I know you think I'm heartless after allowing your aunt to die," Bachas replied. "And I'd agree with you if I could. Sometimes it is better to be heartless. You can't feel how terrible life really is if you don't have a heart."

Theo thought about the night Rose told him he could leave her and nodded.

"But it's not the point of life, is it?" Bachas continued. "Pixies and fairies are very different creatures, but we are alike in many ways. We are even similar to humans at times. But we are not allowed to choose our life's highest ideals. And one of our ideals is the idea of honor."

"Honor?"

"Yes. So if someone saves your life, protecting you from death, you're given a new chance. Our honor demands that while we did not die, we die to ourselves, and serve the one who saved us."

"But sometimes you have terrible masters," Theo reminded him.

"Yes, but it is still a high calling we have, to honor the good of ourselves and our heritage, even if we are unable to stop all the bad from happening."

"It seems a little silly."

"To you. But you know as well as I do there are plenty of things we do that are bad in order to bring about good."

Theo agreed, but did not want to give Bachas the satisfaction.

After Bachas left him, Theo finished burying his aunt. As he packed down the dirt on her small grave, he felt a sense of relief when he laid her to rest. Even though he felt conflicted with her death, and he did not want to go home to his grandfather with the news, he knew that Bachas was right: Annalora had treated Elva terribly, and it was his obligation as a husband to act.

After all, Theo thought as he finished burying her, *I would have done the same for Rose.*

Bachas called out to him a moment later. "Theo."

He turned at the sound of his voice. "What is it, Bachas?" he asked.

"Elva and I are almost finished in here," he said. "But we need you to help with something."

Theo went inside, heading back to the workroom. He was gratified to see Elva had managed to get the bloodstains off the floor. The spinning wheel remained in the heart of the room, but the blue aura was gone. "What is it?" he asked.

"That," Bachas said, pointing to a small, ornately carved box on the fireplace mantle.

Theo glanced down at it.

"We can't touch it," Bachas explained. "It's a kind of power not for us to mess with."

"So I should pick it up?" Theo asked, arching his brow.

"You're not a pixie, so you should be able to," Bachas said.

Theo headed over. Once more, he felt the magical barrier surround him that had saved him before. "I thought this was Annalora's magic."

He reached out, hesitant, and picked up the box. He opened it up to see a large ruby staring back at him. He gasped.

"Woah," Bachas said. "That's one big ruby."

Theo nodded. He touched the ruby lightly. It reminded him so much of the one Amalia had given to Rose. *Is it possible this one also holds dragon's blood? Or does it contain some other power?*

Elva spoke up. "That was the object which canceled out Annalora's power, and mine as well," she said. "It must be a powerful gem."

"It cancels out magic?" Theo continued to stare at the jewel. He suddenly wondered if Rose would be able to use it on her eighteenth birthday.

"At least my magic, and Annalora's," Elva said. "She was at the spinning wheel earlier when you came, and her magic was unable to keep her young."

Theo nodded. "This might help Rose," he said. "Can I have it?"

"She was your aunt," Bachas said. "You're not thinking of using that to fight Magdalina, are you?"

"Well, yes," Theo admitted. "Why?"

"We're going to need more than that to defeat her."

"Rose has dragon's blood," Theo told him. "She's got a crystal like this, too."

Elva and Bachas raised their eyebrows and exchanged a look of surprise.

"Besides," Theo said, "what do you mean 'we?' You and Elva are both free. You don't have to help me and my friends fight Magdalina."

Bachas and Elva linked hands. "We want to help you," he said. "As a way to thank you, for all you've done for us."

"You don't owe me anything."

"It's not a matter of owing someone," Elva said. "We are grateful."

"But you're also in love," Theo replied. "And the battlefield is no place for love."

"That's hardly the truth."

"I'd return the gratitude if you'll let me take this ruby," Theo said. "That is all I would ask of you, for helping me here."

"She was your aunt," Bachas said with a shrug. "Take what you want."

"Thank you." Theo tucked the small box into a pouch on his belt. The magic barrier radiating from the jewel disappeared. "I don't know if it can help Rose at all, but if it's a possibility, I can't leave it here to burn."

Bachas smirked. "If nothing else, it'll give you something to talk about other than how she doesn't love you."

Theo frowned at him, while Elva nudged him with her elbow. "Thanks, Bachas," he said. "Now, let's finish up here. If this is something that can help Rose, we should head out as quickly as we can."

It was only when Theo walked outside moments later that he saw they were not alone.

He stopped in his tracks, just outside his aunt's door, as Everon stared at him, his eyes burning an angry red.

689

9

For the first time in a long time, Rose was looking forward to dinner. She had requested Ethan's favorite foods and Sophia's favorite drinks. She had prepared a special table setting for Isra and Phillip, and they were all supposed to be happy to see each other and eager to get down to business.

Halfway through the night, Rose sighed as she barely glanced at her mostly-full plate of food.

Mary and Fiona chatted happily together over tea at the far end of the table, while Rose alternated glances between Ethan and Sophia, while Isra and Philip seemed content to concern themselves largely with each other.

Of all of them, Sophia was the one who seemed most like her usual self. She at least smiled and seemed somewhat warm toward Rose as they ate and talked.

Her brother, on the other hand, seemed more surly than Rose had ever seen him.

"How was the trip here, Ethan?" Rose asked.

The clinking of their silverware and the small whispers faded. Ethan barely glanced over at her as he shrugged. "It was fine, Rose."

Rose looked over at Philip, who tore himself away from Isra's attention long enough to give her a worried look.

Rose turned to face Sophia. "Did you have any trouble while you were at Einish?"

"Not really," Sophia replied.

"So everyone there is okay?"

"Well, with the exception of Ambassador Rolez," Philip said. "Although Einish does not have a hard prison system, he has been stripped of his position and sentenced to a lengthy term. Once he's free, he will be able to reclaim his wealth, but not his title."

"I'm glad to hear he has been taken care of," Rose said. "I hope Juliette is well?"

"She's doing well," Philip said with a nod. "And the baby is good, too."

"Wonderful," Rose said. She tried not to feel the familiar tingle of jealousy she often felt when women talked about having children.

"We didn't have any trouble," Sophia said. Her mismatched eyes, one blue-green and the other brown, gleamed as she said, "Everything was really lovely, actually. Philip let me hang out in the smithing yard, so I was able to learn some new tricks."

"Glad to hear you were able to have some fun while I was gone."

Ethan snorted.

Rose frowned at him. "What's wrong?" she asked. "Did Penelope decide not to come to Einish or Rhone after all?"

"There's no need to see to my happiness, Rose," Ethan said. "You're too good at destroying other people's."

Rose blanched. "What?"

"Maybe we should talk about something else," Philip suggested quickly. "I hope you don't mind, but I borrowed Virtue to send a letter to Derick before we left Einish."

"Oh." Rose, still shocked by Ethan's anger, slowly nodded at Philip's news. "I was wondering where he was."

"I received Derick's latest letter the day before we left," Philip explained. "Derick said he had quite a few men willing to join your campaign, especially after the news of what you did in the Wandering Caverns."

"You did more than me," Rose replied. She could feel Mary's gaze on her from the far corner of the room. She refrained from mentioning Magdalina's visit to the rest of her friends after telling Theo. From his reaction alone, she had decided it was better that she keep that to herself.

And it is better to forget completely about that, Rose thought. If Magdalina thought she would ever marry Everon, she was dead wrong.

"You are still the most inspiring one of all of us," Philip said. "I know most of the men in question are from near our shared border. Some of them are helping the pixies resettle the caves."

Isra sat forward in her seat. "I can't tell you how many of them thought I was you, Rose," she said with a reluctant smile. "Quite a few were disappointed as we passed through the country. I'm sure some of them signed up to fight at Darkwood just hoping they would see you."

Rose nearly scoffed, but she saw Philip's hand reach out and take hold of Isra's. "I wouldn't say they were disappointed," he said. "I'm more willing to bet they were shocked that it was possible for someone with even more renowned beauty than you to be alive."

Ethan made a face and Sophia rolled her eyes, as the Isra and Philip just stared at each other. Rose had to wonder if their affection was part of the reason that Ethan was unhappy. She would not be able to blame him if that was the case.

Not that she would blame him anyway. Seeing them now, Rose had a feeling both Ethan and Sophia were upset with how she had left them in Einish.

As Isra and Philip began telling Rose about their journey, Rose struggled not to fall into that night all over again.

ONCE UPON A PRINCESS

After watching Theo leave, she had saddled up her own horse and then hurriedly arranged to leave. Sophia had been sleepy and shocked, while Ethan had been upset Theo was not there. Mary had insisted she come along, and that was the only reason Rose had allowed her to come.

Rose barely remembered how she had managed to get through it.

Philip had been understanding, even grateful Rose was not forcing him to leave his home. He promised to come once she sent for him, just to make sure it was safe for Ronan and Isra to come back with them.

"Where is Ronan, anyway?" Rose asked suddenly, looking around for her younger brother. "I would have thought he would want to have dinner with us."

"Ronan's already out hunting again," Isra said. "You know how he is, Rose. He's always hungry for an adventure, and as kind as Queen Utopa was to have us, she was very adamant about how he wasn't allowed to do much more than train with her guards and play chess."

"I'm surprised he lasted as long as he did then," Rose said with a smile. Her brother had often been a force of nature itself when they were younger.

"He snuck out to the town quite often," Isra said. "He'll probably do that now that he's back here, too."

Rose sniffed. "He better not cause us any trouble."

"Roderick is with him," Philip said. "I doubt he'll be in trouble with him around."

Rose thought about the large, ginger-haired warrior who had served in her guard. He had told her before he was the queen's friend, and he took care of things for her on occasion. Rose did not have to guess that included her children. "You're right about that," she agreed. "I guess I can rest easy."

"Have you heard from Theo at all?" Sophia asked softly.

Silence once more descended on the room, and Rose shook her head. She tried to look like her usual self as she said, "No. But I know he's very busy, trying to take care of some family business for his grandfather."

"Hopefully he'll hurry," Philip said. "Reverend Thorne became sick on the way back. He's in the church now."

"Is Thad tending to him?" Rose asked. "I can send the king's physician."

"I don't know," Philip admitted. "But he is very old. He's raised two generations of his family."

"I should go and see them," Rose said. "They've always been faithful to my family, even if the king has been less than kind."

"Must be a family trait," Ethan muttered.

Rose felt her patience snap. "Do you want to say something to me, Ethan? Then just say it. There's no need to spare me."

"No," Ethan snapped. "I don't want to talk to you, Rose."

"Why?" Rose asked. "Because I left you behind, so I could come here and try to take care of my family?"

"You are my family, Rose," Ethan said. "Or at least you were, until you broke us up."

"I thought it was for the best that you stayed," Rose argued. "So you would have some time to rest from the road."

"I'm not talking about that, and you know it," Ethan said. "I know what happened. I know you sent Theo away after he told you he was in love with you."

Dead silence returned to the room as Rose felt the heat rise in her cheeks.

"I heard Thad talking about it," Ethan explained, before Rose could ask him. "And then you left us, because you couldn't face up to what you did. Now we're all here just acting like it doesn't matter."

Rose still said nothing. She noticed that Philip and Isra were avoiding her gaze, while Sophia was openly staring. Even Mary and Fiona had gone silent.

"You were wrong," Ethan said.

Rose managed to find her voice again. "He wanted to go," she said. "He had family matters to take care of."

"He would have stayed if you told him you loved him, too."

Anger finally replaced her discomfort. "I don't want him to love me," she told Ethan.

"What about what happened with the dragon?" Ethan asked. "You were wrong, Rose. You were supposed to choose love. He told you he loved you. He would have given you anything. *Anything*. A family and children, even. I know you want those. All you had to do was tell him you loved him back."

"I'm still cursed," Rose snapped. "I can't promise him that. I still have to break my curse."

"You always do that," Ethan said. "You always deny yourself anything good because you're cursed. You're never going to live like you're not cursed, even if you do break it."

"I don't want to talk about this anymore," Rose said.

"Because you know I'm right."

"No, because we have other things to talk about," Rose insisted, even though she knew she was lying. She was sure everyone else knew she was lying, too.

"May I be excused then?" Ethan asked.

"I was hoping you would stay," Rose said carefully. "It's been a few weeks since I last heard you play your harp." She hoped that he would acquiesce to her request. They would have some more time to talk later, and she wanted to show him she was still on his side.

"I don't want to play," Ethan told her. "If anything, now that we're here, I want to get some training in. I haven't worked any since you and Theo left us in Einish."

At once, Rose knew she had been right. Theo had been teaching him how to fight like a knight, and Ethan was upset that he was not here with them.

"Come on, Ethan," Philip said, trying to add some levity to the situation. "I gave you a few lessons."

"Hardly," Ethan muttered. "Now, please excuse me."

He walked away before Rose could say anything else. She leaned back in her seat, unable to think of anything to say as she watched her youngest friend leave.

"He's been in a bad mood pretty consistently since you left," Isra told her quietly. "I know he's frustrated with Theo's absence as much as he's been with yours."

Rose glanced at Sophia. "What about you?" she asked.

Her squire sighed. "I love you, Rose," she said, "but I agree with my brother."

Rose nodded. "Why don't you go after him?" she suggested. "See if you can help him."

Sophia shook her head. "It won't do any good," she said. "He's upset about Theo leaving, too. As much as he loves you, Rose, he does not have a good history with his father. Theo managed to temper that some. With him gone so unexpectedly, and for the reasons why, you can imagine how he feels."

Rose snorted, thinking of her own father. "That's the truth," she said. "I should have thought about that before. I'm sorry I didn't. Would you tell him that for me?"

Sophia gave her a small smile. "No, you can tell him yourself," she said. "Besides, you're right, too. We have more things to talk about. When do we march on Darkwood Forest?"

Rose thought about the small fairy castle, where Magdalina ruled as their leader. It was three days' ride from Havilah, and while she had never been there, she had heard enough of the tales to be less than enthusiastic for it.

She looked down at the dark ruby on the edge of her sword, looking for reassurance. But Ethan's words continued to haunt her.

She had a feeling he was right. She did not let herself choose to live as though she was going to break the curse. And she missed Theo terribly.

A picture of her children, the ones she so desperately wanted, flashed across her mind. There were two of them, a boy and a girl, playing in the courtyard. Their hair was a dark ebony, and their eyes glittered like emeralds in the sunshine.

Theo's children.

She sighed.

"What is it, Rose?" Isra asked.

Rose shook her head, letting the picture of her children slip away once more. "Nothing."

"You're not nervous about attacking Magdalina at her castle, are you?" Sophia asked.

Rose forced herself to concentrate on the conversation at hand. There would be plenty of time for regrets later, she decided.

"I'm not nervous," she said. "Einish is lending us some troops, and we have enough power here that we could launch a formidable offense. The biggest obstacle is just getting there without giving ourselves away. It is a three-day ride, after all."

ONCE UPON A PRINCESS

"I agree," Philip said. "That's why Isra and I had an idea."

"What is it?" Rose asked.

"We thought we could hold our wedding here next month," Isra said.

Rose looked between the two of them. "You want to get married?" she asked. "Here? In another month?"

It was Isra's turn to blush. "Yes," she said. "We do."

"Aren't you rushing things?" Rose asked. "You're not even seventeen."

"You could have been married for years now, Rose," Isra said. "If you really wanted that."

Remembering some of the princes and dukes she had been forced to meet over the years, Rose nearly choked at the thought. "Don't you want to have a little more time to see the world?" Rose asked. "You could go off and study at university."

"Philip and I have talked about that," Isra said. "We can travel together. In fact," she said with a smile, "we have a list of places we would like to see and things we would like to do."

"I loved your engagement party," Sophia spoke up. "It would be really nice to have another party like that."

"If that's not enough to convince you, Rose," Philip said, "it would be good politics. You can attend the wedding and nobles all over the nation would come and see you standing behind your siblings. Even if the king is willing to present them formally, you can do it, too."

"What about Magdalina?" Rose asked. She crossed her arms. "Should I send her an invitation, too?"

"No. We were thinking that you could use the wedding as a diversion," Philip said. "Attack her castle during the week of the wedding feast."

ONCE UPON A PRINCESS

As soon as he said it, everything came together in her mind. She could use Philip and Isra's wedding to stabilize the nation, secure Isra's place as her heir, and surprise Magdalina at Darkwood Forest. "That's actually a brilliant idea," she said. A small smirk curled up onto her lips. "You're not just using this as a way to get married faster, are you?"

Isra grinned. "I don't see why it can't be both."

"You and your cleverness." Rose laughed.

"So you approve?" Philip asked.

Rose watched as his hand curled into Isra's. "Ethan said I was wrong before," she said quietly. "And I should have chosen love. Well, who am I to stop it now? Yes, I think it will be okay. But we will have to keep it secret."

"We can keep some of the guards here," Philip said, "in case Magdalina does show up here."

"That is the only thing I am worried about," Rose admitted. "But if I can get to her castle and attack her base, I can at least force her hand."

Sophia giggled. "Does this mean I can be part of the wedding party?"

Rose sighed. "I suppose that is the downside to all this," she said. "We are going to have to coordinate a wedding and a battle at the same time. With the three days' ride between here and Darkwood, we'll be stretched for resources."

"But on the bright side," Isra said, "the king should be happy about this. Don't you think so?"

Rose rolled her eyes. "Who knows what he will think? I still have to take care of my uncle, too."

"Yes, why is Uncle Hebert here?" Isra asked.

"He's here because our mother asked him for help," Rose said. "She thought if he knew she was imprisoned, he would come and help her. From what I've seen and heard, he's more after helping himself."

"Can't you order him to leave?" Philip asked.

Rose shook her head. "Hebert was popular in Rhone when he was forced into his arranged marriage. Now that his wife is dead, he's come back here, and it seems he has been reestablishing a lot of his friendships. The king is concerned that Hebert will try to use his power against the crown."

"Do you think he will?"

"If I can get him to leave, I'm sure that would be the easiest way to take care of everything," Rose said. "But I have to get the nobles on my side, first."

"With a wedding, that shouldn't be hard," Sophia said. "When they come here to Havilah, you should be able to convince many of them that their future is more secure with you than with Hebert."

Rose considered it. "That's a good point. But we'll need to start sending out announcements and invitations at once," she said. "We're going to need time if we have to play nicely with the nobles in addition to preparing for battle with Magdalina. My birthday is seven weeks away," Rose said.

"Give us three weeks," Isra said.

"You'll have to allow time for the people around the country to travel," Philip said. "That might be a good cover for my countrymen, come to think of it. They can use the excuse of being in Rhone as a way to protect any travelers."

"Do you think a month would cover it?" Rose bit her lip. It was a longer time than she would have liked.

Before anyone answered, Rose already decided it was for the best. If she was not able to destroy Magdalina's curse, she would at least be able to give Isra her blessing. She would be able to see her sister, often overlooked as they'd grown up,

ONCE UPON A PRINCESS

finally have her day in front of their people. She would be their future queen, and Philip their king.

"Take five weeks," Rose said. "Then we'll have your wedding feast planned out, and all the people will be here. And if all goes according to plan, we'll be able to come back from Darkwood and tell them my curse is broken, Magdalina is gone, and the Magdust trade is crippled."

"It all seems too much to hope for," Sophia murmured.

Isra shot her a glare. "Never say that," she said. "There's such power in hope."

Rose shrugged. "No point in being unrealistic about it," she said. "But this way, at least the throne will be secure, I'll have some time to get rid of my uncle and curry favor with my father's councilors and the kingdom's nobles, and Magdalina and I will finally face each other in battle. And if the worst should happen, and my curse is completed, I will fall asleep knowing I did everything I could do to break it."

ONCE UPON A PRINCESS

10

Theo stared at Everon silently.

It wasn't supposed to happen this way, Theo thought. He had always imagined taking his vengeance on a faceless creature, one with no remorse or pity.

From what Rose had told him of Everon, he had expected someone incapable of sadness or compassion, or anything of the gentler human emotions. Looking at him now, Theo could easily see his heritage. Magdalina had been a half-fairy, the offspring of Queen Lucia and a human sorcerer. Everon's hair and wings were black. He was tall like Magdalina, and seemed to favor darker colors. His eyes, while they gleamed red with angry power, had a background of blue-green that made Theo pause.

The image of Queen Lucia from his childhood, the image on his mother's tapestry, flashed before him. Lucia was known for her beauty, and her various children. As Theo thought about it now, as he stared at his enemy, he realized that Magdalina had originally been a princess of sorts, he imagined, with beauty and goodness in her heart.

What had changed? Theo suddenly wondered. Did her father die, or leave them? Did Lucia leave them? Was it the loss of her mother to Benedict's power that drove her to where she was?

Everon advanced on him. His dark fairy wings folded down against his back as he drew out his sword. "Where is she?" he asked, his voice torn between terrified and taunting.

"She's gone," Theo told him. "She died fighting me."

"Did you kill her?" Everon's voice was full of hurt and anger. He took a menacing step toward Theo.

ONCE UPON A PRINCESS

"Yes." Theo was about to explain he had also tried to save her, but before he could say a word, Everon attacked.

Theo ducked and rolled to the side, wincing as a flash of Everon's power hit him in the arm.

"I'll kill you for taking her away from me," Everon vowed.

Theo managed to pull out his sword. "You killed my family, too," he told Everon.

"Is that so?" Everon stalled a moment, caught off guard by the remark. "So you killed my Annalora in revenge?"

"I tried to save her," Theo yelled, as Everon attacked again. Their swords clashed together as Theo parried with his blows. The cut in his arm screamed in pain, but he kept fighting.

Everon slashed at him again, narrowly missing his leg. "Annalora was my true love," he said. "I have fought against *everything* to be with her—our families, our bloodlines, *everything*—all so we could be together. And you took her away from me!"

"Didn't it bother you that she was a mortal?" Theo asked, jumping back and took a moment to catch his breath. *If I can keep him talking, I might be able to distract him long enough to destroy him.*

"I'm not my mother," Everon scoffed indignantly. "Blood doesn't matter to me the way it does to her. I hid Annalora here for years, trying to keep her safe from my mother."

"She shouldn't have been in the Magdust trade then," Theo remarked. "She was hurting other people with her skill."

"What are other humans to me, and what did I care if she was hurting them or killing them?" Everon roared. "No one should have been able to break through that barrier of hers. You must be a powerful sorcerer, if you managed to overcome her power."

ONCE UPON A PRINCESS

"I'm not a sorcerer," Theo said. "She was my aunt."

It was Everon's turn to step back. "And yet you still killed her?" he shouted, before he charged at him once more.

"She was the one who attacked me," Theo argued through gritted teeth, as their swords clashed.

Everon sent out a burst of power, hitting Theo squarely in the chest, sending him flying back into the cottage door.

Theo grimaced as his head hit the door once more; the small bump on his head from Bachas' earlier strike groaned at the burst of new pain.

He saw the glitter of Magdust on Everon's sword as he regained his balance.

A new idea came to him. Theo reached out and pulled out the ruby from his aunt's mantle. In the palm of his hand, he felt the warmth of the jewel as the magical barrier once more encased him. Theo felt the burning sensation in his arm from Everon's earlier attack dissolve.

It's working.

With new confidence, Theo unleashed an attack of his own.

Theo felt the titanic power clash between the two of them, as he met Everon's strength with his own.

Keeping hold of his sword and the ruby, Theo fought off Everon's power. He met each thrust of Everon's blade with his own, and he could tell Everon was increasingly frustrated as none of his magical attacks hit their mark.

"Augh!" Theo roared in triumph as he managed to knock the sword out of Everon's hands. He held up his sword high, ready for the killing blow.

This is it, Theo thought. *Now, Everon will die.*

The large fairy, still angry, tried to lash out spell after spell, but nothing slowed Theo's blade. He fell back, unable to protect himself any longer.

Then, it happened.

Theo caught sight of his enemy's eyes. They were full of tears—tears of loss and acceptance. Instantly, he felt himself falter.

He is ready to die, Theo realized.

Shocked, Theo slowly lowered his sword.

"What are you waiting for?" Everon asked. "Aren't you going to kill me?"

"I want to," Theo admitted quietly. "You killed my mother. You killed my father. And while you might have loved my aunt, you allowed her to hurt other creatures and other people."

"So kill me for it then," Everon shouted. "Unless you're too scared."

Theo stepped back.

"Go ahead," Everon yelled again, this time more painfully than before. "Do it! Do it, so I can be with Annalora again!"

Theo decided it was not the time to correct Everon's theology. He sheathed his sword, but held onto the ruby as he grabbed Everon's fallen sword. As he held it, the Magdust, twinkling in its pink and green sparkle, disappeared. "No," he told him.

"Why not?" he growled, angry tears in his eyes. He clenched his fists, punching out toward Theo. "Why not end it now? You have me at your mercy!"

Theo twisted out of Everon's reach, using his enemy's power against him. Everon slammed into the ground, and Theo stood over him.

He was right, Theo realized. Everon was at his mercy. Why wasn't he killing him?

His parents, and his uncle, even if they had made mistakes, were still capable of being good people. Everon had taken all their chances for good away, and he rightfully deserved to die.

But Theo knew, even after tonight, even if he killed Everon, he would still dream of his uncle in his last moments. He would wonder if parents really loved each other, and he would wonder what his life would have been like had they lived.

But it no longer held the same power over him. He wanted something more than revenge—something greater than revenge—to live for. Theo knew in that moment, he had nothing to gain from killing Everon. In fact, he thought, in some ways, he had lost himself.

And so much more, he thought, thinking of Rose.

He almost smiled. Rose was the one who would tell him that it was a knight's highest calling to protect the kingdom, and that he should finish Everon before he hurt other people.

He had known for a long time that Rose was more important to him than revenge. Now that he was able to take his revenge, he did not want it. Seeing Everon was also bereft from the loss of his loved one, Theo knew that he had no place here. While delivering the deathblow to his enemy might have given him momentary pleasure, killing Everon in revenge was wrong.

Perhaps it was even too kind, Theo thought, but he took another step back from the fallen fairy.

"You might be at my mercy," Theo said quietly, still holding Everon's sword against him, "but it's not my mercy you should be asking for."

"I'm not asking for your mercy!" Everon yelled. "Kill me. Just kill me now."

ONCE UPON A PRINCESS

Theo stepped back from him. "Not today," he said quietly. "I have somewhere else to be."

Everon cried out. "You will pay for this!" he said. "I swear by the blood in my veins, I will make you pay for what you have done here."

"I already have paid for it," Theo told him, which only seemed to anger the fairy further.

Before anyone else could say anything, Bachas appeared beside him. "Be gone, fairy!" he cried out, his own power beginning to spark between his small fingers.

Everon rolled to his feet, wary at the sight of Bachas. "This is not over," he warned Theo, before he spread his wings and took off.

Theo watched Everon's retreating form disappear from his sight, and then he turned to Bachas. "Thanks for coming."

"I wanted to make sure Elva was safe first," he said. "She wanted to come and fight with me, but I told her no. Everon might have recognized her, and I didn't want her to get into any further trouble now that she is free."

"What kind of trouble would she get in?" Theo asked. "Her life debt is canceled now that Annalora is dead."

"Still, pixies and fairies have complicated relationships with each other," Bachas said. "Annalora's death could easily be seen as her fault, since she did nothing to save her."

"She tried, didn't she?" Theo said. "I was trying to get her out of the ruby's barrier so we could do something."

"I guess so, but you know for Everon, it would never be enough. A pixie has a duty to protect his or her master from unnatural death. If he wanted to, he could accuse her of breaking the code. The penalty for breaking the code is death."

"One day," Theo said, as he sheathed his sword, "I will have to learn your rules."

Bachas snorted. "Don't worry about it. I think we have plenty of other things to concern ourselves with before we get to that point."

Theo gave him a smile. "Good. I'd like to go home."

"To see your princess?"

"Yes." Theo gripped the ruby in his hand, thinking of the power he had just witnessed. "I have a present for her, and I think she's going to like it."

ONCE UPON A PRINCESS

11

Rose knew that there were higher forces at work in her world. She had been fond of church growing up, until she discovered the truth about her curse. She also knew about the magic born into the fairies, and she had seen divine providence in other people's lives enough to know that there was something greater out there, beyond where she was.

Unlike Theo, Rose was not certain of God's goodness, or even the extent of his power. What was he thinking, letting all those people and creatures and even nature itself destroy others? If he was such a good god, why did she still have the curse on her? If he was so powerful, why did he not save her from it?

But, Rose thought as she prayed, she was graciously willing to reconsider all of that, if he would only give her the strength to get through this conversation.

She squared her shoulders, and then headed out. She walked through the courtyard toward the training area, holding up her lantern in the dying light of the day.

The last week or so had been full, she told herself. That was part of the reason she had delayed this conversation. There was a wedding to plan, an attack to coordinate, and her uncle to intimidate. There had been plenty to do, and plenty of things done. She'd welcomed Virtue back, only to send him back out almost immediately to tell Derick to send his soldiers to designated positions. She had informed the king of Isra's wedding, and he had approved, hearing Isra's decision was for the kingdom. When Rose told her mother, Leea had been more ecstatic to hear Isra had fallen in love with her prince.

ONCE UPON A PRINCESS

Hebert, for his part, took the news well. In front of her, anyway. Rose had a feeling he was agitated about the news, and she was glad for his irritation. She hoped that his true thoughts on the matter would prompt him to make a mistake with his friends, and she would be able to capitalize on that to get him to leave.

Yes, Rose thought. *Everything is coming together the way it is supposed to.*

That was probably why she dreaded talking to Ethan.

She watched him as he sparred with another squire in the training field. She saw his good form, never wondering for a moment how well Theo had managed to train him. She saw his movements and immediately remembered how she'd taught Theo herself, several years before.

She bit her lip, thinking about him again. It had been nearly five years since she had set out to find a way to break her curse, as Rhone's youngest knight. Theo had been at her side, unwilling to leave her to her own devices, and unwilling to let himself be guided by the whims of palace life.

He told her he had come to learn from her, but she knew she had learned just as much from him—if not more so.

She did not want to think about the last weeks of her life without him. Even as they were coming back from the Romani territory, being stuck on the road with their galling guide, Natala, had been brightened with moments of his kindness.

When he comes back, Rose thought, willing herself to believe he would, *I will do everything I can to break my curse for him.*

Rose blinked tears out of her eyes as the sudden realization hit her.

That was what he was asking of me, all along, wasn't it?

That she would not just fight for herself, or her kingdom, or for her dreams of having a real future. He had been asking her to fight for him.

And she had pushed him away, too scared to let him down as well as everything else.

Before Rose could once more tell herself it was for the best she had let him leave, once more force herself to lie to herself and everyone else, she saw Ethan was finished with his fight.

He had won, and Rose was glad to see him help the other squire up from the ground.

She walked over to him, once more reminding God of her conditions.

"Good job, Ethan," she congratulated him.

He whirled around at her voice. "What are you doing here, Rose?" he asked, his voice hard and brusque.

"I wanted to talk to you," Rose said.

"You don't want to talk to me," Ethan corrected her. "You just feel like you should."

Rose frowned. "Fine," she said. "You're probably right about that. You know I hate to apologize."

"You know I don't want to hear an apology that's fake."

"I'm not going to give you one." Rose took a deep breath. "I'm going to give you a real apology. You were right. I was scared, and I didn't do the right thing."

He stared at her. At his expression, Rose suddenly felt ages older than he was, even though he was only five years younger. "I'm sorry about Theo," she said, her voice catching in her throat. "I didn't want him to leave, either."

"You let him."

"I know. I was wrong." Rose sighed. "I miss him even more than you do."

"He really does love you, you know," Ethan said. "He tries to hide it because he knows you don't want him to."

"That's not true," Rose said. "I want him to, I promise. I just don't want him to get hurt. That's why I let him leave."

"Isra was right, wasn't she?" Ethan asked. "You hurt a lot of people when you try to protect them."

Rose laughed bitterly. "I guess so," she said. "But I don't want to hurt you, and I am sorry if I did."

"I think everyone gets hurt," Ethan said. "Pain seems to be something everyone feels, one way or another."

"Or multiple ways," Rose agreed. She held out her hand. "Can you forgive me?"

Ethan took her hand and shook it. "I can," he told her. And then he sighed. "You have always tried so hard to support me, Rose. I love you for it. But you really can't decide what's best for other people all the time, you know."

"I'll work on it." Rose gave him a smile as she pulled him into a tight hug. "Some of that comes from being a princess, you know."

"Well, you should know better than most people that some people are determined to suffer, no matter their circumstances."

She said nothing to that, since she was pretty sure Ethan was talking about her. Rose let him go and watched as he ran a hand through his hair, disgruntled somewhat by her display of affection.

Ethan waved before heading off to continue his training.

She almost told him to get to bed instead, as it was already dark out, but she let him go. Rose knew that he had a point, too—with the wedding and the battle at Darkwood both coming up, they had to work hard to be prepared, and that included Ethan.

Well, Rose thought, as she made her way to her own room. *That wasn't as bad as I thought it would be.* She was actually happy about it. She had her friend back, she had made it through the conversation without crying, and she had one less problem to solve.

All in all, Rose thought, it had been a good day. Derick's soldiers would soon be on the way, Hebert was upset, and Isra and Philip had finally learned that their displays of affection were making people either angry or annoyed. They had promised to tone it down some; but seeing that Isra had begun carrying little scrolls around, Rose had a feeling Philip was writing her more poetry.

She turned down the hallway to her room, hoping Mary had sent her some tea before bed.

And then she stopped.

Theo was standing in front of her bedroom door.

Rose rubbed her eyes, making sure she was awake. But there was no change in her vision as she looked at him again.

As if she had wished him into her reality, there he was. Theo—his face tired, grimy, and tanned by his time in the sun—had returned. His hand was raised, ready to knock on her door.

It's just like that night, Rose thought. They had run into each other unexpectedly at the Crystal Lake hot springs, half-naked and in their underwear. After their fight, he had come to her room.

Only to stop, raise his hand to knock, and then eventually step away without a sound.

Rose had seen him from the hallway behind him, having gotten lost on her way back to her room. She had watched in silence as he left, wondering what their conversation could have been like.

ONCE UPON A PRINCESS

Now, Rose felt the same rush of longing, as her heart began to beat faster. She watched as he pulled his hand back again. Rose could not blame him for his uncertainty; part of her wanted to shrink back into the hallway and pretend she hadn't seen him at all, too, like she had before.

Before she could do just that, he reached out and knocked on her door. The rap was short but loud. If she had been on the other side, Rose knew she would have heard it. "Theo?"

At her voice, he turned to face her. "Princess."

Rose suddenly felt a rush of resigned frustration, angry with God and his humor once more. She had prayed for her conversation with Ethan to go well, but she knew this conversation was the one she would really need help getting through.

12

Theo had spent a good portion of his ride back to Havilah practicing how he would act when he saw Rose again. He knew he had been dreading it as much as he had been anticipating it; Bachas and Elva had both complained when he had slowed down his pace the day before. As he stood before Rose once more, at last, he decided he should have gone even slower on the way back.

Not that it would have helped any; he knew there was little that he could have done to prepare himself to be in Rose's presence again.

He allowed himself a long second just to look at her; after all the weeks apart from her, seeing her again was riveting.

But, he noticed, Bachas' seeing crystal had been accurate. She was tired, with dark circles under her eyes, and her face, while she was trying not to blush as she looked back at him, was pale with worry.

He watched as she crossed her arms over her chest. "It's still Rose," she told him sternly. "There's no need for formalities between us."

"Then I apologize … Rose."

She pursed her lips at hearing her name, as if she knew just how much he'd been tempted to call her Rosary. "I accept," she said. "What are you doing here? Were you able to find your aunt? I know Thad had mentioned you were looking for her."

Theo nodded. "I did," he said. "How is Thad? I haven't seen him yet."

"I haven't seen him in the past few days. He's been taking care of your grandfather this week," Rose said. "He caught a chill on the way back from Einish."

"Oh. Maybe I should have stopped in to see them first."

"I'm surprised you didn't," Rose said. "You went to go and see them first last time you were here."

"Well, I guess it hasn't been quite as long since I last saw them," Theo said, giving her a quick smile. The smile vanished as he added, "And I suppose I don't really want to give them the news."

"What is it?" Rose asked, concerned. "What happened?"

"A lot happened while I was gone," he said slowly, "but the short version is that my aunt is dead."

"I'm sorry to hear that." Rose's hand reached for his, and then suddenly stopped.

For a long moment, they both stared at it, and then they looked at each other. Theo watched as Rose's cheeks flushed over, and he knew she was uncomfortable.

Theo decided to change the subject. "So, where is everyone?" he asked. "I saw Roderick and Ronan while I passed through the town, so I know the others are back."

"Oh, yeah," Rose said. "Isra and Philip were having dinner with the king earlier, and I just saw Ethan in the training yard. Sophia's probably still in the smithing yard."

"Where's Mary?"

"Last I saw her, she was in my room," Rose said, nodding toward the door.

"Oh, sleeping already?" he asked with a grin. "Or is she still sleeping? I know she hates to travel on the road more than she lets on."

Rose chuckled softly. "Yeah," she replied. "I don't know, actually. Maybe I should see if she's in the room."

But she made no move to get him to move, nor did she make some excuse to leave him. Theo was comforted by that; it seemed that for all they were struggling through their conversation, she had missed him enough to stay.

Either that, he thought, or she was trying to prove to herself that she could handle talking with him.

"Why did you come here?" Rose asked. "I mean, I am … I was just wondering why … you came to see me."

If the circumstances were different, Theo would have been tempted to tease her, to ask her if there was some reason that he should not want to come and see her. But he knew—and he knew that she knew, too—there was a legitimate reason she was surprised to see him. While they were still acting like friends, all the intimacy of their relationship before their kiss was gone.

"I wanted to see if you could get me an audience with the king. There are some things I need to discuss with him about his brother," he told her. He reached into his pocket for the ruby. "And I wanted to show you this."

Rose gaped at the gem in his hand. "What is this?" she asked. "Is it dragon's blood?"

"I don't think so," Theo told her. "My aunt had it in her house. It's able to take away power from any magic."

Rose's eyes widened. "It cancels out magic?"

"I experienced it firsthand," he said. Part of him wanted to tell her about meeting Everon, about Annalora and her eternal youth, and what he had found out about his family.

But it was then that she placed her hand on his, as she examined the ruby, and he lapsed into silence.

"I wonder … my mother told me about the Rose Ruby, the one that my father had to find in order to marry her. She told that it had the power to stop magic. Do you think this could be … "

He looked over at her as her voice trailed off. He realized she was staring at him. "What is it, Rose?"

Rose blushed, before she stepped back and sighed. "I know this is important. But … I want to talk to you," she said quietly. "I wanted to talk about … about that night you left."

Instantly, his heart lurched uncomfortably. "No," he told her. "No, you don't have to do that, Rose."

"But—"

"It's better if we don't," Theo said. "Besides, everything worked out for the best, right? I managed to take care of my family's business, and you were able to see to yours."

"Theo—"

"Come on, Rose. We can just be friends again, right?"

"We *are* friends," Rose insisted. "But that still—"

This time, Rose was interrupted as Mary came out of the room. "Theo?" she asked, rubbing the sleepiness out of her eyes.

"Hi, Mary."

Instantly, Mary perked up. "You're back!" she cried happily, flying into his shoulder and hugging his arm.

Theo glanced over at Rose, surprised to see her slumped over in defeat. They had lost the moment, he thought, and he was relieved.

"What are you doing up here?" Mary asked. "Did you just get back?"

"Yes, I did. And I was just showing this ruby to Rose," he said, holding up the ruby again.

"Oh, it's beautiful," Mary said. "But you'll have to forgive me if I still don't want to touch it. After Rose got that one, I'm more than a little leery of them."

ONCE UPON A PRINCESS

"Understandable," Theo said. "I'm pretty sure this one doesn't have any dragon's blood, though. So it should be safe for you." He held it up so she could see it more easily. He tried not to feel anything as Rose's hand slipped away from his.

She clapped her hands to her mouth in astonishment. "Oh, Rose," Mary whispered excitedly. "This is it. This is the Rose Ruby!"

"I thought so," Rose said. "The queen told me that the Rose Ruby was able to cancel out magic, and Theo was just telling me about how he saw it work."

"It's as beautiful as I remember it," Mary said, her voice hushed.

"You've seen it before?" Theo asked.

"Of course. The queen had it in her possession when I first met her. Juana would know more specifics about it, but it has been many years since I've seen it. I remember that it was lost, and that was it."

"My mother told me that she'd given it to my uncle," Rose said. She looked back up at Theo. "Can I see it?"

He nodded and handed it to her. "You said your uncle was the one who had it?"

"Yes." Rose's lips tightened with irritation. "I have learned a lot about my family in the last several weeks. Probably too much."

Theo nodded slowly, sympathetic to her circumstances; he knew the realities of that particular situation. But he also knew he had to focus on their present problems. As he watched Rose take hold of the ruby, he was more certain than ever that he had to see the king and inform him of his brother's treachery at the border.

ONCE UPON A PRINCESS

Before he could ask Rose to grant him an audience with her father again, Mary gasped. "Rose, look at you," she said.

Theo jolted as he saw what she was looking at; Rose's appearance was changing as she held the ruby. He watched as the blue faded from her eyes, transforming into a lovely brown. The warmth of her sunshine hair cooled into a dark brown, and even the shape of her face seemed to change.

"What?" Rose asked.

"It's pushing back the fairy magic you and the others gave her," Theo said.

Rose glanced at him. Even though her eyes were different, they were no less expressive. She ran a hand through her hair, which was suddenly much straighter. "Do I still look okay?"

"Uh … " Theo was too busy staring at her to answer. She still looked like herself—determined and forceful, and strong yet compassionate. Still stunning, still enchanting. He decided, in the end, she looked a lot like Isra, only with lighter hair.

He debated whether or not he should tell her that as she frowned at him. She had made her feelings on their relationship very clear, and he did not want to push. Their friendship was already more fragile than he would have liked.

Rose looked over at Mary. "Mary," she asked. "What do you think?"

The small fairy gave her a big smile. "You're still you, Rose," she said. "All our fairy magic did was make your beauty more pronounced. Nothing we did to you changes your personality or who you really are."

"Does this mean that, as long as I hold this ruby, Magdalina's curse is broken from me, too?" Rose asked.

"I don't think it would be broken," Mary admitted. "Our fairy magic will return when you put it down, after all. But she would be unable to compel you to fulfill the curse."

Rose's eyes lit up. "This is wonderful," she said. "No one would ever choose to prick her finger on the spindle of a spinning wheel."

"That would also be a way to defeat her in the end," Theo realized. "All magic has rules, right? If she can't fulfill the curse, her blood spell would destroy her in the end."

"Maybe now we don't have to march on Darkwood," Mary said, squirming with happiness.

"Oh, we're still going to go and attack her," Rose said, making Mary sigh with frustration. "She's still an enemy of the crown. She tried to kill my father, after all, and she's ruined countless lives."

"Was she the one behind the poisoning attempt after we left for the Romani territory?" Theo asked.

Rose shook her head. "No," she told him. "There's a long story attached to it. Her brown eyes softened. "I'm so glad you're here so I can talk to you about it."

She smiled at him as she handed him the Rose Ruby once more. As soon as he took the jewel in his hand, her locks once more burned with sunshine instead of copper, and her eyes lit up in their usual cerulean.

He stared at her again, as Rose returned to her normal self. Theo wrapped his fingers around the ruby, determined to push past the discomfort between them. "Right now, I need to see the king," he said. "I have news from the border he needs to take care of."

"What is it?" Rose asked.

"If you can get me to him, I can tell you both at the same time."

ONCE UPON A PRINCESS

Rose frowned, clearly impatient. "Fine. Let's go and see him now then, so I can hear what's happening."

He sighed at her displeasure. "It's just a matter of timing. I don't want to have to tell the story twice, Rose."

Mary fluttered between them. "I'm going to go and tell Juana and Her Majesty the news about the ruby."

"Thanks, Mary," Rose said. "See you later."

Theo watched as Mary hurried away, almost wishing she would have stayed so he would have some help with Rose. He turned to face her now, as they were once more alone. "So, your mother is still in the dungeon, then."

Rose nodded. "For all it's hardly a dungeon," she said. "Uncle Hebert has restricted access to her, but he has made sure she is comfortable while waiting for her trial. He might be waiting a long time for that, from what the king has told me."

"Is he intentionally pushing her trial back?"

Rose nodded. "He seems to know she's guilty."

"She's *guilty*?" Theo nearly stumbled as they headed toward the council room.

Rose nodded. "She told me she tried to get rid of the king in order to help me."

"Why? How would that help you?"

"I don't know," Rose said. "She says that the king is going mad, as a relapse of sorts from Magdalina's attempt to kill him with Magdust before I was born. She thought if I was queen, the kingdom would be more politically optimistic, and Isra would be safer, too."

"I was glad to hear that the king decided not to imprison them when they returned," Theo said.

"Oh, he thought about it," Rose scoffed. "But I think he knows the truth about my mother. I suspect he's trying to

ONCE UPON A PRINCESS

hold off until my eighteenth birthday. The future is so uncertain for the kingdom right now."

He knew better than most how much that was true. "I guess the last thing he would want would be more problems for his image and the kingdom's politics."

"Exactly." Rose brightened. "Since you're here now, you can help us with our plans."

"Our plans?"

"Yes. Isra and Philip and the rest of us finally have a solid plan for Magdalina," Rose said, suddenly more excited. "And now that you're here, you'll be able to help us attack her castle at Darkwood."

"You know I will do what I can to help you," Theo assured her.

"Good." Rose reached out and took his arm, and it almost seemed as if they were back to their normal routine.

But Theo knew they weren't. There was no disguising how he felt about her, and there was no getting around how she did not want to feel about him. He carefully pulled himself away from her, ignoring the small pout she sent his way. "Maybe I should see to Bachas first," he said, desperate to put some distance between them.

"Bachas?" Rose wrinkled her nose. "You mean that obnoxious pixie? He's still with you?"

"He has a much better temperament now that he's been reunited with his wife, Elva," Theo told her. "Both of them have offered to help with Magdalina."

"Well, I suppose we're in no position to refuse help," Rose said. "And Sophia will likely be glad to hear he's back. She was wondering how he was doing. But you wanted to go to the king now. If it's urgent, we can survive Bachas being back here, even if he's not chaperoned."

ONCE UPON A PRINCESS

Theo nodded. "True."

A few more moments passed as they made their way through the castle. As they walked through the familiar halls of his childhood, Theo wondered if he would ever feel at home in the castle again. He felt a strange sense of displacement.

"How are the kids?" Theo asked. "I've missed them."

Rose slowed her steps down, as they approached the king's council room. "They are doing okay," she finally said. "They weren't happy when I left them at Einish. But they seem to be doing a little better now. They'll be happy to see you again."

"That's a relief," he said. "Maybe I'll go and check in on them, and our other friends, when we're done here. I doubt the king will be happy to speak with me."

"Don't worry," Rose told him with a playful smirk. "I'll be here to protect you."

Theo gave her an uneasy laugh. "That's why I'm nervous," he told her, as they both stepped into the room.

13

Theo is back. He is finally back!

Despite their awkward reunion, Rose felt a surge of relieved happiness inside of her as she stood beside her best friend.

Rose watched as her father straightened up in his chair, listening as Theo began telling him of his journey to the Rhone-Aragonian border. She saw that the king was tired, and, likely overwhelmed, considering he had just had dinner with Isra and Philip to go over their wedding details.

He was probably irritated, too, Rose thought, knowing he had been happy to hear of Theo's absence when Rose had arrived back at Havilah. He had never liked Theo.

"Your Majesty, while I was there, a small mercenary army was also there. They were waiting for their leader to send for them, and then they were to march on Rhone's capital."

King Stefanos narrowed his eyes at Theo. "What proof do you offer?"

"I saw it," Theo said. "I saw it when I went to go and retrieve my aunt."

"Your aunt?" Stefanos' suspicion transformed into outrage. "What are you doing, consorting with that witch?"

Rose stepped forward. "Majesty, you can trust Theo," she said. "He has always been loyal to the crown."

"Your crown more than mine," the king retorted.

"So?" Rose blushed. "He wouldn't lie about something like this."

"I'm not lying," Theo insisted. From his tone, Rose knew he was trying to hide his frustration. She could not blame him for being insulted.

"I was able to find out that the army in question is acting under the orders of the Duke of Aragon," Theo said.

Her eyes widened in surprise. "Uncle Hebert is behind the mercenaries?"

"It seems so. He commissioned an order from Annalora, my aunt," he said quietly. He turned back to the king. "You know of my family's past, Your Majesty. You know that my own mother worked to save your life once. It should not surprise you that my aunt has a different opinion on the matter."

Rose watched as he bowed his head down, waiting for the king to answer. He caught her eyes with his for just a second, and she felt the shock of his admission.

No wonder he never wanted to talk about his family that much, Rose thought.

"I didn't know about my aunt's involvement until we caught Ambassador Rolez of Einish," Theo said. "but since then I am convinced of her treachery." Rose saw his hands tighten as they gripped the Rose Ruby, and Rose stepped forward.

"If you want proof," Rose said, "we have it."

Theo glanced over at her. "We do?"

"Yes," she said. She pointed to the ruby in his hand. "This is the Rose Ruby, isn't it, Majesty?"

Rose watched as her father's mouth dropped open, and she struggled not to laugh. There was nothing he would hate more, she thought, than to acknowledge he had been wrong about Theo.

As Theo handed the gem to the king, Rose smiled. "The queen told me that Hebert was the one who had taken the Rose Ruby when he had to leave for Aragon," Rose said. "He had it in his possession for the past several years. The fact he

ONCE UPON A PRINCESS

gave it to Theo's aunt to make a Magdust tapestry should be all the proof we need to show that he's after the crown. We can finally order him from the castle."

Stefanos stared. "You're right that this is the Rose Ruby," he said at last. "And you're right about Hebert. But it's not so simple, Aurora. Getting rid of him will still be troublesome."

"We can't afford to go into battle with his troops," Rose insisted. "Not when we're only two weeks away from going after Magdalina. You have to stand up to him."

"He still has supporters here, Aurora."

"Who would support him now, knowing that he's a traitor to you?"

"Plenty, I would imagine," Stefanos said.

"Is there nothing you can do to convince him to leave on his own?" Theo asked.

"He's here to make sure Leea receives a fair trial," Stefanos said. "But I can't take her to trial."

"Because you know she did it," Rose said. "You don't want to convict her."

Stefanos frowned. "I didn't know it was her," he said. "But I had a feeling. She would do anything to protect you, Rose, even if it meant killing me."

"I still don't see why she thought she was protecting me," Rose muttered. "It only caused more trouble in the end."

"She meant well."

"But she planned poorly," Rose shot back. "And we have to worry about cleaning up her mess."

"Does Hebert love the queen?" Theo asked.

Stefanos leaned forward and put his head in his hands. "He has always been in love with her," he said. "But now, there's more than just Leea to consider. There is the crown. With Aurora's curse drawing close, and the kingdom anxious about

ONCE UPON A PRINCESS

her fate, he sees a chance to take everything away from me. He would do it, too. He never forgave me for taking the Rose Ruby from him in the first place."

Rose gaped at her father. "Hebert was the one who found the ruby?"

"He and I both headed to the Orlo Empire when we located it," Stefanos said. "On the way back to Rhone, he attacked me for the ruby. I only won the fight, Aurora. Don't look at me like that."

Rose shook her head. "I can't believe it."

"Maybe," Theo spoke up, "maybe you could use his affection for Leea to get him to go."

"She'll want to stay with Aurora."

"But he wants her safe, right?" Theo looked over at Rose. "Maybe you can offer him a deal. If he leaves, you can pardon the queen for her crime."

"And if he refuses to leave?"

"Tell him you'll have to sentence her."

Stefanos scowled. "That's foolish. He would just attack and try to save her."

"But he would give you just cause to fight, then," Theo pointed out. "And with the army's arrival, at least a week's ride from the border, it would be hard to believe that he just called on his people to fight for Queen Leea. You can easily show your people that he is a traitor."

"That's right," Rose agreed. "And you know the queen will agree to it for my sake."

Stefanos considered it, rubbing his chin thoughtfully. "I suppose you might have a point," he muttered disdainfully to Theo. "I cannot ignore your proof, and Aurora trusts you."

Rose felt her heart twist painfully as she stepped back. She watched as her father, for the first time she could remember,

ONCE UPON A PRINCESS

looked at Theo as more than a source of disappointment and hatred.

"Aurora," Stefanos said. "Go and fetch your mother from the dungeon. I think we can take care of this tonight, don't you?"

Rose felt her heart soar. "Yes, Majesty," she said. "I will go at once. Theo and I can also pick up Uncle Hebert, if you'd like."

"I'll send for him," he said. "I'll trust you to fill your mother in on the plan, and secure her cooperation."

"That should be fine," Rose said. "Theo and I—"

"Your friend will stay here with me," Stefanos said. "Now, go."

Rose glanced over at Theo, who ignored her. She looked back at her father. He gestured toward the door. "Go, Aurora."

She curtly bowed her head and then walked off, wondering what her father could possibly say to Theo while she was gone.

ONCE UPON A PRINCESS

731
ONCE UPON A PRINCESS

14

Theo heard the door shut behind him as Rose walked out of the room, followed by one of the valets sent to fetch Hebert.

Theo felt Rose leave, rather than saw her; he knew Rose well enough to know she was unsure of leaving him with her father, but he also knew she wanted to take care of her problem with her uncle.

I'll bet anything she'll be back here in record time with the queen. Theo could not fully suppress a smile at the thought. He kept his eyes off the king and hoped His Majesty would not mistake his amusement for mockery.

Moments passed before Stefanos sighed. "I think it's about time you and I had a talk," he finally said.

"What is it, Your Majesty?" Theo asked, keeping his tone flat.

"You brought me the Rose Ruby back," he said. "Just as I brought it back to Leea's father, decades ago."

Theo nodded, still keeping his eyes on the ground. "Yes, Your Majesty."

"Tell me how you came to find it. In detail. I know of your family's history, and I know your aunt, with your grandmother's instruction, would have been a formidable opponent."

Theo obliged the king, telling him of his grandfather's wish to meet with Annalora, to ask her to stop making the tapestries, after discovering she was responsible for the one Queen Juliette had in her palace. He did not tell the king about Everon, or about how Everon was responsible for the death of so many of his family members. He told him how he

ONCE UPON A PRINCESS

found the ruby inside a box, and how he had been protected long enough by the barrier that his aunt's magic and the Magdust had been unable to affect him.

"Before I left for Havilah, I made sure to take care of my aunt's cottage." There was no need to tell him he had Bachas and Elva place a protective spell on it while it burned to the ground. "Since her tapestry was not finished, the mercenaries are likely still waiting on her."

As he finished his account, Theo glanced up at the king, watching as Stefanos toyed with the Rose Ruby. When the king said nothing, Theo added, "I thought Rose would be able to use the power of the ruby to save herself from Magdalina's curse."

At his remark, Stefanos looked up at him. "I hope you're right," he said. "The kingdom would absolutely rejoice."

"I know she is beloved by her people."

"And you?"

Theo felt the heat rise in his cheeks as he nodded. "She will make a fine ruler," he said calmly.

His answer seemed to satisfy the king, who sat back in his chair. "I suppose after all of this," he said slowly, "I owe you an apology."

"What?" Theo blinked in surprise. "Uh, I mean … excuse me, Your Majesty?"

Stefanos sighed. "After your family saved me from Magdalina," he explained, "I was warned that the relief would be temporary. Over the years, I have noticed that … I have begun to wonder if Magdalina's power was once more taking hold of me. As such, I worried that your family would try to capitalize on my fate."

"You were worried we would take advantage of you?"

Stefanos nodded. "You can't blame me, can you? Especially after you revealed to my daughter the truth of her curse, and then you became nearly inseparable."

Theo decided to say nothing to that. Instead, he changed the subject. "You thought I was trying to get to you through Rose, weren't you? I told her about her curse by mistake, and we became friends. You were worried."

"It was unwarranted, as I see now," Stefanos said. "And for that, I apologize."

Theo clenched his fist and bowed his head in silence. He did not want the king's remorse.

Stefanos did not seem to notice. "As you have brought me the Rose Ruby," he said, "I do believe that I should reward you."

"I don't want a reward," Theo murmured, before he could stop himself. He saw Stefanos look at him, surprised. "Rose's friendship means a lot to me."

Stefanos rubbed his chin again thoughtfully. "You have been by her side all these years. I think it is time to make it official."

Theo felt his breath catch. "You mean—"

"I think it is time you were properly knighted," Stefanos told him. "You have returned the Rose Ruby to me, after all. It is no reward, either, before you object. You have earned the title."

Theo exhaled slowly. "I would be most grateful, Your Majesty, to serve as my father and uncle have served Rhone."

"Excellent. We will need more men like you, with the attack on Darkwood coming up," Stefanos said. "And … I think my daughter will approve."

Theo smiled as he nodded. "Yes," he said. "She will."

"It's settled then," Stefanos said. He turned to his other valet at the far corner of the room. "Bring me my sword, if you please."

Theo watched as the king came around the table and took his sword from the valet. "I have a request, Your Majesty," Theo said. "I would like to wait for Rose to return."

"Alright, I will grant your wish. While we're waiting, you should take this back." He handed Theo the Rose Ruby. "You seem to have good fortune when it comes to roses."

"If you're certain."

Stefanos nodded. "I am. You will need it more than I do, if you are going to fight against Magdalina at Darkwood."

"But what about your condition?" Theo asked.

"I am going mad because of my own choices as well as magic," Stefanos said. "No matter what I do, I will not be able to fight off my fate forever. You might as well keep it, and use it to protect my daughter."

Theo nodded, and before he could ask the king if the ruby would be able to save Rose from Magdalina's curse, the door opened up, and Rose, breathless from dragging her mother behind her, stepped inside the room once more.

"I'm back," Rose said, stepping up beside Theo. She took one look at her father and asked, "What are you doing?"

"Before Hebert gets here," Stefanos said, "I'm going to knight this young man. You are going to be a witness, Aurora, so please take a step back. Once we're done with this, we can get down to our other business."

Theo knelt down before the king, barely listening as Stefanos made a speech about a knight's duty to his kingdom and his reward. He met Rose's gaze as he promised to protect and defend what was his, and swore his fealty to the kingdom unto death.

He felt the blade touch his shoulder, and then the other, and it was over.

"There you are," the king murmured. "Sir Theo the Faithful, of Rhone."

Theo rose to his feet, and he thought it was an odd moment to feel like his life was beginning all over again. He looked over at Rose and smiled.

Her eyes were glassy with pride, but he noticed when he came to stand beside her, she took a small step away from him.

"What's wrong?" he asked her softly, as the king walked back to the other side of the table.

"Nothing," she said. "I'm happy for you."

"Thank you."

She turned away from him for a moment. He thought he saw her rub her eyes before she looked back at him. "See? I told you that you were ready to be knighted."

"All I need now is the promotion to your council," Theo teased.

Rose went still.

"Sorry," Theo murmured, realizing her discomfort.

Before Rose could respond, the door behind them opened once more.

Hebert had arrived.

ONCE UPON A PRINCESS

15

Rose was glad to see her uncle as he entered into the room. Not only was she glad because her father was finally standing up to him, but his arrival drew attention, and she could breathe more freely without Theo's scrutiny.

Almost. Behind her, Rose could feel her mother's gaze lingering on her as she witnessed the awkward exchange with Theo.

Her head was pounding with pain as she relieved the last few moments of her life.

Theo was finally an official knight of her kingdom's court. She could no longer tease him about becoming a priest, letting herself believe he would always have something else to pursue.

He had earned his right to serve at her side.

Just like Benedict, Rose thought, recalling the legend of Queen Lucia. She had chosen Benedict as her love, once he had proven himself worthy. And then, according to the later part of the story, Lucia had pressured him too much, and he had not only left her, but he had imprisoned her in a genie's bottle. He would reign over Rhone alone and look for a new queen among the mortals.

Rose glanced over at Theo and thought about their history. He had been in love with her for so long, and she had been waiting for the moment when she could no longer ignore that fact—waiting until she had to make a decision.

And she had rejected him. *Just like Lucia.*

Was she destined to drive him away? Would that be her downfall in the end?

738

While Rose was standing there, watching Theo say his vows, in partial disbelief as her father actually knighted him, all Rose could think of was how it was not a matter of whether or not he was worthy. It was a question of her own worth, and she knew he deserved much better than she could offer.

She was glad when Stefanos finally began talking. "Hebert," he said. "Thank you for agreeing to come and meet us."

"I'm always happy to be at your service, my brother," Hebert replied. "But I admit, I am confused. What is this? You do not usually have meetings like this, late in the evening, without your other council members. I would hate to think you had me come here just so you could do something in complete secret."

Stefanos faltered for a moment, before Rose stepped up. "It's hardly a secret, Your Grace," she said. "The council knows I have asked for your departure date several times, and you are in the presence of the king and queen, as well as our newest knight."

"Thank you, Aurora," Stefanos murmured blithely, straightening his posture. "Yes, Hebert, I have called you here because I do believe it is time to discuss your departure."

"I have vowed to stay until Her Majesty is fairly tried."

"You worry so much about keeping the fairness of the law," Stefanos said, "I wonder how you would feel if it were applied to you?"

Rose could see the similarity between her father and uncle as Hebert's gaze hardened. There was an unfriendly gleam in his dark eyes. "Of course I believe you to be a just ruler," Hebert said carefully. "I would hate to think you would find me an inconvenience in your court."

"You are not inconvenient, just unnecessary."

ONCE UPON A PRINCESS

"I was invited here by the queen herself," Hebert insisted. "She sent me a letter."

Rose still could not believe her mother had sent for Hebert, hoping that he would help.

"I wanted you to help Stefanos with to keep the nobles assured that there was nothing to worry about," Leea explained. "But ever since you came, you have been hurting our position more than helping it."

"I have been trying to protect you," Hebert said, and for a small moment, Rose pitied him.

While she thought it was undeniable that Hebert was after the crown, it was clear he wanted her mother more. Rose remembered what Rolez had told her before: Hebert had never been a true husband to his sister, because he was in love with someone else. As he looked at Leea now, the anguish in his eyes was palpable.

Leea, for her part, had to turn away from his gaze.

Hebert took a step toward her. "Leea," he said softly, "if you would have me leave, I will leave. I will leave, and I will never look back. But you are the only one I would allow to tell me to take myself away from your side."

He glanced back at Stefanos. "Love demands more than the law," he told Stefanos quietly.

Rose was starting to feel uncomfortable standing there, watching as her parents battled against each other among themselves. She suddenly wondered if she should say something, anything, to get them back to business. *After all,* Rose thought, *why are they worried about love when there is treason to deal with?*

"Love has some very strange demands, too," Stefanos said. "So I think it is best, in this case, that we all abide by the law first."

"You can't hold to that standard with me while negating it with the queen," Hebert demanded. "My heart cannot take such pain, my brother."

Rose watched as her father's face, already wan, paled even further. "We're discussing you here, Uncle Hebert, not the queen."

"Yes," Stefanos agreed. "We know there are hired troops at the western border, Hebert."

"They aren't mine," Hebert insisted.

"I have been shown proof," Stefanos said. "We know that you were conspiring against me."

Hebert frowned. "What proof do you have? I don't believe you really have anything."

Theo stepped forward with the Rose Ruby. "I retrieved this from your contact," he said. "I was there and I talked with her."

Leea gasped. "Hebert!"

Hebert turned to face her once more. "Leea, this is nothing," he said. "It is a fake, I swear."

"It is not!"

"Even the princess has a ruby like this."

"My father gave me that when he died," Leea shouted. "Don't tell me what I don't know!"

"Even if it is the real thing," Hebert said, "there's no reason to think that I was the one who gave it to the witch."

"I just told you," Leea yelled. "I know it is the real!"

"I know it is real, too," Stefanos said. "You should know better than to try to get me to believe it's a fake. We both had it before I gave it to Leea's father!"

"You mean you stole it from me so you could marry her!" Hebert yelled. He took several angry steps forward.

"Stop!" Rose ordered as she stepped into his path. While there was still the table between them, Rose did not want her uncle and father to come to blows.

"I would do as the princess commands," Theo spoke up. He had his own sword free of the scabbard, but kept it at his side.

"She should not be getting mixed up with this," Hebert yelled, rounding on him. "And neither should you."

Rose held her breath as Hebert, only slightly taller than Theo, leaned over him. She was mentally screaming at him to defend himself, but he did nothing.

He looked at Hebert calmly. "You've already admitted your guilt," he said. "There's no need to make it worse."

"I admitted to nothing," Hebert insisted. "You're just saying that because you're on his side." He nodded toward the king.

"How did you know I got the ruby from the witch?" Theo asked quietly.

Rose felt her breath rush out. "That's right," she said. "We never said that. You would only know that because you gave it to her."

"It was your payment," Theo added, "for her to create a banner for your troops. It would have been laced with Magdust and help you win when they came."

Hebert looked flustered. "You tricked me!" he said. "I admit to nothing."

"If you need more proof, Your Majesty," Theo said, "I have a friend with a seeing crystal. I'm sure he would be able to show us just what happened, if we asked for his help."

"You can just as easily ask your friend to lie," Hebert insisted.

"Enough," Leea said. "You said that if I asked you to leave, Hebert, you would leave. And I am asking you to leave."

Rose watched as the anger on Hebert's face crumbled into anguish. "What about us?" he asked. "What about everything we ever were?" He took her hand. "What about everything that we ever could be?"

"There are plenty of mistakes I have made in my life," Leea said. "But I cannot abandon my daughter." She glanced over at Rose. "I need you to leave. Graciously."

"You can forgo the graciousness," Stefanos called out. He leaned back in his chair with a bored expression on his face. "And while Leea is the one who asked you to leave, you're still the one who faces punishment."

"What are you going to do to me?" Hebert asked. "Sentence me to death? You know as well as I do that the nobles in your court would be upset. They're already upset at you for indulging the princess in her adventure fantasies."

Rose scowled at him.

"I'm going to offer you a deal," Stefanos said. "You said you wanted a fair trial for Leea, but now that she's asked you to leave, I have decided that you can leave, too. If you take her punishment."

"What punishment?" Hebert asked. "She hasn't had a trial before the court yet."

"There's no need for a trial if the villain steps forward," Stefanos said. "Claim her actions as yours, and I will let you leave. You will be properly banished, of course, and you will be killed on sight if you step forth in this country again."

Rose felt shocked at hearing her father.

"What is the alternative?" Hebert asked.

"Death." Stefanos glared at him. "I have proof of your transgressions, Hebert. I have all I need to drag you through the public courts and smear you as the villain you are. For all your support here, conspiracy against the crown is not taken lightly, especially when we are about to celebrate Isra's wedding to one of our closest allies. I would hate to send you to the dungeon while all the parties are going on, so you will be sentenced quickly and it will be carried out."

Rose, along with the rest of the room, turned to see Hebert's decision.

"Fine," he grumbled. "I accept your terms, and my punishment."

"Sir Theo," Stefanos said. "Why don't you take him out of the room and see to it that a team of my guards help him pack. I trust your men will cooperate, Hebert, with your orders as well as mine, now that your fate has been decided?"

Hebert said nothing, just glaring angrily at the king as Theo took his arm.

As they reached the door, Rose heard Hebert as he gave Theo a warning. "You'll pay for what you've done," he said. "One day I'll have revenge against you."

"Of all people," Theo said, "I know how revenge does nothing for the soul. I hope you learn the same lesson I have learned."

She frowned. What did he mean by that? Rose wondered.

Rose watched as they disappeared on the other side. Once Theo was gone, with her uncle in tow, she allowed herself a moment to rejoice.

That's one problem solved. For now.

Rose barely listened to her parents as they had their own version of a stilted conversation. She watched as the queen gave Stefanos a loyal kiss on the hand.

Rose felt nothing as her father dismissed her.

ONCE UPON A PRINCESS

She would deal with her father's illness later, she decided, as she headed out. Hopefully, her mother's release would give her some time to do just that.

Rose headed out of the room and began looking for Theo once more.

After a few moments, she saw him walking down the hallway toward the stables.

"Theo," she called. "Wait up."

He turned around and waited for her, as she requested. Rose knew from his expression he was annoyed. "What's wrong?"

"Nothing," he said. "Hebert's in his room, with several of the king's men watching over him. I was going to check in on Bachas and Elva, and then go to the stables to see if there were enough groomsmen to get everything together."

"Do you want some help?"

"I'm fine. I can handle this job, Rose. No need to check in on me already."

Despite the teasing in his tone, Rose bristled. "I'm going to go and watch him leave from my tower," Rose said. "I want to make sure he's gone by morning."

"Please, Rose," Theo said. "Don't worry about it. I can do that for you."

"There's no need for you to waste your first task as a knight on him," Rose argued. "Besides, you're tired, too. Didn't you just ride for several days, trying to get here?"

"I feel fine."

"Well, I feel fine, too."

"Come on, Rose. I am sure someone else can keep watch for us. Get some rest. You look exhausted."

"I'm *fine*," she insisted.

ONCE UPON A PRINCESS

"No, you're not," he said, the first hint of anger in his voice. "I know when you're lying, remember?"

"Just because you're now a knight in my father's court doesn't mean you get to order me around," Rose said as she crossed her arms.

"Knight or not, I wouldn't dare dream that you would ever listen to me," Theo said. "You've made it perfectly clear you only want to rely on yourself."

Rose went silent. He was right, she realized.

"I'm going to go and oversee your uncle's departure. Please excuse me, Princess."

Rose felt slighted as she watched him leave. He was back, Rose thought bitterly, but there was still a great distance between them.

"It's for the best," she said, hating herself more than ever in that moment.

ONCE UPON A PRINCESS

747

ONCE UPON A PRINCESS

16

It was hours later, with the sun peeking out from behind the horizon, when Theo made his way from the castle to the chapel. The last of Hebert's men were leaving, many of them grumbling at the late hour. Several of the king's guards were ready to escort them back to the Aragonian border.

As the last of them finally left the castle courtyard, Theo glanced up at the tower, where he knew Rose was watching.

In the last of the moonlight, she caught his gaze and then abruptly turned away.

"That's about what I was expecting," Theo murmured, as he began walking toward the chapel, where he knew Thad and his grandfather were waiting for him.

But, he hoped, he would be able to get some sleep first. With Hebert out of the castle and headed back to Aragon, and Bachas and Elva settled in a room of their own, he was done with his work. He could finally rest.

He made his way into his old room and fell asleep at once, only waking hours later when Thad appeared in his doorway.

"So, my brother," Thad said. "I hear you are officially a knight now."

"Good news travels fast." Theo rolled over to look at him. "I'm still allowed to come and sleep here, aren't I?"

"Technically, no," Thad said. "You know how the Grand Father is about rules, and we're not supposed to harbor agents of the state. You're no longer in the service of God here, but God and men, and men have much more blood on their hands."

"I can see about getting a room in the castle or in town later," Theo said.

"I wouldn't worry about it." Thad smiled sadly. "With the Reverend Father sick, no one else will pay too much attention to the rules."

"I guess Rose did say he wasn't feeling well." Theo sighed. "It's almost like he knew."

"Aunt Annalora is dead then?"

"Yes."

"I was wondering." Thad shook his head sadly. "Are you able to talk about it? If so, I'd like to hear it."

"Get me some breakfast first," Theo said. He glanced out the window. "Even if it's too late for breakfast."

Thad brought him some tea as he told him the whole story of how he had found their aunt and confronted her.

Thad sipped on his own cup quietly, as Theo finished up the whole story. "I had a feeling, after getting our grandfather to admit to what he knew, that it would be an unusual tale," he said. "But I have to say, that's more surprising than I thought it would be."

Theo nodded. "I was pretty surprised myself, especially when Everon showed up."

"Our mother never talked much about her family, or her sister," Thad said. "At least, not that I can remember much. But after reading up on the notes I found, and hearing our grandfather tell me the truth, I can understand why Annalora was in love with Everon. Or at least, why she was attracted to him. She wanted power."

"The lure of power does seem to be drawback for many people," Theo agreed lightly.

"You're one to talk," Thad teased. "You're a knight now. The king will order you around and send you off to different places, all to establish his own power. You might be more than tempted to take it for yourself one day."

ONCE UPON A PRINCESS

"I have only wanted power to protect others," Theo assured him. He thought of Rose again and sighed. "What little good it might do in the end."

Thad said nothing, and Theo was glad; he had a feeling that his brother could read his thoughts, and he did not want to speak them aloud. He knew Thad had talked with Rose after he had left her in Einish, and he did not want to know how much his brother pitied him.

"Everon told me that he loved Annalora, despite her mortality," Theo said, changing the subject. "And his mother's disapproval. It seems he didn't really want power for himself."

"She was still a skilled weaver, right? Maybe he wanted that from her?"

"I don't know," Theo replied. "I guess we will never know that. Maybe he really did just love her. Bachas told me that he felt Everon's presence again, when he and Elva were burning down her cottage. I wonder if he came to say a final goodbye."

"Maybe you are right," Thad murmured.

"Or maybe he was angry with me," Theo said. "I buried his sword with her. I thought … I thought it was the least I could do."

"Seems too generous," Thad said. "But then again, maybe Everon really did love her. He's an outcast in his own world, so it makes sense that he would find a kindred spirit in our aunt. The Grand Father told me she was always very reclusive. Our mother and our grandmother were the ones who were better at selling their work, even if Annalora was the better weaver."

"He was terribly upset when he fought with me." Theo shifted uncomfortably. "He actually begged me to kill him, when it was clear I was the winner in our fight."

"But you didn't kill him, right?"

Theo shook his head. "No."

"I'm glad." Thad sighed. "I know you don't understand, but I am relieved."

"I know what the church teaches," Theo grumbled.

"Yes, but it's harder to put it into practice," Thad said. "We talk of love and forgiveness, but when we have to go out and do it, there always seems to be trouble."

Theo laughed. "You're quite the cynic, aren't you?"

"A realist," Thad corrected him. "And why wouldn't I be? I'm the one who often sleeps through morning mass here. Between you and me, it's more often than not well worth the penance."

Theo smiled. "Sleeping in is hardly the same thing as killing an enemy."

"There is always a matter of honor with these things," Thad said. "You are sworn to protect others now. I am sworn to serve the Lord, and that means I have made promises that I am not good at keeping. In fighting Everon, I think you handled it with great honor."

"I didn't kill him," Theo said. "He could still hurt others."

"There's no reason to think allowing him to live goes against your calling. He might become a better person."

"Or he might do something even worse."

"From the sound of it, he was delivering fairies who were trying to rebel against Magdalina's rule to Annalora, who ended up killing them to put magic spells on her tapestries," Thad said. "He might actually have to do some work to find something worse to do."

Theo shrugged. A few moments passed in silence between them. Theo looked out the small window and saw the darkened skies. "It rained today?"

"Yes," Thad replied. "Earlier. It's been intermittent, so I know Rose will be glad to see you when you go to the castle later."

"The king will send for me," Theo said. "I don't need to go unless he calls."

"But you're going to go and see Rose," Thad pressed. "You'll want to see her, trust me. She's got all of her plans in place for marching on Darkwood Forest in two weeks."

"I talked with Rose some last night," Theo said. "That was enough for a while."

"Why?"

"Why what?" Theo frowned. "She wants us to be friends. We *are* friends. Friends don't need to see each other every day. She can send someone after me if she needs me, too."

"I take it that you didn't have a pleasant time meeting with her again?"

Theo scowled at him. "It wasn't great, to say the least. But she did get to watch as I was knighted. So while I have decided to forgo my revenge against Everon, at least I did something that made the last four years or so worth it."

"I know you don't mean that," Thad said with a smug look. "But I know you're still in love with her, so I'll let it slide."

Theo glared at him.

"It might help you to know she's been pining for you," Thad went on. "She found a way to ask me if I'd heard from you every time she crossed my path."

"That doesn't mean anything."

"Come on, don't be so cynical," Thad remarked good-naturedly. "You've only had your heart broken once."

"You enjoy teasing me, don't you?"

"Of course, brother." Thad grinned. "You make it so easy to enjoy."

When Theo said nothing, Thad sighed. "Besides, it's so obvious to me, and plenty of others, that she is in love with you. All you have to do is convince her to act on it."

Theo shook his head. "I offered her my heart once," he said. "And she didn't want it. I won't do that again."

"Sure you will," Thad said, as he refilled his cup of tea. "I'll bet anything you will."

"I take it the penance for gambling is worth it?"

Thad grinned at him. "In your case, brother, it most definitely is."

17

"I know it didn't take long for you and Theo to start arguing," Mary said, as she walked with Rose down the castle hallways. They were on their way to meet with Isra and Sophia to help with last-minute wedding details. "But I am surprised, however, to see that you've allowed it to come between you so much. Even when you argued before, you never let it bother you for this long."

Rose rolled her eyes. "I don't want a lecture, Mary," she said. "Besides, it's not like we've had any real issues. Even dealing with Ethan was easy."

"Easy by comparison," Mary reminded her. "He really only settled down more after Theo talked with him."

"He was fine when I talked to him last week. But that reminds me, they're getting some last-minute training in now," Rose said. "Ugh. They are so lucky. I don't want to help with any of Isra's wedding preparations. Nearly all the most important guests have arrived. The castle is full, the town is overrun, and people are starting to get bored and act up."

"You know as well as I do that even though you are going to head out for Darkwood tomorrow, you're not going to get any rest," Mary said. "You might as well help out."

"I suppose." Rose thought of all the work she had already done for Isra and Philip over the past weeks, in between planning and prepping for her attack on Darkwood Forest.

"Besides, it's nice so many people were able to come for the wedding," Mary said. "They really have enjoyed seeing you preset Isra to them yesterday. I know from what Ronan

ONCE UPON A PRINCESS

and Roderick have reported that there's a lot of excitement for the wedding."

"I guess they're making up for my lack of amusement for theirs," Rose said. "It's not like I'll be there for the ceremony anyway. I'll be three days away, hiding in some swamp bushes, fighting with Magdalina."

"You don't have to feel that bad about missing Isra's wedding. She will likely have another one in Einish in a few weeks," Mary said.

"A few weeks after my eighteenth birthday," Rose reminded her glumly. "There's still a good chance I won't make it."

"Rose, we've gone over the plans several times," Mary reminded her gently. "You spent a good deal of time arguing with Theo last night over details."

"Maybe I should ask Bachas to see if he can see what Isra's wedding will look like."

"There's no need to bother him, Rose. I'm sure it will be grand. And so will the one in Einish. You remember how the Dowager Queen was when we were there."

"Yes, she's almost as bad as my own mother when it comes to parties." Rose grimaced, thinking of her mother's suffocating effervescence. In the weeks since she had been released from prison, the news had gone out that Hebert had tried to poison the king and overthrow the crown, creating a new uprising of support for the monarchy. The Queen Mother embraced it and made sure she kept everyone's attention on Isra's upcoming wedding.

In truth, Rose was relieved that the kingdom seemed happier. Their political troubles were assuaged for the moment, as many were distracted with the grand wedding. It

ONCE UPON A PRINCESS

seemed that hardly anyone remembered her birthday was only two weeks away.

As they walked through the halls of the castle, Rose watched as different workers went about, running through with flowers and food and decorations. She had to suppress a groan. While Rose was happy for her friends and her sister, she hated that getting ready for the wedding took up her time to go over the attack plan for Darkwood. It didn't matter if she had already gone over it a thousand times; it was better to plan for it than it was to worry about it.

Or worry about anything else, she thought.

"I think the queen is relieved to have a project like this," Mary said. "After you told her before you would never get married as long as you were cursed, I think she gave up on weddings completely."

"You're probably right, but I would think she is more excited because she is finally free from the dungeon," Rose said. "I don't care how comfortable Hebert made it for her, it was still pretty bleak."

"That's likely true, too," Mary agreed. "Even Juana and Fiona have been tired out from the queen's demands lately. She seems to be making up for lost time."

"You can help them more if you want. It won't bother me if you're busy."

"I like being able to keep watch over you, Rose."

They came to a balcony overlooking the training barracks, and Rose spotted Theo and Ethan as they fenced against each other. She giggled when she noticed Philip was also with them, acting as a moderator. "Looks like I'm not the only one who is tired of the wedding plans."

"Isra is enjoying the time with your mother," Mary said. "They finally have something to bond over, and even Isra's

ONCE UPON A PRINCESS

governess, Ms. Winston, doesn't seem to bother her, while your mother is around to heap praises on how wonderfully mature she's become."

"Well, Isra is in love, too," Rose said, watching Theo parry with one of Ethan's attacks. "She probably doesn't notice those things as much as she used to, especially since I've hardly seen Philip leave her side."

"Fiona says they are really sweet together."

"Probably too sweet. I know quite a few people have made comments about it."

"I know." Mary wrinkled her nose. "You're one of them."

Rose laughed. "True enough."

"At least others are talking about them," Mary pointed out. "So they're not talking about you."

"That is a relief," Rose agreed.

"Yes, especially since there's so much to talk about, in addition to your attack on Darkwood this week," Mary said with a smile. "Your birthday is coming up soon."

"That reminds me, Mary," Rose said. "I have to write some things down. I need to be able to leave my sister the throne if I don't make it."

"You will make it," Mary insisted.

"That pixie hasn't shown you his seeing crystal at all, has he?" Rose asked bitterly.

"No," Mary scoffed. "He's still pretty rude to me. I don't like talking to him if I can avoid it. But I do know Theo told him to put the seeing crystal away. He doesn't want it used around here."

"There are plenty of reasons to fear the future," Rose said. "I don't need to know what it is until it's here though. I still like to believe there's a chance."

"Is that true?" Mary asked.

"Yes, of course it is." Rose frowned. "You just said I would survive my curse. Why would you ask me that?"

"Because," Mary said, "Ethan is still right about you, you know. You have admitted to things, to the secrets of your heart, but you don't act on it."

Rose crossed her arms. "Philip and I have coordinated the attack on Darkwood, and Derick's men are marching this way as we speak. We will be riding out in a day, Mary. I'm doing plenty."

"I mean, why don't you just tell Theo you love him?" Mary asked. "If you do believe you can break Magdalina's curse, why not tell him? He is a knight now. He's worthy of your love, if you wanted to get married."

Rose shook her head. "No," she said. "I couldn't do that to him … if I didn't make it."

"Don't you think it would be better to give him something than nothing at all? Why are you so against it, Rose? You know how you feel about him."

Rose sighed. She stopped and crossed her arms over her chest. "He's already lost so much, Mary," Rose whispered. "He lost his family to Everon, after all. He's spent years with me, training so he could have his revenge. I know he was young when it happened, and I know that something inside of him is just broken, forever. I know because I have that same feeling, that loss of a different future."

Rose glanced over at Mary. "I don't want to be the reason that his heart breaks even further."

"Oh, Rose," Mary murmured. "Stop this. You need to go and talk to him."

"Why?" Rose asked with a huff. "We have already talked about this, just like we've already talked about my curse. This is something we both knew about each other from almost the

ONCE UPON A PRINCESS

beginning. It's how I know God has abandoned me, why I hate him for it, and why I doubt he's even there. Either way, I know my curse would be too much for him, just like dealing with his own loss is too much for him."

She watched as Theo congratulated Ethan on scoring a point against him. She saw him shrug his shoulders and wondered if his dragon scars were hurting him.

Mary sighed. "Don't you know? He ran into Everon while he was with his aunt."

Rose whirled around to face her, shocked. "What?"

"He didn't tell you, did he?"

"No," Rose said, shaking her head. "No, he didn't." Suddenly, she felt insulted. He had been with her for countless hours in the past weeks as they planned the assault on Darkwood. They had talked with Roderick, Philip, and Sophia and many others about information, weapons and soldiers, supplies and strategies. Never once had he mentioned that he had faced Everon.

"How do you know?" Rose asked Mary. "What happened?"

"You should hear him tell the story," Mary said. "I overheard him telling Ethan."

"So it's true. I can't believe it," Rose said. "He finally did it."

"Rose—"

"And I can't believe he didn't tell me!" Rose clenched her fists together.

"He knows you want to focus on the upcoming battle."

"I don't care," Rose nearly shouted, surprised at just how angry she was. "This was *important*."

"Things have changed between you," Mary said.

"Not that." Rose shook her head. "No, we were still supposed to be friends, even after … everything else."

ONCE UPON A PRINCESS

She gazed down at Theo once more, watching as he shook Ethan's hand. Their battle was over. Philip stepped forward; it looked like Ethan was going to fence with him as well.

"That's it," Rose decided. "I'm going to go talk to him."

"Are you sure this isn't just a ploy to get out of working on the wedding stuff?" Mary teased.

Rose barely heard her as she headed down to the training grounds.

As she approached, Philip and Ethan halted their battle.

"Hello, Rose," Philip said with his cheerful smile. "Are you on your way to meet with Isra and Her Majesty?"

Rose lost her determined stride at the question. "No," she said. "Well, I was going to, but I have other things that require my attention."

"That's a shame. Isra was looking forward to spending the time with you, since you will be marching to Darkwood soon. She knows you won't be there for the ceremony so she wanted to get the time in earlier."

"I'll have to make it up to her," Rose grumbled.

"Do you need our help, Rose?" Ethan asked.

"No," Rose replied. "Keep working. I need to borrow Theo for a few moments."

At his name, Theo glanced over at her. Rose saw the displeasure cross his face and did her best to ignore it.

"Well, he's just been through a fight," Philip said, "so try not to make him suffer too much."

"No promises," Rose said.

ONCE UPON A PRINCESS

18

Rose took Theo's arm and dragged him away from the training area, before realizing she had no idea where to go. The castle was full of wedding guests and workers, and she wanted privacy. Ignoring Theo's questioning looks, she began to look for a quiet room.

"What is it? It's not Bachas again, is it?" Theo grimaced as he fell into step behind her. "I've already told Juana that I'm not responsible for him."

"What did he do before?" Rose asked, suddenly curious. She had been so focused on the upcoming battle, she had barely listened to any gossip from around the castle.

"He was making a mess in one of the gardens, apparently. Juana did not like it, and she liked it even less when he came back into the castle tracking in mud. He refused to clean it up when Juana confronted him. Luckily for both of them, Sophia heard them arguing and stepped in, or another round of war might have started between them."

"Well, that's not what I wanted to talk to you about. But speaking of fairies … "

Rose turned to the library and opened its door. When she saw that it was empty, she shoved Theo in and slammed the door behind her.

"What is it?" Theo asked. "What are you doing?"

"We're going to talk, I'd prefer not to have an audience," Rose told him. She crossed her arms and leaned back against the doors, blocking the exit, as she faced him.

"Do we need to do this Rose? Shouldn't you be getting ready for tomorrow?" Theo asked. "We're heading out for Darkwood. I know there's still some things to do for the wedding, but the others will be able to handle that once we're gone."

"This is important," Rose insisted. "It's just as important as the coming battle."

Theo sighed. "What did I do to irritate you this time?"

"You didn't tell me that you fought with Everon," Rose told him.

She was expecting him to repent at once. Instead, he crossed his arms over his chest. "So?"

"So?" Rose felt her anger spark, and she nearly hit him for his flippancy. "That's big news. I want to know about it."

"It doesn't matter."

"*Yes, it does.*" When he said nothing in return, Rose softened and sighed. "Please, Theo. You wanted your revenge, just as much as I want to break my curse. It was important to you, just as Magdalina's curse is important to me."

"It was important," Theo agreed. "But when I finally met with him, it was more a chance of fate than anything else."

Rose said nothing as he told her how Annalora was Everon's lover, how they both worked with the Magdust trade, and how, in the end, he had let Everon go free.

When he finished, Rose just stared at him. "You let him go?"

"Yes."

"Why?" Rose asked. She came up and stood beside him. "He killed your family."

Theo hesitated as her hand rested on his arm. "There's no one reason why," he said. "He has done terrible things. But with my aunt dead, he seemed too easy to kill. In some ways, I robbed him of his own family, of sorts, just as mine was taken from me."

"But that was an accident," Rose said. "You were going to bring her home to your grandfather."

Theo shrugged again. "I know." He gave her a rueful smile. "I had a feeling you would disapprove," he said. "Maybe that was the reason I didn't tell you I've decided to forgive him. Or at least, I've decided to let it go."

"How do you do that?" Rose asked. She shook her head. "I don't know how you do something like that."

"It's no secret that life is unfair," he said. "But sometimes fairness just makes the world a more terrible place."

"I don't know what you mean."

"Do you remember that fight you had with Marsor the day of the jousting competition on Maltia?" Theo asked. "How I stopped you from killing him?"

"Yes." Rose grimaced. "That turned out to be a bad decision."

"But it was still the right one," he said. "It might have been fair, but it would not have been just. I'm not the true judge, in the end. From what Annalora and my grandfather have told me, my parents were not so innocent, either. And while I still love them, I have to come to terms with their choices."

Rose sighed. "I guess it's good to know you still make me mad with all your priestly wisdom some days."

"Well, we are still terrible friends sometimes," he replied, reaching up to toy with a lock of her hair.

At the small, intimate gesture, tension instantly increased between them. Rose stilled, but she allowed herself to remain where she was, as she stared up at him in wonder.

She thought about how Theo had been able to survive his family's deaths, how despite everything, his heart had been able to find the power to forgive his mortal enemy. Was it

ONCE UPON A PRINCESS

possible that he would be able to survive loving her? Especially if she was unable to escape her curse?

He began to step away from her but Rose stopped him. The wall inside of her finally broke, and she knew she had to act. "No. I want to say something."

"Well, I don't want you to say something," Theo told her. "You want to be friends, Rose. I won't fight you on that."

"Ha," Rose scoffed, regaining some of her fire. "You're fighting me now."

"For good reason," Theo told her. "I'm supposed to protect myself from you, remember?"

He tried to push her away again, but Rose slipped deftly between his arms, wrapping her arms around him. She lay her head down against his chest, willing herself to have the bravery to face him, and willing him to have the weakness to let her.

He went silent and stiff as she held him.

"I didn't want to fall in love with you," she whispered.

"So you've told me, Rose," Theo said, gripping her shoulders, trying to pry himself free from her grip. "If you don't mind, would you please let me——"

"I didn't want to," Rose said, "but I did."

He stopped moving. He stopped breathing.

Rose looked up at him, meeting his brilliant green eyes bravely. "I didn't want to," she said. "You were right about me. I was lying before, so I could protect you. I don't want you to get hurt, if I'm not able to break my curse."

She felt him slowly start to breathe again. She could hear her heartbeat thundering in her ears as she waited for him to reply. Standing as close to him as she was, she could hear his own heart starting to beat wildly.

ONCE UPON A PRINCESS

"Why are you telling me this now?" he finally asked. "Is it because I'm a knight, because I'm suddenly worthy of your love?"

"No." Rose shook her head. "No, *I* am the one who was never worthy of *you*."

He did not seem to hear her. "Is it because we're about to go and face Magdalina tomorrow? Or maybe because Isra and Philip are getting married? Why, Rose? Why are you telling me this now?"

If the circumstances were different, Rose thought, she might have laughed at his reaction. He sounded terrified.

Instead, she tightened her grip on him. "Because as much as I didn't want you to love me, and I know I don't deserve it, I know now that I *need* you to love me." Rose felt her face burn as she admitted what she had known, and feared, for so long.

Theo just stared back at her with an incredulous look on his face.

She released him from her embrace, letting her fingers curl into his chest. Rose did not want to force him to stay. She knew he had the right to walk away from her, after everything she had said that night in Einish. "Curse or no curse, I need you. I know it's asking a lot—"

"No."

Rose winced at his response. "Okay, but—"

Before she said anything else, Theo gently framed her face with his hands. "No, Rose," he said. "No. It's not asking anything of me that I wouldn't give you. Willingly."

Then Theo leaned down and kissed her. As Rose felt his lips press into hers once more, the rest of the world faded away. She began kissing him back as his hands pulled her body against his. Her arms slipped around his neck and tangled in his hair.

It was completely overwhelming, Rose thought. The smell of him, the sweat and musk and sun; the taste of him, the feel of his body against hers as she clung to him—all of it was just too perfect.

"I love you," she whispered against his mouth. The words seemed to free themselves of their own accord, and at last, she was content to let them go.

He pulled back from her to catch his breath. "I never thought I would hear you say that," Theo whispered.

Rose pressed into him again, trying to get closer. "I never thought anyone would love me the way you do."

He grabbed her, lifting her off her feet and pulling her against him. He held her there for a long moment, unable to stop himself from running his hands down her back and losing himself in her hair.

He gently put her back down on her feet. "You know, you should have fought me harder, if that was what you were going to tell me when I came back," Theo told her.

"No," Rose said. "I'm glad I didn't say anything earlier. I didn't want you to … "

"Didn't want me to be hurt?" Theo asked.

She shrugged. "Mostly. If things don't go well with Magdalina … I didn't want you to have to worry about me leaving you."

"What changed your mind?" Theo asked. He frowned. "You're not telling me this out of pity, are you?"

"No." Rose shook her head fiercely. "No. When I heard about Everon, and you told me how you were able to … to let him go, after everything … I just thought that maybe you could handle another broken heart."

He cupped her cheek. "My heart can take anything but your rejection. I know the world is not free from pain and suffering and loss, but I would take it, willingly, if it means I get to be by your side. So you should have talked to me sooner."

Rose let out a shaky laugh. "You have to make things my fault with this, don't you?"

"I'll do just about anything to ensure I can kiss you again," he admitted. "And that includes guilting you."

"I don't think it will come to that," Rose told him. She leaned up on her toes and kissed him tenderly. "But even if it does, I deserve it. I know I hurt you before, and I've never been more sorry for anything in my life."

"All I need is you to be here with me, to make up for it," Theo told her. "No matter how little time we have."

At his mention of time, the reality of their situation suddenly hit her all over again.

They were going into battle. In less than a day.

Rose pulled back from him. "I *should* have fought you harder," she said. "We're heading out for Darkwood tomorrow. I shouldn't have sent you away before. We don't have a lot of time left, do we? I'm so—"

"Rose," Theo said, interrupting her. "Everything will be alright."

"How do you know?" Rose felt her heart clench in despair. She had finally admitted she loved him, and they were together. And now, time was really running out. How much did they have left before their big battle? A day? Three? Then there was the matter of her coming birthday ...

"Because everything is already perfect," he told her, drawing her close to him again.

"But I'm still cursed," Rose reminded him.

ONCE UPON A PRINCESS

"Rose." Theo met her gaze. "Tell me this. If I was the one who was cursed, and you loved me, would you let me stop you from being with me, even if we only had three days together?"

Rose rested her head on his shoulder and nearly laughed at her own foolishness. "No," she answered. "No, there's nothing that would have stopped me."

"Then you know why we're going to be okay," he told her. "We're too determined to be together. If that's the case, nothing can stop us."

"What about death?" Rose asked. "Or at least sleeping death?"

"Death doesn't mean that I will ever stop loving you," Theo told her.

"That's not logical."

"It still works. Come on, you know I'm going to win this argument, Rose. Give it up."

"So you think we'll be okay because you said so?"

"Close enough. You're the one who's said before my logic is unparalleled."

"Have I actually used that word to describe your arguing skills?" Rose asked. "I don't think I have."

"I know you're just trying to distract me, because you know I'm right." His arms wrapped around her.

"I think you're cheating now," Rose murmured.

"I don't think of it as cheating," Theo told her, "since I already won."

Rose was not sure if she argued back or not. She was too busy enjoying his kiss once more.

ONCE UPON A PRINCESS

19

As the morning light dawned in the library the next day, Theo felt a surge of amazement inside of him once more, as he held Rose close to him. She was breathing the soft, easy rhythm of rest, as she lay with her head on his lap, curled on the floor. Even though he was sore from sleeping in a sitting position, Theo felt like he could take on the world.

Rose loved him. She loved him.

He ran his hand through her hair lovingly, marveling as he always did at the softness of her short locks.

They had spent a good portion of the night as they always had, talking and arguing, taking care of each other.

Eventually, Rose snuggled against him and went to sleep, telling him as she drifted off she was too tired and happy to care about anything as trivial as sleeping on the library floor.

Theo, with his own desperation to be near her, had been unable and unwilling to argue. He kissed her goodnight before falling asleep himself.

Now, he stared at her, drinking in the sight of her, feeling unbelievably grateful and humbled. He had been waiting for this since he had first met her.

The memories of riding on the road without her, of his half-reluctance to sleep for fear of dreaming of her, were gone. The warmth and comfort of that moment washed them all away, as Rose slept on beside him.

Theo reached down and touched the small pouch on his belt, where the Rose Ruby was tucked away safely, and he wondered if the king had been right about his good fortune when it came to roses.

"Theo? Are you awake?" Rose murmured, as she began to stir.

"Yes," he replied.

She shifted into an upright position, sitting up beside him. "I didn't mean to keep you here. I hope you can move."

"I'll need to stretch," he told her. "But it's fine. It's better than fine." He reached over and kissed her forehead, still staring at her in loving wonder.

He was gratified to see that despite the uncomfortable sleeping arrangement, Rose looked more refreshed than she had been in the last weeks. The dark circles under her eyes seemed to have vanished, and her skin was a healthy glow.

"We better get up," Rose murmured sleepily. "I wanted to say a proper farewell to Philip and Isra before we left. I know they're worried."

"Philip is more upset that he won't be able to help fight," Theo told her. He stood up and stretched quickly, eager to work the soreness out of his muscles.

"He shouldn't have suggested the wedding to go on at the same time, then," Rose said, rubbing the rest of the sleepiness out of her eyes. "But I guess he is a man in love, right? Maybe he wasn't thinking clearly on the matter."

"Oh, I doubt that," Theo said, as he reached down and pulled her into a standing position. "He was just focused on something other than our battle."

"I guess you're right." Rose laughed, and then she grew quiet. "What should we do about us?"

"What do you mean?"

"I was wondering what we should tell the others ... about us."

"What do you want to tell them?"

Rose blushed. "Well ... they already have their suspicions."

"Then let them be the ones who ask," Theo suggested. He thought about Thad, about how his older brother had teased him before. It would not be the worst thing, he thought deviously, to make some people wonder just a bit longer. "We don't have to tell them anything."

"That's true. But between Ethan and Mary and our other friends, it might be better."

He took her hands in his and squeezed them affectionately. "We can do what you want, Rose. I know we have other things to worry about right now," he said. "And I know how you feel about marriage and falling in love. We can take care of one thing at a time, starting with Magdalina. There's no need to worry about everything right now."

"Well, there's no wonder why I love you," Rose said. "You know me so well."

"Yes, and I still love you." Theo smirked before he gave her another quick kiss. He heard her stomach growl hungrily and laughed. "Come on. Let's get some breakfast. It sounds like you could use it."

"I could," Rose agreed. "I hope the others are getting ready."

"We have always been the early risers of our group," Theo reminded her.

"We are supposed to have everyone come to breakfast though, since we're leaving today."

"That might make some of them less enthusiastic to get up, not more."

Rose smiled as they walked out of the library and started walking to the dining hall. "That's true."

Theo took her arm, tucking it around his possessively and protectively, glad there was no longer any remnant of awkwardness between them.

ONCE UPON A PRINCESS

For the first time in a long time, Rose felt rested and ready. It was as though a great weight was no longer pressing down on her as she watched the rest of her friends gather around the breakfast table.

Theo escorted her to her chair before sitting down beside her. Immediately, Rose could see her friends exchanged surprised glances and questioning looks. She ignored them for now. Theo was right; they had to worry about one thing at a time. She had to get through today first, when they were going to start the celebration for Isra and Philip, and then they were going to leave for Magdalina's castle.

Mary came up to her. "Good morning, Rose," she said. "Sleep well?"

Rose nodded. "I'm ready for this battle," she said. Her eyes briefly darted down to the ruby on the hilt of her sword, before she glanced over at Theo. The trouble of her heart was resolved, and now her courage was ready to be tested.

"Isra and I have talked with your body doubles," Philip said to Rose. "We're all ready to go. All we need is for people to see you in your dress clothes, and then we'll have them swap out with you."

"And then we'll quietly leave as the king makes the announcement," Rose said. She had long memorized the plan. "Great."

"You'll have to put a convincing show before you leave," Isra said. "Ronan is worried that you won't be able to pull it off, since you're so serious all the time."

"Those were my exact words, too," Ronan said, as he came into the room.

ONCE UPON A PRINCESS

"Ronan, there you are." Rose stood up and gave her little brother a quick hug. "I don't think I've spoken more than two words to you since you came home."

"That's your fault," he said. "After I was told what I needed to do, I went back to business as usual."

"You always seem to have an excuse not to see the rest of us." Rose gave him a quick pat on the hair, rustling up his dark brown hair.

He ducked and grabbed an apple from her plate. "Hey, I did what you asked. I spread all the rumors to my friends in town, and there's no reason to think that they won't come through for me. So far as anyone would know, you are going to be at the wedding banquet all week along with everyone else."

"Did they give you any other information?" Philip asked. "I have been wondering if there was any news from Isra's uncle. I knew the Duke of Aragon has suffered a tremendous shift in approval lately."

"With good reason," Rose muttered under her breath.

"He might be foolish enough to come and fight," Ronan said. "But not now. He knows about Isra's wedding, of course, but the guards and our loyal guards throughout the country from here to Aragon have been put on alert. They will defend their nation's princess. Nothing has come up in the last weeks."

"Good," Isra said. "I'd hate to think we would need to worry about him in addition to Magdalina with all of this."

Rose glanced over at Theo. "What about his hired men?" she asked. "You were there. You saw them. They wouldn't be likely to give us trouble, would they?"

ONCE UPON A PRINCESS

Theo shook his head. "That's the nice part about them being mercenaries," he said. "They're not likely to fight unless their payment is guaranteed."

"Good point." Rose gave him a warm smile, and everyone else went silent, watching them. When she blushed, she turned her attention to Ethan and Sophia, as they walked into the room. "There you are," she said. "I was wondering where you were."

Sophia stepped up. "Virtue came back," she said, handing Rose a pile of letters. "Here."

"Virtue's back? That's wonderful!" Rose cheered as she sorted through the pile of letters. She immediately recognized King Derick's scrawl and was glad to see that he had sent his own legion of troops out to Darkwood.

"Excellent," Rose said. "Derick's forces will meet us at Darkwood in three days' time. They might even get there ahead of us."

Philip smiled into his cup. "Einish soldiers are known for their riding," he said. "You better hurry once you leave, if you're going to catch up to them."

Rose nodded. Before she could ask Mary if she had enough herbs and remedies packed, Roderick came in.

"Rose," he said. "The queen has started to assemble the family for the official greeting procession. She requests that you and Isra hurry and change."

Rose grabbed another roll of bread. "Alright," she said. "Isra, are you ready?"

Isra sighed and nodded. "I barely had time to eat," she complained.

"You're getting married this week," Rose said. "Mary's assured me that this is going to be nothing compared to

ONCE UPON A PRINCESS

Philip's mother when you have your wedding ceremony in Einish. You might as well get used to it."

Isra laughed. "We'll see."

Theo gave her a knowing look as she headed out of the room. She knew she would see him again soon.

As soon as they were out of the room, Isra squealed with delight. "I knew it!" she said. "I knew you loved him."

Rose blushed. "Come on, Isra," she said. "You're the one who is going to be married soon. Can't you behave like a mature person?"

"Hey, come on. I'm still young," Isra said with a giggle. "Besides, I have been waiting for you to get together since we were kids. Give me a break here, please, Rose."

Rose sighed as Isra put her arm around her. "How did you know about us? Surely just seeing us at our short breakfast wasn't enough to give it away."

"Oh, I'm sure it was. But, if you're going to insist on a better answer, Mary found you guys in the library earlier," Isra said. "She told Fiona, and Fiona told me."

Rose made a mental note to remind Mary not to gossip about her to her fairy friends.

"So, it's true," Isra said. "You told him you loved him."

"Yes." Rose tried not to groan, as Isra hugged her again. "Now we have to go off to battle."

"I don't see why it would be such a difference from before," Isra said. "He's always loved you, you know."

"I guess he did tell me that," Rose said. She had never thought about how much he loved her when they were traveling. All of the fights and hardships in her memory suddenly had a new layer added to them, as she saw his young face, following her around the world, and then his seasoned look, coming home with her.

ONCE UPON A PRINCESS

She sighed. "Great. Now I'm even more terrified of losing him."

"You won't," Isra assured her. "Now, let's go and get our new dresses on. You heard Roderick. Mother is anxious for the party to begin."

Yes, if there is anything the queen is excited for, Rose thought, *it is a party*.

But despite her reservations, and even in spite of her concern for the upcoming battle, Rose felt a burst of excitement as she thought about dancing with Theo at Isra's wedding celebration.

There was never going to be enough time with him, Rose thought wistfully. Now that she allowed herself to fall in love, and now that she had admitted it to him, they were racing against time before their battle, before her curse could be broken.

Rose had never wanted to fall in love. But, now that she had, there was nothing she wanted more than to make enough memories to last a lifetime—even if she spent that lifetime dreaming of it, forced by a wicked sorceress into a deathlike slumber.

20

The long week of the wedding celebration had officially started, and even Rose seemed to enjoy some of it before they left for Darkwood.

But, Theo thought, he knew Rose agreed with him; there was no feeling in the world like rushing off into battle—even if it was the battle of her life, and the stakes were higher than ever before.

As they made their way through the forest of Rhone, Theo allowed himself to think about how, even at the start of the kingdom's biggest celebration in many, many years, Rose managed to outshine everything else.

The celebration started with a fair and a joust. He had been relieved that there was no need to convince Rose not to participate in this one. There were speeches and presentations and the procession line, where Rose, along with her parents, presented Isra and Philip to the kingdom. The procession did not last long, as the king was quickly overheated and had to go retire, but plenty of excited people were able to see the bride and bridegroom.

None of them suspected Rose was currently headed into battle, where her fate, and the fate of the nation, would be decided.

"What are you thinking about?" Bachas grumbled, as he leaned against Theo's back. "I can practically feel your attention wandering off."

"Nothing," Theo murmured, too embarrassed to admit that Bachas had a point. He had been getting distracted several times over the long hours on the road.

"I can use my seeing crystal on your thoughts," Bachas warned.

"As we've discussed before," Theo said, "I don't think you would actually do that."

After a moment, Bachas only shrugged. "I guess it's too much work, now that I think about it. I gave the crystal to Elva, and she's riding along with your lady and her fairy friend."

"Well, that's a relief," Theo replied.

"I figured you were just thinking about your princess again anyway," Bachas said. "You seem to be on much better terms with her today."

Theo nodded. "We're finally about to go and meet Magdalina," he said. "If we can overcome her forces, we can get stop the Magdust trade, and Rose can break her spell."

"Yeah, yeah, I know."

Despite his teasing, Bachas proved to be good company, Theo thought. He saw Mary and Elva, both sitting behind Rose, were also getting along. "Maybe once this is over," Theo said, "we can do something to help pixies and fairies get along better."

"If they keep to themselves, we usually do just fine," Bachas said. "Sure, some of us have terrible masters, and some of the fairies help trick us into life debts. And both of us are very territorial. But for those of us who have no place left to go, we generally get along."

"You don't have a home?" Theo asked. "Is that why you came with us?"

"Not all of the reason," Bachas admitted. "But it would be nice to have good allies. You know, in case I need to be freed from a life debt, or something like that."

Theo might have laughed, if the truth was not so tragic.

They continued to ride along in mostly silence, with conversations sparse through the thick forest. At night, Theo allowed himself to hold Rose close to him, curling against her until she fell asleep. And then, once she was sleeping, he would pray, counting off the rosary beads Rose wore openly on her wrist, hoping with everything inside of him that they would be able to emerge from their fight as victors.

ONCE UPON A PRINCESS

21

Three days riding wore on Rose, but the renewed comradery with Theo, and Ethan, too, helped her as she made her way through Rhone's forest. Theo would talk with her, fight with her, and comfort her, while Ethan would look on them with a sense of approval. While she was glad he was on better terms with her, and Ethan seemed a lot happier now that they were together, Rose felt much better that he did not ask any questions. He even played his harp for them at night, letting her fall asleep on Theo's shoulders, with the lulling music filling her mind.

She was almost sad to see the edge of the forest—and the last of the quiet before the storm—as the sight of Magdalina's kingdom came into view.

Rose felt her sadness disappear the moment she saw Darkwood Castle, leaving only a simultaneous mix of relief and disgust. It was a relief, because after three days of riding, they were going to battle. It was disgusting because Magdalina, for all her own immaculate care with her wardrobe and self-presentation, did not seem to hold her home in the same esteem. The castle sat on a rocky ledge, with a rickety bridge as the only way inside the castle walls. From where Rose was standing, she could see the keep's walls were full of holes, with vines growing out of them, and the fairies who kept their watch.

"What do you think?" Rose asked, turning to Roderick. Theo had taken half of their party to meet up with Derick's troops on the other side of the castle, while Rose stayed behind to scout the area with the others.

ONCE UPON A PRINCESS

"I think we can move ahead with our plans," Roderick said. He had talked with several of the scouts she had sent out in the weeks' prior. "We'll have to be careful, of course, but there's no reason we can't attack successfully."

"You said that Magdalina was supposed to be here?" Rose asked. She glanced over at the keep, looking for any sign that her enemy was home.

"Yes, she is supposed to be here," Roderick repeated. "But she is still capable of magic. Because of this, there is the possibility she might be somewhere else."

"She better be here," Rose grumbled. "I would hate to think we came out this way for nothing."

"Not for nothing, Rose," Roderick said. "It's just like you said before. Defeating her, in any way, will help to slow the Magdust trade, if nothing else. Especially since we know that some of her supplies come from fairies who are trying to overthrow her rule."

"I wish we could find more of those fairies," Rose replied. "That might make defeating her a little more easy."

"There might be some in the castle," Roderick suggested.

Rose brightened at the thought. "Alright," she said. "Let's make that a priority as we go in. Once Theo and Ethan get back from meeting with Derick's men, we can start to move in."

"Rose," Mary said. "We have a problem."

"What is it?"

"I hear music," Mary said, suddenly worried.

"It's fairy magic," Elva further clarified. The small pixie had been relaxed enough on the way over. "It's a lulling spell."

Rose thought about the time she had been with her mother, trapped by Hebert's men in Havilah's dungeon. "Theo," she murmured. He had the Rose Ruby, she thought. Surely if

ONCE UPON A PRINCESS

there was anyone who would be able to see through magic's barrier, it would be him.

Rose pushed her horse into a gallop, hurrying off to find Theo and the others.

If they suspect us, Rose thought, *then we better hurry.*

When she crested over a small hill, the spell the music had cast over her suddenly broke. She gasped as she suddenly saw the raging battle around her.

All at once, she felt her ears pop, and she could hear the sounds of swords clashing, of men and fairies dying, and shouts of anger and surprise all around.

"It's already going on!" she cried, appalled, watching as fairies and other loyal minions of Magdalina's attacked Derick's men.

"Rose!"

Theo called out her, and Rose instantly felt relieved. As he made his way over to her, he had his sword out, fighting as he maneuvered his horse through the crowd.

"Theo," she called back. "What is this?" She brandished her own sword—Queen Lucia's sword—and waded into the battle. She felt another rush of gratitude when she saw Ethan appear just behind Theo.

A fairy with a sword began to attack her, and Rose leapt into the battle right away. She managed to get him distracted enough that he did not see Ethan coming up behind him.

"Didn't you hear us calling you, Rose?" Ethan asked, as he struck down the fairy attacking her.

"No," Rose told him. "Are you alright? What happened?"

"Derick's men were waiting for us," Ethan said. "Once we came over and met with them, we were attacked. The fairies were waiting for the men to be significantly distracted."

Theo came up beside her. "Even Bachas' seeing crystal apparently did not see this," he said. "They've blocked out his pixie magic."

"How?" Rose asked.

Bachas poked his head out from under Theo's arm. "We might be able to cancel out some of it, but it is sorcerer's magic more than fairy magic here."

"So Magdalina is here?" Rose asked.

"I saw her on the battlements," Ethan said. "She's in the castle."

Rose felt a moment of hope. "Alright," she said, pulling her horse's bridle toward the bridge. "Let's get ready to charge into the castle. If we can defeat her, it will be easier to defeat the rest of her fighters."

Roderick came up behind her. "We have your back, Rose."

"Alright," Rose said. "Let's go!" She urged her horse forward, holding her sword up high as they charged through the battlefield.

22

Theo pushed his horse to follow Rose through the throng of men and fairies fighting each other. He was glad that Bachas had come with them; while he had grumbled about being on the road again, he was proving himself a true ally against Magdalina and her forces. He used his magic to protect their small group from the fairies as they headed over the rickety bridge.

"Charlie doesn't seem to like the bridge," Bachas warned him as they quickly made their way over. "He thinks it's going to collapse."

"Charlie?" Theo briefly recalled his horse's preferred name. "Oh, right."

He quickly studied the drawbridge over the abyss, and realized his horse had it right; there was little hope that the bridge would survive if any of Derick's legions stormed the castle.

"Ethan," he called. His squire hurried beside him, while the others pressed on, clashing with the castle guards.

"What is it?" Ethan asked, gripping his sword with white knuckles.

"I'm going to need you to guard the bridge," Theo told him. "It's old and likely won't hold up if there's a charge against the castle."

Ethan frowned. "I doubt the men would try, and there's a reason the fairies are using their wings," he said. "The castle itself will likely fall with any more people inside of it." He gestured to the rocky ledge, from where Magdalina's home jutted out at sharp angles.

"True. But for now, keep guard," Theo said. "Send our men away, and keep Magdalina's forces at bay."

"I will," Ethan promised. He tugged on his horse's bridle, turning around sharply and heading back toward the battle. While Theo watched Ethan return, a rotten plank snapped under his horse's hoof. Worry ran through him, but Ethan recovered. When Ethan was safe, Theo carefully made his way to Rose once more.

As he followed the rest of the soldiers through the castle keep's doors, he glanced back at his squire, who took a firm position in front of the bridge's crossing.

He seems so young all of a sudden. Theo knew there was no time to worry about that. As he came up beside Rose, he made a note to commend Ethan on his bravery later.

"I almost wish Mary was here," Rose said. "She would be able to tell me which way."

"Forward and up," Bachas replied.

Rose laughed. "I guess I forgot I have a new friend to help with that," she said.

"Thank you, Bachas." Theo glanced back at Bachas, who was vigilantly perched on Charlie's backside.

The pixie shrugged. "I'll do my best to protect us," he said. "But there's only so much I can do about sorcery."

Theo nodded as they hurried forward through the keep. When they came to an open atrium, they stopped. Several rows of steps, leading to different rooms and different levels, surrounded them.

"Which way?" Rose asked.

"She's here," Bachas said. "But I'm not sure where. She's circling."

ONCE UPON A PRINCESS

Theo dismounted from his horse, while the others followed his lead. "Stand ready, together," he ordered, but Rose was already running up a nearby stairway. "Rose!"

"I saw her," Rose shouted back.

Before he could chastise her for leaving the small circle of protection that he, Bachas, Roderick, and the rest of their small group afforded her, Theo felt the burn of fire behind him. He glanced over his shoulder, watching as a ball of white fire ruptured over the soldiers, raining an inferno over them.

Several horses jumped, spooked, while the men all hurried to duck from the flames or smother them.

Before Theo could head down to help, Rose let out a loud cry.

"Rose," he breathed. His decision was made for him, as he ran up rest of the stairs to find Rose. As soon as he reached the top, power blew past him, nearly throwing him down the stairwell. He fell to his knees and dropped, keeping his sword up to block any oncoming attack.

But the attack never came. When the attack resided, he blinked his eyes open to see Rose attack Magdalina ferociously. Magdalina shuffled out of her way, as she transformed her staff into a sword.

At the first sight of their enemy, Theo was immediately encouraged. The wicked ruler of the fairies seemed uncharacteristically flustered, despite her efforts to hide it. As she juggled her magic and continued sidestepping Rose, Theo saw their plan to catch her off guard certainly worked.

Seeing Rose had to be terrifying, he thought with a quick grin.

Theo stood up. As he ran over to help Rose, he could hear her taunting Rose. "I always wondered how Rhone trained its

ONCE UPON A PRINCESS

knights," Magdalina said. "Especially since I've managed to kill so many over the years."

Rose scowled. "You won't kill me," she declared, before thrusting her sword into one of Magdalina's long sleeves. Magdalina balked, but rather than retaliate, she stepped back.

It's the dragon situation all over again, Theo thought with a frown. Rose was too intent on winning to see she was losing. He watched, briefly terrified, as Rose stumbled.

Magdalina caught his eye and stepped back, preparing to launch another round of magic at him.

Theo reached into his pouch, grabbing the Rose Ruby. He felt the protective power of its barrier fan out as Magdalina's power soared over him.

Rose managed to land a strike. There was a brutal hissing sound as Magdalina instantly retreated. Theo watched in amazement, as her arm began to smoke, and black blood began to ooze out of her arm.

Magdalina grasped at her arm, trying to heal it with her power.

"Today is the day," Rose told her, "when you finally pay for all your cruelty against my kingdom and my family."

"Now, that's hardly the proper thing to say when you show up uninvited," Magdalina seethed. She scowled and stepped back again, grabbing her arm while she clung to her sword, but Rose did not let her out of her reach.

Theo hurried forward, determined to help Rose. He held the Rose Ruby in his fist along with his sword, using both hands to fight.

A thousand things seemed to happen all at once; Theo could hear the men down in the atrium, dealing with Magdalina's spell and other fairy fighters; he could hear Bachas cackling happily, which likely meant he had found someone to fight. Theo felt the heat of the battle, the sweat on his skin, as he advanced toward Magdalina alongside Rose, carefully maneuvering her into a corner.

"Rose," he called, as it was a chance for them to end it.

She nodded, and Theo lunged forward.

Magdalina was ready for him. She was able to dodge his blow, and she grappled with his sword.

Theo glanced at her in surprise when she knocked it out of his hand.

"Ha!" Magdalina cheered and pressed forward.

But then Theo ducked down and grabbed onto her, the Rose Ruby still in his hand. All her magic around them instantly drained away from the room. The hot flames surrounding the men disappeared.

Down below, Theo could hear Roderick call out orders to fight, now that they were free of any magical entanglements.

"Theo, watch out!" Rose shouted, as Magdalina tried to strike him down once more.

Just as he had with the dragon, Theo prepared himself for another round of pain. But Rose stepped in between them, bringing her blade down on Magdalina in triumph.

Rose struck her in the back, and Magdalina's cry carried throughout the castle. Red blood, the blood of her human self, dripped onto the floor.

"Now for the dragon's blood," Rose said quietly.

At her word, Theo let Magdalina go. He felt the Rose Ruby's power contract around him once more, while the dragon's blood from Rose's sword leaked into Magdalina.

Magdalina gasped in pain, howling as the deadly power scorched through her. She fell to the floor, writhing in pain. She scowled up at Rose. "You won't get away with this," she hissed.

ONCE UPON A PRINCESS

"If that is what you truly believe, then you know your time has come," Theo told her quietly.

"You have killed many humans and fairies," Rose said. "You have caused a lot of trouble for my kingdom, including me and my father, and you have shown no remorse. Your time has come to pay for what you have done."

Theo held onto Rose's shoulder, as Magdalina fell silent and stopped moving.

Her breathing grew labored. "You will still pay for this," she warned. "Even if killing me frees you from your curse, you will pay. I will be avenged."

"You no longer have any power over me," Rose proclaimed.

Theo was just about to agree when Magdalina drew her last breath, and a tidal wave of power burst out from her body. Light and fire flooded the atrium in raging brightness.

Theo shielded his eyes as her power stormed around them, as the castle began shuddered. Beneath his feet, he felt the floor shook, and the castle walls creaked uncomfortably.

"We need to go," he realized as the creaking turned into crumbling. "The castle is going to fall!"

23

Rose was silent with shock as Theo gave the retreat orders behind her. Even in the midst of Magdalina's castle collapsing, all Rose could do was stare at the scene before her.

Magdalina, her lifelong enemy, was gone.

And she, at last, was free. She was certain of it.

The instant Magdalina died, she had felt it, felt the change inside of her. There was nothing left of the despair and helplessness inside of her. A haze had lifted from across her heart.

She was free, and free at last, and there was a bright future ahead of her for the first time in nearly eleven years. She closed her eyes, even as the castle began to shake, unable to do anything but revel in her freedom.

Rose was grateful, as Theo grabbed her hand and tugged her after him. He pulled her back into the urgent reality that they were going to die if they did nothing to hurry. They fled down the stairs and back to his horse. Theo shoved her up in front of him, hardly giving her any time to grab on before he pushed the horse into a gallop.

There was no time for her to find where hers was, as the ceiling began to break and the rafters, already rotting, began to fall.

Rose, still shocked speechless, watched as the other men around her hurried along with them, heading out of the keep.

"Rose! Theo!" Ethan called from the other side of the bridge. "Hurry! The castle is falling off the cliff!"

Theo's horse pounded down on the bridge, and Rose gasped as several of the wooden planks splintered.

ONCE UPON A PRINCESS

"We'll make it," Theo promised. "Come on, Charlie, jump!"

Just as the castle pulled back from the rocky terrain, Rose and Theo arrived safely on the remains of Magdalina's castle grounds.

"Whoa," Rose breathed. She glanced around at what remained. Rose noticed that, with Magdalina gone, the other fairies who had followed her were either quickly running away, or they were celebrating themselves. She would worry about the politics of Magdalina's death later, she decided, as she turned back to Theo.

"Are you alright?" he asked.

In response, Rose reached up and brought his lips down onto hers, in full view of Derick's men and the rest of their friends.

When she pulled back, she nearly laughed. "I'm more than alright," Rose told him. "I'm free. I felt it. I am free, Theo! I'm finally free to love you."

She kissed him once more, and she could hear the men calling out their cheers, several clapping in the background. Out of the corner of her eye, Rose could see the shocked smile on Ethan's face; it was heartwarming, and she had a feeling that they would get along much better from now on, now that she was no longer afraid of being in love with Theo.

"You were always free to love me," Theo pointed out, as he drew back from her.

"But now, I can do it without hurting you," Rose said. "And that's all I want."

He gave her a smile. "Well, who I am to argue with you, Rosary?"

Hearing him call her Rosary again brought tears to her eyes. She was truly free, and she had someone to love her.

ONCE UPON A PRINCESS

She was overwhelmed all over again, she thought, as a rush of joy poured through her. "Exactly," she said, before she kissed Theo again, before laughing once more. She could not contain her joy. "Maybe I should sing."

"Let's wait until we're back at Havilah," Theo said. "Now that you're free, I don't want anyone else to have you, and your singing might convince some of them I could be defeated."

Rose giggled. "Fair enough," she agreed. "Maybe I should wait to sing on my birthday, and make it a solid eleven years between songs."

"You sang to me before," Theo reminded her.

"Oh, that's true." Rose pressed against him, embracing him tightly as the horse beneath them began to shift uncomfortably. "I guess I forgot. Well, you can't blame me. Now I will be able to enjoy my own birthday! I'll be able to see Isra's wedding in Einish, and I'll be able to rule one day. Oh, this is so wonderful. I'll be able to do all the things I never thought I would get to do."

"What about getting married?" Theo asked.

She stilled against him for the briefest second. "Is that your way of asking me to marry you?"

"I guess I can try to do it more grandly," Theo replied, blushing a bit. "I didn't mean to make it sound so clumsy."

Before he could say anything, Rose knew what her answer was. "Either way, or any way, I would say yes," Rose told him, breathless with overwhelming pleasure. "So let's not worry about it now."

"You're not just saying that so you don't have to sit through a parade of proposals from others, right?"

Rose grinned. "You know me so well."

Theo reached down and pulled out the Rose Ruby. "Either way, or any way," he said, "let me worry about giving you something grand to go along with the proposal."

"Oh, Theo," she said. "You should keep it."

"No," he said. "There is no power that will remove all magic from my life, Rose, so long as I have you to love."

Rose flushed. "Thank you."

"And now that you don't need the dragon's blood," he said, "you'll be able to carry the ruby around without worrying about it."

"It's beautiful," Rose said, holding the small gem carefully, as she wrapped him up in another hug. She felt the power inside of it, and she immediately put it in her pocket. As much as she loved the thoughtfulness of the gift, Rose could not imagine a scenario when she would need it.

Ethan came up behind them. "Alright, you two, I think you're making the rest of us uncomfortable."

Rose had a hard time taking him completely serious, as he had a wide smile on his young face. She laughed. "Alright," she said. "I think we should try to get an idea of what we need to do before we head back home, anyway."

"I can't agree more," Bachas said. "I want to get home to Elva and tell her about all of my heroic feats."

Rose jumped down from the horse and hugged him. "Yes," she said. "We are indebted to you for our victory today."

"Augh, watch it," he snapped. "You're still holding the ruby, Princess. I can't be too close to it. You should put it away."

"Oh, right. My apologies, Bachas."

He sniffed, but said nothing else as Roderick came up to talk with Rose.

Rose took hold of Theo's hand, keeping him close to her as they began to work through burying the men who had died, healing the ones who were injured, and finding aid for the fairies who were left behind. There was a lot of work to do, but Rose was determined to keep Theo beside her. She had felt too far from him in the past, and now that there was nothing standing between them, she was eager to enjoy it as much as she could.

As they headed away from Darkwood Forest, Rose could not help feeling like the shadow hanging over her whole life was suddenly gone, and nothing that would ever go wrong again.

In fact, Rose thought, things could only get better. "You know what, Theo?" she said. "We should get married on my birthday."

He gaped at her. "This birthday?" he asked.

"What?" she asked. "Nervous?"

"No," he replied, still stunned. "Just surprised. I know you dreaded your birthday before."

"Not anymore," Rose promised.

He looked at her for a long moment, and then he smiled. "I think it would be a great idea," he said. "In many ways, it would be a way to redeem the day. But only if you're sure. I know you didn't want Isra pressured into marriage. I can wait for you, Rose, as long as you need."

"Well, you're a better person than I am," Rose told him as she snuggled down next to him, ready to go to sleep for the night. "Because I can't wait for you, and I can't wait to start our new life together."

"You know I will do what you ask," Theo said, planting a quick kiss on her forehead. "Willingly."

ONCE UPON A PRINCESS

There were a few moments of comfortable silence between them before Rose said, "I just hope Isra doesn't mind me upstaging her wedding with my own."

"I think we can get away with a smaller one," Theo said.

"You're hoping for that, aren't you?" Rose asked.

"Yes," Theo admitted. "I'm going to be the most envied man in the entire kingdom. You shouldn't blame me for not wanting the extra attention."

ONCE UPON A PRINCESS

24

There was nothing like coming home. After her battle with Magdalina, finally freed from her curse, and ready to marry her best friend and true love, Rose felt as though her world had completely turned around.

Without Magdalina's curse hanging over her, she could dream freely of a future—any future—that she wanted.

As she rode into Havilah and headed toward the castle courtyard, she saw many of the people, still celebrating Isra and Philip's wedding. They raised their tankards to her, they waved, and called out in greeting; while Rose knew they likely had no reason to know the truth of what had happened in Darkwood, she wondered if they sensed the change in her as well.

As she crossed into the castle courtyard, she heard Isra call out to her. "Rose, you're back!"

Rose saw Isra as she ran toward them. Philip was not far behind, either, as they came to see their friends. Mary and Fiona, who had been tending to Isra as throughout the wedding week, also came flying out to them.

As she jumped down from her horse, Isra wrapped her into a hug. "You're back," she exclaimed. "And in only a week!"

"It went more quickly than I anticipated," Rose said. She squeezed Isra's hands. "But I have some bad news for you, sister."

"What is it?" Isra asked, losing her enthusiasm at once.

"It looks like, for now, you will not be inheriting the throne."

Isra stared at her for a short moment, before letting out a cheerful cry. "Oh, Rose, that's wonderful!" she exclaimed, hugging her once more. When she released Rose, she grinned. "I did not want to rule anyway."

Rose shook her head. "I'm not sure how we're related some days," she said with a laugh.

"But you're sure?" Isra asked. "You're sure that Magdalina is gone?"

Rose nodded. "I'm sure."

"I'm sure, too," Theo said, as he stepped up next to them. "And it is not something I would overlook, considering it would dampen the excitement for our other news."

"Other news?" Philip asked, as he finally reached them. "More good news, I assume?"

Theo looked at Rose as she said, with a faint blush on her cheeks, "We're going to get married on my birthday."

Isra gasped and quickly pulled Theo into a hug. "You'll be my real brother at last!" she said. "I knew it!"

Philip hugged Isra along with Theo. "And I guess you'll be my brother too, Theo. I couldn't ask for a better one."

Rose joined the hug. Mary and Fiona, and then Sophia and Ethan, followed her quickly. They were all bundled together, cheerfully talking and joking in celebration. Rose saw Sophia's eyes water at hearing of the news, and Ethan was already asking her if he could play his harp at her wedding.

Once more, Rose felt overwhelmed with joy and happiness. These were her friends, her family, and the people who had never given up on her. She held onto them tightly, knowing she could never repay them for their kindness and support.

The moment eventually faded, and Rose began giggling as she noticed several others were staring at them. "I guess others are getting curious," she said. "We'd better tell them the news."

Theo gestured toward the keep, where Rose saw her father standing.

Immediately, Rose knew that while there was much to celebrate, there was still business she had to complete.

She disentangled herself from their group hug. "If you would excuse me," she said. "I have to go and see the king."

"Do you want us to go with you?" Isra asked.

"No," Rose said. "I need you to help the others. King Derrick's men are not far behind us, and I think they've earned their keep for a few days. Philip, you'll see to that?"

"Anything for you, sister," he said, mimicking Isra's tone in an endearing manner. His hazel eyes twinkled up at her playfully. "This is the best wedding present I could have given Isra, you know, so I must thank you, Rose, for coming to your senses over falling in love."

"Falling in love and being sensible hardly seem possible," Rose said with a laugh. But in her heart, she knew Philip was right. Before he could argue with her, she gave Theo's hand another affectionate squeeze before heading out to meet her father.

As she made her way to him, she saw him disappear back down the darkened castle halls. Rose was not concerned, however; she knew where he was going, and why.

"What is it, Princess Aurora?" King Stefanos looked at her wearily from across his council room table.

Even the council room had changed, Rose thought. Her father's councilors still looked on her with unspoken questions.

"You know why I am here," she said. "I've come for my letter of abdication."

"So Magdalina is dead then?"

ONCE UPON A PRINCESS

"She's gone," Rose said. "By my hand. There is no doubt. Our battle with her is over."

Stefanos nodded approvingly. "I see."

Rose was hoping for more of a response from him. But she saw that he was tired, with a haggard appearance. As he handed her the letter, the one she had signed with her blood the day before she left for the Romani territory, she still looked to him expectantly.

"Here," he said.

Rose opened the letter, recognizing at once her own signature. She felt a new wave of freedom, as she tore it up. The strips of the vellum fell to the floor between them, and Stefanos managed a smile. "So I will live to see you live your life past your coming birthday," he said.

"And the queen will, too," Rose said. "How has she been?"

"We are working together," he said, but the gravity in his voice told her that further questioning would not be welcomed. She would just have to trust that it was something that would get better, and she could commit to seeing things resolved between her parents. Thinking of her other news, she straightened her posture, determined to meet her father's gaze as an equal.

"I have other news," Rose said.

"You've earned your right to speak," one of the councilors said behind her. "Go on, Princess Aurora."

Rose gave the older man a smile. "I would like to get married."

The councilors, old and frail as some of them were, hummed in varying degrees of shock and approval.

"So it is to be your knight, then?" Stefanos asked.

ONCE UPON A PRINCESS

Of all the people in the room, Rose realized that her father was the only one who was not surprised by her announcement.

"You knew how I felt about him all this time, didn't you?" she asked him quietly, so only he could hear her.

He gave her a curt nod. "As much as I might have disdained the thought," he replied, "I knew."

"Then you know I will ask for your blessing."

"And you will do as you wish, no matter what I say," Stefanos said. "Still, Rhone's leaders are known to be knights. And one as faithful as your knight will do. As Isra's choice, I approve."

"Thank you, Father," Rose whispered, before she reached out and hugged him.

It was, Rose thought, one of the only times in her life, especially since her seventh birthday, that she had embraced him. She could feel the weakness of his body beneath her arms, but she still pressed herself into him. After a long moment, he eased away from her. "Go and get him, Aurora, and we will settle this business as quickly as you would like. After saving our kingdom from Magdalina, and bringing hope to our people as well as to myself, there is nothing that I would deny you."

He pursed his lips together tightly. "Even if I have to suffer through another week of wedding ceremonies."

Several councilors nodded in agreement, and Rose nearly laughed. As she headed out of her father's council room, she could only think of how wonderful everything was, and how good everything turned out to be.

803
ONCE UPON A PRINCESS

25

The next week passed in a flurry. In the wake of Magdalina's defeat and the end of her curse, Rose had to wonder if the kingdom had even more to celebrate than she did. She could not understand why that was at first, before Isra told her that the rumors and stories were already flying of her grand love story with Theo. Upon hearing the news, Rose had to grin. There was something about the magic of a love story, as the old rumors of her supposed relationship with Philip could testify.

So many things were happening. Many of those who had traveled to the capital for Isra and Philip's wedding anticipated another week of parties and games and tournaments.

But even on a personal level, Rose knew there were plenty of things to keep her preoccupied, even on the day of her wedding.

Isra, no longer worried about assuming the duties of an heir apparent to the throne, was already planning her first adventure with Philip by her side.

"What did you say?" Rose asked. She was putting on her dress, preparing for the ceremony, when Isra told her of their intent to head off in search of Queen Lucia's bottle.

"Why would you want to go and search for that?" Rose asked. "We had a lot of trouble on the road as it was."

"You know I've always wanted to go on a grand adventure," Isra said. "And Sophia is more than happy to tag along, too."

"You can't steal my squire."

ONCE UPON A PRINCESS

"She wants to be a blacksmith, Rose," Isra told her. "Don't force her into your mold. No one can take your place or do the things that you alone were meant to do."

"I still think more women would like to be knights," Rose said.

Isra smiled over the rim of her teacup. "I'm sure there are, with you leading the charge," she said. "Maybe while you are here, you could do something about that. I'm sure Theo would be happy to help. Of course, he is so in love with you that you could tell him to walk off the edge of the world and, as long as you were with him, he would do it."

Rose laughed. "I think he would likely try to talk more sense into me before that happens."

"True." Isra chuckled. "But speaking of Sophia, she told me that she has the Rose Ruby ready for you. She's down in the smithing area with the bracelet she made for you. I've seen it, and she did a really good job."

"Good to know," Rose said. "If I am going to lose her as a squire, I would want her to have something better to pursue."

"I'm sure that's how Theo feels about Ethan."

"He's gotten better since the battle at Darkwood."

"Yes, but Ethan is still working on a song for your wedding," Isra said. "And he is waiting for the day when Penelope arrives with her family."

"It will be weeks before she's here," Rose said. "I only just sent for her a few days ago."

"Ethan's taken after Theo," Isra said. "He wants to prove himself worthy of her love."

"He's not even fourteen years yet."

"Theo fell in love with you much sooner," Isra reminded her in her most prudent tone. From that alone, Rose knew she had come prepared to argue if she needed.

Rose sighed. "I suppose that is true." She hoped Ethan was not the only one who was worthy of love. She knew that he had been very taken with Penelope on Maltia, and as much as she now appreciated the miracle of love, she hoped he would not get hurt.

Hours after she left Isra, still wearing her new wedding dress, she fiddled with the gem in the heart of her new bracelet. Sophia had pierced the metal around the Rose Ruby perfectly, creating a rare work of art for her to wear, and just in time for her wedding.

Or more likely, a work of art I can keep safe. After all, Rose knew there was no practical reason for her to keep it. But seeing how Theo had given it to her, she wanted to cherish it along with him for the rest of her life.

Examining the bracelet closer, she smiled once more.

Her squire's skills as a smith were growing, Rose thought. Even if her kindness was as constant as it always was. She held the piece of jewelry carefully, careful to make sure its magic did not cancel out the gifts of beauty and grace from Juana and Fiona.

Everything was perfect.

She had a beautiful gown. She had a lovely new bracelet. Her hair was done, her wedding was completely organized. Her curse was gone, her family was here, and her friends were all excited for her. But most of all, she had the love of her best friend, and in less than a few hours, he would declare his love for her before representatives from all corners of the kingdom, committing to her a lifetime of love and honor.

If only the weather would cooperate. She had to smile, knowing it was not the first time that the weather had tried to stop her.

It had not deferred her before, and it would not stop her now.

But it was still unfortunate, Rose thought, as she glanced out the window. A dark storm was heading their way from over the horizon.

"Well," she said with a small sigh, "it's a good thing Theo wanted a small ceremony after all. We wouldn't be able to accommodate the people otherwise."

She thought about asking Mary to see if they could do something that would help hold off the weather. She glanced down at her white gown, knowing it would suffer the most if it would rain.

But just as she decided to head to her room to see if Mary was there, a strange sense of foreboding slipped over her, and darkened her mood with worry.

A second later, Rose watched as all of the guards lining the hallway suddenly slumped over. She stopped in surprise.

"Are you okay?" Rose hurried over to the nearest one, immediately recognizing Lannister, one of the guards who had traveled with her across the continent.

Lannister gave her a shrug before he yawned. "So … sleepy," he murmured, before he fell forward, already sleeping.

Rose dropped his arm and stepped back. "Something is wrong," she said. "Something is terribly, terribly wrong."

"Rose!"

Rose glanced over to see Mary hurrying toward her.

"Rose, you have to move," Mary said. "You have go, quickly."

"What's wrong?" Rose asked, as she followed Mary toward the castle keep. "Something is happening, Mary. Tell me."

ONCE UPON A PRINCESS

"There's a spell on the capital," Mary said. "I'm not sure who is behind it, but everyone is falling asleep. It's part fairy magic, and part sorcery. I can't stop it."

Rose blinked. She looked down at the Rose Ruby, which she saw was now glowing.

Mary sighed with relief. "You're being protected," she said. "Good. You can get out of here safely."

"But I can't protect you," Rose said. "Not with the Rose Ruby. It can hurt you, just like it can affect Bachas and Elva. And I can't just leave you."

Mary slowed, as her wings started to flap more slowly. "Rose," she said, "you have to go and find Theo. You are the ones who defeated Magdalina before."

"Is there any way she is the one behind this?" Rose asked, suddenly nervous.

"*I will be avenged.*" Rose thought about Magdalina's warning and shivered. *No. It is not possible. I know she is dead.*

Rose began to feel the panic in her throat, an impossibly foreign feeling after her last several days of happiness.

"I don't know," Mary repeated, as she yawned and sat down on a nearby window ledge. "I don't know, Rose. It's getting to me."

Rose gave Mary a motherly kiss on the head. "It's okay, Mary," Rose said. "I will do my best to figure out what is going on."

"I love you, Rose," Mary whispered. "Please be careful."

"I love you, too," Rose said. "I'll see you again soon."

As Mary's eyes fluttered shut and her wings flittered to a stop, Rose had to wonder if she was going to be able to keep her promise.

Before she could speculate, she heard Theo call her name.

"Rose!"

At the sound of his voice, Rose felt her stomach clench. He was calling for her. He needed her help.

She put her new bracelet carefully on her wrist, before folding it behind the layers of her gown. If the Rose Ruby was the only thing that was stopping her from falling asleep, she decided it was best to keep it close.

"I'm coming, Theo," she breathed, as she hurried down the hall.

26

Rose felt her heart squeeze as she hurried up the tower steps. She was not sure how she managed to find her way to this place, of all places, but Theo's voice called to her. There was no ignoring it.

Just like there was no ignoring the sinister aura coming from the other side of the tower door.

Rose hesitated for the last second. She felt afraid, more afraid than she had ever felt before.

And then she shook her head and pushed the door open.

As she stepped into the room, she gasped. "Theo."

He stood at the far end of the room, as a familiar-looking fairy with black wings and broad shoulders held him captive on his knees. There was also a wooden spinning wheel waiting beside him.

Rose narrowed her eyes at him. "Everon." She reached for her sword, realizing it was not there. She had left it behind in her room when she had changed into her wedding dress.

"Princess Aurora," Everon greeted her. "I'm glad you were able to join us. And I'm sure your groom is also happy to see you ... aren't you?"

Theo remained still, only letting Rose meet his gaze. There was something somber in those familiar green eyes, and Rose knew at once that they were trapped.

But that did not mean she would not fight.

"I asked you a question," Everon muttered to Theo, before slamming his sword hilt into Theo's torso.

"Stop it," Rose said. "Tell me why you are here."

"You should know why," Everon snarled. "But then, I suppose you must not know, if you have yet to run away."

"I've never run from a battle," Rose said. "And I won't start now." She stepped into the room slowly, trying to find a way to keep Everon distracted while she put a plan together.

"That is good to hear," Everon said. "But I don't plan to battle you."

Rose frowned. "What do you mean?"

Everon, keeping the sword tight against Theo's neck, nodded toward the spinning wheel. Rose could see a glimmer of light shining on the spindle.

She understood at once.

"This is the spinning wheel of my true love," Everon told her. "Your true love, this scum here, killed her without mercy."

"She killed others, and sought to harm plenty," Rose objected. "And you killed his family, too. If you expect mercy where justice is due, you are only going to be disappointed."

"Rose," Theo said. "Please."

She turned to him. His eyes were soft with sadness, and she felt all of her former despair flood her again. "This can't be happening."

"Oh, it is," Everon said, a wicked smile on his face. "And to make sure things work out the way I want them to, I'll need you to get rid of that ruby on your wrist first."

"No," Theo said. "No, just kill me, Everon. Do it and be done with it."

Rose unlatched the bracelet from her wrist.

"Toss it on the floor in front of me," Everon ordered.

Rose frowned. "Let Theo go free," she said.

"Toss me the Rose Ruby," Everon said. "Annalora deserves to have it, not you."

"Don't do it, Rose," Theo said. "Don't do it. Just run and get out of here."

Rose heard a small whimper escape her—before she remembered. "He can't do anything," she realized. "The Rose Ruby will cancel out any magic on it. Even if I can't use it, he can't, either."

"Toss it here then," Everon ordered. His voice was strangely calm, but Rose watched as he pressed the tip of his sword into Theo's neck.

I can't watch him die, Rose thought. She tossed the ruby onto the floor in front of Everon and Theo, and hoped that she would be able to get a hold of it before Everon used any spell on her.

"Good." Everon moved forward. Rose desperately hoped Theo would be able to find a way to get free from him, but as soon as Everon moved, she realized Theo was trapped by more than just Everon's sword. He was under a spell, unable to move.

Rose blanched. She had gambled on being able to free him, and she lost.

Everon held up the sword in his hand. "Before I destroy this ruby, I really must thank you for allowing me to borrow your sword."

Rose gasped as she realized he was wielding the sword of Queen Lucia.

"So you will kill me and the one I love with my own sword," she whispered. "Why? That won't bring Annalora back, or your mother."

"I could care less that you killed my mother," Everon said. "She might have wanted me to avenge her, and I will, but only because Annalora is gone. My mother hated her, but they were both right in the end. The only pursuit worth

ONCE UPON A PRINCESS

chasing is power. If I had more, I could have prevented them both from dying."

If he was not about to kill Theo, Rose might have felt some sympathy for Everon.

She had even less as she watched him use her sword to strike into the heart of the Rose Ruby.

The ruby cracked as the dragon's blood flowed from her sword, blackening as it split into several shards.

Rose glanced back at Theo, who was just as horrified as she was. She glanced back at Everon, as he returned to his position, standing over Theo.

"Now that I've taken care of that," he said, "I think it is time we turned our attention to you, Princess. We have business to discuss."

"I know Magdalina wanted me to marry you," Rose said quietly. "And if you spare Theo, I will agree to it."

"No!" Theo yelled. "No, Rose, don't do it. I'm not worth it."

Rose gasped in horror as he flung himself forward. "No, Theo," she cried.

Everon stepped to the side, jerking the sword out of Theo's way, laughing as Theo fell forward onto the floor, still trapped by his magic. "How noble," he said mockingly. "You have one brave knight here, Princess."

"Please, Everon," Rose said. "We can be married right now. Everything is ready to go. Just let him go, and the kingdom will be yours to rule, and yours to rule rightly."

Rose did not look at Theo as Everon considered her offer.

She was startled when Everon only laughed a moment later. "There is no reason for me to marry you," he told her. "I can take over the kingdom when you are gone. After all, everything is already in place. Everyone else is already asleep."

ONCE UPON A PRINCESS

"Rose, just get out of here," Theo told her. "Run. You can run away and live to fight him another day."

"I won't leave you."

"Yes, you will." Everon told her. "I didn't just bring Annalora's spinning wheel here for show, Princess. It is time that I avenge both Annalora and my mother—for even as much as I despised her, she fought for me, and I should honor her."

"I killed your mother," Rose said. "Her curse won't work."

"Her curse has no power over you," Everon said. "But it will still work. You just have to choose whether or not you would like to sleep forever. Either that, or I can kill your love, and then kill you."

Rose glanced back at the spindle, the small spark glinting in the dim light.

"You know I'm right," Everon said. "And truth be told, I would rather not kill you. Not when I know there are worse things than death. Don't you agree, Theo?"

"No," Theo called out. "No, don't do it, Rose. I changed my mind. I don't want to marry you. I don't love you. I don't want you, Rose." There was an uncharacteristic harshness to his voice, but Rose never faltered.

Before he could say anything else, Rose reached out with her hand and let the spindle slide deep into her forefinger.

As she held herself there, sucking in her breath at the small, sharp pain, she turned back to Theo. "I know you're lying," she told him, as her blood trickled down the silver spindle and drippled onto the floor.

Power and light danced before her blurry eyes, before she fell down in surrender to the power of her curse.

"No!" Theo yelled as his heart tore in two, watching as his beautiful Rose withered and tumbled down. Her hair fanned out behind her, the short locks offering their softness as a small pillow.

He struggled against Everon's hold once more, more desperate and determined than ever to get to her. Theo was briefly distracted as he suddenly found himself free.

Theo glanced up and stared. Burning white light began pouring out of the spindle alongside a shadow; the two shades, one of light and one of darkness, danced together, battling each other, before exploding into pure, bright light.

A half of a second before it exploded through the room, Theo heard Everon scream in agony. He peeked over and squinted over at his enemy. He watched in painful awe as the light was burning him, the darkness was binding him, and then everything went bright and silent.

The silence was terrifying.

Theo felt his heart racing as he opened his eyes once more, surprised to see that he was unaffected by the explosion. He saw the empty space beside him.

Everon was gone.

There was nothing of him left, and Theo could not bring himself to feel anything over it. Everything in him cried out for Rose.

"Rose," he gasped, hurrying over to her. He cradled her gently against his chest, pulling her into his lap. Theo frantically began searching her for a pulse, looking for any sign that she would be alright.

After all, he reasoned, *Everon is gone. Magdalina is gone. The curse should no longer affect Rose ... right?*

ONCE UPON A PRINCESS

He did not want to think about how she was not supposed to fall asleep, how she was not supposed to prick her finger at all, following Magdalina's death.

At his touch, she sighed deeply, and at the warmth of her breath on his cheek, he stilled. "Rose?" he whispered. "Rose?" His hands framed her face, pushing back her hair, allowing him to see her fully.

There was no answer.

"No." Theo felt his heart as it collapsed inside of him, as he waited for a response he feared would never come. He pulled her face to his, laying his forehead on hers. Theo could not stop the rush of tears as he held her close, burying his face into the crook of her neck, seeking warmth where there was only the chill of sleeping death. "Please, God, no."

As he held her, he recalled what Thad had said before, about true love's kiss. Was it possible that it would work?

Theo pressed his lips against hers, tasting nothing of her former warmth. He felt disappointment sink in as he slowly pulled away from her.

Theo could barely see through his eyes, as his teardrops fell onto Rose's cheeks.

"Rose," he said, his voice hoarse, his heart aching. "I'm sorry. I'm so sorry. I love you. I don't know if there was ever a moment, in all the years I've known you, that I didn't love you. I promise I won't stop loving you, not now or ever."

He gripped her hands, surprised to feel a bracelet on her arm. Theo looked to see the familiar gleam of his rosary beads. He touched them lightly, as he had before when she would sleep, praying Rose would dream of him, of all the good times they had with their friends and with each other.

As despair took him, he leaned down and kissed her once more, lingering long enough to taste the saltiness of his tears as they mixed in with the sweetness of her lips.

"God," he whispered. "I don't know why bad things happen. I don't know if there is any true good left in this world. But I know you are good, Heavenly Father, and I know you have the power to set the captive free, just as much as you can give peace that passes all understanding. And even though my heart is broken now, I can only thank you. I didn't deserve her at all, but I was able to have her, to call her mine, for a short time. Thank you, Lord. Thank you, for your gift. For your love. God, I love her so much."

He embraced Rose again, sadness overwhelming him once more. He barely noticed that her body was suddenly warm.

But when she shifted beneath him, ever so slightly, he went completely still.

"Theo?"

Rose's voice was a hushed whisper against the quiet of the room.

"Oh, God, thank you," Theo cried. He could not stop the rush of grateful pleasure as she stirred. "Rose, you're awake!"

Her hands twitched, and then she reached for him. "Oh, Theo," she whispered again. "I am awake, aren't I? But it still feels like a dream."

"Rose." Theo gripped her lightly as he kissed her again, unable to keep himself from her any longer.

She gave him a shaky laugh as she pulled back. "Careful," she said. "I might faint."

"I'm sorry."

"No, don't be," Rose said. "If anything, I'm the one who is sorry."

ONCE UPON A PRINCESS

"What?" Theo glanced up at her, stunned. "You just sacrificed yourself to save me. You have nothing to be sorry about."

She began brushing away his tears, tenderly running her fingertips over his face. "Yes, I do. I'm so sorry. When I was sleeping, I saw Amalia again."

"Amalia? The one who guards the Serpent's Garden?"

"Yes," Rose replied. "She said that she had a message for me."

"What did she say?"

"She told me I would wake up and come back to you, for one," Rose said. "It is really amazing how what we fear turns out to be nothing to fear at all."

"I wonder if she was the one who killed Everon," Theo murmured, glancing over near the spinning wheel.

"She said his time had come for judgment," Rose said.

"I wasn't sure it if the spell had gone wrong, or if it was something more—"

"That's not the important part of what Amalia told me. What is important is that I know now that I never saw past my own curse," Rose explained. "And for that, I am sorry."

Theo kissed her palm, letting her fingers rub into the grainy stubble of his cheeks. "But you did," he protested. "You traveled the world and helped people as you looked for answers. You gave back, Rose, despite having everything you wanted out of reach."

"But I never saw that *you* were cursed, too," Rose told him. "Magdalina was the one who cursed me, but you were the one who was hurt more because of it, and it was because of me. All because you loved me."

Rose pulled him down to her, kissing his chin softly. "I never saw how much you were cursed by loving me—and

ONCE UPON A PRINCESS

even when I did, I pulled back from you, no matter how hard you fought for me, no matter how long you searched for a way past my defenses."

"Every knight of Rhone has to go on a quest," Theo reminded her. "And every moment was worth it, because in the end, I was rewarded with true love's kiss. Or maybe I should say *we* were rewarded?"

Rose returned his teasing smile, before she sighed happily. "Amalia said that you had a gift for me, and it was time to wake up so I could finally claim it as my own."

"I don't really have a gift for you."

"Yes, you do," Rose said. "The gift of yourself—the gift of your heart." She placed her hand over his heart, letting her hand press into the sweaty fabric of his tunic.

Her eyes met his. "I asked before you why God allowed me to be cursed. I knew Magdalina cursed me, but I never realized that, even though I was cursed, I still had his gift right in front of me, the entire time. I see it now. Every step of knowing the truth about my curse, you were always there for me. You are the real beauty in my life. That's the real magic, isn't it?"

"Oh, Rose. There is no magic here," Theo said. "Only love." He kissed her again, pulling her closer. Theo could not stop his hands from running through her hair, running down her back, touching her skin. He had almost lost her, he realized. He had come so close to losing her.

Never again, he vowed to himself, sealing his promise with his kiss.

"Ahem."

Theo and Rose glanced up to see a sleepy Mary at the door.

"I guess everything is okay now?" she asked.

"Actually," Rose said, "everything is better than okay."

ONCE UPON A PRINCESS

"Rose is right." Theo smiled down at her. "Even though I think we are late for our wedding."

"It seems we are all a bit late," Mary said. She saw the spinning wheel behind them. "I will have to hear the story later, when you get a chance, Rose."

As Theo held her arms, lending her support, Rose stood up and brushed her wedding dress off. "Theo can tell you all about it," she said, surprising them. "After all, he is the one who promised me a long time ago that he would write down my legend."

"That is true," Theo told her. His eyes roamed down her body possessively, before meeting her gaze once more. "I guess I should probably write everything down. So I can tell the whole story to my children one day."

Rose's eyes watered with happy tears as she leaned in and kissed him again.

"You two are getting as bad as Isra and Philip," Mary said. "So come on. You'll have plenty of time for that later. Your grandfather was complaining earlier about having to wait so long. I can't imagine he's any better now, even though we all had some unexpected sleep."

"Well," Theo said. "I can sympathize with him for that. I think we have waited long enough, too."

"Yes," Rose agreed. "We have."

Together, they made their way down from the tower, and headed to the main ballroom, where their friends, family, and future were all waiting for them.

821

ONCE UPON A PRINCESS

Epilogue

In the following days and years, the kingdom of Rhone was once more alive. The rest of King Stefanos' reign was marked with Rose's love for life and for her people. Together, with her noble knight, Sir Theo, they cleaned up the Magdust trade and reestablished good relations with the fairies who lived in Rhone, as well as Aragon, despite her uncle's bitterness.

The kingdom continued to grow in contentment, even as Stefanos fell ever more deeply into madness. He abdicated a few years after Rose defeated Magdalina, but the queen was always at his side, tenderly helping him through the worst of it. The king died, peacefully, in his sleep, a few months after meeting his first grandchild, Princess Honora, the newest crown princess of Rhone.

As he promised, Theo did write down the adventures of Princess Aurora, the one who preferred to go by Rose among her friends. He frequently used the tales as bedtime stories for his children, and even sometimes Isra and Philip's; all this would happen while his wife tenderly watched over them from the doorway and listened herself, unable to resist the voice of the man who had loved her so ardently and so willingly. Once he was done with story time, Rose would sing to her children, and kiss all of them goodnight, sometimes staying late. She would watch them as they felling into dreaming, each of them sleeping beauties in their own right, marveling at the wonder of her own life.

More often than not, she would glance over to see Theo watching her, and then she could only smile.

On some level, Rose knew she should not have been surprised that everything turned out so well in the end. After all, Theo still made sure he said his prayers.

C. S. Johnson is the author of several young adult sci-fi and fantasy novels, including *The Starlight Chronicles* series, the *Once Upon a Princess* saga, and the *Divine Space Pirates* trilogy. She currently lives in Atlanta with her family.

ROSE AND THEO
By Julia Mae Busko

AUTHOR'S NOTE AND ACKNOWLEDGEMENTS

Dear Reader,

It is over, and I am so happy, because I love happy endings, and I am so sad, because it is the end of a story, and this time, the end of a saga as well. It's a complicated, joyful kind of feeling. But, much like the other romances that bloom up in my work, I take great comfort in the fact that Rose and Theo have a bright future together, one that will go on even though I have stopped writing their story.

When I first started out writing this novella series, I really wanted to "fix" the fairy tale of Sleeping Beauty. As much as I adored the story when I was younger, and the movie besides, I have never bought the idea that the princess would not figure out the truth about her curse. And, if someone had told her, don't you think she would have avoided a lot of her problems, or at least had a better chance of making her own life?

Maybe that was the driving force behind wanting to update the fairy tale. Well, that and to leave my own twist in place. Who, after all, would have suspected that Theo was the *real* title character in the end? Despite his own struggles, Theo's constancy is the sacrificial love that characterizes all real beauty in the end. It is a seeming paradox that true love endures such ugly things, yet becomes more beautiful because of it.

One of the greatest joys of writing this (besides all the fun parts where I get to feel clever) is that I can see more than ever how stories, even when they are completely made up, show us the truest parts of life. I have often told my students that fairy tales are often the most real stories we have, because of how, in the face of reality, they show us the simple truths of our lives. The necessity of love, the importance of truth, the complication of trust and trying to do the right thing, even when we are unsure of ourselves—these are all things that only add to the human experience.

ONCE UPON A PRINCESS

While I doubt I will end up cursed like Rose, I aspire to have her courage and determination when I am faced with my own demons. In the past, I have learned the value of that courage, and I can only hope I will have it when I need it—but it is a lesson worth repeating, several times over.

It is a great miracle that we can take the stories we hear and the stories that shape us, and make them our own.

Thank you for joining me throughout this saga's journey, and I hope to see you again in my other work. And please, be sure to check out the work of my fellow authors from Dire Wolf Books!

Until We Meet Again,

C. S. Johnson

WORKS BY OTHER DIRE WOLF BOOKS AUTHORS

Wolf Code: A Sheltering Wilderness
Chandler Brett

A college student, Don, finds his dream career is at odds with the ideals his newfound love interest holds, even as his choices affect the survival chances for a pack of wolves. Check for more information at www.direwolfbooks.com.

The Adventures of Shamis and Larry
Jeff Sartini

An off-beat fairy tale adventure ensues as Shamis and Larry head off with a magical mule and a one-headed monkey. Check for more information at www.direwolfbooks.com.

ONCE UPON A PRINCESS

Thank you for reading! Please leave a review for this book
and check for other books and updates!

ONCE UPON A PRINCESS